# OWEN 9

by

George C. Wilson

**DORRANCE**
PUBLISHING CO
EST. 1920
PITTSBURGH, PENNSYLVANIA 15238

Dorrance Publishing Co
585 Alpha Drive
Pittsburgh, PA 15238
Visit our website at *www.dorrancebookstore.com*

ISBN: 978-1-6376-4035-7
eISBN: 978-1-6376-4882-7

# OWEN 9

Many stories about football teams are about champions overcoming obstacles to win. Often, football stories are about lovable losers overcoming impossible odds to win a big game. This is neither of those kind of stories.

# CHAPTER ONE

## THE GREAT WATER HORSE RIOT

Two-a-day practices started on a hot and muggy morning in early August in mid-Michigan. A bunch of boys stood in the parking lot behind Bear River High School. Some of them sat on the hoods of cars. Four or five were leaning on the back door to the locker room. From the other side of the building, a rumbling sound reached their ears as an old GMC one-ton flatbed truck came into view. One of the players yelled, "Hey, it's The Tank!"

Morgan Miller pulled into a spot on the grass next to the row of beat-up cars the other players had driven to practice. Miller's squat body slipped out of the cab of the truck – known to everyone on the team as "'The Tank'." Morg's feet didn't reach the ground from the bench seat in the truck, and he stumbled a little as he hopped out.

"Morg, that hunk of shit of yours is going to leak oil all over the grass," Seth Parker, the team's quarterback, called out as the other players laughed at the chubby kid.

Morg looked up and smiled and said, "Nope – I replaced the gaskets this summer."

Morg approached the players standing near the door. Jorge Martinez lifted his Detroit Tigers ball cap off his head and squinted. "Morg, The Tank's rolling," he said calmly.

Morgan turned and yelled, "Ahh, fuck!" as the truck gained speed and rolled off the grass and across the parking lot. The players howled in laughter as Morgan ran after the truck. He didn't catch it. It glanced off a chain-link fence and plowed heavily into a dumpster. The trash container banged loudly. The crash put a stop to the truck and prevented it from going over the embankment and into the Bear River that ran behind the school.

Someone was unlocking the door behind the players.

1

"What the hell is going on?"

"Oh nothing, Coach," Seth said with a smile. "Morgan's truck is possessed, and it just tried to kill a dumpster."

Coach Mike Reese looked over at Morgan as he parked The Tank yet again. "Set the parking brake on that beast, Morg, before you kill someone," Reese called out.

"I can't, coach, it's broke – I have to leave it in gear when I turn it off. Sometimes it pops into neutral and rolls. I got a block in back of the seat – I'll wedge it behind the rear wheel," Morg answered as he reached behind his seat.

"All right – show's over, guys. Let's get down-stairs and get ready," Reese announced to the gathering throng of players. The players started filing through the door, pushing and shoving until Reese yelled again for them to stop screwing around.

Minutes later, team manager Wash Dryer sat in the coaches' office flipping a football in the air and catching it in one hand. Head coach John Cale sat at a broken-down old teacher's desk sorting through papers. Coach Reese stood in his underwear in front of his locker picking through his duffel bag looking for a pair of Bear River Bears wrestling shorts. Noise from the locker room was building as more players came through the doors on the opposite end.

Without looking up, Cale said, "Shut the door, Wash."

The noise and some of the stench of boy-sweat dissipated.

"Well, it looks like we got about two dozen physicals here, Mike," Cale said to Coach Reese.

"Yeah but there are forty kids on the sign-up sheets, and it sounds like there is about that many out there," replied Reese.

"Maybe some of them have their forms with them today. Wash, go and check." Cale smiled as he looked over at Wash. His manager jumped up and slipped out the door, closing it behind him.

"Christ, best athlete in the school and we can't use him. He can run like the wind and throw a football sixty yards in the air," Cale mumbled.

"He's only got one kidney. His mom – my kid sister – won't let him play contact sports. I can't even have him wrestle for me, and he was a three-time youth state champion before the accident," Reese replied. "Did you see him play baseball last spring? He is going to get some money for school next year – he might even get drafted. The Tigers and the Reds had scouts out to see him during American Legion ball this summer. At least he isn't playing friggin' soccer," Reese continued on to John Cale who was now glancing out the office window at the players getting dressed and horsing around.

Two young men walked into the office. They wore shorts and whistles hung around their necks. Reese smiled. "Look who's here, the lowly ASS sistants, and only forty-five minutes late."

Pat Packer, heavier of the two young men, replied, "Numbnuts here couldn't get his bike started so I had to drive all the way up to Mt. Pleasant to get him." Keith Marker looked up at the two senior coaches and smiled sheepishly. His boyish face under a ragged ball cap belied the well-muscled athletic body that had gotten him a full ride to play football at Central Michigan University.

"You're gonna get killed on that damn thing, Keith," Cale said as he glanced over at the two young men. "How many tickets did you get this summer? Five?"

Marker said quietly, "Only one, but I got pulled over five times. The other cops let me off because they recognized my name from college." Marker had caught two interceptions his senior year playing safety for the CMU Chippewas.

"Jesus Christ," sighed Reese.

"All right – let's get them out on the field," Cale announced, and the four men started out the door.

Reese shouted out in his loud growl as the coaches entered the locker room, "Move it, sweethearts. Don't be the last one out the door!" Boys of every description stood up from the benches in front of their lockers and shuffled toward the back door of the locker room.

"On the hop! Let's go!" called out Coach Packer, his shrill voice only getting a few of the younger players to quicken their pace.

Dressed in various colored T-shirts and shorts and carrying their helmets, the players scuffed along the walkway in their football shoes to the pedestrian bridge over the Bear River. On the other side of the river lay the football field, baseball field and two practice fields. The football field had attractive aluminum bleachers and a nearly new press-box with "Home of the Bears" in bright red letters on a sign over the windows. Two signs were hung below the press-box. A slightly faded one stating "State Soccer Champions 2009" and a brand-new sign with "State Soccer Champions 2015" hung during a ceremony at the end of the prior school year. Off the east end of the football field were the two practice fields. The one to the north looked well cared for – green and manicured. This was the soccer practice field. A nice block field house stood next to it. The field to the south was scruffy and brown and looked overgrown with tall weeds along the edge. This was the football practice field. No yard lines were painted on it yet despite many written requests to have it ready by today. A rusty blue metal pole building stood nearby next to a massive maple tree. A broken-down-looking blocking sled was wedged up against the tree.

On the soccer field, three teams, twenty players on each of them – varsity, JV, and freshman – were stretching. Their bright red shorts and clean matching gray T-shirts stood out in the morning sun. A half-dozen coaches in matching gear patrolled the neat rows of soccer players. John Cale looked out across the scene. "Must be nice to have the school board's president's kid as the head coach," he said in passing.

Mike Reese replied, "Yeah, and the head of maintenance and grounds as the lead assistant. I notice Ben Coffey didn't find time to mow our field since the end of school in June. I think he was busy painting their clubhouse and maintaining the sprinklers on the soccer pitch."

"Humph," snorted Cale in response. "Well, you win a state championship in this town and you get all the goodies. You had everything you wanted when you won your state championship years ago. They have won two in six years. It's a good thing we have to share the game field or we'd never get that mowed and lined either."

"I'll get into the grounds building this evening and grab a mower and do it myself," Reese replied.

"No," said Cale. "Go through channels and request it again in the AD's office. We don't need to start the season with a feud and grievance from the ground crew bunch."

Reese surveyed the fields and said, "Before you were here – twenty-some years ago – I stood up at the school board meeting and told everyone that adding soccer as a varsity sport was a mistake in a school our size. I said it would water down the football and cross-country talent pool and all three programs would be mediocre at best. I was wrong, of course. It only killed us. Half the soccer team does dual sports in cross and soccer, but we can't even get one of those kids to come and kick field goals for us on Friday nights. They started that youth soccer program twenty-five years ago and old Frank Mack the football coach then warned us that sure enough, them soccer parents would demand it be added as a varsity sport before long. It took two years. We haven't had a winning football season since – not that we had that many before." Reese repeated a story he had told Cale many times in the last two years. Cale had talked Reese, the very successful head wrestling coach, into coming back to coach football as his assistant. Reese was drunk as hell at a staff party two years ago when he said he would, and he didn't have the heart to disappoint the young head coach. Many times, over the months since, he wished he'd stayed sober that night.

"Yeah, I know the story," Cale replied. "Let's get 'em on the field for warm-ups." A crowd of players stood under the shade of the maple tree. The temperature was already above eighty. Warm for Michigan at 8:30 in the morning. Seth Parker was throwing passes to two boys. Cale noted as he approached the practice field that not one ball had been caught. He sighed.

Reese yelled, "Put your buckets on! Line up – veterans in front, rookies to the rear. Seth, Jorge, Morg and Junior Schultz, up front in the captain's position." The four boys came forward and faced the mass of the team. Coach Packer started to yell about the sloppy lines. Boys shuffled into place. Coach Marker steered two or three of the JV's into place. He patted a very large boy on the top of the helmet. The boy smiled at the coach. He had the bright smile of a special education student who has just received some praise.

Big Donnie Donnie was the largest kid on the team. He also was the slowest moving and slowest thinking. Donnie was cheerful and friendly to

4

everyone – even bullies. This was his fourth year of football, and he had never really used his size and strength – his lack of aggression made him a target on the field. Opposing teams figured out quickly he was soft, and lighting him up with big and cheap hits was a favorite pastime throughout the league. Unbeknownst to him, Big Donnie Donnie was the feature in many highlight videos for area teams. The laughter of opposing players echoed at end-of-the-season banquets throughout mid-Michigan at images that showed the big kid in the red Bears jersey knocked on his ass. Last year, the head JV coach, a loud-mouthed owner of a local gas station, had called Big Donnie Donnie a "six-foot-six-inch 330-pound tower of duh" during the coach's comments at the Bears own team banquet. Belinda Donnie, Donnie's equally slow-thinking and equally large mother, began to cry and yell obscenities at the coach. Several other parents booed him. The next day the athletic director fired him, noting that he was an abusive jerk and a lousy coach. Both statements were true, Frank Daugherty had one victory in two seasons as a JV head coach and had been thrown out of two games for swearing at officials. Big Donnie Donnie had to play varsity ball this year because seniors were not allowed to play JV. Coach Cale feared for his safety but knew that given the lack of linemen on the squad, Big Donnie Donnie would see significant playing time.

Keith Marker, who had the makings of a natural coach, was brought in to coach JV's this year, but Coach Cale was nervous about him because he was so young, twenty-three. He was unemployed except for coaching and perhaps working as a substitute teacher this fall. Cale was also worried about Pat Packer, who had assisted the JV's the last three years and had turned into a clone of Frank Dougherty, the coach fired last year. Pat Packer, twenty-six, was also a walk-on coach – he had his own car detailing business, and he was the nephew of the Athletic Director and Assistant Principal Clete Packer – known to most of the kids in school as "Fudge." Pat, being the nephew of the AD, Fudge Packer, made it tough on Cale. Pat Packer had expected to become the JV head coach, but then it was pointed out that Keith Marker had played college ball and Packer had ended his football career as a junior in high school when he broke his leg in three places.

Warm-ups began in earnest, and slowly the team began to act as one as they moved through the stretches. "Where's Bobby Slawinski?" called Coach Cale as he looked up from his clipboard.

Seth Parker called back, "His family moved their trailer over to a park in North Star. He's going to play basketball for them."

Coach Reese said to Cale, "That's just great. He is the only kid who caught a touchdown pass for us last year. Sure, it was only one but still."

Cale nodded, "Where's Quentin?" he called out. An unidentified voice from the team answered, "He's running cross this year." Cale turned to Reese and Reese shrugged. Trevor Quentin was one of the better wrestlers on Reese's team.

Reese told Cale, "I'll call him but I doubt he'll come out after last year." Quentin missed the last five football games his junior year with a separated shoulder. He missed a good portion of his wrestling season as well. He reinjured the shoulder at the state wrestling meet and failed to win a medal.

Coach Cale looked down the list. "Where is Marcus?" Several players started laughing. Morg Miller called out, "Tetherboy is in court today!" More laughter. Glenn "Tetherboy" Marcus was the biggest thief and thug in school. He was also the only player on the squad who had both speed and the size to play fullback. He was a violent but very undisciplined linebacker as well. Tetherboy got his nickname his sophomore year when he played football with a tether on his ankle. He was on probation for breaking into cottages on Crystal Lake. The police caught him and his cousin with a van full of stuff lifted from winterized cottages the prior January. Tetherboy got probation because he was a minor and he agreed to testify against his cousin. The cousin, nineteen years old and already a career criminal, got five years in the Pine River correctional facility. Tetherboy missed two-a-day practices his junior year because he was in a young offenders camp after getting caught stealing a neighbor's lawn mower. This last summer he and another cousin got caught shooting deer out of season and selling the meat for two dollars a pound in the trailer park they lived in. Word had it that Tetherboy might actually do some jail time.

Coach Reese glanced at Cale and said, "Addition by subtraction, John. We don't need him. He is nothing but trouble and he steals everything that isn't nailed down. His freshman year he wrestled for me. He got caught stealing the varsity basketball team's game shoes. The idiot tried to sell them to kids on the JV basketball team – right in the locker room the next day. Then in his sophomore year during track, he got caught in the girls' locker room after practice trying to pry open the Kotex dispenser with a butter knife looking to steal the change. He has never finished a season of any sport he has tried. He is either suspended, arrested or academically ineligible. Sometimes he manages to do all three within the course of a season. He only played two games for us last year because of legal trouble and grades. We just don't need him."

Coach Cale glanced down at the ground and twirled his whistle lanyard around his index finger. "I know all that, Mike, but we don't have another option at fullback, and he will be starting at linebacker, too. We don't have the luxury of only coaching the good kids. We couldn't field a team. Besides he isn't the only kid here with a bad record. Hell, you have coached wrestling for over thirty-five years. You know you have to take both the sinners and the saints to make a team." Reese nodded and grunted in agreement.

Coach Cale scanned the practice field. "Let's get into line drills, Mike, but get them water first."

Coach Reese glanced over to the water horse drinking station that sat between the soccer practice field and the football practice field. No one was there. "All right kiddies – get some water!" The boys broke for the water horse in a group. A few sprinted, most jogged. Just then, the soccer team started sprinting for the large PVC pipe water horse that sat on a concrete pad halfway between the fields. In about ten seconds the teams would collide at the station. No one really figured out exactly what happened next, but in a flash, punches were being thrown and bodies were on the ground. A general brawl was in full progress as the football coaching staff and the soccer coaches sprinted into the melee blowing their whistles and shouting.

Coach Reese arrived in the center of the riot just in time to see Jorge Martinez lateral drop the soccer team captain, Liam Pickering, into the PVC pipes of the watering station, smashing the pipes and sending a broad spray of water into the air and across the crowd. Reese almost smiled at the perfect form of the wrestling move Jorge had used. The cold spray of water should have calmed the boys down, but it had the opposite effect. About forty soccer players surged into the pile all at once. The football players made a stand. Reese caught sight of Morg Miller kicking a lanky soccer player in the crotch. The player folded in agony on the ground just as another soccer player threw a haymaking punch at Big Donnie Donnie. The punch landed on his chest.

Then something happened that had never happened before – Big Donnie Donnie got enraged. He plowed into the on-rushing soccer mob. Bodies went flying. One of the freshman football players was standing in the middle of the spraying water blindly swinging his helmet. A helmet can be a lethal weapon in a fight, but most players are smart enough to leave theirs on when it comes to blows on the field because it is also a very effective shield against getting smashed in the face with fists and feet. Soccer players by and large have no knowledge of what an effective tool of combat a standard football helmet can be. Neither do soccer coaches. The flailing, helmet-wielding freshman got in a lucky shot. It caught Miles Kitteridge, the head soccer coach, full in the face as he ran into the fight. Blood squirted from his obviously broken nose, and he collapsed in a heap.

It was over as quickly as it began. Coach Cale knelt down to see how Miles was doing. Not well – the blood was seeping through his fingers and into his mouth, which caused him to spray blood as he breathed. Coach Reese yelled at the top of his voice, "Football players get to the big tree RIGHT NOW!" The football team disengaged from the throng and jogged back to their field with Reese. The soccer team massed around their fallen coach. About a dozen of them had torn shirts and one boy covered with mud stood there with only a jock strap on – his shorts and shirt had been torn away in the fight. Coach Cale had the odd thought that the soccer team even had matching jocks.

There was a commotion to Coach Cale's left. Ben Coffey, the soccer JV coach and district maintenance director, began to scream at Cale, "Your team fund is paying for this! Your thugs started it!" he shouted. He struggled to turn off the main water supply at the station. Slowly, the spraying water ebbed to a trickle.

Coach Cale squinted up at Coffey and calmly said "Shut up Ben and get your boys back to your field." Ben Coffey stood for a moment, his face beet red and water dripping from his shorts. He grabbed his whistle and blew a shrill note. Without a word, the soccer players turned and jogged away. Wash Dryer stood a few feet away from Cale. He bore no sign that he had been involved in the brawl. "Wash go get the kit. We got to stop this blood – I'll call the school office and get some help down here." Miles Kitteridge lay on the wet muddy ground moaning. John Cale reached into his pocket for his cellphone and thought, "This is going to be a long fucking season."

**Overtime**
On the evening of the Great Water Horse Riot, Wash Dryer sat on his back deck at home with his cellphone in hand. He began a text to his dad, Greg Dryer, a project engineer for an oil company. Greg was on-site at a rig in Montana. He had a large crew working for him and he had been out of town for over a month. It looked like he might not make it home until Thanksgiving. Greg sat on the tailgate of his large yellow company pickup truck. He watched as his survey crew played the oil rig roughnecks in a very violent game of what was supposed to be two-hand touch football but in reality was a crashing slugfest. The sun hung low in the western sky and the dust being kicked up by the game lingered in the air.

WashDryer: Knock Knock.
GregDryer: Whose there?
WashDryer: Boo.
GregDryer: Boo who?
WashDryer: Aww… don't cry you big baby.
GregDryer: An oldy but a moldy.
WashDryer: Grandpa always said start with the classics first.
GregDryer: What's up Kid?
WashDryer: Huge fight at practice today.

The rest of the conversation, Wash filled in the details for his far-away dad. When the last message was sent, Greg Dryer watched the final seconds of the sunset. He missed his boy.

# CHAPTER TWO

COACHES' MEETING AND THE THINGS.

The day after the Great Water Horse Riot, the respective coaches explained new rules to the football and soccer teams. No member of either team would be allowed on the other team's field, and they were not allowed to take water at the same time. The boys shrugged it off. The night before the coaches of both teams all had to sit through a school board meeting. Miles Kittridge was even there with his black eyes and heavy bandages across his nose. Both nostrils were still plugged with gauze. He was a little loopy from painkillers, and when he spoke, he sounded like Kermit the Frog with a bad head cold.

Pamela Kitteridge, the school board president, reamed them out for the fight. She wanted to suspend a bunch of football players, but the school district superintendent, Sheldon Knapp, explained that her son, Miles Kitteridge, the soccer coach, would lose players to suspension as well if they decided to go that route. The whole thing was quieted down in typical Sheldon Knapp style. He had two iron-clad rules: 1. No surprises. 2. No headlines. The coaches of both programs shook hands at the end of the meeting.

Calmer heads ruled, but after the meeting, Pam Kitteridge told her cronies on the board that as far as she was concerned, football was "on the way out at Bear River High School because it is nothing but an embarrassment, and the team is a haven for all the worst thugs in the school."

Day two of the season went off without much fanfare. Glenn Marcus showed up in the coaches' office with his parole officer before the morning practice. The officer explained to Coach Cale that Glenn would be allowed to attend school and play football, but if there was just one more incident he would be spending the rest of the fall in the county juvenile hall. Glenn had a stupid smile on his face during most of the meeting. Coach Reese glared at Tetherboy until he quit smiling.

Between the morning practice and the evening practice, Wash Dryer and Seth Parker hung out at Seth's house playing video games. They always played video games at Seth's place because Seth's dad had bought a sixty-inch plasma screen TV to watch videos of Seth's football and basketball games. Seth hated those sessions because his dad, a successful insurance salesman who had never played sports in school, would yell at Seth about mistakes he was making on the field and court.

Seth's left hand was wrapped up – he had gotten spiked in the morning practice during warm-ups when Big Donnie Donnie stumbled getting to his feet and stomped onto the quarterback. The hand was mostly just bruised with a few light scratches. When it happened, Seth had howled and cursed at Big Donnie Donnie. Morg Miller shouted at Seth, "Shut up Dial-a-Pain! You've had worse owies before." Seth had earned the nickname "Dial-a-Pain" in middle school. He was carted off from nearly every football and basketball game with some apparently near-fatal injury only to reappear at practice the next day miraculously fully healed. He had gotten tougher in high school but still would react to every bruise as though it was killing him.

Wash and Seth were locked into full gaming mode and they said very little. Every time Wash bested Seth in a combat move, Seth whined about his injured hand and Wash would remark, "Pussy." The games went on for hours with breaks only to go to the toilet and to snack. Eventually both boys were glassy-eyed joy stick zombies.

At the school, the coaches met in Coach Cale's math classroom. Pat Packer arranged three-by-five index cards taped to the blackboard. Coach Cale and Coach Reese were sitting at a table facing the board sorting through notes. Keith Marker was flipping a can of Copenhagen chew from one hand to the other. He was slouched in a ratty-looking green couch Cale kept in the classroom for his students to relax on. Marker spat his tobacco juice into a half-empty plastic Mountain Dew bottle. The couch was the most popular feature of Coach Cale's classroom, and players fought over it to sit in it all football season during film sessions for the team.

Each index card was printed in bold letters with a position followed by a player's name and vital statistics. On the left-hand side of the board were cards identifying offensive positions. On the right was the defense. With such a small roster, duplicate name-cards appeared on offense and defense, and players were assigned multiple positions on both teams – starting at one position and backing up others.

Behind closed doors, football coaches are often crude. Their observations of their players can sometimes be both brutally honest and decidedly mean. The good ones will keep their comments far away from the kids they are coaching. The bad ones can't keep from eventually acting on their thoughts and treating athletes accordingly.

Pat Packer liked to say he was there for kids, but when he lost his temper, which happened frequently, his shrill voice would go up an octave and he could not or would not keep his true attitudes about individual players from being known. Most of the boys didn't like him, and all learned not to trust him when he was trying to be nice.

Keith Marker was new to coaching, but he carried himself well and kids were drawn to his shy smile and his pleasant encouragements. He also had the rare ability of being a great athlete who could actually teach how to accomplish what he had achieved. In the right atmosphere, Keith Marker could be groomed to be a very successful coach. These two young men would be the junior varsity staff. Keith Marker, despite his inexperience, would act as head coach, defensive coordinator and backs coach. Pat Packer would be the offensive coordinator, special teams and line coach. Coach Mike Reese constantly referred to them both as the "Lowly ASS sistants."

Mike Reese was the old pro in the room. Reese was old-school tough, fifty-nine years old and on his second marriage. He had two grown boys who were both teachers now, but they, like so many other young teachers, had moved out of Michigan to find jobs. Both coached wrestling and taught history at schools in Florida. Both had been state champions wrestling under their father, and both had success wrestling in college. Mike called and talked to his boys every week.

Mike Reese had coached football for twenty-four years before his failing first marriage and the fatigue of losing game after game drove the love of the sport from him. He had played football in high school and was recruited to play at CMU but he chose his first love – wrestling. He had made it to the NCAA tournament as a senior but did not place. Mike spent fifteen years as Junior Varsity head coach at Bear River High School. He had two winning seasons to his credit. These represented the only two winning seasons in JV football at BRHS in the past thirty-five years. This was his second season back coaching football after taking more than a dozen years off. He knew the game and he knew how to handle kids.

Mike Reese had been the head wrestling coach at BRHS for thirty-eight years. He had won a state championship eighteen years ago with a team led by his own sons. He had coached eleven state individual champions. He had won twenty-eight consecutive league championships losing only two league matches in the time span. Reese was, in short, a legend, and he was beloved in the town of Bear River. He taught history at BRHS, and five times in the last thirty-seven years, he had been chosen as teacher of the year by the students. Four times in his career the senior class at BRHS had dedicated their yearbook to him.

The thirty-year-old head varsity football coach, John Cale, had been at Bear River since graduating from Northern Michigan University with a degree in math and two bad knees obtained from four years of being battered on the college football practice squad. He was a true Yooper – a resident of Michigan's

Upper Peninsula and had played on back-to-back state championship teams for the tiny town of Copps Mine. He had made all-state honorable mention as a tailback his senior year in high school in Michigan's smallest football division, Division 8. In the classroom, John was a serious and diligent teacher. The two older math teachers at BRHS would not let him teach anything other than freshman algebra. That was fine because he found working with the most mathematically challenged kids to be rewarding.

John Cale became head coach of the Bears by default. He got the job three years ago when a big-mouthed Texan, Dean Dellencamp, who had been hired over the phone, was fired after one season. He had been hired based on what turned out to be a mostly fabricated teaching and coaching resume. The superintendent of Bear River Public Schools, Sheldon Knapp, could tolerate losing – that was expected of BRHS football – even though Coach Dellencamp did manage to win three games. What would not be tolerated was a resume full of lies and Dean Dellencamp sitting in front of his classroom reading newspapers while watching game film instead of teaching biology.

Before he left town early in that spring, Dean Dellencamp stole the last four hundred dollars out of the BRHS football team fundraising account and sold off a bunch of the team's equipment and pocketed the cash. It seems "The Big Deano," as he called himself, had a small gambling problem, and being posted to a school less than twenty miles from the biggest Native American gambling casino in the state was not a good thing for him. There were a lot of rumors and recriminations floating around the school, but the one thing everyone knew was that the school assistant principal and athletic director, Clete Packer, had dropped the ball badly on the hiring of Dellencamp.

Packer practically ran the school with ineffectual principal, Mike Shanahan, rubberstamping everything Packer did. Clete was responsible for all discipline in the building. He relished being feared by kids. The kids and a good portion of the teaching staff called him "Fudge" behind his back. At a retirement party a few years back, the drunk honoree called him Fudge to his face, and Clete stormed out in in a huff. Principal Shanahan only took part in running the school when it didn't interfere with his full-time occupation – brown nosing Superintendent Knapp. In most school districts, Clete Packer's head would have been on a stick in front of the high school after the Dellencamp mess. Not at Bear River.

Superintendent Knapp wanted the case hushed up to keep the embarrassment contained. No charges were filed against Dean Dellencamp as long as he returned to Texas and did not ask for a recommendation. Clete Packer got a strong verbal warning and had earned the undying distrust and dislike of school board president, Pam Kitteridge. The day of the meeting when they swept the whole affair under the rug, Sheldon Knapp and Mike Shanahan closed the matter quickly and still made their usual 2:00 Wednesday tee time at the country club.

The outcome was a vacant varsity football coach post with no applicants. John Cale applied for the post after Clete Packer promised his full support. John had a few years' experience as a JV coach. In his first year the Bears won two games. In his second year he talked Mike Reese into coming back to football. The Bears finished with one win. This was his third year, and on paper, the team was the weakest roster in school history.

The meeting in Coach Cale's classroom began in earnest as Pat Packer finished placing the three-by-five cards on the board. Mike Reese was first to speak. "The offensive line is horrible," he said.

Cale didn't look up from his notes. "The defense is worse." There was a pause, and Cale looked up at Reese. They exchanged wry smiles. Cale was in charge of the offense. Mike Reese handled defense and special teams.

Pat Packer sarcastically added, "With the lineman we have, Dial-a-Pain won't last past half-time in the first game." The line didn't get his hoped-for laugh.

"Jorge looks like he can play," Keith Marker said as he spit into his bottle.

Reese replied, "Jorge is a hammer – we could use ten more like him." Cale nodded in agreement. "But," continued Reese, "he can only play one position at a time. We have a center who has never snapped a ball in a game. We have a large and stationary right tackle who can't remember whether he is playing offense or defense. Throw in the fact that we are very thin at all the skill positions and huge academic eligibility issues come grade report time, and it is looking grim."

Packer chimed in "Don't forget about our midget left guard – he's a picture window into the backfield."

Reese gave the young coach a disgusted glance. "Morg is better than you think, Pat. Yeah, he's short, but he hustles and he knows his job. And don't let that pudgy body fool you. He has some power and he has a mean streak a mile wide. He's a salty little grubber on the wrestling mat – he won thirty matches last year on guts and guile."

Coach Cale looked up from his notes and said to his three assistants, "We have to coach what we have." Cale then shifted his gaze to Reese and continued, "But I think we are going to have to move Thing One and Thing Two to the varsity."

"Shit." Reese sighed. "John, they only weigh 110 pounds. I need them for wrestling – don't get them killed this fall."

Cale smiled. "Hell, Mike, you can't hurt the Things. They're made out of spring steel and shoe leather held together by Krazy Glue. And they're quick and violent little D backs who support the run defense. They can catch too. Both of them caught TD passes last year."

Again Packer had to add his opinion. "They're crazy all right. They're little pyscho cheap-shot artists. They'd rather hurt someone than win a football game. Both of them got thrown out of the Perrinton game last year." Caleb speared their running back about three seconds after the whistle in the first quarter. And that little turd Noah sucker-punched their wideout in the throat with less than two minutes to play in the game."

Cale was losing his patience with Packer. "Pat, we lost that game 48 to 6. The Things didn't cost the junior varsity the game. You couldn't move the ball at all."

Packer had to have the last word. "Yeah, well, the Things had to sit out the next game against Riverdale on suspension and they ended up passing for 400 yards against us."

Reese took a turn. "Pat, Riverdale beat us forty-five to nothing on JV last year, and I think we had a total of thirty yards on offense so why don't you just shut up." Packer was stung by that – he was the offensive coordinator for the JV. Packer gave Reese a sullen look but said nothing.

Keith Marker calmly added, "Looks like the JV is going to lose the only two kids who actually like to hit."

Cale gave Marker a sympathetic look. "Sorry, Keith, we need the Things on varsity. The two kids we have starting at cornerback have yet to finish a season without being ineligible because of grades, and no one on the varsity has hands to catch the ball like the Things."

Keith Marker nodded in agreement and the meeting went on.

Twins Caleb and Noah Lott were identical at birth. They grew into hell raisers almost immediately. Their uncle – who had been a state champion wrestler for Mike Reese – started to call them Thing One and Thing Two because no one could really tell them apart except for their mother. The Lott family was known for two things: They were prolific – half the phone book in Bear River was related to the Lotts. And the Lott family was prone to multiple births. Thing One and Thing Two were followed up two years later by another set of identical twin boys – Kyle and Conner – known throughout Bear River as Thing Three and Thing Four. There were at least four other sets of twins in the extended Lott family. The Things had cousins ten years older, triplet girls who had been all-state volleyball players in high school. The girls were the stuff of local legend. They were tall, big chested, hot and available. Many of the local young men liked to tell stories about how they went on to become strippers. In fact, only one of them had. The other two became trophy wives for wealthy middle-aged attorneys in the Chicago area. All three sisters had given birth to sets of twins in the last two years.

Caleb was known as Thing One and Noah was Thing Two. Both were five-foot six-inches and 110 pounds. Both were former state and national champion youth wrestlers. Both had earned black belts in Tae Kwon Do over the last year adding to their lethality. As a freshman the year before, Caleb had won a state championship at 103 pounds and Noah was third place at 112 pounds. Before the start of state competition in wrestling they had flipped a coin to see who would wrestle 103. Caleb won. Noah had lost his state semifinal match by one point to a senior with an undefeated record.

14

The elder Things were tough and vicious competitors. The only thing that held them in check at home was their mother's willingness to use corporal punishment and their father's booming voice. Also, there was the fact that Thing Three and Thing Four outweighed them by twenty pounds and stood three inches taller. The brawls between the brothers commonly led to broken furniture in the house and bloody noses on the wrestling mat their father had installed in the family pole barn. The two smaller, older brothers would pair up to attack one of the larger, younger brothers. Then all four would thrash about, applying illegal wrestling holds and hacking away with martial arts moves.

No one could tell Three and Four apart. And if anything, they were even more feared in Bear River than their older brothers. They, too, were accomplished wrestlers and vicious competitors. In addition, they were devious and crafty to the point of extreme danger. They loved fireworks and homemade explosives and were forever blowing up whatever they could find. That is how Thing Two, Noah, became more easily recognized by his teammates and friends. Thing Three and Thing Four had fashioned a soda bottle bomb and planted it in the drop ceiling in their brothers' room. When it went off with considerably more force than expected, a piece of the drop ceiling frame had gouged a small gash in Noah's left eyebrow. The scar was faint, but it was enough to mark Thing Two for easy identification.

Whatever the case, if you saw any Lott brother with a crooked smile on his face and a squared stance, you knew violence was about to follow. Coach Mike Reese loved them as only a wrestling coach could. Football coaches loved them too, but the wild abandon to do bodily harm the Things could never fully control drove football coaches crazy as penalty flags flew through the air every game. Pat Packer was right – football's bursts of controlled aggression drew the Lotts in but it couldn't contain their violent nature. Hell followed them everywhere.

Wash Dryer had been invaluable to the staff all through two-a-day practices. One of the highlights of the period was the day known to all as Christmas. The fourth day of practice is referred to as Christmas because that's when the players get their presents – pads. It is the first day in full gear and the first day of full contact. Wash had put together spread sheets on his laptop for all of the equipment. He and Coach Marker handled the equipment assignments in record time. Coach Cale walked through the equipment room as the process unfolded and he smiled broadly. "Wash," Cale said while laughing at how neat and orderly things were proceeding, "You are the best team manager I have ever even heard of." Wash smiled and kept entering in numbers as Coach Marker handed out the equipment and called out players' names.

The first day in pads saw the first action for the Things on varsity. Thing One hit Randy Jansen so hard during the "Oklahoma Drill" he almost knocked him out. In the process Thing One had dislodged a crown he had on a front tooth – the result of Thing Four smashing him in the mouth with a pair of pliers the previous summer. Thing One popped up after the hit and pulled off his helmet. He reached in his mouth and pulled the crown out. He held it up and recognized it wasn't another lost tooth. Without a word he handed the crown to Coach Reese and got in line on the opposite side of the drill. Coach Cale and Wash Dryer had by then picked up the dazed Randy Jansen. Wash walked him over to the water horse for a drink. Jansen was done for the day.

On the JV side of the field, Pat Packer spent most of the day screaming out orders to the confused younger players. Keith Marker stopped practice and declared that for the next hour, the only thing they would be working on was stances. The groans could be heard by the varsity fifty yards away.

The last week of two-a-days was capped by a scrimmage. An old college roommate of Clete Packer coached football at Levering, a town near the Mackinac Bridge. As a favor to his old friend, he arranged for the Bears to be one of three teams invited to the annual scrimmage when a long-time participant canceled. It was a three-hour bus ride at least. The coaches were less than thrilled, but at least they would be scrimmaging against teams they had never seen before and no one would likely be there to scout them. One major pain to Coach Cale was the fact that Clete Packer insisted that they could only take one bus to the scrimmage. Varsity and JV would have to share the ride. Forty-five kids plus coaches and all the equipment jammed into a sixty-passenger bus would be crowded and stuffy. Not to mention the smell of players just off the field on the long bus ride home. Mike Reese tried to sign out a school van to take the equipment, but Clete Packer nixed it, saying it would cost the athletic department too much money for gas.

The day before the scrimmage, Pat Packer made it known to the kids that the rinky-dink schools 'up north' should be no problem for the Bears. Wrong. The three other schools were in a smaller division than BRHS, but all of them had a long history of winning playoff games and humiliating larger schools.

At the scrimmage, the two Bears teams separated. The varsity would play on the game field. The JV would scrimmage on the adjacent practice field. On the varsity field, the defense got hammered from the get-go. The teams from up north ran power-running offenses. Early on, Jorge Martinez made some great stops from his middle linebacker position, so teams just avoided him. Conversely, it didn't take long for Glenn Marcus to start free-lancing and blitzing into the wrong gap nearly every single play, giving huge yardage in the holes he left behind. Big Donnie Donnie drew double teams until the opposing teams figured out it wasn't needed. All three teams scored at will on the Bears. Thing One did intercept a pass, but it was from a backup QB.

On offense, things were even worse. Seth Parker rolled his ankle on the first play of the scrimmage and spent the rest of the day on the bench with an ice bag on his leg. Randy Jansen filled in for the rest of the scrimmage at QB until he got his eye poked by a linebacker from Brevort, the third and last team the Bears scrimmaged. The only other option at QB for the Bears was Thing Two, who had played backup QB for the JV team the year before. He ran the offense for the final fifteen plays.

Thing Two got sacked every play but one. He bounced up each time without saying anything. On the last play of the scrimmage, he fore-armed a crashing defensive end from Brevort across the facemask after pitching the ball to Thing One going the opposite way on a wing reverse. The blow caught the much larger kid by surprise and knocked him on his ass. After a stunned moment, he got up swinging and swearing, thinking he would throttle Thing Two. It didn't work out that way. By the time the Brevort player got to his feet, Thing One had been run out of bounds. Without missing a beat and as if he knew what his brother was up to, Thing One sprinted back to the center of the field just in time to launch himself like a missile at the head of the Brevort defensive end. Thing Two took the opportunity to sweep the legs of the much larger boy at the same time. The three of them ended up in a snarl on the ground. Just then, the middle linebacker from Brevort ran in to the Bears backfield to help his friend. He almost got there before Morg Miller kneed him in the groin as he ran past.

The fight was brief but intense as the rest of the two squads joined in. Whistles blew and flags flew. The referees and coaches from both teams restored order quickly. The head referee was purple in the face as he told Coach Cale, "Get these boys off this field before I start throwing them out, Coach. They'll have to sit out the first game next week!" John Cale took the gift and hustled his team back to the bus without even stopping to shake the Brevort coach's hand. Cale was hoping to make a quick exit from Levering. When Wash Dryer saw what was going down, he grabbed up the equipment as quickly as he could and had Randy Jansen help Seth Parker to the bus.

Just as Coach Cale was herding the varsity onto the bus, it occurred to him he had to wait for the JV squad. He scanned the practice field and saw that the on-call ambulance was in the middle of the field. He muttered, "Shit." Then he turned to Coach Reese and said, "Get the boys settled, Mike, I'll go see what's up on the other field."

Wash Dryer grabbed the kit and headed out following his coach. As John Cale jogged toward the practice field, he could see a Bears jersey being cut from a player lying on the gurney. "Shit!" he swore again.

On the last play of the JV scrimmage, the Bears center and only competent lineman, Gunther "Gump" Colby, went down. The pileup was typical of the JV scrimmage. All afternoon, the Bears failed to get any positive yardage. Pat Packer was storming mad as he hissed at the offensive lineman, "Get off the freakin' ball!" after every play. The last play ended and Gump Colby rolled off the bottom of the pile holding his left arm. He walked straight over to Coach

Marker, who stood on the field behind the offense, and said with a slight quiver in his voice, "Coach, I think I broke my fucking arm."

Keith Marker looked down at Gump's arm, which now appeared to have two elbows, and said "Yeah, Gump, I think you did."

The volunteer firemen manning the ambulance insisted on transporting Gump to the hospital in Petoskey. Coach Cale looked over at Wash Dryer and said, "Get his emergency card from the kit." Wash gave him the card, and Cale opened his phone to call Gump's parents. After the call, he told Keith Marker to ride along with Gump to the hospital and the Colbys would give him a ride back to Bear River later that night when Gump was released. It was going to be a long night for the young coach.

Keith Marker's night was long – but not as long as what followed for Coach Cale and the rest of the Bears. As Cale walked back to the now-full bus, he said to Wash Dryer who trailed along with him, "Let's get on Big Yellow and get out of here so we can get back home before midnight." He had no sooner said that when Monte Ward, the head coach of the Levering Blue Devils, stepped in front of him.

"Coach," Ward said firmly. "I need a word with you." John Cale didn't like the tone of his voice.

"What is it, Coach?" John Cale asked.

"First," Ward began, "Is your boy going to be okay?"

"He's got a broken arm. His season is done." Coach Cale replied.

"I'm sorry to hear that." Ward continued. "Brevort's coach and I go back a ways – he said your boys took some real cheap shots. I'll be talking to Clete Packer tomorrow. I don't believe we will be inviting you back to scrimmage next year. Besides, I don't think your program is up to the competition."

The last part of Ward's statement stung Cale, but he kept a poker face as he replied, "You do what you like, Coach, but we're not interested in coming back next year anyway. It's too long of a trip." With that, Cale side-stepped Ward and continued toward the waiting bus. He settled in the front seat next to Mike Reese with a sigh.

"Ward give you an earful?" asked Reese.

"Yep," replied Cale.

"I thought so – he's a pompous ass according to some friends I have who coach around here," Reese replied.

"Yeah. Well, let's get out of here." Cale shifted his focus to the bus driver. "Jimbo, take us home."

Jimbo Davis was the best bus driver in the district. He was also the lead mechanic in the bus garage. He had retired from the Marines after twenty years and came to live with his wife in her home-town of Bear River. He still had his high and tight haircut ten years out of the service, and his voice still had a West Virginia twang. "I'm on it, Coach," Jimbo said without looking around. He was all business, and everyone in the district from grade school kids to adults knew that Jimbo Davis was not to be messed with.

The first forty-five minutes of the return trip to Bear River were uneventful. The sun was getting low in the northern Michigan sky. As dusk set in, Jimbo turned the bus onto I-75. Shortly after the bus climbed to highway speed, Jimbo grunted, "Ahh crap!"

The next few seconds were slow motion terror. The deer vaulted out of the ditch on the right side of the road. Jimbo applied the brakes as the deer leapt into the front of the bus and smashed against the windshield. John Cale and Mile Reese both ducked as glass, blood, hair and deer shit sprayed the first few rows of seats. A chunk of deer guts landed in Jimbo's lap and he grunted again. Fortunately, most of the deer bounced off the front of the bus as Jimbo struggled to keep the bus on the road. It was a struggle that even he could not win, and the bus careened into the median. Again fortune helped the driver as the grassy median was flat and not lined with trees on this section of the freeway. Jimbo struggled to brake and steer as a loud snap was heard over the now-shouting mass of players. The front left tire had bitten into the soft turf and had broken away.

Wash Dryer felt his stomach turn as the bus heaved to the left and then lurched to the right. The bus dug deep into the sandy northern Michigan soil and most of the players were tossed forward into the seat backs in front of them as the massive yellow vehicle plowed to a stop. Morg Miller shouted, "What the fuck!" Wash had bounced into the aisle and up to the seat next to Coach Reese. As he came up to a kneeling position, he reached to his face and felt wetness and lumps. He pulled his hand away and blinked at the red deer blood and brown deer pellets that had sprayed onto him.

"Wash!" Reese shouted above the din of swearing and crying players. "Are you okay?

Wash Dryer blinked at him and then came to his senses. "Yeah, Uncle Mike. It's not my blood."

John Cale sprung to his feet and approached Jimbo Davis who was still gripping the steering wheel tightly with both hands. "Jimbo, it's over. It's okay. You saved us, Jim."

"Goddam deer jumped," Jimbo said blankly. "Why do they fucking jump?"

The bus was a mess, but no one was really hurt. The boys started to laugh nervously as they filed down the aisle to disembark. Jimbo and the coaches walked around the front of the bus as Jimbo surveyed the damage. Deer guts were everywhere across the front. Part of the head was lodged in the grille. Bits and pieces of deer were spread down the road behind the bus. The usually noisy and opinionated Coach Packer could only hoarsely whisper, "Wow." A freshman player vomited with a loud retch as he caught sight of what was left of the deer.

Morg Miller shouted out a laugh and said, "Nice!"

It took a few minutes for the state police to arrive on the scene. The boys were busy on their cellphones but were frustrated by the lack of a good signal on the remote stretch of highway. John Cale was able to get through to Clete Packer with the help of the police. A bus was sent to pick up the team. During the wait, the efficient officers got down all the details and took a report from each boy and the coaches. Several times, they patted Jimbo Davis on the shoulder and complimented him on his heroic effort keeping the bus upright.

At about two in the morning, the Bears rolled into the parking lot at BRHS. The longest road trip in program history was over. As the bus rolled to a stop John Cale stood up and announced, "No practice today boys. See you Monday." Some of the groggy boys gave a faint cheer. "But remember," Cale added "Next week is our first game – we have a lot of work to do, so get some rest this weekend."

## Overtime

It was breakfast-time in Montana when Greg Dryer got the text from Wash. Greg was eating with his survey crew at a truck stop. He stepped outside to focus on the conversation with his boy.

WashDryer: Knock Knock.

GregDryer: I was wondering when you going to send me a text. Where you been?

WashDryer: Knock Knock.

GregDryer: OK OK. Who's there?

WashDryer: Armageddon.

GregDryer: Armageddon who?

WashDryer: Armageddon outta here!

GregDryer: Not your best, Wash.

WashDryer: Sorry – I'm tired.

GregDryer: Why?

Wash filled in the story of the long ordeal of the scrimmage and road trip disaster. Greg Dryer was suitably impressed by the account Wash gave.

GregDryer: So what are you up to this weekend?

WashDryer: Seth and I and a few of the guys are heading over to Ludington to Seth's grandpa's cabin.

GregDryer: Be careful. Make good decisions.

WashDryer: Always.

# CHAPTER THREE

## A TRIP TO THE BEACH

After a grueling road trip and barely any sleep, most people would not be looking to take off on another adventure. Most people are not seventeen- and eighteen-year-old boys with a taste of freedom in their mouths. The unexpected day off moved up the timetable for the boys who planned a road-trip weekend to start Friday evening after practice. Extra time isn't always used wisely by teenagers.

It was 10 A.M. on the Friday morning after the disaster scrimmage. Wash Dryer had just finished texting his dad when he heard a commotion if front of the house. He looked out the front window and saw six boys were standing around an ancient and rusty Dodge 9 passenger van covered with NASCAR stickers. Randy Jansen's dad was a huge race fan, and he would load up the van with family and friends and head down to the Michigan International Speedway. Randy's dad was talking about getting an old school bus to replace the van. Randy's mom was talking about seeking advice from a divorce lawyer. Morg Miller leaned into the front driver's window and honked the horn. Morg then yelled, "On the hop! Let's get going, Wash!" The other boys started yelling as well.

Wash waved out the window and then walked into the kitchen. His mother was there standing next to his bag. Laney Dryer was tall with dark hair and violet eyes. She was leaning on her cane. Wash gave her a quick kiss on the cheek. "I'll call you tonight. You going to be okay?"

"I told you that Sharon Reese and I are going shopping at Birch Run today. And tomorrow I am working an extra shift at the hospital." Laney Dryer pushed him toward the door. Wash's mom was a registered nurse and she had been a softball player in college. Wash hated leaving her alone – especially with his dad being out of state on a job. In May, Laney had her hip replaced for the second time since the accident five years ago. The surgery laid her up for a month and she had only been back to work for about two weeks. Wash and his dad wanted her to take more time off, but she insisted on staying active. Nothing much held Laney Dryer down despite the blows life had dished out to her.

Halfway through Wash's seventh-grade football season, Laney Dryer was driving Wash home after a game. His little sister Maggie was in her booster seat in the back of the van. Wash was in the front passenger seat. The last thing he remembered about that rainy evening was three-year-old Maggie yelling, "Mommy!" The impact of the pickup truck smashing into the van just behind Wash's seat was like an explosion.

The big Ford 4x4 was driven by a very drunk local farmer. He had left Sporty's Bar in downtown Bear River a few minutes before, after spending the afternoon and early evening drinking and swapping stories with his cronies. During the trial he couldn't recall how many beers he had drunk. His blood alcohol was twice the Michigan legal limit. It was his third drunk driving offense. The elderly farmer sobbed during sentencing as he apologized to the Dryers. He was given a long prison sentence, but he died in prison after serving four years.

The van was thrown into the air and off the road by the impact of the much larger truck. It flew into a ravine of a creek that fed into the Bear River. Laney Dryer broke her left shoulder, hip and pelvis when the van landed on its side on the bottom of the ravine. Wash broke both arms and his jaw. He had severe internal injuries including a split kidney that had to be removed along with his spleen. Maggie never had a chance.

Wash was in the hospital when they held the funeral. It bothered him lately that he couldn't really remember what Maggie looked and sounded like. The pictures of Maggie that hung in the Dryer family room showed a smiling, dark-haired little girl with her mother's violet eyes. The pictures didn't giggle like Maggie. The pictures didn't reach their arms out and squeeze Wash's neck in a vise-like hug like Maggie used to. Wash remembered that Maggie would squeal his name out and come running whenever he came home from school or a sporting event – he just couldn't remember what that happy squeal sounded like. Whenever he tried to recall that sound, all Wash could hear in his head was her scream of "Mommy!"

Wash Dryer grabbed his duffel bag and gave his mom an embarrassed grin as Morg Miller laid on the horn again in the driveway. Laney Dryer smiled back and said, "I wish you boys were taking a safer vehicle."

Wash replied, "Randy's dad drives it down-state all the time. It looks like crap, but he keeps it running good." Wash had his hand on the doorknob of the back entrance.

Laney gave the traditional Dryer parting. "Make good decisions."

Wash leaned his head back through the closing door and said, "Always."

Wash knew this trip to Ludington with his friends would include drinking. He wouldn't take part. Nor would any of his friends offer him anything – they knew full well why he never touched alcohol or drugs. Wash for his part was a great companion when the boys were partying. He would get loud and obnoxious just like they did, but when the time came to get people home, Wash was a serious and sober driver. It was something that Seth Parker, Morg Miller, Randy Jansen, Jorge Martinez, Rich Lamb and Greg DeVito knew they could count on. Wash Dryer was reliable not only for this trip but in every instance where they had to lean on someone who would "Make good decisions." They all had a quiet unspoken respect for Wash and what he had been through.

Wash threw his duffel bag on top of the pile in the back of the van. Randy Jansen tossed the keys to Wash and climbed into the front passenger seat. Ten miles north of town, the first beers of the weekend were snapped open. Morg Miller produced a pack of Swisher Sweets cigars from his bag. He made a great show of lighting one. Rich Lamb and Greg DeVito each took one from him and lit their own. Randy Jansen yelled out, "Roll down the windows if you're gonna smoke those cat turds in the van!"

Jorge Martinez added, "Yeah, you're drowning out the stench of beer piss and dried barf in this rolling hunk of junk."

Randy replied, "Ha-ha."

Seth Parker put in his two cents. "I don't know how you can smoke those things. They taste like sugared dog shit."

Morg Miller smiled and blew smoke at Seth and said, "Bold talk from Dial-a-Pain. Didn't you throw up after prom when you swallowed a dip of Red Man? That stuff is nothing but dried horse shit."

General laughter greeted the comment. Seth Parker got drunk after prom last May on wine coolers stolen from his grandmother's fridge. Then he topped it off by trying chewing tobacco for the first time. The vomit fest was legendary among the athletes at BRHS.

Wash Dryer exited U.S. 127 and followed the big curve onto U.S. 10 and headed the van west toward Ludington. In a short time, the scenery changed from the flat fields of central Michigan to rolling hills covered with pine trees and red oaks of west Michigan. The van talk shifted from partying to the other topic on every eighteen-year-old boy's mind – girls. The talk was full of bold statements and claims of nailing this girl or that girl. In typical fashion, the description of various hookups got very graphic. Lies were told, but no one called anyone out. Jorge Martinez laughed at the stories, but as was usual, no one could get him to say anything about his conquests. Seth Parker was mostly quiet as the conversation got more descriptive.

"Hey Dial-a-Pain, has Amber given you a blowjob yet?" Morg Miller asked in a mock concerned tone.

"Fuck you," Seth replied. Seth Parker was the only one present who had a regular girlfriend who actually attended BRHS. Most of the really good-looking girls at school dated soccer players or hung out with college kids up at CMU. Amber Taylor was the hot-looking daughter of a Christian Science minister who liked to brag of her vow to remain a virgin until she was married. Amber was also known for swearing off all medications, claiming that prayer had all the natural healing power anyone needed.

"Yeah, Seth, you can tell her blowjobs have natural healing powers, and that way you could get one every Friday night this fall." Rich Lamb added into the conversation. Wash Dryer laughed so hard the Mountain Dew he was drinking squirted from his nose and he had to pull over until he quit coughing and sneezing. The guys decided this was as good a place as any to take a piss break.

The seven boys walked into the waiting trees of the Manistee National Forest east of Baldwin on U.S. 10. Traffic was heavy on the highway, so they moved well out of sight. The boys separated a few paces apart underneath the tall pines. Greg DeVito, who finished his business faster than the others, snuck up from behind and poked Morg Miller in his butt with a stick as he was shaking his equipment free of the last drops of urine. Miller shouted an obscenity and wheeled around with his manhood still not tucked away. DeVito laughed and said, "Wow, it looks like a penis – only smaller."

Morg Miller zipped himself up and began to stalk toward Greg who was backing up laughing. "Come on, Morg, quit your bitching. That's more action than you've had all summer." Greg managed to get the words out as Morg attempted to kick him in the balls. Between the beer he had drunk and the loose footing on the pine needles, Morg missed his first attempt. He was lining up another kick when Rich Lamb hissed a loud warning.

"Shit! It's the cops." The boys froze and turned and looked toward the highway. Reflexively, they ducked even though it was unlikely that anyone on the road could have seen them through the thicket of trees. From their vantage point, hey could barely see the flashing lights on the cruiser parked behind the van. Wash Dryer sprang into action.

"Okay you guys, get down, be quiet and stay out of sight. Jorge you been drinking?" Wash asked quietly but with force.

"I had one beer." Jorge replied.

Wash nodded and handed him two sticks of gum from a pack in his pocket. "Chew this, follow me and don't get close to the deputy. I'll do the talking." Wash shifted focus to the other boys who were now crouched behind a large log lying on the ground. "Did you guys leave any cans in plain sight?" The other five boys all said no. "Good." Wash continued, "Jorge and I will go to the van and see what's up. if things go bad you guys better scatter or this football season might end right now."

With that, Wash and Jorge started picking their way through the trees. "What you gonna say?" Jorge asked.

"Workin' on it," Wash said as he walked ahead. "Just follow my lead."

24

When they emerged from the trees, Wash recognized that it wasn't a sheriff's cruiser at all. It was a Michigan Department of Natural Resources patrol car. Wash waved a hello to the DNR officer.

"What are you boys up to?" the officer asked pleasantly but with a tone that hinted that Wash had better be careful not to lay the BS on too thick.

"We were on the way to Ludington and Jorge here had to go," Wash said with an embarrassed smile as he motioned with his thumb toward his trailing companion.

"There's a roadside park in a few miles, boys, you could have waited that long," the officer replied.

"Sorry officer," Jorge managed a crooked smile and sounded sincere.

"Seriously boys, we have violators taking deer out of season around here that drive vans just like this one. You're not scouting for some late-night early-season action are you?" the officer asked.

"I hunt up near Marquette at my uncle's deer camp," Wash said, and he wasn't lying.

"I don't hunt, officer, my mom hates guns. She won't let them in the house," added Jorge, and he wasn't lying either.

"All right," the officer said, holding up his hand to signify he was buying the stories but not interested in the details. "You need to move this van. It's on a curve."

"Yes, sir," the boys replied in unison.

Wash and Jorge climbed into the van. They made a show of putting on their seat belts. Jorge sighed, "It's a good thing he didn't look in the van. It stinks like beer in here. DNR cops are still cops – we would have been toast."

Wash replied, "Yeah, but I think this guy doesn't want to spend all afternoon checking on us." He glanced in the rear-view mirror. "He's not moving. It looks like he is writing stuff down. We gotta get out of here. Call Randy and tell them to lie low until we circle around." Wash put the van in gear and waited for an opening in the traffic. As he eased into the lane, Jorge dialed the phone.

Randy Jansen answered on the first ring. "Where the fuck are you guys going?" Randy growled.

Jorge Martinez answered back with disdain. "Calm down butt munch," he said. "We'll circle back around and pick you up soon as the DNR cop takes off."

Fifteen minutes later, Wash Dryer pulled up to the spot where they had stopped. In a flash, the five left-behind boys scrambled out of the tree line and into the van. They were barely seated when Wash gunned the motor. The boys were quiet for about a minute. Jorge turned around from the front passenger seat and said, "The DNR cop thought we were poachers. Wash smoothed him over." Jorge filled in the rest of the story. The boys all relaxed, but the event had been enough of a scare that no one reached for another beer.

Wash spoke up. "Let's go right to that beach in Ludington. We can go to the cottage later." All the boys agreed with that plan.

A little less than an hour later, the van was cruising west down Ludington Avenue. In front of them, Lake Michigan shimmered in the afternoon sun. The lighthouse at the end of the pier came into view, and the boys were quiet in the appreciation of the scene. Wash turned north to go up the few blocks to the park entrance.

Rich Lamb spoke up, "This beach is cool – the locals call it G Park."

Morg Miller looked at the entrance, "The sign says Stearns Park."

Rich said, "Yeah, but my dad spent his summers here. He says that the G stands for giraffe."

Morg gave him a puzzled look. "Huh?"

Rich didn't miss a beat and replied, "Giraffe's got long necks – lots of long necking goes on here after dark." Morg gave an appreciative grunt.

"Babes!" called out Seth as the van began the slow crawl south on the park drive.

The boys started yelling and pounding their seats as the van inched along. The park was crowded, and along the drive, cars were parked diagonally. The place was humming with activity. Little kids walked around with parents. Groups of teenagers and college students were gathered around their vehicles waving at friends. The young girls in skimpy bikinis drew the boys' stares. Justin Timberlake music boomed out of rusty Oldsmobile sedan. A blond-haired boy in baggy swim trunks was shouting the lyrics of "Can't Stop the Feeling" and thrusting his hands up and jumping. A well-tanned college girl in a bright blue bikini and sporting a shiny silver belly-button ring passed in front of the van holding up her hand signaling Wash to stop. She moved on after giving Wash a warm smile. "Ahyahyayi," Morg Miller moaned as he dramatically bit down on the heel of his hand. The music and the tan beach bodies blurred past as the Wash drove slowly down the park drive. The boys drank it all in.

"Find a place to park, Wash. Let's get out!" Randy said loudly.

Wash pulled into a spot just vacated by a jacked-up pickup flying a Confederate flag on a pole. Five young men stood in the back of the truck. Lynard Skynard music boomed from the cab. The van came to a stop at the curb. In front of the van, golden sand spread up and down the beach and stretched to the water line. Several hundred people were visible, but the beach didn't seem crowded because of its large expanse. Most groups of people were close to the water about a hundred yards from the parked cars. The lake was a deep blue and the whitecaps of crashing waves sprayed water into the air. No clouds were visible and the sun was high in the sky. The water was dotted with the bodies of swimmers. Little kids played at the water line, several large sandcastles had been built. A stiff breeze accounted for the size of the waves and the seemingly low number of bathers in the water.

Rich Lamb called out, "The waves are up, man! We can body surf!" The boys started to pass bags around the van and dig for buried bathing suits. Their shirts came off quickly and then they struggled to pull off their shorts and pull on their bathing trunks. A sensible person would have grabbed a bag and walked up the beach to the low block building that served as a changing room and concession stand. These boys were not sensible – they were anxious to hit the beach and test the waves.

The boys seemed to pop out of the van in unison. Towels in hand, they walked barefoot onto the sand. The heat was intense, and Morg Miller danced and exclaimed, "Shit!" The sand's on fire!" One of the boys called out "Aaiieh!" The footrace to the water was on. Halfway down to the water, Greg DeVito stumbled and summersaulted back up to his feet without missing a beat.

Seth Parker called out, "Damn it! I forgot the ball!" He turned and sprinted back to the van.

The boys were standing knee-deep in the white-water cascading in the shallows near the beach when Seth came running in. He flipped the football to Wash who caught it and dove into a tumbling wave.

"Wow, Dial-a-Pain, the Miracle Healer showed up and touched your ankle, huh?" Miller shouted to be heard above the roar of the surf.

"Yeah, Dial-a-Pain, it looks like you had another quick recovery from near death," added Rich Lamb. "It wasn't even ten hours ago you limped off the bus like a cripple."

"Blow me!" Seth yelled back as he grabbed his crotch. Wash Dryer threw the football back to the beach and smiled when it rolled right to his towel. Everyone faced the on-coming waves and they began to walk into deeper water. The waves lifted them and the undertow sucked at their legs so each step was getting harder. The first sandbar was twenty yards away, and the boys struggled into the shallow water on top of it. Morg Miller lagged behind and reached the sandbar just as a five-foot wave blasted into him. The force caught him off guard, and he bounced and rolled for fifteen feet before he came to his feet cursing. Everyone was howling with laughter when another large wave broke and knocked them all off the sand bad.

Rich Lamb hollered as he came up on to the sandbar again. "Let's surf!"

Body surfing is not like board surfing. The waves on the Great Lakes don't surge and roll in like ocean waves do. They crash into the sandbar and smash to pieces in a whitewater torrent. Rich Lamb's dad had a picture on his office wall of the Ludington lighthouse that showed a wave cresting over the breakwall with its spray arching fifty feet up and over the light. The wind this day was nothing approaching the violence of the storm that produced that monster, but waves like this were dangerous enough. Lake Michigan was well known for swallowing up unsuspecting novice swimmers who didn't know enough to stay away on days like this. The undertow was fierce, and a rip current could quickly take even strong swimmers out to deep water and drown them. The boys cared nothing of this, they were all accomplished swimmers. Most young men who were born and raised in Michigan bragged to all of their swimming endurance.

Rich Lamb had spent many days in the big lake and he loved to body surf. He turned his back to the next wave and dove forward on its crest. He zipped past the boys in the splashing white water and popped to his feet fifteen yards away. Wash Dryer had never swum in the lake when it was this violent, but after watching Rich grab another wave, he made his first attempt. As usual with any athletic move, Wash was a natural, and he too zipped past his friends, bobbing up after a run just short of what Rich had made.

The rush was on as the rest of the boys took position and timed their dives. Greg and Seth made feeble first attempts and caught rides of only a few yards. Jorge and Randy dove too late and slid out the back of their wave. Morg Miller mistimed his dive and dove too deep in front of a large wave. Morg's head struck the sandy bottom hard, and as his feet arched up over his ass, the curl of the wave slammed him even harder to the bottom. A garbled "Fuck!" was heard by Greg and Seth as Morg bounced past them in the white water. The wave deposited him just off the sandbar where Rich and Wash lifted him up by his armpits. Morg looked stunned. Again he shouted, "Fuck!" Then he let out a war whoop and dove shoulder-first into the next breaking wave. It went on like this for well over an hour.

Back on the beach, the boys toweled off and dropped to the sand. It was past mid-afternoon now, and some of the families with young kids were packing up their stuff and heading to the parking area. Wash watched as a young father walked past with a load of beach toys in one arm and a drowsy dark-haired toddler girl draped over his shoulder in the other. Wash thought of Maggie and how much she loved the beach the summer they visited here before her death. Wash smiled.

Greg DeVito spoke. "What a work out, man. Those waves kicked my ass way harder than gasser runs at practice."

"Yeah. I wish it wasn't such a long drive over here. I'd come every day," Randy Jansen added.

Morg Miller stood on his right foot shaking his left leg and tilting and bobbing his head to the right. He stopped for a second and spoke. "I got water in my ear. It sounds like you guys are talking in a tunnel." He said it to no one in particular, then began his bizarre dance again.

"Don't be such a dork, Morg. There are girls all over looking at us like we're taking care of a short-bus rider," Seth Parker said as two high school girls in brightly colored bikinis walked the waterline nearby and snickered as they glanced at Morg's ridiculous display.

Morg stopped again and said, "Huh?"

"Never mind," Seth said as he watched the girls walk down the beach. "Christ, we might as well have brought Big Donnie Donnie," he continued with disgust.

"Anyone want to walk the breakwall to the lighthouse? There will be all kinds of tourist girls out there walking, and if you pay a couple bucks, you can climb the tower." Rich Lamb spoke from experience. He visited Ludington frequently with his parents and sisters. They stayed with an aunt who lived in town.

Morg, Greg and Randy all agreed to go. Wash, Seth and Jorge begged off and said they would rather lie out in the sand. The four walkers ambled south down the beach. Morg had pulled on a sleeveless Bears football T-shirt. The other three went shirtless. Once on the breakwall, Rich smiled and greeted the girls who walked past. Randy followed suit, but Morg was playing the dork again and saying embarrassing things to old couples as they walked along. Greg insisted on stopping to talk to fisherman who tended their poles and sat in camp chairs on the lower reaches of the two-tiered cement pier. It was almost an hour before they reached the lighthouse. The volunteer keepers were shutting and locking the porthole door when they approached.

"Looks like we missed the climb," Greg said.

"I'm too tired anyway." Morg replied as he sat heavily on the very end of the breakwall. The wind was dying down, but the waves were still slapping the wall with heavy force several feet below his dangling legs. The other three joined him.

Randy asked Rich, "Do people dive and swim here?"

Rich replied, "Yeah, but they're not supposed to, and especially not on a day like today because the waves would smash you to pieces on the rocks and the wall."

Randy followed up. "You ever swim here?"

Rich said, "Nah, but my dad used to. In high school he and a couple of friends dove in and tried to swim to the south breakwall." He motioned with his hand to the shorter light across the way.

Randy asked, "Tried?"

"Yep," said Rich matter-of-factly. "He and one buddy got half way and chickened out. My dad said it felt like the current from the Pere Marquette River was going to drag them to Wisconsin. He said that by the time they turned around, they were a couple hundred yards out in the lake."

"What about the third guy?" Randy continued.

"Well—" Rich said with amusement. "He made it across but didn't have the nerve to swim back. So he had to walk seven miles around the harbor to get back to town."

Morg Miller erupted in laughter. "Dumbass!"

The boys got up and started the trek back to the beach. They moved with more purpose on the return trip, and in twenty minutes they were back where they had left their companions. The towels and gear were still spread on the sand, but the other three boys were missing. A quick scan of the now less-populated beach led the travelers to a group of girls sitting on towels a hundred yards to the north on the beach in front of the concession stand. They spotted

Seth, Wash and Jorge sitting in the sand next to the girls. Even from this distance, they could tell the girls were enjoying the attention of the football players. Two of the bikini-clad teens were tipping their head back in laughter, but the sound wasn't carrying because of the noise of the waves.

Shortly after the boys took off for the lighthouse, Seth and Wash had decided they were hungry, and with Jorge in tow, they headed to the concession stand. On the way up the beach, they passed near a group of eight girls sitting on blankets and towels. One of the girls called out, "Where's your dancing friend?" That was all the opening the three boys needed, and soon enough, they were sitting in the sand next to the smiling and tanned girls.

Seth Parker recognized two of them as the girls who had snickered at Morg Miller's water ear dance. "Morgan and the other guys took a walk to see the lighthouse," he replied as the boys sat.

"He put on a nice routine – I can tell – I study dance," said the smiling blond who identified herself as Toni. She introduced the rest of the girls. There were two Katherines, a Sophie, a Stephie, a Jenny and a petite redhead with green eyes and a dazzling smile named Colleen. The star of the show was a tall brunette with a traffic-stopping body called Liz. Seth made the introductions for the boys and even gave the names of the missing four.

One of the Katherines asked, "So your dancing friend is Morgan?"

Jorge smiled and replied, "We call him Morg."

Seth piped in with, "He's a real window licker sometimes."

Liz the bombshell burst out in laughter, and Sophie asked with a puzzled expression, "What's a window licker?"

It was Wash's turn to charm the girls, and he informed them, "Seth thinks Morg should ride to school on a short bus with the special kids who lick the windows. Actually Morg is pretty smart, but he is a real goofball sometimes." Sophie led the girls with head-tipping laughter.

The chatter and laughter kicked in as the teens started making connections. The girls pretended to be impressed by the fact that the boys played football. The guys were impressed by the fact the girls were all from Chicago except for Liz who came from Indianapolis.

Wash asked, "What are all of you doing in Ludington?"

Toni answered, "We're Epworth brats." And she motioned to the large dune hill covered with trees north of the beach where large Victorian era cottages dotted the shore in a gated summer colony. "Our families all have houses up there. Very snooty place so we like to come down to G for fun." She used the local term for the park.

This time the boys were really impressed. Not only had they gotten a chance to put the moves on the best-looking girls on the beach, they were rich girls as well. Seth and Wash led the charge telling stories of the disaster scrimmage and the Great Water Horse Riot to great effect. The girls howled with genuine laughter at the description of Miles Kitteridge's broken nose, and they were suitably grossed out by the story of the exploding deer. Liz and Toni were the chatty leaders of the girls. Colleen spent most of the time looking deeply at Wash and laughed with particular force when he spoke. Jorge did not say much, but he smiled a great deal and laughed when the girls talked.

Finally Liz paused and asked Seth, "Jorge doesn't say much does he?"

Seth looked over to his friend who was apparently hanging on every word of Jenny's story of her older brother who played football at the University of Illinois. "He doesn't have to say much to get his point across, and for some reason girls like that." Seth replied with surprising insight.

"Hmm," replied Liz. "It is nice to meet a boy who knows how to listen."

Seth knew the Martinez Magic was in play. Jorge was tall, good-looking and he had powerful muscles. His dark eyes twinkled just the right amount when he focused on a girl, and he used his small little smiles to great effect. Other than Wash, Jorge was the smartest boy on the football team. Jorge was quiet by nature but not shy. He had a real physical presence and a confident way of speaking directly to the point. When people met him, they assumed Jorge was older than his actual age of eighteen. Most important, Jorge learned early that applied and attentive silence could win over girls.

The legend of Jorge Martinez's prowess with girls had been etched in stone the previous spring. Jorge and Wash were taking AP English together. It was a tough class, but as usual Wash Dryer was acing everything. They had a major research paper to do, and when they couldn't find all the resources they needed, the librarian at BRHS suggested that they make the short trip to Central Michigan University and use the library there.

The next Thursday evening, Wash and Jorge made the trip to CMU. As they pulled off the freeway, they saw the sign that read "Mt. Pleasant Home of Central Michigan University."

"Ahhh, Mt. Pleasant – which is neither a mountain nor pleasant." Wash made the standard joke about the town that was the largest in the area.

"Dismal flats," answered Jorge, "where good times go to die."

Wash snorted an appreciative laugh. Contrary to what Jorge had just said, CMU was known as a party school. Most CMU students started their weekends and partying on Thursday nights. High school students in the surrounding towns knew this and would flock into Mt. Pleasant looking for easy access to beer and a possible hook up with the opposite sex. The high school boys usually struck out. The girls had a much higher success rate. Wash and Jorge knew that the library would be quiet on Thursday evening, and to ensure further blending in, they both wore old CMU T-shirts that nearly all local high school kids had in their wardrobes.

Jorge and Wash made their way into the library after Wash found a good parking spot. They were able to find a table on one of the upper floors that was nearly empty. Jorge set about looking for his needed information and Wash went to another section in search of his materials. Jorge got back to the table first and noticed a young coed had set herself up at an adjacent table. He exchanged smiles with her and sat down to work. Just glancing at the girl, Jorge made note of the faded CMU sweatshirt she was wearing which did not do an adequate job covering up the fact that she possessed a hot body. She was also very tanned, which was to be expected for a girl just back from spring break.

Wash returned shortly and he gave Jorge an appreciative nod toward the coed. Jorge raised his eyebrow with a smile and a quick return nod. About a half hour later, the coed let out a groan and slapped her pen down on the table. Jorge didn't miss a beat and leaned back in his chair and caught her eye. "Rough going?" Jorge asked with his typical quiet confidence.

The girl responded, "I'm so behind. I blew off everything during break, and now I don't think I'll ever catch up."

Jorge asked, "Where'd you go on break?" The girl was grateful for the respite from her studies, and she launched into an animated description of where she and her friends had gone in Florida the week before. Jorge swung his chair around and fixed his pleasant gaze on her as she talked on and on. Jorge smiled and nodded a great deal and occasionally gave a good but restrained laugh as the girl described the typical drunken mayhem of college students on spring break. Wash didn't look up but he smiled as his friend weaved his magic.

After twenty minutes of eavesdropping on Jorge's quiet maneuvers, Wash gathered up his materials and announced that he had to go downstairs for assistance from one of the librarians. Jorge shifted his gaze to Wash and smiled and gave him a nod. "I'll catch you before you leave," Jorge said and shifted his focus back to the rapidly talking coed.

Almost forty-five minutes after Wash went down to the first floor of the library, he received a text from Jorge.

JMart: I'll get a ride home later

WashDryer: OK Good luck.

The next morning, Jorge called a cousin who lived on campus at CMU to come to the apartment complex east of town and pick him up. The cousin was happy to oblige. She and Jorge had been close since childhood as all the kids were in the large extended Martinez clan. Jorge arrived at the high school during lunch. As he sat down in the cafeteria Wash asked, "How'd it go?"

"Good." Jorge replied without going any further.

Seth Parker sat at the table as well. "Didn't you guys go up to Mt. Pile last night?" he asked, using yet another nickname for the town.

"Yeah," said Wash.

"He didn't come home with you?" Seth asked as he nodded in Jorge's direction.

"My cousin gave me a ride this morning." Jorge cut in before Wash had to commit to answer.

"Ooooh," said Seth with a knowing smile. "You got some college chick action didn't you?"

Jorge gave a non-committed glance at Seth, but the twinkle in his eye was all Seth needed to yell, "Score!"

Wash changed the subject, but before lunch was over Seth told Morg Miller that Jorge had broken through at CMU. Morg went on a campaign of informing everyone he knew about the hook-up. By the start of baseball practice that afternoon, the rumor had gained school-wide headline status, and some of the underclassmen were talking about how Jorge Martinez had made it with three drunken college girls the night before.

For his part, Jorge never responded to inquiries, so the legend grew on its own. People believe what they want to believe. Jorge knew he couldn't control that. The coed, whose name was Marcy, texted Jorge periodically for the remaining weeks of the CMU school year. They met a few more times. Jorge kept his discussion about himself vague and never let on he was a high school junior. Marcy knew what she wanted out of the relationship and she got it. She had a regular boyfriend who was on an exchange program at Cambridge in England.

Marcy Nelson kept Jorge under wraps from her nosy roommates who only caught glimpses of her dark-haired lover. Once near the end of the semester, Jorge did actually meet and talk to Marcy's roommates who had returned from the bar to the apartment early, both drunk and loud. Fortunately, they did not arrive even earlier, or it would have been very awkward instead of just amusingly so. As it was, Marcy was embarrassed and a little pissed off when her roommates drunkenly teased her about cheating on her boyfriend in front of Jorge.

Jorge enjoyed the ride, but when summer came, Marcy went home downstate. Marcy was student teaching near Detroit in the fall, which happened to be where her soon-to-be returning boyfriend lived, so she stopped texting Jorge in June. Jorge had the sense not to pursue it further.

On the beach in Ludington, the four lighthouse visitors found their companions engaged with girls. As they walked up to the group, the people sitting on the sand shifted their attention to them.

"Hiya, Morg!" Liz the bombshell called out and everyone laughed. The four boys new to the party laughed along in a puzzled sort of way. Morg was thrilled that apparently he was the focus of the discussion while they were absent.

"Hi, back at you!" Morg answered.

Sophie asked loudly, "Is it true you lick windows?" More laughter followed. For a practiced clown like Morg, even potentially negative attention is good attention. He glanced at the laughing Seth Parker and he knew immediately how to play the situation. Morg tipped his head down to his left shoulder and tried to bite at it while thumping his right wrist and limp hand into his chest. This was accompanied with Morg emphatically grunting, "Nyah nyah nyah!" Howls of laughter burst from the girls. Morg was very pleased with himself.

A few minutes passed, and the girls started gathering their things. It was after 6 P.M.

Seth asked, "Where are you going to be tomorrow, right here?"

"No," Toni replied. "We're going to go out on Liz's boat if the waves aren't too high." She explained that Liz's father had a large power boat he kept in the marina in the harbor.

Wash said, "We're going to go tubing on the Pere Marquette tomorrow."

Seth added hopefully, "Maybe we can meet up tomorrow evening."

Liz jumped into the conversation, "Yeah, we were thinking about having a beach party at the First Curve and watch the sunset." She smiled at Jorge as she spoke and he returned her smile.

One of the Katherines mumbled to Toni, "We're having a beach party tomorrow night?"

Toni mumbled back, "Go with it – Liz wants something."

Rich proudly announced, "I know where the First Curve is. It's on the road to the state park."

Toni added, "Sure, but we will actually be just south of the curve in the dunes north of Epworth. You can't have a fire on the state park beach but sometimes we have one in the Epworth dunes."

Seth inquired, "What time should we be there?"

Liz replied, "About 7:30, BYOB." Again she glanced with intent toward Jorge.

Morg came in with an enthusiastic, "We'll be there!"

The two groups separated as the girls headed north up the beach and the boys went south. As the girls walked, the little red-head Colleen declared, "OMG, Wash is a babe." Her companions laughed. Liz added with confidence, "I'm gonna score me some Jorge." This time the girls all screamed with carnal laughter.

The boys were not quite out of earshot and Jorge was trailing slightly behind with Wash at his side. He looked over his shoulder. He had a sixth sense that he was being discussed by the laughing girls. As he looked, he caught the eye of Liz thirty yards away. She smiled a bright and knowing smile. Wash didn't look back. He quietly said, "Liz?"

Jorge played it cool with a noncommittal "Mmm."

Wash shook his head and said, "You're a machine."

As the boys approached their van, Rich pointed out to the lake and said, "The Badger's coming in." Everyone shifted their gaze to the big lake. A large car-ferry was approaching the lighthouse. "Let's go watch her come down the channel." The boys leapt into the van, and Rich gave instructions to Wash on how to get to the channel. The boys got out of the van in a parking lot near the municipal marina as the S.S. Badger entered the entrance of the harbor. They watched as the giant ship glided past, heading for her berth in the lake formed by the Pere Marquette River. Morg was jumping up and down and waving at the passengers at the ship's rail yelling "Aloha!" After the Badger sounded its ship's horn with a mighty blast, the boys climbed back in the van.

Morg Miller yelled "Pizza!" Wash negotiated the back streets along the marina to a downtown Italian restaurant. When the boys sat down, their mouths were watering in anticipation of the feast. They wrecked six large pizzas with a ferocity that would have impressed a pack of hyenas.

After their meal, the lethargic boys agreed it was time to get out to Seth's grandfather's cottage. Wash followed Seth's instructions and they found their way to Hamlin Lake. The boys piled out of the van on a hill overlooking the lake eight miles north of Ludington. The boys unloaded the van and started shouting claims to the beds and couches in the musty-smelling two-bedroom log cottage. After the claims were sorted out, they went to the yard and surveyed their surroundings. Across the lake, the Nordhouse sand dunes rose above the water. The pinkish sand dunes were picking up the magenta hues of the sun hanging low on the horizon. A few lazy clouds were floating in off of Lake Michigan to the west.

"Those dunes are cool." Randy noted to Seth.

Seth nodded and said, "When I was a kid, we came over here and a friend of my grandpa took us over there with his pontoon boat. There are usually a lot of boats rafted up over there on the weekend. It's a big party. I ran up and down the dunes and swam until I was all pruned up."

"Can we get over there? Maybe we could go on Sunday before we head back." Randy said hopefully.

Seth shook his head and pointed to an old-looking aluminum fishing boat on saw horses next to a leaning one-car garage. "I don't think that thing would hold us all. The putt putt motor in the garage might not even run – my grandpa hasn't been here in two years since dad put him in the VA home in Grand Rapids. Dad says soon as grandpa is gone, his sisters are going to insist on selling this place and pocketing the money. Besides it's s'posed to rain on Sunday."

"Too bad." Randy answered.

Fatigue was catching up with the boys. With bellies full of pizza, the long road trip and the effects of the workout in the waves, their tanks were on E. As the sun set, they made their way into the cottage. Within minutes, the first snores were echoing in the dimly lit cottage. Morg Miller was snoring with gusto on the couch in the living room across from the smoke-stained fieldstone fireplace. In the back bedroom, Wash finished texting his father. He plugged in his phone and stretched and yawned, lying on the bed. He could hear snoring coming from most of the rest of the house. The ragged snorts emanating from the living room were the most obnoxious noises he had ever heard coming from a human being. The racket was too much to take, and Wash emerged from a back bedroom holding a football. With considerable force and typical accuracy, Wash pegged Morg with a throw that hit the pudgy boy in the chest. Morg grunted and rolled over. Wash smiled at the silence. The snores began again in five minutes. Exhausted, Wash buried his head in the smelly feather pillows on his lumpy single bed. Moments later he was beyond caring.

**Overtime**

Wash texted his dad from the back bedroom of the cottage overlooking Hamlin Lake. His dad received the text sitting at a desk in a field office trailer in Montana.

WashDryer: Knock Knock

GregDryer: Who's there

WashDryer: Carrie

GregDryer: Carrie who

WashDryer: Carrie me home. I'm tired

GregDryer: Nice. Fun day?

WashDryer: The best. Spent all day in the lake. Learned to body surf.

GregDryer: Did you call mom?

WashDryer: Just got off the phone. She spent all day shopping. She is beat. Better call her before she goes to bed.

GregDryer: I will. Good Night Kid

WashDryer: Good nigzzzzz

Greg Dryer smiled as he dialed his wife's cell. They spent most of the conversation agreeing on what a great son they had.

# CHAPTER FOUR

## MAKING BAD DECISIONS

By eight o'clock the next morning, all the boys were up and regretting they hadn't planned ahead for breakfast. After collecting various snacks they had brought to the cabin, they made do with a meal of Chips Ahoy, beef jerky, Doritos, Power-Bars and Mountain Dew. They were tossing a football around in the yard in short order, and Greg DeVito found fishing gear in the garage and made his way down the hill to the lake. The cottage did not have lake frontage, only a view. Greg sat on someone's private dock until a middle-aged woman asked him to leave. Disgusted, Greg hiked back up the hill to where the boys were laying out their plans for the day.

"We have to be at the canoe place in Scottville at 11:00, but we need to stop at a store to stock up for the float," Seth said in his role of quarterback and cruise director.

"We gonna take some beer?" asked Rich.

"Nah," Seth answered. "We only got a case left. Let's save it for tonight at the beach party. Liz said BYOB, and I don't know where we can get someone to buy us more."

Morg Miller was busy cramming the last of the Doritos into his mouth. "That sucks!" He sprayed little orange bits from his mouth as he protested.

The seven football players pulled on swimming trunks and T-shirts. Rich Lamb was pulling on a ratty-looking pair of canvas deck shoes. "Put on river shoes, guys. The stones and sticks will tear your feet up." They were heading to the van when he saw that Morg was barefoot and Randy was wearing flip flops. "You have to have shoes. Randy, those flip flops will disappear in the mud."

Randy shrugged. "It's all I got besides my court shoes, and they're leather."

Morg protested, "I just bought my sandals. I ain't gonna ruin them."

Seth said, "just a second." He returned from the cabin moments later carrying a pair of carpet slippers and a pair of ancient-looking white Chuck Taylor high tops with rusty eyelets and black shoestrings. They were his grandpa's, and like all men in the Parker family, he had long feet. Seth threw the shoes to Morg and the slippers to Randy. Morg shrugged and sat on the ground where he pulled the shoes on over his bare feet. When he stood, the others laughed because the shoes were at least four sizes too big.

Randy examined the slippers, and then he flung them onto the cottage porch. "Pass," was all he said.

Seth answered, "Whatever, dude."

The boys stopped at a grocery store to load up on supplies, and they made the canoe livery with moments to spare. Less than an hour later, they were floating in bright yellow tubes on the Pere Marquette River east of Custer. The float back down to Scottville should have taken just short of five hours. It took the boys almost six. Morg got caught in every fallen tree in the river. Randy lost his flip flops in the first hour. The food and Gatorade were gone by three.

During hour four, Greg and Randy started singing country songs and harmonizing very badly. By the third time they sang "She Thinks My Tractor's Sexy", Jorge had had enough. He floated up to the erstwhile country stars and quietly informed them, "You sing that fucking tractor song one more fucking time and I'll break your fucking necks and leave your fucking bodies in the fucking river." That was about as long a sentence Jorge had uttered the whole day, and, since it contained five emphatic fucks, Greg and Randy switched to classic rock.

They'd had high hopes that they would run into some girls floating on the river. The boys saw three different groups of tubers made up of people in their thirties – mostly drunken rednecks who refused to share their beer when Morg begged them for some. They saw several canoeists who glided past without even acknowledging them. They came across a middle-school-age church youth group floating in old tractor tubes during hour five. In celebration of meeting them, Morg began to loudly yell out filthy limericks. When he got through a rousing rendition of "There once was a man from Nantucket," the youth group leaders pulled their kids from the river and let the football players float well downstream before reentering.

By 6 P.M., the boys climbed back into their van. Morg's ridiculous oversized sneakers oozed river slime from every eyelet. Soggy, muddy, and mosquito-bitten, the football players looked a sorry lot. Everyone but Jorge and Wash, who had sense enough to don sun screen and broad canvas Tilley hats for the trip, was sunburned. Jorge's bronze body showed no effects of sun exposure at all. They stopped at the McDonalds in Ludington for a quick burger and then trekked to the cabin for showers and fresh clothes for the beach party. The boys reeked of body spray when they piled in the van. Wash opened a window and complained of their stench.

At 7:45, the boys pulled up to the First Curve on M-116 at the Ludington State Park. They scanned the beach and saw no one, but Rich informed them they would have to walk south in the dunes toward Epworth. Lugging their beer and pop in an old Styrofoam cooler they found in the garage at the cottage, the boys set forth.

They heard the party before they saw it. They crested a dune and saw thirty or more young people in a depression in the dunes known as a blowout. The blowout had three steep sandy sides and was open to the lake at the water line. A driftwood bonfire was burning. Towels, blankets and coolers were spread across the bottom of the blowout. Rap music was playing loudly from a large boombox hooked up to an iPod. Liz and Toni waved and the boys made a beeline for them.

"Who are all these people?" Seth asked Toni.

"About half are Epworth brats. The rest are townies. They were already here when we got to the beach. This is our favorite spot, so we are sharing it with them. It's cool – we know most of them," Toni answered. She was drinking a wine cooler and she offered Seth one. Seth turned slightly green when he remembered the Prom night barf-fest and informed her he preferred beer.

The Bear football players started to mingle with the diverse group. Liz sought out Jorge and took his hand. "Let's walk up the beach." She said it confident that he would accept the invitation. He did, and in a moment they were walking south along the waterline. The waves were almost nonexistent and the wind was calm. A gentle lapping sound came from the low water ripples greeting the shore. The Epworth hill loomed above them. On the north side it was devoid of cottages and left in its natural tree-covered state.

"No waves today," Jorge observed.

"Perfect for skinny-dipping when the sun sets." Liz added with a smile.

Jorge was thinking of kissing her when she said, "But that's for after."

"After?" Jorge inquired.

Liz just smiled and led him over a low frontal dune to a secluded small shallow blowout. She stopped him in the middle of the little sand bowl and lifted his Bears football T-shirt over his head. They kissed as Liz lowered Jorge to the sand. In the distance the thump of rap music from the boom-box was the only sound that made it to their hideaway.

Some time passed.

Back at the party in the big blowout, the boys had started playing catch with two of the Epworth girls. They lobbed easy passes and the girls fired the football back at them, complaining that they threw like girls. Laughter met their protests. Colleen shadowed Wash's every move, cheerfully commenting on his throws. Other partiers tossed a Frisbee. Three local stoners played hacky sack with a couple of Epworth boys. A young man with shaggy hair and tattooed arms who looked to be in his early twenties sat on an old Army blanket with a chubby teenage girl. They wore matching Kiss T-shirts and cut-off jeans. They drank beer from green bottles. She held a long cigarette in the fingers of her left hand. He tried repeatedly to slip his hand under her shirt, but she kept pushing it away with a giggle. Rap music pounded from the boom-box near the bonfire. The sun would set in about fifteen minutes and the dunes cast long shadows. Smoke from the bonfire formed a haze in the windless air over the blowout.

Greg dove for a pass from Seth but missed the catch. The ball bounced once and struck the green beer bottle next to the dusky green Army blanket, spilling the contents across the U.S.A. imprint. The shaggy-haired man spun around as his girl cussed and slapped at the spreading beer, trying to stop its progress.

"Hey, you assholes! Watch it!" Shaggy Hair shouted at Greg who was picking himself up off of the sand.

Greg apologized.

Wash, sensing trouble, called to Greg, "Offer him one of your beers."

Shaggy Hair shot Wash an angry look. "Is it Heineken?"

Greg answered, "All we got is Bud Light."

Shaggy Hair snarled, "Fuck that horse piss." He then turned back to his girl who was now turning over the grungy blanket looking for a drier spot to sit on.

It was quiet for about two minutes. Morg was on the receiving end of one Wash's perfect spirals. He made a nice catch next to the blanket. In the process he kicked a little sand on it. This time Shaggy Hair was moved to get to his feet. As he rose someone on the opposite side of the blowout yelled, "Watch it!" as an errant Frisbee sailed in and struck Shaggy Hair in the face. He spilled his beer down his front. Purple rage came to his face.

"I told you fucking high school punks to watch it!" he screamed at Morg.

Morg flipped the football back to Wash. "That's not our Frisbee, dude."

"How about I shove the Frisbee and your little football up that fat faggot ass of yours?" Shaggy hair yelled at Morg.

The usual comedic smile faded from Morg's face and his eyes narrowed. "Fuck you," Morg stated flatly.

Shaggy Hair paused and blinked. The switch blade appeared from nowhere in his right hand. Morg muttered, "Shit."

Wash stepped forward with his hands open. "Take it easy, dude."

Shaggy Hair flashed the knife toward him. "I'll cut you both!"

One of the Epworth girls screamed a warning. "He's got a knife!" A mad scramble ensued as the kids ran up the sides of the blowout. Someone kicked over the boom-box. The music stopped.

Shaggy Hair's girl yelled, "Terry, put the knife away!" He ignored her.

One of the townies yelled, "Terry, quit being an asshole!"

"Shut up, Bobby, This is between fat-faggot-school-boy and me!" Terry answered his critic without taking his eyes off Morg.

There is a time to speak up and there is a time to shut up. Morg was not in the mood to make the smart choice.

"Fuck you," Morg flatly repeated.

Terry snarled and stepped toward Morg. Wash moved into Terry's peripheral vision on his right as Morg stepped backwards toward the lake. Again Terry flashed his knife at Wash. "Back off pretty boy, or I'll slice your pretty face!" Terry hissed at Wash. Greg and Rich shadowed Wash a few steps behind. Seth stood further down the beach. His face was white with terror. Randy had backed up the blowout slope and stood alone. Townies were spread out to his left.

Again Morg uttered his curse at the knife-wielding townie.

Terry took two steps forward. Morg took three steps back. They were getting near the water.

Morg's heels were wet when he mouthed more than spoke his last, "Fuck you."

Two things happened almost simultaneously. The townie named Bobby yelled, "Terry! On your left!" At the same time, Wash made a strong feint on Terry's right. The synchronicity of the two sensory inputs froze Terry for an instant. Then the shaggy-haired townie's world exploded.

When the soft thump of the boom-box ended, Jorge was lying naked next to Liz in the shallow bowl of their private little dune blowout. She was naked as well. She was on her left side kissing his neck and sliding her right hand down his abs. She moved with slow deliberation. Jorge thought he heard a scream and he sat up quickly.

"What is it?" Liz asked, alarmed.

"Something's up." Jorge stated as he grabbed his shorts. He was sprinting up the north face of the little blowout as Liz called out for him to wait. He pulled on his shirt at the crest of the little dune. He waved at her to stay put. Jorge then bolted on a straight line toward the larger blowout. He topped the high south face of the big blowout and paused.

Toni, the Epworth ring leader, was on his right. She pointed wordlessly to where Morg stood with his heels near the water's edge. The sun was touching the broad lake horizon. The golden yellow light was tinged with pink on the horizon. The water of the lake had taken on a glass-like sheen near the setting sun. The magical golden west Michigan sunset was at hand. Jorge caught sight of the flash of metal in the hand of the shaggy haired man facing Morg. He started his run down the dune. He moved silently but hoped that Wash could see him coming. Jorge counted on the fact that most everyone else would be focused on the confrontation at the water's edge and that no one would sound the alarm. He was gaining speed as he came off of the dune to the flat of the beach. A split second before impact, he heard the warning yell and saw Wash take a forceful step as he lowered his left shoulder.

Jorge hit the shaggy-haired townie with a perfect crack back block. The townie grunted as he flew through the air, dropping his knife on the beach to

Wash's right. He landed with a splash in the shallow water to Morg's left. The scene froze for a second. Wash swept the knife up with his right hand and he closed the blade.

Terry, the shaggy-haired townie, came to his feet sputtering and cursing. As he approached the dry sand, Wash hurled the knife far into the lake. Terry pivoted and watched the knife splash silently seventy-five yards out. The sun was a half circle on the shining glass of the flat lake.

Terry cursed, "You fuck – that knife cost me $200 in Mexico!"

Wash looked him in the eye, nodded toward the dipping sun and said, "Swim for it."

The sopping wet Terry made a move across the sand toward him. Wash squared his stance and Jorge came to his side. Something flashed in front of them. It was Morg.

In movies and on television, you frequently see a man being kicked in the testicles only to bounce back up after a few yelps of pain. In reality, the blow is usually much more devastating. In a lifetime of cheap low blows delivered for maximum effect, Morg Miller had never timed or aimed a kick better. Morg spun and kicked Terry the Townie squarely in the delicate package between his legs. Morg put his full force with his right foot up and through his target. The air in Terry's lungs left with a loud huff. He collapsed with a squeaking noise escaping his lips. He began to grunt and vomit beer foam on the sand.

Morg looked down at his prone victim. "Fuck you," Morg said firmly. Jorge reached out and grabbed him by the shoulder.

"He's done, Morg," Jorge said as a congratulation and as a call to end the attack.

"Terry!" screamed his chubby girlfriend as she dove to his side in the sand and tried to comfort him. The townie boys and a few of their girls crowded down to the water's edge. The Epworth brats were beating feet for their gated haven. Jorge caught a glimpse of Toni and Liz on the south crest of the blowout. He saw only their silhouettes. The sun had set and light was fading fast on the beach despite the glowing sky in the west.

The girl on the sand looked up and screeched, "Who invited you fuckers anyway?" Terry was dry-heaving next to her and gasping for air. The townie known as Bobby moved up in the gathering darkness.

"That's a good question. Who invited you assholes?" He asked menacingly. A chorus of male voices echoed with calls of "Yeah."

The Bear River boys were now gathered together at the water's edge as well. Jorge's first instinct was to make a stand. Wash quickly processed the numbers arrayed against the Bear River seven, and he calculated the odds that one or more of the players would get seriously hurt in the coming fight. "Move!" he called as he spun and began to run north on the beach. The other six followed in tight formation. Morg was laughing for some odd reason. He pulled even with Wash. Jorge came up on the opposite shoulder. They could hear calls of "get them!" from behind. All seven increased to full sprint speed.

Superior conditioning and a massive adrenaline rush ensured the football players could not be caught. The townies gave up after a few dozen yards.

In what seemed like only a minute, the boys were back at the van. Wash fished the keys from his pocket.

Randy Jansen turned and looked down the darkening beach to the south. "Are they coming?" he asked.

"No," Jorge answered without looking.

"Ah shit!" exclaimed Morg as he climbed into the van.

Greg asked, "What!?"

"The beer!" Morg replied.

"Skip it," Wash said as he slammed the van into gear and hit the gas.

As they approached the north city limits of Ludington, the nervous laughter had faded and it was replaced by teen bravado. His mates slapped Morg's back hard in congratulation.

Morg was shaking off the nervous adrenalin rush, but he had enough beer in his system to trigger the hunger that young drinkers often get so he yelled, "Taco Bell!"

A half hour later, the boys sat in the van in the parking lot of the local fast food Mexican eatery. They grunted pleasure as they mowed through thirty dollars' worth of Taco Bell cuisine. The van stunk of refried beans and greasy cheese. The papers and bags the food came in littered the seats and the floor.

Randy asked, "What now?"

Wash took control. "I don't think it is good idea to hang around town." He said, "Maybe we ought to go out to the cottage." Everyone agreed that was advisable.

Morg complained bitterly. "We don't have any beer."

Seth Parker chimed in. "Grandpa probably has some stuff stashed in the cupboards."

The van was parked in front of the cottage twenty minutes later, and everyone rushed to the kitchen but Wash and Jorge. Seth found his grandpa's liquor in a cupboard above the fridge. They took inventory of the stash. There was a pint bottle of something called "Wild Irish Rose" wine. There was a fifth of sloe gin with twenty years of accumulated dust on the bottle. Seth said, "Wait a minute," and he dashed to the front bedroom. He emerged moments later with a bottle in a purple velvet bag, and he slipped out a fifth of Crown Royal whiskey that had about two inches of liquid in the bottom. "This is Grandpa's sipping whiskey but I don't think he is going to ever be here again so—" The boys all ooohed and ahhhed over his find. They decided to start with the Crown Royal.

Morg grabbed the bottle and unscrewed the top. "To Grandpa!" he toasted. He took a short pull from the bottle and passed it to Seth. Seth took his turn after toasting his Grandpa who was dying of Alzheimer's in the VA home. Greg, Randy and Rich repeated the toast and took a swig. The bottle made one more trip around the room, and it was empty.

43

Next, the cap was taken off the Wild Irish Rose. Randy Jansen took a small sip. "Nasty," Randy declared. Only Greg thought the wine was palatable. He sat in the living room next to Wash and Jorge who were watching the goings-on with rueful smiles. Greg sipped the wine and smacked his lips.

Seth cracked the seal on the sloe gin and took an appreciative whiff of the contents.

"You gottta mix that," Rich said knowingly.

Morg said, "Mountain Dew!"

Rich made a grimace. "Uh-uh. I've got a two-liter of Sprite. It's warm, but it'll do."

Seth found green and yellow glass tumblers in the kitchen. The boys sat at the table. Seth poured two inches of the bright red syrupy sloe gin into each glass and Rich topped them off with Sprite. Morg took a drink, and with a smile said, "Mmm – Red Pop." The boys started aggressively gulping the contents of their tumblers.

Across the main room of the cottage, Jorge looked at Wash and then to the four sitting at the table.

"This won't end well," he said calmly.

Wash nodded. "Yep."

Greg gave a small snicker while sipping his cheap wine. "They'll be okay. We aren't going anywhere."

"Good thing," replied Wash.

Randy said, "Let's play Euchre!" Seth found cards and the first hand was dealt at the same time a second round of drinks was poured. After a game or two, the boys were noticeably drunk. The volume of their discussion was climbing, and the coherence of their statements was dropping. The Sprite ran out after the third round of drinks. The boys at the table took to sipping the slow gin from the bottle.

Amateur teenage drinkers who are used to guzzling beer getting access to hard liquor is not a good thing. Warm sloe gin and room-temperature pop is an even worse combination. The card game degenerated into nonsensical laughing and yelling. Fifty minutes after the first tumbler of the red fizzy concoctions were downed, Randy stood up and made a weaving stumble toward the bathroom in the hall. The noise of his explosive vomiting made the others laugh very hard. In two minutes, Seth made the same trip. When he found that Randy had monopolized the toilet, he threw up in the sink. The red mixture of his Taco Bell food and sloe gin splattered up on the mirror. Seth sunk to the floor groaning. Randy moaned while still hugging the toilet and retched again.

Rich was next. He stumbled to the bathroom and fell into the bathtub where he projectile vomited across the wall and shower curtain. Only Morg remained at the table. He sat the bottle down with a loud thump and looked across the room to the other three boys and with a nearly incoherent slur declared, "What a bunch of pussies!" Morg closed one eye. Three seconds later his head pitched forward to the table and then he slumped from his chair to the floor. In the process, he knocked over the nearly empty fifth bottle which rolled off the table and struck him on the head. Morg grunted and with a cough he vomited up a pool of red foaming liquid and mostly digested refried beans that spread across the green linoleum kitchen floor.

"We better help them," Wash said without emotion.

As Wash and Jorge moved to the kitchen to aid Morg, Greg stood for a moment and then walked out the front door of the cottage. As Wash was picking up Morg, he could hear Greg puking with loud sputters in the front yard. Jorge went to the bathroom, surveyed the mess and his pale sick friends and turned around.

"The john is a horror movie," he announced to Wash who was depositing Morg on the couch in the living room.

"Get them outta there and bring them in here. We don't want to put them in the bedrooms. They'll puke on everything," answered Wash.

Jorge picked Rich up out of the bathtub. Rich was out cold. Barf covered his shirt, so Jorge pulled it off. Seth crawled out of the bathroom crying and apologizing between sobs to his absent grandpa. Wash helped Seth to his feet and then laid him down on the brown shag carpet of the living room. Jorge propped up Rich in the vinyl recliner and extended the foot rest. Rich's head lolled to the side. Red spittle was drying on his face. Wash and Jorge returned to the hall bathroom and pried Randy loose from his death grip on the toilet. Randy groaned and hiccupped over and over again as they laid him out the floor next Seth. Randy rolled over and hugged Seth. The prone quarterback mumbled, "Not now" and turned away from Randy but did not have the energy to push himself away from the embrace.

Greg returned from his private barf fest in the front yard. He was pale and disheveled. He looked down at the two boys cuddled together and then looked up at Jorge and Wash with a smile and said, "They're cute." Greg sat with a grunt in the floral-patterned rocker near the door.

Wash announced, "I gotta piss."

Jorge pointed down the hall. "Not in there," he stated with gravity.

The two boys went to the front yard to relieve themselves. The wind was blowing and no stars could be seen in the sky. As they stood doing their business, Wash said, "Wind's pickin up."

"Gonna storm," Jorge answered. They made their way back in to the cottage. Jorge found blankets to cover their passed-out friends. Wash turned out the lights, and he and Jorge went to separate bedrooms. They fell asleep knowing the morning would not be a kind one.

Sometime around 5 A.M. Morg awoke to the sound of rain pelting the windows and roof. He was still drunk. The dark room spun as he made his way to the even darker bathroom. He dropped his shorts and sat on what he assumed was the toilet. It was the edge of the tub. Morg shit a wet mess into the bottom of the bathtub and urinated across the congealed vomit on the floor. He staggered to his feet clutching at the towel bar. Morg grabbed Randy's beach towel and wiped himself. He dropped the towel in the sink and stumbled bare-assed back to the living room. Morg kicked Seth as he groped in the dark for the couch. Seth whined. Morg pitched face-first into the couch and passed out once again.

Rumbles of thunder and hard rain awoke Greg DeVito at 7 A.M. He groaned as he stood up from the rocker he had slept in. He proceeded to the front porch. He urinated off the porch into the downpour. Then Greg leaned his head under the gushing water flowing from the porch roof. The cool water felt good. Greg shivered and shook his head. He turned his head up to the torrent and took a mouthful. Greg gargled and spat. He massaged his head and rubbed his face under the cascading water for another minute. Greg pivoted and went back through the door. He took no notice of his prone buddies and he set about looking for a towel as he pulled off his wet shirt. When he turned on the light of the bathroom he yelled out, "Holy fuck!" Just then, a flash of lightning lit up the dim cottage and a massive thunder clap shook the building.

Wash and Jorge emerged from their respective bedrooms. Anguished moans came from the direction of the living room. Seth growled, "Dude! Get off me!" and he shoved Randy across the floor. Three of the gin drinkers stumbled into the hall.

"Who shit in the tub?" Greg asked with disgust.

Randy glanced into the foul-smelling bathroom. "My towel!" he exclaimed.

Seth looked in. "Aw, sick, man!" the quarterback declared.

The six boys walked into main room of the cottage. Wash turned on the lights. They were greeted with the vision of Morg's stark white ass shining up at them from the couch. He was still asleep despite the racket and the thunder claps. "Get up, asshole!" Seth called out. Randy threw an empty Mountain Dew can at Morg's head.

Morg sat up and said. "Shit!"

"Yeah, shit. As in, you shit in the bathtub," Greg said angrily.

"Where's my shorts?" asked a dejected Morg.

"Lying in your piss on the bathroom floor, asshole," Randy answered.

The hung-over boys groaned and winced when another close-at-hand thunder clap hit outside.

"Okay, listen up," Wash interrupted. The five pale partiers looked over to their friend who stood in the kitchen. Jorge leaned on the table to Wash's left. All five had bloodshot eyes. The gin drinkers had Kool-aid mustaches like preschoolers. Greg edged away from the other four. He could sense what was coming.

Wash began his soliloquy. "I will drive your drunk ass home. I will run interference with the cops for you. I will bail you out of jail if it comes to that.

I will even keep you from getting killed in a knife fight." Wash paused for effect as he looked at Morg deliberately. Morg took his gaze to the floor. "But I will not—" Wash continued, "Repeat Not! Clean up this mess! And I don't think Jorge is interested in that either."

Jorge shook his head and added, "Nope."

Wash continued. "Jorge and I are taking the van to town and getting some breakfast. Maybe we'll get some donuts and Red Bull for you douchebags. We'll be back in an hour or so, and then we are heading home. You better get this place cleaned or Seth's dad will kill him when he comes here next month to go hunting."

"Coffee!" Morg said with an apologetic grin.

Wash shook his head.

Greg piped up. "I didn't drink that red shit. That ain't my puke. Why do I have to clean it up?"

Jorge held up his hand to stop the protest. Greg stopped and glanced down.

Wash and Jorge found clean clothes and left without saying anything.

The mournful Bears who were left behind set about the grim task of cleaning the cottage after they located some Spic and Span and Windex under the sink. They forced Morg to clean the bathtub. None of them wanted anything to do with that. Randy Jansen kept calling Morg an asshole as he wrung out his beach towel in the kitchen sink. Mostly the boys were silent. The only sound for the next hour was thunder and lightning punctuated with their groans. The boys took turns in the shower after they succeeded in scouring the cottage clean.

Jorge and Wash took showers upon their return. The donuts were barely touched and all but one Red Bull sat unopened. Only Greg drank his as he wolfed down a couple of plain donuts.

Nothing much was said as they loaded the van. The rain had stopped, but thunder could still be heard in the distance. Wash started the van and Jorge took the front passenger seat. Randy didn't protest. Gray clouds hung low in the sky as they began the long drive home.

An hour later, Wash pulled the van into the gas station at the U.S. 131 freeway exit off U.S. 10 near Reed City. He fueled the van while the boys trudged over to the McDonald's. They returned with bags in hand. All except Seth, who claimed that Mickey D's didn't sound good to him. He went into the mini-mart and came out with a bottle of Diet Squirt and an ice cream bar. He called shot gun and Jorge opened the door for his quarterback. Everyone was inside. Seth turned to the boys in the back and sang, "What would you do for a Klondike Bar?" mimicking the commercial jingle. The boys laughed. The food and the cold Cokes were brightening their spirits. Even Jorge and Wash chuckled. Twenty minutes down the road Seth said, "Pull over, man."

Wash knew what that meant, and he looked for a cross-road to turn down. He didn't make it. Seth fumbled with the window crank and stuck his head out

47

the window. The vomit splattered down the side of the van. The outside of the windows on the passenger side were spackled with white glop containing flecks of chocolate. Greg said, "Nice." Morg laughed and called Seth a dumbass.

In another hour, the van returned to Bear River. Randy insisted that Wash pull into a car wash. The boys watched, laughing as Randy made Seth hose down the exterior of the van. Randy then took over the driving duties, and he dropped the boys at their homes. The last one out was Morg, who lived down road from Randy outside of town. Morg's squat mother stood on the porch of the old house at the crumbling farmstead. She did not look happy as Morg marched up the steps carrying his duffel. Randy turned on the radio. Country music blared from the speakers as he backed out of the long driveway. Minutes later he was singing at the top of his lungs as he pulled into the drive at his house. "She thinks my tractor's sexy—"

**Overtime**

Wash texted his father Sunday afternoon when he returned home from Ludington. Greg Dryer was at a picnic at the home of an oil company executive.

WashDryer: Knock Knock
GregDryer: Why didn't you text last night?
WashDryer: Knock Knock
GregDryer: Alright Who's there?
WashDryer: Chair.
GregDryer: Chair who?
WashDryer: Chair you go again asking too many questions.
GregDryer: what happened last night?
WashDryer: Phone Battery is dying. I'll tell you later.

Wash Dryer told himself that he would tell his dad the whole story of the road trip years later after he graduated from college. Greg Dryer would not be thrilled about the story of the knife fight even then. Wash knew he would never tell his mother of it.

Excerpt from The River County Register High School Gridiron Preview
BEAR RIVER HIGH SCHOOL
NICKNAME: Bears
LEAGUE: Mid-Peninsula C
HEAD COACH: John Cale 3rd year. Career record: 3 wins 15 losses.
Assistant Coaches: Mike Reese, Pat Packer, Keith Marker.
Schedule
Week one: Mecosta HS A
Week two: McBride HS H
Week three: Sumner HS H
Week four: North Star HS A
Week five: Perrinton HS A
Week six: Elwell HS A

Week seven: Elm Hall HS H
Week eight: Pompeii Central HS A
Week nine: Riverdale HS H

The Bears return a handful of starters from last year's 1 – 8 squad. Third-year coach John Cale has high praise for Senior Quarterback Seth Parker and returning all-league Linebacker Senior Jorge Martinez. The Bears will feature a pro-style offense and run a base 53 defense. The overall numbers at Bear River are low and if the injury bug hits the Bears this year as it has in the past, they will find it very tough going this season. The Bears open with non-league games at the always powerful Mecosta, and then McBride comes to Bear River for game two. That game is the Bears' best shot to put one into the win column. The Bears beat the Marauders last year for their only win. Starting with game three, the Bears finish out the year with seven straight league games. It is difficult to see how John Cale's gridiron squad can come up with enough manpower to be competitive in the league. The season is capped off with a grudge match game with Mid Pen C powerhouse and heated rival, Riverdale. The Bears and the Beavers go toe-to-toe in every other sport in the league and there is no love lost between the two schools. But this isn't wrestling, soccer or baseball – it's football. The Bears have not beaten the Beavers on the gridiron in twenty-three seasons. The streak will continue this year.

Predicted finish for the Bears: 0-9

# CHAPTER FIVE

## OWEN 1

Coaching is often a profession of quiet desperation. Coaches spend a great deal of time fretting about lineups and personnel decisions. It comes with the job. At a small high school with limited talent, you say a constant prayer during your quiet times as you stare at the ceiling in the middle of the night. That prayer is that injuries and other personnel-robbing problems such as academic eligibility and athletic code violations don't leave your roster cupboard totally bare. This prayer had mostly gone unanswered for every football coach at Bear River for a generation.

Friday afternoon after the disaster scrimmage the football coaches met in Coach Cale's classroom. They viewed films of the scrimmage. The JV scrimmage film was of poor quality. The parent volunteer who filmed it was not familiar with the camera functions and for the most part shot from too far away to be of use. The varsity film was of better quality. An ineligible player had filmed most of it. The quality of play looked even worse on film than what the coaches had observed with their own eyes.

"We can't block. It's worse than I can believe. Donnie is not capable of stopping the D end from blowing up any play we run outside. We have to find someone to play right tackle who understands our blocking scheme," John Cale said with fatalistic certainty.

"Donnie doesn't understand the scheme at all, John." Mike Reese stated the obvious. "GOON is the only hope because we just don't have another player to put at right tackle." Reese alluded to an acronym used to describe a blocking scheme used with novice middle school teams. G stands for Gap. If there is a defensive player in the gap number called – block him. O stands for On. If there is a D lineman lined up on you – block him. O stands for Over. If there is a linebacker lined up over you with no D lineman in front – block the linebacker. N stands for Near. If all else fails, block the defensive player nearest you.

"We're playing varsity ball, for God's sake. We have to be able to trap and run the Veer." Cale protested.

"Hell, John, Junior Shultz had a dozen bad snaps. We can't even start a play right, let alone get off the ball to make assignments. We had false starts every other play. And you can forget about second tier blocks – no one was making it to the linebackers. If Marcus doesn't get the ball he refuses to block. We'll be lucky to gain fifty yards on the ground against Mecosta the way they run stunt," Reese countered. "We either GOON or we never make a first down, let alone sustain a drive."

Cale switched topics. "Glenn Marcus killed us on defense too, Mike. We have to switch him to Will linebacker. All he does is look in the backfield and try to guess where the ball is. Most times he crashes in like every play is going to be a pass," Cale said as he looked at his notes on currently unavailable players.

"In a month, if we get Lenny Shore back in the lineup, that may happen, but until then we're stuck with your boy Glenn," replied Mike Reese.

Lenny Shore was born with a wrench in one hand and a blow torch in the other. His father was a local farmer who dealt late model Dodge and Chrysler parts from the farm. The farm that looked more like a junkyard than anything else. Lenny was scavenging parts at age six and rebuilding MOPAR engines at age twelve. Football and riding dirt bikes were the only activities that remotely held his interest outside of grease monkeying with his dad. Lenny was an aggressively ignorant student. He had failed two classes in the spring and would begin his senior football season on a four-game academic suspension.

On the football field, Lenny Shore was a country-strong thumper. When he was academically eligible, he played strong side (Sam) linebacker his junior year and was a nice complement to Jorge Martinez at Mike (Middle) linebacker. On offense, he played guard and tight end. In the classroom, he was a real challenge to motivate. The teaching staff at BRHS assumed that Lenny Shore would not have enough credits to graduate with his class next spring.

Lenny Shore learned to weld when he was eleven. He developed a little side business in middle school buying up bicycles at yard sales and customizing them in bizarre ways. He specialized in creating ridiculous-looking extended chopper bikes and improvised tandem bicycles. Five years ago, Coach Reese had watched Lenny ride down the Eleventh Street hill on one of his welded-up tandems. Lenny was in front and his obese older sister was on back. Near the bottom of the hill at a high rate of speed, the welds broke apart and Monica Shore slammed into the pavement. She slid for twenty feet in her shorts and tank top as Lenny skittered away in a shower of sparks on the severed front half of the bike. Mike Reese watched with a mixture of hilarity and horror as the obese Monica, sporting severe road rash, picked up the rear half of the tandem and began to beat Lenny with it. Mike Reese loved to tell that story whenever the topic of Lenny Shore came up.

When Lenny Shore got his driver's license halfway through his sophomore year, he lasted two months before he had his first accident. As with most gear-heads, Lenny had an extreme lead foot. After school on a rainy spring afternoon, he and Glenn Marcus were racing around the back roads near Bear River in Lenny's '70s vintage Dodge sedan that had begun life as a police cruiser. Lenny lost control on the crest of a low hill and spun into a roadside sand pit. The car didn't flip, but it did do a crazy 360-degree turn and slammed into the sandy slope of the pit. When the glass stopped tinkling, Glenn, who had strapped himself in minutes before when Lenny took a gravel road corner at forty miles an hour sideways, was shocked to see Lenny lying on his stomach on the hood of the old cruiser. Lenny still had firm grasp of the steering wheel reaching through the hole where the windshield had been. Lenny was stunned but unhurt.

When the cops showed up at the scene, Lenny claimed that there was an oncoming car in his lane and he swerved to miss it. Glenn played along, but as a budding career criminal, the newly nicknamed Tetherboy was stunned that the story worked. He never rode anywhere with Lenny again. Lenny would jokingly offer Glenn rides every day for the rest of the school year but Glenn stuck by his guns. Jorge Martinez witnessed one of these exchanges a month after the accident. Jorge pointed out to Lenny, "If Tetherboy thinks you're too crazy to ride with, then you got a problem."

After the football season the following fall, Lenny had yet another old Dodge police cruiser. This ex sheriff's patrol vehicle was bought at a municipal equipment auction in northern Michigan. The car was still painted black and white and had a large steel grille protector mounted on the front bumper. Late in the evening coming home from a friend's house, Lenny plowed into a deer standing serenely in the middle of the road on a curve. The deputy sheriff offered Lenny the opportunity to keep the deer carcass. Lenny was happy that his car had sustained no real damage, but he was really excited about the free deer. He had been skunked while hunting that season.

Lenny figured that a good deal was worth seeking out again but was disappointed a week later when he struck a deer and did not get the same offer. Lenny happened to be parked on top of the deer in a sugar beet field one hundred yards from the road when the same deputy sheriff arrived on the scene. What Lenny did get was a suspended driver's license and loss of his hunting license for two years.

When the story circulated through school, the football coaches were relieved. Maybe they would get a senior season out of Lenny after all if he would put his time into school. With his driving curtailed, however, Lenny Shore turned to his other hobby – racing dirt bikes. By late in the summer before his senior year, Lenny Shore was gaining a reputation for racing his bright green Benelli motocross bike on various courses in central and southern Michigan. As a result, Lenny did not make it to any weight training sessions during the summer and had only attended a handful of two-a-day practices. The football coaches were not encouraged.

John Cale continued to survey the list of suspended, ineligible and missing players. "What about Tim Manikowski? Don't we get him back in a month as well?" Cale asked Mike Reese.

"Tim has been at practice, and he would help in the backfield on both sides of the ball, but I don't think we should count on him," Reese responded.

"Does Clete Packer have him on the 'get list'?" Cale returned.

"At the very top, I'm sure. In reality I think Tim is just here to scout for new customers," Reese answered.

Tim Manikowski was a decent athlete and a good student who was also a budding entrepreneur in the area of recreational pharmaceuticals. Early in the track season the prior spring, the usually very cautious Tim had a customer fail to show up with cash just before school, so against his normal practice he stashed the packages in his gym locker. Tim hoped to get the stash home during lunch. It was the day of the first track meet of the year, and Tim was scheduled to run hurdles and high jump. As luck would have it, the county drug-sniffing dog team made a surprise visit the first hour of the day. Tim found himself sitting in Clete Packer's office at the end of second hour. Two small baggies of pot were found when the locker was opened. Tim missed the rest of the spring season and would have to sit out half of his next season on an athletic code violation.

After the football season his junior year, Tim Manikowski had announced that he was quitting football to focus on his true calling – basketball. It was widely known by the students that Tim was attempting to avoid missing any basketball this year by serving his suspension during the football season. When he was nailed with drugs, his mother, an administrator at Riverdale schools and a former teacher at Bear River, came to his defense, vehemently claiming that someone had planted the incriminating drugs. She was able to use political connections to finagle a deal with the police in which Tim was not charged with dealing. Clete Packer didn't buy a word of the defense and pushed through the full school punishment for Tim. The battle with Tim's mother had left a bad taste in the assistant principal's mouth, and now Tim Manikowski held the top position on Clete Packer's hit list for expulsion. The rumored pending loss of the main supplier in school had the dopers at BRHS in a sweat, and they were very concerned. The obnoxiously confident Tim Manikowski was not.

"There is some good news for the JV's," John Cale announced. With that, Pat Packer and Keith Marker perked up.

"What's that?" Packer asked in anticipation.

"We have a transfer in from suburban Detroit. A freshman who wants to sign up. Clete sent me an email this morning," announced Cale.

"What position does he play?" asked Keith Marker.

"The email doesn't say. Says his name is Tom Osborne," replied Coach Cale.

"Good football name," Mike Reese added.

"Woody Hayes would be a better one," John Cale said with a smile.

The young coaches looked puzzled.

"You don't know who we're talking about, do you?" asked the incredulous Coach Reese.

Both young coaches shrugged.

"Christ, I have pairs of socks older than you two," Reese said with disgust.

"Problem is, Mike, you wear them every day," Cale said with a laugh. It wasn't really a joke. Mike Reese had old tube socks he had been coaching in for twenty years. He wore two pair at a time – oldest and rattiest pair on the outside. Both young coaches looked on in disgust before every practice when Mike went through the ritual of pulling them on.

"Hopefully, he's a lineman. We need help on the line after losing Gump yesterday," Pat Packer said matter-of-factly.

"You need help everywhere, Pat," Mike Reese replied, not wanting to miss a chance to needle the lowly ASS sistant.

"How is the Gumper?" Cale changed the subject.

"He's having surgery to put pins in his arm this afternoon. I am going to go visit him tomorrow in the hospital. He's done for the season for sure – but last night he kept asking his dad if he could still wrestle this year." Keith Marker filled in the status of the freshman center hurt the last play of the scrimmage.

"Too bad," Cale concluded.

"I'll go with you tomorrow, Keith," Reese said. Gunther "Gump" Colby was the younger brother of Chet "Cheese" Colby who had wrestled four years on varsity for Reese. Cheese Colby also was starting center for two seasons for the Bears football squad. Just before the state wrestling meet last winter, the Colby family learned that the boys' mother, Bea Colby, was diagnosed with advanced cervical cancer. Mike had held the sobbing older Colby brother when he was eliminated from medal contention at the state meet in his last career match. The young boy couldn't focus on wrestling with the tragedy that had fallen on the family and had not been prepared to compete for what should have been a high place.

Everyone loved Bea Colby. She was the president of the Bear River sports boosters. There had been a benefit for her at the high school cafeteria after school in June. Mike Reese had help organize it. Mike Reese and the elder Colbys had been friends long before the boys were born. The whole town turned out and over $7,000 was raised. The Colbys could use it. Chester Colby Sr. lost his job a month before the previous Christmas. He had been a plant manager at an auto parts manufacturer in Saginaw. The factory closed after the product line was moved to a new facility in Mexico. Bea Colby was a school secretary in the Bear River Elementary. Hospice was called in during the third week of July. Bea would not last the year.

"Surgery, huh? Man, the Colbys can't catch a break," Packer said with forced concern.

"There is a black cloud over that family," Reese said with a sigh.

"Anything else for the JV's?" asked a hopeful Packer.

"Danny Short will be at practice on Monday," Cale responded with enthusiasm.

"Whoopee," came the snide reply from Packer.

"Who's Danny Short?" asked Keith Marker. He knew nothing of the boy because Danny had not been to weight lifting or two-a-days at all.

"Danny is great student and a really friendly kid. He is coming back from a two-month-long scouting expo thing out west. He is scheduled to make Eagle Scout this fall," Cale informed Marker.

Packer let out a disgusted groan and his face darkened like it did when he was losing his temper with his players. "I have never seen a worse football player," he began, his voice rising. "The kid is only 100 pounds and is slower than Big Donnie. Worse yet, he will not make contact. We had to play him at safety on JV last year as a freshman for most of the second half of the year. We had to – no one else stayed eligible academically. He didn't make a single tackle, but at the end of every play he would help up the opposing player and say 'Nice catch!' or 'Good run!' He is just flat-out horrible. The kid is a pussy!" Packer said to Marker who looked uncomfortable listening to the description of the sophomore. Keith was learning to not like the way Pat Packer was so bitterly critical of kids in private.

Mike Reese could see that Marker was a little taken aback at Packer's evaluation of Danny Short, so he tried to lighten the mood of the conversation.

"When I was a first-year football coach, I worked under an old hand by the name of Bob Gropp who used to teach shop and was the Future Farmers of America advisor here," Mike began as he glanced at Cale, who gave him a knowing smile in encouragement. "Bob had been coaching for decades at that point – he had been head JV coach for a dozen years. I was just a lowly ASS sistant and one of my jobs was to coach the defensive backs. I had a whole crew of Danny Shorts starting on the JV's that season. After the third or fourth game of the year, we were sitting in a meeting just like this and I was going on about how my D backs couldn't tackle or cover or do anything right at all. We had yet to win a game and we were getting lit up like a Christmas tree every week. And 'ol' Bob let me finish my rant and said, 'Small, slow and friendly is a deadly combination for defensive backs, kiddo. Friendly is what really kills you come game time.' Still, I'd rather teach and coach good kids who stink than complete assholes who can play ball." Reese paused to let Cale lend some knowing chuckles. Pat Packer let out a derisive snort.

"The thing is," Reese continued, "We did win the last two of games that season even though the defensive backfield never really came around. Although, one of my little cornerbacks, John Lemanski, saved the day in the last game on the last play of the year by intercepting a pass on point after attempt in the end zone. We all cheered like we won the Super Bowl. That was the last football play that kid ever participated in. John broke his ankle real bad in basketball and missed out on playing sports for his remaining two years in school. He was my team manager in wrestling his senior year. I still get Christmas cards from him. He's a doctor in the Army now. John did three tours in Iraq." Keith Marker was hanging on every word of Reese's story and he gave Mike a big smile.

"Tell them about the Wuff Game, Mike," Cale said, not wanting to stop Reese who was exploiting a teachable moment with the young coaches.

Mike Reese laughed a hearty laugh and began again, "The smallest and slowest defensive back I had on the team my first year was a hearing-impaired boy named Thorton – Carl Thorton – and when I say hearing impaired, I mean he was stone deaf. He had a full-time sign interpreter following him around school, and he spent half his day in speech therapy at the Intermediate School District. Carl had never played any organized sports, but for some reason he decided he'd like to try football. We didn't see anything wrong with letting him try, and besides, his interpreter was a stone cold fox named Debbie – she ended up marrying Bob Gropp's oldest son. Bob junior was coaching with us part time that year as he was finishing up his degree at CMU. He and Debbie have like six kids, and they live in Arizona now."

"Anyway," Reese went on. "Carl Thorton really didn't understand football and Debbie would follow him around the practice field signing what we were saying. Carl didn't speak much. He was worried the kids would tease him because he had a real bad speech impediment – he was deaf from an early childhood fever and forming R's was something he couldn't get the hang of. I never really could understand much of what he was saying, and he had a way of yelling like some deaf people do because they don't have volume control. Debbie worked hard with him on that. But mostly, she would sign with him and then relay Carl's questions to us if he had any – which wasn't often. Like I said though, Debbie was hardcore, and sometimes she made Carl speak even though he preferred to sign. So a few times, Bob and I would have these bizarre shouting matches with Carl where neither one of us understood what the other was saying. Why we felt it necessary to yell back at Carl I don't know because, like I said, he couldn't hear a damn thing. One thing I remember well, though, is Carl didn't understand that on the field he should call his teachers 'Coach,' so I was 'Mistah Weese' and Bob was 'Mistah Dwopp'." Even Pat Packer laughed at that description from Reese, who was now on an animated roll telling the story.

Reese continued telling his story with his eyes sparkling. "The third game of the season, we were down at North Star, and it had been pouring rain all day so that joke of a field they have was a bowl of soup. In the fourth quarter, we were down by like forty points and Bob Gropp tells me, 'It's time – let's play Carl. If someone tags him, at least the ground is mush, and it will cushion the blow.' The rain had started again and the visibility was shit. I told Debbie to sign to Carl he was going in next defensive series. He had seen no action to this point, and I had told the rest of the team to lay off him a little during practice scrimmage, so really he hadn't had any hard contact at all. We were wearing road uniforms – all white with red numbers – and Carl stood out like a sore thumb as he ran out to the field. Every other player on the field is just covered with mud.

"After the huddle, Carl lines up at safety. He gets in a good stance and he is raring to go. The play goes off, and they run wide left toward our bench. The sloppy footing was slowing everyone down, and I look up and I see this white uniform flash up from the center of the field. Damn it if Carl doesn't have an angle and for a brief delusional second I thought he was going to make a play. Then the North Star fullback comes up and lays a block on Carl that sends him flying. The North Star kid has got a hundred pounds on Carl, so it's just simple physics.

"Carl disappears in the rain and the fog and the play goes past our bench and they score. Everyone was concentrated on the touchdown. Then Carl comes wandering in from the field. He is covered with mud all up his front. Don't ask me how. And he has an enormous clot of turf sticking in his facemask, but it doesn't matter 'cause his helmet is twisted and he is peering out his left ear hole. Bob Gropp stops Carl as he comes off the field and pulls his helmet off him. Carl has got mud in his right eye, mud up his nose, and small chunks of sod stuck to his hair for God's sake. Bob is like stunned at the sight so he doesn't say anything. Carl blinks his left eye – the one that isn't caked shut with mud – and he half yells at Bob, 'Izza wuff game out da, Mistah Dwopp!'"

By the time Reese was finishing the story, he was struggling to keep from laughing, and Keith Marker was laughing, banging his hands on the tabletop and gasping. Packer was shaking with laughter. And Cale had tears running down his cheeks. He wiped them with a Kleenex as he howled. Minutes later the meeting ended. As Cale was locking his classroom door, he stopped Reese and laid his hand on his shoulder. "Thanks Mike, we needed that," was all he said. Reese gave him a beaming smile and walked down the hall to his own classroom.

Michigan state law requires public schools to wait until after Labor Day to start classes. The law was pushed through the state legislature by the tourism industry looking to milk summer dollars as long as possible. For fall sports, this meant that games would start well before the student body was back from summer break. The BRHS Bears had two games scheduled before Labor Day. The first game would be away against perennial state title contenders, the Mecosta High Panthers, on a Thursday evening twelve days before the start of school. That forced the JV squad into a Wednesday night home game against the Panthers squad that likely would have crushed the Bear varsity team. It was the first time in ten years that the Bears would play Mecosta. In that time, the Panthers had won three state championships in Division 7, one division below Bear River who played Division 6 football in Michigan.

Practice the week of the game for both Bears teams was oddly effective. The kids were focused and even the JV's ran their offense efficiently. A few large cracks of impact came from the JV practice, showing that the kids were getting confident in their tackling. The young JV coaches were lulled into believing that they could give the Panthers a decent game.

John Cale knew better and he remembered what the gruff legendary old Mecosta coach, Manny Stevenson, had told him at a coaching conference a few months before the season. John asked Manny what the key was to getting good numbers of boys out for football at his school. The old coach paused, looked at John and said, "Well, we ain't got soccer at Mecosta." Manny Stevenson paused once more to let John know that he knew that soccer was king at Bear River before he continued. "And only a few marshmallows run cross country, so we get just about every swinging dick in the building out on the football field." John Cale laughed in response, but it was a nervous laugh. John Cale knew full well that merely surviving against Mecosta would be considered a victory for both the varsity and JV Bears football teams.

Kickoff for the first JV game of the season was on a hot and windy evening. The home stands on the Bear River side of the field were virtually empty. Only parents and a few varsity players were in attendance. There were no cheerleaders on the Bears' sidelines – the BRHS JV cheerleaders had gone to an away soccer game that evening. The Mecosta crowd was crammed into the much smaller visitor bleachers. They had cheerleaders and a kid in a panther mascot suit sweltering in the late August heat.

The sparse home crowd made no difference to the public address announcer. Big Bill Simon, the Bear River middle school principal, was the PA announcer for all home football games, varsity and JV. As usual he was announcing everything in a booming voice as if it were the Rose Bowl. Clete Packer stalked around the press-box making sure everything was just so. He popped his head into the home coach's cubicle and said, "Look at that crowd over there – this is going to be our best visitor gate receipt total of the year. Just imagine next year when their varsity is here – we'll really do well. That's why I scheduled home and home with Mecosta." Mike Reese and John Cale were setting up and testing the field radio system and trying to get through to the young coaches on the sideline. Mike Reese looked up from the tangle of wires and said with thinly veiled contempt, "Yeah, that's just great, Clete." Packer ignored the slight and rushed over to the opposite end of the well-appointed press box to check in with the visiting coaches to see if they needed anything in their cubicle.

John Cale surveyed the Mecosta sideline and counted thirty-three players. The Panthers would be playing two platoon football – a real advantage on a hot evening like this one. The Bears had twenty JV players suited up with two kids in street clothes – Gump Colby, his arm in a full cast with a sling, and Tom Osborne the slump-shouldered, potbellied freshman who had only just shown up for practice two days ago. Pat Packer had already tabbed him as Gump's replacement at center.

Big Bill announced the Bears lineup as though they were Pro Bowlers. A fuzzy rendition of the national anthem was played over the sound system. The Mecosta crowd was on their feet cheering as the Bears kicked off. The kick was a low line drive that bounced once and landed in the arms of their deep back. Pat Packer yelled in to his headset mouthpiece "NOOOO!" Ten seconds later, the Mecosta boy crossed the goal line basically unmolested. The Mecosta crowd cheered as Packer yelled into the headset, "Damn it, I told him to kick a squibbler to the up backs on our side!"

In the press box coach's cubicle, Mike Reese said into his mic, "Calm down, Pat, and get your kick return set up."

The Bears took the kickoff and managed to return it to their own thirty-yard line. The first offensive play was an end run. When the tailback got to the edge of the line, the Panthers' defensive end snatched the ball cleanly from the Bear player, and a few seconds later, he too was in the end zone. "Auughh!" Packer yelled into the mic.

This time it was John Cale's turn. "Pat – keep it between the tackles until your kids get their feet under them."

The kick return after the second Panther TD was badly handled, and the Bears were pinned down inside the ten-yard line. Pat Packer did as recommended and ordered up a simple dive to the full back. The handoff was fumbled, and the Bear quarterback, tailback and fullback did a good imitation of the Three Stooges as they tried to pick up the ball. A lumbering Panther defensive tackle scooped up the ball, and in three steps he was in the end zone. Pat Packer threw off his headset, and loud enough to be heard over the wildly cheering Mecosta fans, he screamed across the field, "Just fall on the frickin' ball! Cover it up!"

Keith Marker squatted down and plucked some grass from the field. Without looking to the press box, he calmly said into his headset, "This is getting out of hand."

Mike Reese replied, "Keith, get them calmed down – call a timeout."

After the time-out, the Bears had a better kick return – this time they returned it to just short of their own 40-yard line. Packer called for a swing pass to the flats on the Bear's right. Cale spoke forcefully into the headset. "Stay with the game plan, Pat," he said. "Stick to the ground game." The Bears quarterback telegraphed the throw and threw a wobbly ball, which was snatched out of the air by the lanky Mecosta outside linebacker. Running awkwardly with his elbows and knees flapping comically, he proceeded into the Bear's end zone. The Mecosta crowd was wild and laughing.

The Bears got a left-handed gift from the football gods. The PAT went wide left. Less than three minutes were off the clock, and the scoreboard read Bears 0 Visitors 27. Pat Packer held his headset in his hand and looked dejectedly down at the ground. There was a lull before the kickoff, and across the field Packer could distinctly hear the Panthers' head coach call down the sideline to his defensive assistant: "Will you guys knock it off with the getting turnovers for touchdowns! I'd like to run some offense tonight!"

In Michigan, the state athletic association has a football mercy rule. The rule states that if a team is trailing by thirty-five or more points in the second half of the game, clock continues to run and only stops for timeouts, injuries, penalties and scores. Most people refer to it as the Running Clock. Many times during the season for the last several years, the Bears football teams faced the Running Clock. In most cases, the Running Clock was a true act of mercy.

The Bears found themselves down 48 to 0 at halftime. In the second half, the Mecosta Panthers played nothing but backup players. The final score was 66-0 in favor of the visitors. It was still daylight at the end of the game. The temperature was still well into the eighties. From his vantage point in the press box, John Cale watched the post-game talk given by Keith Marker. Even though he could not hear what was being said, he felt compelled to observe. The Bears players were kneeling near midfield in a broad semi-circle. Keith Marker had his hat off and was talking without moving much. Pat Packer was pacing behind Marker and he occasionally stepped in front of the JV head coach and waved his arms and pointed at kids. Cale could tell Pat Packer was not controlling his temper. The sweat-soaked heads of the Bears players were dipped down. Their exhaustion read in their bodies.

"That was a hell of a beating," Reese said as he packed away the field communication equipment.

"We were thoroughly outclassed, Mike. Pat Packer is too impatient calling the offense, but even without turnovers, they just flat out beat our ass," Cale responded heavily.

With the field communication system put away, the varsity coaches headed for the field. The Mecosta coaches were on the opposite side of the press box. They were laughing and talking loudly. Reese and Cale walked past them on their way to the stairs. Cale made eye contact with Manny Stevenson. The twinkle left Manny's eye and he gave John a serious nod. John Cale returned the nod. He read the eyes of the opposing varsity coach. The message was clear – expect more of the same tomorrow night.

Mike Reese caught up with Keith Marker on the pedestrian bridge over the Bear River that led to the back of the school and the locker room. The Bears players walked single file in front of him carrying their helmets and shoulder pads. Keith Marker was quiet but walked with his head up. Mike Reese reached his arm around the younger man's shoulder. "It's a wuff game out there, Coach," Reese said in a fatherly tone.

The day of the first varsity game began with an intense thunderstorm. Power in Bear River was knocked out for two hours. John Cale didn't believe in omens, but the storm had flooded his basement, so by noon, he was already exhausted by the cleanup and not feeling good about the day.

Jorge Martinez started the day with his phone buzzing. His screen showed an incoming text from Eliza Meyer. He was puzzled for a second. He didn't know an Eliza. Then it dawned on him – Liz.

EMeyer: How r u?

JMart: Good. u?

EMeyer: Fine. Getting ready 2 head 2 college.

JMart: I.U.?

EMeyer: Yep. Classes start next week.

JMart: Opening game 2nite.

EMeyer: Good luck. How r your friends?

JMart: Good now.

EMeyer: No one got hurt on the beach did they?

JMart: No. Things got messy l8er.

EMeyer: OMG. Details?

JMart: No details. We all took vow of silence.

EMeyer: Even Morg?

JMart: Especially Morg. Our season would be over if details got out.

EMeyer: LMFAO. I can't get the beach off my mind.

JMart: It was nice – until the fight.

EMeyer: Gotta go. Facebook me. I took an easy schedule. Don't want to start my freshman year working too hard. LOL. Maybe we can meet up for a weekend.

JMart: OK. B careful. Have fun.

Jorge was conflicted about Liz. The connection had been great, but he didn't see a future in it. He reflected on the discussion Wash Dryer had led as they returned from the trip last weekend. Everyone agreed that the only thing that anyone needed to know was that they had fun at the beach and they met some girls from Chicago. And that was all that would be said to anybody – especially parents and coaches. Even Morg made no protest and he kept his vow. Silence seemed to be the best way forward with Liz as well. Jorge decided to tell no one about the contact – not even Wash Dryer.

At 4:40 that afternoon, Jimbo Davis had the bus idling in front of the school. It was loaded with boys and equipment. Coach Cale and Coach Reese stood at the curb. Irritation showed on their faces as a rusty late-model Ford sedan pulled up and Glenn Marcus got out from the passenger side. His mother was yelling at him as he slammed the door shut.

"Sorry, Coach," Glenn said to both men.

"Bus time was 4:30. We're late," answered Coach Cale. "Wash has already put your stuff on the bus."

"Sorry, my Ma was late coming home from work," Glenn continued. Mike Reese gave him a stern look and motioned with his head toward the bus door. Glenn climbed up and looked at the full bus. A few cat calls about holding things up greeted him. He had to sit near the front. Across the aisle were the two players not eligible to play the game sitting in street clothes. Tim Manikowski was listening to his iPod and gave him no notice. Lenny Shore gave Glenn a big smile.

"Gee, Glenn, if you needed a ride, you shoulda called me." Lenny Shore's comment dripped with needling sarcasm.

"Go fuck yourself." Tetherboy answered in a low growl. Lenny laughed out loud.

Mike Reese was the last one on the bus.

"Let's keep it quiet, gentlemen. Focus on the game." Reese commanded and sat across from John Cale in the front seat.

Wash Dryer reached into his duffel bag and pulled out a Kindle e-reader. He turned it on and began reading. Wash had started reading a book called *Watership Down* the night before. He had downloaded it when Greg Dryer suggested the book in their nightly text after Wash had mentioned he was really bored. Wash wasn't sure what to make of it yet. Reading a story about rabbits seemed to be kind of a silly way for an eighteen-year-old to pass his time in the late summer.

The humidity was down after the rains that morning, so the players were spared the misery of a hot and sticky ride. The bus trip across central Michigan heading west was uneventful. Jimbo Davis made up most of the lost time. The tiny town of Mecosta looked deserted. The players soon found out why. Every soul in town was at the football field. It was an hour before kickoff, and the home bleachers were packed. Less than a dozen people were setting in the visitor stands.

The Bears got off the bus and donned their pads and helmets. Keith Marker left the sideline after warm-ups and made his way into the press box. Pat Packer was on the road scouting the next game.

With fifteen minutes left to kick off, Coach Cale assembled the team in the end zone. The PA announcer was loudly explaining the fifty-fifty drawing tickets being sold in the stands. The Bears took a knee in front of their young head coach.

John Cale began his pre-game comments. "What we have been working for all summer is a few minutes away. This is what the long hours lifting was all about – right Jorge?" Jorge Martinez nodded in agreement. "This is what throwing drills in the spring and summer passing league was all about – right Seth?"

"Hell yeah!" The quarterback shouted to the team.

"Yeah!" echoed the team.

"We had a very good week at practice. Let's make sure we keep our edge – get off the ball on the snap. No stupid penalties," Cale continued. "And we have to protect the ball – this is a ball-hawking team – keep it tucked away." He turned to Reese and said, "Coach?"

Reese came forward. "Don't try to tackle that fullback high – he'll carry you for ten yards. They run to set up the pass. Linebackers watch out for the quick release by the tight end. They scored a dozen touchdowns on the dump pass in the playoffs last year, and they love to run it out of double tight formations. No freelancing linebackers. Got that?" Reese looked deliberately at Glenn Marcus. "Defensive ends, you cannot get hooked – if we lose containment, that tailback of theirs will kill us on the edge."

"You ready?" Reese called out to the team.

"Yeah!" the Bears answered in unison.

"One more thing," Reese continued. "Pete, the Old Pigskin Predictor in the Mt. Pleasant paper has Mecosta winning this by forty." Calls of "Bull" and "No Way" came from the Bears. "Ol' Pete's got it wrong – the Panthers don't have a clue what the Bears can do. And I tell you what – my plan is to scrape up some of the Panther crap we scare out of these guys tonight and slip it in between some bread buttered up with Bear grease." The team started to laugh heartily. "Then tomorrow I am going to drive up to Dismal Flats and shove that crap sandwich down Old Pete's throat!" Cheers greeted Coach Reese as he stood with his hands on hips giving the team a defiant smile.

"ARE YOU READY?" Coach Cale yelled.

"Yeah!" The Bears replied.

"I SAID, ARE YOU READY??" Cale shouted once more.

The Bears replied emphatically, "YEAH!!"

Seth Parker stood and shouted, "Bears on three!" The team gathered and shouted their name.

The Bear River Bears were not ready for a team as talented and disciplined as the Mecosta Panthers. For most teams, the first game of the year is always marked with miscues and sloppy play. The Panthers had no first-game jitters. The Bears had plenty.

The Bears started the game on their twenty after the Panthers kicked it through the end zone. Morg Miller lined up at left guard. As he came out of the huddle, he looked across at the Panther defensive tackle. The boy's full beard obscured his face under the helmet's mask. Morg noted that the kid was the same size and shape as the old refrigerator Morg's dad kept in the garage for beer. The purple Panther jersey had the number 76 in yellow across the front. To Morg it looked like a billboard.

Morg started in with his usual line of smack talking. "Hey, big fella – you're kinda cute. Let's get married!" No response. Seth Parker mishandled the snap on a simple dive play. 76 crushed Morg to the ground. Seth recovered the ball for a loss of four yards. Thing One came in the huddle with the play. Trap to the right. As Morg came to the line, he said, "Comin at ya, princess," to 76. No response. This time the snap was clean, and Morg pulled to his right. Morg cleared Junior Schulz at center and was greeted with a large white wall bearing the number 75 in red. The Panther defensive end had stood up Big Donnie Donnie and drove him into the backfield. At the same time, the 76 in purple did as he was trained and followed Morg's pull. Morg got smothered between the two large bodies as the Panther defense piled on the play. Under the pile, Morg jammed his thumb into the ribs of 76. No response.

The Bears gained a total of fifteen yards in the first half. The Panthers moved the ball methodically. Jorge Martinez was able to stop the fullback dive plays so the Panthers exploited the Bears' lack of containment on the outside. Mecosta scored on the last play of the half. The scoreboard read "Panthers 35 visitors 0." Morg Miller tried every cheap trick he knew to get a rise out of 76. The big Panther never answered.

Half time was quiet. John Cale and Mike Reese went through adjustments and instructions. They could read the eyes of their players. The Bears responded positively verbally, but their eyes showed they were already done. Seth Parker had an ice bag on his left elbow. Mike Reese looked over the arm. Seth had a burst bursis sack and the jelly-like mass on his arm was sensitive to the touch. Reese caught Cale's eye and shook his head. Dial-a-Pain was done for the night.

The Panthers scored on their first two possessions of the second half. Both on tight-end dumps that should have been stopped by Glenn Marcus if he had been in position and reading the play. The mercy clock was running late in the third quarter when Manny Stevenson pulled the Panther starters from the game. Morg was relieved when 76 found his way to the sidelines for the final time. But wanting to get in the last jibe, he held his finger and thumb to his face-mask like a phone and said, "Call me, I've got a ring all picked out," as the giant Panther jogged past him. No response.

The lowlight on defense in the fourth quarter should have been one of the few highlights of the night. After a game full of blown assignments and uncalled fruitless blitz attempts, Glenn Marcus finally nailed the backup Panther QB for a seven-yard loss. On his way up from the ground, Glenn gave the Panther player a little extra shove and pointed at him yelling, "Yeah, Baby!" The referee flagged the play for unsportsmanlike behavior. A grim-faced Mike Reese pulled Glenn from the game and simply pointed at the bench when Glenn came running up trying to apologize. Tetherboy did not play the rest of the night.

The Bears offense responded to playing against backups with three turnovers in their remaining possessions. Junior Shultz did not adjust to Randy Jansen taking snaps at quarterback. They combined for six fumbled exchanges. They lost three of the fumbles. Two ended up with the jubilant Mecosta reserves converting the turnovers to scores. At the end of the game, the score board showed 62-0 in favor of the hosts.

The players lined up to shake hands at the final horn. Morg Miller was exhausted and not looking to run his mouth for a change. The huge number 76 towered over him as they shook hands. The giant Panther tackle squeezed Morg's hand tightly and pulled him close. "The engagement is off," 76 said as he released the hand. Later on the bus ride home Morg found himself chuckling at the line. It wasn't often Morg got bested in verbal competition, but he had to admit that the final exchange was funny.

The bus ride home was quiet. A few groans punctuated the silence when the bus hit bumps. Jimbo Davis turned on the interior lights as the bus pulled to a stop in front of the locker room door. John Cale stood and faced his team. "Film session at 9 A.M., boys. Practice will follow. Get in the locker room and get your business done quickly. I don't want to hang around till midnight."

A half hour later, the players were gone. The showers were running but no one was in them. Wash Dryer remained in the coaches' office. John Cale was calling in results to the papers and the TV stations in Saginaw. Mike Reese came in naked from his shower. Reese looked at his nephew and said, "Wash, you can take off, but go turn off the water and pick up a bit. I don't want the night custodian bitching tomorrow." Wash replied with a quick okay and slipped out the door as John Cale hung up the phone.

"Talk to Pete the Predictor, did ya?" asked Reese.

"Yep – he made some remark about how he figured it wouldn't be close," John Cale answered as he rubbed his eyes.

"Man, I would purely love to force Pete to eat at least a couple of shit sandwiches this year. He hasn't picked us to win a game in two seasons," Reese responded with disgust.

Cale shrugged and replied, "Yeah."

Reese smiled. "Come on – I'll buy you a beer."

Cale's face brightened slightly as he said, "Or six."

## Overtime

Wash Dryer was watching the *Football Frenzy* highlight show on a Saginaw TV station as he turned on his phone to text his dad. Greg Dryer had just sat down on the end of his bed in a hotel room when the message came through.

WashDryer: Knock Knock.

GregDryer: Who's there?

WashDryer: Owen.

GregDryer: Owen who?

WashDryer: Owen 1.

GregDyrer: Mecosta pretty tough?

WashDryer: Very.

Wash filled in the lowlights of the first game.

WashDryer: Well that's about it. Going to bed and do some reading.

GregDryer: Watership Down?

WashDryer: Yeah. I don't know. A book about rabbits?
GregDryer: Stick with it kiddo. It's more than that.
WashDryer: OK. Love you.
GregDryer: Love you 2.

Greg Dryer pulled on some casual clothes and headed out the door for dinner. Wash fell sleep with his Kindle on his chest. He dreamt of fearless warrior rabbits.

# CHAPTER SIX

## OWEN 2

Friday morning at nine, the Bears were in film session. Jorge Martinez, Morg Miller and Seth Parker sat on the ugly couch in John Cale's classroom. The rest of the team sat at desks. The room was dark. The only light came from the LCD projector mounted on a post from the ceiling. The sound of food being wolfed down could be heard.

The film session was quiet. Only Coach Cale and Coach Reese spoke. They worked hard to stay positive. A great deal of time was spent going over blocking failures. Mike Reese asked questions of the linebackers. Jorge gave the answers he wanted to hear. Glenn Marcus sat in the front row and knew better than to make a sound. On film, it was apparent to everyone the play of Big Donnie Donnie was horrible at right offensive tackle. He was only marginally better at nose tackle on defense. Donnie didn't pick up on the vibe of the room. He liked watching himself on the big screen in the front of the room, and he sat with a large grin on his face through the whole session. Most of the rest of the team would rather be running gassers than watching this horror movie.

The lights came on. Twenty minutes of Coach Cale illustrating plays on the whiteboard followed. The team was drowsy and unresponsive. Cale was starting to get a little exasperated when Mike Reese broke in. "Looks like you had a hell of a battle with 76 there, Morg." Chuckles greeted the comment. "Did you ask him to marry you?" Morg's game-day banter with opposing players was well known to the coaching staff.

Morg Miller waited for the laughter to fade before he responded, "He shot me down, Coach." Morg did not want to share how the giant kid from Mecosta had bested him verbally as well.

"Too bad Morg. You like them big and hairy, don't you?" Seth Parker butted in. A huge roar of laughter came from the team. Only a confused Big Donnie Donnie and the usually quiet Jay Brau did not join in.

Morg Miller rarely refused to pick up the gauntlet when Seth Parker got in a shot. "How's the elbow Dial-a-Pain?" Morg's retort quieted the quarterback. Morg pressed the attack. "Did you get a call in to the Miracle Healer yet? You better tell him to show up next Wednesday – we play on Thursday."

Seth Parker gave him and angry look. Morg knew he had scored a direct hit.

"That's a good question," Cale broke in. He wanted to regain the focus of the team, but he was grateful Mike Reese had lightened the mood. "How's the elbow this morning, Seth?"

Seth Parker shrugged and said, "The swelling is still there, but the pain is better – my mom scheduled an appointment with the doc this afternoon." Seth's elbow was wrapped in an Ace bandage. It was hard to tell if it was swollen or not.

"The horse doctor?" Mike Reese asked hopefully. One of three doctors in Bear River, Dr. Mark Linehan was a friend of the wrestling program and known for clearing athletes quickly when an injury occurred that could affect the team negatively. Doc Linehan and Mike Reese would go steelhead fishing up north every spring after every wrestling season. Reese had always called him the 'horse doctor'.

"No," answered Seth. "Mom is taking me up to Mt. Pleasant – she has a new doc up there." Marlene Parker was a doctor-shopping hypochondriac with a fondness for mood-elevating drugs. Mike Reese suspected that Seth's mom projected her own medical issues onto her son. Mark Linehan never would divulge any information about his former patient, Marlene Parker, but when Mike brought up the idea with the doc of the psychological disorder Munchausen by proxy, he did not dismiss it out of hand.

The film session ended, and the boys flooded from the room. Mike Reese held Glenn Marcus back. "You owe me twenty extra gassers at the end of practice – forty if I see you dogging it today," Mike Reese said calmly and sternly.

"K, coach," Tetherboy replied, and he ran to join his teammates.

The coaches followed the boys down to the locker room. They were met at the door by Molly Saunders, the lead custodian of the building. She had her custodial cart with her and she was fussing with the contents.

"Mike, that locker room smells horrible. Get those boys to take their dirty clothes home. I'm coming in later today to disinfect the room. I don't want a bunch of mud and crap on the floors. So have them clean their spikes outside for a change. And I'm damned tired of picking up tape and old bandages everywhere. There are trash cans. Make sure those boys are using them for Christ's sake." The gruff old woman with a smoker's raspy voice scolded. She ignored the younger Coach Cale. She barely even noticed him. As far as she was concerned, Mike Reese was the oldest coach, and he was in charge.

"Sure thing, Molly. I'll remind the boys. But you got to promise me something," Reese answered brightly.

"What's that?" The gray-haired matron asked. She and Mike Reese were the same age and they had worked together in the building for decades. Over time, they had developed a teasing banter between them.

"Last dance at homecoming this year is mine. Remember now. I won't take no for an answer." Reese smiled as he jokingly propositioned the old janitor.

Molly Saunders cackled and cursed. The cackle turned into a wet coughing fit. The old woman turned an alarming shade of purple, and then she hocked up a glob of mucus into her waste container on her custodial cart. "Mike," she gasped, "I've told you I don't date teachers. I got enough grief in my life. Besides, you're married and I ain't no trollop like my skanky sister. You just keep your paws to yourself." She laughed and coughed as the two men slid around her into the locker room. The last of the boys were slipping out of the locker room.

"Jesus, Mike, that old woman acts like I don't even exist," said Cale. "And that's fine. She is one scary old broad. How come you and she are always teasing each other?" he asked conspiratorially and quietly. Molly Saunders had the reputation of being an eavesdropper, and even though she wasn't in the locker room Cale wondered if she was listening outside.

"Oh, Molly is harmless – mostly. And she is a damn fine custodian – keeps this building pretty well. But don't be pissing her off. She will make your life a living hell. She is Clete Packer's eyes and ears – something happens around here and a few hours later Clete knows everything. And she is real hard on the women teachers if they don't pass her scratch-and-sniff test. She's kind of a religious fanatic – Catholic Taliban. We had a young math teacher a few years before you got here. She was living with a male teacher from Mt. Pleasant. They weren't married, and the topic came up in the lunch room with Molly listening in like she does. Well, after that, Molly practically hounded the woman from the building. They had a couple of screaming matches in the young teacher's classroom after school. Molly is a busybody but a bit of a hypocrite – she's been divorced twice. Anyway, the young teacher couldn't take Molly stalking her every step and she resigned at the end of the year. Got a job over the phone teaching out in Vegas." Mike Reese related what Cale already knew very well. Molly Saunders was a force in the building, like it or not.

"Man, I wouldn't be flirting with her even to tease her. What would happen if she started taking it seriously?" Cale asked sincerely.

"I used to joke when she was still married to her second husband that all the male staff in the building should send him gift certificates to local bars so he would never have to buy another drink again. His reward for eliminating the one-in-two-billion shot any of us would be married to her," Reese jested. Cale laughed out loud.

"You wanna hear something sort of funny but kind of creepy? She mentioned her sister. Right?" Reese asked.

"Yeah, what about her?' Cale asked.

"See, Molly has this younger sister. Her name is Amanda. She's at least ten years younger than Molly. She wasn't a good student but she was quiet – almost timid. She was in my class decades ago. I was your age when she graduated. She was a 1980s hotty. Pat Benatar hair and the most spectacular set of tits I ever saw in thirty-nine years in this job. Seriously – boys would damn near walk into walls around here ogling her. And I couldn't blame them. She disappeared after graduation – left town. Molly was a young custodian then, and when anyone asked her what happened to Amanda, Molly would sneer that she didn't care. And then she would mumble something about Amanda being a whore. And guess what? That's what she was – probably still is," Reese said.

"Huh?" Cale was incredulous.

"Yeah. In the late '80s, I went to a coaching conference in Chicago and a bunch of us went out bar-hopping after the afternoon session. It was after midnight, and we were in a dive on the South Side and Amanda was there working the johns. She recognized me and came up to me. I was drunk and so was she. She tried to talk me into paying for a blowjob while feeling up my crotch. Creepiest thing I ever had happen. Sobered me right up. I split out of there, but some of the guys I was with took advantage of her services, including old Frank Mack, our head football coach at the time. Crazy old fuck. He caught crabs for his trouble. His wife had passed away a little over a year before of cancer. He wasn't making good decisions, and he was becoming a hardcore alcoholic. He ended up dying of a heart attack a few years later." Reese reflected back on the long-ago incident with regret still in his voice.

"Jesus Christ. He had sex with a former student?" Cale asked.

"Frank was drunk as hell. He didn't even recognize her. He never had her in class. He taught metal shop and small engine repair. But yeah, he bagged her. It never made it back here. I shudder to think what might have happened if Molly had heard about it," Reese replied. The two men grabbed up their whistles and headed for the field.

The post-game practice was 'socks and jocks' or shoulder pads and helmets only – non-contact. The Things dressed quickly and bolted out the door. They were on a mission to commit some sort of chaos. Whatever presented itself would do – they didn't have to wait long. Thing One and Thing Two celebrated the less restrictive uniform requirement by pulling down their shorts and mooning soccer team captain Liam Pickering who was jogging alone on the track around the game field.

Thing One called out, "Hey Picky!" It was a nickname he had had for years, and one that he hated. Pickering turned to flip off his antagonist only to be greeted with the twins' bare asses pressed against the chain link fence encircling the track. They were laughing hard as Jorge Martinez and Jay Brau came jogging off the pedestrian bridge over the river, their bare asses still pressed to the fence even though Pickering was jogging away with his middle finger of his right hand thrust high over his head.

"You guys better not let the coaches see you doing that. The whole team will have to run extra gassers. We're supposed to stay away from the soccer players, remember?" Jorge Martinez said to them calmly as the Things turned and pulled up their shorts.

"Okay, Cap." Thing Two answered as he squinted in the late morning sun. "Whatever you say." The Things had called Jorge Martinez 'Cap' – short for captain – since last wrestling season when Jorge was also a team captain. Jorge liked the respect of the nickname. The Things held him in high regard because he was the only wrestler on the team who could withstand the crazy freshman twins' frequent tag team ambushes before, during and after wrestling practice. Jorge gave as good as he got. The other wrestlers would play dead when attacked for fear that the Things' well-known temper would kick in and then all hell would break loose. Coach Reese had all he could do to keep the Things on a leash, even in practice.

The Things sprinted on ahead to the practice field, laughing. Jay Brau mimicked Thing Two's flinty high voice. "Whatever you say." Jorge Martinez slowed to a walk.

"Watch out for those two," Jorge said seriously to his friend. "You never know what might set them off, and when it happens you have to deal with two of them at once. Four – if their little brothers are around."

"Okay," Jay Brau answered. Jay and Jorge had been friends since ninth grade football. He knew that Jorge was not joking around. Jorge had been the first friend Jay had made at Bear River. Both were good students. Jorge was a much better athlete, but he respected Jay's hard work in the weight room, which had filled out the gangly basketball player's frame in the last year. Jorge had paved the way for Jay being accepted in ninth grade by laughing generously at Jay's gift of mimicry. The other Bears players figured if Jorge thought it was funny, so did they.

Jay Brau came to Bear River the summer before his freshman year to live with his great-aunt and -uncle. Jack Brau and his wife Sally owned a farm a few miles west of town. At one time, the Braus kept a dairy farm, but now they leased the land out and boarded horses. Jack Brau was well-known in the area for his team of Belgian draft horses, which he took to competitive horse pulls throughout the region. Jack Brau was also proud of the fact that fifty years ago he had been the captain of the only Bear River football team to ever go undefeated. He had been a linebacker and fullback, and even now, decades later, he possessed a powerful body. The Braus were childless. They frequently took in foster kids for the county protective services. With their large farmhouse, it was easy to take in siblings, and they were known to be very kind foster parents.

Jay Brau was the only child of Meagan Brau. Meagan had been the victim of date rape in college. She was studying to be a pharmacist. Meagan had been brought up Baptist, and though she had left the faith, she could not bring herself to have an abortion or to give the child up for adoption. Meagan dropped out of school for a year and had the baby. Through hard work and determination, she finished her education and started her career in suburban Detroit. Jay never knew his father. Meagan raised Jay alone.

Meagan finally began dating when Jay was in middle school. Her boyfriend lost control on a curve while driving them to a bed and breakfast along U.S. 12 in southern Michigan. They were killed instantly by an oncoming dump truck. Jay had been staying with a friend when the accident happened. His world collapsed, but as was typical of Meagan Brau, she had planned ahead. Her will set up a trust for Jay and provided for him through college. Jay's grandparents lived in Florida, but neither were in good health, so his great-aunt and -uncle stepped in to provide Jay a home. Jay had visited them frequently as a child, and he had loved the farm where his great-uncle and grandfather had grown up, so it was agreed by Meagan Brau's family that Bear River would be Jay's new home.

Working with his great uncle proved to be just what was needed to get the silent, mourning boy back on track. Jay loved grooming the magnificent draft animals, and soon Jack Brau was teaching Jay to rig the horses and drive the Belgians around the farm. When August came around, Jack Brau suggested that Jay play football. It would toughen up the thin boy and introduce him to new friends before school started in the fall. Not wanting to disappoint his uncle, Jay agreed even though he had never played the sport.

Jay Brau had grown up playing basketball and baseball. Football did not come naturally. And Bear River was no place for a novice football player to be groomed slowly. He was a starter in his first JV game. He struggled, but through hard work he very slowly mastered some of the skills necessary to play the game. Until this season, Jay had played wide receiver, but he agreed to play tailback when no one else was available to play the position. On defense, he played linebacker like his uncle, but he lacked the ferocity necessary to play the position well. Jay had two natural gifts. The first was that he had inherited his mother's willpower and work ethic. The second was that he was a gifted mimic. His fondest memories of his mother were of her laughing as he imitated celebrity voices and the voices of her friends.

After getting more comfortable around his teammates that first school year, he began to share his gift for mimicry. He could do a great Pat Packer. He copied John Cale's Upper Peninsula Yooper dialect flawlessly. Coach Reese's growl was almost too easy. The kids on the team responded to his fun talent and would soon beg him to learn different voices. He mastered most of the teachers in the building by the start of basketball season his freshman year.

On the basketball court, Jay developed a very good outside shot. His junior year, he had made second team all-league. He was the best shooter on the team and was twice runner up in the school-wide HORSE tournament during the winter carnival. He lost two years in a row in the finals to Wash Dryer.

On the baseball team, Jay played right field and pitched on days when Wash Dryer reached his innings limit. Jay did not have the velocity pitching that Wash had, but he could throw a good curve and his knuckle ball was baffling. Last spring, he and Wash led the Bears to a league title. Wash kept a friendly rivalry going with Jay in most things. Jay envied Wash's effortless athleticism. Wash Dryer respected Jay's determination.

In the classroom, Jay Brau was hard working. He was a top ten student in all subjects. The teachers knew his story well and they took a shine to the shy, gangly boy with the crooked nose and curly hair. They even laughed when he mimicked them respectfully. The boys in the school appreciated his sense of humor. The girls liked him as well, but his awkward looks and shy way of talking with them kept him on the friend's-only list. In an insulated community like Bear River, it was tough to gain a place socially in a class of students that had been together since kindergarten. For his part, Jay Brau did not seek out the inclusive connections with classmates that a shared childhood engendered. Jay was slightly set apart from his peers, but he was not lonely.

Jay Brau had been with his boyfriend since last spring. They had attended a Future Farmers of America national conference together. They were both region representatives from the central Michigan area. Freddy Wilkes was from Riverdale. He was a blond-haired boy with blue eyes who ran cross country for Riverdale. Freddy lived on a dairy farm with his parents and his older sister who had Down syndrome. The sparks between Jay and Freddy started the first day. By the third night of the week-long conference, they went from sharing a hotel room to sharing a bed. Jay Brau gave his whole heart to another person for the first time since the death of his mother.

The students and staff at Bear River liked Jay Brau. They did not know of his sexual orientation, and Jay did not share it even with his great-aunt and -uncle. A handful of students in the school were un-closeted homosexuals, but Jay did not seek them out. The most difficult thing Jay dealt with was the general anti-gay attitudes and language of his teammates and friends. It was a burden but one he felt he had to endure. Jay convinced himself that if he kept quiet he could avoid any embarrassing revelations that might come back to hurt his great-aunt and -uncle. Jay loved and respected them, and he had made a deal with himself that he would not come out to them until after he had graduated from college.

The football practice the day after the first game was subdued, and the players went through the motions as though sleepwalking. After an hour of lackadaisical behavior, Coach Cale had seen enough. He blew his whistle sharply.

"Bring it in on me!" Cale shouted.

The boys formed a semi-circle around the two coaches.

"Gentlemen – after the defeat last night I would have hoped for a little more effort this morning. I think we need to do some running to clear the cobwebs," Cale said firmly. Mike Reese grimly shook his head in agreement. The players knew better than to protest.

"Take off your buckets and pull off your shoulder pads!" Reese called out.

"Five laps of the field in twelve minutes or less – and you get twenty gassers. Anyone takes longer than that and it's forty!" John Cale shouted. After the players assembled near the big maple tree on the southwest corner of the field, Reese blew his whistle sharply and the run began.

Jorge Martinez hung back to get Big Donnie Donnie and Phil Long moving and motivated. Donnie was not an enthusiastic runner and would walk as soon as he felt like no one was watching. Phil Long, a junior, was shorter and fatter than Big Donnie and if possible even lazier when it came to running. Most team runs would end with the two of them getting lapped on the perimeter of the field in less than three laps. Phil would take slow, choppy steps and piston his arms back and forth as if he were sprinting. Donnie would take longer strides, but unless someone ran right next to him he would stop and walk.

Jorge Martinez did not know that Phil had eaten a whole box of Apple Jacks and four long john donuts for breakfast washed down with a half-gallon of whole milk. That is not the sort of breakfast that an athlete should eat on a hot morning with running in mind. Jorge pushed and prodded the two lumbering linemen, and for the most part they responded but the pace proved to be too much. On the third lap, Phil Long vomited his entire breakfast up on the fifty-yard line. Coach Cale had Wash Dryer and the injured Seth Parker walk Phil over to the water horse. He whimpered and cried most of the way.

"Phil, you can't drink milk before practice – you know that. What is this, like the tenth time you have thrown up on the field?" Wash scolded the pudgy player. Phil only grunted as he stuck his head under the stream of water at the horse.

"Why did you even play this year, Phil, you don't really like it?" Seth Parker asked with as much sympathy as he could muster but even at that it sounded like an accusation. Wash Dryer gave the quarterback an exasperated look.

Phil Long stood up straight and with sad eyes told Seth, "My dad said that if I finish the season this year I can have his old truck and he'll pay for gas and insurance and everything."

Seth shook his head and said, "Okay."

Phil Long hated football. He hated exerting effort for just about any reason. His freshman year, he quit the team after only two practices. Last year in the second game of the JV season, he had wrenched his left knee early in the game. As he was carted from the field, he smiled broadly. He joyfully announced to Pat Packer, "I don't think I can play anymore this season, Coach!" Coach Packer was dumb-founded. He had never heard of a player getting excited at being injured. Phil's injury didn't require surgery but he stayed on crutches for the remainder of the fall just in case his football-loving father got the idea that he should return to the field. This season, the lure of getting his dad's old pickup truck as a reward was too much to resist, so once again Phil showed up to play the sport he despised. If there was one thing Phil hated more than physical exertion it was riding a school bus. He needed that truck.

The weekend was uneventful except for the Roman Candle Battle involving the Things. On Saturday evening, all four Things visited their cousins. The Lott family was spread out all over the area, but the clan's headquarters was Grandma Lott's farm on the edge of the town of Gratiot. The farm was overgrown with a mix of old apple trees, hay fields and a large forty-acre wood-lot. In the wood-lot was a winding ravine and a creek. On the side of the ravine was a mammoth oak tree. Over the years, various Lott children had built and maintained a rambling tree house in the oak tree. It was four levels, and a roof covered most of it. The highest point of the tree house was a crow's nest platform fifty feet off the ground that hung precariously over the creek. The tree house was a favorite destination for the dozens of Lott cousins and their friends. It was the site of sleep-overs, many wild BB gun fights and general mayhem.

It was another hot August evening – the Things and about fifteen friends and cousins were having a campout. Everyone came armed with BB guns and Things Three and Four brought two cases of Roman candles. Where they got them no one would ever learn, and the younger Things had their secret weapons stashed in a shed behind their grandma's house. The BB gun battle began after they chose teams. Thing One was team leader of the group that held the tree house. Thing Two had his team set up on the edge of the woodlot in the apple orchard. When the BB's started flying, the kids shouted and cursed as they were hit. The battles raged back and forth, and as the sun set, the Roman candles were deployed. The woods were lit up with flaming balls arching up at the tree house. Laughter and howls rang out as Thing One and his cadre of Lotts fled their fortress amidst the flaming projectiles bouncing in and out of the tree house. Thing Two had both Three and Four on his team. They began to chase the fleeing Thing One and a couple of his cohorts through the ravine, stopping only to light Roman candles and then running full tilt with the tubes in their hands aiming at their brother. It was hard to light the Roman candles and run at the same time, and soon they lost their targets in the gathering darkness.

Thing One called to all his soldiers and commanded them to retreat toward the road that bordered the southern end of the wood-lot. The ten members of the squad hunkered down in a deep ditch next to the road.

"Where the hell did those assholes get the Roman candles?" asked Mickey Lott. Mickey was a cross country runner for Gratiot. Taller than most Lotts and very skinny, he could run all day long and never get winded.

"I don't know. They are always getting shit like that somewhere," answered Thing One. "We need to split up and circle around and take them from behind." Thing One motioned to cousin Mickey, who tapped four of the Gratiot Lotts on the shoulder and led them down the ditch to the west. Thing One took the other group east. About a minute later, a siren blared and amplified shouts of "Freeze! Get on the ground right now!" echoed across the woodlot from a sheriff's car loudspeaker.

Thing Three and Thing Four had divided up the remaining Roman candles with their team. They set up an ambush near the road and waited for their brother and his teammates to show. Hearing a noise on the road, they rose up from the weeds a few yards from the ditch with lit Roman candles. The flaming balls bounced off the police cruiser passing on the road and one went in through the driver's side window and struck Deputy Sherriff Jim Mason in the face.

The siren sounded. Kids scattered in every direction. Deputy Mason shouted obscenities through his car speaker. He called a few of the kids by name as they ran toward the safety of their tree house and he caught them in the beam of his search-light. Jim Mason was married to Connie Lott, and he knew full well where those kids were heading. Fifteen years prior he had conceived his first child with his young girlfriend in the tree house after a night of drinking Wild Irish Rose wine.

A half-hour later, the entire group of kids was standing on the front porch of Grandma Lott's old farm house and their cousin-in-law, the deputy sheriff, was lecturing them sternly about fire hazards and what might have happen if some other deputy had been there and drawn his weapon when the Roman candle balls pelted the cruiser. Grandma Lott held Thing Three and Thing Four by their ears as they winced in pain. She would be deploying her wooden mixing spoon on the butts of the young Things in a few minutes.

The week of practice before the second game was short again. The JV's were to play on Wednesday and the varsity on Thursday before the start of the long holiday weekend. Practices went well enough and there were no disruptions. Seth Parker started throwing on Tuesday and by Wednesday he was ready to practice with pads.

Wash Dryer finished *Watership Down*, and his dad was right – it wasn't just about rabbits. He was talking about the book with Jay Brau and Jorge Martinez after practice in the locker room on Wednesday when Morg Miller interrupted and announced, "I read that book!" Wash was not really surprised – he knew that Morg was smarter than most people thought and that Morg's mother wouldn't let him watch TV or play video games until he read at least one book a week. Morg's reading tastes ran to science fiction and fantasy. Dolly Anne Miller never questioned what Morg read just as long as he kept reading. Morg had developed a very good speed-reading technique, and by Tuesday of most weeks, he was happily watching TV and playing video games to his heart's content.

Jay Brau perfectly mimicked Morg's voice and asked, "What did you think of the book, Morg?" Morg's broad smile faded a little and for a second he was lost in thought. He glanced at Jorge and then at Wash. Morg pointed at Jorge and said, "He's Bigwig," recalling the rabbit in the book noted for his heroic and protective nature. Jorge looked puzzled as Morg then pointed at Wash and said, "That makes you Hazel." Referring to the inspirational and clear-thinking leader of the small band of homeless rabbits. Someone across the locker room called Morg, and he wandered off without saying anything else. Jorge and Jay looked at Wash, who just shrugged.

"He's right – you are Bigwig," Wash said to Jorge.

"Then are you really Hazel?" Jay asked Wash.

Wash shook his head as if to say no – he didn't think he was Hazel, and he answered, "Read it."

By the start of the Labor Day weekend, both boys were several chapters into the book.

The second JV football game was on the road the Wednesday before Labor Day. The Bears played well for three quarters, but in the end, the McBride Marauders pulled away. The final score was 34-13. Tom Osborne managed to play the whole game without a bad snap at center. Scott Baier, the JV QB, played well and threw for over 150 yards without an interception. Coach Cale and Coach Reese took the lowly ASS sistants out for beers after the game, and the talk was positive and hopeful for the varsity game the next day.

Pat Packer had a few beers in him when he asked cheerfully, "Did the Miracle Healer show up today?"

John Cale knew exactly what Coach Packer meant, and he said, "Seth Parker is ready to go – the swelling is down and his arm feels fine. He practiced today and not a peep or a scratch."

Packer laughed. "The miracles never stop!"

Reese had heard enough. "Pat, give Seth some credit. Most of the time it's his batty mother that insists on holding the boy out for some minor injury she is convinced will leave him a cripple. That woman is as crazy as a shit-house rat." Packer nodded acknowledging the truth to that statement. Marlene Parker was a high-strung nut case – she had driven Packer over the edge several times when Seth played JV football.

The second game of the varsity season was on the hottest day of a very hot month of August. The bank clock thermometer read ninety-eight degrees. The community pool was packed with swimmers trying to beat the heat in the early evening. Two blocks away, the football field stands were virtually empty. On the visitors side, only the bravest and most dedicated parents came to watch their sons play for the McBride Marauders. McBride was mired in a seventeen-game losing streak that spanned from the second game of the season two years prior. The Bear River Bears beat them 6-0 on a stormy late-August night. The game featured three lightning delays and didn't finish until almost midnight.

The Marauders were being coached by their third head coach in three seasons. Last season, John Cale's squad got their only victory of the year by handing McBride a loss on the Marauders' home field. The McBride Marauders actually did win two games in their league the season before, but they had to forfeit the wins when it was discovered that they had used an ineligible player. The Marauders and the Bears had been playing a non-league game for decades, and during that stretch neither team had put together a winning streak against the other lasting more than two games. Every season this game was viewed as the "Toilet Bowl" by Pete the Pig Skin Predictor in the Mt. Pleasant paper. Pete had the Marauders winning this year's game by fourteen points.

Excerpt from the Pig Skin Predictor column week II

"The Bears are coming off a humiliating defeat at the hands of the Mecosta Panthers. Rumor has it the Bears Senior QB Seth Parker is still feeling the effects of an elbow injury. The Marauders will get Bob Sims – their young head coach – his first career victory. McBride took it on the chin from New Richmond last week 44-12. Look for the final score of this year's Toilet Bowl to be McBride 20 and Bear River 6. But don't ask me how the Bears will actually score – maybe their defensive standout LB Jorge Martinez will return a fumble."

Mike Reese had been on edge all day. Reading the words of Pig Skin Predictor had just about set him off. It was not an uncommon occurrence. Fifteen years ago, in a Mt. Pleasant bar in the late hours after a CMU homecoming game, Mike Reese had buttonholed Pete Petterson, the sports editor and lead columnist for the Mt. Pleasant paper, and explained quite forcibly, "Only a colossal asshole would refer to a football game played by high school kids as a 'Toilet Bowl.'"

Pete drunkenly told Mike Reese, "Lighten up, dickhead," and then shouted some statements about how if Bear River had the ability to hire and keep competent coaches, they wouldn't be such a "fucking joke on the football field!" Mike Reese responded by launching himself at the much larger sports reporter who had been an offensive tackle in his college football playing days. It took a half dozen former CMU football players who were working as bouncers in the bar to restore order. Both men were deposited in the parking lot of the bar into the waiting hands of the Mt. Pleasant police department. Fortunately for them both no charges were filed.

In the years since, the only words exchanged between them were results of wrestling meets Mike Reese called in to the paper during the winter. Every coach in the area knew of the long-running feud between Pete Petterson and Mike Reese. It was a story often told when beers were shared after games. The vast majority of the local coaching fraternity agreed with Mike Reese. Pete Petterson was a colossal asshole.

The game started after introductions and the national anthem. Big Bill Simons shouted the Bears lineup loud enough into the PA system for the swimmers down at the community pool to clearly hear their names over the splashing and little kids screaming. The Bear River marching band, twenty-eight strong – including six pudgy flag corps girls, played a desultory rendition of the Star Spangled Banner and the Fighting Bears Fight school song which was set to the tune of "On Wisconsin." No one in the home stands sang the words to the fight song. It was just too hot and they were parched after singing the anthem. Only three varsity cheerleaders were on the Bear sidelines. Four other girls on the squad sat out a half-season suspension for getting caught drinking at prom the previous spring.

The first quarter was scoreless. Neither team could sustain a drive. On defense Jorge Martinez dominated the middle of the field and Glenn Marcus played a disciplined game for a change. Thing Two intercepted a pass to start the second quarter, but the Bears could not capitalize. After two short runs by Jay Brau and a dropped pass, they had to punt. By mid-way through the second quarter, the heat was really catching up with all the players on both sides. Neither team had dressed more than twenty players for the game. Too many of the kids on both sides had been playing nearly every down.

With four minutes left in the half, a fine haze of dust hung over the field. The dry air was choking the players and no amount of water sucked down during breaks in the action seemed to quench their thirst. It was at this point that the poor choice in pre-game hydration came back to haunt Big Donnie Donnie. There was a mad howling scream coming from the field when Big Donnie went down. Lower leg cramps paralyzed and terrified him as he rolled on the ground pounding up a mini dust storm with his fists. Mike Reese, Wash Dryer and two paramedics from the Gratiot hospital ambulance who sat field side did their best to calm down the giant boy. The screams he let fly were compared to those of a dying elephant by those in attendance. What no one but Donnie and his mother knew was that Donnie had drunk three two-liter bottles of Mountain Dew since lunch that day despite repeated warnings from his coaches not to drink pop on game day – only water. He spent a good deal of the late afternoon pissing away what little water he had in his system, and for dinner he had eaten four grilled cheese and ham sandwiches and a whole bag of pork rinds – washed down with more Mountain Dew. The sugar, caffeine, salt and the dehydration they caused were just the ticket for Big Donnie Donnie's early exit from the game with severe leg cramps.

It was then that the scene got really weird. As Wash Dryer and three Bears players lifted the sobbing Big Donnie Donnie off the field, his mother came down out of the home stands yelling his name at the top of her voice. She presented quite a sight. Belinda Donnie stood well over six feet and she weighed in excess of 300 pounds. On that hot evening, she wore revealing short shorts and a sleeveless shirt highlighting both her belly roll and numerous badly done tattoos. She met the bewildered boys as they set their huge package down on the bench. Mrs. Donnie shoved them aside and held her giant baby boy in her arms as they both sobbed. During the commotion, Marlene Parker took her cue to get involved in the proceedings.

Marlene Parker came down from the opposite end of the home stands from Belinda Donnie. Not many people noticed the thin woman in the light blue sundress as she crossed the track and entered the playing field. Everyone was focused on the show Donnie and his mother were putting on. Marlene had her cellphone to her ear. In the press box, Clete Packer the Bear River A.D. laughed at the sight of Belinda Donnie's hysterics as he reached into his pocket to answer his phone and noticed simultaneously that Marlene Parker's name was on the screen and she was on the field approaching the referees.

"Cletus Packer, you get down here and stop this game immediately – these children are in danger!" Marlene Parker hissed into the phone. This was not the first time she had called Clete during one of Seth's games, but it was the first time she actually stormed the field. By the time Clete Packer got to the field, the Bear River coaches were already trying to separate Marlene Parker away from the referees. Coincidentally, the head referee had briefly been Seth Parker's pediatrician when Seth was a preschooler. Marlene had left his office furious with the doctor who insisted a slight fever and a sore throat were not a reason to have Seth tested for leukemia. Clete Packer arrived to the middle of the group of adults standing midfield under the watching eyes of shocked teen boys taking a knee with their respective teams a few yards away. Marlene Parker was berating the referees, accusing them of child endangerment – risking boys dying from heat stroke. She pulled away from Clete when he reached out to calm her down. Seth Parker felt the urge to run and jump in the Bear River to hide himself.

Dr. Macbeth had had enough. "Ma'am, I am a board-certified pediatrician, and I am fully aware of the dangers of heat exhaustion. The young man is dehydrated, and he will be fine. You have to leave this field, or I will penalize the home team."

Clete Packer turned and said, "Now just wait a minute Doc," Clete knew the doctor well. They were both members of the board at the Gratiot Elks Club.

Marlene Parker pivoted away from Mike Reese who had mostly succeeded in gaining her attention, and she got directly in front of the head referee, her eyes wide with recognition. She snidely questioned him. "Dr. Luke Macbeth!!?" Then she spat with venom. "I should have known it was you. You should have had your medical license suspended years ago you – you – quack!!"

That was all it took. The yellow flag flew high in the air and landed right in front of Seth Parker and Jorge Martinez. Dr. Macbeth blew his whistle loud enough to make everyone close by wince. He turned to Clete Packer and John Cale and announced firmly, "Remove this woman from the field, or I will forfeit this game to McBride!"

"Aw Jesus Christ, Doc," pleaded Clete Packer.

"You have two minutes." Dr. Macbeth replied flatly. He glanced at Marlene Parker who stood a few feet away with her arms folded. Thin-lipped, seething anger played across her face.

Two men approached midfield from the same direction. The potential for the confrontation to get even uglier was pressing down on the participants. All involved eyed the female intruder at midfield wondering what might happen next.

Deputy Sheriff Jim Mason showed up at midfield seconds later. He had been sitting in his air-conditioned cruiser in the school parking lot. With so few people in attendance at the game, he had not expected any crowd-control issues. He was damned if he was going to sweat his nuts off watching Bear River get its ass beat again. A member of the side-line chain gang had walked over to the parking lot and got his attention as the confrontation started to heat up at midfield. Jim Mason was sweating profusely after his jog from the parked cruiser. He had a bright red mark on his cheek where the Roman candle ball had scorched him two days earlier. Coming up behind him was Seth's father, Myron, "Mike", Parker; his face betrayed no emotion. Mike Parker had been shooting the shit with a group of friends at the concession stand when someone came up and said, "Mike, Marlene's on the field causing trouble." Mike Parker said nothing, and he turned and walked deliberately to where his wife was making her stand.

Deputy Mason was about to speak when Seth's father cut in front of him. "Marlene, we have to go now. Let Seth play his game – he will be just fine," Mike Parker said calmly. It was the voice of a man who had talked his high-strung wife off far too many ledges. Marlene Parker began to cry silently as her husband took her hand. The deputy led them both away.

Marlene Parker whispered quietly "Sorry – please forgive me," as she walked past Coach Cale and Coach Reese. Both men looked down at the ground in embarrassment for her.

The Bears were still huddled on one knee ten yards away. Morg Miller took a long drink from one of the green plastic Gatorade water bottles Wash Dryer had brought out after depositing Big Donnie on the bench. He announced quietly to no one in particular, "That is some fucked up shit." Jay Brau looked away from Morg and tipped his head down. He felt enraged at his teammate.

Jorge Martinez instinctively reached out and grabbed Seth Parker's shoulder pads. The quarterback spun to face him. "Keep your head in the game, Seth, it will be okay." Seth Parker's eyes were wide and moist. He shook his head slowly.

Moments later, the game started up. The referees paced off the penalty which pinned the Bears deep in their own territory. John Cale knew better than to put any pressure on his shell-shocked quarterback. He called two consecutive dives to Glenn Marcus. Then Seth Parker did get off a very nice punt, which the Marauders failed to return. The very next play. Morg Miller popped the ball out of the McBride tailback's hands and the ball skipped once before Jorge Martinez scooped it up and returned the fumble to the Marauder end zone. The Bears had scored their first touchdown of the year and they had their first lead.

Mike Reese tugged on John Cale's elbow during the celebration on the sideline.

"John, go for two. We might not get another chance."

Coach Cale nodded and sent in the offense. "I wish we would have put in 'Cheese Stick' this week," he noted to Reese. "It would work nicely here." Cheese Stick was a power I backfield play named in honor of the former team captain and offensive center from the prior season, Chester "Cheese" Colby. The Bears used it in short yardage situations on the goal line for the last two years of his career. Cheese would line up as the deep back and power through the line. Instead, Cale sent in a fake fullback dive left pitch right.

Seth Parker got a clean snap from Junior Shultz. Glenn Marcus executed a very nice fake dive, crashing into the middle linebacker with enough force to send him sprawling. The pitch was clean and Jay Brau had the corner of the end zone in his sights. He crossed the goal line just as the penalty flags flew. Phil Long was subbing for Big Donnie Donnie at right tackle. Phil was flagged for holding the defensive end. When the coaches looked at the film the next morning they both flew into a rage. Phil never even got off the ball, and he never touched the defensive end.

The yardage was marched off, and John Cale sent Thing One in with a play. The ball was snapped, and before Seth Parker could set his feet to throw, the Marauder defensive end shoved Phil Long into the quarterback, causing Seth to fire a pass long and high out of the end zone. Thing Two was wide open, but the ball was ten feet over his head. The attempt failed.

The half ended with the Bears kicking off and the Marauders taking a knee for one play. The mood in the locker room should have been a little higher, but the boys were still a little off after Marlene Parker's showdown with the refs. Seth Parker only nodded yes or no when talked to during the halftime session. John Cale was very concerned that his quarterback might crack up. The third play of the second half, Seth Parker went down with heat cramps. The Bears did not gain a first down the entire third quarter, but the lead was holding up as the fourth quarter started.

With three minutes left in the game, the McBride Marauders returned a punt for a touchdown. Greg DeVito was the backup punter. He kicked a low line drive right to the fastest Marauder. Two stutter step fakes, and he was able to return the punt sixty yards without being touched. The extra point cleared the crossbar on the goal post by three inches. The Bears failed to gain a single yard on offense in their last possession, and the Marauders celebrated as the clock ran out with them in possession of the ball at the fifty-yard line. The "Toilet Bowl" was over, and as Pete Petterson had predicted, the Bears found a way to lose to what looked to be their weakest opponent of the year.

The locker room cleared quickly after the game. Jorge and Wash took Seth out to get a burger. The limping quarterback was silent as they left. Morg Miller watched them leave, and he leaned back on the chair in front of his locker. There were only a handful of players still present. Morg sucked in his breath and announced, "Seth's mom is a crazy bitch." And with a dramatic sigh, he shook his head and uttered, "Mothers" with considerable disgust.

Jay Brau was a few feet away, and before he could stop himself, he threw a shoe at Morg hitting him in the shoulder. Morg stood and spun to face his attacker. He was shocked to see Jay Brau.

"Screw you, Morg. What the hell do you know?" Jay said menacingly.

Morg was almost ready to go after Jay when he remembered what had happened to Jay's mother.

"Hey – I'm sorry man. I didn't mean anything by it." Morg Miller held up his hands and apologized with sincerity.

Jay Brau turned away without saying anything. He fought back tears on the drive back to the farm. When he got into his bedroom after talking with his great-uncle about the game, he began to text his boyfriend from his laptop. Then the tears flowed.

In the coaches' office, John Cale made his calls to the local media. Mike Reese was showering. When he came into the office, Cale was on the speaker phone with the *Mt. Pleasant Daily News*. Cale was consulting his stat book and reading off totals. Reese pointed at the mute button. Cale told the person on the line to hold for just a second and he pushed the button.

"Is that Pete Petterson on the phone? What the hell? Where are his night desk interns from CMU?" Reese fired off the three quick questions.

Cale informed him that because of cutbacks at the paper, all the interns had been let go that week, Pete had to come in to field phone calls on game nights so they could make the deadline for the next day's paper. Cale clicked the mute button.

"Sorry about that Pete. Did you get all the totals?" Cale asked.

"Yeah, that ought to about do it for stats. I got couple of questions though," answered Petterson.

"Okay, Pete, what do you need to know?" Cale asked.

"I understand there was some sort of standoff on the field with a deranged parent in the first half. What can you tell me about that?" Petterson asked, barely keeping the amusement out of his voice.

John Cale leaned back in his chair and inhaled. Mike Reese grew red in the face and began to clench his fist.

"Any information about non-player-related matters will have to be given to you by Clete Packer in the AD office, Pete. No quote from me on this," John Cale said in a measured voice.

"Oh, come on, John. You know damn well that control freak superintendent of yours will clamp down on Fudge before I get to him for a quote. Give me something. We are leading the sports page tomorrow with a story about out-of-control parents on the sidelines. You have to say something on the record." Petterson pressed home his request.

Mike Reese held up his hand, and before Cale could say anything, he said, "Pete, this is Mike Reese. I have a quote for you."

Petterson was slightly taken aback by the sound of Reese's voice. "Okay, Coach, what can you give me?"

John Cale expected the worst, but Reese continued on in a calm voice. "It shows poor judgment on the part of the press to sensationalize unfortunate incidents involving disturbed people, especially when minor children are a major part of the story. Out of respect for the rights of minor children to privacy, Bear River Public Schools officials and coaches will not comment on this incident. Is that good enough for you, Pete? Let me add before you answer that the quote must appear in its entirety in print. Otherwise, the district lawyers will be calling you."

Pete Petterson was not pleased. He replied, "I can't use that, Coach."

"Well then, Pete, I guess there is only one thing left to say—" Mike Reese said with mock pleasantness.

"What's that?" snapped the irritated reporter.

"Fuck you!" And with that Reese pushed the button to end the call.

John Cale rubbed his head and blew out through his lips as he leaned back and sized up his assistant coach. "Six beers?" he asked.

"Maybe twelve." Reese replied with a smile.

**Overtime**

Wash Dryer returned home at midnight. He and Jorge Martinez had managed to get Seth Parker to eat a burger and fries. Jorge and Wash kept the conversation light and even managed to get Seth to laugh a few times. Wash was getting ready to text his dad, and he felt good about getting Seth to lighten up. The loss of the game stung a bit. Wash knew that this would be their best chance at escaping a winless season.

WashDryer: Knock Knock.

GregDryer: Who's there?

WashDryer: Owen.

GregDryer: Owen who?

WashDryer: Owen Two.

GregDryer: Not good. This was your best shot at a win wasn't it?

WashDryer: Yep. Seth's mom came on the field and tried to get the refs to call off the game because of the heat. She got us flagged for delay of game and Seth's dad had to take her home.

GregDryer: Really not good. Marlene is a very fragile person. How is Seth?

WashDryer: He's going to be ok. Jorge and I took him out after the game. He knows his mom has problems.

GregDryer: Finish the book?

WashDryer: Yep. Morg has read it. He says Jorge is Bigwig and I'm Hazel.

GregDryer: He might just be right.

WashDryer: Maybe with Jorge. I'm not an inspirational leader type. G'night I'm all wiped out.

GregDryer: Good night kiddo. You're more Hazel than you know. I'm proud of you.

Greg Dryer made a mental note to reread *Watership Down*. He hadn't read it since college. As he remembered it, Hazel and Bigwig would be the type of sons any father would be proud of. Even if they were rabbits.

# CHAPTER SEVEN

## OWEN 3

The film session the Friday morning before Labor Day was quiet and uneventful. Morg Miller sought out Jay Brau and apologized once more for his degrading talk about mothers. Jay gave him a smile and imitating Coach Cale's Yooper accent he said, "Well, Morgan, when you try your best, good things follow." It was a phrase the coach used frequently when instructing his players. Morg laughed at the mimicry and all was forgiven.

The practice was a typical socks-and-jocks run-through. Coach Cale gave a small speech at the end of practice about being careful during the holiday weekend and reminded the team that there was practice on Labor Day at 7 P.M. The whines and complaints were cut short by Coach Reese who shouted out, "Anyone missing practice on Monday will not start on Friday!"

The practice field cleared quickly, as did the locker room. The team members scattered to the four winds. John Cale worried a little about them as they left but soon was on his way home where his pregnant wife was packing for a trip to the Upper Peninsula. It would be a long trip, but Cale felt the need to see his parents. He was the youngest of four children, and his father would be turning seventy-five years old at Christmas-time. Bob Cale had had a stroke in the spring, and the family was worried that he was not taking proper care of himself.

The elder Cale would not hear anything about it. He insisted on fishing, mostly at remote streams, all summer long and was planning his fall deer hunting. The only lasting symptom of the stroke was a slight limp and an occasional short-term memory lapse. If anyone had the nerve to question Bob and ask how he was feeling, all they got in reply was a terse, "I'm good." Johnny Cale found talking to his dad about his health to be very one sided. Bob would merely laugh off his son's concerns. Barb Cale, John's mother, followed the old man around watchfully – which drove Bob nuts. Their bickering was nearly constant.

John Cale's concerns for the well-being of his players were not wholly unfounded. Three days of the last burst of freedom at the end of a long hot summer offered a wide array of activities for teenage boys. Not all of them safe or legal.

Most of the team spent the weekend with family and friends. Wash Dryer spent Friday afternoon helping his mom weed her vegetable garden and canning tomatoes. Laney Dryer loved gardening and Wash loved eating her canned goods. A large storage room in their basement was lined with canned tomatoes, pickled peppers, canned corn and Laney's famous strawberry jelly.

Jorge Martinez spent Saturday at his family reunion in Midland. Over seventy members of the extended Martinez clan gathered at his grandmother's house. Jorge played whiffle ball with his little cousins in the afternoon. A huge picnic featured wonderful Mexican food prepared by his many aunts. In the evening and late into the night, his uncles and older cousins played guitars and sang songs around a large bonfire. Jorge's cousin Reuben had recently gotten out of prison and was proudly showing off his new Harley and several new tattoos. Reuben had been in prison for assault with intent for beating a rival biker gang member so severely the man was blinded in one eye. It was generally understood that Reuben's new motorcycle was paid for through illegal activities – mostly drug running. Late in the evening, the burley Reuben grabbed Jorge in a headlock and with beery breath whispered to him, "Don't be a pendejo like me. You got brains mi'jo – use them."

Reuben had been a wrestler in high school and had taught the sport to Jorge when he was a young boy. The wrestling sessions helped the grieving Jorge get over the loss of his older brother who was killed in Iraq shortly after arriving there on assignment for the Army. Reuben and Jorge bonded, and when Reuben was not otherwise occupied, he attended Jorge's games and matches – usually a few of his fellow gang members came along. They formed a rather intimidating cheering section. Reuben was proud of his young cousin who was much more successful as an athlete than he had been. Poor grades and bad choices in friends ended Reuben's high school career before his senior year. Coach Mike Reese often said he had coached better wrestlers than Reuben, but none were close to being as tough as he was – with the possible exception of his nephew, Jorge.

Morg Miller spent the weekend working on "The Tank." His dad helped him bleed the break lines and change the master cylinder. On Saturday, they combed local junkyards looking for parts to make the parking brake work, but they were unsuccessful. Morg's dad, George, was over sixty years old, and the years he had spent working as a farmer and factory worker had stooped his back and toughened his skin. He knew the words to hundreds of dirty songs and limericks. Morg followed his dad around like a puppy when he was younger listening to his Dad's friends howl with laughter whenever George shared one of his limericks.

The Things – all four of them – traveled to Chicago with their dad to compete in a Tae Kwon Do tournament on Saturday. All four medaled in their respective divisions. Thing Two lost in his final match of the day because of repeated illegal blows. Otherwise, he would have been the champion in his group. On Sunday morning, they worked out for two hours with weights, and then their father ran them through a wrestling practice on the mat in their pole barn. After an hour of drills they paired off and wrestled matches against each other.

The matches lasted for about an hour, and the Things were getting tired and a little cranky. Thing Three put Thing One in an illegal sleeper hold and was choking him out when Thing Two jumped in and punched him in the ear. Thing Three released his hold and squared off against his older but smaller brother. Several punches and kicks later, both had black eyes and bloody noses. Their father finally broke up their fight. As punishment, he had all four brothers mow their five-acre lawn with two rickety old push mowers and two antique rotary mowers. It was a punishment he used often. In fact, that summer he had barely used his large riding mower at all. The grass was mostly brown and really didn't need mowing, but Ken Lott followed them the whole time in an old golf cart yelling at them if their pace slackened. It took nearly four hours in the hot sun. After dinner, he made them sit at the kitchen table quietly until after dark. The things finally went off to bed and slept until noon the next day. Ken and Jenny Lott enjoyed the peace and quiet immensely.

Greg DeVito spent the weekend fishing on the Muskegon River. He caught several nice trout but released them all. He and his father camped in a tent at the state park in Newaygo. Greg arrived home Monday afternoon with numerous bug bites and a badly sunburned neck, face and arms. The blisters on his neck were the size of half dollars.

Lenny Shore raced his bright green Benelli dirt bike all over the family farm. On Sunday, he took a nasty spill and might have been seriously hurt had he not been wearing his helmet. He slid through some gravel on a tight corner and dumped the bike. As it was, he had many bruises and a bad road rash on both legs – the price of wearing shorts while riding. His mother picked stones and dirt out of his legs for over an hour.

Seth Parker went on a date with Amber Taylor on Saturday night. They traveled to Lansing to see a movie. Jay Brau was on a date with his boyfriend at the same movie. There was an awkward moment in the theater lobby when they met after the movie. Jay introduced Freddy Wilkes as a friend he had met through FFA. Jay kept his cool, but his stomach was doing flip flops. He prayed that Amber and Seth had not seen him holding Freddy's hand during the film. They hadn't. Amber was studying Freddy closely as the boys walked away – he was very cute but she seemed to sense there was something more to Freddy than met the eye.

"I think Freddy might be gay," Amber stated as the couple walked to Seth's car.

"Huh?" Seth said as he settled into the driver's seat.

"I said I think Freddy Wilkes is gay and he has a crush on Jay." Amber embellished her statement.

"J.B. isn't gay." Seth replied with a little disgust, using the nickname the basketball players had given Jay last season.

"I didn't say Jay was gay – I said his friend probably is. Maybe Jay is just clueless," Amber said defensively.

Seth, like many teenage boys, was uncomfortable talking about homosexuality. He was getting edgy as they drove north out of Lansing on U.S. 127. He felt he had to defend Jay Brau's manhood. "Jay is an athlete and he goes out with girls. He took Butter Face Johnson to the prom last spring – we sat at the same table with them." Seth, too, spoke defensively.

Amber flashed her eyes angrily at Seth. "Don't call her that. Roxy is my friend," she said coldly. Roxanne "Butter Face" Johnson was a classmate they had known all their lives. She possessed what all the boys in school acknowledged as the hottest body in town. Puberty had been very generous to Roxanne. The boys teased her in middle school when her breasts began their expansive growth. And while she had a body to make the boys' heads turn, her face was not pleasant to look at. She had a large nose with a prominent bump on the bridge. She had worn braces for years and often had to wear her retainer to school. She had very bad eyesight, and her parents wouldn't buy her contacts, so she wore her oversized thick-lensed glasses everywhere. She never wore makeup, and she tended to cut her hair short. Instead of being shy because of her looks, Roxy Johnson was quite outgoing and popular. She was very bright and involved with just about every school organization. Morg Miller had given her the unfortunate nickname "Butter Face" in reference to the fact she had everything needed below the neck but her face ruined it. The jocks in school laughed about her, but more than a few wondered what she looked like naked. They all assumed Jay Brau had found out in the spring, but like Jorge Martinez he wouldn't speak of his conquests.

Amber was still agitated with Seth. "Yes, Jay took Roxy to the prom, but I know nothing happened. Roxy said that after prom all they did was sit in his car and talk about books they had read. Jay was so shy he didn't even kiss her good-night," she blurted, and instantly regretted having shared a friend's secret.

"Who's gonna want to kiss her anyway?" Seth asked petulantly. His words caused Amber to fold her arms and scoot up against the passenger door.

"You're such an asshole." Amber spat. "You're scared of gay people aren't you? That's why you're so worried about Jay being gay. You're afraid to shower in front of him now, aren't you? Just like the guys in Tommy Klapthorn's gym class when we were sophomores." Amber made reference to a very un-closeted gay boy who last year the girls in school nominated and elected homecoming king as a senior. It was another scandal in a string of small-town dust-ups over Tommy. When Tommy was a junior, the parents of some boys went to the school board to complain about Tommy being allowed to shower after gym class with their sons. It got ugly, and when the parents threatened to get lawyers involved, Superintendent Knapp got very nervous – his golden rule about no headlines was in danger. He quietly arranged for the boys to be transferred out of the class. When word of the coverup spread in the hallways of the school, a group of girls swore they would get revenge somehow. The next fall, nearly all the girls in school voted Tommy homecoming king. Sheldon Knapp was relieved the boy didn't wear makeup and a frilly outfit for the half-time ceremonies. Tommy wore a very nice tux. The picture in the *River County Register* showed Tommy with a beaming smile as the king from the prior year nervously placed the crown on his head.

Seth knew his plan for a make-out session with Amber was in danger. She was pissed off now. "Look, I'm sorry, okay? It really doesn't matter if Jay's buddy is gay. It doesn't matter if Jay is gay – but I don't think he is. It isn't fair either way for us to be talking about them anyway. It's their business, not ours." Seth was surprised at how reasonable and adult his words sounded. He gave his sweetest smile to Amber. He finished with, "I think Roxy is very nice, and Morg's an asshole for calling her that name and I'm just as bad. I promise I won't say it to anyone ever again." He said it with enough conviction that he believed it himself.

The anger drained from Amber's face and she edged over closer to him. In a few miles, he took her hand in his. She clasped it firmly. By the time they passed the Maple River Bridge, she had slid her hand down to his right thigh and was gently stroking it. The passion of the argument had ignited a different kind of passion. Jay turned down a side road by North Star. They parked in a rural cemetery. Amber stayed true to her vow of virginity, but the kissing and groping pushed the young couple closer than they had ever come to breaking that vow.

Seth dropped Amber off at her house before twelve as promised. He made his way home with the evidence of his arousal straining his khaki pants. Briefly, his mind wandered to those commercials on TV with some concern, commercials that advised for erections lasting for more than four hours, seek medical attention. Seth calculated the time as he pulled into the garage. His parents were awake and watching TV. Seth stayed behind a chair as he talked briefly with them, and then he walked briskly to his bathroom. His release was nearly immediate and explosive. He cleaned up and went to bed. Seth couldn't sleep. Less than thirty minutes later, he found himself fantasizing about Amber – but this time her sweet, heart-shaped face was atop Butter Face Johnson's body. He took his time and enjoyed the fantasy, and as he neared completion, he paused and sat up in bed. Seth reached out to his sock drawer and slid out a bright white athletic sock. When he was done, he made a mental note to himself to rinse the sock out before putting it in the laundry in the morning. His mom didn't like surprises.

Rich Lamb spent the weekend at his aunt's house in Ludington. He spent all his time at the beach. He had hoped to see the girls from Epworth, but they were nowhere to be found. Rich returned to Bear River with a sunburn and water squishing around in both ears.

Big Donnie Donnie was engrossed in building models all weekend long. The shelves in his bedroom were lined with dozens of simple snap-together car models. The paint jobs were often bright and garish, but there was never a part misapplied. He couldn't read the instructions very well, but he could study the simple schematics and replicate them. When Big Donnie Donnie was a young boy his mother, Belinda Donnie, had bought up all the Legos she could find at the yard sales where she did almost all of his clothes shopping. Big Donnie Donnie had thousands of Legos, and he built enormous free-form castles in the basement of their ramshackle ranch house on the edge of town.

By the time Big Donnie Donnie reached high school, he switched to model cars. Just about every week, he would present one of his cars to a teacher, classmate or teammate. Most of them accepted the gift with a smile, not wanting to see the giant boy's crestfallen face if they refused. Big Donnie Donnie got upset a year prior when Thing One and Thing Two gave away the cars he'd given them to their younger brothers, who promptly blew them up with dozens of firecrackers in a field near their house. The explosions accidently started a grass fire that required the fire department to extinguish. Pictures of the fire and a short story explaining it appeared in the next edition of the *River County Register*. When the story was explained by his mother to Big Donnie Donnie, his face got dark and he went to find the Things. When he found them he gravely told them, "No more cars for you."

Phil Long attended a hog and corn roast at a neighbor's house on Saturday night. Over a four-hour period of time, he consumed ten heaping plates of barbecued pork, twelve ears of corn, half a large watermelon and a whole strawberry rhubarb pie. He washed it all down with fifteen cans of Coke. He left at midnight and went to bed bloated and very gassy. And even though he made numerous trips to the bathroom Sunday morning before church, he considered the day before his happiest day of the whole summer.

Tim Manikowski visited his cousin in Ann Arbor. The cousin, Jared, was his connection for marijuana and other drugs. Jared Manikowski was in his sixth year at the University of Michigan. His latest major was English. It didn't really matter to him what classes he was taking – he got effortless A's in almost all of them. He was thinking he might actually graduate this year and maybe go to law school. He made plenty of money dealing drugs and enjoyed life in Michigan's most open-minded town. Tim used his cousin as a role model in the much smaller and more restrictive market of Bear River. After going to the football game with his cousin on Saturday, Tim headed north with a duffel bag of product tucked behind the seat of his bright blue Toyota pickup. Tim rarely used drugs himself. Weed made him dizzy and gave him a dry mouth. He liked the money, and he liked the power of being the supplier in school.

Glenn Marcus went cruising Saturday night with his mom's boyfriend. Shawn Boyer was the latest in a long line of men that Shelly Marcus had paraded in front of her three kids as her "soul mate." Most grew tired of her and her three rug rats after only a few months. Shawn was a hard-drinking stone mason if and when he could find work. Mostly he collected unemployment and was working on getting workman's comp for what he claimed was his bad back. When opportunity presented itself for an easy score, Shawn Boyer dabbled in breaking and entering. Glenn kind of liked Shawn – he had hung around for almost a year, and he was good to Glenn's mom – at least he never hit her.

Shawn had been drinking off and on all day, and shortly after dark he threw Glenn the keys to his 1968 Camaro and said with a slight slur, "Let's go get some more beers." Glenn had never driven the car before, but he had admired it for some time so he jumped at the chance. The beer run lasted for two hours with stops at two houses but no party store. Glenn waited in the car listening to the stereo at each stop. Later, as they were cruising by an apartment complex in Gratiot, Shawn asked Glenn to stop and wait but keep the car running. Shawn reached into the glove compartment and pulled out a nickel-plated .38 caliber revolver. Glenn was a little nervous as he watched him enter the seedy-looking complex. In a few minutes, Shawn returned to the car.

"Sum'bitch didn't have the money he owed me," Shawn said clearly – his beery slur was gone and his eyes were suddenly quite clear. He handed Glenn a piece of paper with an address and another number written on it. "Let's go – can you find that place?" Shawn asked. His tone was serious enough that Glenn just nodded and put the car in gear. Soon, Glenn had the car at the address – a house on a golf course on the other side of town.

"Pull over and leave it running while I get out." Shawn commanded, and he left the vehicle. Before he shut the door, he told Glenn to give him the paper. "Go roll for twenty minutes and don't do anything stupid and get pulled over by the cops or nothing. Come by here and I'll be waiting at the corner." Shawn scanned the nearby houses and then walked to the side of the stately home. As he pulled away, Glenn surmised that written on the paper was the access code for the alarm.

Shawn's contact begged off having any of the money he was owed. When Shawn produced the .38 he quickly turned over a "Sure thing." The contact was a handy-man who had worked at the house off and on for years. He had the code to the alarm system. The teary-eyed man assured Shawn that the elderly couple was out of town and they had plenty of easy-to-move stuff and usually had cash on hand.

The couple was out of town attending a funeral. Shawn rifled through the house quickly. In twenty minutes, he was waiting at the corner with a leather bag tucked under his arm when Glenn pulled up. Shawn wordlessly got into the passenger seat. As they drove away, Shawn told Glenn to get on the freeway and drive north. Glenn drove cautiously – Shawn didn't have to tell him to. In just over half an hour, they were sitting outside a party store in Mt. Pleasant. Shawn opened the bag for the first time. "Keep an eye out." He told Glenn.

In few moments, Shawn exhaled and closed the bag. He had something in his hand. "Got some cash and a few gold and silver coins. Some jewelry too, but nothin' too fancy. That shit is probably in the safe. No time to crack that, and it was in the floor in a closet. I got this guy in Saginaw – he'll take the coins and the jewelry – he can remove the stones and melt the gold. He ought to give me a couple grand – gotta be two ounces there." He handed Glenn a fifty-dollar bill and a heavy ring. The ring was set with a cheap-looking green gem and looked like a class ring. The markings read "MSU 1954 Rose Bowl." Shawn smiled and said, "That ring ain't solid gold or nothing, but you're a football player – thought you might like it. Keep your mouth shut about this." Shawn stashed the bag under the seat and opened the door. "I'm gonna get the beers," he announced. Glenn felt the heft of the ring and then shoved it in his front pocket. He then opened his wallet and put the fifty in. Tetherboy was thinking two things as he looked through the store window and watched Shawn pay for the beer. The first was that he kind of liked being a wheel man. The other was that Shawn might be wrong about the Rose Bowl ring – some sports memorabilia was worth a few bucks.

Glenn Marcus was twenty minutes late to football practice on Monday evening. Every other varsity player was there, and they had just finished stretching and warming up. "Mr. Marcus – nice of you to join us," Coach Reese said loudly as he approached the field. Glenn mumbled something about not being able to get a ride and having to walk. Reese held up his hand to stop the story. "Give me five laps now and five more when we're done," Reese said without any kindness in his voice. Glenn took off on his run. He knew better than to let Reese see him dogging it, so he kept a good pace going. As he rounded the field, he watched the soccer teams break a huddle and jog off to their field-house. They were done with their practice. He smiled. Tonight would see the continuation of The Tradition.

As practice started in earnest, Pat Packer waved John Cale over to the JV practice area. "Jesus Christ," Packer hissed. "We only got twelve JV's here." The two coaches stood just out of ear-shot of the teams.

Cale surveyed the JV team as they took a knee in front of Coach Marker. "Did you tell them they can't start Thursday if they miss this practice?" he asked.

"Yeah. Goddammed freshman don't listen for shit." Packer answered.

"Where is Scott Baier?" Cale asked about the freshman JV quarterback.

Packer snorted with disgust and said, "The superstar? His dad called me about an hour ago saying they were just crossing the Mackinac Bridge. Gave me some lame-assed story about having car trouble this morning and Scotty wouldn't be able to make practice this evening. Total bullshit."

A concerned look crossed Cale's face. "Pat, you gotta stay positive with these JV's. Scott Baier is likely to be our starting varsity QB in two seasons, and I think he might be pretty good. Work with him and he might become the leader we need." Cale gave Packer a smile in hopes that he could get his coach to see the possibility.

Packer didn't get the hint. His face darkened. "Yeah, well if Scotty is half the player his old man thinks he is right now, he'll be all-state and get a scholarship to MSU for sure." He concluded with bitter sarcasm.

Cale let it go. He didn't have time to waste scolding Packer about his attitude. He put another check on his mental list of reasons why Pat Packer needed to be phased out of the BRHS football program. "Coach, run your kids through drills, and we'll team up for a few scrimmage plays at the end of practice." He concluded the conversation with a cool and distant tone as he turned to walk back to the varsity practice area.

The players were rusty and tired from their weekend activities. Greg DeVito complained mightily about his sunburn. Phil Long was sluggish and whiny. Lenny Shore's legs bled off and on throughout practice from his road rash. Morg Miller started calling him the "Benelli Bleeder." Lenny flipped him off wordlessly each time but didn't miss a play. Only Big Donnie Donnie seemed to be in the mood to practice hard. When he crushed a couple of JV's with a block during the late practice scrimmage, Jorge Martinez gave him a high five. Donnie was ecstatic.

During the last water break as the players approached the water horse, Morg Miller announced, "Seniors, drink up big time. We're gonna need the fluid." There were some laughs in response.

Practice finished with the sun hanging low in the sky. The temperature was the coolest it had been in weeks. The next day would be the first day of the school year. The boys showered, and the Seniors started to congregate around "The Tank" in the student parking lot. The sun was down and twilight was fading. They watched as the coaches pulled out of the staff parking lot. Keith Marker's motorcycle made a little squawk as he hit the street in front of the school. Coach Marker opened up on the throttle and sped away. Lenny Shore gave an appreciative smile.

All the Seniors were present including Wash Dryer. Jay Brau looked a little nervous – he was uncomfortable with "The Tradition" but didn't want to be marked as a bad teammate. Big Donnie Donnie was there but he was confused about what was going on. Morg Miller announced "Okay, let's go – get on The Tank and I'll give you a ride." The boys clambered onto the flatbed without much noise. Jorge Martinez climbed in the cab with Morg.

Morg guided his hulking truck down the street past the school. After a block, he made a right turn and took the bridge across the Bear River. He made another right past the game field and cruised toward the curve by the middle school. The soccer practice field was in the middle of the curve just south of the middle school. The northwest corner of the field lay a few yards away from the street. Morg parked The Tank on the shallow decline leading to the north of the curve. Darkness was enveloping the neighborhood as the boys dismounted the truck and quietly walked toward the immaculately groomed soccer pitch.

For the last decade, the seniors on the BRHS football teams had ceremonially "watered" the soccer pitch. Originally, this much-anticipated event occurred in the last week of the season, but heightened awareness of the soccer coaching staff and "Fudge" Packer had forced the seniors of recent classes to pick less conspicuous times. The soccer coaches dreamed of catching the football team in mid-act someday. Ben Coffey, the district grounds crew chief and JV soccer coach, usually sat in his Gator utility tractor on the soccer pitch until well after dark the last week of football practice in hopes of nailing the "fucking thugs," as he called the football squad. The whole school knew of The Tradition, but each successive senior class of football players for over ten years had managed to escape getting caught in the act.

The Tradition of urinating on the soccer field was a rite of passage for football players in Bear River. The fact that the soccer team was made up of friends and classmates they had known their whole lives made little difference. Jorge Martinez knew that there were at least a half dozen fellow wrestlers playing varsity soccer this year. Jay Brau and Seth Parker played basketball with several others. Wash Dryer was good friends with four or five players, and he had grown up across the street from Liam Pickering the soccer team's best player and team captain until third grade. Wash's mom had pictures of the two of them playing together as kids. Their smiles gave no hint that in the future they would be on opposite sides in the great Bear River divide. None of that mattered now. This was about the divide between the football team and the soccer team at a school that cared nothing about the fortunes of the former and worshiped the latter. This was about a group of teenage boys bonding against the community that laughed at them and scorned their efforts. The Tradition was a symbolic act of rebellion. None of the kids involved would articulate it that way, but acts of rebellion are a common human instinct of an oppressed social group.

The seniors of the BRHS football team felt tradition and full bladders, adding urgency to their mission. They gathered at midfield and the muted glow of the security light on the soccer fieldhouse roof cast their shadows across the pitch. "Gentlemen," Morg Miller, the official organizer of this year's "watering" intoned with mock gravity. "Let us commence." The boys fumbled with their shorts and soon enough the sound of urine softly landing on grass could be heard. A few dramatic "ahhs" were uttered. Big Donnie Donnie watched with wide eyes as his friends did their business. He made no move to duplicate them.

"Come on Donnie. You gotta do it," Morg said with a fatherly tone.

"Uh uh. My mom says that I can't pee-pee outside anymore." Big Donnie Donnie replied with fear. Tim Manikowski and Lenny Shore snickered at the statement.

"Ah Jesus, Donnie," Glenn Marcus said accusingly.

Jorge Martinez held up his hand to stop Glenn. "Donnie, it's okay – no one will tell your mom."

Big Donnie Donnie giggled and shrugged. In a flash, he had his member out and was squirting the ground with short bursts of piss. As he finished, Morg Miller cleared his throat and spoke again in his official-sounding mock-baritone voice. "One last thing, gentlemen." With that, Morg strode a few yards away from the group and straddled the midfield line. He dramatically dropped his shorts and boxers to his ankles and assumed a deep wrestling stance. With little effort, a very long turd dropped from between his butt cheeks. The end of the act was announced with a loud fart. All the boys, even Jay Brau, laughed out loud but quickly realized that they were being too noisy.

Greg DeVito was nearly gagging when he exclaimed, "Holy shit! It's a new tradition!"

Morg Miller drew up his shorts and announced, "Been saving that all weekend. Hope Picky lands on it in practice tomorrow!" More stifled laughter followed as Morg fished out his cellphone and used the flashlight app to highlight the glistening turd. It was shaped like a long fish hook.

Wash Dryer stopped laughing. "We better get the hell out of here. Somebody might see that light," he announced with authority.

The boys began a brisk walk back to the street. When they got there, The Tank was gone. "Fuck!" Morg exclaimed quietly. There was a moment of panic with whispered accusations and general hushed cussing.

Jorge Martinez started walking fast down the little hill. "Over here," he whispered loudly and pointed to a practice baseball field north of the middle school. The Tank was sitting on third base. The street light on the next corner highlighted its dark shape fifty yards away. There was no curb on the street past the school and The Tank had popped out of gear and rolled silently to a stop on flat ground. The boys dashed to it and pushed the truck out to the street.

Seth Parker was exasperated as they got the truck to the street. "Morg, this fucking truck is nothing but a goddamned disaster waiting to happen." As Morg opened the driver's side door, he turned and shrugged at Seth. The boys laughed nervously as they jumped aboard and made their escape.

A moment later, Jorge Martinez turned to Morg in the cab of the truck. He had a quizzical look on his face. "How the hell can you shit like that on command? And aren't you sitting there with shit in your crack?" he asked in a puzzled way.

"Nope," Morg said proudly. "I always get a clean pinch off as long as I ain't been drinkin'." Jorge laughed in response.

At 6:45 Tuesday morning, Ben Coffey entered Clete Packer's office. He was wearing his soccer warm up and his face was purple with rage. Clete was about to greet him when Coffey began his angry rant. "Those goddamned thugs shit on my field last night!"

Clete Packer got a screwed-up look on his face and loudly replied, "What in the hell are you talking about?'

Coffey explained that he had found Morg Miller's fish-hook-shaped turd at midfield on the soccer pitch when he went to start the sprinkling system at dawn. Then he proceeded to rail on about "The Tradition" and filthy football players messing up the pH of the turf and causing the grass to brown. Clete listened for a few minutes, and during a pause, he told Coffey, "Look, class begins in an hour. I'll get John and Mike down here and we'll see what they know about this." He picked up his phone and hit the all-call code.

John Cale was going over his class lists at his classroom desk. Clete Packer's booming voice erupted from the overhead speakers throughout the building. "Will Coach Cale and Coach Reese please report to the AD office immediately!" John Cale muttered a few choice words and proceeded out his classroom door. He met Mike Reese at the office door. Reese raised his eyebrows, frowned and tipped his head to signify he didn't have a clue either. They both guessed what was up when they looked through the window of Clete Packer's office by the main office desk and saw a bug-eyed Ben Coffey glaring at them.

Before they sat down, Coffey shouted, "Your goddamned thugs shit on my field last night!" Cale shifted in his chair to look directly at Coffey, but before he could speak, Reese jumped in. Cale could tell his easily riled assistant coach was ready to explode. Cale's first instinct was to stop him, but he was angry, too. Class was going to begin in few minutes and he really didn't need this distraction. He let Reese take the lead.

"Just who in the hell do you think you're yelling at, Ben?" Reese began. "What shit are you talking about?" Without pausing, Reese shifted his gaze to Packer. "This could wait until after school couldn't it? John and I teach for a living – we don't mow friggin' lawns!" Reese said without taking the edge off his voice in deference to Packer's authority.

It was Clete Packer's turn to get hot under the collar. "Listen, we all know about the football players pissing on the soccer pitch every goddamned year! This time they stepped over the line, and I intend to get to the bottom of this. This sick little tradition your program has is going to stop right fucking now!"

Reese was not backing down. "How in the hell do you know it was even a football player? Probably some dog took a shit and Coffey couldn't tell the difference when he sniffed it!" Reese jerked his thumb toward the soccer coach without looking at him.

"I know what dog shit looks like!" Coffey shouted at Reese.

Reese paused and looked at Coffey, and with a mocking tone asked, "Did you save it for the investigation, Ben? Maybe the district can do DNA testing of all the dogs in the area. Should only cost us a few thousand dollars."

Coffey's rage was bubbling over now. "Fuck you! I should have thrown it on your field!"

Reese rose from his chair, but John Cale got between him and the soccer coach.

Packer looked out his window and he could see the secretaries ushering Principal Mike Shanahan toward his office door. He decided to calm down the matter quickly. "Take it easy, boys. Shanahan is coming in. Let's not make this a board matter just now," he hissed with urgency. Ben Coffey sat in a chair as Packer stepped around his desk to open the door.

Mike Shanahan stepped through the door. Shanahan was tall and broad shouldered. He was dressed in a $500 suit. His silver-gray hair was perfectly cut. Anyone seeing him for the first time would expect him to be the perfect administrator for the highly visible and often difficult job of high school principal. Everybody who knew him even casually knew that Mike Shanahan was worthless at any part of his job other than sucking up to the superintendent and the school board. "Is there some sort of dispute, gentlemen? You know there are kids coming through the door now. It wouldn't be professional of us for them to hear staff shouting back and forth behind closed doors on the first day of school, now would it, boys?" Mike smiled and spoke in a calm and fatherly tone.

"No dispute here, Mike." Clete Packer answered in an equally calm voice. "The coaches and I were working out some issues about practice facilities. But Coach Reese was just pointing out how he and Coach Cale need to get to their classrooms so—" Packer clasped John Cale's shoulder and held his open palm toward the door. Cale and Reese exchanged pleasant greetings with the Principal as Packer ushered them into the outer office.

Mike Reese was not done. His competitive spirit was in full gear as he headed for the door. He pivoted before he exited the main office door with John Cale. He had a twinkle in his eye and a smile on his face as he stuck his head back into Clete Packer's office. Ben Coffey was just about to exit when Reese began. "Oh, I almost forgot," Reese said with choirboy sweetness dripping from his words. "Apparently, Ben, you must have mislaid the five request forms John Cale sent you since June to have our practice field mowed and lined. Is there any chance you might get to that this week? Have a good first day of school gentlemen." And with that Mike Reese closed the door in front of Ben Coffey and walked out. He could almost feel the icy stare of hatred from Ben Coffey on his back as he left. Now he could start his thirty-ninth year of teaching in a good mood.

The halls were filling with students as Mike Reese made it to his classroom. Several kids greeted him warmly. Despite the cool morning temperatures, most of the kids were still in shorts and warm-weather clothes. Some of the girls wore flip flops. High school kids give up on summer only begrudgingly. When the first bell rang, the noise level rose in the hallway. Kids were crammed together, but everyone was moving toward some destination. A few freshmen students could be seen with panicked and puzzled looks on their faces as they studied their class schedules and tried to read room numbers at the same time.

Morg Miller groaned and cussed as he made his way through the crowded halls. He spied Roxanne Johnson coming toward him. He was getting ready to shout, "Hiya Butter Face," but he was stopped short and left speechless. Next to Butter Face was a tan goddess with jet black hair and deep brown eyes. She was nearly as tall as Butter Face and her beauty was stunning. Morg watched the girls glide past without a word. During the morning, the buzz about the incredibly hot new girl grew. Reports of sightings of her spread among the BRHS athletes, and by lunch-time, the jocks were in full stalking mode.

At noon, Wash Dryer, Jorge Martinez and Seth Parker sat at a table in the cafeteria waiting for the lunch line to shorten. Roxanne Johnson and Amber Taylor walked up to the table with the new girl between them. The three boys stopped their conversation as the girls approached. Roxanne took the lead, "Hi, guys. This is Maricel Arambula. She's an exchange student from Bolivia."

Wash and Jorge rose from their chairs. Seth looked at them as if they had done something weird, and then he realized what was going on, and he stood as well. Maricel greeted them in only slightly accented English. Wash felt a blush coming to his face, and he had the sudden thought that the girl was so pretty that it hurt to look at her. She smiled as she shook his hand. Wash's heart lurched. Seth was careful not to fawn over her. Amber was looking directly into his face as he took her hand. Jorge was his usual cool self, and as he took her hand, he greeted her and welcomed her to the school in Spanish.

Maricel lit up as Jorge talked, and she laughed a soft laugh as she thanked him in Spanish as well. She kept talking to him, noting in Spanish that his accent was unfamiliar. Jorge paused and smiled one of his patented small smiles. He switched to English, "My family has been in Michigan for three generations – mostly we speak Spanglish at home. I have never been to Mexico or South America."

Maricel looked puzzled. "What is this Spanglish you speak of?" she asked as her eyes shifted among the three boys. She was nervous as if she was being pranked.

Jorge laughed his gentle laugh to put her at ease. "Spanglish is American slang. It's a blend of English and Barrio Spanish that Mexican Americans like me use with each other. It isn't as refined as your language at all," he said as he held her gaze. Wash felt the odd sensation of jealousy creeping in. His friend was just too good at this. He had never been jealous of Jorge before, and he was a little ashamed of himself.

Seth burst into the conversation. "We're going to get in line for lunch. Do you girls want to join us?" The girls agreed, and with trays in hand, they returned to the table. A few soccer players, including Liam Pickering, came up to greet the new girl. Seth did his best to make their stay brief. The football/soccer mismatch at Bear River be damned – he was still the quarterback, and that meant he had to control the room.

The conversation turned to the boys and their chosen sport. Maricel was confused about American football and how it was different from soccer, which is what she knew as football. It was Wash's turn to engage her and explain the differences. He only blushed once or twice as she hung on his every word smiling and asking questions. Jorge was talking to Roxanne Johnson as this went on – he respectfully let Wash have his time. He glanced a few times at Wash and then back at Seth. He made a slight gesture at Seth to get him to notice Wash. Seth was clueless as he talked to his girlfriend, Amber. Jorge understood that Wash was charming the girl in a way that was going to be the best opening any of the boys in school would have. He was teaching her about this strange new world she was in. Wash was better equipped than anyone in the building at accomplishing this. The fact that Wash was unaware of his effect on Maricel made it even more entertaining to Jorge. He wondered how long it would be before his friend figured out what was in store for him.

The lunch meetings continued for the rest of the week. Wash found himself still blushing whenever Maricel smiled at him, but he grew more comfortable around her with each encounter. Jorge was confident that before long, Wash would figure it out and realize the opportunity that was presenting itself. Jorge kept quiet, though, and gave no assistance. As with most things involving romance, Jorge Martinez kept his own counsel.

The football team settled into practice and preparations for the coming game with the Sumner Spartans. Most everyone was healthy and ready to play. Tim Manikowski and Lenny Shore were still sitting out their respective suspensions, but the coaching staff was beginning to give them more reps with the starting teams. Tim was running good routes as a receiver and getting a nice rhythm going with Seth Parker. On defense, Lenny Shore would be a significant upgrade at strong side linebacker, allowing Jay Brau to switch to the weak side. When that package was on the practice field together, Mike Reese smiled at the results, but he was guarded in his optimism. Reese knew that when the first grade checks came out, Lenny Shore was very likely to be ineligible. That would come in three weeks. The same time Lenny was scheduled to play his first game of his senior season.

The JV Bears traveled to Sumner on Thursday evening and got thumped. The boys who missed Monday's practice sat out the first quarter. The scoreboard at the start of the second quarter saw the home team up 21-0. Things got worse from there – the final score was 49-0. Scott Baier threw three interceptions and fumbled two snaps. Pat Packer was beside himself on the sidelines, and at the end of the game, he yelled at the defeated and dispirited kids for a full fifteen minutes using profanity more than once. "This game was lost on Monday night because some of you thought this team was not important enough for you to follow through on your commitments. Well, by God, if you can't put this team first in your priorities, then you damn well better turn in your gear!" Packer shouted in his conclusion. Keith Marker cringed when he said that, and he immediately stepped in with some more encouraging and soothing words. He only hoped none of the kids would take up Packer's offer to quit.

The next day, two freshmen turned in their pads and jerseys. After the JV team watched film and did some running at a short practice, the two lowly ASS sistants found themselves sitting in the coaching office with Coach Cale and Coach Reese. Cale explained in no uncertain terms that the last thing the program needed was kids quitting. The numbers were low to the point of being critical. "Pat, damn it. You know grade checks are in a few weeks. Your actions last night put us at risk of not having enough players to finish the JV season. Both those boys are worth putting our effort into, and you better get on the phone with their parents and get this straightened out. Your childish temper tantrums are not an effective coaching tool, and if you can't control yourself, then maybe YOU better find something better to do with your time." The hang-dog look on Packer's face gave Cale hope that the message was getting through.

"Pat, you should call those boys right now and apologize personally for your tantrum, and then Monday you need to apologize to the team. Keith, you call their parents and talk to them about how in the heat of the moment, the inappropriate behavior of a coach was the cause of their kids quitting, and give them assurances it will not happen again – maybe they will send their kids back to us." Mike Reese said after Cale finished speaking. John Cale nodded, endorsing Reese's plan.

"Get it done, Pat. Mike and I don't have time for this shit right now. We got kick-off in less than two hours. If we have another conversation like this this season, I will be asking for your resignation." John Cale concluded tersely. Packer was practically in tears when he left the office. Keith Marker stayed behind.

"I can't coach this team alone, Coach." Marker said sincerely to John Cale.

"Don't worry, Keith. Fudge Packer will never let John fire his nephew." Mike Reese said with a smile. "We just got to get Pat to reign in his temper around the kids."

The varsity game was on a pleasantly warm evening. There were a few more fans in attendance than the prior week. Wash Dryer was carrying gear onto the field a few minutes before kickoff when he glanced up in the stands and caught sight of Maricel sitting with Roxanne and Amber. She stood and waved. Wash blushed deeply and set down his armload and waved back.

The game started with Sumner returning the kickoff for a touchdown. The Bear offense was stifled from the get-go, and they were down 21-0 near the end of the first half. John Cale had called five passing plays in the half. Each time, the left defensive end blew past Big Donnie Donnie and crushed Seth Parker before he completed his drop-back steps.

At halftime, Coach Cale and Coach Reese talked as they walked across the pedestrian bridge behind the team on the way to the locker room. "Mike, I'm gonna start rolling out to the left to pass and we'll tell Seth to tuck it and go unless Thing One is wide open."

"That is the only thing that might work on passing downs. Donnie can't block their left end at all. Jorge can pull and lead and Jay can seal their right end, I think." Reese agreed. They spent most of the time at the half going over the play calling.

The third quarter started with Jay Brau returning the kickoff nearly fifty yards. On the next play, Seth fumbled the snap and the Sumner Spartans had the ball at midfield. It did not look good – the Bears were looking at another miserable defeat and a probable running clock for most of the second half. Two plays after that, the Spartans fumbled in the backfield and Jorge Martinez scooped up the ball and scored a touchdown going the other way. Some cheers rose up from the home side. The scoreboard showed guests 21-7, and John Cale thought hopefully that the Bears could close the gap and maybe even win. If they could find a way to pass the ball just a little.

Seth Parker got off a nice kickoff, but the Spartans set up a wall and it looked like they were going to get another return for a score. Morg Miller shed his block, and as he hit the returner, he punched the ball loose. Thing Two recovered the fumble, and the Bears had the ball at the Spartan 45-yard line. Glenn Marcus turned a dive play into a 20-yard gain on the first play of the possession. Cale could feel the momentum shifting. The crowd was actually on its feet. Most of the band members had left after halftime, but those who remained blew "Charge!" on their horns. Wash caught a glimpse of Maricel standing and cheering. He had a warm feeling of pride.

The next two plays gained no yardage. On the second play, the left defensive end shed Big Donnie Donnie on a veer play to the left. Seth gave the ball to Jay who was stacked up. The defensive end laid Seth out with a cheap shot just after the whistle. John Cale screamed at the refs but no flag was thrown. He signaled to his limping quarterback to run the roll out left pass play. The ball was on the 25-yard line. Junior Shultz called the huddle.

Seth had his own plan. He was pissed and he wanted some blood. He called the play, but before he broke the huddle, he turned to Glenn Marcus and Thing Two. "Glenn, never mind the dive fake. Lay that fucking end out when he blows past Donnie. Cap his ass. Thing, play in tight and crack the fucker from behind." Glenn Marcus smiled and nodded. He was never much for blocking, but a little violence like this appealed to him. Thing Two just laughed.

The huddle broke and Junior Shultz got the snap off cleanly. Morg Miller got away with a cheap chop block on the nose tackle and buried his fist in the big kid's balls in the pile. He was rewarded with a satisfying grunt and a sob. Jorge led past Jay, who effectively sealed the right defensive end. Jorge laid out the outside linebacker just as Seth tucked the ball. Thing One started blocking the cornerback who had him covered. Seth slipped the tackle from the safety and the goal line was wide open. He crossed it and was turning around to celebrate when he saw the flags on the ground.

Glenn Marcus achieved complete surprise. Mostly because he hadn't put any effort into blocking up to that point. As a result, he had successfully smashed the left defensive end in the chest and slipped his elbow up into his throat for good measure. The boy was tumbling backwards and falling. Just then Thing Two launched himself at the stumbling player. There was a horrific helmet-to-helmet collision and the flags flew. Thing Two bounced up unhurt. The Spartan player did not. He struggled to get his feet but didn't succeed. The crowd booed the penalty. John Cale cussed silently to himself. Two Spartan players were on the ground. The nose tackle was clutching his aching balls and howling. The end was barely responsive when his coaches got to him. One of the assistant coaches yelled at the Bear sideline about it being a cheap shot. Reese and Cale ignored him.

Seth called the huddle after the injured players were removed from the field and the personal foul for spearing was marked off. He was angry about the lost touchdown but more than satisfied to watch the now-conscious but obviously woozy Spartan end get led to his bench. The next play was stuffed and the Bears punted. The Spartans scored on their next four possessions. Seth Parker went out of the game in the fourth quarter after yet another sack. He sat on the bench with his left, non-throwing, shoulder under a large bag of ice. The final score was 48-7 for the visitors.

As the teams shook hands, the head coach for Sumner confronted John Cale. "That was some cheap shot, John. My boy has a concussion and will probably miss the next two weeks, maybe longer. And punching in the balls is just bush-league horseshit."

"It wasn't intentional, Coach. Your kid fell into the block," Cale responded un-apologetically.

"Bullshit," the Sumner coach said flatly.

The coaches' after-game comments were brief and supportive. Coach Reese even found reason to praise Glenn Marcus. Wash looked past the players who were taking a knee on the fifty. He hoped to see Maricel. He couldn't locate her in the crowd as it filed out.

**Overtime**

Wash Dryer was sitting sort of watching TV later that night when his dad texted him.

GregDryer: Well?

WashDryer: Sorry Dad I almost forgot. Knock Knock.

GregDryer: Who's there?

WashDryer: Owen.

GregDryer: Owen 3. Right?

WashDryer: Yep – they blew it open in the 4th. Looked like we might make a run at them in the 3rd.

GregDryer: Tough Sledding, huh.

WashDryer: Mostly.

GregDryer: Good night Son.

WashDryer: Yeah. You too.

The next day, Greg and Laney Dryer talked on the phone. Laney mentioned that Wash was kind of spacey since the first day of school and she suspected it might be related to a girl. Wash's Dad replied, "Ahhhh – that explains why he is distracted when we text."

# CHAPTER EIGHT

## OWEN 4

On Monday morning, Jorge Martinez, Wash Dryer and Seth Parker sat in their first-hour business class just after first bell when the teacher made an announcement. Mrs. Conover informed them that starting this morning, a student teacher from CMU would be observing in class and that in two weeks, she would be teaching most of the lessons.

Jorge's eyes went wide with recognition when the young woman walked in the room. He unconsciously slid down in his seat behind the computer terminal as Mrs. Conover made the introduction. "Class, this is Ms. Laurie Starke – she comes to us from CMU and she will be student teaching here for the next twelve weeks and I believe she is assisting with the volleyball team." The tall young woman was quite beautiful, and even though she was dressed conservatively, the boys in class, except for Jorge, were undressing her with their eyes in short order.

Mrs. Conover then said something that made Jorge sweat a little. "Let's have everyone practice a good professional business greeting. When I call your name, please come up to the front of the room and introduce yourself and shake Ms. Starke's hand. Also explain a little something about yourself – one or two sentences will suffice."

Wash Dryer was the third student called forward. He shook her hand firmly and informed her, "My name is Michael Washington Dryer, but everyone calls me Wash, please do the same. I am a senior here at BRHS and I hope to attend U of M next year or sign a contract with the Tigers." He returned to his seat and flashed a silly grin at Jorge who did not respond. Wash sensed his friend was a little off his normal cool.

A million things ran through Jorge's brain as the next few names were called in alphabetical order. For some reason, an unwanted thought popped into his mind. He could just see himself introducing himself to the young woman. "Hi, I'm Jorge Reuben Martinez, and last spring I screwed your roommate! Quite a few times! We've met before, but you might not remember it. When your roommate excused herself to the bathroom after introducing us, you squeezed my ass and tried to hit on me. Of course, you were just back to your apartment from the bar and drunk as hell, so I doubt you remember much of anything. Gee, I hope this doesn't start our professional relationship off on an awkward note."

Jorge managed to get through the introduction. He introduced himself and mentioned something about football and wanting to join the Air Force after graduation. He wasn't sure how he made it through it all. But what he was dead sure of was that Laurie Starke recognized him. What would follow was anyone's guess. Jorge was distracted for the rest of the day. That afternoon, he had the worst football practice of his career. Coach Reese called him into the office afterwards and asked what was up. Jorge begged off an explanation, saying he was not feeling well.

Laurie Starke finished her first day at BRHS, and after volleyball practice, she pointed her late-model Toyota north on U.S. 127, lost in deep thought. Her mind raced for the next twenty minutes as she made her way back to the apartment in Mt. Pleasant where she had squeezed Jorge Martinez's ass six months before. She ate a bowl of ramen noodles and made herself a drink. Her roommates had evening classes. Laurie was all alone, and three Captain and Cokes later, she was getting drunk. She picked up her smartphone and texted her former roommate.

Downstate in a northern Detroit suburb, Marcy Nelson glanced at her phone as it made a beeping noise. She read the text.

L Starke: Call me.

Marcy was busy preparing lesson plans for her first week as a student teacher. She was assigned to a second-grade classroom. Marcy did not want to talk to Laurie. When they first started rooming together in an apartment their sophomore year, Marcy and Laurie were good friends. In the last year, the friendship had cooled to the point where Marcy was considering not including Laurie as a bridesmaid in her wedding the following spring. Laurie had accused Marcy of being a slut during a fight near the end of the spring. She was drinking at the time – alcohol was Laurie's downfall when it came to making good decisions and keeping her mouth shut. Marcy had retorted by calling Laurie a drunken bitch. They had only spoken a few times since Marcy moved out at the end of the school year. The conversations were short and cordial, but not the kind that maintain friendship.

A few minutes passed before the phone beeped again.

L Starke: Seriously this is very important. Call Me!

Marcy's fiancé, Jack, was watching *Sportscenter* and lying on the couch in the living room of their small apartment. Marcy took her phone to the bedroom. Back in Mt. Pleasant, Laurie's phone rang once and she answered.

"I saw Jorge at school today, girlfriend." Laurie announced loudly. Marcy could tell she had been drinking from the tone of her voice. It was a tone she had heard many times over the years. It did not bode well for this conversation.

"What are you talking about?" Marcy asked, not really understanding what Laurie was saying.

"You know. Your Latin luh-ver, Jorge." Laurie laughed loudly into the phone.

"Will you keep it down! Jack is in the other room," Marcy said in exasperation. Laurie howled with laughter. Marcy was close to hanging up. Something stopped her as her mind flashed back to her spring fling with Jorge Martinez.

"What are you talking about? Jorge is a student teacher at the same school as you? He told me he was a business major or something. I didn't know he was an education major." Marcy asked with real puzzlement. The statement was answered with more howls of laughter followed by some gasps and more laughter. Then the phone was silent for a few seconds. Marcy asked, "Are you still there?"

"I need another drink. And I got to get my cigarettes. Just a sec," Laurie answered with a laugh as she fumbled with her purse, and a moment later, Marcy could hear a glass being filled with ice.

"Will you please tell me what the hell is so funny about Jorge being a student teacher in your building?" Marcy hissed the question into her phone. Her fiancé was zoned out in the living room, but Marcy knew he would get up and come in the bedroom if he heard her yelling on the phone.

Laurie took a long drag on her cigarette and then cleared her voice with a cough "No, no babe. Jorge is not a student TEACHER. He's a student. He's a student, a senior, in my first-hour class, as a matter of fact."

"Huh?" Marcy asked with amazement.

"Let me paint a picture for you, girlfriend. Last spring you cheated on your loving fiancé while he was out of the country with a seventeen-year-old high school junior. Is that coming through for you now?" Laurie asked with an edge of smarminess.

"No fucking way!" Marcy said loudly, forgetting about Jack being in the other room.

"Yes, fucking way, girl. You had sex with a child – several times. I think you might be guilty of statutory rape or something." Laurie said with all the seriousness she could muster given her drunken state and how hilarious this all seemed to her.

Marcy could feel her dinner rising in her throat. She choked back a dry heave. "Oh fucking shit, oh fucking shit." Marcy repeated. "What the hell are we going to do?"

"What do you mean we? You screwed the kid – not me. All I did was give his ass a squeeze. This is ALL on you, girlfriend." The last bit of the statement sounded mean to Laurie, and she started to regret her tone even as the alcohol was loosening her tongue. The statement was greeted by several seconds of silence. Laurie thought maybe Marcy was crying. Guilt was creeping in with regret for how the conversation had gone so far.

"Did he recognize you?" Marcy's voice quivered.

"Yes," replied Laurie.

"How do you know that for sure? You didn't talk to him for Christ sake did you?" asked Marcy.

"My supervising teacher went through this exercise where each student practiced their best professional business introduction on me. Jorge looked like he had seen a ghost when he shook my hand. I thought he was going to bolt from the room. I was nearly shitting myself so – yeah, the kid knows who I am." Laurie's voice was slightly slurred as she replied. She stubbed out her cigarette and lit another.

"Oh, fucking shit!" Marcy said loudly. Her fiancé, Jack, stuck his head in the door.

"What's up, Marce? Are you okay? Who's on the phone?" Jack asked with sincerity.

Marcy cupped her hand over the phone and made up a quick lie about talking to her cousin who just had a friend hurt in a car accident. It wasn't a highly successful story given how emotional Marcy obviously looked but Jack gave her space and retreated back to the living room. Marcy quickly turned her attention back to the phone as he withdrew.

"What are you going to do? You can't teach in the classroom with him there." Marcy asked.

"Wait a minute. Do you know how hard it was for me to get a student teaching position close enough to campus that I didn't have to move? Do you think I can just ask for a reassignment now and get one without having to skip the semester and then graduate later? Christ, I can't wait another year to graduate!" Laurie's anger cleared her slurred tongue for a few seconds. The statement was greeted with silence on the other end.

Marcy took a sharp inhale before her reply. "I'm getting married next spring. What if this gets out? What if Jack finds out? How do you know Jorge won't start shooting his mouth off about how he bagged his teacher's roommate for God sake!? You have to get out of there right away. Tomorrow!" Marcy hissed loudly.

"Like hell. This is your problem, not mine! I'm just givin' you a head's up. And maybe you should have given Jack a little more thought before you started fucking a child last spring!" Laurie said without care at how nasty the accusation sounded.

"You fucking bitch! I am—" Marcy started to yell when Laurie hung up. She felt like sobbing, but she held it together. Jack stirred in the other room. Marcy grabbed her purse and slipped out the front door claiming she had to run some errands. She drove her car a few miles holding the steering wheel in a death grip. She pulled into a 7-Eleven and bought a pack of Virginia Slims and a bright yellow lighter. She hadn't smoked since spring break in March. That was before Jorge, she thought bitterly.

In the car, Marcy ripped the plastic sheath off the pack of cigarettes. She smoked angrily for the next hour as she drove the streets of Warren, Michigan. No tears came. Just raw burning anger that made her stomach hurt. Marcy could think of no way out of the mess without breaking Jack's heart and ending their engagement. She decided to keep silent, and she hoped Jorge and Laurie would do the same. Jack called her cell and she made up a lie about going to visit her cousin in Pontiac – she would be late. After another three hours, her cigarette pack was half empty. She returned to her apartment and took a shower. As she slid into bed, Jack stirred but didn't wake up. Marcy did not fall asleep until nearly dawn.

Jorge Martinez had a rough night as well. As he worked it over in his mind again and again, he came to the conclusion that there was nothing to say to anyone about this. He hoped to avoid even talking with Ms. Starke and considered dropping the class, but since it was already the second week of school, drops were not allowed. He left for school on Tuesday morning resolved to wait and see what would happen.

First hour went off without a hitch. Ms. Starke did not interact with Jorge at all. She was observing the class. Wash Dryer noted to Jorge that she looked like she was hung over or sick. Jorge merely shrugged. At lunch Jorge went to watch game film in Coach Reese's classroom. Seth and Amber sat by themselves at a small table. Roxanne Johnson had a Students Against Drunk Drivers meeting to chair. The original lunch group from last week was otherwise engaged, so Wash ended up sitting and talking with Jay Brau, but he kept scanning the cafeteria to catch a glimpse of Maricel. A few minutes later, she entered the room. Every boy seemed to be watching her as she breezed over to the table where Wash and Jay were sitting and she slipped effortlessly into a chair.

"Hola, Wash," Maricel greeted him with a smile.

Wash returned the greeting with a blush. He introduced Jay to her and they made some small talk. Wash felt his heart beating in his chest. She rose to leave, saying she had to meet with a teacher about speaking to a Spanish class in the middle school.

"I have to go," Maricel said, her Spanish accent lilting. "Wash, my host family is taking me to see Lake Michigan this Saturday. They have told me to invite two friends to come along. I have already invited Roxy – can you come too? My host mother says Lake Michigan is very beautiful – I am excited. We are going to a place called Soggy Duck." Maricel's eyes twinkled as she extended the invitation.

Wash was frozen for an instant. Jay Brau spoke up, "The town is called

Saugatuck. I was there a few times this summer with a friend. Your host mom is right – I think Saugatuck is the most beautiful spot on the lakeshore."

Maricel laughed at her own mispronunciation and sounded out the town name, "Sog ah tuck."

Jay laughed and said, "That's it – not Soggy Duck. I think Wash would love to go, wouldn't you, Wash?" Jay rescued his speechless friend. Jay could tell Wash was smitten with the new girl – he was too but not in the way his friend was. Jay was always fascinated by the exotic, and Maricel Arambula was easily the most exotic thing to hit Bear River that Jay could remember.

"Yes, I'd love to go," Wash finally said with confidence. "I was there once when I was a kid." He felt himself blushing again as he met Maricel's eyes. Maricel smiled broadly and thanked him and said they would talk about the details of the trip later.

Maricel exited the cafeteria under the watchful eyes of over 100 boys. Jay Brau looked at his friend and said, "Wow."

Wash smiled. "Yeah – wow." His heart thumped in his chest and his mouth was dry. Wash drank the last of his Mountain Dew. He looked at Jay who was giving him an odd sort of knowing smile. Wash felt like he needed to say something, so he asked, "What do think, Jay, can you do her voice?"

Jay Brau thought for a few seconds, then he said in Coach Reese's gruff coaching growl, "If you try to imitate an angel, God will strike you down!" Wash laughed a loud laugh that was interrupted by the bell ending lunch.

After school, football practice was about to begin. John Cale, Mike Reese and Keith Marker were in the coaching office putting on shorts and gathering up some gear. Someone knocked on the door. A tall, middle aged man stood there with a teenage boy. The boy was Andy Myers – one of the two JV boys who had turned in his gear the past Friday after Coach Packer had issued his ultimatum after Thursday's game. Andy was a tall freshman but soft muscled, with red hair and blue eyes. He played tackle on offense and defense. Of the two boys who had left the team, he was the better athlete.

"Please come in," invited John Cale. "We're about to get out to the field. Are you Andy's dad?"

The man introduced himself. "I'm Tom Myers – Andy's my boy. His mother and I split five years ago and I live up in Mt. Pleasant. I didn't hear about Andy quitting until last night. I think after discussing it with him, he has something to say." Mr. Myers guided his son in front of the coach's desk. He didn't meet John Cale's eyes as he started to speak.

"Coach, can I come back and play? I'm sorry – I shouldn't have quit because Coach Packer yells so much. I really like football." Andy finally met Cale's eyes as he finished.

"That's fine, Andy, we're glad you're back. Wash Dryer is in the equipment room. Why don't you go see him and he'll get your gear for you," Cale said, and the young boy left the room. Just as he stepped away, Pat Packer showed up at the door and excused himself past the visitor. John Cale introduced Packer. "Mr. Myers, this is Coach Packer." Pat Packer's face showed his embarrassment, and he shook the man's hand.

"I'm sorry for any misunderstanding about what happened last week," Packer offered reluctantly as an apology. John Cale's face darkened. Mike Reese angrily stuffed some clothes into his locker as he turned away.

"Misunderstanding?" Tom Myers voice was part puzzlement and part anger. He withdrew his hand. "Young man, I think you need to understand something. My boy Andy has always loved football, and now he wants to quit playing. Now, I know young boys tend to exaggerate, but Andy has told me a few times since the season started that you are always screaming and cussing in practice and games. If half of what he says is true, it ain't right, and it shouldn't be happening around boys this young. Let me tell you, if I hear that you swore at my boy so much as once for the remainder of this season, I'm gonna come down here and we are going to have a talk. But I wouldn't worry too much about that – I might get hot under the collar, but that's about all. Now, if my ex finds out you cussed at her child, you will have some real trouble. She will be on the phone to the superintendent, and if I know her, she will have your ass on the unemployment line in about half an hour. Are we clear?"

"Yes sir, I'm sorry," Packer said quietly as he gazed at the ground.

"Good," Mr. Myers said firmly, and he turned to John Cale. "Coach, good luck this week." Cale thanked him for coming in and escorted him to the door. When he turned to face his coaches, his lips were drawn tight with anger.

"Well, we got one back. I don't suppose you had any luck with Steve Cantor, did you, Pat?" Cale asked curtly.

"His mom wouldn't let me talk to him on the phone and she hung up on me." Pat Packer answered defensively.

Cale glanced at Keith Marker. The young coach offered collaboration, "She won't take my calls either, coach."

"So I understand – Steve is in my algebra class second hour, and he won't talk to me about it either. All he said is his mom doesn't want him to play football anyway." Cale kept his temper as he spoke. It was then that Pat Packer made a serious miscalculation about what the discussion was really about.

"We don't need him anyway. The kid sucks. Hell, Danny Short knocked him on his ass a couple of times in practice last week." Pat Packer's comment was met with icy stares from his fellow coaches.

"Mike, you and Keith get the boys down to the field and start practice. I need to talk to Pat alone," John Cale said without emotion. Keith Marker exited quickly as John Cale sat at the desk.

Mike Reese was slower to leave. He waited as the last kids headed out the back door to the locker room. As he neared the office door he looked at Pat Packer who sat on a wooden chair by the small bank of coaches' lockers. The young man had a defiant look on his face, which filled Reese with considerable anger. "Pat, you better put your listening ears on, son. Because if what I think John is about to say doesn't get through to you, you're just about done coaching for the Bears." Reese exited without further comment.

John Cale drew in a heavy breath and let it out slowly. Pat Packer sat up straight in his chair and looked as though he was getting ready to say something. Cale froze him with an angry look. "Pat," Cale began in even tones. "I really hoped that you would have come back this year having learned a few things about how to handle kids properly. This is your fourth year coaching, and there should be some growth, but if anything you have gotten worse. These are children and you are not Bill Belichick. You're a young coach who hasn't learned you can't scream at kids and get them to respond. If you're not happy working with these kids—"

Pat Packer almost leapt to his feet and Cale stopped speaking as the young coach trembled with rage. "Not happy! What the fuck is there to be happy about! These kids are so soft it makes me sick! You and Reese coddle these kids and then you bring in some superstar coach from CMU who's a kid just like they are and wants to be their pal! If you would have made me head coach instead of Keith these cream puffs would be in shape and learning how to bring the wood blocking and tackling! He has us practicing stances and doing form running, for fuck sake, and we're a month into the season! The kids are afraid to hit and they miss practice and quit and you expect me to kiss them on the cheek and kiss their parents' asses. Do you have any idea how much time I spend studying game film and working on the play book trying to figure out a way to get some sort of production out of this group!? You think your precious CMU stud spends any time at all on that? No! He's up at Mt. Pleasant trying to get in the pants of every skank coed in the bars every fucking night! And still he's the head coach. Well, that's bullshit and it shouldn't be that way and if you don't know that, then this team ain't never gonna get any better!" Spittle flew from Packer's mouth as he shouted at Cale. John Cale fixed Packer with a look that was mixed with anger and pity. Cale knew where this was heading, and there was little hope of stopping it.

John Cale resolved to make one last attempt at a rational conclusion to the argument. "AS I was saying, Pat, if you're not happy working with these kids, then you have some decisions to make regarding your future as a coach here. This isn't about your commitment to winning or your willingness to do the hard work necessary to improve your play calling and make the team more efficient on offense. This is about your handling of kids and being a positive role model for students in this teaching environment. This classroom, if you like. Take the day off and give it some thought. Come up with a plan of action for yourself if you intend to stay and write it down in a letter. I would like to make a suggestion. If you intend to stay, you might want to include some anger management counseling as part of your plan, because as it stands now, your inability to control yourself is a lethal detriment to the program that I as head coach—"

"Bullshit! Don't lecture me about anger management!" Packer cut Cale off again. Cale was about to lose it himself but decided to let the young man hang himself with his own stupidity. Maybe he would just quit and that would make it easier with the administration. Packer continued, "What the fuck do you know? You didn't grow up here – I did! When I played here, being a football player still meant something! Now all anyone cares about is fucking soccer! We didn't win many games, but we damn well knocked some fucking heads out there! My senior class was one of the groups that started pissing on that fucking soccer field every year, you know that? You know what else? Big Deano and I led the group that did it the year before they hired you as head coach. That's right and where were you? Up in your CLASSROOM marking papers. Big whoopee fuck, Mr. Teacher. The kids you were supposed to be coaching were making a stand for something and you didn't even know about it. Some role model you are! These kids are soft because you and that old man who does all your real coaching think you have to baby these players! Bullshit! I can't even show my face around town it is so fucking embarrassing being a football coach at this school—"

John Cale had heard enough. He slammed his open hand down on the desk – one of the leaning legs on the rickety wooden carcass collapsed and papers slid from the top to the floor. Cale ignored them. "IT-IS-NOT-ABOUT-YOU!!" Cale shouted louder than Packer. "All I am hearing from you is Me! Me! Me! Well it isn't about you. It's about these kids, God damn it! And you are not helping them in this classroom! That's right! This locker room and that practice field and that game field and the hallways and the parking lot and the bus we ride to the game are my goddam classroom just as much as where I teach math! If you would like to resign – fine! Let me tell you how it is going to go if you don't. You are not going to be coaching kids on my field. My CLASSROOM! If you come to practice, you can stand on the sideline and keep your mouth shut. You can sit in the stands at the games but you are not to interact with the players, and if I so much as hear you yell once, I will have security escort you out. Your uncle can make me keep you on as a coach, but it is my prerogative as to what you coach and how, and as far as I am concerned, you are done interacting with these kids, you poisonous little prick! You'll get your paycheck at the end of the season, and if they offer you a job for next year, I'll resign and then you can be head coach of the whole shooting match – heaven help us if that happens!" Cale concluded as Packer stood with his eyes bulging in both amazement and anger.

"I'm going to my uncle's office!" Packer shouted petulantly as he strode out of the room. He slammed the door behind him. Another leg on the broken-down desk collapsed, and John Cale sat down with a sigh and planted his face in his palms.

Ten minutes later, John Cale was on the practice field – both teams were practicing together. Mike Reese looked at him quizzically, and Cale shook his head and frowned in response. About forty-five minutes after that, a text message rang through on Cale's cellphone. It was Clete Packer.

CPacker: Come to my office.

JCale: We have not finished practice.

CPacker: Send the boys home I want you here right now.

JCale: I'm on the way.

"Clete wants to see me," John Cale said as he walked past Reese.

"I'm coming," Reese replied.

"You don't have to, Mike. Finish practice," Cale said calmly.

"Marker can finish it – they're just going to get some reps on punt and kick coverage and do some running," Reese answered as he motioned to the lowly ASS sistant.

Keith Marker blew his whistle and sent the boys to the water horse – but first he made sure the soccer team wasn't using it. He trotted across the field and asked, "What's up?"

"I'm going to Fudge's office with John. You finish this out, okay?" Reese said to the young coach.

"Okay, is there going to be trouble?" Marker asked with concern.

"Not if I can help it, but you might be head coach in about thirty minutes," Reese said with a smile.

"Ha-ha, Coach," Marker said nervously.

John Cale and Mike Reese walked from the field. As they headed to the building, John filled Mike in on how it went with Pat Packer. They walked into the office together. Clete Packer was alone. Reese noticed that he did not look happy to see him.

"Mike, this meeting is between the athletic director and the head coach," Packer said officiously.

"I'm not here as an assistant coach, Clete. I'm here as John's union building rep," Reese said with a note of confrontation in his voice.

"This is not about his teaching performance, Mike, or anything about the classroom. This is about the current state of the football program!" Packer was adamant in reply.

"If you will consult the contract, you will note that when a teacher has been called to a meeting with administration concerning anything, he or she is entitled to union representation. That is why I am here, and given the nature of the events that proceeded this meeting and your relationship with the assistant coach involved, it is in John's best interest that I stay. Now if that is not to your liking, we will leave and you may request our presence in the central office tomorrow to have a formal hearing with an official transcript being recorded. Your call, Clete," Reese said. His tone was a direct challenge to the AD.

Reese knew he had the AD over a barrel. He knew Packer did not want to make this a formal action. Clete Packer was looking to intimidate John Cale into reversing his decision. Reese was not about to let that happen. He had had enough of Pat Packer as well.

"Fine!" Packer announced. "Take a seat, Coach." His voice was laced with anger. He turned to John Cale and began, "Now, if you would please tell me why Patrick just handed me his resignation? And while you are at it, would you explain this shit about having him stand on the sidelines doing nothing if he chose to stay on as an assistant!?"

Cale was about to answer when Reese held up his hand, "Clete, if the tone of this inquiry does not change to a more professional manner of communication, I will call an end to this and make a formal request for a hearing myself. John has just spent a half hour listening to your nephew's profanity-laced temper tantrums, and that is quite enough for one day. As head coach, he is entitled to change any assistant's duties to whatever he deems necessary for the good of the program. If you look it up in the coaching contract, you will see the exact verbiage, but remember I wrote that language as the lead negotiator well before you were hired as AD, so I know what I am talking about," Reese replied coolly.

Clete Packer was stymied and his face was red. Little beads of sweat appeared on his forehead as he talked. "Okay, if that's the way you want it, fine, but there is no money to hire a replacement. You're going to have to make do with three coaches. And you better know this, Coach Cale. Your evaluation will reflect this episode of poor judgment on your part at the end of the season."

It was John Cale's turn to respond "Mr. Packer, sir, I am a tenured teaching staff member with nothing but excellent evaluations in my official record. My coaching evaluations are quite in order as well. You should know that – you evaluated me. You also are well aware that your nephew's coaching evaluations for the last two years made specific reference for the need for him to curtail his profane language in front of the players and to put an end to his tendency to fly into rages in front of them. I wrote those evaluations and you signed off on them as AD. This season, your nephew has been nearly uncontrollably angry in practices and at games on numerous occasions. His actions have caused players to quit the program. That is not acceptable, and when I met with him today he verbally assaulted me and claimed I was not competent as a coach. Maybe you feel the same, but I should remind you that you came to me and begged me to take this position. You claimed I would have your full support and that the program would get whatever it needed to turn the corner and be successful. Meanwhile, we can't even get our practice field mowed and lined more than a couple times a season." Cale's voice was firm as he made his case.

Clete Packer leaned back in his chair as Cale spoke, his face red with anger and his eyes flashing back and forth between the coaches. He leaned forward and placed his open hands on his desk as he began to speak, "Young man, I think I can make a very clear case that you are not meeting the expectations for being retained as head coach. Your team has played horribly. The behavior of your players on and off the field has been near criminal. I should have written a letter for your file after the fighting fiasco at the scrimmage last month. I have had formal complaints lodged in writing by your opponents regarding violent cheap shots and late hits. Those shithead Lott twins are bound to get thrown out of a game eventually. And don't get me started about your inability to keep your players from perpetuating the sick tradition of pissing on the soccer pitch. Last week they even shit on the field. Don't bother denying it. You know very well it was them. I have heard it was that little asshole Morgan Miller that led the seniors over there, and it was him that did the shitting, and if I can obtain firm proof of that, I am going to suspend that fucking punk from school for two weeks."

Reese stood and placed his hands on the desk-top, leaning forward to get in the face of the AD, "Clete, I have asked you to keep the tone of this meeting professional, and I can see that is pointless. It isn't difficult to see where your nephew got his negative attitude about kids. I will lodge a complaint with the central office if I hear you refer to a student in terms like you are using ever again. These are children. And as far as your accusations about defecating on the soccer field goes, I think you should know that your nephew just admitted to John that three years ago he and Big Deano led the senior boys to the field after the last practice of the year and they urinated on the field. That sort of revelation should play well if these matters come up in a school board meeting – which is where this is heading unless you start considering your words more carefully. Need I remind you Pam Kitteridge has been after your hide ever since the fiasco of hiring of Dean? And now you are going to undermine your hand-picked successor for the head coaching position – maybe even fire him before this season is over. Well, Clete, why don't you force him to resign today and see what happens. I'll resign too. Who is going to coach these boys? Your nephew? Or maybe you think you can. After all, you were a middle school basketball coach for what? Four seasons? Hey! I know what you can do – have our great gray-haired leader pick up the whistle. Shanahan is always going on about his undefeated freshman football team he coached at Gratiot forty years ago."

Clete Packer was close to completely losing his cool. He began pacing behind his desk. He was about to speak when Reese interrupted him. "Here is a plan of action, Clete, which may work out for the best. Accept Pat's resignation and be grateful, because it was only a matter of time before you would have had parents in this office demanding he be fired. He was coming apart at the seams. I'll be on the sideline for the JV's on Thursday nights. I'll contact some of my former athletes and see if I can't get one to come in as a paid volunteer. I'll pay him for the rest of the season out of my check. Matter of fact, I know just the kid – Chet Colby. He delayed starting college this year because of his mom's health, but he needs to be doing something to get out of the house. As it is now, he is just sitting at home watching his mom fade away. What do you say, Clete? This might be the best way to go forward."

Clete Packer stopped pacing and fixed Reese with an angry look. "How about this? You two get the hell out of my office! Right now! In all my years as an administrator I have never seen—just get the hell out! I'll tell you tomorrow what actions will be taken in this matter."

Reese and Cale exited without saying anything further.

John Cale had a restless night. Mike Reese slept like a baby. He knew that Clete Packer was painted into a corner. Reese was so confident that the AD had no choice but to let Pat's resignation stand, he called Chet Colby and offered a paid position for the remainder of the season. The young boy said he would think about it. Twenty minutes after the call, Chet's dad called and tearfully thanked Reese for the offer. They agreed it could be the best thing for Chet.

The first thing the next morning, John Cale was called to the AD office via the overhead speaker.

Mike Reese met Cale in the hallway. "I'm coming too – just in case Clete blows a gasket. Plus it will piss him off just to see me." Reese smiled as he opened the door to the main office for the head coach. Clete Packer looked out his window. He did not do a good job hiding his anger over seeing Reese leading John Cale into the office.

"Mike, this isn't a formal meeting – I just called John down to ask him a question. You don't need to be here to hold his hand." Clete Packer was less than pleasant in his tone.

"Do we really have to go over the contractual rights of teaching staff again?" Reese asked Packer.

The AD waved his hand signaling that further discussion on the point was unnecessary. "Look, John," Packer began. "I talked to Patrick last night – I think I can get him to agree to rescind his resignation, but first you're going to have to back down on having him standing on the sideline and not actively coaching. I'll help in supervising him, Coach. I'll be at every game – even the away games. If he gets out of line, I'll step in and take care of it."

Cale didn't wait to respond. "Mr. Packer, sir, for the good of the program I will not invite someone with a poisonous attitude like Patrick's back to coach after he had the good sense to resign. His actions yesterday were disloyal to the program, to his fellow coaches and to me personally. I'm sorry, but I will not ask him back, and if you force the situation and reassign him to his former post, I will be forced to resign."

Packer's phony good will faded from his face. "Okay, fine. I just want you to be aware that you and your team are on very thin ice. One more incident – just one, and I am fully prepared to clean house. I don't care what the political outcomes are."

"Have a good day, Clete," Reese said as he ushered Cale out the door. Clete Packer made no response. Reese and Cale talked briefly in the hallway. Reese assured the younger coach that the AD did not have any options. Pat

Packer's resignation would stand. Reese also assured Cale that starting today at practice, Chet Colby would be there to help with the JV's.

At practice that afternoon, gray clouds hung low in the sky and the air was damp. During warm-up, the two teams were combined. There had been a great deal of rumor and speculation about what had happened with Coach Packer. Morg Miller said he had the inside scoop. "Packer had a big fight with Cale yesterday before practice and Cale fired him for being such a douchebag," he knowingly told the varsity players as they walked to the field before practice.

The boys were surprised to see Chet Colby waiting for them at the field. "Hey Cheese! Good to see ya! Gonna put on some pads and practice with us?" Morg Miller shouted as they reached the field. Chet "Cheese" Colby had graduated in the spring. He was stocky and well-muscled. He had deep-set, sad eyes and a dark, heavy beard shadow. He wore a Bear River varsity athletics sweatshirt that looked a bit ragged. He did not answer any direct questions about why he was there – it was what Coach Reese told him to do.

"How's your mom?" Jay Brau asked quietly after all the noise about their old teammate being on the field had calmed down. Chet Colby looked at Jay. His eyes glistened a little, and he was grateful when Coach Reese arrived at the field and interrupted before he could find the words to tell Jay about his dying mother.

"Take a knee boys, Coach Cale will be here in a minute, and he has something to talk about." Coach Reese called out the orders, and as usual, all the boys complied without question. Chet Colby almost followed the instructions out of reflex.

John Cale walked up to the assembled team. Wash Dryer was by his side. Wash smiled and nodded at Chet Colby who returned his nod. Cale began, "Okay, I know there are a bunch of rumors flying around about what is going on with Coach Packer. As of yesterday, Coach Packer resigned his position as assistant coach. The details of the resignation are a private matter, and that is all you need to know. Chet Colby, who you all know, has agreed to lend a hand in his absence. Coach Colby will be working with both the JV and varsity teams. Coach Reese will be on the sidelines for both games each week going forward. For the time being, we will be running combined practices Mondays and Tuesdays. We will work out further details in the coming weeks," Coach Cale informed the players. No one responded as the information sank in. Morg Miller gave a knowing smile to Seth Parker.

Coach Reese cleared his throat and looked at Coach Cale, who motioned for him to speak. "Listen up!" Reese began. "I know that some of you played ball and wrestled with Chet, but from now on I would appreciate it if you call him Coach. He may be your friend, but he has a job to do and you need to respect that. Anyone showing disrespect to Coach Colby will find themselves running until I think you might die. And then you will run some more. Got it?!" Reese growled.

The team shouted out, "Yes, Coach!"

Practice was clean and crisp. The JV's were in pregame mode. The boys were sharp and hustling. Mike Reese was very active and went around high fiving the young players. Chet Colby was quiet – soaking up the feel of the team and learning the names of the youngest players. On the varsity field John Cale had the offense prepare for Friday's game against North Star. He spent a great deal of time on ball security and preventing fumbles. The forecast for Thursday called for rain, and North Star's field was notorious for being in poor condition, so mud would be a factor Friday night.

Thursday evening was rainy, but the downpours of the afternoon had let up. There was a small crowd in the home stands for the JV game. Pat Packer arrived at kickoff and sat alone at the top of the stands below the press box. John Cale saw him take his seat but Packer gave no indication that he saw his former boss. Cale was in the coach's box with a headset on. He forgot about Pat Packer as the game got underway.

The JV's played well on defense. Andy Myers prevented a touchdown on the goal line with a good tackle that forced a fumble the Bears recovered near the end of the half. By the middle of the fourth quarter the Bears were trailing 14-7. Scott Baier had scored on an option play to end the third quarter. The JV quarterback was also the kicker and he split the uprights with a nice PAT. Pat Packer yelled, "Way to go, Scotty!" a few feet below Cale in the press box. Cale noticed that it was the first time he had heard anything from his former assistant. He was relieved that no incident had occurred thus far.

With four minutes left in the game, the Bears got the ball on their own 30-yard line after forcing the North Star Vikings to punt. The few dozen fans in the stands cheered and Pat Packer yelled, "Ram it down their throats!" The Bears moved the ball efficiently down the field with dives and some option plays. With 55 seconds showing on the clock, the Bears fullback ran the ball into the end zone from seven yards out. Pat Packer started yelling, "Go for the win!" loud enough for the whole field to hear. Cale was irritated but he focused on the conversation he was having with Mike Reese.

"Mike, I'm thinking kick it – they look tired on the other sideline. Scott kicked it clean last time. I don't think they can score on you in OT and the boys are clicking in the run game." John Cale spoke through his headphone.

"Yep, go for the tie at home and the win on the road," Mike Reese responded with the age-old football truism.

When the PAT personal lined up for the kick, Pat Packer started walking down the bleachers yelling, "No!"

On the field, the ball was snapped and Scott Baier slipped as he approached the ball. The kick hit the cross bar of the goal post and bounced backwards. The visiting Vikings danced around as the ref waved off the attempt. Pat Packer screamed "Stupid! Stupid!" in the general direction of Mike Reese on the sidelines across the track. Reese did not turn around. He was too busy trying to set up an onside kick attempt.

As the Bears took the field to try to pull off a last-second miracle, Reese spoke quietly into his headset, "Can you get someone to shut his ass up?" He asked Cale. Cale said he would get Clete Packer to get down there to quiet his nephew. John Cale stood and walked out of the coach's box to the main room in the middle of the press box. He caught the AD's eye. "Mr. Packer, can you please try to calm down, Pat? This isn't appropriate behavior for a JV game." Clete Packer looked at Cale for a moment and shrugged his shoulders. John Cale shook his head in disgust and returned just as the onside kick was covered by the visiting team. The Vikings took a knee for one play on offense and the game was over. Final score was Visitors 14, Home 13.

Pat Packer was leaning over the rail near the track shouting, "Stupid call, Reese! Stupid call!" Mike Reese ignored him. Chet Colby and a few players looked his way. Colby shook his head in disgust. The crowd was already filing out. No one approached the former assistant coach.

In the press box, John Cale was putting away the field communication equipment when Clete Packer walked into the room. The AD asked, "Was that Reese's call or yours?" in an accusing voice.

"We both agreed," Cale responded with a flat tone.

"Not a very good one," Clete Packer replied.

John Cale paused and looked the AD in the eye. He knew if he took up the insult that the dispute would get ugly and there were other people still in the press box. He let it go. "Excuse me, Mr. Packer, I have some equipment to tend to." It was the only thing he would give the AD, sensing that a confrontation was what Clete Packer wanted. The older man gave a non-committal snort and left the box. John Cale was coldly furious as he walked back to the school. As he walked, he was thinking it was a pity that it was Thursday night. He could use a drink – several of them.

Friday night was not any better for the varsity as it traveled down to North Star. Glenn Marcus was late for the bus. John Cale informed him that he would be sitting for the first quarter as punishment. Tetherboy did not protest. When the bus pulled up to the field, Mike Reese noted how bad it looked. The midfield area was mostly brown mud. Large puddles of water stood in both endzones even though it had stopped raining in the middle of the night. It was muggy and a foggy haze was rising in the farm fields surrounding the old school and sports complex.

The coaches surveyed the field during warm ups and noted with disgust what bad condition it was in. "That's not the worst news," John Cale said.

"What's the worst news?" newly-minted Assistant Coach Chet Colby asked with concern.

"It's their homecoming game tonight," John Cale replied as he looked at the poorly decorated floats lined up on the old cinder track surrounding the game field.

"Crap. One season when I coached years ago, we played in five homecomings. One of them was the opening game at Sumner, for crap's sake," Mike Reese said with dramatic disgust.

"So?" asked Chet Colby.

"Extra-long halftime and the players on the opposing team are all psyched looking to beat up on an easy mark. Bear River has played as guest in more homecoming games than any ten schools in the area," Reese answered.

The first play of the game on offense, Morg Miller started in on the defensive tackle across the line from him. He was pleased when the player growled, "Fuck you, fag" in response to Morg's request for a romantic date. On the next play, Morg called the opposing player a hottie. The defensive tackle came out of his stance before the snap and smashed Morg on the helmet and then tried to kick him a few times as Morg backed away laughing. Flags were thrown and the player was ejected. The fifteen-yard penalty for unsportsmanlike behavior was the Bear's longest positive gain for the whole game.

In the huddle after the penalty was marked off, Morg was still laughing and said, "Guess he's sensitive, some of those fags are touchy when you tease 'em." Jay Brau gave Morg a disgusted look. Morg Miller didn't notice.

The first quarter was scoreless, but then Glenn Marcus fumbled the ball three times in the second quarter. Both Things got called for late hits and the refs warned John Cale that the next infraction would get them ejected. The Vikings led 14-0 at the half. North Star's half-time homecoming festivities included fireworks. The Bears warmed up on the field for the second half with rockets exploding largely unseen in the fog.

Late in the third quarter, with the Bears trailing 21-0, Seth Parker got buried in the mud face-first when he was sacked after Big Donnie Donnie whiffed on a pass block. He came out of the game with his face covered in thick mud. Wash Dryer spent the rest of the game spraying saline solution in his eyes trying to clear his vision. The final score was Home 28, Visitors 0. The exact score that Pete the Pigskin Prognosticator had predicted in the Mt. Pleasant paper, which did not sit well with Mike Reese. The bus ride home was quiet except for the occasional whine from Seth Parker complaining of his blurry vision.

A thick ground fog surrounded the school when the bus pulled into the parking lot. Coach Cale gave some instructions for the upcoming week and urged the boys to get rest and make sure they were keeping current with schoolwork. Within twenty minutes, the players had stowed their gear and vacated the locker room. John Cale made calls to the local media from the office. Mike Reese stored gear in the equipment room with the help of Wash Dryer and Chet Colby. Reese dismissed Wash and Chet and walked into the office.

"This was not our best effort tonight," Reese said to Cale as the head coach hung up the phone.

"Yeah, Glenn's fumbles didn't help, but on offense, we were just flat," Cale answered.

"Jorge Martinez had the worst game I have ever seen him play," Reese observed.

"He was sleep walking through the whole week. I don't know what the deal was," Cale replied.

"Girl trouble, maybe," Reese offered.

"Umm, maybe, but usually Jorge brings it come game day no matter what. There might be something else going on," Cale replied.

"I know what we need," Reese said with a smile.

"Beer?" Cale said with a sigh.

"My wife got me three cases of lager from that brew pub in Lansing. The bottles are in the fridge in the garage. Why don't you follow me out to the house and help me put a dent in that total?" Mike Reese made an offer he knew Cale could not refuse.

"I'll follow you. I don't know if I can find your place in this fog," Cale said with a smile. Mike Reese lived with his second wife in a log home down river from town. Sharon Reese was an engineer at Dow Chemical in Midland. Their home sat overlooking the Bear River in the woods halfway between their respective jobs. Sharon Reese was a tall, elegant woman in her mid-fifties. Those who knew Mike Reese well said that the marriage was the best thing that had ever happened for him.

"Stay close. I'll call Sharon and let her know we're on our way. She'll put out some snacks and we'll watch the Saginaw station for the *GridIron Round-up* show," Mike Reese said as he picked up his gym bag.

The two coaches emerged from the school into the fog. A dark silhouette stood at the street near a street lamp. It was Glenn Marcus. "Hey, Glennie. You got a ride home?" John Cale called across the parking lot.

"Yeah, Coach. My mom's boyfriend is coming to pick me up in few minutes," Glenn answered.

"You sure?" Cale asked. The coaches never liked to leave kids unattended at the school after hours. In the case of Glenn Marcus, it was not because of what might happen to him but rather what he might do if no one was around.

"Yep," Glenn answered forcefully. Cale and Reese walked slowly to their cars, keeping an eye on the boy. The sound of a loud motor announced the car before it could be seen. A bright red muscle car pulled up in front of the street lamp. Eighties music blared through the open door as Glenn jumped in the passenger seat. The car revved and lightly squawked the tires as it pulled away.

"That is trouble waiting to happen. You ever met Glenn's mom?" Reese asked Cale.

"Yeah, she's kinda rough but you can tell there was something there at one point," Cale replied.

"She was in my class eighteen years ago. She got knocked up with Glenn her senior year – didn't graduate. Before that, she slept with half my wrestling team. If her current boyfriend is anything like the rest of the men in her life, then Glenn likely has found a kindred spirit. Water seeks its own level," Reese said as he fumbled with his keys to his pickup.

"Yeah. We just need Glenn to keep it together for another five weeks," John Cale answered as he opened his car door and immediately felt bad for having written the boy off so glibly.

Two hours later, the two coaches were sitting in the glassed-in porch at Mike Reese's home overlooking the Bear River. After watching the football highlights on the Saginaw TV station, they had retreated to Reese's favorite room of the house. The river was barely visible in the moonlight due to the fog. "Catch much fish this summer?" Cale asked as he looked out at the river.

"A few, but we still can't eat any. The Department of Natural Resources says all the fish in this stretch are too toxic. The oil refinery that closed in Gratiot twelve years ago and the old chemical plant that sat west of town on the river pretty much killed this stream for the next hundred years. Still down here, the river looks good – and as long as you don't stir up the mud it smells okay. When I was a kid in Gratiot, the Bear River was the most polluted river in the region – and that is saying something. We used to set fire to the creek that ran down out of the oil refinery property. And that old chemical plant was just a wasteland of leaking metal drums. The whole town of Bear River stunk something fierce when it was up and running. On a foggy night like this, you didn't dare leave your car out of the garage. The condensed dew residue would eat the paint off the metal. The plant shut down when I was in college. That hit Bear River real hard, economically, but the poison it pushed out came to end. Just don't dig any holes on the west side of town. God knows what might be in the ground out there," Reese reminisced as he opened yet another bottle of beer.

The conversation turned to football and then to Pat Packer. Sharon Reese came in and announced she was heading off to bed and asked if the guys needed anything. Mike Reese was in an animated description of the Packer family. He paused and stood and kissed his wife goodnight and said, "John and I still got some stuff to go over, kiddo, I'll sleep out here tonight. And I'm taking John's keys from him – he'll take the other couch." Cale started to protest as Mike Reese talked to his wife but one look from Sharon corrected him.

"I'll call Amy and tell her it is too foggy to drive," John announced in a slightly slurred voice. He lifted his cellphone out of his pocket and made the call.

When Cale finished his explanation to his wife, Mike Reese took up the conversation and rambled on about the AD and his family. "You know, I've known Clete Packer for twenty-five years. He came here as a business teacher after he bombed as a stockbroker. He was shit in the classroom, and soon as he got a chance, he jumped to administration. He was Middle School assistant principal for a while and then moved over to the high school twelve years ago. He actually does run a tight operation for the athletic department as AD, but he wants to be principal so bad he can taste it. As assistant principal, he's been running things for Mike Shanahan for years. Clete's biggest problem is he just doesn't like kids much. His wife is a sweetheart, though. A friggin' saint for putting up with a blowhard like Clete. I like Betty. Their daughter is married to an Air Force major, and she is a good kid too."

"What about Pat? How in the hell did he end up here?" Cale asked even though he knew most of the story.

"Clete took him in when his dad went to jail for real estate fraud up in Mt. Pleasant. His old man, Clete's older brother, was double-dealing oil leases and got nailed by the feds. Pat came to live with Clete when he was in seventh grade. Pat's mom got killed in a car accident when he was a little kid.

"I coached Pat, ya know – half season in wrestling. I recruited him to wrestle after watching him play football. The kid could play a little – he had a mean streak in him, but he didn't have the stuff on the wrestling mat and he quit on me his freshman year. He might have been all-league his senior year as a linebacker if he hadn't shattered his leg the last football game his junior year. Never got back on the field. That is why he is such an angry little prick. He got cheated out of what he thought was his chance, and he has been pissed off ever since." Reese explained, leaning forward toward Cale who sat on a couch with half-closed eyes. The beer was catching up with him.

"Can we win a game the rest of the way?" John Cale asked quietly. "Maybe just one – Christ I hate losing. I fuckin' hate it."

Mike Reese drew in his breath. He liked his young head coach. He had coached many just like him over the years. Decent athletes with a passion to win, they made themselves better through sheer willpower and hard work. Sometimes that works in wrestling, but Mike Reese knew football. If you don't have the players you don't have the players, and, sometimes no matter how hard you work, it doesn't translate into wins. "Well," Reese began, "We just had our three easiest opponents of the season on paper, and we didn't get it done. It isn't going to get any easier, but you never know. We might catch a break."

John Cale was sleepy as he replied, "We get Lenny Shore and Manikowski back this week. That will give us a boost – I hope."

Mike Reese took on a fatherly tone as he explained the situation to John Cale. "One thing I have learned over the years in coaching is that some kids make bad decisions, and if you count on kids that have a history of screwing up, you will get burned in the end. You never shut the door on them. Give them every chance you can without hurting your team, but never count on them. Lenny could help on defense for sure. I like the kid, but I have talked to some of his teachers – his eligibility is hanging by a thread. And Tim Manikowski is on Clete Packer's shortest of short lists. Clete is going to get that kid come hell or high water, but the boy's mom is not a woman to take lightly."

"You know his mom, don't you?" John Cale asked.

"I've known Julie for years. My first wife and I used to hang around with her and her first husband back in the day. Julie actually student taught for me. She was as sharp as tack. She got hired for a middle school position here at Bear River. Bob Manikowski was a lawyer in Mt. Pleasant for a while. We had a lot of fun with them before Julie caught Bob in bed with his secretary. Bob hightailed it out of town. He's a big-time lobbyist down in Lansing now. Julie got remarried to the chairman of the county Republican Party, Carl Bysshe, after a few years, and we drifted apart. Julie got her PhD and a principal job in Riverdale. She's assistant superintendent now. Dr. Julie Bysshe is hell on wheels when pissed, let me tell you. She went from being a sweet-natured and nurturing classroom teacher to ball-breaking politician administrator in a New York minute. They have a saying over in Riverdale. 'Whatever the Bysshe wants, the Bysshe gets.' She had her husband fix things with the sheriff's department last spring when Tim got nailed with drugs. Clete Packer may be biting off more than he can chew going up against her." Mike Reese told his story, and as he finished he noticed John Cale had fallen asleep.

Mike grabbed a blanket out of a closet and draped it over his head coach. Then he made his way to the couch in the living room. In a few minutes, snores echoed across the house.

## Overtime

Wash Dryer couldn't keep his focus while talking to his mom about his planned trip to Saugatuck with Maricel. He jumped from topic to topic without pause. Laney Dryer recognized the signs. Her boy was completely gaga over this girl. Wash excused himself to his bedroom to text his father about the game.

WashDryer: Knock Knock.
GregDryer: Who's there?
WashDryer: Owen.
GregDryer: Owen who?
WashDryer: Owen Four.
GregDryer: Was it close?
WashDryer: Nope.
GregDryer: Big day tomorrow. What's the weather look like for Saugatuck?
WashDryer: Did you talk to Mom?
GregDryer: Yes I did. Is this girl special?
WashDryer: She's great dad.
GregDryer: Go and have a good time. You know about Saugatuck don't you?
WashDryer: What?
GregDryer: It is the destination resort town for Gays and Lesbians on the lakeshore. Big party town.
WashDryer: So?
GregDryer: Nothing really. It's just the town's rep.
WashDryer: Ha ha Dad. It's not like I'm going unattended.
GregDryer: Be safe. Make good decisions.

WashDryer: Always.

Wash Dryer was sleepless for a long time. His mind wandered back to Maricel. He hoped the weather would be nice. It might be something to see. Maricel in a bathing suit on the beach. Before he finally dozed off, he had a stray thought about Jay Brau. He couldn't quite formulate the question in his mind as to how Jay knew all about Saugatuck.

# CHAPTER NINE

## OWEN 5

Wash Dryer woke a half hour past dawn on Saturday morning. The sun lit up his bedroom wall. He could feel the warmth filling up the room. He was excited – it wasn't raining. Maybe the trip to Saugatuck would include a trip to the beach.

Two hours later, he was sitting in the backseat of a minivan heading west down the M 46 highway. He sat next to Roxy Johnson. Maricel Arambula sat in the middle seat next to the five-year-old son of the Martin family. She spoke Spanish to the little boy. Little Neal Martin giggled and made fun of Maricel in Spanish.

Jimmy Martin and his wife Ellen were in their mid-thirties. Jimmy had recently taken over the family business – a large farm implement dealership east of town. The Martins had been a host family before. Maricel was their third guest student from South America. Ellen Martin had a teaching degree but had never taught. She convinced her husband that hosting exchange students would allow their child to grow up bilingual. From what Wash Dryer could tell, it was working out just that way, but then he only had two semesters of high school Spanish, so most of the conversation was beyond his understanding. He found himself feeling jealous of a five-year-old, and the attention he was getting. During the ride, Wash made small talk with Roxy Johnson about college choices and ACT scores.

The weather was beautiful. The early morning fog burned away quickly and by 11 A.M., the van was on the main street of Saugatuck. The little village had a postcard quality to it. Small gift shops and art galleries lined the street. There were quaint restaurants as well. The Kalamazoo River pooled up in a lake, creating a harbor before exiting down a channel to Lake Michigan. It was late in the boating season, but boats of all descriptions still docked in the marinas. The big lake was not visible from the streets of downtown. A large tree covered sand dune blocked the view.

"Let's get some lunch," Jimmy Martin suggested. He found a parking spot on a side street. Even though it was past Labor Day, the little summer tourist village was quite busy. Mr. Martin noted how many cars had out-of-state license plates. "Lots of F.I.S.H. here today. And a few F.I.P.'s as well."

Wash Dryer was puzzled. "Huh?" he asked as the family and guests walked down the sidewalk.

"Look at the plates – Illinois and Indiana. Some of the locals call people from Illinois "Fu—"

A look of exasperation from his wife stopped him, and he changed his statement with a stutter. "F—Friggin' Illinois Shit Heads." Ellen Martin's face did not register happiness at his quick edit. Jimmy Martin shrugged.

Wash Dryer and Roxy Johnson gave him his desired laugh. Maricel was confused. "And what's a F.I.P.?" Roxy asked.

"Friggin' Indiana People," Jimmy Martin informed them. More snickers came from the teens. Ellen Martin steered the group to a restaurant.

"This is a good place to eat," Mrs. Martin said as they waited at the door for a seat. "Jimmy and I come here sometimes. When I was a kid, my family used to visit my aunt in South Haven for two weeks every summer. She had a cottage near the lake about halfway between here and South Haven. When I was a teenager, my sisters and I would come up here, but my aunt used to scold us about hanging around in Saugatuck. She disapproved of the lifestyle here."

Roxy Johnson asked, "What lifestyle?"

As they were being seated, Jimmy Martin started to explain. "Saugatuck and Douglas, the little burg across the river, are the mecca for gay people looking to spend time on the lakeshore. Lots of the resorts and motels kind of cater to them. It's been that way for a long time. It's kind of funny too, because this part of the state is strict Dutch Christian Reformed. Real conservative – but good business people, and they like the money the gays bring more than they hate the culture."

Wash watched as four well-tanned men about forty years old walked into the restaurant, as if to underscore Jimmy Martin's explanation of the Saugatuck atmosphere. They were dressed in summer casual clothes. They all had sunglasses pushed up on the top of their heads. One of the four was loudly greeting the hostess. Were these men gay? How could he know? Did it matter? Wash was momentarily distracted.

Jimmy Martin read Wash's face, and he tipped his head in the direction of the quartet and raised his eyebrows. Wash widened his eyes and searched for something to say. "I was here once when I was a kid – we went to the beach. But I don't remember much about it."

Maricel Arambula disengaged from her playful patter with little Neal Martin. "Your friend, Jay, says he likes it here," she announced innocently.

If Wash Dryer had been looking at Roxy Johnson, he might have caught the flicker of recognition in her eyes. But Wash knew nothing of Roxy's prom date frustration with his friend Jay. No thought of Jay's visits to Saugatuck meant anything to Wash. His focus was on Maricel.

After lunch, they decided that they would head to the beach. Maricel was excited to see Lake Michigan. They all clambered into the van, and Jimmy Martin guided around the harbor and past the dunes. Oval Beach spread out to greet them as they arrived. Small waves lapped at the shore. There was a light breeze blowing. The beach was not crowded despite the nice weather. The weather of west Michigan is fickle in September. Even though the calendar had not yet turned from summer to fall, beach traffic tends to drop off drastically after Labor Day. Locals on the lakeshore enjoy these days when they can visit their home beaches without fear of being overrun by tourists.

Maricel exclaimed in Spanish at the beauty of the lake. "It is like the ocean!" she said to Wash. "And this is fresh water?"

Wash replied, "Yes." The pride of ownership of the natural wonder of the lake was evident in his face. Many Michiganders have just such pride when showing the lake to first-time visitors. Maricel continued to praise the beach and the dunes as they walked to changing rooms at the concession stand, bags and towels in their hands. Neal Martin sprinted ahead.

Wash, Neal and Jimmy Martin emerged from the men's room and waited for the women. Mrs. Martin came out of the changing room first. Then Roxy Johnson came out. She wore a one-piece bathing suit that fit her voluptuous body in a way that would have turned Wash's head if he was not fixated on Maricel who followed. The yellow bikini she wore shone brightly in the sun, her tan skin in deep contrast. Wash Dryer felt the now-familiar lurch of his heart in his chest. Her smile was so intense that he felt the urge to kiss her. But he restrained himself.

The Martins led the group down the beach to the water line. The sun was high in the sky. If Wash did not know better, he would have sworn it was July, not mid-September. Very few people were on the beach, though, and only a handful in the shallow water steps from the sand. Neal Martin immediately crashed into the water and jumped out yelling, "Cold!"

Wash, Roxy and Maricel walked gingerly into the surf. Maricel called out in Spanish and jumped back. Wash felt the chill of the water. "It's pretty cold – maybe sixty degrees," he informed the girls.

"Well, the wind has been blowing out of the northwest for most of the week. The lake has turned over. All the cold deep water has been pushed in to shore." Jimmy Martin passed along his knowledge of the workings of the weather and how the lake reacts to it.

"In a couple of months there will be ice floating out there," Ellen Martin added.

"I have swam the ocean many times. I have never felt water this cold." Maricel dipped her hands to the water and then she touched it to her lips. "It is sweet," she announced with a smile. She flicked her hands at Wash, sprinkling him with the cold droplets. He danced away.

"Come on! Let's swim anyway. It will be the last time this year," Roxy Johnson suggested, and then she began to wade into the lake. Wash and Maricel followed. The first sand-bar was twenty yards out. Before he got that far, the low waves began to splash Wash's groin. He tried to mask his discomfort. He did not do a good job of it.

Maricel laughed and whispered something to Roxy. Their shared laughter made Wash blush. He scooped up big handfuls of water and threw it at the girls who squealed and began to run down the sandbar kicking up water as they went. Wash followed. Roxy turned toward deeper water and dove in. She came up shouting, "Holy crap!"

Maricel followed with her own graceful dive. When she came back to the surface she screamed, "Madre de Dios!"

Wash had to follow. He braced for the worst and dove. With a few powerful kicks, he swam underwater toward the girls. He emerged between them with a smile. Roxy laughed and pushed him under again. The three teens headed for the next sand-bar farther out in the lake. They had to swim a few strokes through the waves to reach the shallows. Wash could touch bottom, but the girls had to bounce to stay above the low waves.

"It is so cold, it makes me ache," Roxy Johnson said.

"I've gone numb," Wash replied and he dove below the surface. Both girls squealed as he pursued them under-water. When he surfaced Maricel and Roxy both splashed his face. Wash gave them a big smile.

"It is too cold. Let's go in and lie in the sun," Maricel suggested. The other two teens agreed.

On the beach, Neal Martin was building a sand-castle, and the two girls sat on the sand next to him and helped him dig a moat around his creation. The Martins sat in beach chairs soaking in the sun. Jimmy Martin struck up a conversation with Wash about baseball. Jimmy worked as an umpire, and he had called some of the games Wash had played in American Legion ball. The girls finished Neal's sand-castle and lay in the sun on bright beach towels. Wash dug a pit in the warm sand and stretched out between the Martins and the girls. They shared casual conversation.

Shortly before three, the Martins announced they were going to go into town, but that the teens were welcome to stay on the beach for another two hours. Neal Martin begged his father to go to a playground. Ellen Martin wanted to do some shopping. The teens agreed they would rather stay and enjoy what promised to be the last nice day on the beach for the season.

"I'll check and see if the chain ferry is running. You guys can walk to it from here, and it will take you across the harbor to downtown. We'll meet you there where we parked before," Jimmy Martin said.

"What's a chain ferry?" Wash asked, squinting in the sun.

"It is a small ferry that uses a chain and pulleys to bring people back and forth from the town to the beach. It's been running for over a hundred years. Usually it shuts down on Labor Day, but the weather has been so nice, they will run it on weekends like this," Ellen Martin informed him.

"Sounds cool," Roxy Johnson said with a smile.

"I'll call you, Wash, if it is running. Otherwise, we will come pick you up at five, okay?" Jimmy Martin asked.

"Okay," Wash replied. The Martins gathered their things and made their way to their van. Ten minutes later, Jimmy Martin called and said the ferry was running until 5:30.

The teens stretched out in the sand. A few clouds were drifting into the northwest sky. The wind picked up out of the west, and the temperature dropped a degree or two. After a half hour, they decided to take one more swim. The cold water again made them squirm as they walked into the surf. They stood on the first sandbar and scanned the beach. People were picking up their gear and moving toward the parking area.

Wash led the girls for another swim to the second sand-bar. After about fifteen minutes the three teens began to walk to shore. As they reached the sand-bar before the beach, Maricel stumbled and Wash caught her hand. Its warmth and softness felt wonderful. She righted herself, but she did not let go of his hand. Instead she gave it a gentle squeeze to let him know she did not want him to let it go. Roxy Johnson followed a few yards behind. She smiled a knowing smile. Wash and Maricel walked through the shallows to the sand hand in hand. He felt like he could walk on the water.

As they sat on the beach and dried off, Wash looked to the west. What had been a few clouds a half hour ago was now a gray mass blotting out the horizon, and what looked like a low-hanging mist was on the lake. The sun was dipping close to the opaque wall. Wash could guess what was behind it – rain and fog. The ever-changing Lake Michigan weather was about to take a quick turn for the worse. His phone rang. Jimmy Martin advised Wash to head to town ASAP as the weather was going to get wet soon. Wash agreed, and as he hung up his phone the wind shifted. A gust of wind from the northwest blew sand into their faces as they sprung to their feet. Quickly, they gathered up their towels and bags and they began a brisk walk to the concession stand and changing rooms.

When they'd finished dressing, they met outside. The sun dipped below the gray mass of clouds now menacing the beach. The temperature dropped several degrees, and Maricel shivered. Wash took her hand in his and said, "Let's get going." The three turned to the southeast and walked out the park drive. The wind pushed against their backs as they walked. In fifteen minutes, they were at the chain ferry dock. They paid their fare and walked aboard the ornate little craft. As they stood at the rail, Wash watched the gray mist as it crested over the tree-covered dune. Another burst of wind announced the arrival of wet weather.

The mist enveloped the ferry a few feet from the dock. Maricel huddled close to Wash. Roxy cussed softly and wrapped her beach towel around her still-damp head. She stood across the narrow deck from her two friends. Wash grabbed his towel from his bag a draped it over Maricel. She shivered and thanked him sweetly in Spanish. The mist was mixed with droplets of rain. Maricel looked up at Wash and blinked the drops from her eyes. When their lips met, Wash became totally oblivious to the rain and cold.

The ferry ended its short ride across the river, and the teens dashed hand in hand down the street to the van. Jimmy Martin hit the automatic open button and the girls leapt into the van. Wash stowed the bags in the back, and then he climbed in. A violent gust shook the van, and the rain increased to a downpour. "Just made it," Jimmy said as he put the van in gear and pulled away from the curb. "Gotta love Lake Michigan – the weather changes every hour."

Wash spoke up, "I've lived here my whole life, and I've never seen the temperature drop that quick."

"People along the lakeshore see it happen often enough to know when it's coming," Ellen Martin responded. "When I was a kid, I used to love to watch a thunder-storm come in from the lake. It can be more exciting than fireworks."

"We'll stop in Grand Rapids and get some dinner. We ought to get home by 9:30 if you kids want to call your folks." Jimmy Martin informed them. He turned up the heat in the van and windows began to steam up. The girls dried their hair as best as they could and combed out the tangles.

Ellen Martin reached into a large plastic shopping bag and pulled out a pink Saugatuck sweatshirt. She handed it to Maricel. "These were on sale. What do you think?" Maricel thanked her profusely in both English and Spanish. Wash gave her a big smile as she pulled it over her head. Less than an hour later the van pulled into an Italian restaurant parking lot in Grand Rapids. The family and their friends shared pizza and salads.

Wash walked through the front door of his house at 9:15. Laney Dryer could tell at a glance that her son had had a special day. The kind of day someone remembers their whole life. She fought the urge to grill him about the day's events. She waited for him to open up. Within minutes, Wash was telling details of the beach and the weather. Laney Dryer sensed there was more to tell about Maricel, but she did not press.

"What did you think of Saugatuck? Did you recognize it from when we were there the year before Maggie was born?" Laney asked.

Wash answered, "It's a neat town and the beach is very nice – not as nice as Ludington, but real cool. I don't remember much about being there before. Did you know that there are a lot of gay people who summer and vacation there? Jimmy Martin says it's been that way for a long time."

"Yes – that's pretty much common knowledge. Your dad has a childhood friend who lives near there. When we visited him that summer we went to the beach there. He had some negative things to say about all that. We really haven't talked with him and his wife since. That sort of intolerance is difficult to get around," Laney Dryer answered. "Did you and the girls have fun?"

"Yeah," Wash answered in a non-committal way. He blushed just enough to give Laney a hint that romance between her son and the exchange student may be taking a firm root. Wash excused himself and went off to take a shower. The day was drawing to a close, and Wash felt tired but was still elated over the kiss he had shared with Maricel. Wash had kissed girls before. Last year at prom his date – a senior whose boyfriend had dumped her a month before – had insisted they do a little bit more than just kiss. But she was quite drunk and Wash couldn't take advantage of her. When she fell asleep, passed out really, he took her to her cousin's house and helped the older girl put the young inebriate to bed on a couch. Wash reflected on the times he had kissed girls and made out with them. Nothing in his life felt quite like what he was feeling on this night. Eventually he drifted off to sleep.

Across town, Roxy Johnson was tossing and turning. The revelations about the town of Saugatuck and her own thwarted attempts at seducing Jay Brau the prior spring coalesced in her brain. Jay Brau was likely gay, was her conclusion. She wondered who else might know this. She hoped that Jay was prepared to deal with being outed if anyone did.

On Sunday afternoon, the Bear River Bears once again got poked in the eye by the football gods. Wash Dryer and Jorge Martinez were visiting Seth Parker. They were standing in the driveway of Seth's house drinking Mountain Dew and leaning on Seth's car. The talk was of Wash's trip to Saugatuck, but Wash was being evasive about how his day went. Jorge was proud of his friend for two reasons. First, that he knew Wash was making significant headway in starting a relationship with Maricel Arambula. Second, that Wash was not going to brag about any action he had gotten.

The three boys were about to head into the Parker home to play some video games when they heard a high-pitched whine of a motorcycle going at high speed approaching from the west. "That sounds like Lenny's bike," Seth Parker said factually.

"Uh-huh," Jorge noted. The noise got louder and a bright green motorcycle with a rider wearing a jet-black full helmet flashed past them on the street. The bike was doing at least eighty through the subdivision and heading for the open lots at the end of the cul-de-sac.

"That's Lenny, all ri—" Wash Dryer's statement was cut off by the scream of the siren of the sheriff's car giving chase. The boys ran to the end of the driveway just in time to see the cruiser slide to a halt in the cul-de-sac. Lenny Shore's Benelli motorcycle was nowhere to be seen. The boys could still hear the bike, though, and they surmised that Lenny had taken it off-road in to the tall weeds and scrub oaks on the east end of the unfinished subdivision.

"Lenny's fucked." Seth Parker said with regret.

"Uh-huh," Jorge replied as he pulled his Detroit Tigers baseball cap from his head.

"Yep," added Wash.

Lenny Shore had spent most of Sunday morning tinkering on his motorcycle. When he finished, he decided to take it for a test run. After about an hour racing through the fields behind his family farm, he was hungry, so he decided to go to the mini-mart on the west end of town to get a Dew and some Funyuns and Skittles. Lenny's driver's license was suspended, but for the last several months he had been sneaking onto the back roads with his motorcycle. He hadn't once seen any cops, so he was secure in the thought that he would not be caught.

It might have worked out that way, but it didn't. Lenny had just finished his snack and retrieved his bike from behind a dumpster next to the mini-mart. Had he looked up the street before he started the bike, he might have seen the sheriff's car. He was about to pull out of the lot as the cruiser pulled in. Lenny cut in front of the car. He looked in through the windshield and he recognized the deputy as the one who had ticketed him for running down the deer in the sugar beet field less than a year ago. Lenny panicked and gunned his bike, nearly dumping it on the loose gravel as he hit the roadway. In a blink of an eye, he was being chased into the middle of Bear River.

Lenny Shore turned onto Main Street. He gunned his engine, and the howl of the bike echoed down the two blocks of store fronts. The street was largely deserted because the stores were closed on Sunday. He heard the siren just a block behind him as he crossed the bridge over the Bear River. He made a snap decision to take the side streets. As he raced into the subdivision where Seth Parker lived, he formulated a plan to make it to the empty fields to the east. He hoped that with his full-face shield hiding his identity, the deputy wouldn't recognize him enough to figure out exactly who he was. The Benelli had a license plate, but Lenny strategically covered it with mud before starting his trips onto public roads.

Twenty minutes after he had unknowingly raced past his teammates and into the brush at the end of the cul-de-sac, Lenny pulled into the fields behind his family farm and slowly motored across the back forty. He walked the bike through the junked cars littering the acres directly behind the barn. He leaned his bike against a rusty 1970 Dodge Barracuda that he had helped his father pull the engine from the day before. Lenny tossed his helmet into the backseat of the car and walked nonchalantly around the south end of the barn.

There were two sheriff's cruisers and a state police car in the driveway of the large old farmhouse. Their emergency lights flashed. Lenny briefly thought of running and hiding, but just then, his father came out the back door of the house leading three uniformed officers. Lenny's stomach dropped as he lifted his hands and clasped them behind his head. He buckled to his knees as the sheriff deputy approached with the handcuffs. Lenny Shore knew he was well and truly fucked.

Just before seven the next morning, John Cale and Mike Reese were sitting in Clete Packer's office. "I don't know what the dumb shit was thinking. He's got the only neon green dirt bike in town. It's not like the cops around here don't know him well – he's leading all his classmates in moving violations. Well, he's bit it big time now, fleeing and eluding, reckless endangerment and driving on a suspended license. He's all done here as an athlete. Probably won't graduate anyway. He's three credits short as it is," Clete Packer informed the coaches.

Mike Reese had heard about Lenny Shore's mad dash and arrest the evening before and had already gone over what was going to happen with Cale during a late-night phone call. The young head coach could read Clete Packer's face as he ticked off the charges against Lenny Shore. There would be no commiserating about the loss of a player who might have improved the team after sitting out his original suspension. If anything, Cale noted a hint of satisfaction in Clete Packer's voice. Cale and Reese left the AD's office without exchanging pleasantries with Packer.

On that Monday morning, Keith Marker was substitute teaching for the world history teacher. All the JV football players found their way to the classroom to say hi and to exchange jibes with their coach. At the end of second hour, he and Coach Reese stood in front of their rooms talking about Lenny Shore's misadventures as kids passed in the hallway. A couple of football players high-fived Marker as they went past.

"Keith! Is that you?" a voice called out. Marker turned and saw that it was Laurie Starke. She had an enormous smile of recognition on her face as she walked up the hallway to him.

"Hi, Laurie," Keith Marker said with just enough discomfort in his voice to get Mike Reese to notice.

"What are you doing here? Are you student teaching too? I didn't know you switched majors," Laurie Starke commented as she stood in front of him just a little too closely, and he edged slightly away.

"No, I'm just subbing. I coach JV football here, and I'm picking up some extra bucks as a substitute teacher. How are you?" Keith asked with a bit of forced enthusiasm. Keith had known Laurie Starke for three years. His roommate had dated her two years ago. When they broke up, she turned her attention to Keith and was not too subtle in pursuit. Laurie was very good-looking, and if half the stories his old roommate told were true about her willingness in sexual pursuits, then most guys would have at least taken her out. Keith was not comfortable hooking up with a friend's ex – no matter how available and willing she might be. And Laurie's habit of getting wasted and then grabbing at him was not his style. He preferred to be the pursuer, not the pursued. They had bumped into each other a few times since. Keith had always felt awkward around her.

"I gotta go – I got class," Laurie said with bubbling enthusiasm. "Are you eating lunch in the lounge? We can catch up."

Mike Reese read the situation and he threw his Lowly ASS sistant a lifeline. "Keith, we've got some film to watch before practice today."

"Maybe next time I sub we can, but not today, sorry," Keith said with a smile.

Laurie Starke gave a mock pouty frown. "Okay, next time."

As Laurie Starke turned to walk up the hall, she came face to face with Molly Saunders. The old woman's doughy face scowled fleetingly as she assessed the young woman. It had been dislike at first sight for Molly when the girl had shown up to student teach. Everything about the CMU student said skank to Molly. A flighty bouncy little trollop; she knew the type all too well.

"Hi, Molly," Laurie Starke smiled and greeted the custodian.

Molly gave an almost imperceptible nod and low "uh" in return.

Laurie Starke read the body language and the judging looks. She had very little tolerance herself. Except her prejudice was directed at fat old women with no fashion sense sitting in judgment of young people. But she was on her best behavior, and she had been warned by her education professors not to antagonize custodians and secretaries at all costs. She smiled sweetly and passed Molly by.

The bell rang and third hour began. Keith ducked into the classroom after giving Mike Reese a relieved smile. When the bell rang for lunch, Marker walked across the hall to Reese's classroom. Large portraits of the president's decorated the walls. Quotes from each surrounded the portraits. Mike Reese was sitting at his desk trimming his finger nails with a pair of scissors.

"So I take it Miss Starke and you have a history, then?" Mike Reese said as he glanced up at the athletic young man.

"Yes and no," Marker replied, "She was the girlfriend of a roommate of mine a couple of years ago. He was a backup QB."

"And?" Mike Reese asked with a smile. "You didn't do something regrettable did you?"

"They broke up and then she kind of shifted her focus to me and I – avoided getting involved," Keith Marker said with a smile.

"Kind of tough passing up something like that, wasn't it?" Reese continued. He was enjoying Marker's evasive discomfort.

"I had other options," Marker said with confidence. "Laurie was just a little dangerous. One night she started a big fight in the Wayside. She was trying to get my roommate jealous by coming on to a couple of wrestlers. They got a little too aggressive a little too quick and four of us football players ended up toe to toe with them and then the bouncers got involved and – well, a few minutes later in the parking lot, she was laughing and teasing us about getting thrown out." Keith Marker paused. "Let's just say Laurie doesn't always make great decisions when she drinks – and she likes to drink."

"You know what we wrestlers say about girls like your friend Laurie?" Mike Reese asked with laugh.

"What?" Marker asked.

"Let's date em!" Reese replied and as Marker laughed in appreciation he continued. "We fought with football players forty years ago at CMU over the very same thing. They got the good looking ones and when they brought them to the bar we tried to take them away. Matter of fact, that's where I met my first wife. At the Wayside – and she was dating a football player at the time. I didn't get thrown out that night, but I have been bounced out of there a few times – once or twice because of a girl."

On Monday afternoon, the varsity football players stood around the massive maple tree at the south end of the practice field waiting for the start of practice. Seth Parker was telling the story of Lenny Shore's police chase. As the coaches approached, Morg Miller called out to Coach Cale, "Is Lenny suspended?"

John Cale had the players take a knee on the brown scraggly turf. He called the JV players over from their end of the field so he could talk to the whole program. "Gentlemen, we're going to go over this real quick and then we're going to get ready for Perrinton. As you all know by now, Lenny Shore was arrested yesterday. I won't go into details about his legal issues, but we were informed by the AD that Lenny will not be eligible to play this season – which is unfortunate because he is a senior. On a personal note, I want to talk to you about something. I think it is important for you all to remember that playing football, or any sport for that matter, is a privilege. You only have so many games to play in the four short years you are here. I know it doesn't seem like a short time, but if you ask any graduate they will tell you how short a high school football career is – isn't that right, Coach Colby?" John Cale asked his young assistant.

"Very short," Chet Colby answered.

"Each game is a gift." Cale continued as Colby nodded in affirmation. "And it is just plain foolish to waste your opportunity. To give away these gifts because of mistakes that could be avoided with a few moments of clear thinking followed by making good decisions. Let's try to learn from this and move forward as a team," Cale finished, and he motioned to Mike Reese to add his comments.

Mike Reese stepped to the front of the team and began, "I just want to second what Coach Cale has said. And I want to add two things that I have seen over my career. Now, most of you know I have been at this coaching thing for a long time. I have coached your fathers, uncles and older brothers. If I bother to total up the number, I've probably coached well over a thousand student athletes in almost four decades here at Bear River. I see many of my former athletes on a regular basis around town. They tell me one of two things when we talk. First – many talk of how special their memories of playing football or wrestling are to them. We share stories of past glory and games won or lost, but mostly we talk of all the friends they made. I hope you all know that the guys with you on this field right now will talk of your achievements with pride for the shared sacrifice and hard-fought battles you are facing together. That sort of friendship lives well past these years, let me tell you. Those are the kind of friends that will always have your back.

"There is a second group of my former athletes I see around town as well," Reese continued. "Members of this group sometimes have a hard time meeting my eyes when we talk. They talk of regret for having not finished a season because of bad grades or discipline issues. They bitterly complain of being young and foolish for having quit or for not going out for wrestling or football when they were seniors because they thought they had to get a job or the practices were too hard or whatever. And those that can say it without getting too emotional say that they regret that they let their teammates, their friends, down." Reese paused and met the eyes of the players in front of him. Some tipped their heads down. Tim Manikowski and Glenn Marcus held his gaze briefly and then glanced away.

Coach Reese finished, "It is my sincere hope for the players on this field, right here, right now, that they never have to apologize to anyone ever for having let their team down. Now that's about it other than one last thing."

A few of the players, mostly wrestlers, called out, "Yes, Coach!"

Mike Reese grinned broadly and then shouted in his loud growl, "Let's kick some Perrinton Owl butt this week!"

The players stood and cheered. The practice on both ends of the field was as good as any that season. When it was over, the coaches sat in the locker room office watching the players get their gear together and begin to leave. "Whatever was bothering Jorge last week seems to be past. He was an absolute beast out there today," John Cale announced and everyone agreed. Cale closed up the office a few moments later and he walked up to his classroom to correct some quizzes. In spite of the bad news to start his coaching week, he smiled. If he had any inkling of what lay ahead for the Bear River Bears over the next few weeks, that smile would have faded quickly.

On Thursday morning during first hour, two students sat in the chairs in front of Clete Packer's desk. The girl was a freshman cheerleader – very cute but not very bright. She was crying. The boy was a junior. One of Clete Packer's frequent fliers – a kid he had suspended three times in the last two years, once for having synthetic marijuana in his locker. Ben McClellan had a defiant look on his face.

"You know why you're here don't you?" Packer asked in his best stern voice. He knew the boy would be uncooperative, but he was sure he could get the girl to talk and perhaps give him what he needed.

The boy shrugged. Lia Lebowski let out a soft sob. Packer continued, "Look, let's not beat around the bush here, I have it on the surveillance video from the parking lot. The two of you can be seen getting out of Ben's car and entering the building – ten minutes late for class. And Lia you showed up for English class reeking of pot. That's why Mrs. Felix sent you down here. And I can smell it on you too, Ben. I've already called the police. The K9 team will be here in a half an hour." Packer told a small lie. He had no idea if the police would bring the drug-sniffing dogs – probably not. Packer continued, "I'm sure they will have no trouble hitting on your car, Ben. Maybe both of your lockers as well. Is someone going to start talking, or do we have to wait for the police and your parents to get here?"

"I'm not saying nothing," the sullen Ben McClellan replied.

Clete Packer ignored him and shifted his focus to the cheerleader. Her eyes were red – partially from crying. Tears streamed down her cheeks and dropped softly on her cheerleading sweater. "I, – I've never done this before!" Lia Lebowski heaved a heavy, sad sigh and then pointed her thumb at the boy without looking at him. "He talked me into it!" Ben McClellan shot her an angry look. Clete Packer motioned to a secretary in the outer office to come and escort Ben to the chairs by the main desk.

Packer fought the urge to smile. He had his opening. "Okay, Lia. Did Ben tell you where he got the drugs?"

Lia Lebowski cried with more force, knowing she was trapped into telling Packer everything she knew. "I don't know nothing. He said some senior sold him the joints. He said it was supposed to be real mild, and I wouldn't get high or nothing." She managed to tell her story between sobs, and Clete Packer didn't care if it was wholly true or not, but he knew he had to press harder.

"Did he say it was Tim Manikowski?" Packer asked, guarding against letting her in on his joy at the possibility.

"I don't know, maybe, I don't remember who he said. My head hurts. I'm gonna be sick. Can I call my mommy, please?" Lia's voice trailed off sounding like that of a wounded little girl.

Clete Packer deftly picked up the small plastic trash can next to his desk and held it out to the crying girl. He motioned again to the secretary through the window. When she opened the door he asked, "Can you please take Lia to the nurse's office and call her mother? And send Ben in here now please."

Ben McClellan slouched into the chair in front of Packer's desk. He leaned his head back and stared at the ceiling. Clete Packer stood behind his desk chair with his hands behind his back as he spoke. "Ben, this is your second drug offense. You're in a great deal of trouble. I'm not going to lie to you. We are going to search your locker, and I'm sure the police will have a warrant to search your car in an hour or so. You will be suspended for at least ten days, and then we will likely start proceedings to expel you. That might be the least of your troubles. If the police find more than just a joint in your possession, you could be spending some time in juvie at the very least. If there are drugs in your car, they are going to impound it and probably auction it off." Clete Packer hoped that the threat of losing his car might get the boy talking. He was willing to lie a little about what might happen in hopes to get Ben to crack and spill the beans on Tim Manikowski.

Ben McClellan snapped from his slouch to sitting upright. "Bullshit! No one better mess with my car!" Ben was passionate about two things in life. Getting high and his 1999 Toyota Supra, which Ben and his older brother rebuilt and tricked out for street racing. Ben's older brother was in the Marines. At least every other week his older brother sent him an email about the car – which was still in his name. Ben knew the small baggie filled with pot in the glove box was a serious problem. He also knew if he lost the car, his brother would kick the shit out of him when he got home.

"Well, I see we have some interest now in cooperation," Clete Packer said with a malicious smile.

"Man, you better think twice about fucking with my car. It's my brother's and when he gets back from deployment, he'll fuck you up!" Ben threatened.

"Young man, your idle threats mean nothing to me. You had better start giving me names about where the drugs came from or I can guarantee two things. You will be expelled and the second thing is when you get out of juvenile detention, you're going to be walking because that car is going to be sitting in the county impound lot waiting to be auctioned off in the spring," Clete Packer answered the threat in icy tones.

Ben McClellan sneered at Packer. "Maybe you better think about what you'll be driving. That piece of shit you drive ain't going nowhere with sugar in the gas tank and slashed tires. And when my brother gets done with you, you won't be driving shit with two broken arms."

Clete Packer laughed a loud dismissive laugh. He didn't care one iota about the twenty-year-old Mercury sedan sitting in his parking space. It was a piece of shit – it had been his father-in-law's car before he was incapacitated by a stroke a few years ago. He had learned long ago never to drive anything nice to work – not with the better part of four hundred kids hating your guts. Clete kept his 1968 Mustang and his nice F-250 pickup in a pole barn behind his home – under lock and key.

The laugh faded, and Packer looked the young punk in the eyes. "Give me a name. Was it Tim Manikowski?" he asked in flat tones.

Ben McClellan had bought pot from Tim on a few occasions, but not this time. He had traded a carburetor kit he had shoplifted in Mt. Pleasant to Dave Labarre for the pot. Labarre was a fellow gearhead and stoner. Labarre might try to kick his ass, but it wouldn't be anything like what Ben's brother would be dishing out when he got home to find his car auctioned off. Ben was trapped now, and he knew he had to give Fudge Packer something – maybe it would keep his car from getting seized.

"I don't know, it probably came from Tim, but that's not who I got it from," Ben begrudgingly confessed.

"Name," Clete Packer replied.

"Dave," Ben McClellan answered.

"Dave Labarre?" Packer questioned. Ben McClellan nodded. Packer was a little disappointed that there wasn't a direct fingering of Manikowski. Dave Labarre was a tougher nut to crack. He was lazy and shifty but he wasn't stupid. Plus John Labarre, his father, had a pure hatred of Clete going back several years when Packer had suspended Dave's older sister just before graduation for drinking at prom. She got her diploma but wasn't allowed to walk with her class. This mess was getting sticky; John Labarre would stonewall any attempt at trying to get to his son. Clete Packer could feel Tim Manikowski slipping from his grasp. He was not about to let that happen if he could prevent it.

The bell rang ending first hour. Clete Packer knew he had to act fast. He escorted Ben McClellan to the chairs in the outer office. He told the secretary to get Dave Labarre to the office at the start of second hour and to keep it quiet. He exited to the hallway with his locker keys in his hands. Packer only hoped that a search of Tim Manikowski's lockers in the hallway and the gym locker room would produce something to hang him with.

A police cruiser pulled up in front of the school, confirming to most of the student body that the rumors about a drug bust involving Ben McClellan and Lia Lebowski were true. Dave Labarre was making for the exit to the student parking lot when he saw Tim Manikowski talking to a girl in the hallway. The bell to begin second hour was about to ring.

"The cops are out front. Fudge just nailed Ben – I'm fucking out of here," Labarre whispered hoarsely into Tim Manikowski's ear.

"Okay," Tim answered. He felt no need to run. He knew his lockers were clean and his half-empty stash bag was well hidden. After last spring, no one could find so much as a stray seed anywhere in this building tied to Tim. His stash bag was in the rafters of the garage in the backyard next door to his house. The eighty-five-year-old widow who lived there had no idea Tim had a key to her garage, and she was half blind anyway.

Tim ducked into the boys' room and pulled his iPhone from his pocket. He quickly texted his mother at work.

TMan: Mr. Packer is conducting drug raids. One of my friends just told me he is coming after me.

Tim didn't wait for the reply. He turned off his phone. He exited the bathroom quietly and went to his second-hour class. It was after the bell, but he sweet-talked his way out of a tardy.

Clete Packer made his way back from the boys' locker room. His search had turned up nothing. He found a deputy sheriff siting waiting for him in the office. Packer briefed the deputy on the situation. The deputy made a call and then started his interrogation of Ben McClellan.

"Where's Labarre?" Clete Packer asked the school secretary.

"We can't find him. He was in first hour, but he never showed up for second," she replied.

Packer could feel his blood pressure rising. "Did Lia Lebowski's mother show up yet?"

"She works in Lansing – she can't get here until after lunch," the secretary answered.

"Okay. Okay. That's okay. Don't let her leave until I get a chance to talk to her. Where's Mike?" Packer asked after looking into Principal Shanahan's darkened office.

"He's across the street with the super at the central office. I think they're reviewing cut scores for the state tests or something," the secretary answered with disdain for the always-absent principal.

"Yeah, okay. Okay. I'm going to use his office while the deputy uses mine. See if Tim Manikowski is still in the building. If he is, send him to me." Packer ordered.

The principal's office was well-appointed. A burgundy leather office chair was behind the large mahogany desk. Expensive golf clubs in a bag were stored in the closet – the door was ajar. Unread books lined the shelves behind the desk. On the other walls, pictures hung in neat rows. One large picture showed Mike Shanahan shaking hands with President George W. Bush. On the desk top sat a dark computer – rarely if ever used. Mike Shanahan had the secretaries print his email for him every day. A Sudoku puzzle book lay next to the computer with a pencil stuck in as a book-mark.

Clete Packer sat in the principal's chair. If this were any other time, he would scan the room and note how different it was from his office. His space was covered with papers and folders. Sports photos lined his walls. His carpet was threadbare compared to the lush dark carpeting of this office. None of that really mattered now. He had Tim Manikowski in his sights. This office would be his someday, but today was about nailing the school's leading drug dealer. If he could pull that off, it would be a major feather in his cap and sweet revenge on Tim's bitch of a mother.

The secretary ushered Tim Manikowski into the office. Tim was carrying a backpack and wearing a Bears Basketball T-shirt. Clete Packer made no greeting. Tim stood in front of the desk.

"Tim, please put your backpack on the desk and empty your pockets," Packer said officiously.

"Why?" was the short reply. Tim Manikowski's voice betrayed no concern, and his face was as placid as if he were studying in the library.

"You're a clever young man. You know there is a police car here. More on the way, I suspect, after Ben McClellan finishes with the deputy. Probably they will have the dog team with them. Lia Lebowski will be making a statement as well. And I think the sheriff deputies will be visiting Dave Labarre this afternoon. He seems to have left the building rather abruptly," Clete Packer replied.

Tim Manikowski made no reply. He emptied his pockets and placed his wallet and iPhone on the desk. He unzipped his backpack and removed a calculus textbook, a note book, a graphing calculator and a dogeared paperback copy of the *The Sun Also Rises* with school markings on the cover. He spread them all across the large mahogany desk.

Clete Packer surveyed the collection. He picked up the iPhone. He turned it on. "Make any phone calls or text messages since school started? You know these are supposed to be turned off during school hours," Packer observed giving no indication of what he was after.

"Yeah, well, my mom contacted me earlier to remind me about something. But I think that was before first bell," Tim said innocently.

Packer tried swiping his finger across the phone screen. "It's locked," Tim informed him.

"Why?" Clete Packer asked.

"It's against the rules to use it during school hours," Tim made a light mocking of Packer's earlier statement. "Besides if I were to lose it or someone took it from me – well, you know stuff isn't very secure around here. People are always ripping stuff off and no one seems to ever do anything about it in this building," Tim answered with another subtle dig at the man who was in charge of school security.

Packer's eyes flared slightly at the dig. "Unlock it please," he said.

"No," Tim replied quietly.

"Okay. If that's how you want this. I'll just keep this until the deputies need it. You'll open it for them, I'm sure." Packer fought to keep the building anger out of his voice. He was not liking how the interview was going. This little shit was too cool and too smug. He made a show of slipping the phone into his suit jacket.

"That's my private property," Tim said coolly.

"You can get it from the deputies later. I don't think it is advisable given this situation for you to have the ability to contact your contacts at this point. I am well within the rule of law on this. You obviously have broken school code – the message light is blinking on the phone indicating that it was used recently and someone is replying. You took student law last year. Remember *in loco parentis*?" Packer returned with the hopes of making his target squirm a bit.

Tim did not give him the satisfaction of protesting further. He was confident there were no incriminating communications on it. "Look, I told you that message is probably a reminder from my mother. But if you don't want to believe that, fine," Tim Manikowski baited the assistant principal.

"A message from your mother? About what?" Clete Packer was desperate to keep the boy talking with hopes of tripping him up somehow.

Tim Manikowski reached into his back pocket and pulled out a folded index card. He flipped it onto the desk. "This, I think," he said without inflection.

Clete Packer picked up the index card and unfolded it. In large black ink capital letters was printed the word "FUDGE!" Packer's eyes narrowed and his lips thinned into a strait grimace. He had been suckered by Tim and the fury was bubbling in his chest.

"What is the meaning of this?" Clete "Fudge" Packer asked with an audible hiss.

Tim smiled. Direct hit. And now for the kill shot. "My mom wants me to pick up the ingredients. She is making a batch of FUDGE for the church social on Sunday. I don't know why. Personally, I can't stand FUDGE. In fact, I don't know anyone around here who has any use for FUDGE. Even my mom and step dad think FUDGE is worthless. But that's what the ladies on the church social council told her to bring so, that's why my mom is sending me a message. I think she is worried I might forget to stop at the store," Tim Manikowski said sweetly, putting just a hint of sarcasm on the word FUDGE each time.

Clete "Fudge" Packer's hands shook with rage as he discarded the note back to the desk top. "Take a seat. I have to talk to the deputy in my office." He managed to not shout in response. He exited the principal's office and walked quickly across to his own. He stepped inside and explained to the deputy that he was just pausing to get the suspect in his office to sweat a little. He stood clenching and unclenching his fists for a few minutes. Ben McClellan read "Fudge's" eyes. Even he could tell that Tim Manikowski had the upper hand in the other office.

Tim was sitting quietly when the assistant principal returned. "Okay. It's time you got clued into what is happening here today. Ben McClellan and Lia Lebowski have already fessed up to using this morning. Ben has told the deputy that there is an ounce in his car. Which I am sure they are going to impound. He and Lia have named their source, Dave Labarre, who they have made plain gets his supply from you. When the deputies arrest Dave, it will take all of about two seconds for him to rat you out. Then with search warrants in hand, they will visit your house. You're not leaving here until all that plays out. I have got you, my friend. I got you square. So maybe it is time you start thinking about your future and whether or not you can get into college with a drug felony conviction on your record. Maybe if you write up a nice statement right now about your role in this your mother can keep the records sealed as a juvenile offense. You might still get into a community college or something – maybe join the service. But you are done here as an athlete, and you will not be allowed to participate in graduation. Your status as a top-ten student in your class will be expunged from your records." Clete Packer badgered and bluffed his way through the statement. It was a Hail Mary pass trying to get Tim Manikowski to fess up. A long shot.

Tim Manikowski's face betrayed no emotion while Fudge blustered. The chain of evidence from Ben McClellan to him was not strong and he knew it. He also was very confident that his stash was hidden very well so the police would never find it even if there was ever a search warrant issued. Tim paused for a few moments before responding.

"I'm not sure who this Lia Lebowski is. Is she a freshman? I don't think I know her. Ben McClellan is that junior kid with the tricked-out Toyota. Kind of a stoner – not very reliable as a witness. I suppose he would tell the cops his mother bought the drugs for him if they threatened to take that car from him. Of course I know Dave Labarre – we've been in school together since kindergarten. We've never been friends, though. I'm an athlete and a top-of-the-class student. Dave is a grease monkey like Lenny Shore, but he has never played any sports except for T-ball and he stunk at that. I doubt Dave is even going to graduate. Just like Lenny. So, I guess it's going to be their words against mine. Now I know you think because someone planted drugs in my gym locker last track season I have some sort of role in this. I don't and the records will show that I was never arrested for anything last spring, so any college applications I fill out will be fine I guess." Tim gave his response with no sarcasm or defensiveness. That made Clete Packer even madder.

"Listen, my friend," Packer began with anger. "Once the police finish their investigation, this thing is going to snowball on you. If you don't get in front of this and start providing names of students that you have sold to and who your supplier is, the prosecuting attorney is going to have you locked up awaiting trial by about game time tomorrow." Packer launched his most desperate fabrication. He wasn't stupid. He made his play trying to turn Tim, but it wasn't working. His anger would not let him back down.

"Uncle Steve?" Tim Manikowski finally laughed in the face of Clete Packer. "You do know that Steven Thurston is like my stepfather's oldest friend, right? He's the county prosecuting attorney. My stepdad and mother chaired his election campaign. You remember my stepdad is the assistant chairman for the county Republican Party, right? Jesus, that's the best you got? Uncle Steve has already written my recommendation letter for U of M. I don't need it though. I'm a legacy. My mom got her doctorate there and my biological dad is a Michigan Law School graduate." Tim Manikowski could not keep the derisive laughter out of his response. When he finished, he kept chuckling for effect.

As Clete Packer stood a few feet from the snickering student, it took all his willpower not to slap the smug grin off the kid's face. It would end his career, he knew that, but God, he had never wanted to hit a student more than right then. He was formulating his response when Agnes Johns the high school office's lead secretary stuck her head in the door. Clete turned to face her with an exasperated look. "Not now, Agnes!" he practically shouted.

Agnes Johns was an old pro. Anyone who has been in education for very long knows to never anger a school secretary. It is the first thing school administrators learn on the job, and if they don't learn it they don't have their job very long. Agnes betrayed no emotion but she was not going to be yelled at. Any thought of bringing Clete Packer out of the office to give him the message left her mind. "Mr. Packer, the superintendent just called. Timothy's mother is in his office. He would like you to drop what you are doing and get across the street immediately." Agnes Johns shut the door before he could respond and went to her work station, smiling vengefully.

Tim Manikowski held his hand up to his mouth to stifle his laughter. "Can I have my phone back please?" he managed to get out without collapsing on the floor.

Clete Packer's face was blank for a second. He blinked at the boy as he processed the hot mess that was waiting for him 100 feet out the front door of the high school. He regained his composure and pointed at the chairs in front of the main office desk. "Take a seat out there," he said evenly, and he briskly walked out of the office.

As Clete Packer crossed the street, he was oblivious to the light rain that was falling. He did notice the white Lexus SUV parked in the visitor's parking spot in front of the district central office. There was a U of M alumni sticker on the right upper hand of the back window. On the left was a Riverdale Beavers sticker. It was the car of Dr. Julie Bysshe, E.D., the assistant superintendent of Riverdale Public Schools. Timothy Manikowski's vengeful mother was waiting in the Super's office. Clete Packer was quite sure that the helicopter mom from hell was preparing to tear him a new asshole in front of his bosses. And he knew for certain his gutless principal and political manipulator of a superintendent would not lift a finger in his defense. Two hours ago, he had thought that he had Tim Manikowski nailed – now all that was past. He only hoped he could escape this meeting with his dignity and job intact.

Sheldon Knapp was sitting behind his desk when Clete entered the office. He looked calm. He had the same dark mahogany desk as the principal across the street. The rest of the office was even more elegantly appointed than Mike Shanahan's. Julie Bysshe sat in a large guest chair at the right-hand front corner of the desk. She was dressed in a dark blue power suit. Her light blonde hair was tinged with gray and pulled back from her face. She fixed Clete with an intense angry stare. Mike Shanahan stood near the window a few feet to the left of the Super's desk. He had a look on his face as though he was trying to jimmy open the window latch and escape to the city park out the back of the office.

"I believe you two are acquainted," Sheldon Knapp said with his best political smile as he motioned to Julie Bysshe.

"Mr. Packer," Julie Bysshe greeted him coldly.

"Mrs. Mani – Bysshe." Clete Packer stumbled badly in response. Already off to a bad start. Had he been looking that direction, he would have seen Mike Shanahan wince.

"You will refer to me as *Dr.* Bysshe, thank you." Julie Bysshe's eyes narrowed angrily in response. The hatred radiating off her was enough to make Clete Packer avert his eyes.

"Yes, of course, I apologize," Packer offered.

Julie Bysshe wasted no time getting to her point. "Where is my son right now? I have been trying to contact him for some time, and he is not answering his phone."

"Tim is in the office across the street. We are currently investigating an incident of drug use on school property, and your son has been named as a potential participant in the case. I have his phone, and I am holding it until the police request it for evidence," Clete Packer said with as much firmness as he could.

"You have his phone!? Give it to me at once!" Julie Bysshe demanded.

"Dr. Bysshe, as I said, the police are investigating—" Clete Packer began.

Julie Bysshe stood. "I am fully aware of the type of investigating you're capable of, Mr. Packer, and I will not stand for another one of your kangaroo court farces! You will give me his phone right now or the next conversation we will be having will be with my lawyer and the county prosecuting attorney in attendance!" she announced very firmly.

Clete Packer sought the eyes of the superintendent. Sheldon Knapp glanced casually away. "Dr. Bysshe, I have three students who are about to name your son as a supplier—" Packer tried to respond.

"Enough! I have heard quite enough of your slander against my son!" Julie Bysshe cut him off. She shifted her focus to Sheldon Knapp. "Superintendent Knapp, it is high time you reign in this rogue administrator of yours. I will not have him jeopardizing my son's future by rigging some farcical evidence and testimony gotten from the typical Bear River criminals that walk the halls of that zoo you call a high school! No doubt, Mr. Packer has a fine specimen like the boy who led police on a high-speed chase through town on Sunday ready to testify that Tim is the biggest drug kingpin in the state. Just as long as they get off scot free. This has to end or I will be calling Steven Thurston and asking him to investigate your discipline referrals for the last five years. He will find a pattern of administrative indifference, at the very least. Probably more like gross negligence!" Julie Bysshe laid down her threats.

Sheldon Knapp could have stood and met fire with fire, but that was not going to happen. He calculated the political pull that Julie Bysshe had at the county level. He looked at Clete Packer and nodded toward the angry Dr. Bysshe. "Give her the phone, Mr. Packer," he said.

Clete Packer thrust his hand into his suit coat pocket and retrieved the phone. Without saying anything, he offered it to Dr. Bysshe. She snatched it from his hands and opened her leather briefcase to deposit it. As she did, she pulled out a thin set of papers and laid them on the desk.

"I believe you will find these in order. It is a transcript request. We are transferring Timothy to Riverdale effective immediately. I am not interested in letting Mr. Packer conduct a vendetta campaign against my child. I know full well Mr. Shanahan will do nothing to prevent it. And apparently neither will you, Mr. Knapp," Julie Bysshe coolly stated.

Clete Packer felt the need to get the upper hand in some way. "Tim will not be eligible for sports until next spring if he transfers now. The state athletic association will not allow it," he stated with some power behind his words.

"I am fully aware of the rules for participation for student athletes, Mr. Packer," Julie Bysshe answered with contempt. "What you are not aware of, obviously, is that my husband and I own a home in Riverdale. We bought it this summer. I only left Tim here at Bear River because he begged us to allow him to finish his high school education with his friends and classmates. YOU have made that wish absolutely a moot point. I have already talked to the AD as well as the head football and basketball coaches at our high school. They tell me Tim will be welcomed to begin play immediately. A change of residency negates any of your petty protests," Julie Bysshe said defiantly and with finality.

Yet, Julie Bysshe was not quite done. She had learned that when bridges are burned, it was best to make sure no potential enemy could effectively rebuild them. "As far as your little drug investigation goes, you should know this. I will bring all the power I have to bear against any attempt to further ensnare my son. And let me assure you, it will not be related to only this incident. I am the liaison for the state superintendent's association to the Michigan Associated School Boards. I know there are people here that wish to move up or possibly on from Bear River. With the exception of your figurehead principal, of course, who is content to twiddle his thumbs for another two years until he retires. I believe Mr. Packer might find it difficult to get the principalship here if I contact certain people. And he certainly won't get an opportunity to make any lateral moves to any neighboring school districts."

The bald-faced threat stung her target, Clete Packer looked down with a grimace. "And Sheldon, you and my boss both are looking to get interviews for the Midland superintendent's post next spring. I figure you both will be finalists. That won't happen of course if I name you and your administrators here in a lawsuit for defamation of character of my son or if I persuade the county prosecutor to conduct a very public investigation into the discipline referral records of this entire district looking for malfeasance and/or intimidation of students. Don't fuck with me, gentlemen. You have no idea what lengths I will go to in protecting my child." With that Dr. Julie Bysshe left the office without saying goodbye.

The three Bear River administrators watched her leave. The atmosphere of the room was of total defeat. A moment passed. "That did not go very well," Sheldon Knapp said with an edge to his voice as he eyed Clete Packer with anger.

Mike Shanahan took the opportunity to utter his first words of the meeting. "You know what they say at Riverdale. Whatever the Bysshe wants the Bysshe gets." Sheldon Knapp did not look at him as he held up his hand to stop further comment. Knapp kept his withering gaze fixed on Clete Packer.

Knapp cleared his throat. "Clete, whatever is going on across the street, you better wrap it up neatly. I don't want this in the papers. Suspend anyone with drugs in their possession, but that is as far as any of this needs to go. I will call the sheriff and get him to call off any further investigation," the Superintendent said coldly.

"I've got two kids caught red-handed and a third I am sure supplied them. What sort of message are we sending if they only get a few days of suspension?" Clete Packer asked defensively.

Sheldon Knapp kept his temper in check. "Clete, state student count day is next week. We just lost over seven grand in state aid because the Manikowski boy is transferring. If we suspend three more students or expel them, that is even more state aid money out the door. If you want to move into upper administration, you are going to have to pick your battles with a little more care and consider the economic and long-term outcomes of your actions. Our financial margin is razor thin – we can't afford to lose any money. This ends now. Today." Knapp explained his position clearly. Clete Packer hung his head in response.

"Buck up, Clete, Tim Manikowski is transferring. You got what you wanted. You said he was the biggest drug dealer in school and now he is gone. That's a victory, in my book." Mike Shanahan said with forced humor. Clete Packer shot him a disgusted look and Shanahan turned to look out the window once again. Sheldon Knapp dismissed Clete Packer. As he walked back in the rain to his office across the street, he hung his head in total defeat.

By the end of the school day, all the kids in the building knew that Tim Manikowski was transferring to Riverdale. The stoners were despondent. The athletes were not shocked, but the football team now had to deal with the loss of two players in one week. No one was happy – including Tim Manikowski. It wasn't that he wouldn't be graduating with his friends. He really didn't have many to begin with. He was upset that he would now be cut off from his client base. As he sat at home that evening, he contemplated a temporary retirement from drug dealing. Maybe he would get back in it in college.

The JV team played their home game that evening in a steady rain. Just a few parents were in the stands. Pat Packer sat next to Wyatt Baier, Scott Baier's father, in the stands. Both of them were yelling at the coaches on the field to throw the ball more. Pat Packer was confident that their voices were carrying into the press box. He smiled to himself with satisfaction. He knew that in the rain, passing was not in the game plan. He didn't care – he only wanted to agitate his former coaching partners.

Just before halftime, a Perrinton Owl player went down to a serious leg injury. During the timeout, Pat Packer loudly proclaimed, "Wyatt, I think you better think about transferring Scotty to a school where they know how to groom quarterbacks. This staff doesn't know anything about teaching the passing game. Run, run, run and punt – that's about all they know!" A few parents laughed. In the press box, John Cale was coldly furious at his former assistant. He would ask Clete Packer to do something about his loudmouth nephew, but the AD had taken off shortly after the start of the game complaining of not feeling well.

"What in the hell is Pat doing up there?" Mike Reese asked through his field headset.

"Being an asshole." John Cale replied from the press box.

"We can't pass and neither can they in this rain. He knows that," Mike Reese stated.

"He just wants to get under our skin. He is cozying up to Wyatt Baier like their old buddies. He's trying to poison the well on us. The thing is, it is working. I'll bet you ten bucks we get a call from Wyatt about how we're holding back his son's development," John Cale replied.

"It's another super day for the program," Mike Reese observed.

The Bear JV squad ended up losing the game 12-0.

Friday evening the varsity travelled to Perrinton for their game. The festive decorations on the field indicated it was Perrinton's homecoming game. Heavy clouds hung in the sky. Halfway through the second quarter, a lightning strike and a loud clap of thunder drove the teams off the field. The game was delayed for forty-five minutes as the brief thunderstorm passed overhead. The teams returned to the field to finish the last six minutes of the half. Perrinton scored just before the gun to make the score 21-0 in favor of the Owls.

The Bears sat in the visiting-team locker room during the long halftime. Seth Parker was nursing a sore throwing hand. An Owl linebacker had stepped on it. The bruise was darkening and the fingers were tightening up. John Cale made the call. Seth was done for the night.

As the Bears returned to the field, the homecoming floats and the marching band were circling the track. The Bear players had to wait until they cleared. As they got into place for the mandatory three-minute warm up, the clock was already ticking. As Cale and Reese walked to midfield, the head referee blew his whistle and threw his yellow flag. The Bears were penalized for delay of game.

John Cale stood at midfield in front of the ref. "What the hell are you talking about? We couldn't get to the field because of the parade," Cale said in exasperation.

"You should have come down earlier. Perrinton did," the ref replied loudly.

"It's their homecoming for God's sake – they stayed down on the field for the whole show!" John Cale replied just as loudly. His anger was getting the best of him.

"That's enough, Coach! You know the rules. You have to warm up for three minutes, and if you don't start with the timer, then the second half kick is delayed. That is delay of game!" the ref replied as his face reddened.

"That's a chickenshit call and you know it!" John Cale answered back. He regretted it almost immediately. The ref blew his whistle once again and hit John Cale in the foot with the yellow flag.

"Unsportsmanlike conduct! Fifteen yards! And Coach, if you say one more thing, I am throwing you out of this game right now!" The official yelled loud enough for the whole field to hear. Mike Reese ushered his young head coach to the Bear bench.

The Bear players watched the events unfold. "Jesus – Cale is pissed off," Morg Miller observed.

"Yeah, and now we're going to be kicking off from our own end zone, almost," Jorge Martinez replied.

The second half started after the refs marched off the penalties. The Owls returned the kick for a touchdown. Just before the end of the third quarter, one more fast-moving thunderstorm caused yet another forty-five-minute delay. The Bears returned to the field with the score board reading Home 28, Visitors 0.

With four minutes left in the game, the score had not changed. Lightning struck in the western sky. The refs again suspended play. This time the storm lingered. The Bear players sat for over an hour in the locker room listening to the thunder outside. Morg Miller started to share some slightly filthy limericks with his teammates until Coach Cale told him to stop. After ninety minutes, the refs called the game. No attempt was made to reschedule for the next day given the score, so the Perrinton Owls won their homecoming 28-0. The stands were empty but the field lights were still on as the Bears briskly walked to their bus. The rain poured down and distant thunder rumbled.

Morg Miller handed his helmet and shoulder pads to Wash Dryer. Wash gave him a quizzical look. Morg grinned and then let fly with a loud war whoop and jumped the fence of the track. He sprinted to the middle of the football field. His feet kicked up large splashes as he went. The team began laughing. Morg danced on the large blue and white Owl painted on the field at the fifty-yard line and let loose with another shout. Then he sprinted down to the five-yard line and dove head first into the mud puddle that stretched from there through the end zone. Morg hydroplaned, sending up a giant V-shaped wake as he slid past the goalpost. He stood, covered with mud and dripping brown water. Morg thrust his fist in the air and yelled, "That's for Lenny!"

"Miller!" John Cale yelled at the stocky lineman. "That just cost you ten laps on Monday! If your butt is not on the bus in two minutes I will double that!" The team laughed hard and Morg felt triumphant as he sprinted to the bus. After they were underway, Wash Dryer threw a clean towel to Morg who wiped his face and thanked him.

Greg DeVito sat in the seat across the aisle from Morg. He shook his head and looked at his goofy teammate and friend. "Was it worth the ten laps?" he asked with amusement.

"Don't know. Ask me Monday," Morg Miller replied with a grin.

## Overtime

Wash Dryer took a shower when he got home. It was past midnight. The lightning delays during the game caused the late return of the bus to Bear River. Wash considered not texting his dad but then decided he would.

WashDryer: Knock Knock.

GregDryer: Who's there?

WashDryer: Owen.
GregDryer: Owen who?
WashDryer: Owen Five.
GregDryer: Another blowout?
WashDryer: More like a lightning out.

Wash filled his father in on the story of the game, including Morg's antics on the field after. Greg Dryer laughed as he stretched out on his motel bed.

GregDryer: It's getting late there. You better get some sleep. Have fun tomorrow night.
WashDryer: Mom told you?
GregDryer: Yep. Have fun. Make good decisions.
WashDryer: Always.

Wash went to bed. He didn't sleep much. His upcoming date with Maricel on Saturday evening filled his thoughts. On Wednesday when he asked her to go to a movie with him, she squeezed his hand and answered yes in Spanish. During the week, Maricel Arambula had taken up the habit of slipping up behind Wash in the hallways during class changes and taking his hand in hers. It made Wash feel like leaping for joy each time it happened. The whole senior class gossiped about the couple all week long. Wash didn't register the looks of envy he was getting from the boys in school. He wasn't noticing much of anything other than Maricel.

# CHAPTER TEN

## OWEN 6

Wash Dryer went for a long run on Sunday. Several miles more than his usual two. The excitement in his heart was almost too much to deal with if he wasn't occupied with some activity. The date with Maricel was fantastic. They went to eat at an Italian place in Mt. Pleasant, and Wash drove her around CMU's campus before they went to the movie. Wash and Maricel did not watch much of the film. After dropping her off at eleven, he drove home with every atom in his body singing.

On Monday morning near the end of first hour, Clete Packer called John Cale in his classroom. "Please come to my office, Coach," Clete Packer said, giving no hint as to what it was about.

"I can't. I have class second hour," Cale replied.

"I'll send someone down to cover for you for a few minutes. This won't take long."

Shortly after the bell for second hour rang, Cale sat in the athletic director's office. Clete Packer was on the phone. "I'm sorry, Coach, but I had to take that call. Can you explain to me what happened after the game at Perrinton on Friday night?" Packer wasted no time getting to his question.

"Pertaining to what?" John Cale replied.

"Pertaining to a Bear River player vandalizing the football field after the game. Dan Marx, their AD witnessed it from their press box as he was getting ready to turn off the field lights. He called me this morning about it. Who was the player?" Clete Packer asked. John Cale was regretting meeting with Clete without Mike Reese present. But then he knew this meeting was timed, so that was unlikely to have happened. Packer was spreading a trap, and Cale was unsure on how to avoid stepping into it.

"The player involved is facing team discipline at practice today. And I would hardly call what he did vandalism. He slid through a mud puddle on the field as we were heading to the bus. It had been storming all night. Youthful exuberance and stupidity, maybe, but there was no intent to vandalize," John Cale explained.

"I want the player's name," Clete Packer dismissed Cale's explanation.

"Morgan Miller," Cale replied calmly, belying the anger that was welling up in him. He could see where this was heading, and he was not pleased.

"I suspected as much. Young Mr. Miller has exhibited contempt for playing fields recently here." Clete Packer pressed the intercom button as he finished. "Agnes please have Morgan Miller sent to my office," he declared, releasing the button before Agnes Johns could answer.

"Mr. Packer, I don't think—" John Cale began before Clete Packer held up his hand to stop him.

Packer stood and walked out of the office leaving John Cale fuming in the chair. Fewer than five minutes later, he returned. As he opened the door, Morg Miller entered the main office and Packer waved him into the athletics office. Packer laid a yellow discipline form on his desk as he sat. Morg Miller stood next to Coach Cale looking puzzled.

"Morgan, I am writing a referral for you, and you are suspended for the rest of this day," Clete Packer said without emotion.

"What? Why?" Morg asked in disbelief.

"For conduct unbecoming a Bear River High School Student athlete – your willful vandalism of the Perrinton field constitutes improper behavior. Their mascot painting was defaced, and according to their AD, the gouge you left in the end zone required grounds crew to repair it before the soccer game they played there on Saturday. Of course, you know any athlete suspended from school is not eligible to play in interscholastic events for one week. You will not be playing this Friday. Please have a seat in the outer office, I will call your parents when I am finished with your coach," Packer explained.

"Whatever," Morg said as he turned to leave.

"Young man," Packer said forcefully causing Morg to stop and turn to face him. "If you don't watch it, I will extend the suspension to two games. I've had quite enough of your disrespect and your antics," Packer threatened.

Morg Miller silently withdrew from the office.

"Clete, your punishment does not fit the violation and you know it," John Cale said with both disgust and pity.

Clete Packer held up his hand. "Stop right there, Coach! Do not presume to tell me my job! Vandalism either in our facility or at another school is a serious offense, and it is high time a message be sent to the football players that their lawlessness will no longer be tolerated!"

John Cale blinked in disbelief at the AD. "Vandalism? The owl painted on that field was practically washed away from the rain and torn up from the game. That whole field was torn up. Calling what he did vandalism is a huge stretch. I have to wonder if this punishment is even about Morgan – maybe it's—" John Cale paused in his description of Morg's actions. He was treading on thin ice, and he knew it.

Clete Packer's fury was building. he stood and yelled loudly enough that Morg Miller turned his head to watch through the office windows, "Enough! The punishment stands!"

John Cale shook his head sadly and stood. "Mr. Packer, I have an important lesson plan to teach, so, if you don't mind, I am returning to my classroom," Cale said dismissively.

Packer returned to his chair. "One more thing, Coach," Cale paused before leaving. "I am making note of the penalty for unsportsmanlike behavior you received Friday night at the game. I am attaching it to your coaching file. If there are no further penalties on you this season, I will remove the note from your file. It is important for you to know that the final month of this season constitutes the beginning of the interview you will have to go through next spring to see if BRHS retains you in your present coaching position." The AD issued the thinly veiled threat with a straight face. John Cale resisted the urge to repeat Morg Miller's exclamation of "whatever" as he left the office.

As Coach Cale passed Morg Miller in the office, he grasped his young player on the shoulder as a symbol of support. Morg turned his face up to see his coach. The usual goofy grin Morg greeted everybody with was replaced by a look of grim anger. "This is a bunch of bull, Coach," Morg stated plainly.

"I know, Morg, I know – Mr. Packer is on the warpath, and he will not listen to me. I want you at practice and at the game just the same – even if you can't play." Cale met Morg's eyes as he spoke. Morg nodded.

Morg Miller's parents were in the building within the hour. They met with Clete Packer as Morg sat outside the office. The meeting did not go well. Morg squirmed as he watched through the window. His mother was crying, and he could tell that his dad was well and truly pissed off. As his parents left the office, Morg had to grin. He heard his father get in the final word.

"Mr. Packer, I have been a farmer all my life. I know when someone is shoveling big piles of horseshit to bury their mistakes. This is the biggest pile of horseshit I have seen in years. My wife and I are going across the street to talk to the superintendent. This is not through. Not by a damn sight it's not," George Miller growled. He turned to Morg and before Morg could say anything, his dad motioned to the chair. "Stay here," he said sternly.

Sheldon Knapp was standing in the doorway of the Central Office building when the Millers approached. He was on his way out the door. He greeted them and immediately Mr. Miller launched into his complaint. Knapp tried to deflect the anger that was mounting in George Miller's voice. But the volume was climbing, and Morg's mother was beginning to cry again.

Sheldon Knapp finally held up his hands. "Okay, okay. I guess I just need you to tell me what you would have me do at this point," Knapp said without too much exasperation.

George Miller began to calm down. "Mr. Knapp, I'm not saying Morg shouldn't be punished. As I understand it, Coach Cale has a pretty strenuous punishment run set up for him. I just think the punishment should fit the crime. Coach Cale's does. Mr. Packer's doesn't. I know for sure if it was a soccer player involved the coach's decision would not be overruled by the AD. Mr. Packer has had it in for the football program since his nephew resigned his coaching position. My son is paying the price, and any way you slice it that ain't fair." As he finished, George Miller's face was less red and his voice was calmer.

"I'll look into this. Can you wait in my office for a few minutes while I talk to Mr. Packer?" Sheldon Knapp asked with a pleasant smile in hopes of putting the Millers further at ease. The Millers agreed and Sheldon Knapp walked across the street to the high school. He walked past Morg Miller sitting in the chairs without noticing him. Knapp entered the AD's office without knocking. Clete Packer sensed what was about to happen, and he unsuccessfully tried to mask his grimace.

"Clete, what in the hell?" Sheldon Knapp began. "I don't have time for this, so I'll make it brief. Pull in your horns. Let Coach Cale handle the Miller boy and the discipline on this issue. The last thing I need is pissed-off parents right now. You do realize we have a millage renewal election coming up next spring, right? I don't need football parents showing up voting no because you don't think ahead to the politics of the situation we are facing financially. God damn it!"

Packer tried to make a protest as to why it was necessary to send a message to the football team about their behavior, but Knapp cut him off. "Just make this go away! I'm going to go tell the parents to come see you, and you had better find a way to get out of this," the superintendent said as he exited the office.

Ten minutes later the Millers left Packer's office with their asses sufficiently kissed, and Morg Miller was on his way back to class more convinced than ever that Fudge Packer was the biggest dickhead in the world. Clete Packer drummed his fingers on his desk for a few minutes and then he reached into his desk drawer and retrieved a bottle of Maalox. The sourness in his stomach lingered as he emailed John Cale telling him there would be no suspension but that he fully expected Morg Miller to run his chubby butt off.

At lunch, John Cale sat in the teachers' lounge. He was talking with Dan Portland, the head basketball coach. They were commiserating on the loss of Tim Manikowski. Portland was angered about how the boy was allowed to leave BRHS and then play for Riverdale. "Just fucking great – I lose a starting forward and my third leading scorer and Riverdale gets healthy. I'm going to have a hard-enough time beating them this year – they have two all-league players coming back, and their JV team was undefeated last season," the basketball coach complained bitterly.

Xavier "Two Tone" Simpson entered the lounge. The oddly shaped BRHS band director sat at the table. Dan Portland greeted him. Portland played guitar in one of the jazz bands the band director had formed in town. They were drinking buddies. John Cale found the sometimes-caustic Simpson to be amusing but considered him to be a barely competent teacher. The long-legged band director had black hair and a bushy red beard, earning him the nickname "Two Tone," and he had what Cale considered to be the most-foul breath of any human being he had ever met. Whenever Two Tone sat with them at lunch, Cale slid his chair as far away as possible so he could eat without getting nauseated.

"You talking about Manikowski?" Two Tone Simpson inquired.

"Yeah," answered Dan Portland. John Cale took a bite of his sandwich and nodded.

"I guess Clete finally got him – sort of," Simpson noted. "Bad frigging timing, though. He was supposed to be on the homecoming court this year. Now I am a senior short." Two Tone Simpson was assigned to running homecoming court elections every year, and he complained about it all fall long. "He probably would have won the election and been crowned king, too. I know he had all the stoners in school voting for him. Most of the athletes as well," Simpson continued.

John Cale nearly choked on his sandwich, but before he could swallow and respond, Dan Portland beat him to the punch. "Jesus Christ, Two Tone, who gives a shit about homecoming. John just lost a kid who could have helped him turn his season around, and I lost a starter on my basketball team," Portland said, only half kidding.

Simpson normally would have lost his temper with anyone using his nickname, but Dan Portland was a fellow musician and a good friend, so he answered sarcastically, "Yeah, well fuck me for being concerned about something other than sports at Bear River."

Mike Reese was stretched out on a couch across the lounge. Under normal circumstances, he would have been at the table with Cale and Portland, but he knew that on Mondays, Two Tone Simpson would be at lunch. Reese felt Simpson was for shit in the classroom, and eating lunch at a table with him and his stinking breath did not appeal to him. Upon hearing Simpson's exclamation regarding sports he roused himself and ambled to the table.

Two Tone Simpson sensed Reese standing near, and he turned to face him. Simpson was more than a half a foot taller than the coach. And he was more than twenty years younger, but he had always been intimidated by Reese. Simpson had often thought that Reese reminded him of a badger about to mount a ferocious attack. They rarely ever talked.

"Well, Xavier, you are the fourth band director I have worked with at this school. And not a single one of you ever understood one important fact," Reese growled in a low voice.

Simpson cleared his throat a little nervously, "What's that, Coach?" he asked.

"Nobody in this town reads a newspaper on Saturday morning to find out how the band played at halftime the night before," Mike Reese replied.

Two Tone Simpson was not sure how to respond, and Mike Reese did not give him the opportunity. Coach Reese gave a smile to the table and left without saying anything more. Dan Portland laughed a good laugh. Simpson flipped his middle finger up at him. John Cale sat and passively took the last bite of his sandwich. Cale admired Reese's ability to bluntly get to the point.

Jorge Martinez had settled into a quiet routine during his first-hour business class. He would arrive just as the bell rang. He rarely spoke or asked questions, especially when the student teacher Miss Starke was in charge of the class. Wash Dryer sensed something was off with his friend but never broached the subject. Most of Jorge's classmates first hour were used to him being reserved, so they did not make any note of his behavior – with one soon-to-be key exception.

Bethany McCambridge was a junior. She was in her second year at BRHS. She had transferred to Bear River as a sophomore, coming over from a school near Lansing. Bethany played volleyball and was a late bloomer. Most of the boys in school were starting to notice her recently as her body caught up with her good looks. Bethany only noticed Jorge Martinez. She had been nursing a desperate crush on him. Most days during first hour, she spent a great deal of time trying to get his attention or engaging him in one of the business startup projects that the students in class had to run. Jorge was quietly pleasant to her, and she misinterpreted his small smiles as potential interest.

Bethany McCambridge was also one of Laurie Starke's growing circle of student acolytes. There were about ten or so that had Miss Starke either in class or as a coach. The relationship was one of friendship rather than mentorship. At volleyball practice Laurie Starke gossiped and laughed with the girls as if she were still a high schooler herself. It was the sort of mistake experienced teachers rarely make. On Tuesday night of the fourth week of school, Laurie Starke made another mistake that she would soon regret. Bethany McCambridge sent her a friend request on Facebook. Laurie had two rum and cokes in her, and had she been thinking a little straighter, she might have ignored the request. She accepted. Within two days, half the girls in the volleyball program were Facebook friends with the popular young coach.

Jorge Martinez was cautious around Laurie Starke, and as far as he knew, she was keeping their prior encounter solely to herself. Jorge had no understanding of what was ahead for him regarding Laurie Starke. Even if he had some sort of forewarning, there was little he could have done to avoid it.

Wednesday morning was a watershed day for the football program. It was a day that John Cale had learned to dread. The first eligibility report was posted. Any athlete found to be failing one or more classes would be ineligible to compete until the next report. Since the next report was the week after football season ended, it meant any football player ineligible now would be done for the season.

John Cale pulled the large manila envelope from his mailbox early Wednesday morning with a sense of impending doom. It felt like it weighed fifty pounds. He walked back to his classroom. Mike Reese was waiting for him. "How bad is it?" Reese asked quietly.

"Don't know yet – I haven't opened it," Cale replied.

The two men entered the classroom and sat at Cale's desk. Cale opened the envelope. He handed Reese the sheets of paper listing JV players' grades. They both began to flip through the sheets and read. After two minutes, Cale sighed and leaned back in his chair. "We lost Lemanski and Lansing. Shore is on the list too, but that doesn't matter, he was all done anyway," Cale said, and he rubbed his temples.

"Six," Reese replied, referring to the JV list.

"Who?" asked Cale.

"Well let's see," Reese said. "Got one freshman, Caleb Barnes – that's our starting tailback and safety. He also is the backup QB." Cale groaned in response.

"And the sophomores are Brent Quillan, starting left guard, Todd Brancato, starting middle linebacker and right guard, Nick Ryan, starting outside linebacker and tight end, Jacob Hermman, starting nose tackle. And Rick Klemmant, starting cornerback and backup tailback," Reese continued.

Cale sighed in disgust. "Let me guess – all five sophomores are failing tenth-grade English."

"Yep," replied Reese. "It's been that way for twenty-eight years. Ann Van Kampen cuts no slack for athletes or anyone else. It doesn't matter how much we warn sophomores not to miss assignments or hand in things late, every year, it's the same story. A dozen years ago, I lost three starters on my wrestling squad for half a season for the same reason. Cost us a regional championship. And you can forget about talking to Ann – she won't even consider accepting late assignments."

"How in the hell are we going to field a JV team capable of playing anything close to a competent game? We got like fourteen kids left. No one to play linebacker. If Scott Baier goes down we don't have a QB. Christ, what a mess. If anyone gets hurt, we are absolutely screwed," Cale stated with fatal certainty.

"We'll have to spend practice today covering new assignments with the JV's. I don't think Elwell's JV's have lost a game yet this year. With full strength, we might have held them to forty points. As it is now—" Reese's voice trailed off.

"We're going to have to replace Lemanski on the varsity. I don't know how without weakening some other position. There is certainly no help coming from the JV's. Jesus Christ, if we finish the season able to field both teams, it will be a friggin' miracle," Cale summed up his disgust at the situation.

Wash Dryer spent the first half of football practice logging in the gear of the seven players lost to eligibility. He was always puzzled about how anyone could be ineligible. All you had to do was show up and turn in assignments on time and just about every teacher in the High School would at least give you a good enough grade to stay eligible.

On the practice field, the coaching staff scrambled to reassign players to new positions. It is an activity that any coach from a small high school knows all too well. Depth charts are thin with a small squad to begin with so mid-season position switches are not uncommon. If the players possess athleticism, it can work out okay. If they don't, then it usually ends in failure. At Bear River, failure was always an option.

The pressure of coaching wore heavily on the staff. Only Mike Reese was stoic. He had been coaching way too long to let on how disappointed he was. And he knew lecturing the boys who had maintained eligibility about the failures of the former teammates was not a good thing to do. John Cale was tired and felt like he was swimming upstream against a raging river. Keith Marker was disturbed. The meeting they had with each of the suspended players was emotionally draining. Four of the seven had cried at one point or another as they sat in the coaches' office. Marker was having a tough time focusing on the task at hand. Chet Colby was from Bear River. He knew what it was like to watch players go down for any number of reasons. It was to be expected, but it still made him angry at the kids who let themselves get in the position of having bad grades ruin a season.

The players were not enthusiastic about the position switches. Their effort lagged most of practice. To make matters worse, on the last play of JV special teams run-through, a freshman went down after rolling his ankle. Matt Cutler lay on the ground writhing in pain and crying. Keith Marker and Mike Reese knelt on the ground next to the boy on the practice field. The ankle was already swelling and any movement of it caused the boy to scream. Reese knew at a glance it was a bad high-ankle sprain. It might take two weeks or more before the boy could play. Earlier in the practice, Cutler had taken several snaps at quarterback. It was a position he had played in middle school for a few games. He was horrible but he was the only backup QB available for the JV's. As Mike Reese left the school after practice, he could sense the beat down that was coming for the JV's on Thursday night. He knew that despite whatever preparations they might try, there was little they could do to avoid it.

On Thursday morning, Clete Packer emerged from the AD office as the bell to start first hour rang. A knot of kids were waiting at the main desk. Agnes Johns was checking absence slips and parents' notes. She paused and handed Packer a gift-wrapped box. "Someone left this for you."

"Who?" Clete Packer asked, turning the box over in his hands. If felt heavy.

"I'm not sure. It has been so busy the last twenty minutes. I turned around and it was just sitting here," Agnes Johns replied as she turned her focus back to the remaining kids in front of the desk.

Clete Packer flipped open the thank-you card taped to the package. The card read: "Thank you for all you do. BRHS Soccer Moms." Packer smiled and opened the gift wrapping. The smile drained from his face. It was a box of homemade fudge. A Post-It note attached to the wax paper wrapping in the box read: "Enjoy the Fudge!" Packer again asked Agnes Johns who had left it. She shrugged. Agnes was puzzled as to why Clete Packer seemed so angry.

Packer marched into his office and put the package down on his desk. His anger was building. He flashed back to his first year as assistant principal. He had received a chocolate cake anonymously placed on his office desk. Like a fool he ate half of it during the day. He spent all evening and well into the next day on the toilet. The cake was laced with Exlax. Eventually he had to go to the hospital and spent twenty-four hours with IVs attached to prevent dehydration. Packer lost over thirty pounds in three days. The cake had been baked by two girls who he had suspended just before prom for smoking in the bathroom. When it was traced back to them, the girls were expelled.

Clete Packer had never heard of any organization called BRHS Soccer Moms. Packer smelled a big rat with the fudge. A rat with Morg Miller's face on it. Or maybe Tim Manikowski's. He wouldn't put it past the latter having one of his stoner friends drop off the fudge in the attempt to poison him. He resolved to get to the bottom of the mystery of who dropped off the package.

Clete Packer was late for a teacher observation. He had three that morning – one each hour. The fudge would have to wait until he had time to track down the culprit later this afternoon. He contemplated having the fudge tested for drugs. He would expel Morg Miller if it was him. If he could trace it back to Tim Manikowski, he would have the joy of seeing him arrested for it. He smiled throughout the morning contemplating Tim Manikowski going to jail as he sat in classrooms watching teachers and checking off evaluation form boxes. All three teachers wondered why he had a constant smile. It wasn't like him at all, but none thought to ask him about it.

At lunchtime, Clete Packer hustled back to his office. His thoughts were racing about how he might be able to use the video surveillance in the hallway in front of the office to pinpoint who had brought the package in. Packer was surprised to see Mike Shanahan, the principal, sitting in the chair in front of his desk.

"There you are. Agnes said you had observations this morning. I came in first hour to drop off some paperwork on state testing, but you were not here. Do you have some time to look at it now?" Shanahan asked.

Packer glanced at the desk. The package of fudge was open. Several pieces were missing. Packer's eyes went wide and he looked at the principal. "Did you eat that fudge?" Packer asked in a weak voice.

"Huh? Oh, yeah. I had a piece during first hour. Damn good stuff. I snuck in and grabbed two more pieces during second hour. And I just had two more sitting here waiting. I'm sorry was it being saved for something?" Mike Shanahan asked with clueless cheer.

"Oh my God!" Packer said with shock.

"What!?" Shanahan responded.

"Mike, I think that fudge is poisoned – remember when those girls gave me the cake with Exlax in it? I don't know who brought this in and – oh shit, oh shit. Mike, do you feel all right?" Packer felt weak in the knees as he looked at the Principal. He watched as all the color drained from Shanahan's face. Small beads of sweat formed on his forehead.

Mike Shanahan felt his stomach roll. Acid-laced chocolate bubbled up into his mouth. "Why in the good fuck did you leave it out on your desk!?" he almost screamed. A loud belch escaped his mouth. Packer smelled the sickly-sweet chocolate waft toward him. Packer's stomach lurched at the memory of the cake. He had not eaten chocolate since his own poisoning.

"I was going to investigate this afternoon when I got done with observations!" Packer's voice went up a register to almost a whine.

Mike Shanahan groaned and clutched his stomach. A dry heave caused him to sit straighter. Clete Packer reached into his desk drawer and retrieved his always-ready bottle of Maalox. It was nearly full. He had opened it the day before. It was his second bottle this week. "See if this helps!" Packer hoarsely whispered trying to keep his panic down. Shanahan grabbed the bottle and unscrewed the cap. He took four large gulps from the bottle. Another loud belch erupted from his mouth. Packer felt nausea creeping in as the chocolate and mint smell filled the office.

The Maalox was not helping. Mike Shanahan groaned loudly, "I've got to lie down. Get me to the nurse's office."

"Come on." Clete Packer responded as he helped the woozy principal to his feet. They walked past the main desk. Agnes Johns asked what was wrong. "Mike ate the fudge, and I think someone poisoned it. Call his wife!" Packer replied as he led Shanahan into the nurse's office. The office was empty except for an old desk and low, red-vinyl covered examination bed. The district had eliminated the nurse's position years before in a cost-cutting measure. Shanahan flopped on the examination bed. His feet hung over the end. He groaned and belched loudly. Packer knew he was going to be ill himself if the principal didn't stop belching up the foul chocolate smell.

Agnes Johns came running into the nurse's office. "Pauline is in Detroit visiting her mother. I got her on her cell. She wants us to take him to the hospital in Gratiot right away," she said urgently.

Clete Packer was about to protest that he did not want to transport the principal in his car and have him vomit in it. Before Packer could speak, Mike Shanahan yelled, "I'm gonna be sick!" Agnes Johns reached for a trashcan and tried to get the prostrate man to sit up. He didn't make it. The vomit spewed down his chest and stomach. A tan mixture of chocolate and Maalox obliterated Shanahan's red power tie and blue blazer. Chunks of vomit-covered nuts from the fudge splattered the examination bed.

That was the last straw. Clete Packer stumbled from the nurse's office and threw up violently into a nearby trash can. Four students were standing in front of the main desk. One of them screamed. At that moment the young assistant secretary entered the office. Mary Pierce was seven months pregnant. She had just finished her lunch break. The pregnancy had made her already notoriously weak stomach volatile. The smell of vomit and the sound of the AD retching were more than she could take. She leaned over the trashcan next to the main desk and vomited a mixture of Cobb salad and diet Sprite. The vomit smelled of neonatal vitamins. Three of the students ran from the office. One threw up in the hallway. The fourth student happened to be Danny Short, the soon-to-be Eagle Scout and erstwhile starting safety on the JV football team. Danny tried to help the young secretary to a chair, and he told Agnes Johns to call 911.

Agnes dialed the phone with one hand and guided Clete Packer to a chair with the other. Mike Shanahan emerged from the nurse's office. "Gotta go to the bathroom," he mumbled as he weaved past Agnes Johns on his way to the small restroom at the back of the office. Within a minute the sound of him moaning was followed by the sound of a loud fart. "Ungh!" the principal groaned, and wet splattering noises came from the bathroom. Clete Packer and Mary Pierce responded by ducking their heads into their respective trashcans and retching.

Agnes Johns got through to the 911 operator. "Send an ambulance to Bear River High School right away. Someone has poisoned our principal and vice principal!" she shouted into the phone. Agnes was detailing the events when she heard Mike Shanahan retch one more time in the bathroom. A garbled curse came from the small room. Shanahan had thrown up on the floor while sitting on the toilet. He tried to stand but felt light-headed. As he reeled, he slipped in his own vomit. Shanahan pitched forward into the bathroom door striking his head on the coat hook mounted on the backside. He slumped to the floor with a grunt and passed out. His body blocked the bathroom door.

Agnes Johns let loose with a yelp at the sound of Shanahan collapsing in the bathroom. "Oh my God! Mike! Mike!" She tried to open the bathroom door but it wouldn't budge. She hung up the phone and gave the door another push. Nothing. Agnes glanced down at the floor. Blood was seeping under the door. Shanahan had cut his scalp on the coat hook on the back of the door as he fell. It bled profusely. Agnes Johns yelled, "Mike!" There was no response. Agnes Johns turned and looked at Danny Short. "Go and get help!" she commanded. Danny ran from the room.

Clete Packer had recovered enough to help Agnes. He tried to open the bathroom door. It wouldn't open more than a small crack. He kept calling

Mike Shanahan's name. He was slightly relieved when a couple of muffled groans came from behind the door. Carol Christianson, the school librarian, rushed into the office, trailed by Danny Short. "What's wrong? Danny said Mike has been poisoned. Where is he?" the librarian asked.

Agnes pointed to the bathroom door in the back office. "He collapsed in the bathroom and he has blocked the door," she answered.

Clete Packer coughed and held his head. "He's bleeding – I think he fell and cut his head. There's blood on the floor under the door," he said weakly. "Someone poisoned some fudge, and he ate it," he added miserably.

"Oh my Goodness!" Carol Christianson exclaimed. "Danny, run across the street and get the superintendent." The football player exited and sprinted toward the front door of the school. Some kids were starting to congregate in the hallway. They were talking in hushed tones and peeking through the office windows.

Sheldon Knapp entered the building with the police and the fire rescue squad. He could hear the siren squeal of an ambulance approaching. He made his way to the office. Teachers were walking up the hall with concerned looks on their faces. A crowd of people blocked the door. Knapp cleared the way for the rescue workers. The ambulance pulled up on the sidewalk in front of the building. The siren blared once more and died.

"Clete, what the heck is going on – Mike has been poisoned?" Knapp asked, taking note of how pale Packer looked.

Clete Packer nodded. "Some kid probably. I'm certain it was a football player. Left some poisoned fudge wrapped like a present on the desk this morning. I've had it happen before. I put the package on my desk and was going to find out who it was by looking at the video files this afternoon. Mike ate about five pieces of the fudge during the morning. By the time I got back to the office, it was too late."

"What about you and Mary – what happened?" Knapp asked.

"Mary is lying down now." Packer pointed to the nurses' office. "She's pregnant – weak stomach – couldn't handle something like that. I'm okay. When Mike vomited I got sick from the smell. The chocolate – I – I don't like fudge."

Clete Packer slumped into a chair.

"Okay, let's clear this office of all nonessential people, please." Sheldon Knapp began to guide people to the door. Danny Short was the last to leave. The sound of the fire rescue team prying the frame off the bathroom door made Knapp wince. He started to calculate the expense of repairing the damage.

Fifteen minutes later, Mike Shanahan was on the stretcher. "That's a hell of a gash in his scalp. He's going to need stitches. I'm not sure why he is non-responsive. Could be from whatever he ingested, but more likely it is from the blow on the head. He's gonna have a bad headache when he does come around. We'll get him over to the hospital. They'll pump his stomach when he is stable. From the looks of things around here, though, I don't think they'll get much out of his stomach," the paramedic told Sheldon Knapp.

"Well, Agnes, it looks like it is going to be me and you. I'll take Mary and Clete to their homes. Just as soon as the officer is done getting his statement. While I'm gone, get custodial down here and have them clean this mess up. Tell them to use plenty of deodorizer. I'm about to get sick from the smell myself," Sheldon Knapp said with forced cheer.

The phone rang and Agnes Johns answered it. "Mr. Knapp, it's Pam Kitteridge. She wants to talk to Clete," she said, cupping the receiver in her hand. Knapp sighed as he looked at Packer. He was sitting in a chair looking gray and half out of it. The police officer was taking a statement from him and not getting much in response. He told Agnes to put the school board president on hold.

"I'll take the call in Mike's office," Knapp told the secretary. As he walked into the office, he planned how to do some damage control. The last thing he needed right now was the board getting involved before he knew all the answers.

"Pam, it's Sheldon. Clete isn't able to come to the phone right now. Can I help you?" Knapp asked brightly.

"Oh, Sheldon, I was going to stop by and see you and Mike Shanahan in a little bit. The group of soccer moms I just organized is baking up surprises for all the administrators and soccer coaches. I am just calling to see how Clete liked the fudge Sue Pickering made for him. I think her son dropped it off for him this morning." Sheldon Knapp tipped his head forward and rubbed the bridge of his nose between his thumb and forefinger. A headache was starting to build behind his eyes.

"Sheldon? Sheldon, are you still there?" Pam Kitteridge asked with concern.

It was less than fifteen minutes to kick-off of the JV home game when Scott Baier entered the locker room. His twelve remaining teammates were sitting on the benches in front of the chalkboard in the team instruction area. Coach Reese was talking about blocking assignments. Coach Marker placed his hand on Scott's shoulder and guided him quietly to the coaches' office.

"You should have been here over an hour ago. I've been calling your house. Where have you been?" Marker asked calmly. He was angry and concerned.

"I'm sorry coach I – um – took a nap on our back porch. I overslept – I didn't hear the phone," Scott Baier replied. Coach Marker knew the boy was lying but investigating further was not going to be productive. Kickoff was minutes away. Getting the team onto the field was his first priority.

"Get your gear on – make it quick! We have already been on the field for warm ups. Make sure you stretch and throw before kickoff," Coach Marker ordered.

Scott Baier quickly got to his locker and pulled out his pads and game uniform. Coach Reese barked out orders for the team to start for the field. The team was out of the locker room and crossing the pedestrian bridge over the Bear River on their way to the field. Scott Baier caught up as the last boy walked off the bridge. "Where were you? You were with Kelli, weren't you?"

169

asked the boy bringing up the rear of the single-file line. It was Sam Bott – a wide receiver who would be the starting tailback for the shorthanded JV Bears.

Scott Baier laughed in response. "Maybe." Kelli Tenent was Scott's sophomore girlfriend. They had been together since the beginning of the school year. Kelli Tenent had a bad reputation. Or a good one if you were a freshman boy being pursued by an older girl. Scott had been bragging for weeks about their coupling. Kelli had been at Scott's house after school. Any concerns about making it to the locker room on time for pre-game had been very far from Scott's mind until she left.

"Aw, yeah!" Sam Bott said suggestively. Scott Baier laughed again.

The boy in front of Sam Bott in the single-file line was Danny Short. As the line reached the field, Danny grew furious. He didn't like or trust Scott Baier. They were in the same Boy Scout troop. Danny did not think Scott lived up to any part of the Boy Scout Oath. Danny resented how Scott got a free pass on everything just because he was a good athlete.

The JV team dashed across the field as the loudspeakers blared the school fight song. The players lined up after introductions for the national anthem. There were thirteen of them in uniform for the game. The bleachers reflected the team. Less than two dozen people were in the home stands. As the last notes of the anthem played Coach Reese called for the kick-off team to huddle on the sideline. Danny Short walked over to Coach Marker who stood near the far end of the bench.

"Coach, Scott Baier was with his girlfriend. That's why he was late," Danny stated plainly.

Coach Marker stopped fumbling with the field phones and looked at the blond-haired boy. He decided not to engage on the topic. "Danny, we are about to kick-off. You need to get on the field," Marker declared.

"If Scott Baier is playing, I'm not. He was late for pregame. That's a violation of team rules. It isn't right if he plays. He should have to sit out as punishment," Danny Short declared.

Coach Reese yelled for Danny to get back in the huddle with the kickoff team. Danny shook his head. Coach Marker looked at Reese who stood twenty yards away with the rest of the kickoff team and then back to Danny. He was at a loss as to what to do or say. The referees blew their whistles and the side judge told Reese to get his team on the field. Reese signaled for a timeout. He was tempted to walk over to the young coach, but he wanted the JV's to understand that Keith Marker was the head coach. It was a delicate balance.

In the press box, John Cale was talking into the field phones. "What the hell is going on?" Mike Reese shook his head and turned and shrugged at Cale. "Well, we just wasted a timeout, for God sake!"

"Danny, we only have thirteen players dressed tonight. Scotty is our only quarterback. We can't play this game without him. Any punishment will have to wait until tomorrow," Keith Marker explained.

"It's not right. He broke team rules." Danny Short pulled off his jersey and shoulder pads. He walked down the sideline with his helmet in one hand and his pads and jersey in the other. Keith Marker stood shaking his head.

"What just happened!?" John Cale asked into the headset as Keith Marker pulled his own set on.

"Danny Short just quit," Marker replied.

"What!?" John Cale exclaimed.

"He said if Scott Baier was going to play after breaking team rules, he wasn't going to play. Then he walked off," Marker replied.

"You have got to be kidding me! What else can go wrong? Get a sub in for him on kickoff. We're going to get nailed for delay of game." John Cale was as exasperated as he had been all season. He was glad that for one thing, Clete Packer was not here to see this. He was at home – too ill to attend the game.

The Bears kicked off. Danny Short was walking up the steps to the pedestrian bridge over the Bear River as the Elm Hall Rangers returned the kick for a touchdown. Danny did not look back. Neither did the Rangers – they led 48 to 0 at the half. Scott Baier fumbled five times. That did not help matters.

The only bright spot for the Bears was the play of Tom Osborne. The slope-shouldered center/defensive tackle was pressed into being middle linebacker. He actually made a few good tackles and recovered a fumble. More importantly, he was being a leader. He was barking out defensive calls and hustling everywhere. John Cale was impressed as he watched from the booth, and he told Keith Marker to give the boy praise at halftime despite the lopsided score.

Tom Osborne wrenched his knee on the third play of the second half. He was unable to put any weight on the leg, so he was done for the game. The Bears were reduced to eleven players. Things got worse. With the Rangers leading 63-0 late in the third quarter, they still had their starters in the game. Coach Reese was getting more and more angry. They had thrown for the last two touchdowns.

The Bears had the ball on their own 35. It was third and twelve. Against his better judgment, John Cale let Keith Marker call a dump pass. The Rangers called an all-out blitz. Scott Baier was nailed for a ten-yard loss. Coach Reese threw his headset aside and called a timeout. He walked out on the field, but instead of walking to where the Bears were huddled on the 25-yard line he walked the midfield line to within twenty feet of the Elm Hall Ranger's sideline. The Referees started to trot over to where he stopped.

Mike Reese pointed at the young head JV coach for the visiting team. "Are you a teacher?" Reese asked forcefully.

The young coach pulled off his headset. He blinked at Reese. "What does that have to do with anything?" he asked.

"Because, young man, no one trained in education would be calling a blitz and throwing the ball in this situation against an undermanned and demoralized team of kids. You have a 63-point lead – it's not necessary. It's an embarrassment to the game and humiliating to the boys playing on this field. No teacher worth anything would ever do what you are doing."

The referees broke up the discussion before the Ranger coach could respond. "Coach, return to your sideline or I will penalize you and your team." Mike Reese turned to the ref and shook his head.

"Bob, you and I have known each other for thirty-five years. You know damn well what this young 'coach'" Reese spat the word as he glanced angrily at the young man, "is doing is wrong. Apparently he doesn't have a clue. I'm just trying to help him understand what he is doing is hurting kids," Coach Reese explained to the referee. Bob Jameson was a retired teacher from North Star. He had refereed many wrestling matches for the Bears over the decades. He and Reese were not friends, but they had a long-standing professional relationship. In truth, Bob Jameson never had liked Reese much and his patience was wearing thin.

"Coach Reese, look to your own team and let him coach his," the ref said forcefully. The young Elm Hall coached smiled a sneering smile. Reese turned and walked back to the Bear's sideline shaking his head in disgust. The laughter of the Elm Hall players and coaches followed him. On the sideline, Coach Marker was talking via the headset with Coach Cale.

"What is Mike doing?" Cale asked as Reese strode across the field after calling timeout.

"I don't know. I think he is going to go talk to the Elm Hall coaches," Marker replied.

"Oh Christ. I hope he keeps his temper. He is going to get flagged or thrown out of the game," Cale said.

"This is all my fault. Ian Larson is the head JV coach for Elm Hall. He hates me. He was on the practice squad at CMU when I was a freshman. He was a junior and a safety like me. He thought he was going to get a regular spot on the team but when I got on campus, they gave the scholarship to me. We had a few fights in practice that year, and the coaches dismissed him from the practice squad," Marker explained to Cale as Coach Reese was dressing down Ian Larson on the far sideline.

"Oh man, did you tell Mike about this?" Cale asked.

"Sort of, I didn't tell him about Larson starting a fight with me at the Wayside just before the season began this year. He still lives up in Mt. Pleasant. I think he works for one of the hotels up there, and he coaches at Elm Hall for a few extra bucks. Anyway, he started in on me about how bad Bear River was and how he was going to beat our asses. So I asked him if he was going to back it up on the field because he had never done it when he was playing. He swung on me and missed and I laid him out. I got the hell out of there before the bouncers got involved," Marker explained.

"Shit. Looks like Mike is done. No flag. You watch yourself after the game during handshakes. Don't get drawn into anything with Larson," Cale instructed.

"I won't," Marker replied.

Mike Reese looked grim as he came across the field. He was mumbling to himself angrily as he pulled on his headset. "That friggin' punk thinks he is Urban Meyer and this is Ohio State versus Michigan or something. This is going to get a lot worse. Thank God we have a running clock or they might score 100 points," Reese said with disgust to Cale as Coach Marker called for a punt.

"Listen Mike, don't get pulled into any confrontations – Marker has a history with that coach and there is plenty of bad blood between them." John Cale informed him.

"Grand," Reese said flatly.

The Rangers scored two more touchdowns. The score was 77-0 with just over two minutes left in the game when they scored the final touchdown. On the kickoff, the Bear's deep back returned the kick up the home sideline before stepping out of bounds near the forty-yard line. A Ranger player came up and hit him late well outside the line. As the flags flew in the air, Sam Bott ran up and dove at the legs of the Ranger player who was standing over the Bear player shouting taunts. The collision crumpled the kid, and he screamed in agony. Whistles blew and there was a short shoving match among the remaining players. Coach Marker grabbed Sam Bott and walked him away from the brief melee.

The Ranger player was still screaming on the ground. Wash Dryer knelt by him trying to calm him down. Wash was a little sick to his stomach. The boy's leg was broken near the ankle. His foot was flopped sideways. The referee motioned to the Ranger sideline. The Elm Hall coaches and their student manager began to jog across the field. The manager had his med kit with him and was struggling to keep up.

After debating with himself for a minute, John Cale swept off his headset and exited the press box. He headed down to the field, worried that there might be further confrontation.

He was right. But he didn't make it to the sideline in time to prevent what happened next. Ian Larson, the Elm Hall head coach, looked at his prone player as his assistant coach and student manager knelt next to Wash Dryer. The boy with the broken leg was sobbing. Players from both teams were on one knee a few yards away.

"Get away from him!" Ian Larson growled and pulled on Wash's shoulder. Wash stood and apologized and tried to explain he was only trying to help.

"Take it easy, Coach," the referee, Bob Jameson, urged. "The boy was helping."

"Bull! These Bear River thugs are nothing but cheap shot artists. Look at my boy – his season is done!" Ian Larson shouted back.

Mike Reese was about to respond when the young Bear assistant coach, Chet "Cheese" Colby, stepped next to him. "Your player started this – he got what he deserved!" Colby shouted at the Elm Hall coach. Reese watched as blind rage played across Ian Larson's face. Twenty years earlier, Reese would have easily intercepted the much younger man, but Reese was fifty-nine and even he would admit to having lost a step. Ian Larsen brushed past him and seized the wide-eyed Chet Colby by the shirt collar. His fist was drawn back and he was about to deliver his punch when Keith Marker stepped forward and stopped him with an overhand right to the jaw. Ian Larsen fell to all fours. Chet Colby blinked dumbly at Marker as the referees shrilly blew their whistles and once again threw their flags.

John Cale arrived at the bench as Marker threw the punch, and he swept up behind Keith Marker and grabbed him. Marker gave no resistance as Cale walked him backwards. "Keith, you shouldn't have done that," Cale said quietly near Marker's ear.

"I wasn't going to, but he was about to sucker-punch Cheese," Marker replied.

The referees were confronting Mike Reese. "This game is done right now! Both head coaches are ejected!" Bob Jameson was shouting at Mike Reese. "In all my years of officiating I have never seen such behavior on a sideline – clear this field now before I eject all the coaches!"

Mike Reese held up his hand. "Okay, Bob. Let's get this young boy attended to first." He pointed at the prone and sobbing Ranger player as the first responders rolled the ambulance onto the field.

All hell broke loose Friday morning. The superintendent of Elm Hall was on the phone to Sheldon Knapp at 7:00. Phillip Hollings informed the Bear River Superintendent that 1.) He had fired Ian Larson for being thrown out of the game and because some parents of the Elm Hall JV players had been on the phone during the game to Hollings. They were complaining about the lack of sportsmanship by Larson in running up the score against the vastly undermanned Bear River squad – laughing the whole time he was doing it. 2.) Hollings fully expected that Bear River would follow suit and fire their JV coaches for causing the brawl at the end of the game.

Sheldon Knapp explained that he could not easily dismiss Mike Reese who had been coach of the year in the state wrestling association twice, was a legend at Bear River, and was, to Knapp's understanding, not responsible for the punch that knocked out Ian Larson. Phillip Hollings knew Reese well. Twenty years prior, Hollings had been a wrestling coach with four consecutive seasons ending in losses to Bear River in the state tournament. Hollings had a long memory and those losses still stung. The fourth in particular. Hollings was coaching the Trufant Trojans, and he had them ranked third in the state by the end of the season. Mike Reese's Bears were ranked 10th. Reese pulled a couple of lineup switches and bumped his state-ranked 140-pounder up a weight class. The kid pinned a previously unbeaten Trojan wrestler, and the Bears won the match by one point. Hollings was out-coached, but in the years since he had convinced himself that Reese had fudged the weigh-in sheets to allow the 140-pound wrestler to wrestle up two weight classes.

"Goddamn it, Sheldon. Reese is a dinosaur. I heard he confronted our coaches on the field during the game. Bob Jameson nearly ran him then. He helped provoke that final fight and you know it," Hollings complained bitterly.

"Calm down, Phil. I'll dismiss the two young coaches – Marker and Colby. I'll reprimand Reese and Cale. We still have some games to play, and firing Reese will make it impossible to finish the season. You look to your school, and I'll look to mine," Sheldon Knapp replied with mild, exasperated contempt. Elm Hall was a smaller school than Bear River. Knapp was dammed if Phil Hollings was going to get to dictate anything to him. But he was concerned that this was just the sort of incident that would make bad press, and he was determined to get out in front of it if he could.

Sheldon Knapp knew the Mt. Pleasant paper was hound-dogging this story. He was taken aback when no sooner than he hung up with Hollings his secretary informed him reporters from the Saginaw and Lansing newspapers were on hold waiting to talk to him. He stonewalled them by telling the secretary to take a message and to tell them that the school would be making a formal announcement about the matter after noon today, and until then there would be no comment.

Pete Petterson from the Mt. Pleasant paper called Sheldon Knapp on his private cellphone five minutes later. Knapp was pissed off and asked him how he got the number. Petterson refused to say. "Sheldon, give me a quote."

"Mr. Petterson, there will be an official statement made this afternoon to all press outlets. Until then, there will be no comment," Knapp replied icily.

"Okay, have it your way – but you might want to check our website. We have video posted of all three incidents up and the hits are in the hundreds already. This will go viral – major broadcast outlets across the state are already requesting rights and—" Petterson stated with poison in his tone.

"What do you mean three incidents?" Knapp cut him off.

Pete Petterson smiled broadly and caught the note of concern in Knapp's question. It was apparent the noted control freak superintendent of Bear River was not completely up to speed on the story. He paused to savor the moment and to let Knapp stew for a spell. "Well, Sheldon," Petterson began with slight condescension. "It seems a very fine young student in your sophomore class quit the JV team last night – an Eagle Scout, no less. Did it right after the National Anthem after he had some sort of disagreement with Coach Marker on the sideline. Then Mike Reese is on screen standing in front of the Elm Hall bench shouting at their coaches until the referee makes him go back to your bench. It's not hard to connect the dots from that incident to the punch thrown at the end of the game by Marker. The young coach John Cale ran off the staff, Pat Packer, I think he is your AD's nephew, if I'm not mistaken – videoed everything on his cellphone from the stands. Pretty high-quality video too, if I might say so. Good enough for lip readers to make out plenty, I'm sure. Young Mr. Packer also has been a source for some good quotes on just how royally screwed up your football program is. Even by Bear River standards, Sheldon, this season is a shambles, you have to admit. Soon as I'm off the phone with you I will be calling the parents of that young Eagle Scout, Danny Short, and I'll have more than enough background material to form a basis for a full investigative story to run this Sunday. So what do you think? You want to get ahead of this and give me a full interview or wait until I let other people frame this story?" Petterson finished in a professional yet somehow smug tone.

Sheldon Knapp felt the headache building behind his eyes. The urge to tell off the fat sports reporter was almost too strong to pass up. Knapp drew in his breath slowly and paused. "There will be a formal statement issued this afternoon. Until then no comment," he stated flatly, and he pushed the end-call button on his smartphone.

Twenty miles away Pete Petterson reached for his fifth glazed donut of the day with a huge smile on his face. As he was washing it down with his coffee, he watched the counter on the video click over 300. He was sure that Sheldon Knapp was that 300th viewer.

The Bear River superintendent of schools watched the video as he chewed on four bitter extra-strength aspirin. He picked up his desk phone. "Katherine, buzz Clete Packer and tell him to get his ass over here right now."

Katherine Bigelow had been Sheldon Knapp's administrative assistant for eight years. The tone of his voice indicated to her that the day would be one with plenty of fireworks. Two seconds after giving Clete Packer his marching orders, she patched the board president through to Knapp's office line. That phone call lasted fifteen minutes. Clete Packer paced in the outer office while Sheldon Knapp talked to the shouting Pam Kitteridge.

Packer walked into the superintendent's office. Sheldon Knapp's face was purple with rage as he spoke. "This is a Goddamned mess, Clete, a big time Goddamned mess that is snowballing on us. And if it snowballs any larger, the board president is fully prepared to take your head and maybe even mine."

The AD went on the verbal offensive, hoping to deflect some of Knapp's wrath. "I wasn't there last night, Mr. Knapp. I was too ill after yesterday afternoon. But I have written letters from John Cale, Mike Reese and Keith Marker detailing the fight. I think Marker will have to be dismissed and maybe young Colby too, but his mom is so ill that might not go down too well in town. We can put reprimands in Cale's and Reese's folders. Either way I think I can talk Cale into letting my nephew back on the staff so—"

Sheldon Knapp yelled, "Your Goddamned nephew is why this is snowballing on us!"

"Huh?" Packer replied completely puzzled.

"Did you view the videos on Pete Petterson's website?" Knapp questioned furiously.

"Um, I heard about them but I, uh, have not had time to view them yet." Packer fumbled a response, but Knapp could tell that he was lying and the AD knew that the superintendent knew that the videos were a complete mystery to him.

An evil smile spread across Sheldon Knapp's face. "Shut up, Clete, and come look at your nephew's handiwork." He then motioned the AD to take a seat in his very expensive desk chair. Knapp cued up the video on the website and clicked play. As the video buffered, Clete Packer suppressed the urge to squirm in the superintendent's chair. The tension built up but dissipated as soon as the first video segment began to play.

Clete Packer was clueless as to why Danny Short was talking to Keith Marker. And when the video showed Danny pulling off his shoulder pads and walking off the field with his helmet in one hand and pads in another, Packer couldn't keep the look of befuddlement from his face. "Did Danny Short quit the team between the anthem and kickoff last night?" he asked with real amazement in his voice.

"Keep watching," was Sheldon Knapp's calm response.

"Ah, what in the hell is Reese doing on the field?" Packer exclaimed with disgust as Mike Reese could be seen gesticulating at the young coach near the opposite sideline.

"Keep watching," Sheldon Knapp told Packer as the third video cued up. The video had been edited so that none of the play proceeding the punch was seen. Wash Dryer was pushed aside by the young man in the bright yellow coaching windbreaker showing an Elm Hall Ranger on the back. Then the man turned to confront young Chet Colby and seemed to be menacing him when Keith Marker stopped him cold with a well-thrown overhand right. The yellow flags of the referees flying through air was the last part of the video. Much of the sound of the entire video was garbled with crowd noise. Clete Packer recognized his nephew's cackling laugh at the end of the video.

"That's right, Clete, your nephew provided not only those videos from his cellphone to Pete Petterson, but he also gave Pete some juicy quotes on the disastrous state of the Bear River football program – at least according to Pete. So, no, your nephew will not be invited back to coach at Bear River. Not as long as I am superintendent, anyway. And if I hear of him so much as littering in the stands at a game I'll have the sheriff deputy escort him from the grounds, and then I'll have him banned from attending all sporting events for the remainder of the school year." The evil smile had disappeared from Knapp's face as he spoke. The contemptuous glare remained as he motioned to Clete Packer to get up from his chair.

The acid reflux was boiling in Clete Packer's stomach and throat as he glumly stood in front of the superintendent's large mahogany desk. Sheldon Knapp eased his narrow frame into his executive-style leather chair. His face lacked expression as he began to talk. "It's 8:30, Clete. I want you, John Cale, Mike Reese, Keith Marker and young Mr. Colby in this office at 10:15. Get subs for Cale and Reese for the rest of the day – I don't know how long this might take, and I may have them working on statements of their own for the press."

Packer nodded and began to withdraw.

"One more thing, Clete," Knapp announced, and the AD stopped and faced him once more.

"You better find some time during all this to get in touch with your nephew. Tell him to cool it with the press. He better disappear, as far as they are concerned. And if you can't convince him to do that, start working on your resume. Because if Pam Kitteridge comes looking for your head this time because this thing snowballs further – I'm going to let her take it." Knapp issued the threat without raising his voice.

Clete Packer slipped meekly from the office and made a beeline to his own office and his much-needed fresh bottle of Maalox in the upper right-hand drawer. He chugged his fourth swallow with his cellphone to his ear. Pat Packer's voice mail message played, and when it ended, Clete Packer began forcefully. "Patrick, this is your uncle. Call me before you talk to anyone about last night's game. Especially Pete Petterson! Knapp is looking for a fall guy to give to Pam Kitteridge, and he is sizing me up for the frame job. DO NOT talk to the press! DO NOT post anything online! Come and see me this afternoon at the latest."

Packer glanced out his window into the front desk area trying to make eye contact with the secretary, Agnes Johns. She wasn't at her desk, so he got up and walked into the deserted room. Packer could hear crying coming from Mike Shanahan's office. The door was slightly ajar, so he stuck his head in. Agnes Johns and Mary Peirce were holding each other and crying.

"What is wrong?" Clete asked a little too officiously. Mary Peirce glanced away and dabbed at her eyes with a Kleenex. Agnes Johns grief-stricken eyes clouded over with anger in an instant.

With thin lips, Agnes announced, "Bea Colby was taken to the Hospice Center in Gratiot at midnight – she's dying, Clete."

"Oh, look. I'm, uh, very sorry to hear that. She was the best, uh, president of the sports boosters I ever worked with but—" Clete Packer stammered as he struggled to put the proper amount of care into his voice.

"But what? You pompous ass!" Agnes Johns said furiously.

"Agnes, I'm very upset as well, but the business of this district can't grind to halt because Bea Colby is dying," Packer said plaintively. As soon as he said it, he regretted it.

Mary Pierce let out a racking sob and slid past Packer on her way to the bathroom to throw up. Packer stepped further into the room past the threshold.

Agnes closed the principal's door behind him with a forceful jolt that made Packer flinch. Clete Packer knew that he was about to receive his second brow beating of the morning. This one was shaping up to be worse than what Sheldon Knapp laid on him. Agnes Johns took a firm hand-full of his suit jacket above his elbow and spun him around to the front of the principal's desk. And although she was a foot shorter and well more than 100 pounds lighter, she aggressively closed the gap between them, and for an instant Packer thought she was going to strike him. Agnes stopped short and thrust her balled-fist close to his face.

"You listen close, Mister!" Agnes shouted in a rage. "Bea Colby was a thousand times more valuable to this school district than worthless empty suits like you or Sheldon Knapp or that complete turd Mike Shanahan could ever hope to be. She was the best secretary I have ever seen. I worked next to her for eleven years at the middle school before she went to the elementary and I came up here. I never once saw her miss an appointment or misplace a file. I never saw her forget a child's name. Over 300 kids in her building and she knew each one by name. Every. Goddamned. Year. For over two decades! Can you say that you fat faced slob?! Hell, Mike Shanahan can't even remember the names of his faculty!

"Bea Colby is my friend and she is dying. In five minutes, I am going to leave this office for an hour or so to go say goodbye because she will likely not last another day. The rest of the administrative assistants and secretaries in the district will rotate out for the rest of the day to at least go pay their respects. Mary will be leaving when I get back. Did you know that Mary is Bea's cousin? No, I suppose you wouldn't. You're just another in a long line of mostly worthless transient suits that have sat in the principal's chairs and superintendent's chair for the last twenty-five years. I swear to God, we have not had a decent administrator in this district since Richard Wing retired as super in 1987. Now there was an administrator. He was the super for nearly thirty years. Raised his family here and he and his wife are buried in Holy Name cemetery not six blocks from this damn office. He's probably spinning in his grave watching you assholes tear apart what he built." Rage was succumbing to grief as Agnes lost her train of thought. She paused. A sob escaped her lips.

Clete Packer made another miscalculation. He reached out to Agnes Johns. She slapped his hand away. Resolve filled her eyes. "The business of this district will get done today just like it gets done every day. We won't miss a beat." Agnes swept her arm toward the secretary desks in the outer office as she said the word "we." She continued, "So you empty suits can go sit your fat asses in your luxury office chairs or go stroke each other's egos in one of your never-ending parade of ridiculous frigging meetings. You shitheels are always running away to the Central Office to hide in a meeting while we actually do your work! All while we are doing our own work and wet-nursing teachers, bandaging scraped knees, kissing boo boos of sobbing children calling for their mommies and generally making sure that every Goddamned brick of every Goddamned building in this district doesn't slide into the Goddamned Bear River!"

Without saying anything else, Agnes Johns left the office. Clete Packer felt a bit nauseated. It wasn't the nausea his bottle of Maalox could help. He felt heartsick. He knew he had handled the Bea Colby situation badly and that he had further upset both Agnes and Mary Pierce. He made a mental note to wait until after the funeral and then apologize to Agnes and Mary with a nice card. Maybe he would include some flowers or something. It always worked when his wife went on one of her tirades – at least the ones that he caused.

Keith Marker answered his cellphone on the third ring. Clete Packer was brief and curt, "Be at the superintendent's office at 10:15." For an instant, Keith considered asking why but discarded the idea as Packer hung up without saying goodbye. Keith knew what was coming. One of his friends had called him at 6:30 to tell him about the videos posted on the Mt. Pleasant paper's website. In the time since, five other friends had sent him the link via Twitter. Keith knew he was about to be fired. He was surprised that a state police cruiser hadn't yet pulled into the driveway of his rental house. He thought maybe there might be an assault charge warrant coming his way as well.

Clete Packer walked down the hall to John Cale's classroom. Packer was marshaling his anger. He felt that if he could gain the upper hand with John Cale and Mike Reese before the meeting it might play well with the superintendent. Packer had always felt that he was skilled at applying anger to badger underlings – it was a dramatic management tool that he relied heavily on. It was also a tool that earned him contempt from those who worked with and for him. That never really bothered Clete Packer. That is because he often mistook silent contempt for fear and respect.

Cale was demonstrating some algebra problems on his white-board. Packer walked into the classroom unannounced. "Coach, I need to talk to you – now." Packer made an abrupt hand gesture pointing to the hallway.

John Cale was taken aback by the rudeness of interruption as well as the unprofessional way in which Packer had spoken to him in front of the students. Cale knew what this was about, and his anger was starting to get the better of him.

"Can this wait until class change?" Cale said with some irritation.

Clete Packer's face grew quite red. He repeated his hand gesture toward the classroom door.

"Okay, let me give the students some instructions—" Cale said and Packer's face darkened even more.

"I said NOW!" Packer barked.

Cale was supremely angry, but he held it together. "Mr. Packer – sir – I will join you in the hallway just as soon as I give my students instructions on what problems to work on while we talk. After all, you and Mr. Shanahan just talked to the teaching staff about making sure students are always on task in the classroom." John Cale could not keep all the sarcasm out of his last sentence. The students picked up on it. Sam Bott was sitting in the front row of desks. A place he had earned about three days into the school year due to his inability to keep his mouth shut for more than a few moments. Sam chuckled slightly, and he may or may not have mumbled "Fudge Packer" as Clete Packer shut the door loudly as he exited the classroom. Cale let the comment pass. He felt no urge to defend the name of the assistant principal. Cale gave his class a set of problems in their textbook to work on. He cut off Sam Bott's dramatic moan with a withering glance before following Clete Packer into the hall.

Cale did not wait for Packer to begin. "Mr. Packer, sir, I will thank you not to address me in such an unprofessional manner in front of students ever again. You should know better, and I certainly deserve better." John Cale issued the statement with thinly veiled contempt.

"Do not presume to lecture me about proper etiquette in front of students, son, I have been in education longer than—"

"Don't call me son!" John Cale interrupted forcefully.

"Huh – what?" Packer was fumbling now, his flop sweat beading up on his forehead as John Cale's anger began to surpass his own. It was a very righteous anger, and Packer was now getting clued into how his own stage anger may have pushed this confrontation into a bad area. Packer knew that a bell could not be un-rung. Nor could a man's buttons be un-pressed. Clete Packer, for the third time in less than an hour and a half, had pressed the wrong buttons on the wrong person. He was about to catch hell for it.

"You heard me," John Cale said menacingly. "I have a father. Do not presume to call me 'son.' My father ran his own business for over forty years. Everyone who walked in to his heavy equipment garage got respect and fair treatment. My father never made a lot of money, but when he retired a few years ago, truckers and construction company owners from all over the Upper Peninsula showed up at his retirement party. To a man, they said my father was a man who understood that to be respected you needed to treat people with respect. They praised him for his knowledge and good work, but most of all, they praised his sense of honor and respect. So, Mr. Packer, do not ever call me 'son.' My father is the only man alive who gets to call me 'son,' and I am proud every time he does. When a lesser man calls me 'son,' it cheapens the word. It cheapens my father's honor. I won't allow that."

It occurred to Clete Packer as John Cale finished his emphatic statement that he really was an imposing figure. They were the same height, about six feet tall, but where Packer's frame ran to fatness, John Cale had lean, rip-cord steeliness wrapped around a body that was now fully tensed. His veins and muscles competed for space in his neck. His large hands were clenched by his side. Cale focused his gray eyes on Packer, not in blind rage but with lethal intent. The AD knew that the way he chose to respond now would have consequences.

The brightly lit hallway was empty. Neither man had raised his voice significantly. No one had poked their head out of a classroom to watch the confrontation. Clete Packer was confident that the younger man would not express his anger physically. But he was not 100 percent sure. He chose to diffuse the confrontation.

"Look, John," Packer began in a calm and respectful voice. "We got off on the wrong foot – and that's on me. There was the poisoning of Mike yesterday and then today the super chewed a big chunk of my ass off about the game last night. And then Agnes Johns got all emotional over Bea Colby a few moments ago and gave me quite an earful – rightfully so. I was out of line." Packer talked a little faster as he laid out his litany of excuses. "I'm a little on edge, and I apologize if I came across as disrespectful. You're right. I should know better." Packer smiled a forced smile. Cale's face remained unchanged for a few seconds and then softened slightly.

John Cale gave a small nod to Clete Packer. He did not feel the need to verbally accept the apology. "I suspect the super wants to talk, then," Cale said without emotion.

"Yes, I came down to tell you and Mike there is a meeting at 10:15 in his office. We have to discuss—"

"Mike's gone." John Cale interrupted the now fast-talking AD.

"What? Where? This wasn't a prearranged absence. He didn't put in a request." Anger crept back into Clete Packer's tone as he responded.

John Cale did not respond in anger – he was more quietly exasperated than anything else. "Mr. Packer, Mike got the call from his wife about Bea Colby shortly after we got here this morning. He left to go be with the Colby family. He's coached Cheese and Gum – Chet and Gunther – since they were toddlers. He's known their parents for even longer. Remember, it was he and Agnes that put on the benefit for the family this last summer. There was no way he was staying here. Mr. Shanahan is out and you were in a meeting with the super, so he arranged for a substitute with Agnes. She runs the office and handles the subs anyway. Anytime we ask you or Shanahan about subs, you always say go talk to Agnes. So he talked to Agnes and I'm sure he will file the proper paperwork on Monday. He had other more pressing business, you know."

"Yes, yes, of course." Clete Packer was now dismissive and abrupt. "We'll just have to proceed without him, then, I guess. Mr. Knapp wants to have a press release ready by noon about last night's altercation. Half the news outlets in the state are hounding us on this. Bea Colby picked a very bad day."

John Cale did not respond. He was reminded once again what an asshole Clete Packer truly was. Responding to his asshole statement might escalate the confrontation back to the point where it had been only moments before. Unlike Clete Packer, John Cale was quite sure that physical violence might occur if he was pushed once more. Lately there was something about Clete Packer's face that made John Cale want to slam his fist into it even on days when the AD wasn't a total douchebag. And those days were few and far between.

The meeting would begin in about an hour. John Cale normally would have had the council of Mike Reese in a meeting like this, but Mike was unavailable. Cale thought of Sue Irwin, the president of the local teachers' union. When he volunteered to be on the contract bargaining committee last year, Sue Irwin had taken quite a liking to him. They had developed a playful banter where she would play like she was a Cougar, an older woman on the make for a younger man. And while she looked the part, Sue had graying blond hair, leathery skin and pronounced bags and crow's feet around her eyes; nothing could be further from the truth. Sue Irwin was a lesbian.

Sue Irwin was a year older than Mike Reese. The fact that she was a lesbian was generally well-known. She had been married when she first was out of college. It was a marriage of convenience. He was a gay man. After she got married, Sue went to work teaching in Bear River. Kevin Irwin went to work on destroying his liver through alcohol abuse.

Shortly after Sue turned thirty-five, her three-pack-a-day cigarette-loving mother died of lung cancer. It filled Sue with resolve to make some changes. First she quit smoking. She became a vegetarian. She became a dedicated distance runner. And although she had competed in marathons in twenty states in the decades since her life-changing decisions, Sue Irwin never lost the raspy voice of a smoker.

After two years of dedicated clean living, she moved Kevin Irwin out of her life. The divorce was uncontested. Kevin drank himself to death by the age of forty-five. Sue attended the funeral and consoled the funeral director who had been Kevin's closeted lover for more than fifteen years. Few other people were in attendance.

At the age of forty-six, Sue Irwin became the lover of a middle-aged woman who remained in the closet until her twin sons graduated from college. Karen Mortenson was a veterinarian and an adjunct professor in the animal husbandry department at Michigan State. Together, they restored an old farmhouse north of St. Johns halfway between their two jobs. They ran a dog rescue for abused and neglected basset hounds on the old farmstead. Several times a year, they hosted Karen's sons and their young families in the rambling farmhouse. Sue never had children, but Stephen and Robert came real close to feeling like her own boys. And the fact that the boy's children called both Karen and herself 'Grandma' filled Sue's heart with a joy she never thought possible.

Sue Irwin had begun her teaching career as a third-grade teacher, but just before her mother had died, she became the district reading specialist. And she was a damn fine one. Over the years she had helped hundreds of struggling young readers master the skills to be successful learners. Every year, she went to graduation and was filled with quiet pride when many of her ex students were announced as having received a college scholarship. A few of them even became teachers. One of them taught down the hall from her office. Every year since Christy Caulkins was hired, a bright red poinsettia plant appeared on Sue's desk at Christmas time with a note saying "Thanks Teach" and a gift card to Starbucks.

Over the last twenty years, Mike Reese and Sue Irwin alternated as president of the local chapter of the teachers' union. It was a friendly rivalry.

183

The two were acknowledged as the best teachers in the district. They had a genuine respect for each other. When Mike Reese lost by two votes in the last election, one of his longtime supporters complained pretty bitterly when he announced that he would not be running for the position again. The middle school teacher was not a fan of Sue's lifestyle. Mike knew that, and rather than dress down the busybody teacher for bigotry, he calmed her down saying that if anything, Sue Irwin was a better-prepared and more skillful negotiator than himself. Still the bigoted teacher pressed on. She questioned Mike as to why he didn't see it as a dishonoring thing and why he was so accepting of his defeat.

Mike Reese paused for moment and then he spoke. "Candy, you have taught history for almost as long as I have and maybe you can recall General Sherman's words about Mary Ann Bickerdyke, the long-serving and tireless volunteer nurse and soldier's health advocate during the Civil War. Do you remember what Sherman said?" The puzzled teacher shook her head. Mike continued, "I look at it this way, Shelly, when it comes to Sue Irwin and our union. Like Sherman said of Bickerdyke, 'She ranks me.'"

Sue Irwin was sitting at her desk when her phone rang. She looked at the information screen and smiled when she saw that it was John Cale. She picked up the headset, and in her husky voice she seductively said, "Johnny you can't call me on this line – people are starting to talk."

John Cale gave a short laugh. Sue Irwin was a wonderful teaser. "Sorry Sue, but this is strictly business."

"Okay, John, what's up?" Sue's raspy voice became serious.

"I don't suppose you heard about what happened at the JV football game last night," Cale answered.

"John, the only thing being talked about here is Bea Colby. Everyone is pretty down," Sue replied. Cale could hear the grief creeping into her words.

"Here, too. Mike Reese left a while ago to be with Chet and Gunther," Cale stated quietly.

"Mike Reese is a treasure in this town. Bless his heart," Sue said with conviction. "I visited Bea two days ago at the house. She was so very frail, John, very frail. She is ready – the only thing holding her here are the boys. She spent most of our visit talking about them. She is a very proud mother. She only got teary when she spoke of you and Mike working with Chet coaching football. She was so happy that he has something to do besides sit at her bedside watching her die." Emotion caused Sue's voice to grow thin as she spoke.

John Cale heaved a heavy sigh. "Well, Chet is involved with what is going down. The game got out of hand last night. There was an incident in front of our bench with less than a minute to go. There were some late hits, and one of their players got his ankle broken pretty badly. The opposing coaches came over to check the boy out, and Chet got in a shouting match with Elm Hall's head JV coach. The guy went after Chet and grabbed him, but my head JV coach, Keith Marker, decked him before he could do much. Mike and I did what we could, but it all happened too fast. It's all on video and all over the press this morning. I've got a meeting at 10:15. Normally, Mike would be with me, but he is with the Colbys, so—"

"So you need me to be with you in an official capacity as union prez. Let me guess, Sheldon Knapp is shitting giant concrete bricks fending off the press and Pam Kitteridge, and he's got that worthless Fudge Packer doing the dirty work looking to chop some heads. That about the size of it?"

"That's it precisely," Cale said with some relief.

"10:15 in Sheldon's office – I'll be there. This was shaping up to be a pretty boring morning, but now I get to piss off Packer, Knapp and Kitteridge just by showing up. Things are looking up. I just hope those dipshits have the sense to leave Chet alone. Firing him as his mother is dying – not even Fudge would be that callous and stupid – I hope," Sue Irwin declared confidently.

At a little after ten, Sue Irwin and John Cale stood in front of the superintendent's office building. Keith Marker pulled up on his motorcycle. It was a bright and clear morning. Fall was in the air. Leaves were still on the trees, but vibrant red and yellow colors were starting to dominate much of the landscape. Marker wasn't wearing a helmet. He pulled off his sunglasses and nodded a greeting. "Hi, Coach."

Cale looked Marker up and down. The young man was wearing jeans and a leather jacket over an un-tucked flannel shirt. He had ratty-looking court shoes on his feet. His hair needed combing. "Kind of an important meeting, Keith. Maybe you should have dressed up a little." Marker said with a smile.

Keith Marker smiled back. "Not going to make any difference, Coach. Besides – I'm going to resign." Marker replied.

John Cale started to protest, but Marker cut him off. "Coach, you and I both know they have to let me go. I'm all over the internet laying out an opposing coach. The video is going viral. Rather than let them fire me, I'm going to resign. My letter is typed up and signed. I'm going to turn it in and leave. Hopefully I don't have a warrant out for my arrest."

John Cale glanced down at the ground. When he looked up, the sun made him squint. "What are you going to do now?" Cale asked with genuine concern.

"I'm heading out west. I was going to at the end of the season anyway. I got a cousin out in Colorado who flies for the U.S. Forest Service. He flies smoke jumpers into the backwoods and up into the mountains. He said he can get me a job as a Forest Service firefighter out there. I might get my pilot's license, too." Marker said with genuine excitement.

John Cale smiled. He opened the door for Sue Irwin and his young friend. He knew that Keith Marker would succeed in whatever he chose to do. He almost envied Marker. Right about now he wished he was a firefighter and not the head coach of a disastrous football program.

Clete Packer stood in the outer office. His face was dark and foreboding. It grew darker when he recognized Sue Irwin. He did not like her, and he was sure the feeling was mutual. Without greeting the guests, Packer pointed at the lounge area in front of the secretary's desk. "Take a seat, John." He then pivoted to face Keith Marker. "The superintendent and I will see you first," Packer said curtly as he made a thumb point gesture toward the office door. The sign on the door read: "Sheldon Knapp Superintendent of Schools."

"Good morning to you too, Cletus," Sue Irwin rasped brightly.

"Look, Sue, it's been a difficult morning. I know you are here to represent John. But this one," Packer motioned toward Keith Marker, "is not a member of the bargaining unit. He is an at-will employee. Mr. Knapp and I will deal with him accordingly," Packer said officiously. Keith Marker's eyes flashed with anger at being referred to in such a manner. He was not about to be treated like a student being called to principal's office.

"This one will save you a little time then, I guess," Keith Marker said with restrained anger as he reached into his jacket and produced an envelope, which he handed to Clete Packer.

"What the hell is this?" Packer demanded.

"It's my letter of resignation." Marker replied in the same forceful tone.

"Oh no you don't, young man! You are not taking the easy way out! You will answer some questions, and by God, you will contribute to the official press release! And then we will work out the details of your termination! You will not dictate the terms of this – your actions last night put this school district into some considerable hot water and you will be held accountable! If you resign, I will see to it that you will not substitute teach here any longer, and you will not get the remainder of your coaching paycheck! And if you think for one minute you will get anything but a poison-pill recommendation from this district on further employment, you are sadly mistaken, young man!" Packer's face was turning crimson as his voice rose.

Sheldon Knapp opened his office door, a very cross look on his face. "Clete, there is a time and a place. The place is my office, not in a public waiting room!" Knapp said curtly.

Keith Marker made a decision – clean or no, he was making the break. He turned to John Cale and shook his hand. "Thanks, Coach. You know despite the losing, I really enjoyed the opportunity to work with you and Mike. Thank him too, please." Marker smiled. Cale could tell something was about to happen. He just wasn't sure what.

Keith Marker looked back to the AD. Packer was standing next to Sheldon Knapp. "You want a statement from me? Okay – here it is. I stand by everything I did last night. Period. I would pop that punk Ian Larson again if he went after a kid like Chet Colby in front of me. Football is as much about honor and loyalty as it is about blocking and tackling. Where I come from and the way I was taught to play this game, honor means something. And when one of your teammates is about to get hammered with a cheap shot, you help him out. But quite frankly, here at Bear River with people such as yourself running things, honor and loyalty are out the window. You are an embarrassment. So do me a favor. Take my remaining paycheck and your precious letter of recommendation and shove them up your ass," Marker said clearly and quietly, and he turned to leave.

Keith Marker's hand was on the door when Clete Packer roared in anger. "STOP RIGHT THERE! JUST WHO IN THE HELL DO YOU THINK YOU ARE TALKING TO!?"

Marker stopped and faced him. "I know exactly who I am talking to. So long, Fudge," the young coach said and he exited the building.

"Why that insolent little bastard!" Clete Packer charged forward to the door. Sheldon Knapp grabbed at his jacket sleeve. Packer shrugged him off. John Cale stepped in between Packer and the door. Cale intercepted the charging AD, and although he was fifty pounds lighter, he picked the older man up off his feet and walked him backwards to the superintendent's door.

"You go out and try to get physical with him, Clete, and he'll break you in half. And I'm in the mood to let him do it. It's time for you to sit and calm yourself down," John Cale uttered hoarsely as he muscled the AD into the office. Cale put Packer down on a chair in the superintendent's office as he heard Keith Marker's motorcycle roar to life.

Sue Irwin watched the events unfold with a twinkle in her eye. Sheldon Knapp was as flustered as she had ever seen him. Physical confrontations obviously terrified the skinny twerp. And Fudge was so enraged he was practically crying. Her boy, John Cale, was controlling the show. It occurred to Sue that John would make a fine administrator someday if he had a mind to do it. But then that would be such a waste of teaching talent. She sensed it was her turn to take over.

"Sheldon, I think it's best if we take a few minutes before we continue," Sue Irwin said as sweetly as her gravelly voice would allow.

Sheldon Knapp would never admit it to anyone, but Sue Irwin owned him in negotiations. He didn't like that, but it was the truth. Their professional relationship was marked with some bitter disputes over the years. Rarely did Sheldon Knapp feel like he even stayed even with her let alone get the best of her. At this point, though, he was so shook up that he was grateful for her offer to delay the meeting. "Yes, yes, let's meet here in thirty minutes."

John Cale and Sue Irwin excused themselves.

"That was very exciting, Johnny," Sue Irwin said to Cale as they walked out onto the sidewalk in front of the building. "He'll break you in half, and I'll let him do it!" She paraphrased the young teacher. "Very exciting stuff. For the first time in over twenty years, I feel like I want a cigarette," Sue chuckled.

"So what do we do now?" Cale asked.

"Let's walk over to the 7-Eleven and get a cup of joe. It's a nice day and the walk will do us good. That will give Sheldon some time to pour a bucket of ice water on Fudge. Maybe he'll sort this out in his head and I won't have to hold his hand as we negotiate a good conclusion. I doubt it though. You know for his hot shit-reputation for being a control freak, Sheldon sure can't seem to avoid caving in. I know all his tells. The man lives in panicked fear of the press airing the district dirty laundry. He would agree to almost anything if I couch it in those terms. He's a spineless twerp masquerading as a tough talking sheriff. Like Don Knotts in those ridiculous cowboy movies from years ago. He even looks a little like Don Knotts, don't you think?" Sue Irwin talked without pause and barely gave Cale the opportunity to get in answers to her many questions as they briskly walked several blocks to the 7-Eleven. He found that he almost had to jog to keep up with her.

Thirty minutes later, John Cale's belly sloshed with coffee as he and Sue Irwin came back into the central office building. He noted that his calf muscles were burning from the stress of keeping up with the much older but fabulously in-shape woman. Sue didn't even appear the least bit stressed by the mile power walk. Sheldon Knapp welcomed them into his private office. Clete Packer was conspicuous by his absence.

"I sent Clete back to his office. Mike Shanahan won't be back until Monday, and with all the secretaries trying to go visit Bea Colby today we are a little short-handed." Sheldon Knapp said in a desperately casual way, as though dismissing the AD was not a big deal. Sue Irwin suspected Knapp chewed the fat man's ass pretty good before he was banished. She was fine with Packer's absence. His temper was a wild card. Nothing she couldn't handle, but one on one with Sheldon was preferable.

"I understand, Sheldon," Sue said agreeably.

"I've watched the videos, but I need you to put everything in context for me, Coach. What more can you tell me of the events last night?" Knapp asked without being confrontational. Sue Irwin could tell this was going to break totally their way if she just nudged Sheldon to the proper conclusions. She smiled sweetly as John Cale began a detailed description of the game and the three incidents. Sue regretted that Keith Marker had been so adamant about resigning – she was sure she could have talked Sheldon out of dismissing the lad.

Sheldon Knapp listened and nodded as John Cale went into detail about the three videoed incidents.

"I know this Danny Short boy. Excellent student. Good parents. What possessed him to quit in the manner he did? I mean walking away just before kickoff?"

"I have a meeting scheduled with him and his parents right after today. Danny has a very keen sense of honor. I think once we talk it out, he will return to the team," John Cale answered earnestly.

"I am not pleased with the actions of Coach Reese. Clete Packer wants to suspend Mike for tonight's game. And I am inclined to agree. Elm Hall's superintendent, Phillip Hollings, was very angry about Reese goading his coaches into the eventual confrontation." Knapp shifted the subject to the second incident caught on video.

188

"Phil Hollings? Seriously, Sheldon, you're going on the say-so of Phil Hollings?" Sue Irwin interjected before Knapp could complete his thoughts. "There is a reason Phil Hollings is the super at a rinky-dink school like Elm Hall. He's a dullard. He is the classic example of a coach retiring from the field to misadventure as an administrator. More is the pity. They are getting ready to terminate his contract over there anyway – he's incompetent." She patted John Cale's hand as she took a shot at coaches. Cale knew she wasn't including him in the grouping. She continued, "And according to Mike Reese, he wasn't even good at coaching. We had a hell of a laugh two years ago when he got the appointment to Elm Hall. Mike said Hollings couldn't coach his way out of a wet paper bag. Mike owned his ass in wrestling. That's what this is about. Phil Hollings is carrying a grudge from the old days. You can't go on what he says, Sheldon. You can't suspend Mike Reese. He has thirty-eight years of excellent service to this district. That just isn't done," Sue concluded.

"Well, uh, yes I suppose not, and with the resignation of the JV coach, it would leave John here with a very thin staff for tonight's game, I guess." Sheldon Knapp stumbled through his capitulation, and then he felt the need to assert some control. "I think a temporary letter of reprimand in his coaching file would suffice. We'll remove it at the end of the season if there is no further trouble—"

"We will grieve that letter formally and request a hearing at the next school board meeting, Sheldon." Sue Irwin interrupted him yet again. "I don't think you want a public hearing on this, Sheldon. Do you really want to try to reprimand a legendary coach who was not even penalized during the game? Do you want it to come out that you decided to reprimand him after he was not able to appear at this meeting to defend himself because he was attending to the needs of the Colby family? Pretty bad form, Sheldon." Sue Irwin's calm tone belied the threat in her words.

Sheldon Knapp's expression was a mix of anger and exasperation. "Okay, then, no letter, but certainly a verbal reprimand."

"From who, Sheldon? Clete Packer? You think he will do any better than he did this morning with young Coach Marker? Certainly not Mike Shanahan. Jesus, Sheldon, the man gets lost walking from his office to his car every other day at the end of school. And I don't imagine you feel it is worthy of your position. Do you really want to establish the precedent of the superintendent managing the coaching staff directly? Over such an inconsequential matter?" Sue Irwin maintained her calm, direct manner. She could sense he was preparing to cave at any second. John Cale was in awe of her effortless control of the situation.

To save face, Sheldon Knapp engaged John Cale directly. "Coach, I would like you to discuss this with Mike Reese. Inform him that the administration of Bear River Schools expects nothing but the best examples of sportsmanship from the coaches who represent our school. Please send me an email upon completion of this verbal rep—" Sheldon Knapp paused as he glanced at Sue Irwin. She arched her eyebrow and began to lean forward. Knapp cleared his throat with a cough, "This, um, discussion – when it is practicable to hold a meeting with him, given the events of this day. Perhaps by next Tuesday or so."

"Certainly, sir," John Cale replied.

Sue Irwin relaxed but not completely. There was still the matter of Chet Colby.

"Now about that final confrontation on the field, I believe—" Sheldon Knapp began, knowing full well that Sue Irwin would likely interrupt. And she did.

"Sheldon, the Colby family does not need to deal with any disciplinary action taken against young Chet. For the love of God, don't do something that will make their way any harder. I can't imagine the blowback from the community. Bea is beloved. If you take action against her son for standing up to an out-of-control bully of a coach – well, it won't go well. You have the resignation of Coach Marker. Button this up and move on," Sue said in her most assuring voice.

"If you would allow me to finish, Sue, I was going to say that any official action regarding Chet Colby can wait until a time appropriate to the situation. In fact, I think Coach Cale can handle this as well when he meets with his coaches at the end of the season to give them their evaluation." Sheldon Knapp struggled to get this statement out without sounding totally defeated.

Sue Irwin smiled confidently. Total victory. John Cale suppressed the urge to bow down to her right there in the office. Sue prepared her coup de grace, "Sheldon, would you like coach and me to help in the preparation of the press release? We'd be more than happy—"

It was Sheldon Knapp's turn to cut off Sue Irwin in mid-sentence "No, no, that won't be necessary. Thank you for the offer."

As they exited the building, John Cale couldn't restrain himself. He gave Sue Irwin a hug. "Sue, you are amazing!" Cale effused.

"Oh, Johnny, it was almost too easy. Sheldon Knapp is no Richard Wing. My first tour on the negotiation team years ago, Wing took me to school in that very same room. He had me turned around seven ways to Sunday. That old buzzard nearly had me in tears off and on through three dozen meetings. Then my mother up and died just after we signed the tentative contract agreement. Richard Wing drove all the way down to Battle Creek to go to her funeral. Old buzzard indeed. I bawled like a baby when he hugged me at the church. I cried just as much at his funeral not ten years later. The key to mastering anything, Johnny, is to learn from the greats, and I was blessed early in my career to work with a few." Sue Irwin was wistful in her response. She squeezed John Cale's hands tightly and wished him luck in the game that evening. John watched her walk briskly to her car.

Back in the superintendent's office Sheldon Knapp leaned back in his $800 leather office chair and massaged his forehead with the tips of his fingers. He had taken three Excedrin just before the meeting. They were not even making a dent in the headache. Knapp wished it was like the old days. Some of the supers he worked for early in his career kept a full bar in their office. He thought of his home overlooking the Bear River. In his study was a glass wall that had a lovely vista of vibrant colored leaves spread out across the river valley to gaze and wonder at. More important, there was a fully stocked bar. A bottle of Johnnie Walker Blue Label scotch was waiting there for him. Oh, how he wanted to sip the contents of that bottle well into the weekend. It would have to wait. What a hellish week it had been. It wasn't over yet.

Knapp leaned forward and pressed the intercom button, "Karen, buzz Clete Packer. Tell him to get his ass over here."

Shortly after noon, Karen Bigelow knocked softly on the superintendent's door, and she slipped quietly into the room. Sheldon Knapp sat in his big chair. He was dictating a statement to Clete Packer who was hammering away on a laptop computer. Knapp could tell at a glance – Karen had bad news.

"Is it Bea?" Knapp asked his executive assistant delicately.

Karen Bigelow nodded. Tears ran down her cheeks. "Mary Pierce just called Agnes. Agnes called me. Bea passed twenty minutes ago."

Sheldon Knapp sighed. Clete Packer set aside his laptop and grabbed a handful of Kleenex. He passed them gently to Karen.

"Okay, Clete, scrap that statement. I've got to compose a new one. But first I have to send an all-user email blast to the district about Bea. Tell you what, head back across the street. I'll email you a final draft about last night and you put your name to it. Fax it out. If it's later than the deadline, so be it." Sheldon Knapp had taken on a mournful tone. He was well-practiced at it. He learned early on to be not only the CEO of the school district but also the Mourner In Chief. Nearly every school year provided at least one opportunity to don a black suit and to make an appearance at the funeral of someone connected to the district. It wasn't a total waste of time, either. Good political connections can be made and reinforced at funeral parlors. The mournful voice was part of the package. It really wasn't an act this time – at least not totally. Like everybody else in the district, Sheldon Knapp had a real affection for Bea Colby.

Less than twenty minutes later, every in-box in the district received the standard Sheldon Knapp condolence email. It began with the all-too-familiar phrase: "It is with a heavy heart that I have to inform you of the passing of our friend and colleague—"

Shortly after two in the afternoon Pete Petterson was handed a fax from a CMU intern working for nothing at the cash strapped daily newspaper. Pete was greatly irritated. He couldn't help thinking, "Who the hell faxes anything anymore? What about a text or a tweet? Even an email is preferable to a fax." Then he thought. "Oh yeah. Schools still fax shit all the time."

Finally, he was going to get something on the record from Bear River. Pete Petterson had been frustrated for hours. Pat Packer wouldn't answer his phone. The parents of the Boy Scout who quit after the national anthem at the previous night's JV game stonewalled him, saying they were meeting with John Cale after school. Petterson desperately wanted to update his blog. More people read his blog on Friday afternoons before the start of varsity football games than at any other time of the week in the fall. He wanted a juicy lead-in story on Bear River. He wanted to announce his exposé article that would appear in Sunday's edition of the paper.

Petterson cleared away the potato chip and cookie crumbs from his desk and from his lap, the remains of his midafternoon snack. As he read the communiqué from the Bear River athletic director's office, his face turned red. "Well, I'll be go to hell – son of a—" The big man mumbled crossly to himself.

Due to the untimely death this morning of Veronica "Bea" Colby, longtime Bear River Public Schools employee and president of the Bear's Sports Boosters, after an exhausting battle with cancer, there will be no detailed report at this time on actions taken by administration regarding the unfortunate incidents that occurred in the junior varsity football game between the Bears and the Elm Hall Rangers. The only information available at this juncture is that we will confirm that Junior Varsity Head Football Coach, Keith Marker, has resigned citing that he accepts all responsibility for the events of last night's football game. We have accepted Mr. Marker's resignation and agree with him that his resignation is for the good of the program.

We thank you in advance for any condolences you may wish to send forth to the Colby family and to those in the Bear River school community who are mourning the loss of a valued colleague and friend.

Clete Packer

Assistant Principal/Athletic Director

Bear River High School.

Twenty minutes after updating his blog, Pete Petterson managed to get Clete Packer on the phone. "Clete, in all my years of reporting, I have never seen such a bullshit shedding of responsibility and avoidance of accountability. You people seriously just hid behind a dying woman to avoid answering questions about your out-of-control football program. Unconscionable!" The bloated sports reporter spat out the last word with contempt.

"Now hold on, Pete, we're not hiding anything. You have your story – Marker resigned. And he has taken responsibility for everything in his resignation letter. Run that Marker resigned and leave it at that," Clete Packer forcefully replied.

"No, I am not leaving it at that. Did you read my blog update yet?" Petterson's anger was still in check but not by much.

"Pete, I have better things to do today than read your blog. We are dealing with a tragedy," Packer responded in disgust, and before he could continue to berate the sports reporter using the death of Bea Colby, Petterson interrupted him.

"I ran your bullshit press release verbatim in my blog. With your signature, by the way."

"Huh, I, ah, I don't see how that was necessary, Pete. You have the Marker story. The rest is just—" Packer reached into his desk drawer and extracted his Maalox bottle.

"Let me guess, Sheldon Knapp wrote the press release and told you to sign your name to it – didn't he?" Petterson inquired with disgust and disbelief.

The question was answered with silence.

"Man, you are just dumber than a sack of hammers, Clete. Knapp played you. He got a fall-guy gift-wrapped when Marker resigned. He clamped down on your nephew – probably threatened you to do it. He swept the whole mess up and hid it with the timely death of a staff member who just happens to be the mother of one of the coaches involved in the brawl. Probably used the mom's death to avoid firing the boy. And then to top it off, he sticks you with the whole stinking mess of the cover-up. You are the one looking like an asshole right now, Clete, not him. Most people with half a brain will see through that heinous press release and see it for what it is – cheap and shoddy avoidance using the death of a woman to buffer the district from proper oversight from the press and the public. It stinks, Clete, and the stench is all over you while Sheldon Knapp slides out the back door to go play golf with his cronies. Jesus!"

"It's not that way at all – ah, Pete – you see I, uh, I—" Packer tried vamping until something popped into his head to say to deflect the very accurate account of the situation.

"Clete, you're just an ignorant tool, you know that?" Petterson uttered with total disgust, and he ended the call.

Clete Packer glanced at his computer screen. In the last five minutes, he had received thirty emails. The beeping notices distracted him during his call. A sense of dread began to creep into his thoughts.

After school Jay Brau was weeping as he sat dejected on the large sectional couch in the living room of his great-aunt and -uncle's house. He came home to rest before the team bus was scheduled to leave for Elm Hall. He desperately wanted to talk to Freddy Wilkes, his boyfriend. He wanted to hold him in his arms. He wanted Freddy to tell him everything was going to be all right. But Freddy was at cross country practice at his school in Riverdale.

When news came that day of the death of Bea Colby, Jay Brau took it very hard. He really didn't know her well. But Cheese Colby was his friend and he had been tutoring Gump Colby in algebra for over a month. Jay was a member of the National Honor Society and he volunteered to tutor underclassman struggling with academics. Jay had taken a liking to the younger Colby, who was quiet and respectful but unfocused in the classroom. Who could blame Gump for being unfocused and falling behind in class – he was consumed with fear of losing his mother. Jay's heart ached for the boy.

After each tutoring session, Jay found himself freshly remembering how bad it was to lose his own mother. Long talks with Freddy Wilkes were the cure for pulling Jay out of his funks.

Jay and Freddy Wilkes had traded several texts during the afternoon. Much love was professed as Freddy sought to comfort his boyfriend. Jay reread the text string with tears running down his cheeks. He was grateful he had the house to himself. There was a note on the large oak kitchen table that informed him that his great-aunt and -uncle had taken the two foster children staying in their home to Mt. Pleasant to do some clothes shopping. The two foster children were sisters who had been placed in foster care that summer when their meth-head mother had been jailed for running a drug-cooking lab in their double-wide trailer. The mother had got caught when the trailer exploded in a ball of flame. Fortunately, no one was home when it happened, but for the second time in recent years, the two Trammel sisters, Crystal, sixteen, and Angel, thirteen, found themselves wards of the state as their mother sat in jail.

Jay texted Freddy: "I love you, Muffin. I want to run my hands through your hair. I want your lips pressed to mine. I need to feel your body next to mine. Please tell me we can be together tomorrow night. I'll be home by 10:30. Call me."

Jay glanced at the old railroad station clock his great-uncle had mounted on the wall of the living room. It read 4:35. The bus was leaving the school at 5:00. Jay sprung to his feet and ran to his room on the second floor. He grabbed a clean Under Armour shirt from his dresser. He was packing that and some clean clothes for after the game into his big black Bear River football duffel bag when the house phone rang. He dashed down-stairs to answer it. It was the chairman of the county fair board looking to talk to his great-uncle. Jay hastily took a message, grumbling to himself about the fact that the answering machine sat unplugged next to the phone. Jay's aunt had been dusting and unplugged it. It was something she frequently did. It never failed to exasperate Jay's great-uncle when it happened.

By the time Jay finished the phone call, he had less than ten minutes to make the bus. He pulled his late-model Dodge sedan into the student lot and ran to the bus parked at the curb in front of the gym. The door swung open and Jay entered the bus. He apologized to Coach Cale for being late. Cale told him to take a seat. Cale was concerned, because it was very unlike Jay Brau to be late or to violate any team rules. Jay found a seat next to Phil Long, who grunted as he slid his wide body close to the window. Jay was harried and distracted and sad. Had he been his usual collected self, he might have realized his cellphone was sitting on the cushions of the couch back at his great-aunt and -uncle's house. As it was, he wouldn't realize it was missing until the next morning.

Most of the members of the Bear River Bears football team were surprised when Cheese and Gump Colby showed up during warm ups before the game at Elm Hall. They were with their father, Chester Colby Sr. Mike Reese and John Cale knew that they would be there. Reese had been present when Bea Colby passed away. He had talked to Cale when they were sitting in the coaches' office as the boys trickled into the locker room before the bus left.

"I think Cheese will be there tonight," Mike Reese stated without emotion, but John Cale could tell the events of the day had weighed down his assistant coach with considerable grief.

"What makes you say that?" John Cale asked.

"His mom told him to go to the game before she died," Reese replied with a slight tremor in his voice.

"Huh?" John Cale was a little embarrassed at the incredulity in his response.

"Well, I wasn't in the room, but Chet Sr. told me about it. Bea was fading fast and he came out of her room to where the boys and I were sitting in the family lounge area sipping on Cokes. Jesus John, those boys. I don't know, I mean, I was in my forties when my parents passed within days of each other. I was devastated but – can you imagine what it is to a teen to watch your mother get hollowed out by cancer in a few months—" Reese shook his head to clear it. "So, Chet Sr. takes the boys back to the room. Less than an hour later, they came out. Gump was sobbing and Cheese was holding him trying to calm him down. I hugged both the boys and held them for a minute. Their dad took me aside and told me how the last few minutes of her life went." Mike Reese was visibly shaken as he spoke. He paused and splashed some water from the rusty sink in the office onto his face and neck.

"Chet Colby is a strong man, John. Very strong. Heroic even. I don't know how he has held it together. I swear, I don't. He was so calm as he told me—" Reese struggled to get the words out. He paused and then continued, "Bea was fading but she insisted on sitting up and talking to the boys. Cheese explained he wanted to stay with her in the room this evening but she insisted that he had responsibilities to the team. Chet said her voice was barely above a whisper when she told him, 'You need to go to that game, Chetty, and take the Gumper with you.'"

Mike Reese cleared his throat. "You know she never called him by the nickname Cheese – she didn't like it. But she called Gunther 'Gump' because that is what Cheese called him when he was born. As a four-year-old, he couldn't pronounce Gunther. The name stuck. We didn't start calling Chet Jr. 'Cheese' until he was in middle school wrestling. I don't remember how exactly he got that nickname but—" Reese paused again and heaved a heavy sigh. "So, anyway Bea patted Cheese on the hand and drew him close and kissed his cheek. She told him again that he had to go and that she was going to take a nap but not to worry, she would be there when they got back. She dozed off and passed away twenty minutes later." Mike coughed and cleared his throat as he finished. John Cale felt the tears welling up in his own eyes, and he wiped them away with a towel.

One by one, the members of the team paused during warm ups and came over to shake Cheese Colby's hand. They all called him "Coach." Even Glenn Marcus – who was very sad about Mrs. Colby's death. He remembered numerous times when she was very nice to him when he was in elementary school. She gave him cookies every year on his birthday. As far as he knew, she was the only adult in that building who even knew when his birthday was. Glenn had tears in his eyes when he shook Cheese Colby's hand.

Jay Brau made it a point to shake Gump Colby's hand. He quietly leaned in close and told the sad-eyed boy, "If you need anything, Gunther, just let me know." Gump Colby shook his head slightly and whispered a thank you.

In a feel-good movie about a high school football team facing tragedy, the team would go out and win the game for their bereaved young assistant coach. But this was the Bear River Bears. No such thing would happen on this night. The Elm Hall Rangers laid a massive butt whipping on the demoralized squad from Bear River. The final score was 67-0 in favor of the hosts – the raucous homecoming crowd cheered the first four touchdowns. After that, if the crowd noticed, mostly laughter rang down from the stands when succeeding scores were put up on the scoreboard. Seth Parker jammed the wrist on his throwing hand on the third play of the game and "Dial-a-Pain" sat the rest of the night with an ice bag on his lower arm and hand. In the third quarter, Morg Miller took a vicious knee to his groin. It was a retaliation shot delivered by an Elm Hall lineman that Morg had knee-dropped in the balls late in the game the prior season. Morg was done for the night, and he was nauseated from the ache well into the next day.

It was Jay Brau who suffered the bloodiest injury of the game. Late in the game with the mercy clock running, Jay got stood up in the backfield when Phil Long and Big Donnie Donnie were pushed back into him as he took the handoff on a first down play. Jay was in the process of spinning away from the congestion when Glenn Marcus hit him from behind and the defensive end from Elm Hall lowered his helmet into Jay's facemask as he stepped in to make the tackle. Jay's helmet popped off his head like a watermelon seed. Jay felt the impact of the lower bar of his own facemask against the bridge of his nose. An explosion of pain seared his face. Blood spilled from the open wound on his nose into his eyes. He never lost consciousness, but he was hyperventilating and panicky when Wash Dryer and Coach Cale got to him. Because of the proximity to the eye and the bloodiness of the wound, the paramedics insisted on loading Jay into the ambulance and taking him to the hospital in Gratiot. His great-uncle followed the ambulance in his large Dodge dually pickup right up to the emergency room entrance.

Jay and his great-uncle left the emergency room almost four hours later. Jay had five stitches covered by a small gauze pad on his nose. He was a little loopy from the pain meds as he sat in the front seat of the large pickup truck. His great-uncle settled into the driver's seat as Jay flipped down the passenger visor mirror. He gingerly lifted the gauze pad. The black stitches stood out in a field of red puffiness and yellow-tinted topical ointment. The blue to black and purple half-moon under his right eye hinted at the shiner that would be in full bloom in the morning. Jay groaned and slumped into his seat.

"It's not all bad, Sport. Women dig a man with scars and interesting stories to tell about them. When you get to college next year, tell the chicks you got in a knife fight," the old man said cheerfully.

Jay's voice sounded wounded and miserable when he replied. "I look like Frankenweenie."

## Overtime

Earlier in the evening, Wash Dryer was about to text his father when his phone chimed.

GregDryer: Hi son. I know Owen Six was about to knock so we can skip the formalities.

WashDryer: Did you talk to mom? Did she tell you about Cheese's mom?

GregDryer: Yes. Bea was a very special woman. Your mom was pretty emotional. Are Cheese and Gump Ok?

WashDryer: I don't know. I guess so. Uncle Mike was with them all day.

GregDryer: Your Uncle Mike is as good of a man as I have ever known.

WashDryer: Are you coming home for the funeral – I think it is Tuesday.

GregDryer: Son – I checked on flights. The company won't pay for these things unless it's a family member. Your mother and I agree we just don't have $2000 to spend on tickets on such short notice.

WashDryer: That's Ok. I understand.

GregDryer: I need you to stand in for me. Will you do that? Be strong for your mom – take her to the visitation and funeral. Give the boys and Chet my condolences.

WashDryer: Yes I can do that.

GregDryer: I love you son.

WashDryer: I love you too dad.

Though they were more than a thousand miles apart, the Dryer men simultaneously went into their respective bathrooms to splash water on their faces to wash away their tears.

# CHAPTER ELEVEN

## OWEN 7

Revelations and Another Homecoming.

Morg Miller was nauseated when he woke up on Saturday morning. His nuts ached. He had taken shots to the groin before. Over the years, guys he had slammed, kicked and elbowed in the crotch had retaliated in kind. But he had never been caught so unaware and so squarely. He grimaced as he stepped into the shower. As he gingerly washed his lower extremities, he should have given some consideration to changing his cheap-shot tendencies. He didn't.

Jay Brau woke from a dreamless sleep at the same time Morg was dealing with the consequences of his injury. His hand immediately went to his nose. He drew back the gauze pad slowly and felt the jagged and stiff stitches. An ache radiated from his abused nose. Jay felt stinging tears coming to his eyes. His nose was already no prize to look at. It was long and crooked. Now with a scar, he was going to look like a thug in an old gangster movie. Freddy was so beautiful – how would she ever stay with a scarred piece of meat like me, Jay mournfully considered as he lay in his bed with tears dripping down to his pillow.

At ten in the morning, Jorge Martinez and Wash Dryer picked up Cheese and Gump Colby. They went over to Seth Parker's house to play video games on the giant plasma screen television in his family room. Seth's right arm was in a sling. His mother hovered near the boys for hours, waiting on their every need. Tears were in her eyes often as she talked to the Colby brothers. Seth was embarrassed.

Mike Reese picked up Chet Colby Sr. shortly after the boys left the house. The two of them talked of the weather as they drove to the funeral home in Gratiot. It was windy, and bright white clouds were being pushed in from the northwest in small bunches. Chet Colby mentioned that a month from now, they might see snow come with a wind like the one that was blowing. Mike sat calmly as the elderly funeral director guided his widowed friend through the process of arranging for services, casket and burial. Mike was staggered at the cost quoted. Bea had a small death benefit from work, but no other life insurance. The Colbys had no savings to speak of, and the money Mike and Agnes Johns had helped raise in the summer at the benefit was mostly gone. Chet had been looking for work for so long – where would the money come from? Mike thought of this as Chet Colby pulled out a credit card from his wallet.

"Can you put $1800 on this card? That will max it out. Bea's brother will be arriving from Texas on Monday. We will stop by first thing, and he will pay you the remaining $5,000. I'll be able to pay him back, and he won't charge me interest," Chet Colby said somewhat absent-mindedly.

The funeral director nodded and replied "Certainly, sir. Now this covers the cost of the burial, but not the plot or monument. Where did you say you have a plot?"

"At Holy Name in Bear River – the old section. Bea's great-grandparents, grandparents and mother are buried there. There are a ton of aunts and uncles in it as well. Her dad is buried somewhere in Florida. He ran off when Bea and Brian were kids. That's when Bea's Ma switched their name back to Anderson. Brian says we can have the last grave in the old family plot. He and his wife are going to be buried in Texas when the time comes." Again, Chet Colby's statements wandered in a distracted way. Mike Reese thought of shell-shocked soldiers he had read about over the years.

The funeral director efficiently wrapped up the transaction and guided Chet and Mike to the door of his office. Gentle platitudes were given and firm handshakes closed the proceedings. Mike and Chet walked out to Mike's pickup. Chet sat in the passenger seat. His eyes were hollow, and his gaze was on the horizon.

"I'd like to go look at the plot, Mike. Is that okay?" Chet said without looking at his friend.

"Sure, Chet, we can do that – no problem," Reese replied.

In a few minutes, Mike Reese wheeled his truck through the gates at Holy Name Cemetery. It was easily the most beautiful spot in Bear River. Not the new section, of course, with its flat grave markers and treeless grounds. But the old section which covered several acres of a large hill facing the Bear River a half mile distant. It was like something from a movie set. Mike Reese – when he was younger and could still run distances without his back and knees aching for days after – liked to jog through the old section of the cemetery. Towering oaks and maples competed for space with the old head stones and pinnacle monuments made of limestone covered with dark lichens. The oldest graves at the top of the hill dated back to the 1820s.

The rest of the town of Bear River was shabby. Like so many small towns on the fringe of America's rust belt, Bear River was played out. The main street downtown was filled with mostly empty store-fronts. Small deteriorated houses at its core spoke of a time when local jobs were plentiful and a working man could have a small town lot and a little two-or three-bedroom home. Maybe even a tiny garage in the back yard. The school buildings and grounds four blocks from downtown were well-kept, but the surrounding buildings showed their age badly. A few old Victorian-era gingerbread homes lined the main streets, but they too were either in disrepair or badly restored with pitted aluminum siding of mid-century vintage, or worse yet, cheap modern vinyl cladded over old-growth timbers hewn from the magnificent trees that covered the landscape along the Bear River more than a century ago.

The river that gave the town its name meandered through the heart of the city. A small dam was north of downtown. The pond it created was narrow and backed up for about a mile or so. The former chemical plant property covered the longest stretch of the pond frontage. No buildings remained on the site, only the tell-tale mound of the clay cap placed there to contain the oozing poisons below. Nobody from the town ever swam in the pond. They went out of their way not to touch the pond and the river.

The city of Bear River had some hills because of its proximity to the river, but it was surrounded by flat fields common to the topography of central Michigan. Decrepit and unkempt farmsteads were spread across the back roads. A modern sort of tenant system had emerged in recent decades in rural Michigan. Former successful family farms had been gobbled up by large corporate interests. Land was rented out or sold off in chunks by the families that had been on the farms for generations. Little plots of land sporting old farm houses with a few mostly unused and falling-apart outbuildings and barns was a common sight. East of Bear River, sugar beets dominated the agricultural fields. Elsewhere nearby, corn and beans were planted. Some cookie-cutter-looking modern homes dotted the rural landscape – these were owned by the few farmers who had managed to succeed at the modern model of farming. Closer to Bear River, there were newer homes in recently built small subdivisions serving families whose breadwinners needed to travel more than an hour to find decent wages. But these buildings lacked charm or real beauty. Those lucky enough to have homes on the river – like Mike Reese and Sheldon Knapp, had nice views. But they knew as everyone in the area did that the Bear River was still laced with poison salted into it by the long-defunct chemical plant and the more recently closed and demolished oil refinery in Gratiot. Both ventures died wheezing unprofitable and ignoble deaths that stole away the economic life-blood of the community as they sank into disuse.

It was a sad locally known fact that for miles in any direction, only the cemetery on the hill had any real beauty. But as a monument to the dead, it served mostly as a reminder to the community that the city of Bear River used to matter. That was its real function. The cemetery reminded the local residents that Bear River used to be a place to build a thriving business. It used to be a place to raise a family on good local wages. Bear River once had a piece or two of the industrial might of Michigan's glorious past. But that past was gone, and it would never come back. The town was too small and too far from the urban islands of southeast Michigan to be of any real consequence and still too large to blow away like a western ghost town. Now nothing identified Bear River to the outside world but a ZIP code and a school district. It had ceased to be anything like a thriving community quite some time ago. But it did have a beautiful picture-postcard-quality old cemetery.

Guiding the full-sized pickup through the narrow lanes of the old section of the cemetery would be a daunting task. Mike parked his truck in the flat newer section, and he and Chet walked the hundred or so yards up the hill to the Anderson family plot. As they transitioned from the flat ground to the slope of the back side of the cemetery hill, Mike glanced down and saw the flat gravestone that read: "Wing, Richard G. 1920 – 1997." A U.S. Army medallion was attached to the stone.

Mike Reese flashed back to a happier time in Bear River. It was at the end of his first year of teaching. He attended the Bear River public schools staff golf outing. Nearly every district employee was on the course at the country club in Gratiot. Richard Wing had heard that Mike could drive a ball a country mile off the tee so he recruited the young teacher and coach for his foursome. Mike even rode in his cart. The superintendent of Bear River public schools wore a broad Panama hat and carried a deadly accurate putter. The whole way around the course, Wing smoked horrible-smelling cigars. After Mike had a half dozen beers in him, he finally accepted one from the old man. It tasted better than it smelled.

They tore the course up that day. It was a scramble format tournament and the superintendent's foursome won by two strokes at fifteen under par. Mike still had the cheesy little trophy they all got for finishing first. Mike also won the longest drive contest. The fifty bucks was quite a boon, given he and his ex-wife were trying to make it on his first-year teacher's pay.

Richard Wing usually arranged to stack his team and win the yearly event. No one ever complained, because after the golfing was finished he hosted a barbecue at the country club and put up the money for door prizes. The partying lasted well past dark every year.

It was after midnight when Mike Reese found himself sitting on a patio at the golf club with a few of the party holdouts, including Richard Wing. Three of the older teachers were telling stories of their service in World War II. Mike was enthralled – what young history teacher wouldn't be, no matter how many beers he had in him. One of the veterans cracked a joke about worthless officers. But then he froze and looked at Richard Wing. "Sorry, Captain. Present company excepted, off course."

"Ahhh, don't worry about it. That was almost forty years ago." Richard Wing dismissed the slight with a minor slur in his voice. Wing then began to tell his own stories. He told of landing as a second lieutenant at Omaha Beach and being the only officer in his unit to survive uninjured or not to be killed in the next forty-eight hours. He talked of the brutal fighting in the hedgerows of France where he earned a Bronze Star and found himself promoted to first lieutenant. He talked of Paris and girls giving away their virginity to him. He talked of making the rank of captain shortly after turning twenty-four. He talked of the bitter cold of the Hurtgen Forest and of his Silver Star and Purple Heart. He talked about riding a hospital ship back to the states with a painful million-dollar wound. Mike Reese quit drinking, and his mouth went dry. He sat silent and respectfully listening until the club steward ran them off the property at nearly 4 A.M.

Over the next several years, Mike Reese had the veterans on staff speak to his history classes of their experiences during the war. Richard Wing came in every year even after his retirement. They all did. And they were all dead now. Mike Reese felt a physical pang of regret at the thought of that fact as he and Chet Colby approached the grave site. He refocused his attention on his friend as they stood at the only empty plot in a row of headstones marked with the name Anderson.

"This is where we will put you, honey," Chet Colby said to his absent wife. "Right here, next to your ma. Maybe when I go, the boys can spread my ashes here. Otherwise we can't be together. There's no room up here on the hill," he concluded, almost in a whisper. Colby paused and ground the heels of his hands into his eyes. He snorted back the wetness in his nostrils. He turned and glanced down the hill, and he pointed to the far corner of the cemetery. "My dad is buried down there on the flat ground, Mike. He's been gone since before Chet Jr. was born. My ma remarried and moved to Arizona. Her Alzheimer's is so bad that when I talked to her a couple of months ago on the phone and tried to tell her about Bea, she didn't even remember that I was married. No use in bringing her home for the funeral. She won't remember the boys and that will break their hearts, Mike." Reese let his friend ramble on. He could sense that Chet Colby was reaching his breaking point. Maybe he could talk his way through it.

Chet Colby continued his impromptu guided tour of the grounds. "Look over there. See that tall obelisk across the lane? That's Bea's great-great-grandfather's grave. Miller Krumrie was his name, Mike. Owned the biggest store in town in the 1890s. He sold off the farm he grew up on to the company that built the chemical plant there on the west side of town. Took the money and built the Krumrie house. Remember that big old Victorian on the corner of Locust and Nelson that burned down twenty years ago? That was it. Bea and I stood on the sidewalk the next day looking at the ruins. She cried telling me stories her grandmother had told her about growing up in the house. That lot is still empty. There aren't any Krumries left in town that I know of. Not many Andersons either." Colby's voice was uneven as he swept his hand toward the row of Andersons. "At least not any who are relatives of Bea. They're all dead. More than a dozen of them up here. They all worked for the chemical plant, you know. All of 'em died of cancer. Bea's ma included. My dad worked there when I was a kid – he died of cancer. Bea grew up in a house right next to the main gate of the plant. Back in the '80s, the EPA bought it and plowed the whole thing onto the grounds of the chemical works and covered the entire area with twenty feet of clay. Like that does any God damned good. Now Bea is dead."

Chet Colby drew in a ragged breath and tipped his face to the sky. The shattering scream of anguish came up from the very bottom of his soul, "FUCKING CANCER!!!" The scream echoed across the deserted cemetery but died quickly in the low roar of the wind rushing through the tall trees on the hill. Colby stumbled slightly forward and fell to one knee. Mike Reese encircled his friend from behind with one arm. Colby leaned heavily on it. A silent gasp of a sob froze in his throat. His body shook with effort to release it. When it broke loose it came out with a primal *Ahhhh* sound. Colby drew another ragged breath and repeated the raging sob and again over and over for several minutes.

Mike Reese clung to his friend even though his back was starting to protest. He thought of how long he had known Chet Colby. Since his first year teaching when Chet was a senior. He didn't wrestle, but he was a hell of a football and basketball player. Mike never had him in class as a student, but they knew each other through football. Chet joined the Air Force after high school. When he returned home, he married Bea Anderson and they bought the little bungalow next to the house that Mike and his first wife owned on the south side of town. The Colbys babysat for the Reeses often in those days. The Colbys tried mightily to start a family of their own. Finally Chet and Bea ended up traveling to California to meet a doctor who was able to help. Bea gave birth to Chester Colby Jr. at the age of thirty-five. It was a difficult pregnancy and delivery. The fertility doctor told the Colbys that there was no chance that there would be another child. She was wrong. Without actively trying, Bea Colby got pregnant and effortlessly gave birth to Gunther 'Gump' Colby four years later. They named him Gunther after Chet's dad. Chet Jr. called him 'Gump,' and soon the whole town followed suit. Everyone knew the younger, roundish Colby brother with his mother's smile as 'Gump.' He looked like a Gump.

During the busting up of Mike Reese's first marriage, it was Chet Colby who took Mike out regularly to get him ripping drunk to blow off steam. Chet would sip one beer as Mike pounded down several. At the end of the night, Chet would deposit the blitzed coach back at the apartment he was renting in Gratiot. Mike was grateful – Chet Colby helped Mike avoid a few drunk-driving charges in those days.

Chet Colby took over the Bear River youth wrestling program for Mike when no one else would take the non-paying job. And even though he had been a basketball player as a boy, he brought up his own sons in the sport of wrestling. When they got older, Mike Reese went to work to turn them into champions. Bea's recently diagnosed cancer prevented Chet Jr. from focusing on a medal run the last season. Chet Jr. had placed third in the state as both a sophomore and junior. Gump held real promise. He looked like a soft round puppy, but he was surprisingly agile and powerful. If anything, he was a better wrestling technician than his brother. He had multiple youth state championship medals to prove it. If Gump's broken arm would heal, Mike thought he might get him back at mid-season. He needed a 160-pounder. Gump could qualify for state. He might even medal as a freshman. That would be impressive in a senior-dominated weight class like 160. Getting Gump to focus on wrestling might be a very good way to help the boy manage his grief. Mike had seen that work before with other kids over the years.

Mike Reese thought of all this as the racking sobs of Chet Colby Sr. lessened in their fury. The sleeve of Mike's Bear football windbreaker was soaked through with Chet's tears where his arm crossed the grieving man's chest. Mike's own tears had stopped flowing several minutes before as he gazed numbly at the leaves blowing loose from the branches above. The wind was picking up. Heavier gray clouds were racing in on it. It would be a dreary and chilly late afternoon and evening. Finally, only the rushing wind and the crackling of the leaves could be heard. Chet was done. His grief wasn't abated. That would likely take years, but it was momentarily exhausted. Mike silently helped him to his feet. The two men began the trek down the hill to the truck. Both of them were quiet. Both focused on thoughts of returning in a few days to lay Bea Colby to rest near the crest of the only really beautiful hill in the mostly flat and featureless county.

Glenn Marcus met up with his sometime-girlfriend a little after five in the afternoon. Kelsey Smith was a year older than Glenn, and she had dropped out of high school without getting a diploma. She was as dumb as they come but hot in a trashy sort of way. Glenn liked that about her. She also was skilled with her mouth. Although Glenn found the whistling sound her two nose rings somewhat of a distraction when she was engaged below his belt.

"Hey, Babe, hop in, I got Brad's car for the night," Kelsey said, popping her gum. She had pulled up into the front yard of the Marcus's double-wide trailer in her older brother's mid-'90s Nissan. Glenn grunted a greeting as he slid into the front passenger seat.

"I thought Brad said he wouldn't let you borrow his car anymore," Glenn stated with barely any interest in her reply.

"Yeah, well, I gave him the last of my stash. It was mostly stems and seeds anyways. He was bitchin' about how shit has dried up around here lately," Kelsey stated brightly. Glenn Marcus grunted again and he made some rudimentary economics and marketing connections to the recent demise of the Manikowski pipeline. He snorted with a little pride as the light bulb went off in his head.

Kelsey ignored his monosyllabic utterances. "Let's scoot down to Lansing – I got a girlfriend there who can hook me up. Uh – you got some cash?"

Glenn protested honestly that he had only a few bucks to his name. Kelsey pouted for a few moments as the car idled. "I know!" Kelsey practically shouted. "Tara said the next time I was going to Lansing she wanted to tag along. I can get her to front the gas money and maybe if we get her high she might help out a little later, ya know?" To emphasize her bolt of logic, she grabbed playfully at Glenn's manhood. "You suuuure you can't get some money?" Kelsey teased seductively.

The thought of a three-way had never occurred to Glenn before. So what if Tara Malcaitus was a fat version of Kelsey – except dumber. Two chicks – that was definitely doable. Tetherboy smiled broadly. "Hold on, I got something," he announced, and he exited the car and bolted up the rickety metal steps into the double-wide trailer. Moments later he was back in the passenger seat. The lump in the front pocket of his jeans was the size and shape of a large class ring. "Let's roll!" he commanded.

A half of an hour later, Kelsey Smith had the old Nissan pointed south on U.S. 127 driving though a heavy mist. In the backseat, the very chubby twenty-year-old Tara Malcaitus was smoking a cigarette. She reached into her large brightly colored purse and pulled out a pint bottle.

She unscrewed the cap and took a drink.

"What's that?" Kelsey asked in her usual chirpy way. She glanced in the rearview mirror at her friend in the backseat.

"It's called Wild Irish Rose – it's wine!" Tara chirped back.

"OMG, where'd you get it?" Kelsey questioned, laughing and chirping in even a higher register. Glenn was starting to get irritated at the sounds they were making.

"Ya know, I been like cleaning houses for some extra cash an' stuff. Well, I found two bottles of this in Mrs. Abrahamson's bar cabinet. They were tucked behind about a dozen different gin bottles her old alcky husband had in there. He's been dead for like two years an' she had a stroke or somethin' a few months ago so it ain't like she's gonna notice. So I took 'em a few days ago when I was cleaning her house," the chubby girl stated with pride at having committed the perfect crime. "Here have some." And she passed the bottle to Kelsey.

Kelsey took a large swallow while keeping one hand on the wheel. "Oooh, that's really sweet!" she said with pleasure in her voice. Tara took the bottle back and downed another swallow herself, making a cooing noise as she did. She passed the bottle forward to Glenn and made a nodding gesture at him to have a drink. Glenn blocked the bottle with his hand and gave the fat girl an annoyed look.

Tara shrugged and petulantly declared, "More for us then."

Glenn looked at Kelsey as she accepted the bottle back from her friend. "Hey, don't be getting' drunk. I don't want to be pulled over – they might search me," he said with forceful irritation.

"Maybe you oughta drive, then," Kelsey said with hope that he would say yes.

"No, I need you straight. When I go in, you need to keep the car running." Glenn 'Tetherboy' Marcus said sounding as authoritative as the experienced criminal he thought he was. If his mom's boyfriend knew what he was planning, he would hit him across the nose with an ax handle.

"So, what's the big secret? What you got that's gonna get us some partyin' money?" Kelsey chirped and sounded accusatory at the same time.

Glenn reached into his front pocket with one hand and flipped on the dome light of the car with other. He opened his hand and displayed the MSU Rose Bowl championship ring.

"Izzit gold?" Tara questioned as she leaned forward to look. The foul sweet wine on her breath made Glenn wince.

"It's a class ring. That ain't gonna get us shit," Kelsey said in a mopey voice.

Glenn was irritated. "It ain't solid gold, but its valuable. it's a MSU Rose Bowl championship ring from the '50s. Sports collectors will pay real money for shit like this," he said dismissively to the girls who obviously had no clue about the quality swag he possessed.

"Where'd you get it if it's so valuable?" Tara queried from the backseat as she fished into her cavernous purse for the second bottle of wine.

"My mom's boyfriend gave it to me," Glenn replied as he turned the ring over in his hand admiring it.

"Where'd he get it?" Kelsey asked.

"I dunno," Glenn lied.

"So what's the plan – who you gonna try to sell it to?" Kelsey asked with confusion.

"Well, I figure MSU is in Lansing, and there are all kinds of fans down there. I think one of the pawn shops on Michigan Avenue might give me at least $200 for this. Like I said, sports collectors buy this shit up." Glenn laid out his plan, such as it was.

Tara was finishing the last of her second bottle of wine as Kelsey pulled the Nissan into a municipal parking lot off Michigan Avenue east of downtown Lansing. It was dark and a gray mist hung in the air. The amber street lights give the area a weird glow. If it had been clear the dome of Michigan's capitol building would have been visible – lit up with white spotlights a dozen blocks to the west. As it was, just the glow was visible. Tara was smoking and chatting non-stop. Glenn ignored her.

"So, what's the plan?" Kelsey asked Glenn.

"See that store?" Glenn pointed across the street. Vintage neon signs in green and white flickered. The store was called Spartan Town Pawn. A red neon sign of newer vintage brightly announced: "We Buy Gold." The red light illuminated a large placard in the window. The placard read "Quality Sports Memorabilia Bought & Sold." Kelsey nodded at Glenn signifying that she understood he was going to hock the ring there. The excitement read in her face. Visions of cash and partying filled her empty head.

"You keep the car running. I'm going in, and if I don't like the way it looks, I'll come out and you swing across the street and I'll hop in and you drive off. Keep your phone ready. Don't be callin' anyone. If I need to give you different instructions, I'll text from in there." Glenn talked loudly so he could be heard over Tara who had started singing a Rihanna song – badly. Glenn was too focused on his plan to even be annoyed at the drunken fat girl.

Glenn opened the passenger door and as he slid out, Tara belched and hiccupped stopping her song. "Cutie, you go score us some partyin' cash and me and my girl here are going to rock your world tonight!" Tara announced drunkenly. Both girls burst out in laughter. Glenn buttoned his black jean jacket and ignored them. There was some traffic to dodge as he made his way across the street.

The electronic bell that announced his entrance was sickly sounding. The store had a creaky wooden floor. A fat security guard sat on a stool near the door. A young couple was looking at rings. An enormous black man was opening the case to pull out the tray full of jewelry. The man stood well over six feet tall and weighed about 300 pounds. He didn't look fat – he looked like an athlete. Glenn wasn't worried about the fat guard – also a black man. The really big man, who was obviously in charge, made Glenn regret the choice of this particular pawn shop for an instant. But then Glenn saw the wall of sports memorabilia.

Michigan State jerseys from several sports hung on the wall – spotlights on the ceiling made the green and white display look like a shrine to all things Spartan. A large 'Go Green' banner covered the top of the wall. Several pictures were spaced in among the jerseys. A poster-size picture of the man behind the counter showed him in younger days. He was standing on the MSU campus next to the giant bronze statue known as "Sparty." The green and white football jersey the man wore had the number 78 on the front. Glenn knew at a glance that the shop owner was a former football player, not just a fan.

Glenn stopped to admire an even larger poster on the wall. It showed MSU basketball legend Magic Johnson throwing an alley-oop pass to somebody whose jersey identified him as Kelser. Both athletes had signed the poster. The large price tag read $1,595.00. Glenn smiled. There was real money here and he was going to get something good for the ring.

The young couple didn't buy anything. They exited the store after the giant man behind the counter told them "Come in again," in a low, rumbling voice.

"Is there something I can help you with this evening, young man?" the giant behind the counter asked pleasantly. Glenn liked the voice. It was deep and warm and it made him feel welcome. Any second thoughts about his choice to sell the ring here evaporated.

"Um, the sign says you buy sports memorabilia, I got something I need to sell." Glenn smiled his best smile, and the man behind the counter returned it as he spoke.

"What do you have?" the big man asked politely.

Glenn reached into his pocket and produced the ring. He held it out to the gentle giant.

"My goodness, that looks like a Rose Bowl ring." The man behind the counter sucked in his breath in appreciation as he held the ring. He looked closer at it with a squint. "1956, I met some of those guys. They had a thirty-year reunion back in my playing days. That was a good team. One of Coach Duffy Daugherty's best." The ring looked small in the giant's hands. He placed it down on the counter.

"Where'd you come across this?" the man asked.

Tetherboy had a whole elaborate story to tell but most of it fled his brain at that moment. "My mom gave it to me. She got it from her step-dad when she was young," he answered tentatively. Then he quickly added, "She died last year and said to sell the ring if I ever need the money. I got a job offer in Texas and I need gas money to get there."

"Uh-huh." The big man rubbed his chin, taking in the story. "Well, I got to tell you I have never seen one of these in the store before. Kind of hard to put a price on it." Glenn tried hard to not let his disappointment show. The man seemed to sense this. "I sold a 1979 NCAA basketball championship ring a few years back – one of the bench players brought it in to me and I found a buyer for him, really. So all I got was a broker fee. That buyer paid eight grand for the ring. Now this isn't a national championship ring, but I think the same guy might be interested. He comes in here a couple times a month to check if I have anything new. Usually drops a few bills before he leaves. I'll give him a call. He doesn't live too far from here. If he isn't busy he could be here in less than twenty minutes. What do you think?" The big man's soothing voice showed no strain but Glenn started to get nervous.

"I don't know. Can't you just give me what you think it is worth and then deal with him? I'm kinda in a hurry." Glenn glanced to the door as he replied. The tubby security guard seemed to be sleeping. Glenn calculated the chances that he could grab the ring and run. But before he could do that, the big man behind the counter picked up the ring and held it close to his eyes again. He pulled out a jeweler's loupe, fitted it to his eye, and hummed the Michigan State fight song quietly as he examined the ring.

"Son, I don't like to keep the kind of money on hand here on the weekend to cover the cost of this ring. It's Saturday night. Keeping that kind of cash around would put Franklin and me in danger of armed robbery." The big man motioned to the security guard as he spoke. The guard was still.

Glenn was unsure on what to say. He blinked at the big man and tried to smile. A giant smile was returned.

"I can't give you a low-ball offer of a few hundred bucks. That sort of deal would ruin my reputation and that's bad for business. And I'm not going to lie to you. Sometimes I get people bringing in knock-off championship rings in here and I've been burned a few times. My man is an expert collector – he'll give you a good fair offer. Could be north of two grand – if he thinks it is the real deal, and I think he will. I tell you what, I'll even knock down my ten percent broker fee to five. How's that sound?" The big man's eyes twinkled as he spoke. Alarm bells were ringing in Glenn's head.

"Uh, I guess okay," Glenn said thinly.

"Have yourself a seat and I'll get my man on the phone," the big man said cheerfully. He still had the ring in his hand as he pulled an iPhone from his pocket. He stepped back toward his office as he spoke. Glenn strained to hear but caught nothing of the conversation. He was distracted by the security guard who ambled his way.

"You wanna Coke or something while you wait?" the fat man asked. His voice was high and reedy in contrast to that of his boss.

"Yeah, I guess so," Glenn said as he retrieved his cellphone from his pocket.

Glenn texted Kelsey: "Bring the car in front. Text me when you get there." He made up his mind to run even if he didn't have the ring.

The drizzle had stopped and the wind was calm for the first time all day. Kelsey and Tara were standing outside the car smoking when the text came through. "Get in, Glenn's coming out," Kelsey commanded, and the girls threw their cigarettes to the ground. Tara climbed in the backseat. She was laughing and stumbling. Kelsey gunned the motor and pulled out of the parking lot. She went up a block and took a left turn into another lot and wheeled the car around to take a right onto the busy street. She glided the car into a space in front of the store. An old van was immediately in front of her.

In the store, the security guard returned with a can of Coke and opened it for Glenn. "Here ya go." Glenn nodded a thank you, and the guard walked back to his post. The creaky floorboards protested his steps.

The cellphone vibrated in Glenn's hand. He glanced at the screen. Kelsey texted she was in front of the store. Glenn set the can of Coke on the counter. He put his phone away. He glanced into the office. The big man flashed him a smile and held up the okay sign with his left hand. Glenn paused for a second. He brought the Coke can to his lips and took a gulp. His eyes shifted to the door and the fat security guard. When he brought his eyes back to the big man, he noticed the smile was gone. The big man's eyes went wide as he read Glenn's intent. Tetherboy dropped the can and bolted for the door.

The big man came out the office door and boomed out in the loudest voice Glenn had ever heard, "Franklin! Stop him!"

The fat security guard moved quicker than Glenn thought possible. He jumped up and bolted the security dead-bolt on the door. Glenn hit the fat man on a dead run with the best shoulder block he had ever thrown. The fat man grunted but didn't budge. Glenn bounced off him and was stunned that the guard didn't go down. The fat man reached out and grabbed Glenn by the left wrist. The grip was vicious and painful. An adrenalin burst powered Glenn's next move. He twisted his arm free and head butted the guard. This time the fat man went down. Blood seeped from the split eyebrow Glenn had given him. Glenn reached for the dead-bolt. The crashing footsteps of the big man running across the store sounded like bombs going off. Glenn fumbled with the bolt. He didn't make it. The giant swept Glenn up off his feet with a crushing bear hug. Glenn felt his bladder give way as the big man shook him like a dog might shake a chew toy. Glenn had never known such powerlessness and pure terror.

Wetness flooded down Glenn's legs and he let out a mewling cry. The big man roared, "You come into my store trying to sell stolen goods and you assault my employee and now you go and piss on me!" He threw Glenn with tremendous force to the floor. Glenn was knocked nearly senseless, but the big man wasn't done. He reached down, grabbed Glenn again and pulled him to his feet with one hand. Glenn's eyes went wide with terror anticipating a smash to the face with the opposite hand. The blow didn't come.

The giant plucked Glenn off his feet like he was a toddler. With a thrust he pinned him up against the frame of the door. "Here's what's gonna happen, you little pissant. You're gonna lie down face first on the floor and Franklin is gonna sit on you until the cops get here." The fat security guard stood behind the huge former football player. Blood trickled down his face from the split eyebrow Glenn had given him. The unpleasant smile on his face told Glenn that he was not going to enjoy the experience. The giant placed Glenn down and pointed to the floor next to the door. Glenn meekly assumed the commanded position. He groaned when the fat guard sat on his back.

"Like dat, muthafucka? Mebbee next time you best think about who you be fuckin' whit'," the fat man with the high reedy voice snarled. To emphasize his point, the guard shifted his weight back and forth across Glenn's torso. Glenn moaned and let loose a sob. Breathing was difficult, and he couldn't even draw enough breath to beg for mercy.

It was at that moment that Kelsey crashed into the locked door at the front the store. She had watched the beginning of the fight from the car. She screamed something unintelligible to Tara. She let out a cry of "Glennie!" and she jumped from the car. She watched dumbfounded as a huge black man shook her boyfriend like a rag doll and then threw him to the floor. She ran three steps but then back pedaled. Her mind was frozen. She didn't know what to do. She yelled at Tara to get out of the car, but the fat drunk girl only gaped at her. Finally, Kelsey bolted toward the pawn shop door.

The giant black man barely acknowledged Kelsey as she screamed and kicked uselessly at the locked door. She screamed some racial epitaphs and

211

started to pound the security glass with her fists. The security glass muffled the yelling but there was no doubt about what she was calling the two store employees. "Franklin, you sit tight, you hear? I'm gonna go get some ice and a towel to clean you up a bit. Not too much, I want the cops to see what he done. You understand?" the big man rumbled calmly.

"Uh-huh," Franklin answered. He shifted his weight again and Glenn sobbed.

"I mean it, sit tight and ignore that bitch – the cops will be here in a minute or so. If that dumb white trash don't know enough to split, then they can arrest her too," he instructed.

Tara was about to get out of the backseat when the two police cruisers with lights flashing but no sirens blaring pulled up in front of the store. Seeing them, she slid down in the seat and tried to disappear. Kelsey stopped her assault on the door and ran to the lead cruiser. A tall, white female officer got out the front passenger door. She looked to be forty years old. Her dark blue jacket had sergeant chevrons on the sleeve. Her partner, a shorter, younger black man, got out on the opposite side. The two officers in the trailing cruiser were black. The passenger-side officer emerged while his partner sat behind the wheel and talked on the radio.

"Those – guys – are killing my boyfriend!" Kelsey wisely edited her speech to exclude what she was just calling them seconds before. "They got him locked in the store and the fat one is crushing the life outta him right now!" Her voice climbed a register to hysteria. Kelsey stamped her feet and pointed vehemently at the locked door.

"Calm down, ma'am, we have a report of a white male trying to sell stolen goods here and just now the owner called to say he assaulted a guard." The tall woman focused her clear blue eyes on Kelsey and spoke firmly.

"Bullshit!" Kelsey screamed. "Glennie didn't steal nuthin'! His mom's boyfriend gave him that ring!"

Kelsey pivoted away from the officer and ran up the steps to where the giant store proprietor was opening the locked front door. He closed it in her face. She crashed her shoulder into the door. She let out a yelp of pain. Kelsey began to jump up and down and was crying as she clutched her separated shoulder. "Get offa him you fat bastard! He can't breathe!" she cried as the female cop's partner got between her and the door.

"Mike, put this girl in the cruiser. Looks like she's messed up her shoulder but you better cuff her. She's probably involved with the theft," the tall sergeant commanded. The younger partner led the sobbing girl to the parked car as yet another cruiser pulled up outside of the parked Nissan where Tara was hunkered down crying to herself and trying not to be noticed.

The door of the store opened yet again, and Glenn was thrust through the door by the big owner.

"What you got there, Jim?" the tall sergeant asked the big man.

"This one tried to sell me a hot Rose Bowl ring. I recognized it from the sheet last month. Got to be pretty damn dumb to fence something like that a couple of miles from campus like this. Then to prove how dumb he is he gets all hinky and tries to bolt – lays into Franklin and splits his eyebrow with a head butt. I got to him before he got out the door," Big Jim answered. Franklin stepped out the door clutching a red-stained towel filled with ice over his right eyebrow.

"Hi, Officer Cyndi, glad you guys finally showed up. I wuz getting kinda tired sittin on my boy here. Blood kept gettin' in my eye, too. That stings like a bitch!" Franklin joked.

The tall officer laughed, "I know it does." She looked Glenn up and down. Glenn wouldn't look at her. He looked pathetic. The wet front of his blue jeans showed that he had thoroughly pissed himself. He winced with every breath. Probably got himself some separated ribs, too, Cyndi thought.

The tall police sergeant looked at Glenn's ID. "Looks like you just turned eighteen, young man. Trying to sell stolen goods and assault – if I don't miss my guess, I bet you got yourself a nice juvie record. Well, looks like you got your first adult charges coming. If you're smart, you'll cooperate. Might help some," the sergeant said with a motherly tone as two officers wheeled Glenn around to handcuff him.

Tara peeped over the edge of the car window. All of the officers seemed to be in front of the store looking the other way. With surprising agility given her drunken state and size, Tara wormed her way over the back of the front seat of the small car. The keys were in the ignition. She turned the key and the little car barked to life. The officers all pivoted to watch as Tara tried to navigate the space between the last-arrived police cruiser and the old delivery van parked in front of the car. The grind of metal was enough to spring the officers to action. One jumped at the passenger door. Two more tried to dash to the opposite side.

The officer at the passenger door opened it as sergeant Cyndi yelled, "Didn't any of you think to check the car, for Christ sake!?"

"Get out of the car!" shouted the officer at the passenger door. Tara looked at him and frowned and shook her head. "Now!" he shouted even louder. One of the other officers smashed the driver's side window with his baton. As the glass shattered, Tara panicked and threw the car into reverse. The car flew backward and tagged the patrol car behind it. The car's siren chirped. Tara slammed the shifter into drive and gunned the motor. The officer that shattered the window howled in pain as she ran over his foot a split second before ramming the large van in front of her. The Nissan conked out. The officer with the broken foot began to shout obscenities and hopped to the sidewalk. Tara was frozen at the wheel.

"Get her out of there," Sergeant Cyndi commanded. The officers swarmed the car. The sergeant helped the officer with the broken foot who was sitting on the sidewalk cursing.

213

"Get out of the car! Now!" Cyndi's partner, Chris, yelled at the fat girl behind the wheel. The officers unclipped their side arms from their holsters.

Tara clung tighter to the steering wheel. She shook her head back and forth. The usually chatty drunk was too panicked to even look at the officers now. Tears flowed from her eyes. Mascara ran darkly down her face.

"Jesus Christ, Chris, don't shoot her! Give her the juice if she won't get out!" Sergeant Cyndi shouted with exasperation.

Chris calmly holstered his weapon and motioned to the other officers to back away. "Young lady, get out of this car or I will tase you. Do you understand?" Tara did not even look at him. Her eyes were wide with panic as she reached for the ignition. Officer Chris drew out his taser. "Do not try to start this car!" He shouted the order. Tara turned the key. The Nissan sputtered to life, but before she could put it into gear, 50,000 volts coursed through her body. Tara shrieked and bucked as her muscles locked. After the charge dissipated, she slumped on to the steering wheel and the horn sounded.

Tara evacuated her bowels and bladder as she was pulled from the car. She yelled incoherently as the officers cursed at the stench she had created. Officer Chris reached in and turned off the car. As they dragged Tara to the sidewalk, something happened that Tara had honestly always sworn she had never done. Tara loved to drink large amounts of alcohol and goad her friends into trying to keep up. When they got sick, she would laugh at them and call them little baby bitches. That record was over. For the first time in her life, Tara vomited. Two pints of Wild Irish Rose wine and a whole frozen Tombstone Pizza exited her mouth with alarming force. The bulk of the puke splattered down the legs of Officer Chris.

The police officer danced away shaking his legs, and even though he prided himself on never cursing on the job, he howled, "Fuuuuuck!"

A few minutes later, ambulances were on the scene. A lieutenant on watch showed up, and Sergeant Cyndi quit barking out orders and deferred to the senior man. Cyndi backed away toward the door of the pawn shop. Big Jim had gone inside and returned. He was now wearing a satin Michigan State football jacket. He pulled a large cigar from his pocket and removed the wrapper. He put it unlit into his mouth and fumbled for his lighter. Cyndi beat him to it and she offered hers. He thanked her as he watched an EMT administer to his security guard. Franklin was hitting on the young woman. Jim smiled as he lit the cigar.

"A hell of a mess, Jim. Just one hell of a mess. I don't know how I'm gonna write this one up." Sergeant Cyndi removed her watch cap and scratched her blond hair as she looked up at the even taller black man.

Jim paused and looked west toward the capitol dome. The clouds had blown away and the dome stood brightly lit in the distance. He glanced down at the officer and gave her a beaming smile. "Oh hell, Cyndi – just write it up as a typical Saturday night on Michigan Avenue." His deep baritone voice rumbled with affection.

Jay Brau moped around most of Saturday. Freddy Wilkes had a cross country meet, and if Jay had been in better shape he might have gone to watch his boyfriend run. Freddy had a perfect stride, and he smiled as he ran while most of the other runners grimaced or had blank faces. It was one of the many things about Freddy that gave Jay a secret thrill.

Jay searched the house for his cellphone. It was nowhere to be found. He convinced himself he left it on the bus. Coach Cale called Jay on his cell at 11:00 and got Jay's voice greeting. He wanted to check up on Jay. Cale suspected that the young man was having trouble with memories of his own mother's death brought up fresh by the passing of Bea Colby. And the injury to Jay's nose warranted a check-in.

At noon after leaving two voice messages on Jay's phone, Cale called the Braus' landline. He was relieved when Jay answered the phone. "Jay – everything all right? I tried your cell but it went to voicemail."

"Sorry, Coach, but I can't find my phone. I think I left it on the bus last night. I was going to call Wash to see if he found it, but I don't know his cell number – I just say his name and it rings automatically."

They talked briefly of Jay's injury. Cale got a laugh out of the boy by describing a similar injury he'd had in college that was far bloodier and assured him that the scar would fade in time like his had. Jay's spirits lifted a bit. Cale gave Jay Wash Dryer's cell number.

Wash Dryer was playing video games with the Colby Boys, Jorge and Seth, when the call came through.

"Wash, this is Jay – I'm on the landline." Jay Brau identified himself, thankful that his friend hadn't ignored the call because of the unknown number.

"Yeah, JB, what's up?" Wash passed his controller to Gump Colby and motioned him to take over as he spoke.

"Did you find my phone on the bus last night? I'm sure that's where I left it," Jay said anxiously. For the first time, it occurred to him that his phone was likely unsecured and if someone were to examine his text message log, that would be very bad.

"No, dude, I never saw your phone. Maybe it's still on the bus wedged in a seat or something. We can go check Monday at lunch when all the busses are in the garage," Wash assured his friend.

Jay thanked him and hung up the phone. His great-aunt made him eat lunch so he could take a pain med. Jay ended up sleeping most of the afternoon. When he finally called Freddy that evening, he had convinced himself that his phone was definitely on the bus wedged in a seat. Freddy was very chipper on the phone. Because they were on the landline the conversation stayed mainly on sports. Freddy was concerned about Jay's nose. Jay downplayed the injury and used Coach Cale's story to explain to his friend that such injuries rarely left a permanent scar. Jay left out his now fully blackened right eye. He kept the topics light. When Freddy announced that he would like to come over on Sunday evening, Jay begged off, claiming he had a paper due on Monday that he hadn't even started yet. Jay did not want Freddy to see his face with a swollen nose and blackened eye. He hoped in a few days the shiner would at least fade. Then he could face Freddy. Either way, he knew Freddy would get all teary-eyed when he saw the jagged stitches on the bridge of his nose. Freddy cried sometimes when they drove past roadkill. Just one more thing Jay loved about him.

At the same time that Jay finished his phone call with Freddy, and at the time that Glenn Marcus was getting the shit shaken out of him by an angry giant in Lansing, Heather Kline, the freshman cheer squad captain at Riverdale High School, angrily answered her cellphone.

"Look, I don't know who the fuck this is, I don't recognize the number! Stop fucking calling me! If you're some freak stalker or something you better know my dad owns like fifty guns, fucker!" The blonde fifteen-year-old announced into the phone. Heather Kline was known for two things in Riverdale. She could out party and out-drink any boy in her class. And she had the foulest vocabulary of any cheerleader in the last ten years at the school – or so said the Riverdale cheer coach who had already suspended the foul-mouthed girl for two football games that fall for shouting obscenities at her teammates when they blew a routine.

"Calm down, bitch. It's me, Crystal." The elder of the two Trammel sisters spoke flatly into the phone.

Crystal Trammel was hiding in the little hired-hand apartment in the lean-to part of the huge old dairy barn on the Brau farm. No one had actually lived in the quarters since the early 1950s. It was filled with old crates and tractor parts. A broken-down wooden office chair was the only furniture in the two-room apartment. Crystal liked to hide in there from the Braus and her annoying little sister. The only light in the room came through the dirty window. The bright yard light cast creeping shadows in the dingy room. Crystal sat in the broken chair smoking a cigarette in the shadows.

"CC! Holy shit! Did you get you get a new phone! Goddammmm!" Heather's demeanor changed, but not her vocabulary.

"Yeah, well, I guess you could say that." Crystal kept her voice down. She knew the Braus and her sister were in the house watching TV, but she was still cautious. Crystal Trammel was a silent, sulking, angry and mean-spirited bitch. She had been that way since birth. At least that's what her worthless drug-addled mother would shout at her in her lucid moments. Crystal started believing her mom's assessment of her personality quite some time ago. She became the bitch she had been labeled by the one person in the world who should have looked out for her own daughter who had started life as a timid young girl devoted to her mother.

Crystal hated everything about Bear River. She hated not being in Riverdale where her few friends were. She hated foster care. She hated her

216

stupid little sister. She hated being in eighth grade even though she was sixteen. She hated the gangly, pimple-faced twenty-year-old clerk at the mini-mart west of town who gave her three packs of cigarettes for his weekly hand job in the store's back room. She hated the Braus because they were so damn nice to her. She hated the fact that protective services forced her to turn in her cellphone after she wouldn't stop harassing them with messages and texts demanding to be placed in a home in Riverdale. She hated her meth-head mother for blowing up their trailer and all of her stuff. She hated Jay Brau because she couldn't seduce him into letting her use his cellphone. A few weeks ago, she had offered to suck him off for five minutes on his phone – just five freakin' minutes. And now she knew why he turned her down. When she found his phone sitting on the cushions of the couch the night before, all the answers to her troubles came into clear view.

At first, Crystal thought of blackmail, but that meant keeping Jay engaged and compliant. He wouldn't even talk to her anymore, the big fag. No, what she had to do was to blow the fucking thing up. Poison everything so that the Braus, as nice as they were, would have to send her back into the system. Then she could bully the workers at protective services into placing her somewhere in Riverdale. Maybe even work it so Heather's mom and dad would take her in. She could give two shits about her stupid sister. There was no better option than publicly outing the Braus' beloved grand-nephew. Super Jay who was so smart and so nice and who tutored her half-retarded sister. Yes, Crystal thought to herself, Jay Brau's outing would be her ticket back to Riverdale.

Crystal hushed her string-cursing friend and then spoke. "The nephew of my foster parents stays here too. Remember I emailed you about him being all stuck up and shit. Wouldn't even loan me his cell when I offered to give him a BJ – remember?"

"Yeah, so?" Heather answered.

"Well, Super Boy left his phone behind when he went to his football game on Friday and I swiped it. Figured out his access code. It's written on his desk in his room. And guess what?"

"What?" Heather answered in a tone that signaled she was losing interest.

"He's a bone smoker," Crystal replied sneeringly.

"Huh?" Heather answered.

"He's gay, you dumb bitch. And get this – his boyfriend is Freddy Wilkes," Crystal said with smug pride.

"Get the fuck out!" Heather replied with a howl of laughter. "Ya know, all the girls on the JV squad have been talking about him all fall. He is so hot! But the varsity cheerleaders all say he won't even hardly talk to them. They all say he's just shy. Ha! Guess we fuckin' know why now! What proof you got?"

"The texts between 'em are all hot for each other's junk. Fruity love confessions and everything. And the pictures! Jesus, there's a couple pictures of Freddy in a tight bathing suit on a beach where he is practically flashing his junk to the camera. There is another where the two of them are holding hands on a beach with the sun setting behind and Freddy is looking up at Jay like he's the greatest prom date in the world. I'm tellin ya, they are in luh-uh-uh-uh-uv!" Crystal said with snarky contempt.

Crystal informed Heather of her plan to out Jay and Freddy in the attempt to get a foster placement back in Riverdale. Heather didn't need much convincing – besides, having such a juicy bit of gossip to share with her friends excited her. The two planned a social media blitz with Heather's connections in Riverdale. Bear River was less than ten miles from Riverdale. The two girls knew there were many relationships with boys and girls from schools interacting socially and dating. It wouldn't take long for both boys to be outed. Less than a day, they thought. Then Crystal would confront the Braus' and they would send her back into the Protective Services system in retaliation for having hurt their golden boy. Once Crystal was back at the county youth facility, Heather could go to work on her parents about getting Crystal placed with the Klines.

Shortly after noon on Sunday, Clete Packer informed John Cale by phone that Glenn Marcus was in jail and would likely be there for a while. Cale called Mike Reese to tell him that Glenn wouldn't be playing any more football. As was typical, Reese was stoic as Cale cursed the stupidity of the young career criminal. Reese was also too classy to make any "Told you so" comments to the frustrated young head coach.

By two in the afternoon, most of the football players at Bear River knew of Tetherboy's boneheaded fencing operation in Lansing the night before. The Things were texting everyone they knew telling the story related to their father from his sheriff deputy cousin about the raid that morning at the double-wide home of Glenn's mother.

At 2:15 Thing One texted Morg Miller.

CLott: So Glenn's mom's boyfriend has all this stolen shit hidden in her trailer and when they slap the cuffs on him they tell him how Glennie gave him up. He goes like ape shit cursing Glenn and telling his mom how he's going to kill her retarded son.

MMiller: Tetherboy is fukked. He's going to jail and if his mom's BF is there he'll stick him with a shiv.

Sunday afternoon the social media connections of the Riverdale student body were blazing with the gossip about Freddy Wilkes and his boyfriend from Bear River. Pictures of the two of them, hijacked from Jay's phone, were on popular photo-sharing sites. Intimate messages between the two young lovers were ripped from the text history on the phone and posted with the pictures. Even though most of the commenting text from Riverdale students was on how it was nobody's business, the photos were shared rapidly.

Freddy Wilkes left church at about one in the afternoon and drove up to visit his grandmother at a care facility in Mt. Pleasant. He put his phone on silent when he was with her. They talked of the weather and of Freddy's Down syndrome sister and her recent Special Olympics success. When Freddy returned to his home north of Riverdale, his youth minister from the Riverdale Calvary Baptist Church was standing on the porch with his parents. His mother had obviously been crying. His father had a look of pure fury on his face.

As he approached the porch, the youth minister looked at Freddy and held up a Bible in his right hand, and in his left, he held the picture of him and Jay in the sunset. For an instant, Freddy was confused about how the minister had gotten hold of the picture. The two of them had an older gay man in Saugatuck take it of them a few months ago during the height of summer. Then he remembered Jay's phone had been lost.

"Young man, you have to choose. Walk with the Lord and live, or die with the sin of immoral lust!" The minister intoned with righteous condemnation. Freddy tipped his face to the ground. Tears began to flow. When he looked up again, the tears nearly blinded him as his father came down the porch steps. The first blow the powerfully built farmer gave his son was a clubbing chop to the base of Freddy's neck and left collarbone. Freddy fell to his knees. The pain of the broken collarbone took his breath away. He was unable to ask for forgiveness as the slaps and punches rained down on him. In a detached sort of way, Freddy heard his mother scream out his father's name. As he lay on the grass in the front yard of the farmhouse, he slipped in and out of consciousness. He watched the youth minister back his father away. Freddy blinked and faded.

Freddy woke with a start. The pain in his shoulder was competing with the pain in his face. His ears were ringing. His mother was wiping his face with a dish-cloth. She was crying and repeating his name over and over. Freddy could hear his father and the minister praying but it seemed like they were miles away. He faded out again.

When Freddy came to again, his mother and the youth minister were placing him in the backseat of the minister's minivan. Freddy could hear his sister crying and his father was sobbing and shouting, "Forgive Me Lord! I have struck my own child! Forgive me!" Freddy passed out again as the van pulled out of the driveway. His last sight was of his sister chasing the van down the slight hill in front of their house.

Roxanne "Butter Face" Johnson got a text from her cousin in Riverdale at about the same time Freddy Wilkes was being admitted into the emergency room at the Gratiot hospital. The cousin ran for the Riverdale cross country team. He told Roxanne to check out the stuff he just got sent on Tumblr.

Roxanne felt tears stinging her eyes as she glanced at the photos. Her friend's smile and the obvious devotion the two boys showed to each other in the photos stood in stark contrast to what was waiting for them. Jay Brau was being publicly outted in a very brutal way. She knew that most kids in school would know the whole story by tomorrow morning. She felt the need to talk to Jay – she wasn't sure what she would say, but she had to act. Roxanne borrowed the keys to her mother's Jeep and drove out to the Brau farm.

Jay Brau was cleaning and polishing horse tack in the barn when Roxanne got there. Jay's great-uncle took her into the barn.

"Jay! Roxy's here to see you," Jack Brau called into the cavernous barn. The bright light of the fall afternoon silhouetted the two of them standing in the large opening of the overhead barn doors. Jay emerged from the tack room. He had a puzzled look on his face as he crossed the main floor of the barn. Jack Brau excused himself with a smile. Roxanne couldn't help but show concern as Jay approached.

Jay was self-conscious. Roxy always made him feel that way and the condition of his face only made it worse. He touched his nose. "It looks worse than it feels." Jay managed an embarrassed grin as he addressed what he assumed was the reason for Roxy's look of concern. "I hope the black eye goes away soon – I look like Frankenweenie." Jay almost sounded lighthearted.

"Did you get that at the game?" Roxy asked.

"Uh-huh. Spent a couple hours in the emergency room afterwards, too," Jay replied.

"Jay, I – I need to talk to you but I'm not sure how to—" Roxy's voice started to quiver.

Jay sensed that his face wasn't the reason for Roxy's emotional state.

"Is something wrong? Are you okay?" Jay asked with real concern. He reached out to Roxy and grasped her right forearm.

"You haven't been online or on your phone, have you?" Roxy asked.

"No. I lost my phone on the team bus Friday. I haven't been on the computer today either." Jay answered. He was getting very nervous. Something very serious was breaking and he felt dread creeping in.

Roxanne Johnson connected the dots immediately. "Jay, someone got your phone and they posted your texts and pictures on Tumblr and probably on Facebook too. My cousin in Riverdale texted me about it just before I came here. He runs cross country with Freddy Wilkes – and, and – oh—" Roxy turned her head away from her friend and tears welled up in her eyes. The drops fell from her face onto the dusty barn floor.

Jay Brau was numb. He could hear and feel his pulse in his ears. His throat constricted and he coughed to clear it. He still held Roxy's forearm. He reflexively drew her tighter to him and she hugged him and sobbed. His own tears began to flow. They held each other for a moment. Finally, Jay's head cleared. A galvanizing thought seized him. Freddy!

"Oh my God! Freddy! His folks – his dad will – oh – I have got to talk to him!" Jay burst out.

"Do you need my phone?" Roxy asked as she broke the hug and wiped her tears.

Jay answered in the affirmative, and Roxy watched him as he paced the barn floor. His face was anguished as the call went to voice mail. "Maybe he won't answer because he doesn't recognize the number. I have to go see him!" Jay said anxiously.

"I'll drive you. You're too upset to drive," Roxy announced. She said it with such authority and confidence that Jay agreed. Jay wiped his face and strode from the barn. Roxy started her mother's jeep as Jay's aunt talked to him on the porch. Roxy wondered what he was telling her. Jay bounded down the steps of the porch and leaped into the old jeep SUV.

"What did you tell your aunt?" Roxy asked.

"Huh? Oh, I told her you and I were going to help a friend who is in trouble," Jay answered.

Jay gave her directions to Freddy's house. They drove in silence. Jay's mind was racing. He had no idea if Freddy knew what was going on or not. In fifteen minutes, they were pulling up the driveway at the Wilkes farm in Riverdale. Annie Wilkes sat alone on the front porch on a glider bench. She clutched two dolls in her arms. Jay and Roxy got out of the Jeep and approached the young woman. Roxy noted the almond-shaped eyes and high forehead of a Down syndrome case.

"Jay Jay! Your face is hurt. Did daddy hitted you too?" Annie Wilkes blurted out.

Jay Brau was crestfallen. He knew the question meant that Freddy's father had freaked out and struck his son.

"Is Freddy here, Annie?" Jay asked as soothingly as he could.

"No. After Daddy hitted him, Pastor Jimmy and Mommy took Freddy away. He's hurt bad. Daddy left too. He told me to wait here on the porch until Mrs. Griggs comes." Annie Wilkes mentioned the neighbor who used to babysit Freddy and who taught him piano.

"Did your mom take Freddy to the hospital?" Roxy asked.

"Uh-huh," Annie replied.

"Where did your dad go, Annie?" Jay asked, masking his anger. He felt the need to confront Freddy's father even though the powerfully built farmer would likely snap him in half if Jay tried anything.

"He said he was going to talk to a policeman," Annie replied as she fussed with her dolls.

"Okay, Annie. Wait for Mrs. Griggs. We have to go," Jay told the young woman.

"Bye-bye, Jay-Jay," Annie smiled as she looked up from her dolls. "When Freddy comes home I will tell him you were here."

"Bye Bye," Roxy replied to the smiling woman.

As they climbed into the jeep, Jay asked Roxy quietly, "What do I do now?'

"You can't go to the hospital. You're not family. They won't let you see Freddy." Roxy answered the unspoken part of Jay's question.

Jay began to cry. Real tears and anguished sobs followed as Roxy drove him back to the Brau farm. It was late afternoon. Jay and Roxy sat in the driveway in the jeep for a while. The glare of the low-hanging sun filled the passenger compartment of the jeep with harsh light. Roxy looked deeply into Jay's eyes. "Jay, whatever you need, you can ask me. Do you want me to go check and see if Freddy is okay and report back to you? My aunt works at the hospital. She can find out if she is working."

Jay nodded silently.

"Are you going to talk to your aunt and uncle?" Roxy asked softly.

Jay again responded with a nod.

"What about school and football? Are you going to school tomorrow?" Roxy continued.

Jay paused and drew in a deep breath. He exhaled. Roxy watched as a look of resolve filled his face. With his black eye and swollen nose, he reminded Roxy of an old boxing movie her father made her watch with him last summer. It wasn't too bad, actually. An overmatched boxer named Rocky Balboa fought the world champion to an almost draw, and even though Rocky was beat to a pulp, he gave as good as he got. Her friend Jay was tapping into his courage reserves just like Rocky Balboa had. For the first time since she broke the news to him about his outing, Roxy felt confident Jay had the strength to make it through this.

"I'm going to school. I'm going to live my life," Jay said clearly and firmly.

"Okay." Roxy replied, and she gave him a powerful hug.

Jay got out of the jeep and walked to the house. Roxy pushed the urge to weep out of her head. She had a mission to complete. She pulled out of the driveway and made a beeline to the hospital in Gratiot.

Sally Brau was sitting at the kitchen table clipping coupons from the Sunday newspaper when Jay entered the house.

"Jay, you missed dinner. There's some pork roast and potatoes on a plate in the oven," his aunt said cheerfully. The cheer drained from her face as she read her nephew's body language.

"Jay, honey, is everything okay?" Sally Brau asked with concern.

Jack Brau came in from the living room. "What's up?" he asked his wife.

Sally Brau shushed her husband. "Jay, is there something wrong?" she asked the young boy as he pulled a glass from the cupboard and filled it at the sink.

"Freddy's in the hospital," Jay stated flatly.

"Oh my, what happened? Is it serious?" Sally Brau asked.

"His dad assaulted him. I haven't heard yet how bad it is," Jay answered quietly.

"What!?" Jack Brau ejected. His wife held her hand to her mouth in shock.

Jay felt stinging tears on his lower eyelids. He blinked them back. "Freddy was beat up by his dad," Jay said more firmly.

"That doesn't sound like something Tom Wilkes would do. He's a good man. He's on the fair board with me. He's kind of a religious nut but not the sort that would beat his child to the point where he would need medical attention," Jack Brau said with angered wonderment.

Sally Brau was in her late sixties, but the world had not passed her by. She knew in her heart that her nephew had more to say. Her mind flashed back to the summer before he came to live with them. His mother and Sally had sat up late the last night of their visit to the farm. They told stories and laughed and drank too much wine. Meagan Brau loved her son deeply and during the third bottle of wine that night, she confessed to Sally that she was quite sure that Jay was very likely gay, even though he wasn't really clued into it yet fully himself. Sally agreed with Meagan that it made no difference. Jay was a talented and loving child. He was special.

Sally Brau again told her husband to shush. She turned to her nephew and studied his face. He was struggling with something to say. She could tell.

"Go ahead, Jay, it's okay. What are you trying to say?" Sally Brau asked calmly.

"Someone got my phone and posted pictures and texts from it online. His dad saw the pictures and he beat up Freddy. The pictures were of Freddy and me. He's my boyfriend. I love him. His dad went nuts and tried to kill him because Freddy loves me. I'm the reason Freddy is in the hospital." The last part of his statement sounded like a wounded confession.

Sally Brau crossed the kitchen and took her nephew by the hand. "No, Jay, no. Freddy is in the hospital because his father is sick in his mind. You didn't cause this. Freddy didn't either."

"Why didn't you tell us, son?" Jack Brau asked in quiet confusion as he sat heavily at the kitchen table.

Sally Brau gave him a stern look, but his eyes were cast down, and he missed it.

"Jay, you have nothing to be ashamed of, you know that right?" his aunt asked with conviction. The message was as much for her nephew as it was for his uncle.

Jay nodded and he swallowed hard. "I'm not ashamed, but I am sorry it happened this way. I was going to tell you after I graduated college. I didn't want you both to be embarrassed by – Freddy and I agreed we needed to let our families know after – uh, well, things just didn't work out the way—" Jay stammered with emotion and his aunt squeezed his hands even tighter.

"Love is very powerful. If you try to stop love from happening, you just end up hurting people," Jack Brau announced clearly to everyone and no one in particular.

Jay and his aunt Sally shifted their attention to Jack Brau. His gray blue eyes were focused out the window of the door to the farmyard. The last remnants of the day's sunshine glowed in the west. He paused and then looked at them.

"I don't think I ever talked to either of you about this. It's about the last conversation I ever had with Will Bayley. He was a guy I grew up with, Jay – a farmer like me. You never met him. He just died a while back. Sally probably remembers him, though. He was a regular at the Elks Club back when we used to belong. Will wasn't really a friend. I never trusted him. Will Bayley was a self-serving prick. We played football together in high school. If his talent matched his mouth, he would have gone to college to play ball. As it was, he inherited his father's farm and spent his life running that into the ground.

"Will always made a big show of volunteering in the community, but only on his terms. He would get on this committee and that, and then he would go on a power trip trying to run everything on his own, and more than once people around here accused him of dipping funds from various organizations he belonged to. One time, he got himself elected to the school board. He pulled his usual political shit and got his ass recalled.

"Will got married right out of high school. A timid little girl who bought his constant self-serving pile of BS hook, line and sinker. They had a son and a daughter. Will turned the town little league committee upside down trying to make his son a star. The boy didn't have any talent, but you couldn't tell Will that. He got on the board of the little league association of the county and then got thrown out when it was proved he rigged the all-star team selection process to get his son on the team.

"When his son got to high school, Will Bayley fought with his coaches and teachers all the time trying to get more playing time or better grades. He totally ignored his daughter – who it happens was a fine athlete. She was all-league in three sports. Little Bobby Bayley got all the attention. Until he went off to college, anyway. When he came home at Christmas break, he announced that he was gay and he was quitting college to go to San Francisco with his boyfriend. Well, Will went off his rocker with that. Beat the hell out of his son and threw him out of the house and forbid him from ever coming back. Which he never did – Bobby died of AIDS five years later. Will's daughter and his wife went to the memorial service out in California. Will wouldn't go.

"The daughter ended up marrying another gal last year when it was made legal. They live in Oregon. Will's wife left him and moved to Florida. Will took to drinking real hard. Racked up a few DWI's. The last time I talked with him was about five years ago. He buttonholed me in the bar downtown. Drunk as usual. He was telling lies about his football playing days to some fellow drunks and wanted me to back up his stories. I walked him away from his group and bought him a coffee instead. I don't know why. Normally I wouldn't have spent the effort on him. I asked him about his daughter. He started to cry. You know like some drunks do. He said she wouldn't talk to him. Every time he tried to reach out to her, she hung up the phone. His letters were returned unopened. He confessed to me that he had been wrong about his son and about his daughter. He had destroyed his own family. And then he said his biggest mistake was thinking he could stop his children from loving who they wanted to love. He said you can't stop love. It's too powerful. You only hurt people when you try.

"Two weeks later he was driving drunk when he T-boned Laney Dryer's minivan. Killed her little girl outright and nearly killed Laney and your friend Wash. Will Bayley died in prison not too long ago. But he was in a prison of his own making well before he went to jail."

Jack Brau paused for several seconds as he looked intently at his nephew. Something of a smile came to his lips, then he glanced to the floor. The pause lingered. Finally he looked back up at his wife and nephew who stood in front of the kitchen sink. Their faces showed both bewilderment and relief.

"Don't ever feel ashamed for loving someone who loves you, Jay," Jack Brau concluded.

With that the old farmer looked out the window again.

Jay drew in his breath and let loose a shuddering and emotional sigh. Sally Brau felt a surge of love for her husband of forty-five years, and she silently walked over to him where he sat and she draped her arms around his neck. Gently, she kissed the bald spot on top of his head.

"Well, faggot, I'll guess you'll be wanting this back now." Crystal Trammel walked confidently into the kitchen and tossed Jay's smartphone to him. He was stunned but he instinctively snatched the phone cleanly out of the air.

"That's right, I was eavesdropping on your precious little family meeting. Hard not to, the way the old man shouts like everyone is as deaf as him."

"It was you?" Jay asked incredulously.

"Yeah, you big homo, it was me." Crystal was defiant in reply.

"Oh, Crystal, why would you do such a hateful thing? A boy is in the hospital. His father might be going to jail," Sally Brau was nearly in tears as she spoke.

"I'll tell you why. I hate it here. I hate this house. I hate this town. I hate the school. I want to go home, and there is no way Child Services was ever going to let me out of here unless I made you want me to leave. So, yeah, I outted Jay. I fucking hate you and him. Now, if you will excuse me, I'm going out to the barn to have a smoke. Don't want to stink up your lovely home." Crystal finished sarcastically, but most of the statement was cold and nasty.

Jack Brau stood and threw his chair into the table with a hard slam. Crystal jumped at the noise. For an instant, a little fear showed through her icy features. It quickly passed. "Go on, old man. What do you think you are going to do?" she asked with a sneer.

"Well, young lady, I'm going to make your dream come true. First thing in the morning, I will call the county and have you removed from this home. And don't think for an instant they are going to place you anywhere in Riverdale. You see, I know all the foster parents in the system. I chair the protective services citizens advisory board for the county. I can pretty much guarantee you will be cooling your heels in a group home somewhere downstate for the next two years. No family will take you in after I make it known what you did here." Jack Brau's tone was matter-of-fact.

Rage showed in Crystal's face and she spat, "Fuck you!"

Jack Brau gave her a look of real concern, "I'm sorry your mother was such a horrible person. I really am. But plenty of kids grow up with a bad parent and find a way to not hate the world. Some even thrive and become good people in spite of their bad parenting. My wife and I took you and your sister in because no one else in the system would touch you. Our own fault for not realizing just how far gone you actually are. If you really did listen in our conversation, I hope you heard the last part well. You are going to end up in a gutter somewhere or maybe in a jail cell or worse yet, an early grave. Like Will Bayley, you are putting yourself on that track. A person filled with as much hate as you rarely pulls out of their nose-dive. You can still do it if you try," the old farmer said, ending with a note of hope and pity.

Crystal said nothing in reply. The rage in her eyes burned. She slipped her cigarettes out of her pocket and placed one in her mouth. She opened the door to the farmyard and walked down the steps, but instead of walking to the barn, she headed down the driveway. As she walked she lit her cigarette.

Sally Brau watched from the window in the farmhouse door. "Jack, she's walking away," she said in a defeated voice.

"Yeah, that's what I figured. I'll call the sheriffs – they'll pick her up pretty quickly. Her sister is at church group this evening – we better go get her and prepare her for her sister leaving. She's going to be upset," Jack Brau said quietly.

A few minutes after Jack Brau got off the phone with the sheriff's office, the house phone rang. Jay Brau picked it up. It was Roxy calling from the hospital.

"Freddy has a broken collarbone and some bad bruises and cuts. They think he might have a concussion as well. They are waiting for the neurosurgeon to make sure it isn't a more serious head injury, but they don't think there is a skull fracture or anything. My aunt is on duty in the ICU and they just took him in there. He is drugged up and pretty out of it. I haven't seen him. My aunt will get in trouble if you tell anyone. She swore me to secrecy. She said the hospital social worker is contacting protective services and making sure his father is picked up by the police," Roxy informed Jay.

Jay was silent.

"Are you there – is everything okay?" Roxy asked anxiously.

"Yeah… it's all right. My aunt and uncle are being really good about everything. It was Crystal, the foster kid staying here – she took my phone and uploaded the pictures and texts to a friend of hers in Riverdale. They spread it on Tumblr and Facebook." Jay's words sounded sad and far away.

"Why would she do that?" Roxy asked with disbelief.

"She hates me, and she hates it here, and she wanted out so she figured this was the best way to get my aunt and uncle to throw her out. Now she's run off, and they have the police looking for her," Jay finished distantly.

Roxy asked again whether he was coming to school in the morning, and he assured her he was.

Jay took his pain meds and fell asleep on the couch shortly afterwards. His aunt Sally covered him with an afghan. She was grateful he was resting.

The rumors floating around Bear River High School the next morning were numerous. Glenn Marcus and Jay Brau dominated the conversations. When Jay Brau arrived at school, Roxy Johnson and Amber Taylor met him at the door. Amber made a big deal about his black eye and stitched up nose. They formed a shield between Jay and everyone else although Jay was keenly aware of the stares and hushed conversations of people nearby. When the first bell rang, Jay headed to his class. No one spoke to him. Between first and second hour, he had an awkward encounter with Tiffany Short, Danny Short's cousin, the leader of the school Gay Strait Alliance. She stopped him in the hallway and invited him to come to the next meeting of the alliance Wednesday after school. Jay awkwardly declined, citing that he had football practice.

John Cale and Mike Reese were called down to Mike Shanahan's office at the end of first hour. Mike Shanahan looked pale and haggard. The events of the prior week had taken their toll. Clete Packer was in attendance as well, and he was subdued. Shanahan rambled on about school climate and creating a welcoming learning environment for all students regardless of background. Cale and Reese knew that the point of the meeting was the outing of Jay Brau, but they were not sure if Mike Shanahan knew how to bring it all together. For a while, he digressed into a story of how he was bullied as a child.

Clete Packer waited for Shanahan to wrap up his story. Then he turned to the coaches and said plainly, "We spoke with the superintendent a few minutes before the meeting. I assured him that you are both fully aware of the state's laws on bullying and that you would work to make sure that Jay Brau was accorded every protection from harassment, given the news spreading now about his sexuality. I expressed full confidence in your abilities to keep this from being either a problem for Jay or for your team and this school district. After all, this isn't thirty years ago. Gay students have no reason to fear persecution at Bear River."

The meeting was over quickly after Packer relayed the message. John Cale spoke to Mike Reese in the hallway as they returned to their classrooms "That's our first meeting with Clete in over a month that didn't end in a shouting match. I don't think we will have any problems with the boys on the team about Jay. I can't say the same for some of the parents. What do you think?"

"Well, John, I think Jay Brau is a great kid and his teammates will respect his privacy for the most part. I think Clete Packer is shell-shocked after last week, so he is being quiet out of necessity. I think Mike Shanahan should retire

227

and be tested for early onset dementia. And the one thing I know for sure is sometime soon, we will be in a meeting with at least one asshole football parent ranting about their child being forced to shower with a gay teammate. Clete Packer may think it's the 21st century in Bear River, but for a lot of people around these parts it's still 1955."

Jay Brau was nervous as the bell announcing the start of lunch rang. He wasn't sure if he could face sitting in the cafeteria with everyone staring at him and gossiping. As he walked down the hall with a bag lunch and a can of Mountain Dew in his hand, he half considered finding an open classroom to duck into. He ignored all the homecoming week decorations hanging everywhere. He shook off the urge to run and hide, and he walked into the cafeteria and sat at a table. Soccer players were congregated a few tables down. It was a large group and some stood and some sat close by at other tables. Jay felt their eyes on him. As he sat, he thought he heard the word "fag," but laughter from the table was so loud he couldn't make it out for sure. He felt his face turning red.

As Jay opened his lunch bag, Jorge Martinez sat down across from him. "Nice eye, dude, does it hurt?" Jorge asked nonchalantly.

"Unh, not really, the stitches on my nose itch though," Jay answered softly.

Wash Dryer slid into the seat next to Jorge. "So you going to be able to play this week?" he asked with concern. Maricel sat next to Wash as he asked the question. She gave Jay a sweet smile as she settled in.

"The emergency room doc said he thought I should avoid contact until the stitches are out, but if I thought I could take it, to go ahead and play," Jay answered, his voice brightened slightly.

Seth Parker and Amber Taylor sat down on Jay's right. "That's some black eye, JB," Seth Parker noted.

"Yeah, it looks worse than it feels," Jay smiled.

The soccer players were laughing and talking loudly when Liam Pickering walked into the cafeteria. He stopped at the table where the ring-leaders sat. Jorge Martinez watched the table carefully. The laughter suddenly quelled. Pickering pointed at a teammate, a student who had transferred in at the start of the school year. Jorge had trouble making out what Pickering said. It ended with, "You're an asshole. Knock it off."

Liam Pickering walked to the football players' table and stood next to Wash Dryer. "Man, JB – they said you took a hell of a shot, but that looks pretty bad. You gonna be okay?" Pickering asked. Jay assured him he was fine. Jorge Martinez nodded at Liam. He nodded back, and he walked on.

Roxy Johnson came to the table and stood quietly behind Jorge Martinez. She felt pride for her friends. She placed a hand on both Jorge and Wash's shoulders. Wash turned slightly and gave her a small smile. She caught Jay's eye. Nothing was said. Roxy was sure she saw something that looked like relief in his expression.

Morg Miller dragged a chair to the end of the table at sat down heavily. Jay Brau was talking to Seth but he sensed Morg staring at him. He paused and turned to look at Morg whose chin rested in the palm of his right hand, his right elbow on the table. He was glancing up and down at Jay's face. He was silent. Finally, Jay raised eyebrows at Morg and jiggled his head slightly and asked. "Yeah?"

Morg Miller picked his head up off his right hand and smiled as he said, "Jesus, Jay, you look like Frankenweenie!"

There was a slight pause. Jay Brau began to shake and giggle. The giggle turned into a full laugh, and his teammates joined him. Amber Taylor let out a squeal as her laughter pierced the lower rumble of the football players. Roxy Johnson playfully yelled scolding, "Morgan!" as she joined the laughter. Jorge Martinez banged on the table as the laughter took over his full being.

The laughter died down. Jay Brau wiped his eyes with a napkin. He looked Morg right in the eyes. In a perfect mimic of his friend's voice he loudly stated, "You look like Frankenweenie!" Again the laughter rang out. Two tables away, the members of the soccer team fell silent. A few of them got up and walked away. The rest ate their lunch quietly as more rounds of laughter came from the football players.

Monday's football practice started with a film session in Coach Cale's classroom. Cale started the meeting with a talk about remaining focused during homecoming week. There was a brief statement about Glenn Marcus and making bad choices. The players were informed of adjustments in playing assignments to cover for the absence of Glenn for the remainder of the season. They watched the scouting film of the Pompeii Central Pumas. The Pumas looked fast but not very big. Coach Reese spent most of the film stopping and rerunning their read option offense. The Puma quarterback wasn't much of a thrower but he was fast and he carried out his fakes very well. Their tailback was much slower. He fumbled several times. Morg Miller called him a dumb-ass butterfingers after the fourth time he fumbled on film. Everyone laughed and other boys made similar comments.

The film ended and the lights came on. Coach Cale quieted the boys down. "Well, Morg, number 23 does have butterfingers, but we won't see much of him on Friday. They brought him up from the JV for the last month while Jake Herrick sat out his suspension. Herrick will be back in their lineup this week starting at tailback and middle linebacker on defense." Cale relayed the bad news. The smiles turned to frowns quickly. Seth Parker moaned and let loose with a curse word, which got him a stern look from Coach Reese.

"Yep, boys, the roider is back!" Morg Miller called out loudly. Over the last two years Morg had lost many wrestling matches to Jake Herrick. Both wrestled at 215 pounds. Short and pudgy Morg looked like a little boy wrestling with a full-grown man each time. In the dozen or so matches they wrestled, Morg was pinned each time – usually within a minute of the start.

Herrick stood six-foot-two-inches and played football at 235 pounds. He cut down to 215 for wrestling. The result was a chiseled-out-of-granite body that was like something from a weightlifting video. Herrick was incredibly fast and powerful. As a junior he had been all-state in football, state champion at 215 pounds in wrestling and he had finished second in both the 100- and 200-meter dashes in the state championship track meet. When he lost the 200-meter race, he went into a rage on the track and threw some hurdles across the infield. The Pumas lost the state track meet by one point, the point the team lost as a penalty for Herrick's unsportsmanlike conduct.

Every athlete in the area was in awe of Jake Herrick. Most talked about how he was a steroid- and HGH-user. The rumors were unfounded. Off the field, Jake Herrick was quiet and a very good mechanic. He rebuilt old cars with his grandfather. On the field, he was a holy terror – an angry shouting menace. He had numerous scholarship offers from major college football programs to play linebacker. He envisioned being a tailback, and so he accepted an offer from Iowa State to play in their offensive backfield. When he was suspended from school and the football team early in the season, rumors flew about how he was going to lose his scholarship. He hadn't lost it yet, but the Iowa State staff was watching him closely.

Seth Parker had bad memories of Jake Herrick. Last season, Herrick sacked him seven times, and the Bears lost the game to Pompeii Central by fifty points. When they were freshman in a JV game at Pompeii, Herrick hit Seth so hard as he was running out of bounds that Seth flew all the way across the bench and onto the track. Seth's mother screamed, "They're killing my baby!" from the stands and passed out. The EMT's had to take her out on a stretcher when smelling salts didn't bring her around.

"Just what in the heck did Herrick do to get suspended for a month?" Seth Parker asked with a mix of disgust and fear.

"I know. Can I tell them, Coach?" Morg Miller asked with pride.

"Go ahead Morg, but make it quick. We got to get on the field." Coach Cale gave permission.

"So like, you know how it's been like real quiet about what happened. But my cousin goes to Pompeii, and she told me everything on Saturday when we were at her house for my grandma's birthday dinner. She knows Jake pretty well. In fact, she and her boyfriend went to their prom with Herrick and his date last spring," Morg began excitedly.

"Is she hot?" Greg DeVito chimed in.

"Huh?" Morg asked with irritation.

"Is your cousin hot?" Greg asked with a mocking laugh.

"How the hell should I know? She's my freakin' cousin. In my family we don't go to reunions to pick up chicks like your family does." Morg answered in the same mocking tone. The team burst out in laughter. Even Coach Cale and Coach Reese laughed.

"Wrap it up, Morg," Cale said when he finished laughing.

"Anyway," Morg began again, "Herrick rebuilds old cars with his grandpa. The old man is like famous for his muscle-car rebuilds. I guess he even sold one to Jay Leno like twenty years ago. The grandpa found an old 1971 Chevelle SS convertible on the web when Jake was a freshman. It was a basket case, ya know, but like, those old Chevelles restored are worth the bucks. The old man tells Jake he will buy the car and they will rebuild it together and then Jake can sell it or keep it if he wants." Morg rolled on in his story. The room was quiet. Most of the boys were at least mildly interested in hot cars, and Morg was an enthusiastic story teller.

"They take two years to rebuild this car. Jake worked in the shop for free to offset the cost of the parts. Total restoration – frame off. Full body strip and metal work on the rust, not just Bondo. They put in all new glass. All the chrome gets redone. They end up painting it red. Like a ten-grand paint job. New white leather upholstery and white top. Jake's dad bought him a kick-ass sound system for it for Christmas last year. The grandpa buys this monster 454 crate motor to put in it 'cuz the original motor is shot anyway. They spend huge money on custom rims and top-of-the-line tires. This thing is like beyond cherry when they get done with it this last June. Before Jake gets the keys, the old man puts it on a trailer and takes it to a car show in Indiana. Some guy there offered him sixty grand for it, but he says no 'cuz he built it with his grandson; it's his car." The serious car guys in the room were moaning and whistling at Morg's breathless description of the car.

"Jake loves this car, man. Polishes it with a cloth diaper before and after every drive and he only drives it on days with perfect weather – Jake's got a Dodge pickup he drives most days. And all summer long, this guy from the car show in Indiana keeps calling jacking up his offer for the car. By late August, he's up to seventy-six grand. Now Jake is like thinking about it. He knows he's got a football scholarship, but going to college with a pocket full of cash is better than going there broke like everyone else. He starts telling everyone when he signs a pro contract in a few years he'll have his grandpa build him something even better. Just after Labor Day, the guy from Indiana calls and offers seventy-nine grand. Jake tells his grandpa to say yes but only if Jake can keep it for another few weeks while the weather is still nice. The guy agrees to the terms and sends Jake a check for five grand in earnest money." Morg's eyes flashed when he talked about the money. He was as impressed as his audience was.

"A month ago on the Saturday after the second game of the year, Jake takes his baby out for what he figures is his last drive with her. He stops at the Meijer grocery store up in Mt. Pleasant to pick up some stuff for his mother. He parks the Chevelle all the way across the parking lot from the front of the store. There isn't another car parked within 100 feet of it. And he dashes to the store. He figures it will take him ten minutes tops to get this stuff," Morg continues

"Oh, oh, oh! Man I remember this! That was Jake's car?" Greg DeVito interrupted again.

"Shut up, man, let him finish!" Seth Parker yelled.

Morg ignored them both and pressed on. "Jake gets in the store and Pete the Pigskin writer is in there shopping with his wife and he gets ahold of Jake and starts interviewing him about the game the night before and why Jake didn't sign with MSU to play linebacker. It ends up taking Jake forty-five minutes to get out of Meijer and as he comes out the front door he looks across the parking lot. There is a bunch of emergency vehicles with lights flashing near where his car is. He sprints like a mad man across the lot. Drops his bags. He hears a dog barking and whining. And something that sounds like an old woman screaming. Smoke is rising up from the middle of the street in front of the store. He looks and it's his Chevelle burning. It's crushed up under an oil rig service truck in the middle of Pickerd Avenue and it's on fire. Fireman are hosing it down but the car is totaled." Everyone in the room groaned at the demise of the perfect muscle car.

"So Jake is yelling like a crazy man. Screaming about what happened. He sees cops talking to an old man standing next to a beat-up rusty Ford pick-up from like the 1960s. The old man has a gauze pad pressed to his forehead, and it's soaked with blood. Jake realizes the truck is sitting almost exactly where his car had been. The front of the truck is smashed in and steam is rising off the flattened radiator. An EMT has the passenger-side door open and a really fat old woman is in the seat screaming about her legs being broken and her nose is gushing blood. There's this raggedly-looking mutt of a dog barking and whining and dragging a badly broken front leg, running around the wrecked truck with a couple of state troopers trying to catch it. It's just chaos, man, and Jake is running and yelling so a couple of sheriff deputies grab ahold of him. What Jake doesn't know is the old man pulled up to the front of the Meijer to get out and grab a prescription for his wife who is so old and fat she is like a cripple. He leaves the truck running and gets out. Their dog jumped up on the steering wheel and his paw slipped down and popped the truck in gear. Apparently, the idle was set real high, and so this truck takes off like a shot with the old woman screaming and the dog barking. The old man turns and runs after the truck, but no chance he's going to catch it. He trips and falls and cuts the hell out of his scalp as the truck bashes a cart corral to hell and shoots across the open lot to the Chevelle. Hits it going at least forty. The Chevelle vaults over the grass median in front of it and into the traffic on Pickerd Avenue. A Sodus Brothers Oil Rig Service truck plows into it going fifty. You know those big frigging green trucks you see up in Mount Pile all the time? Boom – that's all she wrote for the Chevelle." Groans and laughs at the chaos described filled the room.

Morg drew a dramatic breath and continued, "This is where it really gets bad for Jake."

"Did the cops tase him? They tased his ass didn't they?" Greg DeVito interrupted yet again.

Morg ignored Greg and continued. "So Jake is all fired up and these two deputies are trying to get him to calm down and he yells at the old man 'What did you do to my car?!' and the old man shakes his head and says 'I only got out for a second and the truck was running. It's hard to start so I left it running – and the dog must of jumped up and—' and Jake starts to go ape."

Seth Parker was really into the story and he shouted, "Morg, just tell us what happened, for frig sake!"

"I'm getting to it." Morg answered. He continued, "So Jake starts shouting 'Your dog!? Your dog? What the freak do you mean, your dog?!'" Morg looked at the coaches and said, "Only Jake didn't say 'freak.' He dropped a big ole F bomb. Just as the state troopers finally caught the dog and it bit one of them. I guess they had to put it down and test it for rabies or something later"

John Cale was exasperated. "Morgan, we really need to get to the field! Let's wrap it up!"

"Anyway," Morg started again building to his climactic finish, "Jake is screaming 'YOUR DOG!' over and over again and he breaks loose of the deputies and he grabs the old man by the collar and pins him up against the pickup truck. Then the cops swarm on him, but they can't get him to let the old guy go. One of the deputies smashes Jake in the head with his night stick. Jake drops the old man and spins around to go after whoever just whacked him. Man, I could have told them just smacking Jake in the head with a stick ain't gonna do anything but piss him off –and—" Morg stopped and wheeled to look at Greg DeVito and with a dramatic finger jab toward his teammate he announced, "That's when they tased his ass!"

Laughter raised the ceiling of the classroom and even Jay Brau was howling. In the back of the room, Thing One and Thing Two laughed along. They looked at each other as only twins can and a whole conversation took place with a single glance. The twinkle in their eyes spoke volumes. Friday night couldn't come soon enough for them.

As the team exited the room, Seth Parker, still disappointed that Jake Herrick would be chasing him down yet again this Friday night, asked loudly, "I don't get it – how come he only got a month suspension? They should have ended his season. Assaulting cops and an old guy? How does he get off the hook for that?"

Morg was walking next to Seth as they ambled down the hall to the locker room. "Yeah, well, Jake's dad is the president of the Pompeii School Board. Guess he cut some sort of deal to get Jake enrolled in an anger management program. He even begged Iowa State not to take his scholarship away. Jake is on probation for the rest of the school year – if he so much as gets a penalty flag for a personal foul, he is all done for the season – wrestling and track too. If that happens, then he can kiss that scholarship goodbye," Morg informed his quarterback.

It seemed as if the entire town of Bear River was packed into the Episcopal Church located down the block from the high school shortly after noon on Tuesday. The schools were closed at lunchtime. All the district employees were at the funeral. Bright sunshine poured into the church intermittingly as the cloud cover broke during what was yet another blustery fall day in mid-Michigan.

Mike Reese and his wife sat with the Colbys in the front pew. A closed casket was situated at the front of the altar. John Cale sat a few pews back with his pregnant wife and their two small sons. Sue Irwin and her partner sat next to the Cales. Jorge Martinez sat with his mother in the same pew with Wash Dryer and his mom. Both boys wore dark suits. Every varsity football player was in attendance.

Bea Colby knew everyone in town. No one had an unkind word for her alive or dead. That was the gist of the minister's brief sermon. Chet Colby's voice quivered only once or twice as he gave a eulogy for the love of his life and mother of his boys. Cheese Colby held his younger brother tight as Gump cried quietly in the front pew. Agnes Johns spoke briefly telling of her long friendship with Bea and of her friend's love of children.

When Mike Reese spoke, he started with a gentle joke about how horrible at golf Bea Colby was. Then he told about the time she accidentally hit a hole in one at the staff end-of-school-year outing a few years back and the comical, all-night drinking celebration they had after her stroke of blind luck. The laughter from the gathered mourners sparkled and lifted everybody's spirits. Even Gump Colby laughed when Coach Reese talked about how Bea spent a whole paycheck on having the ball mounted in a presentation case that sat next to her desk in the Bear River elementary school office.

After the laughter died down, Mike Reese continued, "You know, in thirty-nine years as a teacher I have never met a school secretary that wasn't great at the job. It just isn't the sort of job that allows for incompetence. That isn't true for everyone who works at a school. If you are at this business for any length of time, you realize that a teacher can be out sick or at a conference, and the school day is pretty much the same. Heck, administrators can be out of the building for weeks and some people might not even notice. But if the school secretary takes an extra-long lunch to run to town to do some banking, it takes about five minutes for the school to fall into total chaos." Mike smiled as his line brought knowing and appreciative laughter from the teachers in the audience. Clete Packer sat five pews back and frowned. Sheldon Knapp was sitting a pew behind – he laughed, but no humor showed in his eyes. Mike Shanahan sat next to Knapp looking at his watch absent-mindedly.

Mike Reese changed his tone as he concluded, "Bea Colby was my friend. She helped me through difficult personal times. She was the best babysitter for my boys I could have ever wished for, and both send their condolences. They teach and coach a hundred miles apart in Florida. Sean, my eldest, said Bea was the best teacher he ever had. I pointed out that Bea was a school

234

secretary not a classroom teacher. And he said, 'Dad, I'm not talking classrooms and curriculum. I'm talking about really teaching children the most important things in life, like taking care of yourself and being mindful of others. Mrs. Colby taught every kid she ever interacted with. She taught her lessons with love and respect. I only wish I could do as well.'" Mike Reese paused and watched Agnes Johns and Mary Pierce vigorously nod in agreement. He shifted his gaze to the casket holding the remains of his longtime friend. "So long Bea. Thank you for the lessons you lovingly taught us all."

Most of the congregation paused to dab their eyes when Mike Reese finished. Soaring piano music began to ring out. Maddy Long, the church pianist for over thirty years, played the opening chords of Dvorak's Largo from his New World Symphony. John Cale was struck by the beauty of the music, though he did not recognize it. Classical music and religion were not Cale's long suits. Cale felt out of place in the church. Other than weddings and funerals, he had not been to church since he was young. One summer afternoon shortly after he turned eleven, John played hooky from vacation Bible school at the church where his mother attended services every Christmas and Easter, towing her children along freshly scrubbed and clothed in their best. When Johnny showed up several hours late having spent the day fishing for brook trout with some friends his mother was very cross, and she was in mid-rant about the sin of disrespect when his no-nonsense father interrupted, "Look, the boy doesn't get anything out of it so he took off. You only go to church twice a year – what's the big deal? Leave him alone." John Cale never went for religious study again. His mother gave up the pretense of holy day attendance not long after. When asked about matters of faith, he simply stated he did not participate. He found teaching in a small town wearing the label of Atheist was too much of a hassle.

As if from nowhere, Maddy Long's grandson, Phillip, appeared at her side at the piano. John Cale was puzzled but then Phil Long – the laziest and most difficult-to-motivate athlete John had ever coached, an athlete John had largely given up on and barely even noticed any longer – began to sing:

Going home, going home,
I'm a going home.
Quiet-like, some still day,
I'm just going home.
It's not far, just close by,
Through an open door.
Work all done, care laid by,
Going to fear no more.
Mother's there, expecting me,
Father's waiting too.
Lots of folk gathered there,
All the friends I knew.

Cale marveled at how Phil Long's rich baritone voice blended with the music his grandmother played. As he sang the verses of the spiritual set to classical music, Phil would sometimes tip his head toward his grandmother and her eyes met his. They didn't smile but their faces shone brightly. The look they shared was one of harmony and peace. John Cale was moved. Not by a religious epiphany, but rather by the lessons his friend Mike Reese had reminded the congregated that were the lessons of Bea Anderson Colby's life.

After the well-attended graveside service marked by dazzling shafts of sunshine bursting through gray cloud cover as the final invocation was given, John Cale sought out Phil Long. He walked next to the lumbering fat boy as they walked down from the only beautiful hill in the area. "Phil, I just want you to know that your singing today was absolutely great. What a special thing it must be for you to have that connection with your grandmother. It was just wonderful to watch." John Cale said with quiet sincerity.

Phil looked up at Cale with a shy smile and replied, "Thanks, Coach."

They walked on with the throng to the flat ground. They made small talk about homecoming week and the upcoming game. As they parted, John Cale shook Phil Long's hand. Cale settled into the rear seat of Sue Irwin's SUV. He had sent his wife and kids home after the church service. The boys were getting antsy.

Sue Irwin and her companion settled in the front seat, but before she buckled in, Sue turned to John and in her gravelly voiced tinged with emotion exclaimed, "What a beautiful service! Can you believe the way the sun broke through at the end? Bea was smiling down at us telling us everything is going to be all right. And oh how that Phillip Long sang! Such beauty!"

John Cale gave Sue a sweet smile and agreed, "Yes. Yes he sang wonderfully." Cale felt pride for his young student athlete. He didn't bother to refute the presence of the spirit of the deceased. Charming and comforting as such belief must be for the faithful, Cale's lack of faith was not changed by meteorological happenstance. He was pleased, however, to acknowledge to himself that Bea Colby's examples could still be learned from and the lessons she taught about engaging all children equally were of great value even though she was gone forever.

Coach Cale and Coach Reese only had to wait until after practice on Wednesday afternoon for Reese's prediction to come true that they would be visited by an asshole parent complaining about a gay player on the football team. Rodney Rosa was waiting outside the coaches' office in the locker room.

Cale had been in good mood all through practice. Jay Brau had returned to the field and showed no signs that his nose injury was impairing his play, and Seth Parker was very sharp all through practice as well. Phil Long almost approximated something like hustle during the workout. He jumped on a Jay Brau fumble during the scrimmage at the end of practice, and, as he stood, he flipped the ball to Jay and said, "Here, JB, you might want to take this with you next time." Everyone on the field laughed. Phil Long beamed with pride at the response he got, and for the first time in his unwanted football career he felt a connection with the team. With all that, as soon as Cale saw Dave Rosa's father standing by the office door, he knew his good mood was about to be spoiled.

Rodney Rosa owned a carpet-cleaning business and a small storage facility south of Bear River. He was overweight with a large stomach hanging over spindly legs. He was balding and had a poorly trimmed graying mustache. Under his weak chin was a huge fat deposit circling his neck like a reversed life preserver. It looked as though his head was floating on a pillow of fat. He wore a cheap blue blazer and gray polyester slacks with frayed cuffs. His olive drab shirt matched neither his jacket nor his pants. His red tie had a recent soup stain below a silver cross tie tack. His American flag lapel pin was twice the size of any John Cale had ever seen before. Rodney Rosa had been a lay preacher at a church housed in an old warehouse situated between the towns of Bear River and Gratiot for several years, and five years prior he had gained some local notoriety by becoming a vocal leader of the county Tea Party. Recently Rosa bragged to all that he was going to make sure that Donald Trump was victorious in mid-Michigan and the rest of the state in the upcoming November election. But in the primary season he was a vocal Ted Cruz supporter who gave quotes to the Mt. Pleasant paper on how a goofy game show host had no business being the GOP nominee for president.

"Coach, I need to talk with you about something very important!" Rodney Rosa announced urgently in a voice both hoarse and nasally. John Cale was carrying a bag of equipment, and he set it down. Anticipating the topic, he stuck out his hand and greeted the insistent visitor. "Mr. Rosa, our door is always open to any parent with a concern. Can you please wait until Coach Reese and I handle some business with the boys and then we will be more than happy to sit with you in the office." Rosa took his hand and shook it firmly.

"Coach, I have a busy schedule this afternoon and church council dinner meeting – I don't have a great deal of time," Rosa answered with irritation showing in his small dark eyes.

"This will only take a few minutes while we square away some gear and pass out some scouting films," Cale answered politely. On cue Mike Reese entered the locker room from the hall door carrying a small box filled with game film DVDs. He assessed the situation at a glance. He nodded a greeting to the visitor "Rod, how are you?" Reese used the name by which Rosa was known as a high school student twenty-five years prior. He then ignored the stout and irritated visitor as he began to shout out names of players and passing out the videos.

True to Cale's word, fifteen minutes later he was sitting at his desk with Rodney Rosa in a chair across from him. Mike Reese was sitting at a stool in front of his locker. Even though the conversation had not yet begun, there was tension in the room and Rosa's ridiculously fat neck was sweating and bright red. "I'm gonna get right to the point here, Coach. I understand that this Jay Brau boy is a homosexual. Are you gonna dismiss him from the team?" Rosa elongated the word "homosexual" with disgust.

"Jay Brau's private life is exactly that, private. There is no reason to dismiss him from the team. That would constitute harassment, and it would potentially put this school district in legal hot water. But that doesn't even matter. Jay Brau is a valued member of this team, and he is a fine example of a student athlete. I have always been proud to be his coach and nothing recently has changed that." John Cale struggled to hold his temper in the face of such blatant ignorance.

"Don't give me none of that PC liberal crap! I'm not gonna stand by quietly as they push their gay agenda into this community and into our schools! Kids' wellbeing is at stake here! I don't want this faaa – ho mo sexual – showering with my boy! It's disgusting! He's made his choice to lie with boys – that makes him ineligible to be on this team with decent Christian boys like my son, as far as I'm concerned!" The red showing in the fat above Rosa's collar swept up through his face and spittle sprayed as he shouted.

John Cale felt his anger rising with the bile in his throat. He was formulating a response when Mike Reese rose to his feet. "Who the hell are 'they', Rod? What agenda are you talking about? We are talking about a young man who has had his private life invaded! We are obligated to protect him from harassment in this school and on this team. It's the law. That includes shielding him from assholes like you sticking their noses in where it doesn't belong!" Reese had both ice and disgust in his voice as he addressed the meddlesome parent.

Rodney Rosa rose to his feet and pointed at Mike Reese. "You will address me as Mr. Rosa – I pay your goddamned salary with my taxes! You know full well who they are! Liberal faggots and dykes riding the coat-tails of that illegitimate Kenyan in the White House! Well, the American people have had enough! Things are gonna be changing soon! Don't you dare quote me laws about harassment and bullying! I'll tell you who's getting bullied – good God-fearing Christians who made this country great, that's who! We are taking this country back, you understand, we ain't gonna put up with this liberal shit anymore. First thing we're gonna do is get this country back to its Constitutional roots! The Founding Fathers gave us a beautiful gift that you frigging liberal commies have poisoned with your Godless education and indoctrination schools and your liberal activist judges! After the Tea Party cleans up Lansing and after we run that – gentleman – out of the White House we are gonna empty out this cesspool you call public schools! You're all a bunch of bleeding heart tree-huggers and union thugs stealing away our tax dollars and poisoning our kids' minds!" Rosa's voice was shrill and loud as he raged through his threats.

John Cale imagined the obese man was close to having a heart attack. He briefly considered that if that if Rosa did stroke out, he and Reese wouldn't administer CPR even though an AED device was in a case in the hall between the locker room and the gym.

Reese was incensed and his vengeful reply was cutting to the bone "Rod, thirty years ago you struggled to get a C- in my freshman civics class! I can see nothing has changed. You're still a pig-eyed willfully ignorant sack of racist shit. Don't talk to me about the Constitution! I've taught it for thirty-nine years. I have a master's degree in history and a master's in education. You bombed out of community college half way through your first semester and married a girl whose dad had enough money to buy you a business even a dullard like yourself couldn't screw up so his little girl wouldn't spend her married life on welfare. Tea Party my ass! You're nothing but a hate-spouting small-town redneck bully. Now get the hell out of this office before I throw you out!"

Rodney Rosa's mouth opened and closed several times. Pure rage read in his face, but no words came to him. He started to turn and go, but John Cale couldn't resist getting in one more shot. In for a penny in for a pound. "One last thing Mr. Rosa," John Cale mustered something of a solicitous tone. The angered parent paused and looked at Cale in confusion and fury. "You mentioned Jay Brau chose to not be a heterosexual. Just when did you make your decision about who to be attracted to? Do you actually recall someone asking you; 'Do like girls or do you want to suck dicks?'" Cale asked mockingly.

Rodney Rosa was thoroughly overmatched. He wasn't even smart enough to leave while the getting was good. He narrowed his eyes and looked back and forth between the two coaches. Words finally came to him, "Fuck the both of ya!"

"Oh, I see," John Cale said knowingly, "You still haven't made up your mind. Well I think I can speak for Coach Reese in saying we really can't help you out there. But if you were to go online and search the right websites I'm sure you could find a fat middle-aged man like yourself to help you experiment so you can make your final choice. Good luck in your search."

Rodney Rosa growled something unintelligible and slammed the office door as he stormed out of the meeting.

"He's not through. Not by a long shot," John Cale said fatefully.

"To hell with him. He'll likely storm off to Pam Kitteridge. They went to school together. Pam's a grade A bitch, but she isn't stupid. As board prez, she went through the same stuff we did on bullying. Let her deal with Rod. She'll holler at Clete to holler at us for being rude to a parent. Like we haven't had him on our ass all season. Big deal. Rod's gonna make his son quit, though, just watch," Mike Reese offered his disgusted response.

Mike Reese began to laugh, real gusts of laughter. John Cale was puzzled as he looked at his assistant. Reese paused and looked at Cale with a twinkle in his eye. "Do you like girls or do you want to suck dicks!? Man that was beautiful! If I hadn't been so pissed off, I would have been on the ground laughing!" Reese wiped his eyes with a towel as he spoke.

"Yeah, well, that was kind of unprofessional, but I was pretty pissed myself and it was either belittle him or kick his ass, so—" Cale blushed. Reese renewed his laughter.

When the assistant's laughter died down, Cale asked him sincerely, "Do you know many homosexuals?"

Reese paused. "A few, I guess. There's Sue Irwin, of course. My ex's first cousin, they grew up together. They were closer than brother and sister. He played cello for the Detroit Symphony. Great guy – big sports fan. He had season tickets to the Tigers and Red Wings. I used to road-trip down there all the time and we'd go to games and then go out and get drunk. We went to a Series game in '84. Man, could he drink. He died of AIDS in '91. I think losing him is why my ex started aching to get out and see the world. And she didn't want me or the boys to follow, I guess." Reese was quiet for a few seconds after he made his final observation. He brightened, "How about you?"

Cale shrugged as he started to speak. "Yeah, one of my roommates in college. Tony is his name. He played offensive tackle. Huge. Not tall but really thick and strong as an ox. Hairy as hell – he looked like a walking carpet. A freakin' short Wookie, ya know? Funny too. Jesus, he was always running his mouth. Drove the coaches nuts. He wrecked his knee when we were juniors. Started dating one of the physical therapists rehabbing his knee – a guy. They live in Louisiana now. Got a couple of kids they adopted. Tony was a groomsman at my wedding. We still talk online and swap Christmas cards, still one of the funniest guys I ever met, but I haven't seen him a few years. He and his partner run a dating website for big hairy gay men. Kind of a hobby thing but they make some money."

"No shit?" Reese asked casually.

"Yeah, I guess that's a thing," Cale responded. The two men collected their personal gear and left the office.

Dave Rosa turned in his jerseys, pads and helmet at the start of practice on Thursday. John Cale talked to him in the coaches' office. Cale decided not to press the issue. He could see the young man was despondent and embarrassed by his father's actions. Dave started to cry when he tried to explain that his dad was making him quit and that he personally had nothing against Jay Brau. Cale consoled him telling Dave everything was going to be okay. Wash Dryer put away the equipment when Cale told him to without asking why. Everyone on the team already knew what was up. It was all the varsity team talked about during the day with each other. Everyone agreed the situation sucked and that Rodney Rosa was an asshole.

The JV game was played at Pompeii Central. The weather was awful. Rain mixed with snow fell for most of the game. The Bears lost 24 to 0. Late in the third quarter, the Bears were flagged for too many men on the field. Mike Reese asked the referee for a conference to talk about the call. The referee refused, so Reese called a time-out and talked to the young man in the white hat standing near midfield. Reese noted that the scruffy, bearded ref was very young for a crew chief even in a JV game, Rather than yell at the kid, he decided to take a different tack. The young ref had a very cross look on his face. "Coach, see to your team. There is nothing to discuss," the young ref said officiously.

Mike Reese felt his anger rise, but he held it in check. He began calmly, "Mr. Referee, can you count? Because I can. I just counted to two. That's how many players I have on my bench. Both with their helmets off. One has an ice bag on his ankle. The other has been throwing up since the end of the first quarter. So unless a Puma player snuck out and found one of our uniforms to wear there are only eleven Bears on the field because we only dressed thirteen tonight."

"Coach! I am giving you one last warning! See to your team! The call stands!" The young man's voice cracked a little as he shouted at Reese who maintained an amused but forced smile.

"Look, I have coached more games than you have seen in your entire life. You've made a mistake. It's okay to reverse it. No one is going to evaluate you down at the end of the season on the referee review sheets if you correct your mistakes. I'll talk to the Pompeii coaches so they won't ding you, and you'll keep your white hat for next season and the bigger paycheck," Reese said but could not keep the condescension from his tone.

The yellow flag hit Reese in the leg. "ONE MORE WORD COACH AND I WILL THROW YOU OUT OF THIS GAME! NOW GET OFF THIS FIELD!"

Reese casually sauntered back to the bench and placed the headset back on his head. "Damn it, Mike, don't get thrown out of the game. Not after all the shit we had last week," John Cale urged plaintively from his post in the press box.

Later on the bus ride home, Cheese Colby sat next to Reese. Colby had been quiet most of the night, but he managed to get through his coaching duties despite his lingering grief. "Coach, did you know that the referee was Greg Miles? Remember he wrestled for Riverdale? He was a senior when I was a sophomore."

"That was Miles? The name didn't register when we shook hands at the beginning, and I didn't recognize him with that fuzzy beard. I guess that explains why he was so pissy with me tonight," Reese laughed.

"What are you two talking about?" John Cale asked from the seat in front of his two assistants.

"Kind of a funny story, John, the ref for tonight's game used to wrestle for Riverdale. Greg Miles. Pretty damn good wrestler. Three years ago when Cheese was a sophomore I bumped him up at the league tournament into Mile's weight class. Cheese upset him in the finals and Miles was going for his fourth consecutive league individual title. I have had a handful of four-time league champs – Cheese was one. Riverdale has never had a four-time champ. Miles tore apart the locker room after Cheese beat him in overtime. He punched a locker and broke his hand. Missed the state tournament. Could have been a state medal winner. Too damn young to be a white hat. Even for JV's. Must have been filling in for someone," Reese said with amused irony.

John Cale responded, "Man, there isn't a coach or ref in ten counties you haven't had pissed at you for something or another."

"Seems that way sometimes, don't it," Reese replied.

The varsity football team wore their game jerseys as they sat on The Tank tossing bubble gum and jaw breakers to little kids as it rolled through the streets of town in the homecoming parade. Morg Miller's dad was driving – and honking the horn at the few people braving the cold winds to watch the parade. Morg and Junior Shultz had painted the old GMC flatbed red and white with poster paint for the occasion. The team sat on two large round hay bales that George Miller had loaded on the flatbed with his forklift. The truck had started life as a stake truck with a dump bed forty years prior. The stakes were long gone. The Tank was held together with baling wire and spot welds. It looked right at home in the pathetic procession.

Behind The Tank, the Bear River marching band – twenty-two strong for homecoming, not including the flag twirlers, stumbled through repeated playing of the school fight song. Behind the band a half dozen convertibles held the homecoming court. The lead car held Liam Pickering the odds-on favorite to be named homecoming king. With him was Roxanne Johnson – dressed in a very nice gown befitting her courtly status. Roxy smiled and waved enthusiastically as she tossed candy at the handful of elementary-aged kids standing on the corners. Liam was hunched down complaining bitterly about the cold wind as the sun was setting. Roxy grinned sweetly and said, "Quit whining you big baby, At least it isn't raining. Now toss some candy and smile."

A couple of cars back the only football player in the homecoming court, Seth Parker, rode with his girlfriend, Amber Taylor. They were cheerful and smiling and enjoying the experience. Amber even talked about what song they would dance to at the homecoming dance on Saturday night when they were presented as homecoming king and queen. In her mind, logic dictated that the quarterback of the football team would naturally win homecoming king, and being his girlfriend, she should win queen by default. It was a pleasant if unrealistic thought.

Thing One and Thing Two each tore a handful of hay from the large bale they were sitting on. The hay was damp so it clumped up nicely when they made balls of it to throw at the little kids waiting for candy. "Knock it off, you two. I got to deliver these bales to my little cousins tomorrow afternoon. Their step-dad just bought them a horse to ride around their farm. He'll bitch at me if the bales are all torn to shit." Morg Miller scolded the two happy-go-lucky psychopaths. Normally, scolding the Things was a dangerous proposition, but when they wheeled to toss hay at Morg, Jorge Martinez was sitting next to him on the other bale. Jorge arched his eyebrow at them. The Things smiled and shrugged and dropped the hay.

Mike Reese stood next to John Cale. They had their backs to the cab of "The Tank" standing on the flat-bed. They waved mechanically to some of the little kids and the put-upon parents that escorted them. Reese knew that without the handfuls of candy being tossed, there would be virtually no one to watch the parade. It wasn't that way a generation ago when he was a young coach. Homecoming was a big deal in Bear River then. Each high school class sponsored a float for the parade. All the churches in town had floats as well. The stores downtown had painted windows decorated for the occasion by the middle school classes who competed for a $500 prize sponsored by the Chamber of Commerce given to the class with best window design. There was a huge community bonfire on the night before the game. Fireworks were shot off.

Reese could remember when the homecoming pep rally was a big event taking up the entire afternoon of the day of the game – not the lackluster twenty minutes of the present day featuring an anemic playing of the school fight song by the marching band during which no one sang because the kids never bothered to learn the words. That was followed by a few weak cheers from the mostly disorganized cheer team. The homecoming court sat quietly in chairs at mid-court in the gym as they were introduced – a few catcalls from their friends in the audience made them blush. Someone yelled "BUTTERFACE!" when Roxanne Johnson was introduced, and most of the senior girls booed the heckler and then pointed out the culprit – who was escorted from the gym by Principal Shanahan. The fact that the principal did anything at all shocked the teachers, most of whom were leaning on the gym wall near the entrance.

When John Cale introduced the players on the team, some of the potheads in the crowd began chanting, "We want Manikowski!" they cheered for their lost drug connection and former football player. Laughter broke out in the crowd and the cheering for Manikowski increased. Clete Packer turned beet red as he charged into the bleachers in search of some of his usual suspects. He then escorted three of them out of the gym. The bell for the end of the school day rang before Cale was done announcing all the players' names as he called them to join him on the gym floor. The vast majority of the kids got to their feet and filed out the gym doors even as Cale finished, and the band made another attempt at playing the fight song. The whole affair was pitiful, and it soured Mike Reese's stomach.

Reese knew why the homecoming traditions were falling to the way-side. The local economy tanked with closing of the chemical plant and the refinery in Gratiot. The jobs went away. The downtown stores went bankrupt or were closed when the owners died. The city Chamber of Commerce, or what was left of it, got absorbed into the country chamber. Class prizes disappeared. The varsity football team became mired in yearly failure. Clueless school leadership let the traditions fail – they didn't fight to keep any of it going. Homecoming became a shadow of its former small-town spectacle. There was a rumor floating around town that Pam Kitteridge, the school board president, not only wanted to make a soccer game the focal point of homecoming week but that she wanted to eliminate the football program as an embarrassment to the school and the community. Reese felt fury rise whenever he allowed himself to think about a Homecoming soccer game.

The homecoming parade ended about forty-five minutes before kickoff. The Bears rushed through their pregame routine. As they warmed up, Wash Dryer scanned the biggest home crowd of the varsity football season. More than 200 people, he estimated. He found Maricel sitting next to his mother. Both of them were bundled up in winter coats because of the harsh wind blowing from the northwest. Over the last few weeks, his girlfriend became great friends with his mother. The situation made Wash both sort of proud but also embarrassed. Maricel was sweet and funny, and Laney Dryer was becoming very fond of her. The fact Wash and Maricel had also recently started a very physical connection in their romance had led to some close calls when they were only partially clothed and almost interrupted by his mother. If Laney Dryer was aware of the intensity of the relationship, she didn't let on. But Wash didn't delude himself. He knew his mother was aware of the fact that he and Maricel were more than just hand-holding boyfriend and girlfriend.

Wash waved at his girlfriend and his mother. Most games, he might have been able to yell out a greeting, but not tonight. Two student council members had commandeered the PA system for the field and they were blasting music that could be heard more than a mile away. They mixed up the playlist and played songs typically heard in sports arenas as well as recent dance hits and the like. The noise was deafening, but the overall effect was to elevate the event to an almost excited level. Unfamiliar territory in the football stands at Bear River – except when there was a soccer game being played.

The excitement ended abruptly when the Pompeii Pumas returned the opening kickoff for a touchdown. The Bears were pinned inside their ten-yard line on the subsequent kickoff. The crowd barely noticed when the first offensive plays gained no yardage and the Bears punted. Seth Parker got a nice wind-aided punt off and the ball bounced down to the Pumas' 25-yard line. No return. Thing Two downed the punt. He picked up the ball and flipped it to the ref. As he did, he got in front of the Pumas' superstar, Jake Herrick, just back from suspension. Thing Two pulled out his mouth guard and barked, "Woof! Woof!"

Herrick was puzzled at first, but then Thing One repeated what his brother did. "Woof! Woof!" followed by more dog yips. Jake Herrick's infamous temper kicked in, but he said nothing. On the next play, he took the hand-off and ran through a tackle by Junior Shultz who was starting at linebacker in place of the absent Glenn Marcus. The Things caught Herrick on an angle on the Bears' 20-yard line. He dragged the two smaller players to the end zone for the touchdown. His celebration was short-lived, however, as the two Bear players began to sing "How Much is that Doggie in the Window?" to him.

Herrick took a step toward his bench, but then he turned and ran toward the Things. They didn't back down or flinch. Herrick stopped short and pointed at them "Just shut up – read the scoreboard! We are going to stomp you!" The Things began to dramatically whimper like wounded puppies. The officials ran into the end zone and separated the players.

"Boys – we'll flag any taunting. You understand?" the linesman said firmly.

Jake Herrick looked at the official. "Tell them, not me!" he complained with almost a whine.

The official pointed toward Herrick's team bench. "Clear the end zone for the extra point."

During the huddle for the extra point try, Morg Miller was laughing. "You two are going to get him really pissed if you keep this up. He's gonna kill you." Neither of the Things said a word. They only laughed. Herrick scored on the two-point conversion.

The rest of the half was more of the same. The Things never passed up an opportunity to start barking. Morg Miller and Junior Schultz joined in taunting the Puma all-state player. A bark here and a yip or whine there, and soon the whole Bear squad was either joining in or laughing about it. And if Herrick's play had anything to do with it, the taunting was backfiring on the Bears. Jake Herrick was playing like a man possessed. He scored two more touchdowns on long runs. He had just shy of 200 yards rushing on offense as the second quarter drew to an end. On defense, he sacked Seth Parker five times in the first half, and the quarterback was getting pissed. He called timeout with just seconds to go before the clock ran out. Coach Cale was angry on the sideline. He had signaled for Seth to take a knee rather than risk a turnover deep in their own territory with a third down and twenty yards to go after Herrick had sacked Seth on the prior play.

Jorge Martinez signaled for the huddle and asked Seth, "What's up? We don't need a time-out to take a knee."

Seth Parker cut him off with a wave of his hand. "Everyone get in here!" Seth yelled. The Bears drew in close. Seth pointed at the Things. "Knock the shit off! Quit the goddamned barking and laughing! He's fucking tearing us apart, and he's going to cripple me or Jay so just fucking stop it! I gotta do the damn homecoming program at half, so I can't go in the locker room with you guys. If I did go in there, I would handle this then, but I can't," Seth said with enough anger for everyone to take it seriously. The music from the PA was almost louder than Seth could yell in the huddle. The two students selecting the music played something with every break in the action. The song playing during Seth's unscheduled timeout was "Rock Around the Clock." Big Donnie Donnie loved that song. He used to sing it with his grandma before she died. He wasn't sure why all the guys were agreeing with Seth, but he shook his head right along with the team. Actually he was listening to the song. He wished they would always play loud music during every game. It was fun.

The halftime show focused on the crowning of the home coming king and queen. The convertibles circled the field on the track. Seth Parker limped to midfield after meeting Amber Taylor at the bench when her car pulled up. "Don't touch me, you're covered with mud!" she scolded her boyfriend, who had taken off only his helmet for the ceremony.

The court was introduced and greeted by the king and queen from the prior year. The new king was announced first. Liam Pickering was announced as the winner. Some cheers and clapping rose up. When Roxanne Johnson was announced as queen, she blushed and felt tears come to her eyes. Amber Taylor ran to her friend and hugged her. Real cheers rose from the girls in the crowd. The band played a few songs as the crowd dissipated from the stands. Fewer than 50 people remained as the teams took the field for the warm ups for the second half. The two students running the PA didn't care. They kept blasting music.

The Bears took the kickoff. The ball sailed through the end zone on the kick. The first play on offense, the Bears ran an option wide left. Jake Herrick smashed through his blockers and crushed Seth Parker as he pitched the ball. The ball bounced out of Jay Brau's hands and the Pumas recovered. Seth Parker rolled on the ground yelling – he had a shoulder stinger. He was done for the night. He watched from the bench while Wash Dryer packed his aching shoulder in ice as the Pumas started on offense.

The next play was one of the most memorable plays of the year. And the fallout from its outcome stretched from Bear River, Michigan to Ames, Iowa. The Pumas attempted a double reverse. Somehow, Phil Long and Big Donnie Donnie were able to shed their blocks and get penetration, so when Puma wide out came back against the grain of the play, they forced him deep into the backfield. Jay Brau read the play and was giving pursuit when he grabbed the Puma player a good ten yards behind the line. Jorge Martinez and Morg Miller came in to finish him off, but Jake Herrick rushed to help and he clipped Morg. Jorge got the job done. Flags flew on the clip as the play completed.

Thing One and Thing Two rushed into the backfield as Morg jumped to his feet. "Cheap shot, Jake!" Morg yelled at the star.

Thing Two yelled in support, "Personal foul there, big guy, hope they don't see that in Iowa!"

Thing One chirped in, "Bow wow big boy! Looks like you lost your scholarship!"

Jake Herrick stood silent and shocked as the refs picked up the flag. He was frozen in panic at what had just happened. He didn't know that his coaches had sought the referees out at halftime and complained about the Bears taunting and trying to draw Jake into a confrontation. The refs agreed to be vigilant on the behalf of the area's star player and only division-one football recruit. The refs huddled together. They were getting ready to wave off the call. But that's when fate intervened.

In the press box, the two students playing music hit the play button on the iPod hooked up to the PA as they had for every lull in the game up to the point.

"Who let the dogs out?!"

"WOOF! WOOF! WOOF! WOOF! WOOF!"

On the bench, Seth Parker exclaimed, "Oh no!" to Wash Dryer. Wash looked at the quarterback with puzzlement. "Not this song – not now." And he pointed at the field. Wash turned and watched.

The opening strain of Big Donnie Donnie's all-time favorite song rang out. He sang it with his mother all the time. He had since he was a kid. The second line of the song played and Big Donnie Donnie jumped up and down, gleefully shouting "WOOF! WOOF! WOOF! WOOF! WOOF!" in response. It was as the last WOOF! escaped his lips that Jake Herrick leveled Big Donnie Donnie with a punch to the back of his head.

Big Donnie Donnie went down, and Jake Herrick jumped on him and began to pummel him. Phil Long, feeling his oats after having helped make a good play, jumped on the back of Herrick. Both teams joined in the melee. Flags flew and the whistles pierced through the strains of the song playing on the PA.

After everything was sorted out, Jake Herrick and Phil Long were ejected from the game. Herrick for his ambush of Big Donnie Donnie – the refs had no choice. Long for his retaliation, which as every player knows, will get you flagged every time.

The game ended with the final score of Pompeii Central 32-Bear River 0. Phil Long got high fives in the locker room after the game from just about everyone on the team. Coach Cale talked to him alone and explained that while standing up for a teammate is important, it is retaliation that always leads to trouble. Coach Cale had to inform Phil that because he was thrown out of the game, he would have to sit out the following week, according to state athletic association rules. Phil was not upset about that. He was sort of upset when Coach Cale told him that he would still have to practice all week. All in all, Phil Long felt good about himself as he wolfed down an entire large Meatlover's pizza at the Pizza Hut in Gratiot. His parents took him out after the game. His father scolded him for getting thrown out of the game, but he smiled the whole time.

Jake Herrick rode back to Pompeii with his father and grandfather. He sat in the backseat of his grandfather's 1969 Plymouth Barracuda. He sobbed uncontrollably all the way home.

**Overtime**

WashDryer: Knock Knock.

GregDryer: Who's there?

WashDryer: Owen.

GregDryer: Owen Who?

WashDryer: Owen Seven.

Wash relayed the whole story of the homecoming game loss and the Jake Herrick story. Greg Dryer expressed concern about Herrick potentially losing his scholarship. Wash agreed.

GregDryer: Big date for the Homecoming dance tomorrow?

WashDryer: Yep.

GregDryer: Your mom says Maricel is a special girl.

Wash felt his face turning red. He was unsure how to respond.

GregDryer: Don't be embarrassed son. Treat her with respect. Make good decisions.

WashDryer: Always Dad.

# CHAPTER TWELVE

## OWEN 8

### TAKING FALLS

Jake Herrick's father was on the phone first thing Saturday morning. When he was finished talking with the recruiting coordinator for the Iowa State football team, he swore bitterly. Jake's scholarship had been rescinded.

At two in the afternoon, Morg Miller and Junior Schultz drove "The Tank" down south of North Star to his aunt and step-uncle's little farm. There was a heavy mist falling. The moisture was tough on the old truck. Twice it stalled out at stop signs. Morg cursed as he tried to start the vehicle. Each time, he was forced to spray ether into the carburetor to get it to fire up. That meant he had to remove the air filter and put a screw-driver in the butterfly valves. Each time, the truck started with a loud backfire. Morg's hands were covered with the scarlet poster paint he and Junior had painted the truck with before the parade yesterday. The rainy mist had turned the dried paint into sticky glop. Morg got it on his hands and clothes opening up the hood and climbing into the engine compartment.

Morg and Junior pulled into the farm at just past three. Calling it a farm was generous. It was five acres. But it did have a small barn with a horse stall. Morg called the little girls staying there his little cousins but in fact they were the daughters of his step-uncle's son. Their parents had been killed in a motor cycle accident a little over a year before. Morg had taken a real liking to the girls, and a few times he had baby-sat them. They were smart and sad, but he could always get them giggling by tickling them.

Heather and Becca called Morg on Wednesday evening jabbering a mile a minute about the horse their grandfather had gotten for them. Heather was seven and Becca had just turned four. They finished each other's sentences.

Both of them chirped on the phone, "Morgy, you have to come see our horse. His name is Prince! Grandpa says Uncle George will bring some hay for him. Can you bring it instead?"

Morg promised the girls he would bring them two big round bales of hay on Saturday. It would work out perfectly – the football team would ride the bales through the parade on Friday evening and the horse would be eating the hay the next day.

When Saturday rolled around, Morg called Junior Shultz and asked if he would ride along down to North Star to deliver the hay with him. Junior Shultz was a year younger than Morg but they had known each other since they were toddlers. They were wrestling partners every winter during practice. Morg liked Junior because he laughed at everything that Morg said. Not a fake laugh. Real gut-busting laughs. Morg loved a good audience. He told dirty jokes all the way to North Star and Junior laughed enthusiastically even though he had heard most of them before.

"Shit! That doesn't look good," Morg exclaimed as they pulled to a stop in the farmyard.

A pickup truck with a cap on the box was parked in front of the barn. On the side of the windowless cap bright red letters announced: Mallon's Large Animal Veterinary. 24 Hour Emergency Service. Below that was a phone number and URL. Morg knew his step-uncle was notoriously cheap. If he called the vet on a weekend, it was bad.

He and Junior could hear the little girls crying as they entered the barn. Becca came running to him and practically knocked him over jumping into his arms. "Morgy, Prince is going to die! The vet just gave him a shot! He's gonna die now!" Morg picked up the distraught girl who locked her arms around his neck in a powerful hug. Her body shuddered with sobs. Morg waited for his step-uncle to emerge from the horse stall.

"Goddamned gopher hole. Broke his goddamned leg in a goddamned gopher hole. Heather was riding him. I don't know how she didn't get thrown. The horse screamed and came limping back to the barn." The old man Morg called Uncle Chuck was disgusted as he greeted the two boys.

The vet, a very good-looking woman, was talking seriously to the older sister. "Heather, he was in so much pain. And he won't hurt any more. We have to let him go." The young girl nodded gravely and some tears dropped from her face to the barn floor.

The vet handed Morg's step-uncle a card. "Give these guys a call they'll come right over and pick up the carcass. They're reasonable. I'll see what I can do to discount your bill. I'm sorry. I've known this horse since he was a colt. The girls should have been riding him for a lot longer than just a few days." Genuine sadness clouded her eyes.

The vet left. Becca stopped crying and whispered in Morg's ear. "Prince is in heaven with Mommy and Daddy now." That almost made Morg cry as he gently placed the girl down. Heather took Becca's hand, and they walked to the horse stall alone.

The old man cursed again. "A thousand bucks for a horse. Five hundred on saddles and tack. Vet bills. Probably a couple of hundred to dispose of the damn carcass. Christ, what a fiasco."

Morg and Junior talked to the old man and the girls for a few minutes. Morg's aunt pulled into the driveway. She had been visiting a friend in Grand Rapids when her husband called with the sad news. The two girls rushed to their grandmother, sobbing.

"Look boys, I don't need the hay anymore. I'm out of the horse business. At least until next summer. I just can't afford it. Tell George thanks for me, will ya?'" the old man said, and the boys shook his hand. Morg stopped to give his aunt a hug and he and Junior climbed in the truck to leave. It wouldn't start. The mist had turned into a heavy fog. Morg climbed out of the truck and went through the procedure to fire up the engine. The girls jumped and let out little screams when the truck backfired to life. Morg felt guilty for having frightened them.

"You going to go dump the hay bales back in your barn?" Junior asked.

Morg contemplated the work involved and the now thoroughly waterlogged bales. The thought didn't appeal to him. "Nah, it can wait to tomorrow. It's gonna be dark soon, and this fog is like friggin' soup. Besides, we gotta get back and get cleaned up for the dance." Morg was subdued in his response.

"Gonna look real cool pulling up to the school with a load of hay on this rig and dripping poster paint everywhere," Junior said sarcastically.

"Fuck it," Morg answered.

The boys were mostly silent as they rode into the gloomy fog back to Bear River.

A notable exception to the downward spiral of homecoming at Bear River was the annual homecoming dance. It was the social event of the fall season. The student council put up thousands of dollars to decorate the school gym and to cater the dance. A top of the line deejay was hired, and he brought first-class sound system and event lights and effects including a fog machine. The money for the big event was greatly aided by donations from the four professional photographers in the area and from a tux rental shop in Mt. Pleasant.

The student council advisory chairperson was also the school business teacher, Nancy Conover. She put out a call for money each fall with a promise that Bear River students would only use the services of businesses that supported the homecoming dance. The photographers wanted the senior portrait business. One year, one of them tried to only give $500 instead of the expected $1,000. He got only three BRHS students as clients that year. The tux shop was owned by a Bear River grad. She was very generous, and as result, nearly every spring every BRHS boy rented their tux there come prom time – even though there were other shops closer to town.

A smattering of smaller donors and the student council usually had over $5,000 to spend on the dance and party.

Laurie Starke showed up in the gym in the early afternoon. She had volunteered to help supervise the dance committee as they transformed the utilitarian gym into a ballroom. This year's theme was Disney Princes and Princesses. Ms. Starke and her supervisory teacher, Nancy Conover, were overseeing a crew of two dozen girls setting up Disney-themed posters and a few mannequins dressed in Disney Princess finery. The streamers required a portable man lift to attach the bright paper decorations to the gym rafters. One of janitors was manning the lift. Molly Saunders was a chain-smoking and grumbling woman of fifty-eight earning double time for working on a Saturday, but she was still in a bad mood about having to work on a day off. She had noticed the young CMU student teacher her first day in the building. She had taken an immediate dislike to Laurie Starke. She felt the way the young woman dressed was wholly inappropriate, and she had heard the boys in the building talk about the worst sort of smutty things in reference to her. Janitors tend to fade into the woodwork, so kids speak as though no adult was within earshot. Clete Packer exploited this, and Molly was often in his office giving him the lowdown on what the student body was talking about. In return, Clete looked the other way when Molly violated the tobacco-free campus rules and ducked out to the loading dock behind the cafeteria to chain smoke two butts after lunch.

Molly was watching from the lift as a clot of girls gossiped with the young woman they called "Coach Laurie." That level of familiarity angered the janitor to no end. It was wholly inappropriate to her mind. The girls were talking about boys – as was almost always the case, Molly noted with weary disgust. The girls were mostly sophomores and juniors, and they discussed the features and hotness of senior boys. One of the girls accused a sophomore of being hot for Morg Miller. The girl stuck her finger in her mouth and made a retching noise. The group burst into gales of laughter with the student teacher laughing the loudest. Molly subtly released the hydraulics on the lift and lowered herself to only fifteen feet over the girls – none noticed her.

Sydnee Smith, the self-anointed leader of the pack, made mention of Wash Dryer. A couple of the girls called out simultaneously, "Babe!" Laughter ensued again.

"Yeah, but he's all into that Maricel bitch. She's such a phony with that accent and making like she don't know what to say. Bet she's got Wash all turned around," Meghan Maleckis said with a sneer. A couple of girls made affirmative noises in agreement.

"That comes from the girl who chased Jay Brau around a year ago trying to get into his pants! How'd that work out, Meggy?" Bethany McCambridge asked with mock accusation, prompting a middle-finger response from Meghan and more laughter but no rebuke from Little Miss Hot Pants student teacher, Molly Saunders noted from her overhead perch. She was disgusted.

Another girl called out, "Liam!" referring to Liam Pickering, the captain of the soccer team.

Sydnee Smith was not able to fight back the bitter sarcasm "Oh sure, Liam is all that and a bag of chips. But no one will ever love him more than he loves himself." Sydnee had briefly been Liam Pickering's girlfriend of the month a year ago. No one laughed because they all knew Sydnee was still angry over being dumped a week before her birthday and then was treated to rumors of how Liam bragged about how much money he saved by not having to buy her any gifts.

Bethany McCambridge called out, "Jorge!" in a lull in the laughter. "Super babe!" someone shouted. Squeals of teenage lust-fueled laughter followed. Molly Saunders squinted with contempt. She caught sight of Laurie Starke. A hint of a blush was on her cheeks, and suddenly, she wasn't laughing with her little pack of sex-crazed witches. Molly focused tightly on the student teacher.

"Oh, sure, Jorge is like hashtag hot, but ain't no one here on dat." Meghan noted forcefully with an emphasis on the knowing slang. The girls stopped their carnal laughs. Some agreement was given. "I mean, like, he is all about the college ladies. Remember last spring everyone was on about how he had a whole train of college bitches. He was up at CMU all the time – I do know that cause my sis goes there and she told me about it. She saw him a whole bunch of times. Different girl every Thursday night at the Wayside. Guess he must have a good fake ID or something." Meghan embellished the story wildly, enjoying the attention and safe in the knowledge that no one present had the ability to refute it. Laurie Starke glanced away. Bethany McCambridge made a pained grimace. Molly Saunders thought she saw the blush deepen on the student teacher. Her eyes bored deep into the young woman, trying to read her body language. And soon she displayed a knowing, sly smile.

"What about that, Coach Laurie, did you party with Jorge Martinez last year at the Wayside? Come on, fess up!" Sydnee Smith laughed through the joking accusation. Girls tittered appreciatively. Laurie snapped her head around quickly from where she was distractedly looking. The red glow in her cheeks crested to a high fever pitch.

"Unh – what? I'm sorry – um – did you ask me something, Meghan – I mean Syd? I-uh – was looking at that wall over there. It needs more decorations." Laurie gestured too emphatically to the north wall of the gym.

"Yeah, Laurie, I asked you did you run across Jorge at CMU last spring when he was working his thing on the college hos?" Sydnee dropped the pretext of calling the young woman "coach." The question was lighthearted, mostly, but the increasingly flustered Laurie Starke fumbled badly in her response. She visibly had to compose herself.

"Uh, you mean Jorge Martinez, that, uh, quiet boy in my second – um, first hour? I, uh, never saw him on campus up there. I mean, he's a high school student and – besides I was so busy last semester. I, uh, took an overload of classes, and I like had no – um, social time at all, really." Laurie finally made it through her disclaimer.

Her stomach felt like it bounced off the floor and up into her throat. The girls barely noted her discomfort – they had moved on to another topic halfway through her fumbling response. Except for Bethany McCambridge – she stood dazed. She looked at Laurie and then at her feet. Her teenage mind couldn't quite formulate a reaction to the clues that Laurie Starke was sputtering out.

Fifteen feet overhead, Molly Saunders wasn't struggling at all. Her lips were drawn tight in an evil grin. Her eyes flashed with malicious and twisted joy. It didn't take someone with a college degree to figure out Laurie Starke was exactly what Molly surmised her to be at first glance. The girl was a wanton whore. Screwing young boys like a hedonistic tramp. Icy thoughts of watching the girl twist in the wind galvanized Molly's mind. She reflexively touched her cellphone in her pants pocket. Clete Packer might well buy her a celebratory carton of smokes for this bombshell bit of information. She would wait, though, until she had some confirming evidence before visiting Clete in his office.

An hour or so later, Laurie Starke watched as her posse of young girls assisted with the placement of the food and drinks on the buffet tables on the west side of the gym. She was impressed. This was no cookies-and-punch dance like she experienced as a young student. The two elderly ladies catering the event had decades of experience working with the school district food service before the current superintendent decided to privatize the department a few years ago. That forced the "Two Old Gals," as they referred to themselves and ultimately called their business, to start out on their own. They knew how to feed a lot of people well and quickly. They bantered sweetly as they instructed the young girls providing the labor how to set up the spread of food and drinks. There were hors d'oeuvres of all kinds. A complete array of lovely decorative and tasty sweets was set up around a giant chocolate fountain. Trays of white cake and marshmallows were on a separate table ready for kids to dip in the fountain. There was plenty of pop, name brands, not cheap store sodas, and a ginger ale punch tumbling out of a serving fountain that Laurie thought was champagne by the look and taste of it. The "Two Old Gals" provided all this at cost to the dance committee. They claimed it was for old time's sake, but there was hardly a graduation party or wedding in town that they didn't get the catering contract for, so everyone knew the "Two Old Gals" were really smart self-promoters.

The deejay was testing his system as Laurie Starke made her way to the teachers' lounge and the staff bathroom attached to it to change from her jeans and Bear River sweatshirt and into the dress she had brought to wear while she chaperoned the dance. Molly Saunders was sitting in the staff lounge eating her dinner out of an old gray lunch pail. The industrial-sized lunch box and thermos had been her ex-husband's. Her second ex-husband's. She had taken that dumb bastard for everything in the divorce. Truth is, he told his friends that he would have even given up the clothes complete with the boxers he wore to court and walked nude from the courtroom if it meant he would be "Free of the Hell Bitch."

"Hi Molly, working the long day today, huh? You got cleanup duty as well after we are all done?" Laurie asked nicely as she collected up her garment bag from the decrepit coat rack by the lounge door. She got a bad vibe from the bag-lady looking custodian, but the director of student teacher placement had met with her recently and reminded her to be courteous and friendly to all janitors and secretaries, so Laurie made a point to always say something cheerful to them. But the intended effect rarely carried through. Laurie Starke didn't effectively fake sincerity. Most of the older women in the building judged her barely more sincere than the worst of the teenage entitlement princesses they dealt with throughout their careers. Molly barely kept her face from going into full scowl, and she answered with a non-committal grunt. Laurie slipped into the staff bathroom, closed the door and turned on the fan. "Bitchy old witch," Laurie sneered to herself. The mature women in the building were not far off in their assessment of the young would-be teacher.

Twenty minutes later, Laurie Starke emerged from the bathroom freshly made up and hair nicely arranged. She wore a red dress just a shade darker than the standard Bear River red. She felt proud to have something just the right color for a homecoming dance. Good school spirit and all. Her three-inch heels clicked on the tile floor. She had thought maybe it wouldn't be a good idea to wear her strappy five-inch "fuck me" pumps to a school function. The dress revealed some cleavage, but the hemline was mid-thigh. The dress clung nicely on the young student teacher's frame. Molly Saunders looked up from the newspaper. Her lips pursed and she let loose with a dismissive snort.

"Excuse me?" Laurie knew instinctively that the old lady was judging her.

Molly flashed her eyes quickly up and down the frame of the young woman and then looked away with contempt. "Who would wear such a thing to school function? Teachers should dress more appropriately," Molly intoned nastily. The judgmental accusation was meant to cut the target deeply. Molly could almost hear the hurt gasp coming as she brought her eyes back toward the young skank.

The hurt gasp didn't come. Laurie wasn't hurt – she was however pissed off past the point of good judgment.

"Oh pleeeze!" Laurie jabbed back with sarcasm. "Could you be a more old biddy grouch lady if you tried?"

"Young lady, poor taste in clothing is—" Molly was usually so very efficient at verbally cutting people down to size, but she had underestimated her target, and it had her uncharacteristically searching for the right cutting remark. When it came to aggressive verbal asides, Molly had never been bested. At least not for many years, and now it seemed as though perhaps this little floozie could dish it out pretty well.

Laurie didn't wait for Molly to regain her ground. "What would you know about fashion, anyway? I doubt you ever had a shred of fashion sense. You certainly don't now but how could you with a body like that. You still got those polyester bell bottoms from ninth grade? Yeah, you do. Bet they don't fit though, do they? Not even close. Have a few dozen more doughnuts, you old sow." There was no regret or letting up as Laurie cut the old janitor with cool contempt.

Pure fury played across Molly Saunders' face. "You cheap skank! You dress like a street walking whore! You look like a two-dollar-a-throw whore! Trying to get those teen boys all lathered up aren't you? Going to pick off another one tonight, skank?" Spittle and little bits of food ejected from Molly's mouth as she went on the attack.

"What the hell are you talking about, you old bitch? Seriously, you're just a crazy bitch. You never had it so you hate everyone who can look this good." Laurie gestured with sweep of her hand to her body as she made her capping statement. It had gone beyond anger now. Laurie Starke was enjoying the rage bubbling up from the old janitor. Had she been more attuned to what Molly Saunders was saying about trying to attract young boys, maybe she could have prepared for what was coming.

"You'll see, you skank, you'll see. Think you can come to this school and play the whore and no one will do anything about it? Well just wait, skank. You're going to find out what happens to people like you around here," Molly grumbled hoarse threats as she gathered up her things and marched past the young woman out the door.

Laurie wasn't about to miss a chance at getting the last word. As Molly waddled past, Laurie looked down her nose at the dumpy old janitor and uttered one more dismissive "sow" to send her on her way. She felt a surge of anger-fueled triumph as she heard the heavy footsteps as the old woman stalked down the hall. It was a premature judgment on her part that she had bested the janitor.

Laurie made her way to the gym a few minutes later. It was beginning to fill with students dressed in nice suits and dresses. The football and soccer coaches were manning the door and handling security around the school. It was a key to the success of the homecoming dance every year. All the athletes were on their best behavior under the watchful eyes of the coaches. In fact, it had been a dozen years since any incident had disrupted the dance. That was about to change.

The girls in the gym made their way to the young woman they called "Coach Laurie." Many commented on her dress. Most of the boys in the gym began to eye Laurie Starke. Notable exceptions to that were Phil Long and Big Donnie Donnie. Phil was piling a plate high with hors d'oeuvres at the buffet table. Donnie was dipping marshmallows in the chocolate fountain and popping them one after another into his mouth. He had a slight smear of chocolate on his left cheek and unrestrained joy in his eyes.

Morg Miller and Junior Schultz walked into the gym together. Morg wore a white jacket with a tuxedo T-shirt underneath. Bright purple pants and red high-top Chuck Taylors completed his outfit. Junior was dressed more conservatively. Morg was playing the clown and high-fiving football teammates.

"Check that out," Greg DeVito said knowingly as he gently shoved Morg with one hand and pointed at the hot young student teacher.

"Jeez zus!" Morg exclaimed loud enough for anyone nearby to hear. He then bit down on the heel of his left hand and dramatically grunted a carnal growl. Junior Schultz led the laughter. It was loud enough for a good portion of the kids in the gym to pause and look toward the group of football players near the entrance.

The deejay began to play music. The dancing began. The first ones on the floor were the dance committee volunteers. They enticed Laurie Starke to come out with them and they danced in a circle. The form-fitting dress shimmered in the effects lighting. The young student teacher was getting into the song. The young boys in the gym were increasingly mesmerized. Wash Dryer nudged Seth Parker and tipped his head toward the dance floor. Wash raised an eyebrow in the style of his friend Jorge. Amber and Maricel had excused themselves to the bathroom. The four of them had been sitting at one of the tables near the dance floor. They were waiting for Jorge and Jay, who had to go pick up Roxanne in Jay's car – her mother's old jeep wouldn't start.

"Holy shit," Seth said flatly. "If all the women teachers looked like that—" He couldn't find the words to complete his thought. He and Wash used the absence of their dates to focus on the show on the floor. The song changed to a faster-tempo house beat. The deejay was enjoying the show as well. Laurie Starke had a well-earned reputation as a party girl. Her party instincts kicked in – she lost herself in the beat. Her supervising teacher was not in the gym. The football coaches were touring the parking lot checking to make sure there were no on-the-side drinking parties starting tail-gate style. Only the head soccer coach, Miles Kitteridge, was on hand to watch. And all he did was watch.

Liam Pickering led a group of soccer players into the circle of dancing girls. The beat of the music was now matched by the pelvic thrusts of a dozen teenage boys. Molly Saunders emerged from the girls' locker room. She was pushing a mop bucket and she was pissed off. The dance wasn't even an hour old, and someone had spilled a Coke all over the floor by the row of toilets near the showers. It took all of three seconds for Molly to take in the scene and her level of agitation increased greatly. As fast as her stubby legs could carry her, she rushed to Clete Packer's office, abandoning her mop and bucket.

The volume of the music was loud enough that Clete Packer could hear it from his office. More accurately, Clete was able to feel it, really, as the drum and bass vibrated the whole school. The homecoming dance was the one social event during the year that he didn't have to watch like a hawk. The coaching staff being in the gym allowed him to spend most of the evening in his office. He hated loud music, and it was his plan to only pop into the gym about every hour or so. The overweight AD shifted his bulk in his office chair and began to rise. Something needed to be done before the neighbors called the cops. He was more than just a little agitated that the adults in the gym did not realize that.

As if from nowhere, Molly Saunders appeared at his office door and her red face and raging eyes immediately clued the AD that something was going wrong in the gym. He imagined it would be her typical complaint of the students making pigs of themselves. Someone probably spilled a Coke or some such thing. Clete Packer cultivated a relationship with Molly Saunders out of necessity. She was his eyes and ears in the building. In fact, she was an enthusiastic and thorough spy. But in truth, Clete found her as unpleasant as everyone else did. Her smoker's rasp and stinky camp-fire-smelling work shirts grated on him. All this was able to play out in Clete's mind because the pudgy janitor was out of breath and apparently uncharacteristically at a loss for angry words. Clete had a fleeting thought that if she collapsed, there was no way he would administer mouth-to-mouth.

"That – young tart – is a dirty – tramp!" The flustered and out-of-breath janitor finally issued her gasp-interrupted proclamation. The nascent emphysema her doctor had warned of last year was effectively stealing her ability to launch a righteous tirade against Laurie Starke. She was too angry to be concerned about health issues just then. Recently, however, while saying her nightly rosary she had broken down and wept, contemplating a life in an oxygen mask and being deprived of her beloved Camels. Most days, just dust mopping the hallways at the end of the school-day left her winded. When the task was completed, she had to sit for a half hour in her cramped little office/closet next to the boiler room, rocking and twisting in her ratty desk chair, all the while coughing and hawking sputum into the custodial floor sink. Since the beginning of the school year, she had been in denial about the blood spots she occasionally saw in the sink as she washed her dark sputum down the drain.

"What?" Clete Packer asked, agitated.

Molly Saunders gulped in a breath and began her indictment. "That horrible little tramp of a student teacher is down there in the gym dancing like a whore! She's already bagged one of the boys, and now she's on the prowl for more. She's got half the soccer team dancing and grinding their hips like dogs on a bitch in heat. Which is what she is anyway! She's got a skimpy dress painted on her and she is shaking her ass like a stripper!" The last two lines were mixed with gasping breaths as Molly's anger played out and caused her face to turn from ashen gray to reddish purple.

"Miss Starke is dressed inappropriately? Dancing with boys? Where is Nancy Conover? And what are you talking about, she's bagged a boy? Is she being familiar with the student?" Clete Packer was confused as he fired off the questions.

"Familiar?! Clete, Holy Mother of God! She has bedded Jorge Martinez and who knows who else on the football team and now it looks like she is parading her ass out for the soccer team as well!" Molly Saunders declared triumphantly.

Clete stood still and quiet but with his brow furrowed as Molly described what she had overheard from the scissor lift in the gym during the setup of the dance. She did not separate the truth from the half-truths or guessed-at suppositions. In her angered state, she didn't know exactly what she had heard and what she filled in for herself. She said it all with such conviction that by the time she was done relating her version of the affair the wanton woman had carried out with Jorge Martinez, she believed it as gospel. Clete believed it as well. In his years of using Molly Saunders as a spy, she had always been accurate and thorough. She had left out the confrontation she had with Laurie Starke in the teachers' lounge before the dance, so Clete did not see how her passion may have clouded her reportage.

"Molly, I'm going to get to the bottom of all this. Right damn now!" Clete said firmly. Molly followed him from the office but had difficulty keeping stride with the taller man. Clete arrived at the gym as Laurie Starke's supervising teacher was pulling the young woman from the dance floor. Nancy Conover had a very serious look on her face, and she held Laurie by the elbow as she spoke. Clete Packer came between the two. He nearly had to yell to be heard over the music.

"I'll take it from here, Mrs. Conover. Do something about the volume of that music!" Clete declared as he pointed at the deejay. Nancy Conover made her way across the gym floor to the mixing board where the deejay was dancing as he cued up a new song.

Timing is very important. It's true on the football field, and the Bear River Bears rarely achieved it. It's true in very many things in life. Clete Packer had struggled with proper timing his whole career. Tonight would be no exception.

As Mrs. Conover was instructing the deejay to turn down the music, Clete Packer was engaged with Laurie Starke.

"What you are wearing is not appropriate for staff to wear at a school function," Clete proclaimed loudly. Some students nearby stopped what they were doing to watch as words were exchanged.

"What are you talking about, Mr. Packer?" Laurie Starke willfully answered. She could see Molly Saunders standing a few feet away with a look of snarky triumph on her face. Laurie was furious. The old bitch was the cause of her troubles. Now her supervising teacher and fat idiot of an assistant principal were scolding her about her dress when half the girls in the gym were similarly attired. Her face became a defiant mask.

Clete Packer was not about to let some bimbo of a college student tell him how to run his school. Anger welled up. The music was pounding. If he had been more in control, he would have quietly escorted the young woman to his office but that wasn't going to happen now. He read the defiance in Laurie's face, and his temper began to crest.

More students began to focus on the confrontation. The deejay and Nancy Conover were still half shouting back and forth when he finally got exasperated and prepared to hit the volume kill switch. Clete's inherent bad timing kicked in.

The first few words of his angry response to Laurie Starke drew the attention of two dozen students near them on the floor. "Young lady, you cannot dress like this while supervising kids!"

The defiance in Laurie's face increased and she started to protest. "Half the girls in here have dresses more revealing than—"

Clete Packer cut her off, shouting even louder. "Half the girls in this gym are not prospective teachers! You don't look like a teacher. YOU LOOK LIKE A WHORE!"

The last five words of his outburst coincided with the stunning silence of the sound system being cut off. His booming words were heard by nearly everyone in the gym. About 200 students gasped. Big Donnie Donnie stopped mid-chew of his fifty-third chocolate-covered marshmallow. Phil Long nearly gagged on a shrimp. Wash felt his jaw dropping in amazement. Jorge, Jay and Roxy Johnson had just entered the gym and they stopped dead in their tracks. Even Molly Saunders cringed reflexively.

Time froze for a second. Clete felt his heart in his throat. Laurie Starke's defiant expression changed to rage. But she was at a loss for words. Then the booing started. Clete felt paralyzed. The escalation of the booing to shouting level forced him to move toward the deejay station – he needed to regain control of this situation immediately. He needed the sound system and the microphone.

The sudden stoppage of the music and the rising sound of booing from the gym caused John Cale and Mike Reese to rush to the gym from the parking lot. Whatever was happening, it had a disaster-like sound to it. The booing was not just because the music had stopped. There was real anger behind it. Mike Reese couldn't help but to think that somehow Clete Packer was at the center of it all.

Laurie Starke followed close behind Clete as he seized control of the microphone. She found her voice. The booing was so loud she had to shout. "HOW DARE YOU! YOU'RE THE ONE BEING INAPPROPRIATE! YOU'RE ALWAYS UNDRESSING ME WITH YOUR EYES, YOU DISGUSTING OLD PIG!"

Some of the students near at hand began to laugh. Clete shouted at Nancy Conover and pointed to Laurie Starke, "Take her to my office right now!" The booing crescendo rose even higher as students realized that Laurie Starke was being escorted out of the gym.

Mike Reese and John Cale were making their way through the crowd of students now pushing forward toward the deejay station when Clete got the microphone to work.

"THAT'S ENOUGH! Stop this right now! I will cancel this dance and empty this gym!" Most of the students had experienced his imperious, take charge voice before and quieted significantly. The booing decreased. BRHS students had seen enough of Clete Packer in action to know his threats were not idle. But not quite all of the students were intimidated by him. Some had a pure hatred of the man. That element was about to be heard from.

The gym quieted significantly. From somewhere in the crowd of students – no one was exactly sure from whom, although several claimed responsibility later there came a loud shout. "SUCK IT, FUDGE!"

Gales of laughter filled the gym. Mike Reese was standing near Morg Miller. It wasn't Morg who shouted at Packer. But Morg was leading the bulk of the football team cheering and whistling in appreciation of the put-down.

Clete Packer's eyes popped. His neck wattle turned purple, and the color was spreading to his face. He opened his mouth. No sound came from it. Laughter increased. John Cale walked up to Clete Packer and took the microphone from the stunned man. He laid it on the table. He motioned with his head to Mike Reese to pick it up.

"Mr. Packer, sir, let Mike and me handle this." John began to steer Packer toward the hallway leading from the gym to the office.

"No – I—" Clete tried to assert himself.

"We can handle it. If you cancel this dance, it will cause a huge problem. Parents will go nuts. The super and the board will step in. It will get in the paper. Sheldon Knapp will have a shit fit. It will be a fiasco," John Cale whispered firmly in the big man's ear as he moved him out the door.

As they walked down the hallway, chants of "We want Manikowski!" began to rise above the laughter. There were enough of the former school drug lord's clients in attendance for the chant to grow quite loud. Clete Packer froze. He pin-wheeled and began to walk back to the gym. For a second, John Cale almost let him go. Let him commit career suicide, he thought.

"Clete! No!" Cale hissed. The AD paused. "If you go back in that gym, those kids are going to start a riot. How's that going to look when you apply to take Mike Shanahan's job? A riot during a homecoming dance on your watch? Let Reese handle it – you know he will get those kids quieted down. They respect him."

The implication that Reese was a more effective handler of students than himself did not suit Clete at all, but he let it slide. Packer threw a hostile glance at Cale but said nothing. The chant died down.

"All right then. You two find that young soccer coach and you get those kids dancing and having a good time so their frigging parents don't helicopter in and sue because their precious babies didn't get their homecoming dance," the disgusted administrator said sarcastically. "I've got bigger fish to fry." And with that, he stalked off to his office. Cale wondered what he meant, but not having seen how Laurie Starke had dressed for the evening and knowing nothing of the whirlwind of accusations and sexual innuendo his best football player was about to get snarled into, the football coach made his way to the gym.

Mike Reese was talking to the crowd of students on the sound system when Cale entered the gym. "Okay, people, I don't know about you, but I came here to have some fun tonight. And to eat some of that food!" The crowd laughed a little. "And from the looks of it, I better make my move before Donnie and Phil pick the tables clean!" Reese pointed to the food tables and the crowd looked over. Big Donnie Donnie had chocolate on his cheek and another dripping marshmallow in his hand. Phil had a red Solo cup poised at his mouth. He stopped and shrugged. Most of the crowd laughed now. Reese turned to the deejay, a former student of his from twenty years ago – kind of the Morg Miller of Bear River circa 1996. "Bobby, lay down some tunes. Morg came dressed to dance, and an outfit like he's got on has to be on the dance floor!" Some cheers went up as the music started up again, but the buzz in the gym was about Clete Packer and his confrontation with Laurie Starke.

"What happened before we got here?" Roxy Johnson asked loudly over the music. "Was there some sort of fight between Mr. Packer and Miss Starke?"

"Yeah, Ole Fudge was super pissed," Seth Parker said.

"Why?" asked Jay Brau.

"Uh, Miss Starke was dressed a little um—" Wash Dryer was at a loss as to how to describe the situation, especially with Maricel listening intently.

"She was dressed freakin' HOT!" Seth said brightly. "She has a freakin' body, man! I mean holy crap, she was dancing and practically twerking, and her body was—" Seth felt Amber's icy glare before he looked her in the eyes. He turned and faced her. The anger flashing in her eyes told him everything he needed to know about the fight that was coming.

Jorge Martinez couldn't keep his troubled thoughts from his expression. Jay Brau was puzzled. "You okay?" he asked his friend.

"Yeah, I'm fine." Jorge smiled a little. "Kind of hungry, though, I'm going to get some food." He excused himself from the table.

The deejay cued up an oldie from the '80s. "Girls, grab a boy and make him kick it old school!" Bobby Walker shouted in the mic. Roxy Johnson grabbed Jay by the hand and dragged him to the floor. He was blushing. But he was happy because she was happy and so he would dance. Roxy was the rock of his life right now. Freddy Wilkes was out of the hospital, but his mother would not let Jay talk to him and she had his cellphone. It was Roxy who sat with Jay in her car after school the day before as his voice quavered when he explained about how he was not being allowed to contact his boyfriend.

Maricel squealed a little and she grabbed Wash. "Let's dance!" Wash didn't have to be asked twice. They followed Jay and Roxy to the floor. Seth looked at Amber, she sat with her arms folded, glaring at him. She got to her feet and began to walk away.

Jorge watched as Seth followed Amber out the front doors of the gym making pleading gestures with his hands. It didn't take too much guessing to figure out what was being said in that conversation. Seth was being shut down for sure.

Teenage dramas are a constant presence in high schools. And hardly a homecoming dance happens anywhere when a fragile young heart or two is not broken. Down the hallway from the BRHS gym, however, in the office of the assistant principal, a very different drama was playing out. The outcome of that drama would be very serious.

Nancy Conover sat with Laurie Starke waiting for Clete Packer. Laurie's face was flush with anger and no matter how Nancy tried to appeal to reason, the young woman got defensive and raised her voice to an almost-shout. In the last few weeks, Nancy had been making a case in her mind that Laurie Starke lacked the maturity necessary to be a teacher, and events of the evening only confirmed that supposition. What really concerned Nancy this evening was that the young woman had seemingly no control over her emotions. To create a scene with an administrator, to show him up in front of a group of students – what in the hell was the girl thinking? That wasn't just a lack of maturity. Nancy now questioned Laurie's mental stability. She had hoped that as Laurie's tour in her classroom ended, that she and the CMU student teacher advisor could counsel the young woman into selecting a different career. Now Nancy was pretty sure that Laurie was finished as of this evening. She felt weary. She wanted this to be over. Sitting there next to the seething young woman, she resolved not to take on another student teacher for the remainder of her career.

Clete Packer entered the room. To Nancy's surprise, he seemed very composed. She had expected him to come in raging. Laurie Starke did not read his mood at all. She stood and began jabbing her finger at Clete. "You have no right to treat me like this! I am an adult! Not some child you can bully! If you disrupt my student teaching assignment, I will sue your ass! I will bring harassment charges so fast it will make your head spin! My uncle is a labor relations lawyer for the UAW! You are in huge trouble, you pervert! Wait until I testify about you stalking me and ogling me all fall long!" she vehemently threatened. Nancy cringed. Partly because of how Laurie was behaving, but also because she fully expected Clete Packer to unleash an equally heated counter-attack. Again, she was shocked. No tirade was returned.

"Please sit down, Miss Starke," Clete said evenly. Laurie froze. She expected a shouting attack as well. She remained defiantly standing but quit shouting. Clete ignored her refusal to sit. "I've had a few minutes to compose myself after our confrontation in the gym. I had hoped perhaps sitting in here with Mrs. Conover would have given you time to cool off as well. And for the record, you are correct. My shouting at you in the gym was unprofessional of me. I think, however, you may not be fully cognizant of what is playing out here—"

"You uptight jerk! You don't like my dress. Big deal! Half the girls in the gym had dresses cut with more reveal than this!" Laurie Starke was building to a full-on rage.

"Your dress is not the issue, young lady!" Clete allowed his voice to climb in volume. Laurie paused and shot him a quizzical, angry look. Clete pressed on. "If it was only the dress, I would have a sit-down with Mrs. Conover and we would draw up a letter to send to the student teacher placement director at CMU. And perhaps we would consult with you on proper attire rather than dismiss you from our school district. No, this is a much more serious issue, and given your agitated state and the threats you have made to me regarding creating a legal situation, I have decided that we need Mrs. Conover present as a witness as we discuss your behavior prior to this evening."

"What the hell are you talking about?" Laurie asked with anger and puzzlement.

"I'll get to the point. Have you had physical relations with students while here on assignment as a student teacher? Specifically, have you been intimate with Jorge Martinez?" Clete asked directly. Nancy Conover felt her stomach sink and she turned to face her student teacher. The shock played across her face.

"WHAT!?" Laurie Starke screamed in response. "What the fuck – who— " Confusion and panic mixed with anger as Laurie began to shake as she spoke. Clete let his questions sink in. From long experience, he knew that when dropping a bombshell like this in an interrogation, letting the interviewee react and shout was often the source of the best information. Laurie's mind was racing, and then it hit her like a bolt of lightning. "WHAT HAS THAT LYING ASSHOLE TOLD YOU?" Laurie assumed, wrongly, that Jorge was the source of the information behind Clete Packer's accusing questions.

Clete held up his hands with open palms in front of the young woman. He wasn't prepared to say anything yet because he was sure that the young woman was going to incriminate herself if he let her rage on.

"That scuzzy little fucker has been going around bragging to all his buddies that he got into my pants! That's it, isn't it? And now every kid in this building thinks he is a love god! What a bunch of bullshit! That isn't what happened at all! Yeah, I met Jorge Martinez last spring. Only once! And we didn't even talk, let alone anything else! My roommate, Marcy, picked him up somewhere just after spring break. She was screwing around on her fiancée. I thought Jorge was a CMU student. She wouldn't even introduce us using his real name. She was keeping everything hidden because she was cheating on her boyfriend. The little bitch! I didn't even know his name until I showed up here! For Christ's sake, Marcy had a meltdown when I told her about it on the phone. She's living with her fiancée now and student teaching in Detroit. Jorge never told Marcy he was a high school junior. Not that it would have mattered to that bitch – she was in heat!" Laurie rushed through her denial flushed with anger and disgust. Of course, she left out the part where she tried to drunkenly seduce Jorge behind her friend's back.

"I have not yet interviewed Jorge on this matter. I have no idea what he has said to others about any relationship you and he have had. I will see him on Monday. As will the police, I assume." Clete was cool as he issued the threat of police involvement. He hoped it might panic the young woman into a confession.

"WE NEVER HAD A RELATIONSHIP! YOU ARE NOT LISTENING TO ME! I HAVE BEEN AVOIDING JORGE SINCE I FIRST GOT HERE!" Laurie continued screaming. He did not like her adamant denials. It dawned on him that perhaps there was a kernel of truth in her rants.

"Look, obviously there are two sides to every story; I am going to place a call to Superintendent Knapp. We will handle this as an internal matter initially, but the authorities will have to be brought in. It's a matter of law. We have no choice. Jorge is a minor and your student." Again Clete played it coolly.

"Fine! Fuck it! Call the cops right now! I want to take a lie detector test! AND I WANT THAT LYING LITTLE FUCKER TO TAKE ONE TOO!" Laurie Starke was enraged, but she was starting to seize the offensive and Clete Packer could feel his flop sweat starting. He thought briefly of the Maalox in his desk drawer. He couldn't take a big gulp of the cooling green lifesaver just now. He had to get the two women out of his office to get away with that.

"Mrs. Conover, please take Miss Starke to the outer office while I try to contact Superintendent Knapp." Clete Packer dismissed the two women. As they left the room, he reached for his Maalox bottle and quickly downed one large gulp. He retrieved his cellphone from his pocket. "Call Knapp," he intoned slowly to the phone.

Sheldon Knapp had just poured his second scotch of the evening when the call came through. He was watching college football. He had spent the day tagging behind his wife as she combed the aisles of antique stores in Bay City. He did his best to be impressed with her finds. He hated antiques as a general rule, but he loved his wife and it gave her happiness to pick up a bargain. And if he had to sacrifice a Saturday afternoon to ensure that he could watch a football game on Saturday night and Sunday afternoon unbothered by his wife, then it was a deal he was willing to make. When he saw it was Clete Packer calling, he considered muting the phone and letting the call go to voicemail. Knapp then remembered it was the night of the homecoming dance. The likelihood there was an emergency at the school was high. Sheldon Knapp heaved a sigh and set the scotch aside. He answered his phone.

"Clete, what is it?" Knapp answered his phone curtly, forgoing a hello. It was his usual demeanor on the phone with underlings.

"Mr. Knapp, we have a situation here at the high school. I think you're going to want to hear about it right now, and I think you will want to come here to address the issue in person," Clete Packer announced.

"Make it quick, Clete, I'm about to down my second scotch." Knapp made no attempt at keeping his impatience out of his reply. Clete Packer filled in the superintendent. Sheldon Knapp felt the pressure of a headache begin behind his eyes as the story played out.

"Are Nancy Conover and Miss Starke still there?" Knapp asked officiously when he sensed Clete Packer was through.

"Yes, they are in the outer office," Packer answered.

"Keep them there. I'll be there in fifteen minutes. And do not say anything further to Miss Starke until I get there, you understand?" Knapp answered.

"Do you want me to call Mike Shanahan?" Packer asked.

"Hell no!" Knapp replied and hung up the phone. The last thing he needed to do was try to guide his increasingly fuzzy-headed high school principal through something like this case. He eyed his scotch. It was tempting to down the two fingers he had just poured. But it was Johnnie Walker Blue, and that was pure sipping scotch, not a guzzle. He took the time to carefully empty the contents of the glass back into the decanter behind the Art Deco bar in his office. The bar was one of the few antiques his wife had purchased that he had an appreciation for. The decanter set was crystal. Also one of her finds. He walked to the living room and informed his wife that there was trouble at the school. Through long experience, she knew not to ask anything before he was ready to tell. She simply looked up from the book she was reading and nodded as he pulled on his long camel hair coat and wrapped a tartan scarf around his neck. As he exited into the garage he pulled on his calfskin driving gloves. In a few minutes, he was driving his Mercedes down the river road.

A half of a mile past Mike Reese's house on the river road and only about three miles from school, the sheriff's car flashed its lights and chirped its siren. Sheldon Knapp cursed as he pulled his car over. The flickering emergency lights of the cruiser created a multi-colored shimmering glow in the heavy fog. A search-lamp beam cut through the gloom and bathed his car in intense but diffuse light. In a minute the young sheriff's deputy came to his window. "Sir, do you know how fast you were driving?" he asked as Sheldon Knapp lowered the window.

"Officer, I may have been over the speed limit but I assure you it was with good cause. I'm superintendent of Bear River Schools and we have an emergency at the school I have to attend to and—" Knapp began his irritated and hasty excuse.

"Is it a life-threatening emergency? Because I've haven't heard anything on my radio about an emergency reported from the school, and I am the lead car in this district. I would have been called to the scene. And in these conditions with this heavy fog, only a life-threatening emergency would give anyone cause to exceed the speed limit," the young deputy cut off the Superintendent assertively.

Sheldon Knapp was exasperated and it showed. "No, it's not life-threatening, but it could be very serious." Knapp offered, but not as assertively as the young officer. In the process of responding, he handed the officer his license and registration.

"I see," the officer answered with knowing condemnation. "Sir, I have you clocked as going sixty-five miles per hour. This entire stretch of road is marked forty-five miles per hour. And you were weaving a little bit," the deputy continued.

"Weaving!?" Knapp said with disgust. "Well, maybe if the county would resurface this road and do a better job at maintaining it I wouldn't have to dodge potholes! I drive this road every day, and quite frankly, it is in absolutely shit shape!" Sheldon Knapp picked the wrong time to get short-tempered.

"Sir, I would think knowing the condition of the road combined with the weather, you would have been much more careful of your speed on this stretch." The response was an indictment. "Mr. Knapp, have you been drinking this evening?" the officer asked in measured tones as he read the superintendent's driver's license.

"What!?" Sheldon Knapp blurted.

"Mr. Knapp, I smell alcohol on your breath. I am going to have to ask you to exit your vehicle," the officer stated with authority.

"Officer, I have had one drink today!" Sheldon Knapp asserted as he noticed a second patrol car pulling in behind the first. "I really must get to the high school. There is a situation developing that could be very detrimental to my district!" Knapp couldn't keep the desperation out of his voice.

"Exit your vehicle. Now!" There was no give whatsoever in the command. Knapp complied.

Five minutes into the humiliating roadside sobriety test, a state police car pulled up behind the two county patrol units. All three officers studied Knapp as he made his way through the alphabet without a stumble. All the dexterity tests were completed without a single misstep. And fifteen minutes later, Sheldon Knapp was handed a speeding ticket for twenty miles per hour over the limit and a citation for driving too fast for road conditions. The stern warning about dangerous driving on foggy nights from the young deputy, barely half Knapp's age, rang in the superintendent's ears as he slowly pulled up to the high school. No parking spot was available, so Knapp double parked in the school driveway by the main entrance, blocking the drive and ignoring the signs warning to keep the fire lane free. The amber glow of the security lights surrounding the building hung close to the ground in the dense fog. Knapp cursed to himself as he glanced at his watch. It was almost 9:30. More than forty-five minutes since Clete Packer had called. The lost time would play out in ways the Sheldon Knapp couldn't begin to fathom.

While the superintendent was completing his field sobriety test, Laurie Starke sat fuming in the outer office of the high school. She texted her uncle, the labor relations lawyer, and as she waited for his response, she grew even more angry. Nancy Conover desperately wanted the whole evening to be over. She sat in the school secretary's chair, and calculated the high cost of buying, at this late point in her career, two more years of service time so she could retire at fifty-five instead of fifty-seven. For the first time since her grandchild had been born, she felt regret at having taken three years off in her late twenties to have two kids of her own. Occasionally, she made eye contact with her young student teacher. Laurie Starke gave her a look of pure hatred at each glance.

Clete Packer was pacing in his office, and, when he saw that the two women were not watching, he quickly downed another slug of Maalox. He knew if he called Knapp again, the superintendent would snap. And his instructions were to not talk to Laurie Starke. It dawned on him that perhaps he should interview Molly Saunders one more time. In an evening of calculated missteps, that decision would be his worst.

In the gym, Morg Miller was hit by a thunderbolt at about 9:15. It came to him as though sent from divine messenger. He walked up to Greg DeVito and Junior Shultz. He had a broad evil grin on his face. They instinctively smiled back at him.

"What's up?" Greg DeVito asked with anticipation, shouting to be heard over the music.

"Let's sell Fudge's house!" Morg declared with glee.

Greg and Junior high-fived Morg. "That's a fucking great idea!" Greg shouted.

Over the next few minutes, word spread across the gym. In an unprecedented act of in-season cooperation between football and soccer it was agreed that shortly after the king and queen danced at 9:30, the athletes would start exiting the gym in small groups to begin the collection. Small groups would be necessary because a mass exit would arouse suspicion. More than a dozen football players and a slightly larger number of soccer players declared they were in. By the time Roxy Johnson and Liam Pickering finished their ceremonial dance as homecoming king and queen, a half dozen cross country runners had begged to be included.

Word of the house selling prank had spread to the non-athletes as well. Two of the school's most notorious stoners eased out the door with the last of the athletes. Josh Gruelich and Todd Donheiser had been two of Tim Manikowski's best customers. The only thing they were interested in was partying and cruising the town on their longboards – usually with spray cans in their backpacks looking to tag an old abandoned building or a rail car or two. They came to the dance high and ready to eat. They almost matched plate for plate with Phil Long. But when they heard Fudge Packer was going to get his house sold, they wanted in. They'd hated him even before he had cost them their most reliable drug supplier.

Had Nancy Conover been in the gym she might have noticed that the gym was emptying a little earlier than usual. Most years, kids would not leave until the deejay stopped playing music at 10:50. But Nancy was engaged in the high school office.

Between the communities of Bear River and Gratiot, which was only two miles to the west, there were at any given time approximately two hundred properties for sale. The last time a group of students "sold" a staff member's house was late in the preceding school year when two disgruntled band members planted three dozen "For Sale" signs stolen from various yards in the area in front of Xavier "Two Tone" Simpson's house very early one Sunday morning in late May. The band director had cheated the two seniors out of the John Phillip Sousa Award given to the most deserving senior band member. The award was voted on by members of the band, but Two Tone rigged the election so his teacher's pet would receive the little trophy. The two musicians took their revenge and snapped quick digital pictures of their handiwork and posted them on social media. Clete Packer only needed about half a day to track down who did it. The two senior boys were suspended and not allowed to walk with their class at graduation later the next week.

Morg Miller was one of the last of the "Realtors" to leave the gym. Junior Schultz, Greg DeVito and Seth Parker left with him. Seth asked Jay to come along on the adventure but he begged off. He claimed he and Jorge had to make sure that Roxy got home, but Jay wasn't sure where Jorge was just then. Seth didn't bother asking Wash. He was dancing with Maricel and the way they were latched on together, there would be no separating them. Seth grimaced at the sight because it made him miss Amber and regret fighting with her.

As the four football players edged out of the gym, they caught sight of the superintendent talking with a deputy sheriff while an ambulance pulled in front of the school. The boys shrugged at each other as they surveyed the emergency vehicles casting a riot of swirling lights into the dense fog. An ambulance, two sheriff's patrol cars and a fire department rescue truck were parked near the front door of the school. It was the large fire truck that really drew their attention. It looked like it had tangled with the gray Mercedes in the front drive. The Mercedes bumper and the driver's side front quarter panel lay several feet in front of the car and wires hung from the stripped front end of the car.

Morg glanced at his cellphone. The time read 10:05. He motioned to the other three to head to the parking lot behind the school where the football players traditionally parked. The murky lighting behind the school contrasted with the brightly lit front of the school. Junior jumped in The Tank with Morg. Seth got into Greg's old Buick. Morg couldn't get the truck started. He cussed as he climbed out and went through the familiar routine of spraying the carburetor with ether.

"Come on man! Get that hunk of shit rolling!" Seth Parker called from the passenger window of Greg's car.

269

"It's this damn fog. The moisture keeps stalling the truck out. This is like the fifth time today I've had to hit it with ether," Morg explained.

"We got less than an hour to grab some signs and get to Fudge's house. The dance ends at 11:00, and he won't hang around long after he has driven the last kids out of the gym," Seth replied.

Morg nodded at Seth and motioned to Junior to turn the ignition key. The truck reluctantly turned over, but the engine caught with a slight backfire. In a few moments, they were easing out onto the street in front of the school. The lights of the emergency vehicles swirled behind them.

Sheldon Knapp leaned against the passenger door of his wrecked Mercedes reflecting on the events of the last hour. He contemplated how much his insurance rates would jump as he ignored the ambulance pulling away with a chirp of its siren. He didn't notice The Tank rumbling down the street. His eyes were burning a hole into the fog like a laser. He had his third ticket of the night folded neatly in his left hand.

Ten minutes before Sheldon Knapp walked into the high school office just before this latest run-in with the law, all hell was already breaking loose. Clete Packer called Molly Saunders to his office on her cellphone. When Molly entered the outer office, she locked eyes with Laurie Starke. A glint of triumph flickered in her eyes. Laurie's eyes flashed with realization and pure fury. In an instant she was on her feet and she closed the distance between herself and the pudgy custodian. Nancy Conover reflexively reached out to the younger woman and mouthed a silent "No." It was too late.

"YOU MISERABLE OLD SOW BITCH! YOU TIRED OLD BAG OF SHIT! YOU WERE THE ONE, WEREN'T YOU? YOU OVERHEARD THAT LYING LITTLE BASTARD BRAG ABOUT GETTING INTO MY PANTS DIDN'T YOU? WELL HE DIDN'T, YOU FAT SOW!" Laurie Starke screamed into the face of the shorter older woman, but Molly Saunders didn't back down from her accuser.

Fury matched fury as the two women stood close to each other.

"BACK OFF, SKANK! YOU BEST BACK OFF IF YOU KNOW WHAT'S GOOD FOR YOU!" Molly Saunders hoarsely shouted into the face of the young woman confronting her. "You come into this school parading around like a whore, and now you're going to get what is coming to you! You don't belong in a classroom with kids! You belong on a pole dancing for fat old men and giving them hand jobs for three bucks a pull!" Molly continued.

Nancy Conover got between the two women as Laurie Starke brought her hands up to claw at Molly Saunders' face. Laurie missed and Nancy pushed her back with one hand. The shove caught Laurie off guard and she stumbled slightly as her heels caught in the carpet.

"YOU FUCKING OLD CUNTS!" Laurie screeched as she scrambled to regain her momentum. Sheldon Knapp heard that scream as he entered the front door of the building. He began to run toward the office. He noted that the music was booming in the gym, so he was hoping no kids heard the outburst.

"THAT IS ENOUGH!" bellowed Clete Packer as he slammed his office door. He reached out and seized Laurie Starke's upper arm and he squeezed his fingers around a surprisingly powerful bicep. Laurie tried to wrench away from his painful grasp. The sleeve of the dress pulled loose at the shoulder seam. Reflexes guided Laurie, and she kicked backwards, gouging Clete with her heel down his right calf. The pain made the vice principal let go of the woman's arm. He was reaching down to feel what he was sure would be blood seeping through his pants leg when Laurie Starke spun around with all her force and struck him in the left ear with her cupped right hand. The young woman's rape and assault defense training paid off. The staggering pain of his eardrum being burst forced the fat man to his knees.

Clete Packer's wounded-animal grunt was drowned out by Laurie's shout. "KEEP YOUR FUCKING HANDS OFF ME, YOU FUCKING PIG!"

Sheldon Knapp entered the office to the sight of the young woman pulling free of the vice principal and spinning to strike him. Knapp froze with his mouth open as the young woman screamed at Packer. Physical violence terrified the slightly built superintendent. It always had, ever since high school when he was a bullied clarinet player in the band who suffered through innumerable toilet swirlies and underwear-tugging snuggies from the jocks who stalked and tormented him. His voice came weakly to him. Like a nervous old woman he cried, "What the hell is going on?!"

Nancy Conover backed Molly Saunders away as Laurie Starke began to advance toward them.

Laurie Starke paused and her eyes narrowed in recognition of Sheldon Knapp. She had only met him once at the beginning of the school year. "I'll tell you what's going on!" she stated firmly, and to Nancy Conover's surprise, quickly mastered her rage from only an instant ago.

"That nasty backstabbing old-biddy – has been spreading lies about me based on the completely false bragging by boys around this building." Laurie Starke pointed at the stout custodian.

"BULL! I heard you with my own ears admit you a relationship with Jorge Martinez! YOU LIE! You – awful – skank!" Molly Saunders turned purple with anger and began to cough during the last few words of her accusation.

"YOU ARE THE ONE LYING!" Laurie Starke shouted back at the custodian, who was struggling to gain her breath.

"Mrs. Conover, can you please tell me what is going on here?" Sheldon Knapp's voice was still high and nervous.

"Mr. Knapp – I – uh—" The teacher and the superintendent were distracted by Clete Packer. The assistant principal groaned and heaved himself up to a standing position, using a desk as support. His left eye was tearing up and he touched his ear tenderly. He pulled his hand down and stared dumbly at the thin watery drop of blood on his index finger. The room spun slightly and he closed his eyes to stop the vertigo.

"This old bat is the liar. Oh, and this one just struck me in the chest!" Laurie Starke used the pause to go back on the attack and she pointed at Nancy Conover. The supervising teacher's mouth dropped at the accusation.

"And Mr. Packer just tore my dress and wrenched my arm." Laurie Starke turned her body and tugged her sleeve to show the angry red welts in the pattern of the sausage-like fingers of the assistant principal. No bruises were raised yet, but Sheldon Knapp knew from the look of it there would soon be. "So, I will be pressing assault charges and I will be explaining to the police that Mr. Packer has practically been stalking me since I got here at the start of the semester. He is always undressing me with his eyes, and earlier tonight he called me a whore in front of the whole student body. He shouted it. There are 250 witnesses to that." Laurie Starke smiled a thin-lipped smile as she spun her version of events.

"I had to defend myself when he grabbed me from behind, and if I did it right, I probably just burst his eardrum." Laurie Starke's thin smile turned into a broader sneer of triumph as she explained herself to the superintendent. She took a second to enjoy the look of shocked bewilderment tinged with fear playing across his face.

Clete Packer fought off the vertigo and gathered himself and spoke hoarsely. "Sheldon, that is not what happened at all – Miss Starke was attacking Molly and Nancy when I reached out to stop her. She has been totally inappropriate this evening with students and some serious charges of student – fraternization – have come to my attention, so—"

"I TOLD YOU THERE WAS NO CONNECTION BETWEEN MYSELF AND JORGE MARTINEZ! THIS FAT SOW IS MAKING SHIT UP! SHE IS FUCKING CRAZY!" Laurie Starke cut off Clete Packer. Sheldon Knapp winced and felt his knees buckle a bit. Clete Packer's vertigo returned with a vengeance and he fought the urge to collapse in a chair. It occurred to Nancy Conover that Laurie Starke was not emotionally unstable so much as she was likely a raging sociopath. She had seen students behave like this over the years, but never an adult.

Molly Saunders stopped coughing long enough to rasp, "Keep it up, Skank! You're all done! You – you – cheap – whore!" another coughing fit racked her whole body as she made her point. Nancy Conover steered the now-gasping woman to a chair and sat her down.

Sheldon Knapp moved to take charge of the situation. "Miss Starke, you have to understand that when accusations as serious as these are made, we are obligated to investigate thoroughly, and of course you will be given due process, but—"

"DUE PROCESS?! I WILL TELL YOU WHAT THE PROCESS IS GOING TO BE. I ALREADY HAVE CONTACTED MY UNCLE! HE IS

A LAWYER FOR THE UAW! HE IS GOING TO COME IN HERE AND SUE ALL OF YOU! AND WHEN I LEAVE HERE I AM CONTACTING THE POLICE TO COME AND ARREST THIS FAT PIG FOR MOLESTING ME!" The volume of the statements did not mask the calculating intent behind Laurie Starke's words. She owned the room. No one else there was willing or capable of matching her energy. And certainly no one was now enjoying the confrontation as much as she was. She had no idea if there could be assault charges brought against Clete Packer. She didn't care about how her own behavior had put her in this situation. She was winning. She knew it. And it was damned exciting. But now she realized that leaving while she was in control was vital.

"Please, Miss Starke, we need to talk this through like adults and—" Sheldon Knapp was gaining his composure quickly and even some anger was starting to come to the surface.

"Fuck off! You can talk to my uncle. He'll be in touch," Laurie Starke said dismissively. And she moved past the superintendent toward the door.

Molly Saunders stopped coughing. She looked at the young woman and exclaimed, "Child rapist! Whore!"

Laurie Starke stopped at the door with her hand on the handle. "Go fuck yourself, you crazy old sow bitch. Better yet, why don't you do everyone a favor and just drop fucking dead," she said coldly looking over her shoulder at the tubby custodian sitting in a rolling office chair. She slipped through the door and began a brisk walk toward the gym. Jorge Martinez was down there somewhere and he was going to hear from her before she left tonight. She was going to do her best to shut that lying little prick down.

Molly Saunders marshaled her remaining strength and propelled herself up out of her chair and out the door. Sheldon Knapp made a broad motion with his hand. "Nancy, please go stop Molly from confronting the girl again. Maybe it is best if we just let Miss Starke leave the building at this point." Knapp's anger was building behind his request. Nancy Conover nodded and left the office as the superintendent began his dressing down of the assistant principal "Clete! Damn it! I told you not to talk to her unless—"

Molly Saunders was moving as fast as she could, but the much younger woman was disappearing into the gym at the end of the hall when she heard Nancy Conover call her name. Molly looked over her shoulder at the teacher and then refocused on the gym doors 100 feet ahead. She took two more steps and a thunderclap of pain hit her in her mid-back. Molly let loose a gasp and pitched sideways into the lockers in the hall. The clash of the metal lockers was drowned out by the thumping music in the gym. The tubby woman slid to the floor fighting for breath.

Molly Saunders' last conscious thought was one of anger at letting the young skank get the last word in. Her eyes had lost their focus as Nancy Conover knelt down and grabbed her wrist calling her name. There was no pulse as far as Nancy Conover could discern. She cursed the fact that her cellphone was in her purse. She looked back at the office and then toward the gym. Just a few weeks ago, she had completed training using the AED device. It was in a case next to the gym door. She bolted down the hall.

Mike Reese was watching Laurie Starke scan the crowd in the gym. She looked like she was on the warpath, and if he wasn't mistaken, her dress was torn at the shoulder. He was looking for John Cale to draw attention to what he assumed was a budding problem when he heard Nancy Conover shout his name over the loud music. He looked to the hall door of the gym where she was frantically waving at him, and then she began to unlatch the AED case. Reese shouted to John Cale and pointed at the door. They both got there at the same time.

"Mike! Molly Saunders has collapsed down the hall. I can't find her pulse!" Nancy Conover said urgently. She was loud enough to be heard, but she was trying not to draw too much attention. Out of the crowd, soccer coaches Miles Kitteridge and Ben Coffey appeared. John Cale was puzzled. He hadn't seen Ben Coffey all night – however, he noted that Coffey had some BBQ sauce on his tie, so he surmised the district grounds and maintenance director had likely been surfing the internet on the custodian office computer and shoveling food in his mouth from the banquet tables. Cale then focused on helping Mike gather up the AED. The five briskly made their way down the hall to the fallen woman. John Cale called 911 as Mike and Nancy got the AED ready to throw a charge into the prone body of Molly Saunders. Cale noted her ashen color. He suspected they were too late.

Nancy Conover thought of Superintendent Knapp as the first shock was administered. "Ben, go down to the office and get Mr. Knapp. He's in there with Clete Packer." Ben Coffey nodded and ran down the hall.

Coffey entered the office and took in the scene. Sheldon Knapp was pacing back and forth. His back was to the door. He was nearly shouting and gesturing with his hands. "And what if she does sue, Clete? Did you think of that? We don't have the money for that! Honestly, Clete, I promise you, if she sues this district, I am going to make sure you never even get a chance to be a building principle at a dog obedience school!"

Clete Packer's right eye was closed and his hand was gently pressed to his right ear. He winced every time Knapp's voice climbed up an octave to a shout. He nodded agreement with every point the superintendent made. But Ben Coffey noted his color wasn't much better than the custodian's receiving heart shocks in the hallway.

"Mr. Knapp, sir—" Coffey interrupted.

Sheldon Knapp turned toward the door, his face flashing from puzzlement to angry recognition. "What is it Ben!? I'm busy!" Knapp curtly snapped.

"Yes sir, but Molly Saunders has collapsed in the hall and we can't get her pulse and—" Ben began his explanation.

274

"Jesus Christ! Did someone call 911?" Knapp cut off Coffey as he made a move toward the door. Coffey and Packer followed him into the hall.

Shortly after Molly Saunders had her last conscious thought, Laurie Starke approached Jorge Martinez from behind at the mock-champagne fountain. He had just filled a large Solo cup with the liquid. It was his second. He had forgone the small clear cups set out by the fountain. It wasn't that he particularly liked the punch. He had cotton-mouth and his mind was racing. The confrontation between Laurie Starke and Mr. Packer had unnerved him. He couldn't help but think that there was trouble ahead. He was right, and he was about to learn how much.

Laurie Starke grasped his elbow firmly. Jorge flinched slightly. "In five minutes, I need to see you in the staff parking lot. Do you understand?" she said with forced calm. The music all but drowned out her word, but she knew from Jorge's body language that he understood.

Jorge bobbed his head gently twice. "Okay." He answered without looking at her.

"Be a man. Come alone. We need to settle some things right now. Wait two minutes after I leave and follow me," Laurie Starke continued in the same tone.

"Okay." Jorge replied and he gave the young woman a brief sideways glance. He couldn't read her face at all and she did not acknowledge his glance. She produced her own Solo cup and filled it in the fountain. She took a slight sip and then walked calmly through the front entrance of the gym. Holding her cup, she glided silently out the door, ignoring a friendly wave from Meghan Maleckis.

Almost no one noticed the exchange between Jorge and Laurie Starke. Bethany McCambridge did, and she got Meghan Maleckis to follow as they skulked behind Jorge when he left the gym. The staff parking lot was tucked into an area between the building and the Bear River, which ran behind the school. The two girls hid in the shadows next to a cardboard recycling dumpster. Laurie Starke was leaning on her car sipping ginger ale punch from a red cup. Jorge approached her quietly. The girls could see her face but not his. They strained to hear what was being said but the school heating system blower was roaring on the roof, and it blocked out the conversation.

Jorge was unsure what was going to be said as he approached the visibly angry woman. He had nothing to say. He had kept his distance. He hadn't spoken to anyone about having been with Laurie Starke's roommate the previous spring.

"This is going to be quick, and you had better listen closely. I'm all done here at this school. I will be taking legal action against the administration and maybe some others." Laurie Starke spoke in the same forced, calm tone she had used when she approached Jorge in the gym. She tried to read his face, but he remained calm. He nodded that he understood.

"You see, that crazy old sow custodian has been telling stories to that fat bastard Clete Packer about you and me. And I don't have any idea where she might have got the idea that you and I have had a relationship unless she overheard you running your mouth to all your little buddies about how you fucked both my roommate and me!" Laurie's voice rose to a higher level. Jorge held up his hands to signify he was not guilty.

"Miss Starke, I never mentioned having met you before this semester. I never talked to anyone about the – the relationship I – uh – had with Marcy. I have been—"

Laurie had come prepared for what she expected would be a lying denial from the boy. That is why she had a full cup of punch. Usually beer worked better, but ginger ale would do in a pinch. It was a method she had started to perfect when she was in high school. Before Jorge could finish his denial, she threw the contents of her cup into his face. Jorge backed away a step, sputtering and wiping his eyes.

"HAVE I GOT YOUR ATTENTION NOW!? GET THIS STRAIGHT, YOU LITTLE SHIT! YOU'RE JUST A LITTLE BOY WHO BRIEFLY GOT TO SWIM IN DEEP WATERS! YOU GOT THAT!? IF I HEAR OF SO MUCH AS A FUCKING PEEP FROM YOU ABOUT HOW YOU GOT IN MY PANTS I WILL COME TO THIS SCHOOL, FIND YOU, AND CUT YOUR BALLS OFF! KEEP YOUR FUCKING MOUTH SHUT FROM HERE ON OUT, YOU UNDERSTAND!?" Laurie Starke shouted harshly, but it was mostly a calculated act. She expected that Jorge would be called in to give his side of the story. It was better that he be scared into silence as far as she was concerned.

Jorge Martinez did not reply to her threat. He stood silently in the foggy parking lot, dripping ginger ale punch, as she got in her car, slammed the door, gunned the engine and pulled away. The two girls very clearly heard the shouting student teacher. They melted away and headed back to the gym. Jorge stood still for several minutes. Tears washed the sticky pop out of his eyes.

Laurie Starke made her way out of Bear River. She paid no attention to the flashing lights of the two fire department vehicles pulling out of the fire station as she passed by. She had just dialed 911 and was acting out a terrified mini-drama for the operator complete with little sobs as she described how Clete Packer had molested her and torn her dress.

When the first responders entered the school, Sheldon Knapp was instructing Miles Kitteridge and John Cale to go back to the gym and to keep the kids there. He didn't want a crowd of students gawking at the custodian as they tried to revive her. Knapp did not hear the grinding of metal as the large pumper truck tore away the bumper and front clip of his Mercedes. Two first responders displaced Mike Reese and Nancy Conover from beside the body of Molly Saunders.

"I've got a pulse! It's weak but it's there. Let's bag her," the younger of the two firemen said.

His older partner began to pull out the necessary material to begin full resuscitation. The young fireman pulled the leads of the school AED from the chest of the custodian and he looked at Nancy Conover. "Your work?" he asked. Nancy Conover nodded and pointed at Mike Reese to indicate both of them had deployed the device. "Good job," he smiled, knowing better than to say anything about the low likelihood that ultimately Molly Saunders would survive for very long. He had seen too many cases like this to be very hopeful.

More firemen came. One called, "Anyone here own that gray Mercedes out front?"

"It's mine," Sheldon Knapp said reflexively.

"You shouldn't have parked it there. That's a fire lane," the fireman stated.

"Did you scratch my car!?" Sheldon Knapp asked heatedly.

"Oh, it's more than a scratch. The pumper rig is forty feet long. Kind of hard to thread needles on an emergency run. They mark fire lanes for a reason, you know. Didn't hurt the truck none but it looks like you will be walking for a while," the fireman replied matter-of-factly.

"What the hell!" Sheldon Knapp called out as he danced around the gathering clot of emergency workers heading for the door. He ignored the snort of contemptuous laughter from the fireman.

Sheldon Knapp was greeted by an ambulance pulling up to the front of the building. He ignored it. He began to shout at two firemen near the pumper truck. "Why did you do that!? You couldn't enter from the other side of the drive?! This is going to cost thousands to repair!" He pointed at the bumper and quarter panel lying in the elliptical drive in front of the school ten feet in front of his car. It was obvious that the fire-truck's bumper had neatly hooked the front of the Mercedes above the left front wheel well and surgically snapped off the parts lying on the ground. Sheldon Knapp had been proud of the money he had saved when he paid cash for the used Mercedes last year. And since he didn't finance the purchase, he got the highest deductible insurance he could. After all he was a safe driver – nothing was likely to happen. To repair the Mercedes was going to cost him $2,500 out of pocket. Not to mention how much his insurance would go up.

Sheldon Knapp wasn't done. "Do you know who I am? I'm the superintendent of this school! I was responding to an emergency! The parking spots were all full! I have a right to park here!!" He shouted. One of the firemen waved him off as he held the front school door open for the ambulance gurney.

"You see, that's where you're wrong. Only emergency vehicles can park in a fire lane." The statements came from a calm, authoritative voice from behind. Knapp recognized it immediately.

Sheldon Knapp turned to face the young deputy who had ticketed him just a few minutes ago. The deputy had parked behind his wrecked Mercedes and the emergency lights of the cruiser blended in with the rest of the vehicles and their flashers.

"Officer – uh—" In his anger Sheldon Knapp drew a blank.

"Doolittle, Mr. Knapp," the deputy finished the statement.

"Oh yes, I remember now. Very aptly named," Sheldon Knapp snapped at him. He was angry and getting petulant.

Deputy Bryan Doolittle gave the superintendent a wan smile. Sheldon Knapp continued, "This was uncalled for!" Knapp pointed at his wrecked car.

"I agree, Mr. Knapp, this is uncalled for. You never should have parked here," Doolittle agreed as he pulled out his citation book and began to write.

"Oh no! You are NOT going to write me a ticket for this! I am the superintendent here! I have to have access to the school! I was responding to an emergency! Knapp angrily confronted the deputy.

Doolittle ignored him and finished writing the ticket. He calmly walked to the wrecked Mercedes and placed the ticket under the wiper blade.

"Look, young man, I think you should know I know the county sheriff very well! I donated heavily to his reelection campaign and I have played golf with him for years! I was in his foursome in his campaign golf outing the last two elections! And I will be calling him tonight! Not tomorrow! Not Monday! Tonight!" Sheldon Knapp spewed petulant threats.

The deputy laughed gently and shook his head. "Yeah, the sheriff loves to golf. He's damn good, isn't he? I mean, I have never beaten him, and he always gives me a few strokes."

Sheldon Knapp was not getting the response he wanted at all, and he paused. He was unsure how to proceed.

"So you are going to call the sheriff tonight? Do me a favor and remind him his daughter and I will be over early to watch the Lions before dinner tomorrow. Tell him we will be bringing the kids so he should put up the baby gate." Deputy Doolittle smiled a little cruelly as he spoke.

Sheldon Knapp blinked. He opened his mouth but nothing came out.

"Say, would you like to see a picture of his newest grandson?" The deputy continued with obvious mock familiarity. He fished into his back pocket and produced his wallet. He flipped through some photos and held up a picture of the county sheriff, in uniform, holding what looked to be a one-year-old boy and smiling broadly. "Some people say he looks a lot like the sheriff, which is cool because we named the boy after him. But then some others say he looks more like me. What do you think?" The cruel smile did not fade from his lips. Sheldon Knapp got the distinct impression he was not the first person to receive this treatment from the deputy. He said nothing.

"I'll tell you what. I'll give you a break. You could, if you like, go back into the school to look after your staff member as they bring her out to the ambulance. And while you are at it, you might want to arrange to have a tow truck come and take your car to a body shop. Because if it is here when I cruise through town later this evening, I am going to call for a truck to take it to the county impound lot. That will get a little pricey for you." The deputy

278

continued to smile. Sheldon Knapp felt his face reddening. He didn't respond. He stood looking at the deputy and trying to formulate a response.

"Or you can continue to stand here and debate with me, in which case I will write you your fourth ticket of the evening for obstructing emergency personnel. What will it be?" The smile disappeared from the deputy's face and his words had a hard edge to them. Sheldon Knapp backed away and turned to walk into the school. He pulled his cellphone from his pocket and dialed the number for AAA road service. As he entered, Molly Saunders was being strapped into the gurney. Clete Packer was being examined by a paramedic.

Clete Packer looked miserable. He met Sheldon Knapp's eyes and spoke in quiet tones. "They say I need to go to the emergency room, but I can't drive because of the vertigo. Can you give me a lift? My wife is on a church retreat down-state."

"Not hardly, Clete, my car is torn to pieces. Have Ben Coffey drive you. I have to wait for a wrecker, then my wife will come to take me home." Sheldon Knapp spoke in defeated tones as well. He was going to go home and get blitzed. Not on the good scotch, though. He was going to demolish a fifth of the cheap rotgut he broke out when his wife's idiot brothers came to visit. He followed the gurney out the front door and walked to his wounded vehicle. He leaned on the passenger side door. He ignored the small group of students outside the front entrance of the gym who were gawking at the emergency vehicles. As he ran his fingers through his hair and rotated his stiff neck to release the stress with a few pops and cracks, he wondered what else could go wrong this evening. Had he been clairvoyant he still wouldn't have imagined what was still in store for the Bear River Schools staff that night.

The story of the confrontation between Jorge Martinez and Laurie Starke swept through the remaining students in the gym. The two witnesses couldn't keep the story secret – it was just too much. Upon hearing the story third-hand, Wash, Jay, and Roxy began a frantic search for Jorge. It would be a while before they would find him.

Out on the streets of Bear River, the two-vehicle caravan consisting of Greg DeVito's Buick and The Tank was cruising through the fog looking for Realtor signs to appropriate for the "sale" of Clete Packer's house. Being late to the hunt, the boys were frustrated. Seth had pulled one sign and tossed it into the trunk of the Buick. The Tank sputtered as Morg coaxed it up the 16th Street hill. At the very top of the hill it gave a muffled backfire and stopped. Morg cursed and slipped the floor shifter into creeper gear, which served as a makeshift parking break when the truck was stalled. The fog was so thick he couldn't even see the taillights of the Buick. He didn't want to honk his horn and alert the neighborhood.

"Sit tight. I'll get it," Junior Shultz offered. He hopped out the passenger door with the screwdriver and can of ether in his hands. Morg was relieved to see Greg's Buick pull up. The car's headlights helped Junior see to pop the hood on the truck. He climbed the front bumper and removed the air filter. Morg could hear him jamming the screwdriver into the carburetor and spraying the ether. He also heard the doors of the Buick close.

"What a hunk of rolling shit," Seth said as he walked to the driver side window.

Morg cranked the window down. "Leave The Tank alone. Don't be saying bad stuff to it. It's sensitive." Morg made light of the situation.

"Hit it," Junior said as he climbed off the bumper.

Morg turned the key. The engine didn't catch. Morg tried again and the starter made a clicking noise. On the third attempt no sound could be heard.

"Aw, fuck," Morg swore.

"What the hell is wrong?" Junior asked.

"The starter is fucked," Morg grumbled, but he resisted cursing his truck. He never did that. He did think the old flatbed was sensitive. In the two years since he and his father had rolled it out of the old chicken coop on the farm and got it running after ten years sitting idle, he had only said nice and encouraging things to the rickety bucket of rust. When his friends teased him about the forty-year-old truck, he noted that at least he had a vehicle and he didn't have a car payment. Also, he noted frequently, his dad had it registered as a farm vehicle so the insurance was real cheap. The simple fact was that Morg Miller loved The Tank in the way that every teenage boy loved his first vehicle.

"Can we give it a jump?" Greg had joined the other two boys at the window of the truck.

"No – it's not the battery. The starter is dead. It's been stalling so much we just wore it out or something." Morg said as he climbed down out of the cab.

"What now? Can we bang on the starter? Sometimes that frees it up," Junior Shultz said hopefully.

"No. I think we would have better luck push-starting it," Morg replied.

"That truck weighs five tons – and it's got those two hay bales on it. Those got to weigh a ton a-piece after being out in the rain the last two days. No way are we push-starting that hunk of shit," Seth whined. Morg waved him off with a frown.

"We can use the hill. We just got to turn it around. Greg, you got anything like a tow strap in the trunk?" Morg took charge. He was a farmer's son. Boys raised on farms know how to get vehicles running, but familiarity can lead to a callous attitude when it comes to safety.

"Yeah, I got one, but it's buried under a shit ton of stuff," Greg answered.

"You two give him a hand, and I'll put the air filter back on The Tank. We got to get rolling or we won't be there to see everybody putting the signs in Fudge's yard." Morg gave instructions to Junior and Seth and he climbed up on the bumper of the old flatbed.

In a minute, Morg twisted the wing nut on the air filter cover and jumped backwards off the bumper. The trucked rocked on its mostly worthless shocks and squeaked a little in protest. Morg swept the hood prop away from its catch, and he caught the hood before it crashed down. He could hear his friends grousing about the amount of things in the trunk of the Buick.

"Jesus, Greg, do you need two spare tires? And why do you have two sets of golf clubs." Seth was whining again.

Morg thumped down the hood of The Tank and pushed himself away from it as he heard the latch catch. What he didn't hear was the soft thunk of the truck slipping out of its creeper gear. The truck rocked gently as he spun around and began to question his friends. "What the hell is taking so long?" The other three boys were making a racket unloading the large trunk of the mid-80s vintage Buick sedan.

Morg walked back to the trunk of the Buick. Junior popped his head up. He was holding his cellphone. He had the flashlight app on, and the glare caught Morg in the eyes and he blinked and waved his hand at his friend to put it down. When Morg blinked away the glare he looked Junior in the face, Junior's face was a frozen mask of pure terror.

"Morg! The Tank's gone!" Junior sounded the alarm.

Morg spun around. The Tank had been about ten feet in front of the Buick. He looked and the only thing he could see was a brightly lit patch of opaque fog where his truck had been seconds before.

"OH NO!" Morg's voice cracked in a scream. The Tank had begun its last trip without him. He was paralyzed for a second. Then he began to sprint into the fog.

Xavier "Two Tone" Simpson was the band director at BRHS. He was thirty-six years old. He had been hired shortly after Christmas as a long-term substitute teacher over a decade ago when the previous band director, a young teacher by the name of Malone, had run off with the sixteen-year-old daughter of another staff member. The event preceded the tenure of Superintendent Sheldon Knapp. The resulting scandal precipitated the resignation of the superintendent at the time who had hired the young man – his nephew. The whole mess played out in the papers across the region. When Knapp was hired the following summer, it was because he had skills in making problems go away quietly. Knapp had been an administrator at a community college down state. He was skilled in education politics. He was not experienced at all in hiring teachers. One of his first acts as superintendent at Bear River was to offer a regular teaching contract to the gawky young band director.

Two Tone Simpson was an odd-looking man. He stood over six feet five inches tall with narrow shoulders and long skinny legs. In the middle was a pot belly that looked like he swallowed a whole watermelon. This caused his shirts to be perpetually untucked. Two Tone was a gifted musician who could play any instrument, and he played trombone in a couple of local swing and jazz bands. He also sang beautifully and headed up the choir at St. Luke's Lutheran Church. His mouth was filled with crooked coffee-stained teeth and his breath was notoriously foul. He was not a gifted teacher. He was prone to outbursts of sarcastic anger directed at his students. He always played favorites and kept teacher's pets. As a result, rarely did more than four or five students in any senior class complete four years of high school band.

Normally, someone with breath as foul as Two Tone's would have gotten a nickname like "Stinky" or "Trash Can Mouth," which is what his roommates in college called him behind his back. And that might have been the case in Bear River had he not grown his beard to look older for job interviews shortly after graduation from college. With whiskers in place, the most prominent feature Two Tone possessed was his bizarre hair. He had jet black hair on his head styled in a 1980s mullet. His beard was large and bushy and bright orange red. With his pasty white complexion the effect was startling and comical. Shortly after he was hired, kids and staff members started to refer to him as "Two Tone." It was not a nickname he liked, and he would blow up at any student in his class he heard using it.

Two Tone Simpson lived at the bottom of the 16th Street hill in a two-story Victorian cottage, which his wife had meticulously restored, putting the young couple deeply in debt. Sharon Simpson was the plain-faced and humorless secretary of St. Luke's Lutheran Church. She also played organ at every service, but not very well, much to Two Tone's dismay. Two Tone and Sharon had been married for ten years. They had two elementary-aged daughters named Charlotte and Beatrix who had both inherited their father's crooked teeth, pasty complexion and black hair. Most unfortunately – they inherited their mother's sour disposition.

The house at the bottom of the steep 16th Street hill was home to an overflowing menagerie of pets. The Simpson family had two skittish cats named Puff and Fluff that were supposed to be the daughters' pets but in fact spent most of the day hiding in the attic, causing the girls to whine as they endlessly searched for them. Two Tone spent hours tending the well-stocked sixty-gallon saltwater fish tank that sat in front of the large picture window at the front of the house.

The noisiest animals in the house were three birds. One was a Citron Cockatoo named Bunny that was high strung and depressed to the point that she plucked out most of her feathers. Bunny looked like a bleached, skinny, half-plucked chicken. Bunny had a very limited vocabulary. Mostly, she whistled and shrieked, but when she was highly stressed, she would shout, "Balls!" This was Two Tone's favorite curse word for home use since the children were born. And with a temper like Two Tone's, it was frequently heard. Bunny was five years old. She was a Christmas gift from Sharon's eccentric grandmother who kept over a dozen birds in her home until the last year when she passed away in her sleep watching TV. Sharon Simpson inherited her grandmother's prized pair of African grey parrots, Samson and Delilah. The three birds had large cages in the front parlor.

The greys possessed expressive vocabularies picked up from cowboy movies that Sharon's hard-of-hearing grandmother had showing on her TV sixteen hours a day at high volume. When family was around they were treated to Samson squawking "Reach for it, Mister!" Delilah would then call out sounds imitating a six-gun shootout. When no one was around or if they were in other rooms, the last few months the greys had taken to imitating Bunny's shrieks and whistles until the frustrated Bunny would scream "Balls!" To which Samson and Delilah would call, "Balls! Balls! Balls! Balls!" sometimes for more than twenty minutes, and all while the anxious Bunny plucked at her few remaining feathers. Two Tone had begun to plot ways to eliminate the birds.

To escape the squawking parrots, Two Tone would sit in a lawn chair in the backyard garage where he kept his man cave. He would spend as much time as possible listening to old vinyl jazz records on his large stereo system in the garage with his favorite animal in the Simpson menagerie. He had bought T-Bone, his black lab, shortly after college, and he was very attached to the dog. His wife loved the old dog too. Sharon Simpson loved all animals – it was one of the few pleasant things about her. She fussed over the aging dog and fed it too much. The fat old dog was happiest lying on the floor near his master, and when Two Tone wasn't home, T-Bone napped on the large front porch waiting for him to pull up in his old Volvo station wagon. At night, T-Bone slept at the foot of their bed emitting unpleasant smells caused by the rich food Sharon always stuffed him with. Every other Saturday night, T-Bone would find himself banished to the oak floored hallway in front of their bedroom door.

Sharon Simpson found sex with her husband to be an unpleasant necessity. She believed providing him with release twice monthly fulfilled her Christian duty as his wife. It hadn't been that way at the start, but after delivering their second child six years ago she found her sex drive gone as if it were never there. She still loved Two Tone – or so she convinced herself, but it was getting harder and harder to approximate arousal as he put on weight, and she had always found his breath to be obnoxious. There were measures she could take to cure that problem. The dog simply could not be in the room while she consummated her marital obligation. She could stand her husband's rotting breath for a few moments as long as she faced the other way and as long as it was not combined with the stench of lingering dog farts.

On this Saturday night, Sharon dosed her young girls with Benadryl two hours after dinner to insure their sound sleep. Besides the obnoxious smells in her bedroom, she could not bear the thought of her girls interrupting the biweekly ritual. At 10:30 P.M., Two Tone led his faithful dog out of the bedroom. Sharon came in from the bathroom and wordlessly accepted the advances of her desperately aroused husband. T-Bone would not have to wait long. The flatulent old Labrador heaved a heavy sigh on the hall floor as their antique bed began to rhythmically squeak.

As Two Tone neared his climax a few moments later, The Tank was gaining considerable speed as it rolled quietly backwards down the 16th Street hill. Morg dashed through the heavy fog as the truck rolled away. He was not keeping up, and he loudly hissed, "Fuuuuuuuuuck!!!" Junior, Seth and Greg followed their friend down the hill. They could hear Morg, but they could not see him or The Tank. There was an eerie five seconds of silence followed by a shattering crash. Screams both human and animal followed.

The Tank had veered off the center of the street at the bottom of the hill. It struck the curb in front of the Simpsons' lovely two-story Victorian cottage and vaulted into the air. In the glow of the large aquarium's lights in the front parlor Puff and Fluff were enjoying the lack of the Simpson girls dogging their every step. They were nestled together on the antique settee glancing back and forth from the birds to the multi-colored tropical fish with malicious intent. The Tank slashed through the shrubs to the right of the heavy concrete and brick steps and slammed violently to a halt halfway up the stairs. The large round hay bales broke free from their restraining straps, slipped swiftly off the flat bed and snapped off a porch support column as they headed for the large plate glass window.

Several things happened almost simultaneously. A wall of hay, salt water, tropical fish and broken glass obliterated the Victorian-era antique furniture in the front parlor. The cats were buried under mounds of wet hay. The birds screeched as their cages were sent crashing. Bunny the Cockatoo screamed one last emphatic "Balls!" and then she died of a heart attack. Upstairs in the hallway, the usually sedate T-Bone sprang to his feet howling and ran shitting and pissing up the hall to the spare bedroom. Two Tone Simpson was at the height of his orgasm shudder when the thunderous collision shook the house under his feet. A fleeting thought crossed his mind that perhaps he was dying of a stroke like his uncle had at an early age.

The screaming howls of his dog, his children and his wife brought Two Tone somewhat back to his senses, but now adrenalin took over his body. The secondary crash as the porch roof gave way was the trigger to send him into spastic action. He pushed himself violently free of his wife's shapeless backside. Sharon Simpson was propelled across the bed and fell to the floor screaming his name. Two Tone snagged his boxer shorts and was hopping into them as he stumbled into the hallway. He managed to put his left leg through but as he struggled to put his right foot through, his big toe got caught in the fly hole. He hopped twice on his left foot trying to extricate his toe and pull on his shorts in hopes of keeping his daughters from seeing him naked and aroused. Too late – Char and Bea were standing ten feet away in the hallway crying. What they saw next stayed with them their whole lives.

On the second left-footed hop Two Tone landed squarely on one of the enormous turds T-Bone had squirted free in his haste to hide whimpering under the bed in the spare bedroom. His foot slipped out from under him and with his right big toe still caught in the fly he pitched forward toward the top of the stairway. Two Tone reached out his left hand to catch himself on the bannister near the top of the stairs. He wasn't able to stop himself, and as his big toe tore his boxers free, he flew naked into the stairwell. His right arm wind-milled into the wall at the landing six steps from the top. His hand smashed a hole through the ancient plaster and lath, breaking his wrist and forearm. His downward momentum pulled him free of the hole in the wall dislocating his right shoulder. A violent yelp of pain escaped his lips as he tumbled through the corner of the stairs at the landing. With his arm disabled, he was not able to catch himself as he gained speed and he struck the lower steps face first. The blow dislodged teeth in his upper and lower jaw. The explosive pain and the concussion of the final strike caused him to lose consciousness. It was the only mercy he was granted that night.

When the first responders arrived on the scene he was still out cold and lying naked in a pool of his own blood. Upstairs T-Bone whimpered and howled in anguish. Puff and Fluff extricated themselves from their wet tomb of hay and scrambled out the broken front wall of the house. Neither cat was ever seen again. Sharon and the girls sat sobbing on the stairs next to Two Tone Simpson's prone body. Their sobs were nearly drowned out by the grey parrots shrieking "Balls!" repeatedly in the wrecked front parlor.

As Deputy Doolittle was taking Morg Miller's statement, the paramedics loaded Two Tone Simpson into the ambulance. Morg was broken-hearted. Not about Two Tone, although he did feel bad that he had inadvertently hurt someone. No, it was the condition of his beloved truck that had him despondent. A simple glance at The Tank told him all he needed to know. The frame was snapped in half and the cab was crushed against the flatbed. The firemen sprayed foam all over the wreck and the front yard of the Simpson house because gas was leaking everywhere. The next stop for The Tank would be the junk yard. The deputy lectured Morg about endangering people with poorly maintained equipment and lack of precautions on the stalled vehicle. Morg shook his head glumly in agreement and accepted the citation without complaint. Junior, Seth and Greg had disappeared into the fog before the cops arrived. Everyone agreed that four boys at the wreck site would look very suspicious. Morg felt profoundly alone as he called his father on his cellphone. It was not an enjoyable call. His night was over and other than pictures on social media, he didn't even get to see the sixty-plus for sale signs planted in Fudge Packer's lawn.

Jorge was walking through downtown Bear River when his friends caught up to him. He had stood in the fog for some time outside the school. Eventually he began to walk. He didn't pick a direction, and in the fog he wasn't really sure where he was at when Wash and Maricel pulled up next to him on the street. Maricel called Roxy. She and Jay were searching as well. Wash coaxed his friend into the car. They met up with Jay and Roxy at a diner near the freeway in Gratiot. By the time they left, Jorge had explained everything about his predicament. He was feeling better by the end of it, and his friends were very supportive, but he knew that it wasn't over yet. He resolved to speak to his parents.

At 11:15, Josh Gruelich and Todd Donheiser glided up to Clete Packer's house on their longboards. They were half wasted. After leaving the school they sat in the play structure at the park near the dam on the Bear river and smoked a couple of bowls. Only high teenage boys would think a foggy and damp fall evening would be a good time to skateboard through town. In fact, as long as there wasn't snow on the streets, the two of them usually travelled by longboard. They laughed as the cross country runners placed the last of the "For Sale" signs. Then they got to work.

Clete Packer's tri-level home sat mid-block on a street in the nicest part of town. The lawn was flawless. All the hedges were perfectly trimmed. It was a large lot with an elliptical drive. An additional two-door pole building sat in the large backyard. An above-ground pool was back there as well. The boys didn't care about that. In fact, it was so foggy they could barely see the house, let alone the back yard. They arranged a perfect line of for-sale signs on the sidewalk in front of the home. All the athletes were gone, so no one questioned what they were up to. Once they were satisfied they fished out the paint from their backpacks. After a brief consultation on which color to use where, it was settled. Josh used a florescent orange on the signs in front. Todd went to work on the large brown garage door under the family room of the tri level. Josh finished first. Then he added some orange flourishes to the large white and fluorescent lime green ornate lettering Todd was masterfully creating on the garage. Then they emptied their cans on the cement drive with just a few more parting words. It took almost a half an hour. They worked silently. No one noticed them. They benefited because on the gloomy night, few people were out. And, of course, Clete Packer was indisposed. They glided off into the fog together heading to the mini-mart west of town to get some Twinkies and Double Stuff Oreos.

Shortly after midnight, Clete Packer was sitting sullenly in the waiting area of the emergency room of the Gratiot hospital and Ben Coffey sat next to him playing Angry Birds on his iPhone. Clete was not shocked when shortly after he got there they rolled Molly Saunders out to the helipad for an air-lift to the hospital in Lansing. When they rolled Two Tone Simpson in a little while later, it was a more disturbing scene. The band director regained consciousness in the ambulance and became combative. He was ranting as they brought him in the ER. Blood sprayed from his mouth with each shout. Less than two minutes later, Sharon Simpson came through the door dragging her crying girls behind her. The girls were in their pajamas. Sharon looked shell-shocked. Clete tried to get her to explain what had happened to her husband, but she got hysterical. She started shouting about her ruined home and her dead bird. Clete gave up and texted Sheldon Knapp.

Sheldon Knapp was in no mood to deal with the situation at the hospital. He had been home long enough to drink two tumblers of McMaster's scotch. The dull iodine taste made him grimace with each gulp, but he truly did not give a shit. Knapp replied to the text, "I'll deal with this tomorrow." And he turned off his phone.

Deputy Bryan Doolittle came up to Clete as he sat uncomfortably in a chair in the ER waiting room. "I thought you might still be here. They still haven't got to you, huh? Saturday nights are busy in the ER."

Clete Packer agreed glumly.

"We just got notified by the Isabella County sheriff's office that they have a woman, a Laurie Starke, in the ER in the Mt. Pleasant hospital who has sworn out an assault complaint against you. I'm here to take your statement," Deputy Doolittle explained. He then told Ben Coffey that he should go sit elsewhere. Ben got up and walked to the other side of the waiting room.

Clete Packer felt a lump in his throat. The vertigo tumbled back into his head. "That's rich," he replied. "She's saying I assaulted her? Christ, I'm sitting here with my head spinning and a burst eardrum, and I assaulted her? I was trying to keep her from attacking Molly, you know, the woman they just airlifted out of here an hour ago? Laurie was trying to scratch her eyes out when Nancy Conover and I stopped her. I hold that evil little – woman – responsible for what happened to Molly Saunders. She kept taunting the poor old girl. Did you get a look at Molly? I think she's not going to make it. Laurie Starke is an evil little witch. She's a student teacher this semester. Or was. As far as I'm concerned, she doesn't belong anywhere near students. We were investigating an allegation of – of some serious improprieties involving Miss Starke and a student when she freaked out and attacked Molly and me. Yes, I grabbed her by the arm, but if you would have been there, you would have done the same if you saw the rage she was in." Clete rambled on in a low, hoarse voice. Once or twice, he glanced at the deputy, trying to read his eyes. He didn't see anything that looked like sympathy.

Officer Doolittle wrote Clete's statement on his yellow pad. "So you say this Molly Saunders and Ms. Starke were having an altercation and you stopped it?" he asked, glancing at Clete.

"Yes," Clete answered.

"And it was related to an allegation that Mrs. Saunders was making about Miss Starke?" Doolittle continued.

"Yes. Molly overheard Laurie Starke talking with some students before the dance tonight. Molly was very concerned that students might be in danger. But with Molly – well, I don't think she will be testifying to anything. And the kids will clam up, probably. They always do. So the little – well, anyway, Miss Starke probably will never have to refute anything – officially." Clete sounded weary and fatalistic.

"Can you speak to what improprieties Mrs. Saunders was alluding to?" Deputy Doolittle asked.

"Not really. Molly was not feeling well most of the evening. Horrible coughing fits. And she was in quite an agitated state. I was not able to get details from her before she collapsed," Clete Packer lied. Before he left the high school with Ben Coffey, the superintendent told him specifically that the police were not to be included in any investigation until he gave the information to them in a neat package.

"Well, any complaint against Ms. Starke for improprieties, whatever Mrs. Saunders might have been referring too, is going to be a complicated case, no doubt. Hearsay testimonials of improprieties are difficult to build a case on. Your situation is different. This is a 'she said, he said' accusation of assault. Both of you have physical injuries. We will have to take the statement of the other teacher present and Mr. Knapp, of course. I can't tell you where it will land. You might want to get your lawyer up to speed as soon as possible," Doolittle explained as he flipped his yellow pad shut and put his pen away.

"Mr. Packer, we have a spot for you now." A young nurse presented a wheelchair and motioned Clete to it as she spoke.

Clete nodded and got into the chair. Ben Coffey walked toward him as they headed back, and Clete waved him away with a sour look on his face.

A bald and world-weary doctor a little older than himself examined Clete a few minutes later. He explained to the now-exhausted assistant principal that it was in fact a burst eardrum. He packed Clete's outer ear with cotton and covered it with medical tape. He advised that Clete keep the ear covered in that manner for a few days. Clete was told not to go scuba diving for the next six weeks. The doctor waited for a laugh. He didn't get one. So the doctor gave him a prescription for pain and nausea should the vertigo cause any. The doctor further advised that that if the vertigo persisted, he should see his regular physician. He also advised against driving for twenty-four hours. Clete asked if he could go to work on Monday. The disinterested doctor assured it would be all right as long as he avoided sharp and loud noises.

At about the time Clete Packer was seeing the ER doctor, Nancy Conover was in bed lying next to her husband. He listened patiently as she listed the steps that needed to be taken for him to withdraw money from his retirement account to finance the purchase of the two service years necessary for her to retire from teaching at the end of the current school year. He knew better than to object at this point. His wife was emotionally spent from the evening's events. He hoped that after a few weeks he would be able to persuade her to stick it out a few more years.

As Ben Coffey was walking Clete Packer to the parking lot of the hospital, Sheldon Knapp was passed out on the leather couch in his home office. His wife tucked a heavy Western Michigan Bronco football blanket around his skinny neck. Knapp turned away on the couch and mumbled, "Clete, you asshole." Marie Knapp had only a sketchy idea of what had put her husband into such a state. Sheldon snapped at her when she had the temerity to try to get details on the night's events and why his car was wrecked. As she walked to the master suite on the other side of the house, she was thinking about contacting her cousin in Lansing. She was a very successful divorce attorney.

As Ben Coffey drove the silent Clete Packer back to Bear River, he noted the fog was lifting. Packer grunted an uncaring response. Also at about that time, Laurie Starke was on her fourth rum and coke and halfway through a pack of cigarettes as she pecked away at her laptop's keyboard posting increasingly profane and descriptive social media rants about Clete Packer, Molly Saunders and Nancy Conover and her former roommate, who, in Laurie's estimation, was responsible for everything because she had been a raging slut who seduced a high school junior. No one was responding yet. But in the morning, plenty of cross-posts would add to the storm building in Bear River. Laurie was not mindful of the fact that she friended more than just a few BRHS students and they in turn had hundreds of friends – including parents and school staff members.

In Lansing, Molly Saunders occupied a bed in the cardiac intensive care unit at Sparrow Hospital. She had already coded once since arriving there. During a bed check, a first-year nurse patted her hand and whispered to her, "Come on, Granny, Hang tough, those grandkids want another Thanksgiving and Christmas with you." The nurse was not aware that Molly had lost her only baby in childbirth over thirty-five years prior and she was never able to conceive another child.

As Molly was being encouraged by the young nurse, fifty miles to the north Ben Coffey pulled up to the Packer house. He stopped short halfway into the drive, and the headlights from his Dodge pickup flashed across the sea of For Sale signs in the front lawn. Clete Packer sat bolt upright and exclaimed, "What in the fucking hell?!" as he read the message left in bright paint on the front of most of the signs. In clean letters the message read: "SUCK IT FUDGE!!"

Packer bolted from the passenger door as soon as Ben Coffey completed the turn into the drive. The headlights illuminated an ornate and very large spray-painted gang tag on the garage door exclaiming: "FREE MANIKOWSKI!"

Clete Packer stormed to the signs tagged with his hated nickname. With a grunt, he pulled the sign with the letter F painted on it from the ground. He spun and heaved it into the street like a discus. As it clattered across the pavement he yelled, "FUCKING PUNKS!"

His head was spinning but he grabbed the sign with the "U" painted on it and tossed it to the street shouting, "GODDAMN FUCKING ASSHOLES!" He repeated the action and the curses with each lettered sign. And then he moved on to the dozens of other signs, uprooting them and cursing at the top of his lungs. Ben Coffey was frozen standing in front of his truck taking in the scene not knowing what to do. The headlights made his shadow appear huge on the garage door. Neither man noticed the lights of neighboring houses coming on and curtains being pulled back at the windows.

The vertigo began to get the better of Clete Packer fifteen minutes into his rage. As he slowed down, Ben Coffey summoned the nerve to approach him. "Clete, man, somebody is gonna call the cops. You got to settle down or you're going to get airlifted to Lansing and get a bed next to Molly." The younger man pleaded with him. And the fat assistant principal finally stopped. About three dozen signs were plucked and discarded across the yard and drive and into the street. Many more remained firmly implanted in the well-manicured lawn. The truck lights and the street light on the corner barely lit the scene but there was enough light to see that the job of knocking down all the signs would be beyond the endurance of Clete Packer. His head was swimming. He could feel his pulse in his wounded ear. His breath came in short panting gulps. He put his hands on his knees and bent over. Ben Coffey thought perhaps he might collapse. But the older man stood upright. His eyes were fixed on the garage door.

"Fucking punks." Packer said more quietly. "They are going to pay. It's those fucking punks on the football team. You know it. I know it. I'm going to fucking bury them. I don't care if we have to forfeit the last two games of the season, I'm going to suspend each and every one of the disrespectful vandalizing bastards. I am going to start with the lead shithead, Morg Miller. I am going to bust the cocky little creep."

"No doubt it was football players," Ben Coffey agreed enthusiastically. He thought back to the shit on the soccer pitch and the broken water horse and everything else. "I'll help you nail them, Clete, I will. But we got to clean up the mess in the street. Then I'll come over first thing tomorrow with my truck and we'll gather up these signs and take them to the school. And I'll have my wife contact the Realtors. She's in that business and she knows most of them in the area. They can come get their signs on Monday. Hell, I got some great graffiti removers at work, and I'll help you get that shit cleaned off your garage door too. I mean soon as we can. We're going to need it as evidence to hang those little bastards. But now we got to pick up those signs you threw into the street. The cops will have a shit fit."

Deputy Bryan Doolittle turned on the flashers as he glided up to the house. The noise of a For Sale sign being crushed on the pavement under his wheels announced his arrival. Clete Packer and Ben Coffey both turned and faced a swinging spotlight beam. Coffey winced and held up his hand to shield his eyes.

"Hands where I can see them!" the deputy curtly commanded from the speaker in his car. Both men lifted their hands above their heads. Clete Packer felt a lump in his throat again. Ben Coffey felt terrified. His stomach churned.

"Mr. Packer? Mr. Coffey? What are you doing?" Deputy Doolittle asked with amazed disgust. He had exited his cruiser and shined his heavy-duty flashlight on the pair. The two men brought their hands down slowly.

Clete Packer swallowed hard and with a voice higher and a little more anxious than he would have liked he exclaimed as he swept his hand broadly at the mess in his yard, "This is my house! Those little snots on the football team put all these For Sale signs here and vandalized my house with graffiti. I want them arrested. I want them charged and convicted!"

"Why are there signs in the street and what is all this shouting your neighbors complained about? It's after two A.M., Mr. Packer." The deputy did nothing to mask his irritation.

Ben Coffey found his voice. "We just got back from the ER and we discovered this and – well – Clete kind of lost it. He's had a very rough night, officer, and I was in the process of calming him down and suggesting we get the signs out of the street when you pulled up."

"Lost it? Shouting obscenities at two in the morning? Creating a traffic hazard? I should be citing both of you for creating a public disturbance." The deputy's tone was one of exasperation, but both men got the sense that there would be no tickets issued. "Okay, let's take a look at the damage." Bryan Doolittle swung his flashlight toward the house. The front door was spray-painted in orange letters. "Fuck you Fudge!" was written on the deep purple door.

"Who's Fudge?" Deputy Doolittle asked. Clete Packer's voice caught in his throat.

"Um – that's what some of the kids at school call Clete. It's disrespectful," Ben Coffey answered.

The deputy suppressed a knowing smile at the crude humor. The three men made their way to the garage door. As they approached the drive, a tall, elderly man dressed in galoshes, pajamas and a heavy bathrobe walked into the headlight beams of Ben Coffey's truck. It was Dick Purple, Clete's eighty-five-year-old neighbor. He was a notorious busybody to the point of being a rude jerk. He was roundly despised in town. He owned a good portion of vacant storefronts in downtown Bear River, and his refusal to sell the buildings at any price had some civic leaders furiously claiming Purple was holding up redevelopment of the city.

Clete Packer did not like his neighbor. Dick Purple had sued Clete in a dispute over property lines involving the removal of a large maple tree between their yards. This happened just after Clete bought the house. What should have been a simple dead tree being cut down ended up costing Clete thousands of dollars. Their relationship never improved in the years since. When Clete's nephew Pat Packer visited the house and he saw the neighbor in his yard, he would always ask his uncle with mock inquisitiveness, "Is that Dick Purple?" To which Clete would answer, "Nah, it's just the way the light is hitting him." And the two of them would enjoy a laugh at the old man's expense.

"Clete Packer, what is all this commotion?! It sounds like Sherman marching to the sea, and now the whole street is cluttered with trash! My wife needs her rest! She is having knee replacement surgery on Monday and you people are carrying on like Negroes on government check day!" The old man was imperious as he addressed his neighbor. Before Clete could answer, the deputy took charge.

"Sir, are you a neighbor? What is your name?" Deputy Doolittle asked.

"I'm Richard R. Purple. I live next door. My company built most of the houses on this street over forty-five years ago. And I can tell you, when they sold then we did not have this sort of thing going on in this neighborhood. Shameful behavior." Dick Purple answered the deputy in a manner that indicated he expected to be treated with dignity.

"Well, Mr. Purple, as you can see, your neighbor has had his home and yard vandalized. Did you or your wife notice anything earlier this evening?" Deputy Doolittle asked without sufficient deference and Dick Purple shot him a look. The deputy ignored it.

"No, we did not hear a thing. We try not to be involved in the goings on at this house. That ridiculous hotrod he keeps in that awful metal shack out back. We should have made those buildings illegal in the neighborhood association covenant." Dick Purple sniffed in response. "I told Norah years ago that when teachers started making too much money and a few of them bought houses on this street that the neighborhood would be ruined. No better than drunken college kids. Shameful behavior. Vandalism indeed. These people attract the worst sort of trouble." Dick Purple made a dismissive gesture toward Clete Packer.

"Yes, if that's the case, then can you please return to your residence while I finish my investigation? Thank you, Mr. Purple." Deputy Doolittle dismissed the crotchety old man.

Dick Purple was not about to let the impertinent deputy have the last word. "Young man, turn off those flashing lights! This is a quiet, respectful neighborhood, and this sort of disruption in the middle of the night is not acceptable!" Dick Purple thrust a boney finger in the direction of the deputy's cruiser.

"Mr. Purple, you need to go to your house now." There was an edge to Deputy Doolittle's voice. "I will turn off the lights when the street is cleaned up, not until. Those signs in the street present a traffic hazard."

"I am a former chairman of the county Republican Party, young man! I will be calling your boss, the sheriff, in the morning! Perhaps he will keep a tighter rein on you young badge-happy types when I explain the political impact of your unacceptable behavior!" Dick Purple said indignantly.

"Mr. Purple, the sheriff, my father-in-law, by the way, had support of both Republicans and Democrats the last two times he was reelected. The reason being is that he has a very good record and he does not let political pressure interfere with the exercise of his or his deputies' duties. So, if you please, return to your home and let me complete my duties here." Deputy Bryan Doolittle's voice was even and firm.

"Unacceptable! Clete, expect to hear from my lawyer on this!" Dick Purple exclaimed as he walked away. Clete Packer glanced down at the driveway. He shook his head and grimaced. More graffiti was painted there – "Fuge is a assho." Apparently they had run out of paint mid-insult.

Ben Coffey began to collect the real estate signs littering the street. Deputy Doolittle took the rest of Clete's statement. "I'm sure it was the members of the football team. They are totally out of control. And the leader of the worst of them is a boy named Morgan Miller. Find out where he was, and you will solve this case." Clete Packer sounded angry and weary.

"I know where Morgan Miller was tonight. His truck stalled on 16th Street and it rolled away on the hill. It crashed into a house owned by Xavier Simpson. The house sustained heavy damage. Simpson was seriously injured and the truck was totaled," Deputy Doolittle explained. "So I'm guessing he wasn't involved in this unless he did it before he had the accident. But supposedly, he was at the dance at the high school until only a half hour before the accident. Witnesses will likely collaborate," the deputy informed Clete.

"That's what happened to Two T – Mr. Simpson? He's our band director. I saw them bring him to the ER, but his wife was too emotional to explain what happened. She was raving about the house and a dead bird." Clete was filling in the blanks, but he was incredulous.

"I ticketed Morgan for failing to maintain a safe vehicle. No parking brake. And reckless driving as well, but if he fights it, he will beat that one. He wasn't driving – the truck rolled away without him in it. His father drove him home. From the conversation they were having as they left, I'm thinking Morgan may be having a rough few days," Deputy Doolittle concluded.

Ben Coffey deposited the last of the signs from the street in the back of his pickup. The three men conferred for a few more minutes and parted ways. Ben drove away first. Clete went to bed. He made a mental note to himself that on the first warm day of spring he would get his Mustang out of the pole building and spend at least two hours with it in the driveway running and gunning the motor as needed to irritate his obnoxious neighbor. As Deputy Bryan Doolittle turned off the cruiser lights and began to drive down the street, he saw Dick Purple standing in front of his house. The old man had a video camera and was filming the scene. The deputy considered stopping, but he had been in Bear River for long enough. As he turned off the street, he made a mental note that when he rotated back to days, he was going to ask his father-in-law to assign him to the southern half of the county. The people in this town were fucking crazy.

Social media exploded Sunday morning. Students were texting back and forth. Someone got a picture of Morg Miller's beloved truck wedged into the front of the Simpson home. That picture was roundly shared. The bulk of the gossip was about Jorge Martinez and the student teacher Laurie Starke. Innuendo buried facts. It was generally thought that Jorge was actively having an affair with Laurie. News of the scandal swept among the parents and staff by early afternoon.

After his mother got back from early Mass, Jorge sat with his parents at the kitchen table of the Martinez house. Jaime Martinez had rebuilt the derelict two-story house halfway between Bear River and Gratiot. He moved his young family into it over twenty years earlier. His oldest son died in the second Iraq War. Jaime Martinez, Jr. was in a vehicle destroyed by a roadside bomb. He had only been in Iraq five days when he was killed. Jorge was a second-grader when his brother, his hero, died. The family took a very long time to recover from the loss. Jorge's two older sisters had graduated from college and both had careers in the medical field. Maria was a surgical nurse and Rosa was a radiology technician. Jorge was the youngest.

The discussion about the events of the prior evening and the relationship he had with the college student the prior spring pained his mother greatly. The hurt in her eyes made Jorge heart-sick. He felt tears come to his eyes several times but blinked them back as he explained what had happened. As he finished his explanation, Carlita Martinez reached out and touched his arm. The hurt in her eyes was replaced with love.

Carlita Martinez worked for social services. She was a caseworker for abused and neglected children. She and her family had moved to the central Michigan area as migrant labor when she was a small girl. Her coworkers and friends had great respect for Carlita. They considered her a woman of fierce loyalty and strength. She began with an even tone. "Jorge, you must not blame yourself for the erratic behavior of the young student teacher. But you used poor judgment in having a relationship with the college girl. I know boys your age are too often ruled by their passions, but we didn't raise you to be a Don Juan. You must—"

"He is not a boy," Jaime Martinez interrupted his wife. "He turned eighteen in January. He is a man. He is almost the age Jaime Jr. was when he died. And Jorge knows better than to be a braggart about women he has been with. What that young woman is accusing him of is false. He is taking responsibility for his actions but she is not." Interrupting his wife was not something Jaime commonly did. He was known for being a man of few words. He was the son of a man who traveled north to Flint, Michigan from Texas during the early days of World War II to work in a defense plant. When his best friend was killed in the Pacific War, Juan Martinez joined the Marines and was wounded on Okinawa. He returned back to Michigan and got married and started a family. He worked for forty years for General Motors. He had ten children. A week before he was set to retire, he died of a heart attack in the parking lot of the GM plant where he worked. All his children were known to have inherited his strong work ethic. Jaime Martinez Sr. had been a shop manager for a company that manufactured building trusses. He lost his job in the Great Recession when the company he worked for went out of business. He had been working as a handyman carpenter ever since.

Carlita Martinez deferred to her husband. She took the lead in raising their daughters. Jaime Martinez was in charge of the sons. He was calm and steady. A stern look from him did more than any shout could accomplish. Above all, he trained his boys to take responsibility and to tell the truth. Jorge spent the rest of his day helping his father finish some drywall at a neighbor's house.

They took a break at 3 P.M. and sat together on the porch drinking iced tea. It was pleasantly warm. Almost an Indian summer sort of day. Without prompt or pretext, Jaime Martinez began talking. "Your mother is right. Jumping from one woman's bed to another does not make you a man, cabrón. Take your time and pay attention to what a woman has to offer you beside just physical pleasures. Stay away from women who can't or won't make good choices in life – no matter how enticing they may be, their problems will become yours. You are smart. Smarter than me. Smart like your mother and sisters. And you are strong like your brother, Jaime, and probably stronger than that. He joined the Army because of a girl – to get away from her. She was not right in the head – like this woman who you dealt with last night. But she was a great beauty. I wish every day that he had not chosen to run from her, that he had faced his problems and to put her aside. But he thought he loved her. She was not capable of returning the kind of love he was prepared to give her. She broke his heart – more than once – and finally he joined the Army to get away from his broken heart. I'm not sure that he ever did get away from it. He was so young when he died in that pointless war." Jorge nodded in acknowledgement of the truths his father was speaking.

"Be strong and smart, Jorge, and don't let people who can't be strong and smart ruin your life." Jaime Martinez spoke his final words and remained silent the rest of the afternoon. His son worked alongside him, equally quiet. Jorge thought mostly of his brother. He was only eight when his brother died. He knew nothing, until this afternoon, of why his brother joined the Army. Jorge never knew his grandfather, but family legend was that before they entered military service, he told his sons and grandsons that death was not a game for the weak and that savagery was a tool that once embraced could then be easily put away. He advised against joining the infantry or the Marines. Juan Martinez always told his male offspring to join the Air Force. Jaime Martinez Jr. did not receive the benefit of his council. He was a small child when his grandfather died.

At 1 P.M., Bear River School Board President Pam Kitteridge sat at Sheldon Knapp's desk. She sat in his chair. Three men stood in front of the desk. The superintendent, the high school principal and vice principal were slowly turning on her roasting-spit. Mike Shanahan had just returned from visiting Two Tone Simpson in the hospital. The band director was highly agitated but unintelligible – his mouth was stuffed with cotton. Sharon Simpson informed Mike that they were waiting to consult with an orthopedic surgeon and an oral surgeon. It was likely he would need to have pins inserted in his broken wrist. The likelihood that his teeth could be saved was dim.

"Gentlemen, I have spent the last three hours on the phone with many upset parents and community members. I want to know what the hell happened. I want to know what the situation with this Laurie Starke person is. I want to know what caused a violent confrontation between her and Molly Saunders, who I understand is in the cardiac care unit in Lansing and may not survive. I want to know why Sheldon's car was demolished in front of the school last night. I want to know why our band director is in the hospital with serious injuries. I want to know why that old fussbudget Dick Purple is on the warpath about out-of-control staff members. I want to know everything. And Sheldon, if you expect to ever get this chair back from me, you had better come up with something more than just your usual tap dance. Apparently this school and the town was a goddamned war zone last night! I want answers and I want them right now!" Pam Kitteridge's dark eyes sparkled with malice as she glanced from face to face asking her probing questions.

Sheldon Knapp gave a concise but legalese-blanketed explanation of the possibility that a student teacher may have had improper relations with a student, but that without Molly Saunders available to give direct testimony, they would have to take some time talking to students to fill in the blanks. And he explained the young student teacher's lawyer may be involved before long. Knapp glossed over his run-in with Deputy Doolittle and the damage to his car.

Mike Shanahan bumbled his way through a description of the events at the Simpson house. He made note of Sharon Simpson's anger over the death of her bird. He then said that he was going to request a copy of the police report, but that it sounded like it was just a freak accident.

Clete Packer had dark circles under his eyes and he spoke in low tones. He gave his interpretation of what had happened in the office between himself and Laurie Starke. He traced it back to Molly and the confrontation in the gym over the student teacher's outrageous attire and her behavior. He explained that he had contacted his lawyer about the assault charge pending against him and that they were considering making a counter-charge. He dismissed the complaints brought by Dick Purple and complained bitterly about being targeted by students, likely football players, vandalizing his house.

"Do you see the common thread here, gentlemen? All these incidents can be traced back to the football team. I have had all I can take of that team. When this season concludes, there will be changes made. To tell you quite frankly, I think it is time we consider eliminating the sport entirely. The team is an embarrassment to the town. It has been for years. And it is the haven for the worst sort of outlaws in our district. Save your objections, I don't want to hear them. When we convene a board meeting on this after the season, you can make your case, but the simple fact is, I have been working on building a consensus among the board members. The events of this weekend may well be the straw that breaks the camel's back." The board president smiled an icy smile.

"Pam, I think it's premature to link anything concerning the Laurie Starke case to the football team. Yes, the student in question is a football player, but that is not germane to the issue. And the unfortunate incident at Xavier Simpson's house wasn't anything but an accident. It could have been any student. Morgan Miller is a football player, but any student might be involved in something like that. And as far as the vandalism at Clete's house goes, we will investigate and any student – athlete or not that—" Sheldon Knapp watched the fury building in the face of Pam Kitteridge. He knew he was pressing his luck, but allowing her to set the agenda on the brewing controversy went against his instinct to control any and all potential problems before they got out of hand.

Pam Kitteridge did not wait for him to complete his statements. "Stuff a sock in it, Sheldon! You have my word I am looking at three men who have career-disrupting problems on their immediate horizon! Do you understand?! What you need to focus on is this runaway student teacher sex scandal, Sheldon. Make it go away. You other two better keep a lid on that collection of criminals you call a football team! If anything else happens involving those thugs, I will hold you both personally responsible. Got it? I am done here. Good day, gentlemen." And with that, the school board president rose and left the room.

After Pam Kitteridge left, the three men waited a few minutes and followed. Clete Packer sensed his career warning lights blinking. He knew Pam Kitteridge wanted to make him the fall guy for the trouble on the football team. Sheldon Knapp was grim-faced. He made a mental checklist of people he needed to talk to. Jorge Martinez was first on that list. Mike Shanahan wasn't sure why Pam was so mad at him. He hadn't flattened Two Tone Simpson's house.

Late in the afternoon on Sunday in suburban Detroit, Jorge Martinez's college girl, Marcy Nelson, sat crying in a half-empty apartment. Laurie Starke's late-night drunken social media blitz had caused a storm not only in Bear River but elsewhere. She posted about being accused of having an affair with a student when it was Marcy all along that was screwing around with a high school kid. Some of Laurie's online friends were also friends with her fiancé. The result was that they had a huge fight and he removed his belongings and stomped out of her life.

Monday morning at 8 A.M., the parents of Jorge Martinez sat in the office of the superintendent. Sheldon Knapp welcomed them and introduced the high school principal and vice principal. Mike Shanahan greeted them poorly in badly accented Spanish. Jorge's mother gave him a weak smile in return. Jorge's father did not acknowledge it.

297

The superintendent began, "There is no delicate way to put this, so I will be direct. Your son has informed you no doubt that he has been named as a student who has had an inappropriate relationship with a young woman who was assigned here as a student teacher. It is unfortunate that the staff member who has made this claim is currently in the hospital in Lansing and unable to provide details at this point. But this is a very serious, even grave situation, and we must press on to reach the truth. There has been more than enough innuendo and hearsay floating around already on this, and we regret any difficulty that may be causing. That being the case, we need your son to relate his side of the story so that we may proceed, if necessary, to inform the authorities that an improper liaison occurred between an adult and child here at our school. Of course you, as his parents, will be in the room as we question Jorge." Sheldon Knapp kept his eyes on the impassive faces of the Martinez's. They betrayed no emotion.

"No," Jaime Martinez answered directly.

"Ah, excuse me – I don't understand." Sheldon Knapp was flummoxed.

"Jorge is not a child. He is a man. He turned eighteen this last winter. A man does not speak of his relations with women," Jaime Martinez stated matter-of-factly. Clete Packer began to nervously shuffle through Jorge Martinez's student records file. He found the date of the birth. It was correct. Jorge was eighteen. He would turn nineteen in a few months. Clete thrust the file in front of Sheldon Knapp and pointed at the date-of-birth line. Sheldon Knapp gave a brief glance of pained fury to Clete Packer.

"Yes, well, Jorge may be eighteen, but a staff member and a student cannot be involved in a relationship. That is a – a very serious –um, breach – of the law. This district cannot – uh – I understand in your culture that a – Jorge is honor – bound to uh—" Sheldon Knapp was floundering badly. Jaime Martinez did not change his facial expression at all.

Carlita Martinez came to the superintendent's rescue in damning fashion. "Mr. Knapp, we do not know what this young woman or anyone else has claimed. We don't care. My son has assured us that he has not been alone with her – other than when she accosted him in the staff parking lot Saturday night and briefly last spring in the apartment she shared with another girl Jorge had dated. Jorge informed us he has gone out of his way not to interact with this woman since she came here in September. You may have an out-of-control staff member, but that is not the concern of my husband, my son or myself. So at this point I believe this meeting is over, and I will thank you not to bring us in on this matter again. And you are not to question our son on this matter at all. If you do, we will be contacting our lawyer. Good day to you." With that the Martinez's got up and left the room.

Clete Packer felt an ache in his wounded ear. Sheldon Knapp fixed him with an icy glare. "Clete, you asshole! Don't you think knowing all the pertinent facts is important before convening a parent meeting is important? What the hell? I have to find out Jorge Martinez is legally an adult during the meeting?! Right now all we have is a bunch of hearsay and the word of a comatose custodian. What are we going to do when Laurie Starke's lawyer shows up? Say sorry – our bad? We are not going to ever get anything out of the Martinez's and our dicks are swinging in the wind. That assault charge may be the least of your worries," Knapp vented cold fury at the vice principal.

"Mr. Knapp, sir, I was acting in good faith on the word of a trusted employee. You saw how Miss Starke was dressed Saturday night. Wholly inappropriate. And Molly was – she was just looking out for the kids, sir." Clete Packer felt nausea creeping in as he scrambled through his response.

"Did it occur to you that Molly Saunders had an axe to grind about Miss Starke? Did it occur to you that perhaps the story we have received from both her and Jorge's mother is closer to the truth. Jorge Martinez boinked the roommate, not the student teacher. And now it turns out that he was eighteen when he had her, so really we have no case against Miss Starke or anyone else, and now there is a giant window of liability for not only you but for this district. Clete, I expect sometime this morning Miss Starke's attorney uncle will come crashing through those doors looking for some scalps. I'm going to make damn sure he takes yours before he gets mine. You better go get your resume in order." Sheldon Knapp was lethal in his remarks and Clete Packer cringed and he pleaded for mercy. None came and he meekly retreated from the room. Mike Shanahan looked blankly at the superintendent until Knapp waved him to the door with a dismissive grimace.

It wasn't a long wait. At 11:05 that morning Sheldon Knapp was trying to massage a headache out by rubbing his temples vigorously with the middle fingers of each hand. He was interrupted by his intercom. "Mr. Knapp, there is a Mr. Van Boren here to see you. He's an attorney with the UAW." Katherine Bigelow sounded puzzled. She knew that there were storm clouds brewing, and she had gotten the entire lowdown on the supposed sex scandal from other staff members, but why an attorney for the giant automotive union would be here she hadn't a clue.

"Yes, Katherine, please see him in." Sheldon Knapp was trying to get his game face on. His tone with his administrative assistant was calm.

Jim Van Boren came through the doorway, and the first thing Sheldon Knapp thought was "Lawyer." He looked the part – down to the expensive Italian shoes, tailored suit and $200 haircut. He was tall with black hair with just the right amount of gray flecks. His deep blue eyes were bright and the smoothness of his face belied his age. "He's had work done," was Knapp's second thought.

He greeted the superintendent with a pleasant, unforced smile. "James Van Boren. Call me Jim, everyone does."

"Please come in, Jim. I'm Sheldon Knapp, superintendent of Bear River Schools. Call me Sheldon if you like," Knapp mirrored the convivial spirit of the initial greeting.

"Not Shelly, then?" Jim Van Boren asked in amusement.

"Not since I was six." Knapp assured him.

"That's when they stopped calling me Jimmy," Van Boren's smile broadened in response.

Sheldon Knapp nodded and gave him a smile in return. He motioned to the desk. "Please have a seat, Jim. I know there is a great deal we have to discuss."

"Indeed. But first I have to ask – is your custodian, Mrs. Saunders, doing better this morning? I understand she is in critical condition at Sparrow Hospital." The lawyer spoke with just the right amount of sincere concern. Sheldon Knapp felt his blood chill slightly. This was no low-level ambulance chaser. This was a lawyer who never took a meeting or sent a document without doing all the possible groundwork needed to dominate a case. Knapp's mind was racing as he tried to figure out what else he might know.

"Well, as of this morning, we have not been informed of any change in her condition. Of course, we are extremely concerned," Knapp lied a little. He had no knowledge of Molly Saunders' condition. He suspected that his adversary probably knew more than he did at this juncture.

"I will keep a good thought for her," Jim Van Boren replied.

"Of course," Knapp agreed.

"I'll give you a little background as to what I see this situation being, Sheldon. If you don't mind if I start?" Van Boren asked.

Sheldon Knapp nodded in agreement. He was beginning to regret that he didn't ask for the school board's attorney to be present. He had calculated that keeping this story stifled would be the best outcome. Two lawyers in the room might lead to a dick-measuring contest, not a quiet resolution.

"My niece, Lauren, is my younger sister's only child. Maryanne spoiled the child. The father has been out of the picture since the girl was very young. He's in jail. I won't go into the details, but he won't be out in time to visit any young grandchildren. I am childless myself, so I have been complicit, perhaps, in indulging her a bit too much. I have been the father figure in her life when I have been available. She is willful and high spirited. I will admit that. But I have never known her to be dishonest. She has assured me that some very unfortunate and patently untrue allegations have been made about her here at Bear River. The sort of allegations, if they proved true, that not only would disrupt her intended career but in fact could put her in grave legal trouble. I assume, Sheldon, that you understand we will be contesting these allegations to the fullest if and when Mrs. Saunders is available to bring something other than hearsay evidence to bear?" The lawyer spoke calmly and efficiently. Sheldon nodded cautiously in response to the last question.

Jim Van Boren continued, "Now, I know that no firm corroboration of Mrs. Saunders' accusations exists. If any corroboration existed, this district would have already brought the police in to investigate. You would have done that yesterday. Even on a Sunday. So I know you are aware that this story is very probably one of mistaken identity, if you like. Someone somehow became privy to the fact that your student, Jorge Martinez, was involved with my niece's former roommate, a Ms. Marcy Nelson, in the spring. The particulars of that romance are not pertinent to the issue with my niece other than the fact that young men tend to have loose tongues when it comes to their sexual conquests. And it is a simple universal truth that most young men will embellish those stories to the point where second- and third-hand recipients of the stories are not presented with anything like the actual truth. The unfortunate Mrs. Saunders was in that loop of second- or third-hand information, and for whatever reason, who knows, maybe out of spite, she relayed it on to your Mr. Packer. I know my niece said she had what could best be described as a contentious relationship with Mrs. Saunders. That is neither here nor there. My niece is high spirited and sometimes she rubs her elders the wrong way. But, if you have been thorough – and I have no doubt you have been – you have likely, by this time, conferred with Jorge Martinez's parents." The lawyer paused with a slight chin-tipping nod to indicate that the superintendent should respond. Sheldon Knapp gave him a single nod in response.

"You have done your work diligently. And unless I miss my guess, the parents of the boy, Mr. Jaime Martinez and his wife Carlita – probably offered you nothing to go on regarding their son, Jorge. You don't have to confirm or deny that. In fact, I would guess that Mrs. Martinez's experience in social services probably led her to be very professionally cordial with you, but she likely told you if you continued down the path of implicating her son in anything, you would be talking to the family lawyer next. And since young Jorge turned eighteen before the rumored liaison with Ms. Nelson, any trump card you had regarding his status as a minor was rendered unplayable," the lawyer continued with ultra-pleasant professionalism.

Sheldon Knapp was astonished and he struggled not to show it. Whatever the UAW was paying Jim Van Boren to be a lawyer they were getting their money's worth beyond a doubt. It was unnerving to be left so naked in a negotiation. Sheldon Knapp had nothing to put into play that Jim Van Boren couldn't return with topspin. He needed a break. "Where are my manners, Jim. Can I offer you some coffee?" Knapp asked, trying but failing to sound as pleasantly dispassionate as his office guest.

"No. No thank you. My doctor has me on a strict one-cup-a day limit," Jim answered pleasantly.

"Some water perhaps?" Knapp asked. He was still vamping for time as he tried to take in everything that was playing out.

"Yes, that would be just fine. The doc says I need to drink more of that," the lawyer smiled gratefully in response.

Sheldon Knapp rose and went to the refrigerator behind the office minibar. "Would you like sparkling or still?" he asked as he open the fridge door.

"Sparkling! Let's live a little. Early in my career, I worked with a bunch of old boys who would break for a martini right about now. Now that is living. The good old days will never come back. Pity." Jim was enthusiastic in his jovial response. Sheldon Knapp had to admit it – despite how this meeting was going and the complete cock-up that led to it, he was finding himself liking Jim Van Boren. He knew he was being played, but it was almost an honor that a master like Jim would play him as if he were a CEO of an auto company.

"I prefer scotch to martinis, and if my wife found out I had a drink this early in the day, I'd never hear the end of it," Knapp remarked lightly as he handed the lawyer a bottle of Perrier water.

Jim Van Boren made a little show of enjoying a deep draft of his water. Then he began in again, "My niece is naïve. She thinks somehow she will extract a pound of flesh from Bear River Schools for the disservice that has been done to her. I have been counseling her that the best course of action is to arrange a clean break. I told her given all the gossip and tall tales being spread here that completing her student teaching assignment isn't practicable. That isn't to say, of course, that I am telling her to tuck her tail between her legs and run away; far from it. So at this point I am going to propose some conditions for a clean break for my niece and some important liability avoidance for your school district." As he completed this statement, there was an almost imperceptible shift in the tone of the lawyer's voice and the sympathetic twinkle in his eye was extinguished.

Sheldon Knapp sipped at his bottle of water. "I am ready to listen and to work with you for an amicable solution to this situation." Knapp tried to hold an edge in his words, but as soon as he said them, he and the lawyer knew it was a total capitulation.

Jim Van Boren tipped his head to the left acknowledging that he was ready to proceed to dictate the terms.

"Laurie will withdraw from her student teaching assignment. We will provide CMU with a hardship withdrawal request based on the health of her mother. Maryanne has been struggling with Lupus for some time and recently she has suffered a severe flare-up requiring Laurie to help her at home. CMU will grant it. Laurie will receive a refund of her tuition and her transcripts will be marked with a withdrawal – not a letter grade or an incomplete. In return, I would expect letters of recommendation from your high school principal, Mr. Shanahan, and her onsite supervising teacher, Mrs. Conover. I'll trust that you will see to it that the letters are quite laudatory of Laurie's strengths in the classroom. Is that suitable?" The lawyer asked in a way that indicated he expected immediate acceptance.

Sheldon Knapp agreed, "Yes, I can make sure that those letters are filed immediately with the placement office at Central Michigan. The director of placement and I go way back. There will be no problem and no question." He was already composing the letters in his head. Shanahan would sign anything the superintendent put in front of him. Nancy Conover might be a harder nut to crack, but a discussion about a potential reassignment in her teaching post to seventh grade would certainly motivate her to be compliant.

"Good. I'm glad we see this the same way. Now regarding the matter of the complaint against your Mr. Packer, my niece rashly filed before consulting with me on Saturday night. I think I can see a way out of it as well." The sympathetic twinkle was back in the lawyer's eyes along with a return to his most pleasant voice.

"How so?" Knapp was inquisitive but almost regretful about Clete Packer getting off the hook.

"Mr. Packer's lawyer, Thom Markle, and I have served on some committees together for the state Democratic Party. He called me this morning as I made my way here. I believe he is prepared to make sure Mr. Packer does not counter file against my niece in the assault matter. And sometime this afternoon my niece and I will go to the courthouse in Isabella County and work on withdrawing her assault complaint. The district attorney for the county is a law school classmate of mine. I think we can work this out," the lawyer explained.

Sheldon Knapp was again very impressed by the smoothness of his office guest. He struggled to keep a tone of total gratitude out of his voice. "I have been in consultation with Clete Packer since the unfortunate incidents of Saturday night. I can assure you he has been castigating himself for his unprofessional handling of the events of the night. I know him – he is beside himself that he misread your niece's intentions in the heat of a confrontation and reached out to stop her."

"Mistakes were made. It is best to move past them. At least at this point. But please convey to Mr. Packer my solemn promise that if he ever so much as mentions my niece's name in casual conversation with a fellow education professional, or if he should make the mistake of replying to any written inquiries about her posting here, or if he should ever, say, bump into my niece's car in a shopping center parking lot, I will find out about it and I will end his career as a public educator quicker than kicking dirt from my golf shoes. Make him understand that, Sheldon. I am deadly serious. I have been counseling my niece against a career in education. I think she would make a fine lawyer. But her grades – well, it has seemed at times she attended college to major in excitement. Anyway, law school graduates are struggling to start careers these days. Law schools keep pumping newly minted JDs at an alarming rate. Yet there is a shortage of teachers on the horizon. Even though, the Michigan Republican Party, with its towering lack of foresight and just nonexistent basic common sense, is killing education as a career choice in this state. Either way, if Clete Packer impedes my niece's career in any manner, I can and will destroy him. Drive that home, Sheldon, drive it home." The lawyer seemingly meandered through his threat. He never lost his pleasant tone or the sympathetic twinkle in his eye. It made the threat even more chilling.

In an instant, Sheldon Knapp knew that Clete Packer's lawyer was the conduit for all the inside information at the disposal of Jim Van Boren. Sheldon Knapp cursed himself for not putting a complete muzzle on his underling. What a setup. No going back at this juncture. And besides, later today he was going to relish letting Clete in on what was waiting for him if he should ever cross paths with Laurie Starke and her uncle again. Knapp barely masked letting Van Boren know his personal pleasure in relaying the message, "I will certainly explain your message to him fully, Jim. I will see to it this afternoon when Clete is done with his supervision duties at lunchtime."

"Excellent," Jim Van Boren responded as he stood to leave. "How about this weather, huh? This late in the fall and it's shirtsleeve temperatures."

"Yes, and the weather was so foul just two days ago," Sheldon Knapp agreed.

Jim Van Boren reached out and shook his host's hand. "You know, I considered a career in education. I even student taught – well, for about two weeks. I was posted to Flint Central High School to teach government. I was not cut out for the classroom and those kids picked my bones clean – I got out while the getting was good. I withdrew from the education department and signed up for the LSAT. Scored pretty well and got into law school at Wayne State. Got a job fresh out of law school with the union. But, sometimes – well, I wonder. I'd be retired now if I stayed with teaching. And summers off to play golf – what a gift that would have been. Or maybe I'd have gotten into your game, administration. I might have my own school district by now as a superintendent. Leading teachers – touching the future educating kids, making a difference. Oh well. The roads less travelled – or some such thing." Jim Van Boren had a faraway smile on his face as he spoke. Sheldon Knapp mirrored his guest's smile.

"It has been a great career for me but it's not for everybody. Leadership can be lonely at times," Knapp replied.

"Oh, and here is my card. Please have your secretary call my assistant with any update on Mrs. Saunders. I certainly hope there will be good news very soon," Jim Van Boren said as he walked through the door that Sheldon Knapp held open for him.

"Certainly, Jim. As soon as we hear anything you will be our first call," Sheldon Knapp lied effortlessly. Both of them knew that Molly Saunders' health had no impact whatsoever on what was just arranged.

"Have a good day, Sheldon. I'm off to take my niece to lunch." The lawyer made his way to the outer door.

"Take care, Jim. Travel safe." The superintendent's sincerity was unforced as his guest left.

Monday was a rough day for Jorge Martinez. He felt eyes on him at every turn. Every whisper and every conversation just out of earshot seemed to be about him. The only respite was at lunch. He sat with his friends and Wash and Seth kept the conversation strictly about the Detroit Lions. Another loss and more missed chances. Seth mentioned that his grandfather had attended the game last time the Lions won an NFL championship in 1957. Amber and Roxy sat at the table and they chatted about classes and an upcoming math test. It was as if Saturday night never happened.

Saturday night was all Morg Miller's tormenters wanted to talk about. Jokes about the demise of The Tank and offers to sell him cars he met with wry smiles. Band members he barely knew gave him high fives. The complete story of the injuries suffered by Two Tone Simpson was not known. All the band students were told was that he would be out for some time as he healed. An elderly substitute teacher with no experience in music took over the class. It was an out-of-control zoo in a matter of minutes. Consensus among the band geeks was that it was the most enjoyable practice anyone could remember in a while.

In Lansing, a hospital social worker was trying to locate the next of kin of Molly Saunders. Ex-husband number two told her to go to hell and hung up. Ex-husband number one wanted nothing to do with the situation but did provide the social worker with some names of cousins in Gratiot. Through them, the social worker was able to get the name of Molly's estranged younger sister who lived in Chicago. The social worker left several messages on her phone but none were returned. The cardiac care unit staff workers were the only people at Molly's bedside. No friends or relatives even called to check on her status. Late in the afternoon, a secretary from Bear River Schools called for an update. No change was noted. Molly Saunders was in a coma and doctors were not sure how much of a chance she had of coming out of it.

Football practice started badly in that only nine JV players showed for practice. One of the freshman linemen was at home with pneumonia. He wasn't expected back for at least a week, according to his mother. Two other boys were in school but not at practice. No one knew where they might be. One boy was still on crutches from Thursday's game. The coaches had no choice but to run a combined practice. The order of the day was to work on a Power I formation for the offensive backfield. The featured play was called "Cheese Stick," so named because the current assistant coach Chester "Cheese" Colby had been the featured player using the formation last season. Normally a lineman, Cheese Colby was rewarded for his efforts his senior year with the chance to run the ball from the deep back in the I formation on a few plays. It was one of the few highlights of the last season. In his last game, he scored a touchdown and converted a two-point try in his last football game. The Bears still lost badly.

This year's featured senior back would be Jorge Rodriguez. The formation and the play was still called "Cheese Stick." Jorge was grateful for the respite football practice offered in taking his mind off the troubles of the last few days. He enjoyed lowering his pads and running a simple dive play. The contact felt good. Carrying the ball felt good. He found himself smiling – really smiling – for the first time since Saturday. Morg Miller called him "Twinkle Toes" as they practiced the dive play at the goal line. Jorge bounced out of the called one hole next to the center. His blocking got stacked up by Phil Long submarining Junior Schultz on the snap. Jorge scrambled to the outside and danced around a freshman defensive back to gain the end zone.

"Jorge, stay in the hole called. You won't find the edge all that generous against a varsity lineup," Coach Cale smiled as he gently scolded his best player.

"Sure thing. Coach, Phil took my hole away, though." Jorge smiled at the tubby player who was suspended for this week's game as a result of getting thrown out of the game Friday for fighting.

"Phil's making a late bid for all-league D tackle, Coach. Twinkle Toes was lucky to escape with his life," Morg Miller added. The ensuing laughter felt good to all, players and coaches alike.

The two missing JV players were caught stealing beer from the mini-mart at about the time practice ended. Their season was done. On Tuesday morning, John Cale and Mike Reese met with Clete Packer. The meeting was brief – the outcome was that the two remaining JV games were cancelled. The JV players remaining would suit up with the varsity for the last few days of the season. John Cale felt weary as he left the meeting.

"Look, John, there is nothing we can do. We have to be as positive with the kids as possible. We let on how disappointed we are and the kids are going to read it, and it is going to affect how they play," Reese counseled his young head coach as they walked back to their classrooms.

"I know, Mike, but I don't know how many more seasons I can keep doing this. We never catch a break. We can't get the numbers we need to be competitive. Sometimes I think Pam Kitteridge is right. Football is played out in this town. Hell, the town is played out. Maybe it's the water. The whole town is poisoned as it is—" Cale answered dejectedly, his voice trailing off.

Reese didn't contest his young friend's utterances. He had been in the same place over the years. It drove him from coaching football once. With a few beers in him, Reese would admit that a fundamental difference between coaching football and coaching wrestling was that as a wrestling coach, he could make an effective wrestler out of a small kid or one who was not a great athlete. As long as he had several of those types of kids and two or three well-groomed studs coming up every class or two, a small school like Bear River could be very competitive – even dominant against other small schools. But with football, the simple fact was that small and/or slow kids in low numbers was an impossible hurdle to overcome. In a season like this one, he knew the best coaching was done by keeping kids focused and working together no matter the outcome on game day. Losing hurt. It always did. But walking away from kids who needed him hurt even more.

On Wednesday, Clete Packer suspended Todd Donheiser and Josh Gruelich when they refused to cooperate with his investigation into the vandalism at his home. Miles Kitteridge had given Clete their names after talking with his soccer players. Miles was aware that it was very likely his soccer players along with football and cross country team members had been involved in the "selling" of Clete's house. He hoped Clete would be satisfied. He wasn't. Miles informed his mother about what might happen if the soccer team was gutted by suspensions. Pam Kitteridge informed Sheldon Knapp that he should call off Clete before headlines were made. On Thursday morning, Clete Packer sat in yet another meeting where his superintendent cut his legs out from under him. "You got your two hides tacked to the office wall, Clete. Wrap this up. Taking a look at the records of these two, I think maybe it's time to counsel the families to send them to alternative education. Neither of them is close to graduating on time. We had them here for the fall count day so the state will give us the large portion of their aid dollars. Let's get them the hell out." Sheldon Knapp made no pretense of giving Clete any satisfaction in holding any more kids responsible for the vandalism he suffered. Thursday afternoon, he used the graffiti removal cleaners Ben Coffey provided to wipe the paint off his garage and front doors. He used a pressure washer to clean the paint off his drive. He could taste bile in his throat the entire time. He denied himself the relief of chugging some Maalox.

On Thursday evening, John Cale and Mike Reese took Chet Colby out for dinner. With no JV game to play, they had the time. They spent the time talking about sports and counseling Chet about starting college now that his mother was gone. Chet was buoyant, but his eyes told a story of ongoing grief. All three coaches agreed that JV players should not be starting on the next evening even if they were better than the varsity starter. No one said anything about the almost certain outcome of the upcoming game. Owen Eight was a lock.

Friday was yet another mild day. The temperature at game-time was fifty degrees. Mike Reese pointed out as the bus pulled out that Pompeii Central was hosting a homecoming game. "Five consecutive homecoming games – this is just great," John Cale answered.

The Pompeii Central Vulcans had yet to win a varsity football game. Their JV team was having a good season, though, and with the cancellation, they like the Bears were combining both squads for the night's game. Pete the Pigskin prognosticator had posted a report that freshman quarterback sensation, Matt Ness, would be making his first-ever varsity start. With that in mind, he made the Vulcans a four-touchdown favorite. Pete got it wrong. The Vulcans thumped the Bears 66-0.

The score was not the story of the game. Seth Parker's injuries were. Seth had yet to finish a game as a varsity quarterback. His season and football career came to a crashing halt late in the first quarter. On a play at midfield on first down, the Bears ran a triple option play to their left. The Vulcans stuffed the play effectively and Seth Parker reversed himself and rolled back to his right. Junior Shultz had slipped in his blocking assignment on the option play and he picked himself up while reading what had happened, and he tried to lead his quarterback on the improvised reverse. Big Donnie Donnie was standing like a statue in the Bears backfield, not making contact with anyone. His presence forced Junior and Seth deep behind the line. The Vulcan safety and left-side linebacker closed ground quickly to force the play even wider toward the Bears sideline.

Seth Parker pointed at the linebacker to give Junior Schultz instruction to block him. Junior launched himself at the player. He missed. Seth stiff-armed the linebacker with his left hand near the out-of-bounds line. His fingers got caught in the opposing player's facemask. Seth spit out his mouth guard to scream as two fingers suffered fractures and dislocations. What happened next was frightening.

The Vulcan's safety, Doug Watkins, was the largest and fastest player on the Pompeii team. Standing nearly six-foot-five and weighing 230 pounds, he should have been a linebacker, but the coach of the Vulcans liked his "eraser speed," as in he had to ability to erase mistakes. He erased Seth Parker with a violent but still legal hit. Seth was propelled through the air into the heavy wood and steel bench on the Bears sideline. The back of his helmet crashed into the bench. Seth bit through his tongue and his teeth slammed violently together. His mouth guard hung uselessly on his facemask after his initial injury. His tongue was nearly severed and three teeth were broken. Seth suffered what would be diagnosed as a grade three concussion as well as a compressed neck vertebra. Seth "Dial-a-Pain" Parker would not be getting a free pass from the "Miracle Healer" for some time.

The Bear River Bears were silent, kneeling on one knee as the first responders strapped their quarterback and friend to a backboard before loading him into the ambulance. Seth was unconscious for several minutes. When he came to, he was crying and spraying blood from his wounded mouth. Wash Dryer tried to calm Seth but his friend was panicked by the blood, and his head injury had him disoriented. Wash fought back tears and his own panic to stay at Seth's side. Even Morg Miller was silent and mortified as Mike Reese led the Bears down to an end zone to warm up after a nearly thirty-minute game stoppage. Junior Schultz sat on the bench weeping as Chet Colby wrapped his arm around the center, trying to convince him that he wasn't at fault. John Cale followed and stayed with his quarterback until the ambulance doors closed and the unit left the field. Seth's father followed the ambulance to Gratiot. No one mentioned it, but everyone thought it was a small blessing that Seth's high-strung mother was not at the game. Marlene Parker was attending the wedding of her college roommate's daughter.

The Bears stumbled through the rest of the game. Tom Osborne took over at center for the emotionally shattered Junior Schultz. Randy Jansen went down with a bad ankle sprain in the third quarter. With their second-string varsity quarterback down, Cale and Reese conferred and decided to put their own freshman quarterback-of-the-future into the game. Scott Baier played the last three offensive series. He didn't play well. Each series ended with him fumbling the ball. The last fumble was returned for a touchdown by Doug Watkins. No one was talking of a bright future for Bear River football at the end of the game. The bus ride home was the most silent one Mike Reese had experienced in nearly four decades of coaching.

## Overtime

Wash wanted to go to the hospital to check on Seth, but his mother called to check on the condition of his friend, and she was informed that Seth had been transferred to Lansing for a neurological and spinal examination.

WashDryer: No knock knock tonight dad. Seth got hurt real bad in the game. They had to take him to the hospital.

GregDryer: Broken bones?

WashDryer: Fingers probably – but he really took a bad hit. He has a concussion for sure. He was knocked out for almost ten minutes. Maybe a neck injury too. They strapped him on a board to put him in the ambulance.

GregDryer: Are you ok son?

WashDryer: It scared me pretty bad. I had to help Seth. He was really confused and frightened. A bunch of us are going to the hospital first thing in the morning.

GregDryer: Let me know how he is, please, as soon as you know for sure.

WashDryer: Yes – I will. BTW it's Owen Eight.

GregDryer: I surmised that it would be. I love you son.

WashDryer: I love you, dad.

Greg Dryer sat at a desk in a hotel room in Montana. Tears came to his eyes as the worst homesickness of the three-month long assignment came over him. He missed his son terribly.

# CHAPTER THIRTEEN

## OWEN FOREVER

### THE TWO BATTLES ON THE BRIDGE

Saturday at noon, Wash Dryer, Jorge Martinez, Morg Miller and Randy Jansen picked up a morose Junior Schultz at his home. They had Randy Jansen's dad's old Dodge van. Randy was on crutches. His ankle was purple from his heel to lower calf. The med center in Gratiot had identified it as a severe high-ankle sprain. Randy would not be getting a visit from the "Miracle Healer" in time to play the final game of the season. As they drove to Lansing to visit Seth Parker in the hospital, the talk was about how bad Seth's injury was and whether or not Scott Baier would be capable of playing a whole game as a varsity quarterback. The consensus was grim.

"Did you see him in the huddle last night? He was scared shitless. No way Scott even plays next Friday. He'll get hurt in practice just enough to make an excuse not to play," Morg Miller guaranteed his teammates. No one called him out as wrong.

"Maybe J.B. can play QB, or one of the Things," Randy Jansen offered without much hope.

"Which one?" Morg asked.

"Thing Two took some snaps in the scrimmage, didn't he?" Randy answered.

"That was Thing One, wasn't it?" Morg replied.

"Does it matter?" Junior asked no one in particular.

"Man, Junior, you got to let it go. It's not your fault Seth got hurt. I blew the block on the front of the play. Big Donnie stood like a tree in your way. And Seth never should have reversed back off that play anyway. He was supposed to pitch or keep it and follow the block. You were at least trying to protect him – the rest of us didn't even get involved." Jorge

Martinez sounded wise beyond his years as he counseled his younger teammate and fellow wrestler.

"He's right," Morg informed his good friend gravely.

"Yeah, but every time I close my eyes I see him strapped to the backboard and I—" Junior trailed off.

Morg Miller handed Junior a cold Mountain Dew. Then he punched Junior in the arm. It was as close to a hug the two wrestling practice partners would exchange. Junior gave him a wan smile and popped open the can.

"Jay could handle being QB but I don't think Coach Cale wants to lose him at tailback. I bet he uses Thing One at QB if Scotty tanks it," Wash Dryer took the subject back to its original point.

"I thought it was Thing Two," Morg answered brightly.

"Whatever," Randy Jansen called out with exasperation.

The scene at the hospital wasn't pretty. Marlene Parker had arrived at Seth's bedside in the middle of the night. She was hysterical, ranting at the nurses about how much pain her son was in and calling for the neurologists to run a CAT scan every half hour because she was quite sure that Seth had a major injury that had caused dangerous clotting in his brain. Three times before mid-morning, the nursing staff had threatened to have her forcibly removed from the hospital. Finally at 11 A.M. Seth's mom screamed herself into near catatonic rage when a nurse was two minutes late answering the call button. Security was called. Marlene Parker threw an IV stand at the security guards and leapt on them, kicking and screaming. They restrained her, and Seth's father, at the advice of Seth's neurologist who witnessed the attack, had them take her to the hospital psych ward for sedation and observation.

Seth's girlfriend, Amber, met the boys outside of the hospital. She had been praying most of the morning in the family waiting room. Amber was a Christian Scientist. The hospital was a totally foreign environment to her. No one in her family had ever been to one. When she was born, her mother delivered at home with the help of a midwife. Amber warned them that Seth was not himself, and he had had a very rough night. She left out the part about Seth's mother being led away in restraints a couple of hours earlier. The boys proceeded to the ward where their friend was being treated. Myron "Mike" Parker, Seth's father, agreed to let them visit one at a time.

Junior Schultz insisted on going first. He held himself together. The room was dimly lit. No TV was allowed. Seth looked at Junior blankly as Junior apologized for missing the block. Seth blinked his eyes slowly at Junior as if to say "Apology accepted." At least that is what Junior assumed. Seth's wounded tongue was stitched up making speech impossible. His left hand was in a traction device holding his damaged fingers in place. Seth's neck was in a brace, and he was propped up in bed. Junior left the room with damp eyes, but he was greatly relieved to have had the chance to apologize. Each boy spent just a minute or two in the room where Mike Parker hovered near the bedside quietly telling his son who was visiting.

Mike Reese and John Cale passed the boys as they exited the hospital. The coaches exchanged concerned greetings with the players and thanked them for being good friends and teammates. On the trip back to Bear River, the boys exchanged their observations on Seth's condition. Wash was skeptical about Seth's return to play even a few games of the basketball season, what with the hand injury and the serious concussion.

"I did a paper for English last month on the new NFL rules on concussion clearances. Seth has the highest level of concussion, and that means about a six month recovery time," Wash informed them seriously.

"Check out the big brain on Dr. Dryer," Morg Miller teased. Junior Schultz laughed. Not his usual gut wrenching laugh when Morg was being witty, but it was a start. Morg felt the best he had all day. Jorge Martinez gave Morg a knowing glance and a small smile. Morg beamed a large grin back at him.

Talk turned to plans for the evening.

"I've got a date with Maricel," Wash happily informed his friends.

"That's a freaking shock," Randy Jansen answered dryly. Morg and Junior laughed.

"She turns nineteen tomorrow. I'm taking her to a sushi place in Saginaw for a birthday dinner," Wash continued. He didn't inform them of their plans to stay in a hotel room that her aunt had reserved for them. Jorge knew about it. He was Wash's beard. Wash told his mother that after the birthday dinner, he was going to meet up with Jorge and they were going to stay at Jorge's grandmother's house in Midland to dog-sit while she was down-state visiting a terminally ill cousin. Jorge really was dog-sitting, but he didn't need Wash's help with that. Maricel's aunt was going to pick her up at her host family's house. Miriam Arambula was a graduate student in international studies at Michigan State. She told her niece's host family that she and her niece were going to spend the evening together for a birthday celebration and that she would return Maricel the next day so that she could have cake and ice cream with their son. The plan for the evening had been in place for almost a month.

"Junior and I are going bowling tonight," Morg offered.

"That's sweet. You buying?" Randy asked Morg.

"Fuck you," Morg answered

"Shouldn't you save yourself for Junior?" Randy countered.

"No thanks – take all you want." Junior answered with a laugh. The rest of the van riders joined in with the laughter.

The mail was waiting for Jay Brau when he finished working in the barn early Saturday afternoon. There was a letter with no return address but Jay recognized the tight and delicate handwriting. It was from Freddy. Jay took the letter to his room. His hands were not steady as he opened it. He began to read.

**Jaybird:**

By the time you get this letter I will be in Missouri. I have enrolled in a prep academy. I can't tell you its location – I don't want you to try to follow me. My uncle has convinced my parents that a change of scenery is all I need to get you out of my system. Their first idea was to send me to one of those horrible Pray the Gay Away programs. My uncle is much more understanding. He has come out of the closet to everyone but my parents. I only need to finish a semester at the prep academy and then I can graduate early. I plan on enrolling in community college in St. Louis as soon as I am done with high school. My uncle lives near St. Louis so I will have family nearby.

You are and will always be my first love but I can't stay with my parents any longer. And that means I can't stay with you, my love. The strain of me being at home is too much on my mother and sister. My father needs time to figure out whether he wants to be a part of my life in the future or not. I don't know if he can change that much. He hurt me very badly. I want to forgive him. I want my family to be whole again but I can't be near him just yet. I want to forgive him but I don't trust him. And as badly as he treated me, my mother and sister need him. I doubt that I will be home anytime soon. I won't live in fear of my own father. I can't ask for you to wait. You have to live. Be the beautiful Jaybird of my dreams. Take care of your aunt and uncle. I hope this was not too much for them to bear. I never ever want to hurt you, but I can't be with you. Please forgive me.

**Freddy**

Jay felt the walls of his room closing in on him. He threw himself to his bed. He buried his head in the pillows. Tears spilled from his tightly shut eyes onto the cool cotton pillow case. He cried silently. His breath was ragged but he stifled his sobs. His phone vibrated in his pocket – he ignored it. Time passed, but time made no sense to him. The ache in his heart was all-encompassing. Nothing meant anything to Jay – no sounds registered in his ears, no physical feelings were present as a meaningless sense of weightlessness settled over him. No thoughts crossed his mind other than the hole in his existence left by Freddy's absence.

Eventually, Jay became aware of his own breathing. Then the ticking of the antique alarm clock his mother had bought him penetrated his senses. He opened his eyes. A word popped into his head. Move. Jay sat on the edge of his bed. The shadows on the wall told him it was late in the afternoon. He heard his aunt and uncle stirring downstairs. His phone buzzed. Jay mechanically brought it out of his jeans pocket and looked at it. The time was 5:15. Roxy Johnson had called four times in the last several hours. He punched in his new security code and answered the call. It was Roxy.

"Jay, is everything okay? You told me to give you a call today and see if you were up for a movie," Roxy said brightly, doing a good job masking her concern.

"Movie? I uh – I don't feel like a movie. Can we just go somewhere and talk? I need to talk to someone," Jay answered. His voice was hollow.

"Do you want to meet at the diner?" Roxy asked, referring to the restaurant near the interstate.

"I really don't want to see anyone from school – except for you – and I—" Jay found it hard to form words.

"I'll pick you up in a half hour and we can go up to Mt. Pleasant. We'll find someplace quiet to talk," Roxy sounded concerned but firm in her decision.

"Okay," Jay answered.

Jay made his way downstairs. He begged off dinner, explaining that he and Roxy were going to the movies in Mt. Pleasant. His aunt and uncle were concerned but hid behind a jovial mask. A little over an hour later, Jay and Roxy were sitting in a booth at a drive-in restaurant near the CMU campus.

"Jay, you can't follow Freddy. He's right. What he has to do is for him alone," Roxy finally said after listening to Jay explain Freddy's letter on the ride up from Bear River.

Jay nodded solemnly in response. His eyes were red, but he had not cried since he left his bed before making the trip with Roxy. His emotions were frayed and his voice quaked at times, but he wanted to explain everything to Roxy without bawling and carrying on.

"I haven't ever had a relationship as intense as the one you and Freddy have had. I can't really say how I would react. But people do survive broken hearts. Freddy wants you to live your life. He has to live his. You told me when you got outed that you were going to live your life and go to school – play football. I thought it was the bravest thing anyone could do. But you have always been brave. You survived your mom dying, coming here to live, finding a way to fit in and make friends. I like to think I understand the strength you have, but I'm not sure. But Freddy understands doesn't he? He is being strong just like you. You two were a good match." Roxy looked directly into his eyes as she spoke.

Jay's wounds wouldn't magically knit shut. He knew that from raw experience. He willed himself to reward Roxy's honesty with a thankful small smile.

"I won't follow Freddy. I could never abandon my aunt and uncle. They saved me. I was so alone when my mom died. They gave me somewhere to stay, but it was more than that. They let me heal. They let me have the chance to live a normal life. Freddy opened my heart. My mom did the same thing. But my aunt and uncle did it too, and they were the ones who did it when I thought my heart would never open again. For me to leave them now would break their hearts. There has been too much of that already." Jay's voice gained strength as he spoke; enough strength that he and Roxy both took comfort.

"Jay, I love you. You're my best friend. A year ago I thought my attraction to you was romantic. It isn't. I don't think it ever was. I love you because you are the best person I know. I only hope that when I need to be strong, I can be as strong as you are." Tears rested in the corners of Roxy's eyes as she spoke. Jay clasped her hands across the table. Roxy blinked and the tears rolled free down her cheeks.

Jay and Roxy ordered some food and ate their meal. They made small talk about their friends – mostly about Jorge and his recent troubles and about the heated romance of Wash and Maricel. After the meal they went to Roxy's car and they began to drive back to Bear River. As they exited the freeway at Gratiot, Jay looked to the west. A bowling alley was just a few blocks down the street.

"I know this is going to sound silly, but would you go bowling with me? My mom and I used to bowl all the time. Even when I was small she would take me bumper bowling. Freddy would go bowling with me too even though he was terrible at it. The whole time he would just smile at me and throw gutter ball after gutter ball. He can run like a gliding dream but skills like bowling—" Jay's voice wandered off as the memory of their last date grabbed at his consciousness.

"Sure! I love bowling! I carried 160 average in the church league last winter," Roxy answered with enthusiasm.

Jay snapped out of his daydream as Roxy pulled into a gas station to turn around. They were laughing as they walked through the door of the alley. The place was busy. Morg Miller and Junior Schultz were just in front of them in line as they approached the counter.

"Sorry JB, we just got the last lane. You want to roll with us?" Morg Miller smiled at his classmates.

Although Morg had often made her the butt of cruel insults over the course of their time together as classmates, Roxy didn't carry a grudge. Often she gave as good as she got. She smiled at Morg.

"You two can't handle us! We'll kick your ass," Roxy replied.

"Oh baby, it's on! My man here would be the lead bowler on the varsity team if he wasn't a wrestler!" Morg replied as he massaged Junior's shoulders. Junior smiled sheepishly. It was true. Wrestling and bowling were both winter sports. Junior tried to participate in dual sports his freshman year, but the bowling coaches kept insisting that he drop wrestling. One of them, a young layman coach who wasn't a teacher, called wrestling a "fag sport" because of the tight singlets wrestlers wore. Junior told him to shove a bowling ball up his ass and quit the team just before regionals. He was easily the best bowler in the school.

Jay found himself almost smiling as they began to bowl. Morg, as always, was playing the clown, and Junior twice had to stop to catch his breath from laughing during their first game. Roxy was a good bowler as advertised – she rolled a 155. Jay was skilled as well – he rolled a 161. Junior, despite being distracted by Morg's jokes and antics, rolled a 194. And Morg for all his clowning was ultra-competitive. Jay marveled at how Morg could completely shut down his mouth and antics to gain focus in just a couple of seconds and roll an accurate if oddly delivered ball. Morg rolled a 160.

In the second game, it looked early on that Morg and Junior were going to start to dominate. Morg was matching his partner almost pin for pin. But Roxy was bowling even better than her first game. Then Jay got on a roll. He threw five consecutive strikes to end the game. Morg was impressed. After the fifth strike, Morg called out, "The Jay Bird is on fire!"

The crashing of balls on pins echoed across the alleys. Jay froze before turning back to his friends after his follow-through. His heart came up in his throat. Jaybird had always been Freddy's pet name for him. Jay swallowed hard. As he came back to his seat next to Roxy, he nodded at Morgan.

"En Fuego," Jay growled in Spanish at Morg. Morg howled with laughter. Roxy patted Jay's arm. He found a way to smile at her. The game continued.

As Jay was finishing his hot streak, Wash Dryer was opening the door to the hotel room for Maricel. As the door closed, they locked in an embrace. She whispered passionately in his ear in Spanish. Wash was too engaged with his physical needs to translate. In minutes, they were naked on the bed. This was their first time being totally naked together with no fear of interruption. And while their encounters had been remarkable in their passion, they had yet to completely engage as lovers. The heat of the foreplay was catching up to them both, but Wash paused.

"I brought protection. Are we going to—" Wash asked a little nervously.

"Si – yes please, yes." Maricel smiled with sweet passion as she bobbed her head up and down.

She helped him with the condom wrapper. At first, Wash proceeded awkwardly, but an athlete is an athlete, and as he gained confidence and began steadying his rhythm, their passion rose. It was over quickly.

The night was not over, however. Maricel proceeded to teach Wash just what kind of athlete she was. They fell asleep an hour before dawn. They awoke in each other's arms and were soon again engaged in lovemaking. Checkout time crept closer. With moments to spare, they showered and exited the room. Wash was thinking a million and one thoughts all at once. Maricel was quiet and smiled a powerful smile as they walked down the hall together. Wash glanced sideways at his girl. Had he made a good decision? It would take a team of lawyers to persuade him that he hadn't.

On Sunday, Junior Shultz got back from church at 12:30. He had done some sincere praying for Seth Parker. Junior still blamed himself for Seth's injury. His cousin Pete called him on his cell. Pete was in eighth grade and played football. He was already a bigger and better lineman than Junior. John Cale was looking forward to having him anchor the line when he got to high school. Mike Reese was watching Pete develop into a very good heavyweight and was already penciling him into the varsity wrestling lineup by the time he was a sophomore.

"You coming over? I'm gonna sight in my new .22." Pete asked. Junior's uncle, John Shultz, farmed for a living and dealt guns at shows for a hobby. Uncle John had taught Junior to shoot at an early age, and last year he had taken him hunting in the U.P. with Pete. All three had taken very nice bucks near Ontanogan.

"I'll be there in twenty," Junior answered. He wanted to sight in his 30.06 before deer season started in three weeks. The sun was high in the sky and the temperature was over fifty degrees. The prolonged Indian summer weather had lulled most of mid-Michigan into believing a mild winter was possible. There were still brightly colored leaves on the trees out on the farm when Junior pulled in. Uncle John had built a nice shooting range facing a hill on some remote acreage well behind the farmhouse and outbuildings.

The boys rode out to the range in a Kawasaki Mule quad. Uncle John was already there setting up targets. There were two tables set up on hay bales down range from the targets. The boys chatted about the upcoming deer season as they set up their gear at one of the tables. Junior turned and walked back to the Mule to get a bottle of Mountain Dew. The shot rang out and Junior stumbled forward smacking his head on the side of the ATV.

It was never really determined how Pete's .22 discharged. He said it was slipping off the hay bales when he tried to catch it and it went off. More than likely, he had ill-advisedly leaned it up on one of the bales. The bullet passed through Junior's left bicep just nicking the bone. The bullet tumbled forward and struck a rib but did not pierce the chest cavity. Instead it traveled underneath his skin across his chest lodging near his right collar bone. When Junior pitched forward into the ATV, he gashed his scalp badly, and that wound was much bloodier than the gunshot.

Pete Schultz rushed to Junior's side. From the sight of the blood gushing from the torn scalp, he assumed he had shot Junior in the head and that his cousin was dying. He began screaming. Junior was lying on the ground looking up at his cousin and feebly trying to wipe the blood from his eyes. As he began to lose consciousness, Junior wondered what all the screaming was about and why his left arm wouldn't work.

Uncle John ran to his wounded nephew as he calmed his son. John Schultz had served in the first Gulf War as a medic in the Army. He had seen his share of battle wounds. He assessed the wounds quickly and efficiently and began to administer what first aid he could to stop the bleeding. He knew his nephew was badly hurt but not critical as long as he didn't go into shock.

"Pete – he isn't dying. Calm down. You have to drive the Mule. Go slow." John Schultz gingerly placed Junior in the back of the ATV and squatted over him. Pete navigated the fields back to the farmhouse. John Schultz used his cell to call 911. They were met by the ambulance in the driveway. In less than forty minutes, Junior Schultz was in surgery in the Gratiot hospital where he had been born seventeen years before.

Near midnight, Junior's mom emerged from his hospital room and greeted John Cale and Mike Reese. Her eyes were red. It had been a very difficult and exhausting day. Her ex-husband, Junior's dad, was speeding back from where he lived in Iowa. Jim Schultz couldn't get a flight, and his outbursts of anger at her and his brother were laced with profanity as he continued to call from his cellphone.

"The doctors say he will be okay. He is awake but groggy. He keeps asking for his dad. Can you come in and talk to him? Maybe it will calm him down," Naomi Schultz asked, looking directly at Mike Reese.

Mike Reese nodded and motioned to John Cale to follow him into the room. It was dimly lit. Junior was in his bed with the head slightly elevated. The TV was on but no sound came from it. Junior's eyes were half open.

"Daddy?" Junior stirred and turned his focus from the TV.

"No, son, it's Coach Reese and Coach Cale," Naomi Schultz replied. Reese and Cale gently greeted their player. Reese touched his arm. John Cale surveyed his injuries quickly. Junior's head was wrapped in bandages. His left arm was in a sling and lying on his lower abdomen. An IV tube was in his right arm and an oxygen tube hung loosely under his nose. As Junior's mother fussed with the oxygen tube, Laney Dryer entered the room. She was dressed in her nurse's uniform.

"Let me get that, Naomi," Laney insisted. Junior's mom backed away. Junior mumbled something nonsensical as Laney adjusted the oxygen flow and the hose.

As she was leaving the room, Laney Dryer tugged John Cale's elbow. He turned to face her. "John, the whole football team is in the lobby including my son and a bunch of other students – I've told them Junior will be okay, but they won't leave," she whispered.

"I'm on it," Cale replied quietly and followed her out of the room.

Junior Schultz's eyes suddenly opened wide. "I'm sorry, Coach – I missed the block," he said, focusing on Mike Reese. There was real anguish in his eyes.

Reese forced a smile. "It's okay, son, it's okay," he answered.

"Is Seth hurt bad? I missed the block. I'm sorry." Junior's eyes were closing as he spoke.

"Everything's fine, Junior. Your dad will be here when you wake up in the morning." Mike Reese tried to calm the boy.

"Did we win, Coach?" Junior mumbled as he drifted off.

Mike Reese's eyes glistened as he touched Junior's right arm. "Yes, we did." He softly told the sleeping boy. "Boy did we ever." He continued on as he smiled with relief toward Naomi Schultz who clasped Reese's hand in a wordless thank-you.

In the hospital lobby, John Cale spoke quietly to a very distraught Morg Miller. Morg desperately wanted to see his friend. Cale explained that it wasn't possible and Junior needed his rest. Morg stumbled out to the parking lot, fighting back tears. He sat behind the wheel of his mother's Ford Taurus for a few minutes before breaking down and sobbing.

Shortly after noon the next day, Mike Shanahan and Clete Packer were sitting in Superintendent Knapp's office. They had just finished an hour-long conference call with the school board president who wound up the call with a profanity-laced diatribe about how the football program was going to have to be eliminated as an embarrassment to the town and the school. Pam Kitteridge was deadly serious as she almost shouted the list of fiascos of the season.

"This team is a fucking train wreck! They caused a riot the first day of practice, for God's sake! They broke my son's nose and he still has headaches from that! They got dismissed from a scrimmage!" She hissed and half shouted. Clete Packer wondered how she had heard about that. Pam Kitteridge wasn't even close to being through. "Those sick little thugs shit on the soccer field!" Packer winced visibly. "There was a sex scandal with a student teacher who apparently was in some fucking love triangle with one of the players and her roommate!" Pam Kitteridge embellished those stories, but no one pointed out the exaggerations.

"The coaches are as bad as the kids, for Christ's sake. Your own nephew got booted by Coach Cale, Clete, and then another assistant punched out an opposing team's coach. Which your fucking nephew videoed and then thought it would be hunky dory to leak to the press. What a fucking nightmare that all was." The board president was on a rant and there was no stopping her.

"To top that, one of the players was outed as gay! Followed by a parent protesting about gay students playing sports, and during that meeting the football coaches throw him out of their office. And then the parent spends three hours screaming on the phone at me! There was a player arrested after a high speed chase! One for fencing stolen property! One of the players was the biggest drug kingpin in town! Oh! Oh! And let's not forget the football player running his truck into the band director's house in the middle of the night and nearly killing him and his wife and kids! You had to suspend the JV football season because the whole fucking team was ineligible!" More exaggerations, but the assembled men let them pass, too.

"And let's not forget the wonderful record of the varsity football team. What have they won in the last five years? Huh? Three or four God damn games? Thanks to that piece of shit thieving Texan you hired, Clete, and then you hired a kid who isn't even qualified to coach little league! This whole friggin' town is sick of this embarrassment of a team! They have not even been close to winning a game this season and Riverdale is likely to beat us by 100 points this Friday! That is if they can even field a team because now the football players are shooting each other, for the love of God!" Pam Kitteridge concluded, her voice rising to a scream by the time she finished.

"Pam, we will weather this quietly if we can keep our heads. We'll talk with the coaches today," Superintendent Knapp smoothly assured her.

"Blow it out your ass, Sheldon!" Pam Kitteridge replied. "When I get back to town from this conference, I am going to convene a special board meeting next week. Heads are going to roll, gentlemen! They will roll! And if you will excuse me, I have a meeting to attend now." There was an audible click on the speaker phone as she hung up.

"Get John Cale and Mike Reese over to this office right now, please." Sheldon Knapp commanded Mike Shanahan. The high school principal blinked twice and looked at his assistant principal.

Clete Packer gave Shanahan a look of contempt. He knew that the principal had no idea where either man was or what they were currently teaching. Clete thought briefly that if heads were going to roll, then Shanahan's ought to go first. "I'll get them – Reese has prep hour now and Cale is teaching Algebra 1 – I'll see if I can get someone to cover for him," Clete said efficiently, hoping the superintendent would realize who actually had a clue about the high school schedule. Knapp made no sound, and he waved his hand to command that the action get done.

Ten minutes later John Cale and Mike Reese were in the district central office, which was located across the street from the high school. Sheldon Knapp called them into his personal office and motioned that they sit down. John Cale was not quite sure why he had been pulled from class, but he was a little irritated. Mike Reese could smell what was coming the instant they were called to the super's office. This was shaping up to be a lynching followed by the administrators playing a desperate game of ducking for cover.

"Gentleman," began Superintendent Knapp in a very direct voice. "We have just spent a rather long time on the phone with Board President Kitteridge and I'm going to be very direct here – she is of the mind that the current state of the football program is unacceptable. And to tell you the truth, in my thirty-five years in education, I have never seen any sports program in more serious disarray." Sheldon Knapp paused and shuffled some papers on his desk. "Now she wants to call a special board meeting next week and we're not just talking about forcing some resignations – she is calling for the football program to be eliminated."

John Cale shifted nervously in his chair as he tried to formulate a response. Mike Reese didn't wait.

"Before I respond further to the board president's unrealistic plans," he said, "I want to make note of how disappointed I am in you as administrators. The very first thing this meeting should have started with is you inquiring about the health and welfare of two injured student athletes. Let me save you the trouble. Seth Parker spent the weekend in the hospital. He has a very serious concussion, a neck injury and broken and dislocated fingers that will likely require surgery. He will be evaluated by specialists this week, but it may be that his athletic career hangs in the balance. He may have long-term consequences to deal with. And Junior Shultz is recovering from his gunshot wound and will likely be able to join the wrestling team mid-season if all goes well. This morning, I spoke with his mother and his doctor, a personal friend of mine, and they both assure me his injuries were bloody, but a full recovery is expected. John and I spent the evening at the hospital last night with his mother. I noticed none of you were there. In my career, I have often heard administrators speak of putting kids first. Maybe you have too. Does it really mean anything or is it just another slogan for newspapers and PTA meetings?" Mike Reese said in measured tones.

"Now, Coach, we are all grateful that yesterday's tragedy was not as severe—" Sheldon Knapp said before Mike Reese cut him off.

"Don't talk to me of tragedies. I have seen plenty in thirty-nine years in the classroom. What happened yesterday could have been tragic – thankfully it is going to turn out okay. But I have seen real tragedy. I have seen way too many students injured and killed in car accidents. I have watched two of my student's die of cancer. I have sat in emergency rooms with anguished parents. I have delivered eulogies at student funerals – several of them, as a matter of fact. All while a parade of principals and superintendents sat dutifully in church pews glancing at their watches and calculating whether they could make it to some meeting or a tee-off time. I have worked teaching and coaching and counseling kids who lost parents to disease and accidents and messy family-destroying divorces. It cost me my first marriage and nearly my own family because of the time I invested in the kids of this district. So please do me a very large favor and don't talk to me of tragedy. If any of you had spent any more than the bare minimum in a classroom before putting on a suit and becoming an administrator, you might have a clue about what I am talking about," Mike Reese said with resolve, holding anger out of his voice.

"Now wait a fucking minute, you sanctimonious motherfu—" Clete Packer was red-faced with anger as he started his reply to Mike Reese. Superintendent Knapp cut him off with a raised hand and a steely look, but before he could respond, Mike Shanahan uncharacteristically spoke up.

"Coach, you have no right to lecture us on what it is to be an educator and to deal with student tragedy. We have all been there just as often as you," Shanahan said gravely.

Mike Reese paused for a few seconds. "Yes, you're right. I apologize, Mike. I'll get off my high horse. These last few days have been pretty stressful, and I should have chosen my words better."

"I'll make note of your apology in the reprimand for insubordination I will be placing in your file," Mike Shanahan said officiously, hoping to take command of this meeting back for the administrators. It was a serious miscalculation. Sheldon Knapp cringed a little as his underling spoke.

"Seriously?" Mike Reese turned his focus fully to Shanahan. "Is that where you really want to go with this, Mike?" The mock incredulity in Reese's voice was apparent to all.

"Let me clue you in how this is going to go," Reese continued. You so much as start typing that letter for my official jacket, I will file a grievance so quick it will spin your gray-haired head off your shoulders. You're not playing intimidation games with some first-year kid teacher fresh out of college here. I have been president of the local union three times. I have been the union building rep for the high school for thirty years. If you even think of putting a letter of reprimand in my folder, I will call the union headquarters in Lansing and have a half dozen lawyers here in less than twenty-four hours." Mike Reese was fully back on attack mode now, and he was about to go out on a pretty thin limb.

He shifted his gaze to Sheldon Knapp and went in for the kill. "I'm pretty sure the super here does not want a messy headline-producing grievance filed over an unsupportable reprimand. This is a legitimate professional dispute. I have made no statements that would read otherwise. I know fully what constitutes insubordination and how hard it is to prove in a he-said, he-said, dispute with no official transcripts and multiple conflicting witnesses. But I don't think Mr. Knapp wants an ugly grievance fight right now – not if he wants to move on to another higher-paying super's job – say the Midland superintendency, which is opening up next spring, I understand. He'd have a hell of a time getting an interview for that position if this meeting and some other key administrative dealings become part of the public record. I'm pretty sure he'd like to finish his career in a nice high-paying job so he can retire to his waterfront condo and boat in Florida – that's what I think. Maybe I'm wrong. Either way I'm fully vested in my retirement, so if you boys want to play hard-ball, throw the first pitch." Mike Reese made no attempt to cushion his contempt.

Both Mike Shanahan and Clete Packer were open mouthed in amazement as Mike Reese finished. John Cale was still as a stone. Only Sheldon Knapp showed a willingness to say anything in response. His cheeks were flushed as he began to speak. "Coach, you have a long record of good service to this district and no one is going to dispute that. I think some words were said in haste here today, and perhaps it is best if we walk this back a bit and—"

"I'm not quite through, Mr. Knapp." Mike Reese cut the superintendent off again.

"Now, you said that Mrs. Kitteridge wants to kill off the football program. Well, maybe you had better 'walk her back a bit.' Tell her that I will be resigning next week as a football coach. That should satisfy her penny ante bloodlust. But also tell her if she comes after the program or John Cale, she will have a fight on her hands like she has never seen. I am going on the record right here and right now to tell you what I will be telling every news outlet in the area if she makes a move in that direction. John Cale is as fine a young coach as I have ever worked with. I would put him up against any coach in this school's history in any sport. And that is saying something, because I have worked with some very fine coaches over the years – with two very notable exceptions." Reese paused and glanced at Clete Packer whose reddening face betrayed the fact that Reese's point had hit home.

Reese continued, "I will not stand idly by as Pam Kitteridge pillories John. Remind her who she is up against. Two of the current board members are former wrestlers of mine. I stood as godfather for the board vice president's first child. The mayor of this town and three members of the city council are former athletes of mine. I have probably been at the weddings and funerals of family members of about 80 percent of the electorate in this district. If there is some sort of public meeting to call the question of eliminating football in this district, tell her who will be showing up and who is really going to be calling the shots. Tell her to go there and then watch the recall election start the very next day. Pam Kitteridge had better be satisfied with my football resignation, boys, cause that's all she's gonna get. Then tell her she only has to wait a couple of years, and I'll retire. I'm going to win one more wrestling state championship – some of the boys on this football team are going to help win it for me and this school, and then I'm gone and Pam Kitteridge can kiss my ass."

All three administrators sat quietly as Reese rose to his feet. John Cale followed him out of the office, not having said a word.

"Of all the fucking nerve! Someone needs to take that prick down a peg or two. Don't tell me that what he said is not insubordination – like hell!" Clete Packer sputtered with anger as he ranted.

"What he said may well have been insubordination, which is, as he noted, hard to prove in a grievance situation. But what he threatened, gentlemen, is something he is fully prepared to follow through on," said Sheldon Knapp with certainty.

"But for Christ sake, he can't say something like that and walk out of here without repercussions!" Clete Packer exclaimed, looking at the superintendent.

"Do I have to spell things out for you yet again, Clete? You want to be principal when Mike here retires, right?" Sheldon Knapp slowly stated to Clete who nodded yes in response. Mike Shanahan sat quietly with a scowl on his face. He didn't like being talked about as if he wasn't in the room.

"Well," Knapp continued, "Mike Reese has it completely right – if we press him on this and he causes a huge public shit-storm, you're not ever going to be principal and I'm not going to get the Midland job or any other one when my contract is not renewed when this stinking pile of crap hits the public fan. Do you want that to happen? Because I don't. We have to pick our battles, gentlemen. And we have to pick wisely. I think we better spend some time figuring out how to keep Pam Kitteridge from blowing this situation up like some hormone-enraged female Kamikaze pilot."

Early Monday afternoon, Molly Saunders' sister, Mandy Polhuis, sat in a consultation room next to the critical care unit in Sparrow hospital. She was hung over. She could feel the shakes coming on. A hospital social worker and a doctor were droning on about her sister's condition. She couldn't care less. She needed a drink and a smoke. The drive over from Chicago the day before had been grueling – she made the whole trip without a drink. She was tense the whole way. Her driver's license was under suspension in Illinois for driving under the influence, and the thought of spending time in a Michigan jail did not appeal to her, so she made the trip sober. Besides she had at least three outstanding warrants she knew of, and if she got busted for drinking and driving a check of her records would likely get her sent back to Chi-Town in cuffs. She spent the evening in a fleabag motel off the interstate getting blitzed on Relsky vodka and warm orange juice. The only ice machine in the motel was broken.

Mandy borrowed her boyfriend's car to make the trip with the promise that she would turn a few extra tricks for him this weekend. "Boyfriend" was how she referred to her pimp. Mandy was in her fourth decade as a prostitute. As she neared fifty years of age, no amount of makeup could cover the ravages of life on the street. She looked and smelled horrible as she sat in the tight confines of the consultation room. Her hosts were rushing through their informative presentation. The woman reeked of booze and stale cigarettes.

"So what you're saying is, she ain't waking up? Is that about it?" Mandy Polhuis interrupted the doctor.

"It is still too early to make that call. There is some brain function, but more concerning is the condition of her heart. She is much too weak for any surgical procedures. And with her heart only functioning at about ten percent of efficiency her kidneys are barely functioning. And fluid is building—" The doctor maintained his professional demeanor but the reeking barfly was barely tuned into his prognosis.

"So pull the frigging plug," Mandy interrupted again.

"It isn't as simple as that, ma'am. We can't do that. Unless, of course, she has a living will. We checked for a primary care physician in hopes that she would have paperwork on file. Apparently she doesn't have one, or at least none that we know of. If we had a do-not-resuscitate order, we could just ease her passing. But without that, we are compelled to keep her alive," the social worker informed the broken-down prostitute.

"Look, I ain't been real close with Molly since Ma died twelve years ago. I don't know what her wishes are. She probably does got a living will. After all the shit we went through with Ma, I'm sure Molly put one together. She is ten years older than me. She insisted on handling everything with Ma. After it took five months on life support to drain the last of Ma's money, she finally died. No will. Not much left over but a few pieces of jewelry. Maybe Molly has her own medical instructions in her lockbox. I can go check if you like." Mandy Polhuis spoke with a little more concern. The whole intent of this trip was to get to Molly's lockbox. Mandy knew full well Molly had all of their mother's jewelry locked up there. Probably some other valuable stuff, too. She was about to tell the social worker to drop dead on the phone on Friday when the phrase "difficult-to-reverse coma" was discussed. Opportunity knocked. The ugly old bitch ripped her out of her inheritance when Ma died. Mandy wanted to even the score.

"Well, that might make things easier, yes," the social worker agreed.

"You got her keys and stuff?" Mandy tried to be as innocent as possible as she asked.

"I have her personal effects in a safe. I can see what is there," the social worker said with a little relief that the meeting would be drawing to a close.

In less than an hour, Mandy Polhuis was driving north toward Bear River with the keys to Molly's trailer. Still cold-sober, but now a sense of purpose helped her fight off the shakes. A sense of purpose and bubbling-up repressed hatred. She hated Bear River. She hated everything about her childhood there. Mandy had been the miracle baby born after five successive miscarriages. Ten years younger than her sister and born a month after her father died falling through the ice late in the winter on Saginaw Bay fishing for walleye. Her mother had always pressured Mandy to consider taking her vows and becoming a nun. Three years of sexual molestation at the hands of the parish priest put an end to Mandy ever taking any religious vows. When she tried to tell her mother of how the sainted priest had abused her, Ma refused to believe her and Molly called her a skank for seducing the padre. She was seventeen. Within two years she was selling her body on the streets of Chicago.

Ma had been gone for over a dozen years, and now Molly was soon to follow. Mandy chain-smoked and slammed down several Diet Cokes as she drove. The last time she had seen Molly was at the wake after Ma's funeral. They had a screaming match about Ma's jewelry. Molly called her a heartbreaking disappointment to their mother and a cheap whore. When Mandy called Molly a dried-up and barren old cow, her sister threw a large glass ashtray at her head. A general melee ensued. Three dozen drunken cousins and friends of the family brawled outside the old American Legion hall south of town. Molly's second husband ended it by retrieving his shotgun from his truck and firing warning shots over the brawlers. That happened just as the sheriff cars pulled into the parking lot. Mandy's pimp boyfriend snuck her out the back door of the hall and they hightailed it back to Chicago. Mandy still had a scar above her scalp line from the ashtray strike – and no jewelry from her mother.

When Mandy got to Molly's sagging double-wide trailer, she had the road jitters. The trailer was in the mobile home community next to the industrial park in Bear River. It took her five minutes to find Molly's lockbox. Sure enough, there was jewelry. Mandy took a quick inventory – it included her parent's' wedding rings, a string of real pearls that had been her mother's, Molly's two cheap and gaudy wedding rings, various earrings and bracelets, but nothing really noteworthy other than an antique cameo brooch that had belonged to their paternal grandmother. It wasn't much, really – hardly worth the trip. Mandy searched through the trailer for other things of value. In a spare bedroom she found a collection of six porcelain dolls all dressed in infant's clothes with names pinned to their collars lined up in miniature cribs. A gold-plated crucifix hung on the living room wall. Molly's Pink Coral rosary beads were draped on a nightstand drawer handle in her bedroom. Mandy hastily put all these things into a storage tub after dumping the clothes found in it on the living room floor. As an afterthought she went back to the lockbox. Mandy flipped through the paperwork. As predicted, there was a medical living will form with a do-not-resuscitate order paper clipped to it.

Mandy tossed the folder with the DNR order into the tub with her haul of Molly's possessions. She checked the fridge. Molly had an unopened carton of Camel cigarettes tucked away. Mandy hated the brand, but a carton of smokes was a carton of smokes. She grabbed it up. There were three cans of beer in the fridge as well. She threw the smokes and beers in a paper grocery bag. She was backing her way out the door with the tub and bag when she heard someone behind her.

"You're the sister, aren't you? I can see the resemblance." Mandy turned to face the person. The voice was high and effeminate. She was surprised to see an elderly man standing there. He wore a white shirt and tie with a well-pressed suit jacket of 1980's vintage. He had a gray muzzled wiener dog with only one eye on a leash. The dog was growling.

"Yes. I'm her only sister," Mandy answered cautiously.

"She said something about having a sister once. I'm Stephen. I live next door. This is Mandi. She's Molly's dog. I came and got her out of the trailer the day after Molly collapsed. I have a key. Molly wouldn't trust anyone else around here with one." Mandy looked at her namesake dog. Hatred welled up in her. "Poor thing," the old man continued, indicating he was speaking about the dog. "Molly was – is a difficult person to warm up to. And she used to yell the most obscene things at this poor poochie. Especially after Mandi was a – um – put in a family way by a mixed breed down the street. Molly had her ex drown the pups. But that was a long time ago – almost ten years. Mandi was barely more than a pup herself. I never could understand why she kept the dog. She seemed to hate it so. But after her Neal, her husband – second husband – left, she was alone, and I guess yelling at a dog is better than being lonely." The fussy old man meandered on and on, well past Mandy's point of being engaged.

"Look – I, ah, got to get on the road." Mandy could not keep the scorn out of her voice.

"Yes, I understand. You want to get back to your sister. I understand she is still in a coma. Such a pity – she is still a young woman. It's the cigarettes – they kill so many good people too soon. My very good friend, Carl, well, he just couldn't quit them. Died at sixty over twenty-five years ago. Lung cancer. We had a shop together but everything was in his name. I got nothing when he passed. Nothing to do but retire here. His family took it all and—" The old man had a faraway look in his eyes as he droned on. Mandy brushed past him.

She threw the bag and tub in the backseat of the Cadillac. As she climbed into the Caddy, the old man approached the car. "I'm sorry. I didn't get your name," he said much more clearly and directly.

Mandy reached into her large purse and pulled out a long cigarette. She lit it and took an aggressive pull. She looked at the dog with disgust. "My name is Amanda." She brought her gaze up to meet the eyes of the old man. The sun made her squint, but she saw the recognition in his eyes. She exhaled her smoke at him. He waved it from his face.

"What should I do with Mandi? I can't keep her. I can't afford a pet on my Social Security. She's so old. And she – well, she doesn't control herself very well and she's so gassy." The old man had a very pained expression bordering on panic as he complained.

"What the hell do I care. Take her to the pound," Mandy sneered in reply.

"But they'll just put her down. The poor old girl," Stephen whined in response.

"Big deal – have 'em put the bitch down. I'm going to have the docs do the same to Molly," Mandy replied without remorse. She put the car in drive and gunned the motor, spraying some gravel. The dog barked and whined.

The three beers from Molly's fridge didn't help mellow Mandy's nasty mood. Going against her own better judgment, she downed them in less than twenty miles. Rather than heading to the hospital, Mandy went in search of a pawn shop. On Michigan Avenue east of downtown Lansing, she found a place. The giant black man behind the counter gave her $380 for the jewelry. He suggested taking the cameo broach to an antique dealer to get a better price. Mandy insisted he take it off her hands for fifty dollars. He refused to give her anything for the porcelain dolls. He claimed they were cheaply made modern collectables and of no use to him. The rosary and crucifix got her an additional thirty dollars.

Mandy chucked the tub of dolls into the backseat of the Caddy. She called her pimp boyfriend on her cell and explained that she only got $200 for the jewelry. He was furious. "Bitch! That ain't even going to cover the gas money! Get your ass back here! You been out two days already! It ain't good for business!"

Mandy whined about being too drunk to drive and not wanting to get pulled over. She promised she would be back by noon the next day. She drove the Caddy up the avenue toward the capitol. Mandy found a parking lot and paid an overnight fee. She wandered up the street to the first bar she could find. She had over $200 to spend, and for the next several hours, she only drank from the top shelf. She spent the night in the apartment of a half-witted john she picked up when the money ran out. He gave her a ride back to the lot to fetch the Caddy. It was almost noon when she got there. Booze sweat was pouring from her body even though there had been a serious drop in the temperature. Before she got in the car, she threw up.

An hour down the road, she pulled into a truck stop on Interstate 94. She bought a large coffee, black, and a pint of Jim Beam bourbon. She sat in the Caddy dreading the ass-whipping she would get for being late, but her hangover was too great to continue. In a half hour, the whiskey and coffee were gone. Later in the afternoon, she woke up still in the driver's seat of the Caddy in the lot next to the truck stop. The radio was blaring country music. She purely hated country music. She angrily turned the radio off. Light snow was falling. She fished around in her purse and found a bottle of Excedrin. She downed three, dry-swallowing the chalky, bitter pills.

She climbed out of the Caddy and swore bitterly as the wind cut through her. She went into the truck stop to use the bathroom. Coming back, Mandy walked with the wind. As she approached the Caddy, she looked in the backseat. The tub with the porcelain dolls was there – open. The folder with her sister's DNR form poked up above their blank, smiling faces. Mandy opened the door and grabbed the tub after making a half-hearted attempt to close the lid. She glanced around the lot. An overflowing dumpster sat behind the restaurant. Mandy walked to it and tossed the plastic tub onto the heap of garbage bags. The tub tumbled off the piled-up garbage. The top sprung loose. Two dolls tumbled out. Their porcelain heads shattered on the cement. Two name tags – one reading "Tiffany" and the other "Michelle" blew across the lot with the contents of the medical records folder. Mandy ignored the bitterly cold wind and watched the paper sweep into the weeds at the end of the parking lot.

"Fuck the dried-up old cow. Let her rot away like Ma," Mandy sneered at the wind.

In five minutes, she was on the freeway heading west to Chicago. She knew an epic ass-whipping was waiting for her, but she had a wicked smile on her face as she contemplated never having to see Bear River ever again.

Football practice on Monday started after a meeting between the coaches and father of Scott Baier. John Cale welcomed Wyatt Baier into the coaches' office. Mike Reese knew what was coming, but there wasn't a thing that could be done.

"I'm gonna get to the point, Coach. Scott won't be suiting up this week," Wyatt Baier stated flatly.

"Is he hurt?" John Cale masked his disappointment effectively.

"No, and that's the point. He isn't going to risk his career and his college scholarship playing behind that joke of an offensive line. The only decent lineman you got you have lining up as a fullback now. Your starting center is a freshman because Junior Schultz is in the hospital. You got a giant retard starting at right tackle. I don't know who the hell you are going to start at right guard. Morg Miller is the smallest left guard in the league. And Phil Long is the worst left tackle I have ever seen. Period. And Scott ain't going to risk everything playing behind that shit," Wyatt Baier explained with disgusted passion.

"I want you to know that I hadn't considered starting Scott at QB this week, Wyatt, but he would have seen a great deal of time on defense. As you pointed out, the roster is depleted. I am sorry you have such a low opinion of his teammates. I don't think Scott does. He has many good friends on the team and the boys like him. He has potential to be a team leader on varsity – if not next season, then surely when he is a junior. As it is, with another varsity game under his belt, with some playing time, he would have qualified for a varsity letter. We don't often give those to freshman. Four-year letterman is an accomplishment to be proud of. I was proud of my four varsity letters." John Cale was disgusted, but he mastered his tone so as not to provoke a confrontation.

"Yeah, well, Scott is just a boy and he doesn't always see the handwriting on the wall. In fact, I'm giving serious thought to transferring him over to Gratiot for next year. We have the house on the market. We will buy something there just as soon as we sell. This town is circling the drain. The school is getting sucked down with it," Wyatt answered with dismissive sarcasm.

"Handwriting on the wall?" Mike Reese spoke up for the first time. "In over twenty years coaching football and nearly four decades coaching wrestling, I have met a few parents that could read the handwriting on the wall. Most of them were college athletes themselves, though. Did you play college ball, Wyatt?"

"I joined the Army after school. First Gulf War vet. I was second team all-league for Dowagiac, down near the Indiana state line, two years back in the '80s," Wyatt answered with defensive puzzlement.

"Quarterback?" Reese asked looking him directly in the eye.

"No, I was a linebacker and a tight end." Wyatt answered with an edge to his voice.

"I played football and wrestled in high school – for Gratiot high school. CMU invited me to walk onto both the football and wrestling teams. I chose wrestling. I got a partial scholarship my second year and a full ride for my last two seasons. Worked my ass off, and I had some success in wrestling, but in football I just would have been cannon fodder for the practice squad. John here walked on at Northern in football after high school. I'd have him roll up his pant legs to show his knees, but it really isn't necessary. He has four years of college practice squad experience and three surgeries worth of scars all for the right to suit up for home games as a senior. And he don't let on, but I know he is struggling some days with pain in those knees. But he loved the game. He still does. Probably loves it more than anyone in this building – adult or child. And that is one of the great hurdles he faces here as a football coach. Until a dozen students in each class raise their passion for the game to meet his, it will be a long time before Bear River turns the corner on the field. Until that time, he and I are committed to making playing football at this school a learning and growing experience for the boys. And for their parents as well in some cases." Mike Reese spoke in fatherly tones.

"I fail to see how your experiences affect—" Wyatt Baier began angrily. But Mike Reese cut him off by talking in the same fatherly tone.

"You talk of reading the handwriting on the wall. Let me help you a little. Because I think your vision might be impaired. I have almost four decades of coaching experience. In that time I have coached eight college-scholarship-winning athletes. Seven in wrestling and one in baseball decades ago – two of the athletes were my own sons. They started wrestling before they could ride bikes. And they both won two state championships. All that got them was a partial scholarship at a Division II college. The three wrestlers I sent onto Division I wrestling college programs were all preferred walk-on athletes. None of them stuck it out. They were accomplished wrestlers, but they didn't have the passion for the business of college athletics. Now, in the twenty-five years I've coached football here, we have sent some boys on to small college ball. One or two of them worked their way onto starting at Gratiot College. We had a nice kid who ended up playing for a Christian college in Illinois and was second team All- American as a center in Division III back in the early '80s. He disappeared in South America on a mission trip about twenty years ago – plane crashed in the jungle. Steve Genter – good man—" Mike Reese was engrossed in his story for a moment and then he read the eyes of his audience and saw no softening, just disgust and impatience.

"Well, look, I see you are not interested in my going on, so I'll get to the point," Reese said with a little weariness.

"Your son is not likely to be a college quarterback – even at a very small school. He lacks speed and size and his arm strength is questionable. It's as simple as that. Oh, he might get a walk-on invite somewhere at a small college. But Scotty will find the business of college football to be pretty brutal. Maybe if we had a full four years of working with him we might have instilled the work ethic and passion necessary to meet the challenge that John mastered as an undergrad, but then John came from pretty exceptional stock. I know one thing for sure – if you go around taking Scotty off the field every time things get a little dicey, he isn't going to learn the resilience necessary to be a college athlete. So go ahead and pull him off the field this week. Shop around for another high school to enroll him in. These days, there are plenty of coaches willing to play your tune and coddle Scotty until he is virtually worthless anytime the chips are down," Reese concluded. John Cale braced for an explosion.

"Pat Packer was right. You're nothing but a washed-up old windbag who loves to listen to himself talk. Seriously, you two are running the worst football program in the state and you haven't got a fucking clue. Scotty is done here at Bear River! Go to hell – the both of you!" Wyatt Baier stormed out of the office.

The silence hung in the air. John Cale took in a deep breath and let it out slowly. "He's right about our O line. It's a shambles," the young coach said quietly.

"Yes it is," Reese responded. "And if anything we are in worse shape on defense. Other than the Things, I haven't a clue what to put out there in the backfield. We will have to use them at safety. That leaves us with inexperienced underclassmen at corner. Bob Pease runs that four wide passing tree stuff. We got no pass rush. No pressure, and that QB of theirs will take us apart. And even if we do manage to hold coverage, he can tuck it in and run with the ball better than any quarterback in the league. They might hang a hundred on us – payback for all the times my wrestling teams have drubbed his. I wouldn't put it past Pease to run up the score. I've ended his wrestling season nine consecutive years in the district final. He always has some good kids. He never quite fields a solid lineup all the way through, though. And his kids just aren't that good at wrestling. He thinks he's hot shit on the football field though. He's won the league seven times in the last fifteen years. Made the playoffs a bunch of times, but he always gets bounced by some school from the Grand Rapids area in the second round."

"Coach Pease's vendetta is a worry I'll save until Friday night. Right now, we have to piece together an offensive backfield," John Cale answered wearily.

"Jay Brau can play QB. We can rotate the Things at tailback and some wingback and use Sam Bott there if we have to. Jorge is really a decent fullback. He hits the hole hard and he punishes the first kid that makes contact," Mike Reese said with confidence, belying the situation.

"Jay's arm is erratic and he doesn't know our passing game very well," Cale replied.

"Coach, the only throwing we will be doing is to the tight end. Maybe we might try a screen pass or two because we won't have time to throw downfield. The O line is a mess. Pass blocking? Not very likely. We have to stay on the ground and we will have to simplify everything in the running game. I think if we want to keep the offense on the field long enough to keep Pease from running up the score, we have to run Cheese Stick. We might be able to grind out some first downs in the power I with Jorge running hard." Again Reese's voice betrayed no defeatism. He stated everything plainly.

"Double tight and power I?" John Cale asked.

"Cheese Stick. And more Cheese Stick," Mike Reese affirmed.

The Bear River Bears players all sensed doom waiting at the end of the week. On Wednesday, Coach Cale dismissed the Bears practice twenty minutes early. It was a reward for the hustle he claimed they had shown. He was being generous. Jay Brau stayed on the field with Tom Osborne practicing the snap and exchange from center to quarterback. Jorge stayed so Jay could practice handing the ball off. John Cale and Mike Reese watched and encouraged. Reese dismissed Thing One and Thing Two and told them to go shower up.

They trotted toward the pedestrian bridge to the school. A cold wind blew gray clouds across the sky.

Things One and Two saw and heard the commotion on the bridge and they quickened their pace. They knew their younger brothers were hanging around campus. They instinctively knew that their brothers were in the middle of the throng on the bridge. The middle school football season had ended a week before. The eighth-grade team had managed to win two games. A good year by Bear River standards. Things Three and Four played tailback and fullback on offense and linebacker on defense. Free time after school was rarely put to good use by the Lott brothers.

The First Battle on the Bridge started with a bullying incident. Members of the soccer team had confronted Kenny Lott, the Things' cousin, on the bridge. They teased him because he was fishing in the Bear River. Kenny was nineteen years old with bulging eyes and pale skin. He had Asperger's syndrome and a deep fascination with ichthyology. One of the soccer players grabbed Kenny's fishing pole away from him as he was explaining to them why the fish in the Bear River had to be studied to understand what long-term pollution had done to the fishery. When the pole was taken from Kenny he stopped and began to keen in a high-pitched whine and slap his hands into his own cheeks. Liam Pickering was approaching the bridge from the field side of the river. The soccer team had ended practice early as well.

"Hey, you assholes! Don't mess with him. He doesn't hurt anybody. Give him his pole back." Liam Pickering was mildly pissed off at his teammates. It had been a bad practice and the state district tournament was starting soon. Liam, as team captain, had lectured the team about not being focused just before they left the practice soccer pitch.

The soccer players stopped laughing when their captain jogged up the steps of the bridge. Kenny Lott was still slapping himself, and he began to sob. Kyle and Connor Lott, Thing Three and Thing Four approached the bridge silently from the opposite end of the bridge. "Better give him that pole back, dickhead," Thing Three said maliciously but with an eerie calm that made the bulk of the soccer players back away from the boy holding Kenny Lott's fishing pole. They knew even though the younger Things were only middle school kids, they were absolutely not to be messed with.

The stocky boy with heavy eyebrows and piercing blue eyes holding the fishing pole was not as familiar with the legend of the Things. He grinned a snarky grin as he taunted Kenny Lott by extending the pole to him and then snatching it away. Micah Showalter had transferred in from the Catholic school in Mt. Pleasant. He had been an all-state soccer player for them but had been booted from school after a sexting scandal. Most of the Bear River soccer team only tolerated the transfer because of his gifts on the soccer pitch. Liam Pickering didn't like Micah, but to win a state championship, he would put up with the asshole.

"Give it back." Thing Four used the same tone his brother had as they cleared the steps to the elevated pedestrian bridge. Things One and Two were jogging in from the football practice field when they glanced at the bridge and recognized their brothers confronting the dozen or more soccer team members. Without saying anything they began sprinting. They closed the 60-yard distance quickly.

"Who the fuck are you?" Micah Showalter asked Things Three and Four. He ignored their squared stances and didn't recognize the intent in their eyes. Violence was going to ensue no matter what by this point, but then the transfer student really sealed the deal. "If fishboy wants his pole, let him fish for it."

Liam Pickering shouted, "Micah don't!" But it was too late. The bully dropped the pole into the Bear River a dozen feet below the bridge. Before the fishing pole sank three feet to the rock and garbage-strewn river bottom the young Things were upon him. Kenny Lott began screaming at the top of his lungs. Things Three and Four rained kicks and punches down on Micah Showalter, who fell backwards toward the terrified soccer players. Things One and Two waded into the crowd from the opposite end of the bridge. Silently but with massive grins, they began to sucker-punch the soccer players from behind.

Liam Pickering was shouting and trying to separate the young Things from the battered bully. Panic on the bridge was rising as the soccer team realized they were being attacked by Things from all angles. Two boys jumped over the bright red railing of the bridge and splashed into the waist deep Bear River.

"What the fuck!" Liam Pickering yelled as he spun around just in time to catch a kick to the stomach from Thing Two. Without missing a beat, Thing One followed it up with a punch to the face of the soccer team captain. He collapsed to the deck of the bridge. He was too woozy to protest as Things Three and Four scooped up Micah Showalter and threw him over the railing. The heavy splash put an end to the screaming of Kenny Lott, who then began to giggle.

Nine soccer players drew close together near their fallen captain. One or two pleaded with the Things as they silently squared their stances and leered at the terrified boys.

"Micah! God damn it! Find that pole and bring it up here before they kill us!" Laboring from the stomach kick, Liam Pickering struggled to yell as the wind returned to his lungs. The three soccer players were struggling and stumbled in the river, but they found the pole surprisingly quickly in the icy cold and murky water. They brought it up the steep bank and then onto the bridge. A red welt was already turning purple around Micah Showalter's left eye. Blood and water dripped from his split lower lip. He said nothing and averted his eyes as he handed the pole to Kenny Lott. The autistic boy stopped giggling and he ran down the steps of the bridge, thanking his cousins as he disappeared around the corner of the high school only fifty feet away. The Things didn't move. They didn't say a word.

Liam Pickering stood hanging onto the bridge rail. Nausea was bringing bile to the back of his throat. He swallowed it back down. The three soaked soccer players were starting to shake in the cool breeze. The four Lott brothers had half the varsity soccer team trapped between them. "Are we done?" Thing One finally asked his brothers and the soccer team captain.

"We're done," Things Three and Four said in unison.

Liam Pickering nodded. "Yes."

Thing Two closed the distance between himself and Micah Showalter and grabbed his chin, tipping his face up to examine the damage. The bully whimpered.

"You're lucky my brothers didn't knock teeth down your throat. You understand? Usually they don't stop until someone needs an ambulance ride." He pushed the face back down. Micah Showalter stifled a sob.

Thing One spoke up. "No one talks about this. If Fudge finds out anything—" He stopped and tried to meet the eyes of all the soccer players on the bridge. "My brothers and I are going to find out who talked and someone really will be needing an ambulance ride. You guys understand?"

One of the soccer players replied, "Yes, we understand." Liam Pickering nodded agreement and leaned over the bridge railing to vomit. The entire episode took about five minutes.

By mid-evening, social media was buzzing. No soccer team members contributed anything to the dialogue online. Morg Miller texted both Thing One and Two. They claimed ignorance of any fight. And yet, most of the story with a good many details about who said what and did what was widely known by the student body.

The next day, rumors continued to spread quickly about the battle on the bridge. Even without his eyes and ears, Molly Saunders, Fudge was onto the story. Shortly after lunch, Clete Packer started searching through the video footage from the security cameras mounted on the back of the school. Only one of the cameras was working, the one trained down-river toward the practice fields. He saw who he assumed were the older Lott twins running on the far side of the Bear River. Then after a few minutes, the gawky outline of a tall boy carrying a fishing pole flashed in the lower frame of the video. Nothing else could be seen. The video from the camera trained on the bridge was dark. It was enough for Fudge to move forward. He wanted to hurt Mike Reese where he lived. What better way than to suspend wrestlers – maybe even have them expelled.

Packer called the captain of the soccer team to his office along with the Showalter boy. Myles Kitteridge, the soccer coach, came as well, but he was puzzled. This was the first he had heard anything of a brawl on the bridge. The injuries to Micah Showalter's face suggested that the rumors of the brawl were true. But neither Liam Pickering nor Micah Showalter would admit to anything other than Micah taking a soccer ball to the face while he and Liam were getting in some extra work on the game field after practice. The AD was getting frustrated.

At two in the afternoon, all four Things sat smiling sweetly in front of Packer's desk. The two younger boys were sent from the middle school at his request. Their "yes sirs" and "no sirs" caused Clete Packer to glance at his desk drawer, coveting the fresh bottle of Maalox. They admitted only to talking to their cousin on the bridge and telling him to go home because it was cold and getting late. Finally he dismissed the four boys, glad to be shed of their flinty voices and smiling faces.

Clete Packer called John Cale and Mike Reese to his office just before they were about to start football practice. They wearily sent Cheese Colby down to the practice field with the boys and they walked to the AD's office.

"You know what this is about, right?" Reese asked the young head coach.

"Fudge is on the warpath about some sort of fight that the Things and some soccer players got in," Cale answered with a sigh. "If he suspends them, we will have to forfeit on Friday. We can't play a game dressing only fifteen kids, half of them JV."

"Yeah, but I think if he had the goods on them he would have suspended them already," Reese concluded. "It's that shithead Micah Showalter – even the soccer players don't like him. He bit off more than he could chew with the younger brothers. Apparently Micah was bullying Kenny Lott – the autistic cousin. Kyle and Connor caught him and beat his ass – threw him off the bridge. Our two Things helped finish it. Liam Pickering got his ass whipped, too. Or so I've been told. Noah and Caleb just shrugged when I talked to them today."

Clete Packer's neck was red – it matched his eyes. He motioned the two coaches to sit. "I'll get right to the point. I am preparing paperwork to suspend all four of the Lott brothers effective tomorrow. It will be for two days. The older twins will not be eligible to play Friday. You'll have to make do without them. Don't think for a minute I will endorse a plea for a forfeit. By my count, you will still have enough players to field a team. Make do." The fat administrator almost sneered at the two coaches as he finished his statement.

"You going to coach them, Mr. Packer? Because if you think I will put a team of fifteen boys – six of them freshmen JV players – on the field come Friday, you're mistaken. Even with the Lott boys we are badly undermanned. Without them, we have no offensive or defensive backfield. It's a no-go. I'll refuse to coach under those circumstances, and I think Mike will too." John Cale stood and pointed his finger at the fat AD as he spoke.

"Sit down and shut up! If you were any kind of coach, you wouldn't be in this situation. You can't control your team – hell, if you had the roster of the Detroit Lions you couldn't put together a game plan to win a JV game." Clete Packer's temper and voice rose. John Cale squinted at the big man but said nothing. For an instant Mike Reese thought punches might fly.

"Wait a minute, Clete. Just what grounds are you suspending the four boys on?" Mike Reese asked forcefully.

"They ambushed the soccer players on the bridge yesterday and threw Micah Showalter in the Bear River. And two other boys too, I think. The younger boys started it. The two older twins assaulted Liam Pickering when he tried to intervene to stop it. I am pretty sure I can not only have them suspended but in the case of the two younger ones, I think it would be best if they were expelled from Bear River schools. They have a dozen or more serious discipline letters in their files already for fighting. So I'm guessing not only the football team will be without their services next year, but maybe you will have to reconsider whether or not you need to hang around any longer to coach wrestling. You're not going to have the manpower you think to win any more state titles," Packer concluded coldly.

Mike Reese reached across the desk and picked up the phone. Packer shot him an icy glare. "What are you doing?" he asked darkly. Mike Reese held his hand up to the AD. He punched in a four-digit code.

"Hi, Katherine. Is the super in his office? I need to talk to him. It's urgent. Tell him Mr. Packer is about to piss away a quarter million dollars in state aid. We are over in his office right now and he is talking about starting an expulsion hearing on the Lott brothers. Yes, I'll hold." Mike Reese looked straight at Clete Packer whose face got even redder.

"What the fuck!" Clete Packer growled. "You insolent motherfucker! I'll have your job for this!" he blustered on.

"I doubt it. But you may want to start thinking about what life will be like trying to make it on the wages of a Walmart greeter," Mike Reese answered calmly.

"What? Okay, we will wait for him," Mike Reese hung up the phone. "The super is on his way over," he announced. Clete Packer began to pace behind his desk.

"You think you're so goddamned all-powerful around here! You think you are untouchable! Well you're not! Grievance or no, I will have you up on insubordination and—" Packer was exasperated and hoarse as he spit out his words.

Sheldon Knapp walked forcefully through the office door. He nearly slammed it on Mike Shanahan who was following close behind him. "What in the hell is going on? What is this about losing a quarter million in state aid!?" Knapp was nearly shouting.

"I am trying to get to the bottom of a serious brawl that occurred yesterday. The Lott brothers – two sets of twins with a history of violent confrontation – assaulted members of the soccer team on the bridge yesterday afternoon. Some boys got thrown in the river. The four Lott boys used karate moves to attack several boys. I called the coaches down to solicit their help, and Coach Reese overreacted to the indictments – and—" Packer started to run out of steam in his story spin. Reese and Cale stood shaking their heads in anger.

"What happened? Does the security video show anything?" Mike Shanahan asked in a rare bout of clarity.

"Well, there is a problem. One of the cameras isn't working properly so the actual fight isn't on video. But I can clearly see the two older Lott twins running up to the bridge. And then a shadowy figure is seen running away a moment later and—" Clete Packer was desperately controlling his words to not show panic.

"You have no video and second-hand information about a fight that may have happened on the bridge after practice yesterday. And on that you're threatening to expel students?" Mike Reese asked with anger and incredulity.

"IT HAPPENED. THE WHOLE DAMN SCHOOL KNOWS THOSE LOTT BOYS THREW MICAH SHOWALTER OFF THE BRIDGE!" Clete Packer shouted.

"Jesus, Clete! Keep it down, will you?" Mike Shanahan was assertive once more. Mike Reese thought it was the clearest communicating he had heard from the befuddled principal in two years.

"Clete, if you are going on rumors, why don't you share what you and I both have heard. Kyle and Connor Lott stepped in to keep Micah Showalter from bullying their autistic cousin, Kenny. He is a student in the special education program in Gratiot but he lives here in Bear River. That's who you see running from the scene on camera, no doubt. The boy can't handle confrontation very well. He wrestled in my youth club a decade ago before he was diagnosed with Asperger's. He sobbed when we tried to get him to wrestle matches. Kenny is smart as a whip about fish and reptiles, practically a PhD, but he doesn't fit in well with kids his age. His cousins have always been pretty protective of him. Showalter is that punk we took in from Sacred Heart after he got nailed in the sexting scandal last year. If that is the case, Showalter was going after Kenny, and I can't blame the boys for stepping in even if things might have gotten out of hand. Showalter is a punk and a bully." Mike Reese was much calmer in reply than the AD.

"We can't know what caused that fight! But I do know the Lott brothers are violent and a danger to the student body as a whole as well as a ticking time bomb on the sports teams. We need to—" Clete Packer was in mid-reply when Sheldon Knapp slammed his hand down hard the AD's desk.

"Will someone please tell me how a quarter million dollars of state aid plays into this!?" Sheldon Knapp asked.

"It's real simple, Mr. Knapp," John Cale answered calmly. "There are about three dozen Lott and Campbell and Maguire children enrolled at Bear River schools. They are all related, a huge family. I think there might be fifty Lott last names in the phone book. Hell, I think my wife is related to the Maguires somehow. If you try to expel Kyle and Connor Lott, the whole bunch of them will show up at the next board meeting and protest. Push them too hard and they will pull their kids and head over to Gratiot. There's another three dozen

Lotts over there. That works out to about a quarter million in state aid right there. This year and for the next several years. I think that's what Coach Reese is referring to."

Mike Reese nodded emphatically.

"Mother of God! Clete! Make this go away right now! Unless you have video showing what you claimed happened, this has to go away. If we lose 200 grand in state aid I'm going to recommend to the board that we eliminate the assistant principals in every building to make up the difference!" Sheldon Knapp threatened in a near panic, and the AD was visibly shaken by the threat. He opened his mouth to reply but nothing came out.

"Coach, don't you have practice?" Mike Shanahan asked John Cale directly. He and Reese agreed that yes, they had better get to it. Sheldon Knapp sat heavily into the chair behind Clete Packer's desk. He rubbed the bridge of his nose as the coaches slipped from the office.

"Holy shit, Mike. Was that Shanahan in there? Where the hell did that come from? He hasn't been that lucid and forceful in months – years," John Cale stated as the coaches walked down the hallway to the back entrance of the school.

As they exited out the door, Mike Reese spoke of his former father-in-law. "My ex-wife's dad had been a pilot in the Korean War and then he flew for the airlines for over thirty years. He failed a flight physical a year before he was due to retire. Mild dementia – no one talked much about Alzheimer's back then. He passed about five years later. But he had some days – even near the end – when he was the lucid captain of old. I see Mike Shanahan on a day like this, and I see the captain."

John Cale listened as they crossed the bridge over the Bear River. Kenny Lott was walking toward them up the steps on the field side of the river.

"Hi, Coach Reese," Kenny said shyly.

"Hi, Kenny, how's fishing?" Reese asked, pointing at the pole the young man was carrying.

"Not good today," Kenny answered "But yesterday there were three big ones in the river by the bridge."

John Cale held back his laughter.

Thursday was a quiet day at school. Wash Dryer got up early and went to the gym to work on his off-speed pitches. Morg Miller came in early to catch for him. They talked about Junior Schultz and Seth Parker. Junior had come home from the hospital the day before. It would be at least a week before he could come back to school. Seth was scheduled to have surgery on his fingers, but the doctors wanted to wait until he was recovered from his concussion. The surgery might have to wait a few more days. At lunch, Jay Brau sat in Coach Cale's room with Jorge Martinez watching Riverdale game film. The boys ate their lunch and watched the Beavers' defense destroy the Perrinton Owls and the North Star Vikings. Jay fought to keep from showing fear. He didn't want

Jorge to know how scared he actually was. He was having trouble sleeping. Between thinking of Freddy and worrying about the game, Jay was frazzled.

Things One and Two walked hallways at lunch. Twice, soccer players saw them coming and turned to walk the other way. In the lunch line, they caught the eye of Micah Showalter. He quickly glanced down to the floor. If he had had a tail, he would have tucked it between his legs.

Thursday afternoon, Sheldon Knapp sat in his office crying. On his desk were divorce papers served to him shortly after he ate lunch at his desk. At 1:30, he told his secretary, Katherine Bigelow, that he was going to leave for the day – he claimed a monstrous headache was building and he needed to lie down. Knapp stopped on his way home for a little Dutch courage. He grabbed a cheap bottle of scotch at the Walmart in Gratiot. He resisted the temptation to crack the seal. He would wait until he got home. He had quit trying to get his wife to answer the phone after twenty unanswered calls; his last message to her ended with a bitter "Fuck you." When he pulled up to his house, boxes covered with a plastic sheet sat in the driveway. A light drizzle was falling. Knapp could see his golf clubs under the plastic as well. His wife had changed the security code on the garage door, and his key would not open the front door. There was a note taped inside the storm door. It was in his wife's neat handwriting.

Sheldon,

I am out of town for the next few days. I do not want to see you or talk to you. If you need to communicate with me I suggest you get a lawyer. My cousin, Sherry, will be handling my affairs. Your wardrobe is neatly packed in the boxes under the tarps. Please take your things and leave. I have already filed a restraining order. After today if you are in my home or on the property I will have you arrested for violating it. Remember the home is in my name. You insisted on it for tax purposes. I am through dealing with your emotional abuse and your bitterness. Seek help. Or stew in scotch if you like. I don't care.

The note was unsigned. Sheldon Knapp sat in his rental car for a while. His Mercedes was still in the shop being repaired after the damage done to it by the fire truck. Finally he cracked the seal on the scotch bottle. He took a large gulp of foul, cheap liquor. He wiped tears from his eyes with his coat sleeve. He mumbled a few curse words and got out of the car. He loaded what he could fit into the car. He left behind several boxes marked "Summer Clothes" and his golf clubs. An hour later, he returned for the remainders. The house was still dark. He had nowhere to fit more boxes in the hotel room he had rented in Mt. Pleasant. He drove to the school to stash the remaining boxes in his office closet. As he pulled up, he noticed that Katherine Bigelow's car was still in the lot. He didn't want to deal with his administrative assistant just then.

Sheldon Knapp pulled his rental car into the high school staff parking spot across the street. The staff lot sat on the elevated south bank of the Bear River. The leaves had fallen from the scrubby trees on the river bank, and Knapp could see across the river to the game field. The drizzle had stopped and a few stray snowflakes fell from the gray fall skies. The football coaches had the rag-tag remainder of the Bear's football team on one knee at the fifty-yard line. Knapp could see John Cale in front of the half-circle of players. He closed his eyes, hoping it would stop the tears from welling up again. It didn't.

The pre-game practice hadn't been particularly crisp or promising, but it was time to end it. As usual, they held the final special teams practice plays on the game field. It served as the last conditioning of the practice to run through kick-off and kick-return ten times each. John Cale looked at his gathered team. Their faces were tipped up to him as they knelt on one knee. Steam rose up from their sweaty heads. Their heavy breathing produced steam as well. Mike Reese, Cheese Colby and Wash Dryer stood behind the head coach. Cale felt a small lump in his throat. As much as the season had been an unmitigated disaster, he couldn't help feeling a strong connection to these boys. Most of them had performed heroically against overwhelming odds week in and week out. And yet, here they knelt in front of him. Tired but smiling. Their season of defeat and multiple failures didn't show in their faces. He saw only young men looking up to him with expectation. He knew he had to say something. It didn't have to be profound. But he had to say something to draw this to a close.

"I am trying to find words to say to you as we get ready for the last game of this season. I wish I had the motivational talents of Coach Reese, but I don't," Cale started. Some players chuckled. Reese smiled and glanced down to the turf. He felt a lump building in his throat.

"I wish I had Wash's ability to rise up to challenges and excel. I wish I had Coach Colby's courage – just a tenth of it." Cheese and Wash looked up and smiled at Coach Cale. Cheese Colby had a tear on his cheek.

Cale continued, "I don't have the gifts that some have, but I have hope and I have the ability to grow. The one great thing I know I do have – what we all have is this: we have each other. We have been through a lot. And it has not been easy. The ones who wanted it to be easy are all gone. Hell… they didn't even show up for the season. And we have lost some good young men recently to injury. They are not here right now, but Seth and Junior gave it their all. I know they wish they were on this field with you right now. If they were, they would probably tell you what I am telling you right now. I am proud to be a Bear River Bear." The players nodded in agreement.

Morg Miller called out, "Thanks, Coach!" Other players joined in. Several thanks were shouted.

John Cale turned to his assistant coaches. "You want to say anything?" Colby and Reese shook their heads.

"Jorge, break them down," Cale said to his senior leader.

Jorge Martinez stood up and raised his fist in the air. "In on me!" The team gathered tightly around their captain. "Loud enough for Junior and Seth to hear it! One! Two! Three!" He shouted clearly.

"BEAR PRIDE!" the team answered. The team broke for the locker room. Some of the young players sprinted. The seniors lagged behind.

John Cale and Mike Reese walked in front of their seniors. "I've been coaching a long time, John. What you just said was exactly the right thing to say. I've got nothing on you when it comes to motivational speaking. Nothing." Reese spoke with emotion in his voice.

John Cale stopped and they shook hands and then they crossed the bridge to the school.

Morg Miller, Jorge Martinez, Wash Dryer and Jay Brau mounted the steps to the bridge to the school and Morg stopped at the top. He turned silently to look at the field. The other boys did too. No one said anything. After a minute they turned and crossed the bridge.

Friday morning was cold and still, but the skies were clear. The students milled around the school before the first bell. Talk was of the weekend. No one mentioned the final football game of the season. Other than the players, barely a soul in the building was aware that the dismal football season was ending that evening.

Wash Dryer held hands with Maricel. They stood near the entrance of the library talking with Roxy Johnson. Jay Brau had come to school early to sit and watch game films in Coach Cale's classroom with Jorge. Morg Miller sat in the cafeteria telling jokes to some freshmen. Laughter rolled into the hallways as the bell rang to signal first hour was about to begin.

The day progressed. Lunch came and went. Jay Brau was startled when the bell rang at 2:35. The school day was over. His mind was elsewhere. He was running plays through his head. He actually was grateful for something to think of besides Freddy Wilkes.

Each Bear football player killed time in his own way for the few hours after school. Morg Miller went to visit Junior Schultz at his house. He felt great joy after making Junior laugh for most of the time they spent together.

Wash Dryer got to the locker room early and set out the red game jerseys and gray game pants. He sorted through the equipment for the sidelines including the med kits and communication gear. Cheese Colby helped him. They talked of Gump and how he was struggling since the passing of his mother. Wash could see that his friend was also struggling, so he changed the subject to girls. Wash asked Cheese who he was dating. Cheese was noncommittal, but he was grateful for the change in subject. Cheese teased Wash about Maricel. Wash smiled and said nothing. Cheese returned the smile.

John Cale was sitting in the coaches' office correcting math papers when Mike Reese came in at about 4:30. Reese looked disgusted. "Did you see this shit?" Reese tossed a folded newspaper down on the desk in front of his young head coach. Cale looked at the headline of Pete Petterson's high school football predictions column.

"Riverdale Beavers Ready Themselves For Another Playoff Run Tonight Against The Woeful Bear River Bears."

The bulk of the column was made up of praise for the Riverdale team and its coaching staff. Before the listing of picks of area games, Petterson editorialized on the status of the Bear River football program.

"While the Riverdale Beavers are enjoying another typical season of successful football, the Bears are putting a cap on a very bad season. For several decades now, football at Bear River has been an afterthought. Failed season after failed season has piled up. Bear River remains the only team in the area and one of the few in the state to never amass enough wins in a single season to qualify for the playoffs. In the two decades-plus since the state expanded the playoffs to include teams with as few as five wins in a season, the Bears have yet to qualify. And even by Bear River standards, this season has been dismal. Not only have they not won a game, they have not even been competitive. Blowouts were the norm, and tonight should be the worst of the season.

"The only player of consequence on the Bear football team has been senior linebacker and guard, Jorge Martinez. And tonight he will see duty as a fullback in the depleted Bear backfield as senior tailback Jay Brau takes his first-ever snaps as a quarterback. Such is the nature of football in some schools where there is no tradition of winning and no expectation that it will ever change. Inadequate coaches shuffle mostly inadequate players into positions for which they have no chance for success. The Jorge Martinez's of the world, despite their talent and dedication, play in futility for schools destined to lose. Expect at least a sixty-point spread. It isn't inconceivable that the Beavers roll up eighty or more points on the Bears tonight. And it is doubtful the injured and undermanned Bears will mount any sort of offense. Truly, this is a game for which the state athletic association created the mercy rule. It will get ugly quickly.

"As a final note, tonight may be the last-ever varsity football game played in Bear River. There are strong indications that the school board in Bear River is not only thinking of cleaning house with the firing of head coach John Cale and lead assistant Mike Reese, but additionally, the football program may be eliminated altogether. When I contacted Bear River School Board President Pamela Kitteridge on this topic, she only would say that immediately following the season, the football program will come under close scrutiny."

"Mmm," John Cale said after reading the column.

"And here is the best news of all. That fat prick will be here tonight to cover the game for the Mt. Pleasant paper." Reese spit out the words with contempt.

"Yeah, well, the Beavers have the only undefeated team in the area. I think the Gratiot radio station is going to broadcast the game as well," John Cale replied calmly.

"Great. Pete and those two buffoons who can barely talk let alone convey sports action on air will sit on the opposite end of the press box from me. They will probably interview that fat piece of shit at halftime. All the while they will be stuffing their faces with pizza and pop brought to them by Fudge Packer who will spend all game checking with them and kissing their asses," Reese said.

"No doubt. Clete will suck around trying to get on the radio as well," Cale observed. "It will be the highlight of his season. Probably spend the whole interview praising the soccer team, too. Nothing we can do about that," he concluded.

"Listen John, I might blow a gasket up there if I so much as see Pete Petterson, let alone have to talk to the prick. I know we planned on having me up in the box tonight, but maybe we better put Cheese up there. I mean, I punched that fat face years ago in a bar fight. I'm too old to be brawling with anyone, but I really would like to knock that fat fuck's teeth down his throat one more time before I retire. I just don't think tonight would be a good time," Reese explained.

"I think perhaps that is a good plan. Cheese can handle being the eye in the sky. And besides I think the Things have got their dander up. It might be a good idea for you to be on the sideline to keep a close watch on them. If they get thrown out of the game, we will be in dire trouble. And then they will have to sit out your first wrestling match as well in a month or so." Cale acquiesced to the request.

The Bear football players were milling about the locker room. They had their game pants on but not their shoulder pads and game jerseys. Greg DeVito called out to no one in particular, "Is Tim Manikowski suiting up for the Beavers tonight?"

Wash Dryer set down a box of gear and answered. "Yeah, he played some last week, too. He isn't a starter or anything like that."

"What about that punk Calvin Schmidt? Isn't he on the JV's? No way he made varsity," Morg Miller asked Jorge Martinez.

Jorge smiled and replied, "He starts for their JV's at center. Declan McCormac is their varsity center. He signed an early letter of intent with Western Michigan. He used to wrestle in middle school, remember?"

Morg nodded. McCormac had pinned him several times in middle school wrestling matches. Even then McCormac was an overpowering force. His football career had been stellar. He was at the end of what looked to be his second all-state honor football season. Morg knew McCormac was going to do a lot of damage tonight, but he was more interested whether Calvin Schmidt was going to be on the field.

"Yeah, but do you think they will play their JV's at all since there wasn't a game last night?" Morg asked.

"That's likely. I saw the program they printed for tonight's game. It's got like fifty-five names for the Beavers on it. I know they only have thirty on the varsity team. I don't think they included their freshman team, though. They play a whole separate schedule because no one else in the league has a freshman team," Wash Dryer answered.

"Jesus, I hope they don't put their JV's on the field. If they do, it's likely because they are blowing us up with their starters," Greg DeVito noted morosely.

"Whatever. I want another shot at that punk Schmidt," Morg answered. "He's a whiney little bitch."

Morg had wrestled Calvin Schmidt three times last year when the then-freshman was supposed to be a super-stud-rookie-215-pound wrestler on the Beaver varsity wrestling team. In fact, the kid was a one-dimensional wrestler – a head-thrower and a punk-ass whiner, as far as Morg was concerned. Morg beat him twice easily. The second time by injury default when the kid started crying as Morg put the leg splits on him.

The third time Morg Miller and Calvin Schmidt met on the mat was in the blood round at the individual district tournament. The winner of the match would continue on to the regional tournament the following week. If the Riverdale wrestler lost, it would be his last match of the year as the Bears had defeated the Beavers in the team district finals three days earlier.

Morg Miller wrestled in the 285-pound weight class at team districts. He beat the Riverdale heavyweight in overtime to start the meet. When it came around to the final match at the 215-weight class the Riverdale Beavers were leading by five points. If they could hold off a pin, they would beat the Bears on the wrestling mat for the first time in sixteen seasons. The North Star gym was packed. Both the Bears and Beavers had disposed of their first-round opponents easily. The Bears were ranked fifth in the state in the division, but many in the area claimed the ranking was based on past success, not the current team. The Beavers were honorable mention in the state rankings.

The Bears had beaten the Beavers during the regular season by ten points and had won the league tournament the prior Saturday by three points. But the Riverdale team actually placed more wrestlers in the league meet than the Bear River team. They had two starters who missed the first matchup of the season nursing injuries. Fans from both schools packed the little North Star school gym. Pete Petterson was there to cover the event for the Mt. Pleasant paper even though he considered wrestling a minor sport. After some close matches to start the meet, the Beavers surged ahead. At 171 pounds Cheese Colby stopped the run by pinning his opponent. Junior Schultz bumped into the varsity lineup and won a decision at 189 pounds. That pulled the Bears within striking distance. The best wrestler on the Bear team was Jorge Martinez. But he was bumping up a weight class to 215 pounds. The gym was buzzing. All Calvin Schmidt had to do was avoid being pinned. He stalked around behind the Beaver bench roaring and stomping. Jorge walked quietly and purposefully to the corner of the mat and waited as the freshman high-fived all his teammates and then rushed to the scoring table to check in. Jorge shook Coach Reese's hand.

"Take care of business, Jorge. Watch his throws. If you get him on his back, end it," Reese said calmly.

Wash Dryer was sitting at the scorer's table keeping the official book. He nodded at Jorge as his friend came up to the referee in front of the table.

"Martinez, 215, Bear River," he said without emotion. His eyes met Wash's. He returned the nod.

The match was over in forty seconds. Jorge took the freshman down with a clean inside step single leg. After riding him for a few seconds, Jorge broke Calvin down with a chop trap, and when the young wrestler tried to regain his base Jorge methodically jammed a bar arm and half nelson. Using his powerful legs, the two-time state medalist powered the over-matched freshman to his back and it was done. The referee slapped the mat signifying a fall. Six team points. The Bears won. Calvin Schmidt jumped to his feet and protested that his shoulders were not down. Jorge waited calmly in the center of the mat as his teammates called out his name and cheered lustily with the Bear River fans. The referee walked the upset freshman to the center of the mat. Jorge held out his hand to shake and Calvin petulantly slapped at it and spun away. The referee grabbed him by the wrist and forced him to properly shake Jorge's hand. Then the young wrestler stormed out of the gym crying. Jorge was swept off his feet by Morg Miller and the rest of the Bears. Pete Petterson wrote in his match report, "Jorge Martinez was calm and collected as he dispatched the hot-headed youth from Riverdale. If he isn't the best wrestler in the region, he certainly is the most imperturbable."

A few days later, Riverdale hosted the individual district tournament. Calvin's family numbered fifty-strong in the gym that day, and they led the partisan crowd cheering for their favorite freshman. Morg lost in the second round. He was battling stomach flu as he wrestled back through the hard road of the consolation or "losers" bracket at 215 pounds. Calvin Schmidt lost his semifinal match by one point and dropped to the losers bracket. He and Morgan would meet in what wrestlers always referred to as the "blood round," – the consolation-bracket semifinals. Riverdale fans smelled blood. They had been complaining all day that the Bears bumped Morg away from their stud freshman at team district because old man Reese knew Morg couldn't keep beating the hard-charging and improving freshman. Morg Miller was nothing but a fat pud. That is what they claimed.

The gym went crazy when Calvin put Morg in a headlock and threw him to his back fifty seconds into the match. Morg fought the pin for over a minute in the first period. The hometown crowd stood and cheered. Down 5-0, Morg was not surprised when the cocky freshman chose neutral to start the second period on his feet. Morg knew what was coming. The taller and stockier freshman bull rushed Morg on the whistle. Morg slipped his right arm into the armpit of the oncoming boy and neatly executed a perfect lateral drop. Morg locked down hard on the panicked and struggling freshman after landing him on his back. Twenty seconds into second period, the referee slapped the mat and Morg ended Calvin Schmidt's season by pinning him. The hometown crowd went deathly silent. Some Bear River fans cheered but then the fans gasped as they watched Calvin Schmidt refuse to shake Morg's hand. Instead, he ran cursing from the floor – pausing to throw his headgear into the gym rafters. The referee threw the freshman out of the tournament. It only served to cost the boy his first JV baseball game of the spring season.

Football coaches often say the longest hour of the week is the last one before kickoff. All the preparation and all the worrying and planning have been accomplished. Coaches and players are keyed-up, and nervous energy has players pounding each other's shoulder pads during pregame drills. At least that is the case across the high school football world in most situations. Certainly the Riverdale Beavers were up for the game. Their rhythmic clapping and shouting during their formal warm ups had the Bears distracted, and the young JV players on the team were greatly intimidated. The Bears were listless as they went through pregame warm ups. Defeat hung in the air.

Thing One and Thing Two were shagging wobbly passes from Jay Brau during warm ups. They spotted Tim Manikowski doing the same for his new team, the Riverdale Beavers. His mother insisted on him playing football for the Beavers. Tim tried to beg off, saying he only wanted to play basketball. The former teen drug kingpin of Bear River wanted to lay low in his new school, but his mother had other plans. She wanted to rub it in Clete Packer's face that he had not won. Just as she said, Tim, by relocating to the Riverdale district, gained immediate eligibility.

Clete Packer stood in the press box. He glanced across the field and saw Julie Bysshe. She sat in the middle of the group of Riverdale parents on the visitor's side of the field. She was talking and gesticulating excitedly. He mumbled a few curse words to himself. He scanned the program for the roster of the visiting team. He found the name quickly – Tim Manikowski, End, #89. Packer curled his lip in contempt. He had heard that Manikowski had only gotten a few minutes in garbage time for the Beavers in the last two games. But still it rankled him that the snotty kid and his bitch of a mother had gotten the best of him.

"Hi, Timmy!" Thing One called to their former teammate.

"How's business?" Thing Two chimed in. His brother barked out a loud laugh.

Tim Manikowski dropped a pass on a simple curl route. His position coach yelled at him to focus. Manikowski was a little afraid of the Things, but he doubted they would spend much time on the field together, so he covertly flipped them off.

"See you soon, Timmy," Thing Two cheerfully called.

It was Senior Appreciation night. A short ceremony was held honoring the senior football players, including Wash Dryer and also one cheerleader and five band members. The loudest cheer went up when Jorge Martinez's name was called. In a crowd of about 100 people, a full third of them were Jorge's relatives. His gang-leader cousin Reuben, the one who had taught him how to wrestle in those anguished days after Jorge's brother was killed in Iraq, was in the stands with over a dozen of his fellow bikers. He had texted Jorge earlier in the week saying he would be there. He didn't want to miss Jorge's last game. And since Jorge was now a feature back in the offense, he wanted to see him score a touchdown. Jorge blushed when Reuben and his mates chanted his name.

John Cale had bought flowers out of his own pocket for the seniors to present to their parents. Wash Dryer handed a rose to his mother, Laney Dryer. She had tears in her eyes as she hugged him. Maricel was with her. She gave Wash a kiss. Wash blushed. Morg Miller gave his mother a rose and high-fived his dad awkwardly. Jay Brau hugged his great-aunt and -uncle. The old man gave him a tight squeeze. He quietly spoke in his nephew's ear. "I'm proud of you, son. So very proud." Jay felt tears come to his eyes.

The Bear River band took the field to play the fight song and the national anthem. Two Tone Simpson was still convalescing from the disaster that befell him the night of the homecoming dance. He'd had two long and painful dental surgeries in recent weeks, and his arm was in a rigid cast all the way up to his shoulder. The dental surgeries left him unable to talk clearly, so he was on a medical leave of absence. After two days of a completely inept substitute teacher causing chaos, the school found a young music graduate from Gratiot College to substitute for the unpopular band director. The young man was enthusiastic and cheerful where Two Tone was not. The band was responding to the better leadership. They still lacked numbers, but their performance was as crisp as anyone in attendance at the game could remember.

The cheerleading squad was down to three members. They tried to rally the home crowd for a pregame cheer. The crowd was largely unresponsive. It numbered just over 100 fans – about a third the size of the crowd on the visiting side. The cheerleaders had a hard time finishing the cheer. Reuben Martinez's gang rushed to the rail in front of them and began to whistle and cat-call at them. The bikers were drinking from Pepsi bottles, but the contents were liberally cut with whiskey. It was going to be a long night for the cheerleaders.

Pete Petterson sat in the press box next to the radio crew from the Gratiot station. They had a press cubical to themselves. They finished their pregame pizzas. Petterson ate a large one by himself. He was wiping grease from his face with the sleeve of his CMU sweatshirt when the Bears kicked off. With fifteen seconds off the clock, the score was Beavers 6 and the Bears 0. Petterson chuckled at the hapless home team. The Beavers missed the extra point try. It was to be their only misstep of the evening. As the obese newspaperman predicted, things got ugly and they got that way quickly and relentlessly.

The Bears fumbled the ensuing kickoff. The Beavers recovered it on the Bear 15-yard line. On the next play, the Beavers scored. They made the two-point conversion. The score was 14-0. On the next four possessions, the Bears netted only three plays with positive yardage. Cheese Stick dive plays out of the power I formation with Jorge Martinez dragging four and five Beaver players with him for two or three yards. Every other play was stopped at the line of scrimmage or for a loss. The two pass plays the Bears attempted resulted in sacks as Jay Brau was unable to even complete his three-step drop before being hit.

Jay Brau expected that the Beavers would be riding him about his sexuality and the scandal involving one of their classmate's. Freddy Wilkes had told him that if anything, Riverdale was even more backward than Bear River; with a few exceptions. One of which was Declan McCormac. Besides being the best athlete at Riverdale, Declan had been a friend of Freddy for years. They led their church youth group. So while there was no overt shouting of anti-gay epithets, Declan wouldn't have allowed it, plenty of quiet ones were uttered in the ear-hole of his helmet every time Jay ended up on the ground on offense or defense. They were ugly and vicious, and some were very personal about Freddy. Jay struggled to keep his focus as the game wore on.

Bad punting from freshman Sam Bott put the Beavers on a short field every possession. The Beavers ran only ten plays on offense in the first half. Every passing play exceeded twenty yards. Three TD passes were virtually uncovered by the young JV players that the Bears were forced to start at cornerback. The Things made some daunting open field tackles at the safety position, but there was only so much they could do. Mike Reese dialed up the pressure and blitzed his linebackers. The tall and athletic Beaver QB eluded all of them but one. Jay Brau and Jorge Martinez hit him for a 10-yard loss. On the next play he scrambled away from Tom Osborne and scored on a 40-yard run dragging four Bear defensive backs as he crossed the goal line. He scored on a 20-yard run on the next possession.

Just before the half – with less than forty seconds remaining, the Beavers had the Bears pinned back on their 12-yard line 4th and 23. Tim Manikowski came into the game for his first play of the night. He lined up as a defensive end. On the punt attempt, Manikowski sidestepped Big Donnie Donnie, and he blocked the punt. The ball bounced once cleanly. It landed in his arms just after he stepped across the goal line for a touchdown. As he raised his hands to celebrate, Thing One and Thing Two hit him high and low. Penalty flags flew. Manikowski popped up cussing, but when he saw the Things, he backed away and hid behind some Beaver linemen. Thing Two asked, "What you afraid of, Timmy?" Manikowski didn't answer, and he sprinted to the visitor's sideline. After the extra point, the score read Riverdale Beavers 49 and the Bear River Bears 0. There were twenty-nine seconds left on the clock.

The Bears fumbled the kickoff inside their own 5-yard line. The Beavers recovered the fumble. There were fifteen seconds left on the clock, and the

Beavers called timeout. Mike Reese was pacing on the sideline and mumbling into his headset. "That fucking Bob Pease is going to run a play. Just watch." On the other end of the line, Cheese Colby denied it. "No, he won't take a knee. He called a timeout for a reason." And then he called his defense to the sideline to talk to them.

"Okay, it's gut-check time. They called a timeout to run a play, not take a knee. Stop them. Put everything into it. Stop them," Mike Reese growled at the Bears. Steam rose from their bodies as the temperature dropped steadily from the high forties at sunset into the mid-thirties. The wind was still. John Cale called the players to break down on him.

"This is your field. They have beaten us but they haven't broken us. Don't let them disrespect you like this! One! Two! Three!"

"BEARS!" The team replied. And as they jogged to their positions to defend their goal line, some players stopped short and stared in disbelief.

Because there had been no JV game, the Beavers had their JV football team dress for the varsity game. The visiting fans began to cheer as a totally fresh team took the field. The uniforms of the Beaver JV players were unblemished with dirt or stains. "Those motherfuckers!" Morg Miller said pointing at the young Beaver football players as he grabbed Jorge Martinez by his jersey sleeve. Then they hustled to their positions. Morg Miller recognized the Beavers' JV center. It was Calvin Schmidt.

Morg went into a stance in front of Calvin Schmidt as he placed his hand on the ball.

"Hiya, punk bitch," Morg said with icy contempt.

"Fuck you, loser. Read the scoreboard," Calvin Schmidt replied as his quarterback came up to place his hands at the ready to take the snap. The signals were called. Morg launched himself at the legs of the Beaver center who dropped back to pass block. The Riverdale JV QB took a short drop and pump-faked to freeze the linebackers and then scampered around the end for an easy touchdown. The Bear cornerbacks never touched him.

Calvin Schmidt dropped hard down onto Morg Miller, driving his elbow into the back of Morg's exposed neck just below his helmet just as the QB was taking off on his run. It hurt like hell, but Morg didn't miss a beat, and he surged up from the ground while the Beaver JV's were cheering themselves for the touchdown they had converted. Morg Miller grabbed at Calvin Schmidt's groin and got hold of his intended target. A hard twist got the response Morg was seeking. Calvin Schmidt let loose a high-pitched panicked scream.

"You fag! Quit grabbing my balls!" Schmidt shouted, and then he charged at the Bear River defensive tackle. Morg backed away as the flags flew. He knew that the retaliators often took the penalty in a situation like this. He couldn't care less about giving up the touchdown. He wanted to get Calvin tossed from the game. It didn't work. He and Calvin Schmidt were flagged for personal fouls. Offsetting penalties cancelled each other out, and the

Beavers converted the extra point. The first half ended. The score was Riverdale 56 and Bear River 0.

The radio station went to a commercial at the half. Billy Plank, the play by play announcer, pulled his headset off.

"This is ridiculous. Fifty-six points. Jesus. And now the Bear River players are cheap-shotting?" the announcer said with disgust.

Pete Petterson flipped open another pizza box and extracted a congealed slice of cold pizza. He paused before cramming most of it in his mouth. He pointed to the Bears as they retreated across the bridge over the Bear River to go to their locker room. "If those kids had any brains they would keep on going and not come back for the second half. Bob Pease is going to hang 100 points on them if he can fit it in with the mercy clock running."

The Beavers retreated to their bus parked near the soccer practice pitch. Julie Bysshe made her way to the concession stand and restrooms. She hoped she would see Clete Packer. She just wanted to stare him down. He would get the message. But Packer was in the girls' locker room in the school. He had gone there during the second quarter to get some half-time drinks and a snack for the referees. They used the girls locker room as their base of operations on game day. Today's crew had driven up from the Lansing area. It was their first-ever visit to Bear River.

The head referee thanked Clete for the drinks and snacks, but he looked cross. "It's getting chippy out there, Mr. Packer. Your boys are over-matched but there is no call for some of what is going on," he intoned seriously.

"It's been a long season, and quite frankly, we have been poorly coached. We are going to address the situation next week. Our board president wants heads to roll. I think she is absolutely right," Clete conceded, leaving the impression that his head was not on the chopping block as well. None of the referees knew any differently.

"Poor sportsmanship reflects badly on everyone," the head referee added pompously.

Clete agreed whole-heartedly and said he would talk to the coaches before the second half kickoff.

The Bears emerged from the locker room led by Coach Reese and began their jog across the bridge. Clete Packer intercepted John Cale who trailed behind his team as the Bears trotted across the span.

"John, I need a word with you," Packer announced seriously. Cale stopped his jog. Mike Reese was already leading the players to the field.

"Mr. Packer, can't this wait? We have another half to play." Cale was more than just exasperated in response. He was becoming quite angry.

"No. This will happen right now," Packer said forcibly. "I just talked to the head referee. He has informed me he is prepared to eject players for any further unsportsmanlike behavior. And I am holding you personally responsible for the conduct of your players," the AD continued without letting the coach get in a word.

"Meaning what?" Cale asked icily.

"Consider this your only warning. I'm not just talking about coaching. I'm talking about your career." Clete Packer quickly turned away before Cale could respond further, and he walked briskly toward the school.

John Cale paused briefly on the bridge. Anger beyond anything he had known in his career played through his mind. He quickly discarded the idea of chasing down the older man. He could accomplish that very easily, but he knew if he did, it wouldn't end well. Assaulting his boss and beating the shit out of him would give him great pleasure for a fleeting moment, but Cale had a wife and children to consider. An attack would end his career and probably land him in considerable legal trouble. He shook thoughts of violence out of his head and jogged briskly to the home side of the field.

Mike Reese was waiting when Cale approached the bench. The players were beginning their halftime warm ups. The temperature was dropping rapidly. Clouds of icy breath rose in the still evening. Reese looked very concerned.

"What did he want?" Reese asked.

"Oh, he just wanted to tell me that the referees have the boys on double secret probation and that my career is on the line if we get any further unsportsmanlike penalties. You know – the usual crap." Cale was attempting sarcasm, but Reese could read his body language. He suspected the fat administrator had no idea how close he had just come to having his dick knocked into the dirt by John Cale.

"Back stabbing piece of." Reese mumbled as he went to monitor the Bears as they went through the end of halftime warm up stretches. The echoes of the Beavers shouting their stretching cadences drowned out the weak voice of the Bears. In the press box, the PA announcer, Big Bill Simmons, was reading through announcements concerning the upcoming winter sports signups as though it were the voiceover for a movie trailer. No one paid any attention.

The third quarter featured four Riverdale Beaver touchdowns on passing plays. The fourth one was to Tim Manikowski. Thing One dragged him down in the end zone. As he did, he rabbit-punched the taller and heavier boy in his kidney. Manikowski fell and writhed in agony. The pain was excruciating. In the stands, his mother gasped and held her hand over her mouth. Some of the Riverdale fans booed loudly and called for a penalty flag. The refs did not see the blatant cheap shot. No flags flew. The Beavers coaches hauled their recent transfer to the bench where he spent the rest of the game hunched over with an ice pack on his back.

Julie Bysshe made her way down from the visitor stands and crossed the track to the rail behind the Beavers bench. She tried to get the attention of her son, but he sat still and unresponsive. She finally got an assistant coach to come talk to her. He assured her that Tim had taken a bad shot but that he would be all right. Julie Bysshe felt her fury building. She looked across the football field to the press box on the opposite side. She could not make out who was inside, but she knew that Clete Packer was up there somewhere. Rather than try to find him there, she decided to confront him as he crossed the bridge back to the school at the end of the game. She was going to hold him accountable for the abuse of her son. She would tell him that she would bring all her power to bear to make sure he would never be anything but the lowly assistant principal of a third-rate high school.

The fourth quarter was underway, and as Julie Bysshe took her station at the bottom of the steps on the north end of the bridge, the Riverdale Beavers scored their fifth touchdown of the second half. After the extra point was kicked, the scoreboard read 91-0 in favor of the visiting team. The clock read 3:38 remaining in the game. Some of the students in visiting stands began to chant "100! 100! 100!"

On the Riverdale bench, the head coach, Bob Pease, called his assistants to him. He knew that they would have liked the opportunity to score 100 points. There wasn't enough time for two offensive possessions. It was time to call off the dogs and let his youngsters get some good game experience.

"I'm pulling the varsity. JV takes us home. Make sure they keep the shut-out, though," Pease commanded.

The JV kickoff special team for the Beavers took the field. The Riverdale students cut loose with a few boos. Some Riverdale parents made their way to the students and told them to stop chanting and disrespecting the hosts. The stands were quiet as the Bears returned the kick to their 28-yard line. Jay Brau dropped back for a pass on the first play of the series. He was able to get some time and he threw a nice spiral to Thing Two. The play went for a 15-yard gain. The Bears had their longest play of the night and had gained their first first down of the contest.

The next five plays were run with no huddle. Jorge Martinez gained at least five yards on each play running out of the power I formation. Each time, Jay Brau called the Bears to the line and yelled, "Cheese Stick!" Each play, Jorge crashed into the JV players from Riverdale and kept his legs churning, dragging four and five young Beaver players forward.

The Bears crossed the Beaver 20-yard line with just under thirty seconds to play, and they called their second time-out. It was third down and with two yards to go. John Cale called the team over to the bench.

The Bears were silent. There were no high-fives and or self-congratulations for their effective drive. They knew it was against JV players. They wanted a score. They wanted to avoid a shutout. Cale looked at them and smiled. "Let's take it in. Jay, call Cheese Stick loudly at the line of scrimmage. But fake the hand-off and run wide right. See if we can catch them crashing the middle with their linebackers."

Jay Brau nodded. The Bears broke their huddle on the sideline, and as they turned to go on the field, they were greeted by the sight of the Beavers defensive starters coming back into the game.

"Fucking dickheads," Cheese Colby announced into the field communication headset. "They won't let us even have the dignity of getting a score."

Mike Reese answered, "Pease hates my guts. This is about the times we ended his wrestling season early."

The Bears lined up. Jay Brau called out "Cheese Stick!" The Beaver starters had been sitting for a few minutes, laughing and gulping Gatorade as their JV's played. They were cold and stiff by the time they were sent back in the game. But the Riverdale linebackers had heard the audible enough to know what that meant. On the snap of the ball, they slammed the middle of the line. They stopped Jorge Martinez cold. But Jorge was carrying out the fake. Jay Brau glided around Beavers' left side. He started on the angle to the pylon at the goal line. The few fans in the Bears stands that were not fooled by the fake began to cheer.

John Cale sprinted to the edge of the coach's box as he watched the Beavers' safety try to cut off Jay. The Bears quarterback sidestepped the safety at the two-yard line and launched himself to the goal. He grazed the inside of the pylon, and John Cale began jumping up and down and cheering as the back judge signaled touchdown.

The small Bear crowd cheered as loudly as they had all season. They didn't notice as the sideline judge on the home side came running up to the goal line and waving his arms. But John Cale knew what that meant.

"WHAT! NO!" Cale shouted and he ran up the sideline out of the coach's box.

The sideline judge emphatically began pointing at the out-of-bounds line three yards up-field from the pylon. "He stepped out!" he shouted.

"NO! He wasn't even close!" Cale shouted as the head referee walked forcefully to him.

"Coach! You are out of the box! Get back or I will flag you. And instead of first and goal from the three, you will be on the 18-yard line," the gray-haired head referee announced with authority.

"There is no way he was out!" Cale protested.

"Coach, you are seeing it with your heart not your eyes. Now, get back to your bench." The head referee shifted his tone to that of a stern father scolding a teen. John Cale clenched his fists and wheeled around because he anticipated getting flagged if he said anything further. He silently strode back to the bench. He could hear the home crowd booing. Reuben Martinez's friends shouted curses and threats in Spanish as they moved down the stands close to the goal line.

The referees paused and looked up at the dozen or so bikers surrounding Reuben. It was a rough-looking crew, and a casual glance would tell anyone that they had been drinking. The head referee was a retired sheriff's deputy. Two of his crew were still on active duty as Lansing city police officers. They had all heard enough Spanish curse words in their careers to know what was being shouted.

354

Tension filled the air, but Reuben calmed his mates. He made a show of it and smiled at the referees. His boys complied. And a silence settled over the field.

On the Bear bench, John Cale paced and shouted encouragement to his players. He wanted a score badly. He expected it might be the last plays of his coaching career. It wasn't much of a victory, but it would take the shutout away from the Beavers if they could just score. Mike Reese waved to his agitated head coach to come in close. The referees signaled they were ready to end the official's timeout

"Call Cheese Stick, John. I think Jorge can take it in. Their starters are stiff from sitting," Mike Reese advised.

"Yeah, we got thirty seconds left and one timeout. If he doesn't make it, call timeout quick and we will try a dump pass," John Cale replied in a hoarse voice filled with keyed-up anger.

Cale hand-signaled Jay Brau, who lined up the Bears and yelled, "Check one! Check!" which the Bears had not used as a signal call all game. They had worked on it as an alternate call to Cheese Stick all week. The instructions from the coaches had been to use it only at the end of the game, anticipating the current situation. The Beavers began hurried calling their own audibles on defense. The noise confused and paralyzed Big Donnie Donnie as the snap went off when Jay shouted "Check" a third time. Donnie was slow getting out of his stance. The rest of the Bear line surged forward a fraction of an inch. Jorge was stacked up, and he shoulder-rolled to his right down the pile of bodies, keeping his feet pumping as hands grasped at him. He bounced into Big Donnie and rolled further to the right. A slice of an opening appeared, and Jorge lowered his shoulder and carried a cornerback across the goal line. Whistles blew and referees came running in and signaling a touchdown. The celebration was short-lived. A yellow flag arched high into the air. As the players stood up and looked around, the tallest Bear player on the field was lying in the end zone. Big Donnie picked himself up. Under him was a Beaver safety. After Jorge bumped off of Donnie, the large man-child stumbled forward and tackled the safety crossing over to fill the gap the Bears fullback had exploited. It was a holding call.

John Cale went red line in a heartbeat. Every frustration of the season boiled over as he ran onto the field yelling, "Nooooooo!" The head referee didn't wait a second, and he launched his flag, which struck John Cale in the chest as he ran toward the center of the field. Cale stopped short and reached down for the flag. He turned and hurled it as hard as he could downfield in the opposite direction.

That was all the provocation the head ref needed. He made a sweeping overhand gesture and yelled, "You're out of here, Coach! Get off this field! Immediately!"

"Bull! You're a bunch of flag-happy jerks! Let these kids play, for Christ sake!" Cale answered with exasperated anger.

"Coach, your team is as undisciplined as you are. You should be embarrassed. It was an obvious hold. Your right tackle tackled the safety. There are no gifts handed out to bad teams for just showing up. Now get off this field!' The pompous head ref shouted at the young head coach.

John Cale was starting forward to the ref when Mike Reese grabbed him from behind and began walking him to the sideline. "John, this is going to get real bad if you don't leave. Don't give Fudge anymore ammo than he already has." Reese felt all the energy and tension release from his friend as he spoke earnestly in his ear. Shouts and boos rained down from Bears stands. The rage in John Cale abated.

"Okay, Mike. I'll leave. It's over. It's all over," John Cale said clearly, and when he got to the sideline, he jogged to the track and kept jogging around the west end of the field on the track heading for the bridge over the river to the school.

Except it wasn't over. There were still eight seconds on the clock. Mike Reese called a timeout as the referee marched off the holding penalty yardage and then called the dead ball personal foul against the Bears bench. Reese was talking to the Bears as the ref placed the ball on the Beavers' 28-yard line.

In the press box, an enraged Clete Packer paced furiously behind the PA announcer. He couldn't take it anymore, and he bolted through the door of the broadcast booth section of the press box. The slamming door startled the radio announcers, but Pete Petterson knew exactly what was up.

"Where you off to, Clete?" Petterson asked knowingly.

Clete Packer stopped and focused on the fat sports reporter. His eyes were red with anger. Sweat was beading up on his forehead even with the chill in the air. "I'll tell you where I'm going! I'm going to fire that little asshole! Right now! Tonight! And his goddamned cocky mentor! Mike Reese has coached his last Bear River contest! He's all done. I'm going to force him to resign from wrestling, too! The insubordinate motherfucker!" the AD furiously yelled.

Pete Petterson smiled broadly. The broadcasters were in a panic trying to muffle their mics. Most of the tirade went live over the air. Back in Gratiot, the minimum-wage college student sitting in the booth didn't know how to hit the dump button to prevent it.

Clete Packer chugged down steps of the grandstand as the Bears broke their huddle on the sideline. He didn't notice it at all. Nor did he notice the huddle Reuben Martinez had called with his gang. They broke their huddle and moved around Packer and headed toward the bridge. A man in control of himself might have read the situation. Clete Packer had no idea what was ahead of him.

In the Bears huddle, Mike Reese had called a pass in the flat to Thing One. He encouraged the team, hoping to get them to refocus after watching their head coach get ejected. He could sense they were out of it. He called for them to break. They did. But the defeat in their voices was evident.

356

The last play of the season was at hand. It was a doomed attempt. Even if the Bears managed to complete the pass, the Beavers' defensive backs were lined up deep to protect the goal line. Thing One was not likely to elude them. Tom Osborne, the Bears center, snapped the ball cleanly to Jay Brau, who set up in the shotgun. Jorge Martinez picked up a crashing defensive end who blew right past Big Donnie untouched. Jay stepped up to throw just as the Beaver left end jumped up over Phil Long at left tackle. He batted the ball up into the air. It landed in the hands of the Beavers' all-state center and linebacker, Declan McCormac.

Jay Brau saw the large Beaver player come around the end of the line with the ball cradled in his big hands. The linebacker took an angle to the Beaver sideline. Jay Brau gave chase. He dove at McCormac as he crossed the fifty-yard line. The linebacker powered through Jay's grasp and crossed the goal line a few seconds later. Jorge Martinez, only steps behind, was unable to get down-field quickly enough to stop the score.

Time should have expired, but the clock-keeper was slow at the switch, and two seconds showed on the game. Bob Pease looked at the scoreboard and smiled slightly. He looked across the field at Mike Reese arguing with the head ref that time had expired. Reese knew what was coming. With time left, he expected Pease to go for the two-point conversion. The Beavers called timeout, and Pease sent his starting offense out to the field. They lined up for a two-point conversion. Their quarterback rolled to his right and faked a pass and walked into the end zone. The score was 99-0 in favor of the visitors. Two seconds remained on the clock and the teams lined up for the final kickoff. The Beavers squibbed the kick. The ball bounced off one of the freshmen Bears, and the Beavers recovered it. The game was over. It was the worst defeat in the wretched history of the Bear River football program. In the stands, Jay Brau's great-aunt wept bitterly as her husband held her.

Mike Reese felt the bile in his throat. It was the most despicable thing he had ever witnessed an opposing coach do. Going for two up by ninety-seven points – nothing could be more classless.

The Bears players lined up dejectedly to shake hands with the Beavers. Jay Brau was last in line. Immediately in front of him was Morg Miller. The Beavers had smiles on their faces. The Bears mumbled "Good game" as they passed down the long line of Beaver players. Near the front of the line Declan McCormac shook Jay Brau's hand firmly. "I thought you had me. Great effort, man," the big player said sincerely. Jay Brau gave him a sheepish smile and nod.

Further up the line in the middle of the Beaver JV players, young hotheaded Calvin Schmidt was waiting. As he slapped away Morg Miller's attempt at handshake, he spoke. "Came up a little short, didn't ya, you dick-grabbing FAG!" Morg was a little stunned. But Jay Brau wasn't. And he had had enough gay-bashing slurs.

Jay threw a well-targeted right-handed punch to the Beaver sophomore's face. The punch broke his nose and he stumbled backward, spraying blood. Time froze for a brief instant, and the teams were on each other at midfield. A full-on brawl was on. Big Donnie crashed into a pile of surging Beaver JV players who were trying to rescue their fallen mate. Thing One and Thing Two went after the Beavers' quarterback, who tried to scramble away from their spin kicks and punches. Morg Miller kicked one of the Beavers' linebackers in the balls and was rewarded with a painful grunt as the player went down. He was stalking another victim when several Beaver players jumped and began to pummel him. Jorge Martinez grabbed at the Beavers swarming on Morg and began to throw bodies away. Phil Long was locked up with a Beaver running back and they were trading blows back and forth. Tom Osborne smashed a Beaver player with an overhand swing of his helmet. In the press box, Pete Petterson was gleefully focusing his smart-phone video camera on the brawl in the middle of the field. Then he resolved to go down and get a better view.

Mike Reese joined his opposing coaches who were attempting to break up the fight on the fifty-yard line.

They were unaware of the near riot ramping up on the bridge over the Bear River.

The second Battle of the Bridge started with harsh words exchanged between Julie Bysshe and Clete Packer. It began as Clete approached the bridge, attempting to chase down John Cale as the last plays of the game ran out. Julie Bysshe intercepted the fat AD as he mounted the field-side steps up to the bridge.

"Clete Packer, I need a few words with you!" The assistant superintendent from Riverdale was imperious in tone.

Packer was not even focused on her as he lumbered up the steps. "Huh? Jesus Julie, I don't have time for your shit right now!" Packer dismissed her angrily.

"YOU WILL MAKE TIME, YOU RIDICULOUS BUFFOON, AND YOU WILL REFER TO ME AS DR. BYSSHE!" the angry woman commanded.

"Get the hell off of my back, you – Look, whatever this is about, take it up with my boss. You're not my boss, so I don't have to take any shit from you." Clete Packer was direct and not the least bit solicitous of the administrator from Riverdale. His tone did not sit well with Dr. Bysshe.

"And just where in the hell is Sheldon Knapp this evening? Why isn't he here?" Dr. Bysshe growled with an icy sneer.

"Mr. Knapp took a personal day today. He is out of the district," Packer answered dismissively as he looked at the back doors of the school, hoping that John Cale was outside watching the end of the game across the river. Cale was not there.

The game had ended, and the referees exited the field on a jog. They approached the bridge and made their way past the two bickering administrators. They weren't interested in intervening in the dispute.

"And what about Mike Shanahan? Surely they wouldn't leave you on duty by yourself. You can't even tie your own shoes unless one of them tells you how to do it." Dr. Bysshe pressed on in an increasingly sarcastic tone.

Clete Packer felt his rage building even higher. He wanted a piece of John Cale, but if that had to wait a minute, so be it. Dr. Julie Bysshe was about to gain his entire focus. And damn the consequences, because he was through taking guff from the meddlesome helicopter-bitch of a mom. He turned to the woman, drew himself up to his full height and glowered at her.

"I don't know where Mike Shanahan is," he answered gruffly through clenched teeth.

"And I'm sure he doesn't know where he is either. The three of you are a perfect team. You're all idiots and incompetent. You three couldn't run a lemonade stand, let alone a school district." Dr. Bysshe met his threatening tone with dismissive insults.

"Listen you bitch, why don't you go and f—" Clete Packer's curse was cut off by a loud yell and a splash as a body plunged over the railing of the bridge and into the water of the Bear River. In a flash, the brawl on the opposite end of the forty-foot-long bridge engulfed the two bickering administrators.

When the referees jogged across the bridge, they found their way blocked on the south end by Reuben Martinez and a dozen of his biker gang members. The referees tried to thread their way through the clot of bikers. One of them was shoved into the railing. Words were exchanged. And then punches were thrown. The bikers outnumbered the refs, and it had been Reuben's plan to jostle them a bit and try to intimidate them. He didn't know that the head ref was a retired sheriff's' deputy and that two others were active duty police officers. The bikers had the numbers and just enough booze in them to be ready for a brawl. The refs were trained officers not prone to backing down from a confrontation.

The violence escalated quickly. And these were not boys in a shoving match after an exhausting night of football. These were men who knew how to fight effectively and to strike with skill. The first body over the rail was the out-of-shape head referee who made the mistake of grabbing Reuben Martinez by the collar of his biker jacket. The blows that followed were many but no matter how skillfully the referees fought, they were outnumbered, and they came tumbling backwards into the steps on the north end of the bridge and right into Clete Packer and Dr. Julie Bysshe.

Dr. Bysshe went down first. A referee crashed into her and knocked the thin woman down three steps to the cement sidewalk at the base of the bridge. She suffered a badly broken wrist and was concussed when her head was stepped on a moment later, quieting her outraged screams. Clete Packer tried to help a referee but took a punch to the face. He fell onto the rail. One of the bikers grabbed him by his belt and heaved the fat man over the rail and into the shallow water near the north bank of the river. In the process, his pants tore free from his expansive ass. The biker tossed them in the air and they landed in the river. The pants floated downstream.

Parents and a few teachers from the visiting school who had parked on the school side of the bridge reached the brawl. The added numbers did nothing to quell the violence. In fact, it escalated. It was at this time that the sheriff deputy and the part-time city patrol officer working game security joined the fray. The two young officers had spent most of the game standing by the concession stand drinking complimentary Cokes and chatting with the fans. They were almost to the street north of the field and ready to direct traffic when the fight between the two teams broke out. They had first run onto the football field to try to stop that brawl when they noticed the near riot on the bridge. As they sprinted to the Battle of the Bridge, the sheriff's deputy called for backup on his hand-held radio.

On the field, the fight between the two teams abated as Mike Reese and Bob Pease corralled their boys with shouts and scolds. Reese stood a few feet from his longtime opposing coach. The scorn in his eyes burned brightly. Pease did not look away. He met the gaze with equal contempt. Reese resisted the urge to tell the Beavers' coach off for the ridiculous way the game concluded. The going for two in that situation was contemptible. But he had his boys to attend to, and there was a near riot occurring a few hundred feet away.

"I'll see you in January, Bob," Reese said icily, referring to the ass-whipping he planned to bring down on the Beavers on the wrestling mat. He did not offer his hand to shake.

"We've got playoff games to keep us busy – January will take care of itself," Pease replied dismissively.

"For the next week or two anyway," Reese noted, referring to the Beavers ten-year run of getting knocked out of the playoffs in the second round.

Bob Pease waved the back of his hand at Reese. "Boys! Get on the bus!" he commanded. And the Beavers jogged off the field.

"Take a knee," Reese commanded to his squad. He walked several paces toward the far sideline, surveying the skirmish at the north end of the bridge. He wondered if John Cale was involved.

"Holy shit! What do you think started that – us?" Greg DeVito asked as Wash Dryer handed him some ice to put on his hand. His knuckles were swollen badly from a punch he threw early in the fight.

"Nah, something else I think," Wash Dryer said with awe.

"Yeah, like what though?" Morg Miller asked innocently.

"Reuben," Jorge Martinez replied quietly.

360

Three miles west of Gratiot, deputy Bryan Doolittle was finishing writing up a speeding ticket when the call came in from dispatch. He shook his head ruefully and muttered to himself as he flipped his logbook closed. "Shit – not Bear River again."

Deputy Doolittle and three state police cruisers raced to the school. They arrived as the bikers were beating a hasty retreat. Most of them got away – including their leader, Reuben Martinez.

One of the last injuries of the Second Battle of the Bridge was Pete Petterson. He was filming the dissipating skirmish on the football field when his reporter's instincts kicked in and he made his way over to the bridge, all the while filming it with his phone camera and keeping up a running commentary. In his mind, he was already selling the video to state news outlets as well as some national ones.

The overweight former college football player bulled his way onto the bridge through a throng of people. He yelled, "Make way! Press!" He pushed people aside as he filmed his progress. Just after he crested the steps on the north end, he took a kick to the stomach. He spun away to the railing. As he leaned over, his phone fell from his hands into the dark water. He retched and vomited fifteen pieces of pizza and two liters of Coke. His puke splattered close to Clete Packer who sat in his muddy underwear and torn Bears' jacket on the bank of the Bear River. He was dejectedly wiggling a loose tooth, trying to be careful to not dislodge it and wincing as his lip swelled to comical proportions. He miserably glanced up at the source of the projectile of vomit. There was a brief flash of recognition in the two men's eyes before the sports reporter slumped to the deck of the bridge.

About twenty minutes after the police arrived in force, Mike Reese led the Bears off the field. They were met on the bridge by John Cale. Little was said as the players threaded their way through the gauntlet of police officers and the people answering their questions. In the parking lot next to the back door to the locker room, three ambulances were loading. They didn't recognize Dr. Julie Bysshe as Tim Manikowski's mother. She was quiet and goggle-eyed lying on the gurney as they silently walked past. One of the referees was being loaded onto a gurney as well. He was bleeding profusely from his nose, victim of a shattered cheek bone.

Morg Miller caught a glimpse of Fudge Packer leaning on the front of a police cruiser shivering and wrapped in a gray blanket marked "Bear River PD." Muddy water dripped from his knobby old-man knees. Morg almost burst out laughing. It was the funniest scene he had ever witnessed at the school, and he wished he had his phone to snap a shot of it.

The Bears made their way into their locker room. They silently took showers and then one by one they stopped by the coaches' office to thank John Cale, Mike Reese and Cheese Colby. The young players promised to be back next season. The Things eagerly asked Reese if they could begin practicing for wrestling on Monday. Reese told them they would have to wait a week at least. The seniors talked to the coaches about how much they had wanted to do better for them and the team. John Cale apologized to each player personally for his behavior on the field during the game. It was emotional and heartfelt. Morg Miller started out cracking wise, but by the end of his visit, he had tears in his eyes. Wash Dryer sat through it all.

Jay Brau was glum as he apologized for his poor play as the team's quarterback and for throwing the punch that started the brawl on the field at the end of the game. "No, Jay, you were given an impossible task," John Cale explained. "There are very few young men I have ever known that would have taken on the challenge we gave you. You were nothing short of heroic tonight. I'm surprised you were able to control your temper as long as you did in the face of the hate those boys from Riverdale spewed tonight. You have no reason to apologize. I am proud of you, and every member of this team owes you a debt of gratitude and all the respect in the world. Jay, you possess exactly the sort of qualities that I hope my sons have when they grow up. You're responsible and courageous," Cale concluded. Mike Reese nodded and grabbed Jay's hand to shake it. The shake turned into a bear hug.

Jorge Martinez was the last Bear player to enter the office. When Jorge apologized for his cousin and his gang ending the season by causing a riot, Mike Reese hugged him and assured him that he was not responsible. The best player on the team broke down in sobs. Wash's heart ached for his friend.

"Jorge, you are not Reuben. And you are not your brother. May he rest in peace. You are the finest young man I have ever had the privilege to coach. And come the first Saturday in March, I will hand you your championship medal at the top of the podium at the state wrestling meet. I guarantee that. Now let's put this season behind us and focus on that goal, okay?" Mike Reese's voice was calm and reassuring as he talked to his captain.

Jorge smiled and wiped his eyes. "Yes, Coach," he answered quietly. John Cale stood up from his desk chair and extended his hand to Jorge. They shook hands and then Cale brought the young man in for a hug.

"Jorge, you will do great things in your life. I know you will. When I end my career many years from now, people will ask what my proudest moments were as an educator. I will have a nice list, but I fully expect the first thing I will answer will be 'I coached Jorge Martinez.'"

"Thanks, Coach," Jorge answered, his voice quivering.

After Jorge left, Mike Reese announced he needed a shower and he excused himself to the grungy stall in the coaches' office bathroom. Wash left to go look for stray equipment in the locker room. Cheese Colby announced he was leaving to meet some friends for pizza. John Cale called his wife.

Clete Packer was able to find some extra-large Bear River girls track sweatpants to wear. They were tight, but at least they were dry and warm. And then he spent a full half hour getting lambasted by the head referee in the girls locker room as the referee's crew prepared to leave – minus one member who was in the emergency room in the Gratiot hospital. Clete hung his head glumly for most of the tirade. As the old referee's fury abated, he said something that really hurt.

"I'm not sure how a school gets to the low level this one has. I really don't. But there must be a sickness here. It must be marrow deep. It's not just poor leadership, and there is plenty of evidence that is fully in place. There is something deeply wrong here, and I have no inclination to figure it out. But I do know one thing for sure: My crew and I will never take an assignment here again – and good luck finding crews from the Lansing area to come up here in the future, because after word gets out about the events here tonight, not a single crew will come. Good day, Mr. Packer. I hope to never hear from you again." The pompous but soggy old man intoned his condemnation and turned away before Clete Packer could respond.

Packer stood dumbly for a moment, pressing an ice bag to his swollen lip as the referees left. His recently damaged eardrum sang a high-pitched wail. As he walked away from the girls' locker room, his pace quickened as though he was on a mission. He made a beeline for the boys' locker room. Each step he took raised his fury another notch. He had scalps to take, and he was going to take them tonight. The football coaches had embarrassed him and this school for the last time.

More than an hour after the end of the worst defeat in Bear River High school football history, the last of the football players were cleared out of the locker room. Coach Mike Reese was emerging from the shower in the coaches' office wrapped in a towel and wearing shower sandals. John Cale was hanging up the phone. He had just completed a call to his wife explaining how he had been ejected from the game. He was thinking of calling his father at home in the U.P. but thought better of it. Cale looked drained and exhausted. Wash Dryer was still picking up things in the locker room. Bits of athletic tape and Band-Aids were strewn everywhere. Clete Packer walked through the open coaches' office door. He had discarded his ice bag. His swollen lip looked comical, but neither Reese nor Cale was in the mood for smiling.

Packer's voice rose from a hoarse whisper to near shouting, the swollen lip gave him a slight lisp. "That was a God damn embarrassment John! Giving up ninety-nine points! Getting tossed out of the game!! I warned you! I did! So now it's time to take action! You two are FIRED! Do you understand? And John, I expect your resignation from teaching to be on my desk on Monday morning. AND I better see that you have filed for immediate retirement at the same time, you insubordinate prick, or I will bring the matter to the school board myself and have you suspended! You have coached your last game, Mike, and your last wrestling meet!"

"Shut the fuck up, Fudge," Reese said calmly. His use of the hated nickname made Clete Packer sputter with rage as he turned his full focus to

363

the assistant coach, his mouth hanging open with a small spit dribble hanging from his lower lip. Reese continued, "If John wants to resign as coach, he will give it in writing to the superintendent after the team banquet next week, I already told you I was resigning. So you better just turn around and walk out of here." Packer stood blinking at Reese. He pivoted on one foot and started to leave. "And one more thing, Fudge," Mike Reese said as the fat man packed into too-tight sweatpants crossed the threshold of the office door. Packer turned to him with a scowl. "You had better stay away from my wrestling room this winter, or I'll make sure it is your resignation on the super's desk come spring."

Packer threw open the door dramatically and reentered the room pointing his finger at Reese. "You don't have that kind of power. You talk a good game, but you're all wind, you sanctimonious insubordinate over-rated has-been." Packer tried to growl, but with his fat lip it sounded like a cartoon character issuing threats.

Mike Reese shook his head in disgust. "You're nothing but a back-stabbing vindictive asshole, Clete. The kids hate you and your staff doesn't trust you any farther than they can throw your fat ass. The worst thing that ever happened in this school is when you walked through the door. Get out of here. I can't even stand to look at you." Reese was as calm. He reached into his locker to grab a clean coaching shirt and a pair of wind pants, turning his back on the fat man.

Clete Packer was looking at the back of Reese's head and he didn't like it, so he paused. Mike Reese pulled on his pants slowly – not looking at Clete Packer. When he did look, he held up his hand to stop the administrator. "I'm done talking to you, Clete. John is too. Get out."

Packer was furious at the dismissal. "I AM NOT FINISHED! DAMN IT! WHO DO YOU THINK YOU ARE TALKING TO? I AM YOUR BOSS! You do not run this school! I run this school! You are just an old man who doesn't know the time has run out and, and uh—"

The mini tirade caused the fat man to become winded. Reese watched as he struggled to gain his breath. His look was one of pity. John Cale stood and walked around the desk. There was slight pause. Cale looked first to Reese and then to Packer. He expected the fat man to explode when he regained his breath. He could see Clete Packer trying to formulate some sort of response. His mouth opened but nothing came out.

The AD slowly regained his composure. He locked eyes with the two coaches. "This isn't over," Clete Packer threatened with a lisp. He then turned to leave and stepped into the half open office door. The thud of impact was followed by a moan as Packer staggered back a step. Reese and Cale reached out to catch him but he stopped short of falling into the coaches. He made a wet sputtering noise and reached up to his face. He spat his previously loosened front tooth into his hand.

Clete Packer's face was a mask of horror and pain. He groaned and mumbled something unintelligible. Cale reached out to offer assistance and Packer waved him off angrily. He then staggered out the now fully open door. Dripping blood as he left.

Wash Dryer entered the office. He watched and heard the entire exchange from only a few feet away through the window to the locker room. He looked back and forth between the two coaches with wide eyes. "Holy shit Uncle Mike," was all he could think to say. Mike Reese looked at his nephew, paused and then rolled his eyes and shook his head. He then gave a rueful smile to his nephew and to John Cale and he said, "So ends another super season for the Bear River Bears."

## Overtime

Greg Dryer was watching TV in his hotel room when the text came through later than he expected.

WashDryer: Knock Knock.

GregDryer: Who's there?

WashDryer: Owen.

GregDryer: Owen who?

WashDryer: Owen Nine.

GregDryer: How bad?

WashDryer: Dad, you're not going to believe it when I tell you.

CPSIA information can be obtained
at www.ICGtesting.com
Printed in the USA
BVHW041145171221
624363BV00019B/149

9 781637 640357